THE
WILD ISLES

PATRICK BARKHAM is a natural history writer for the *Guardian*, and is one of a generation of British authors who have revitalized British nature writing. His books include *The Butterfly Isles*, *Badgerlands*, *Islander*, *Coastlines* and *Wild Child*, and he has been shortlisted for the Ondaatje Prize and the Wainwright Prize. He is currently writing the biography of acclaimed naturalist Roger Deakin. He lives in Norfolk with his family.

Also in the anthology series

THE
WILD ISLES

An Anthology
of the Best of
British and Irish
Nature Writing

CHOSEN BY

PATRICK
BARKHAM

An Apollo Book

First published in the UK in 2021by Head of Zeus Ltd
This paperback edition published in 2022 by Head of Zeus Ltd,
part of Bloomsbury Publishing Ltd

9 7 5 3 1 2 4 6 8

A catalogue record for this book is available from the British Library.

ISBN (PB) 9781803287409
ISBN (E) 9781789541397

Chapter-opening linocuts © Sarah Price
Typeset by Adrian McLaughlin

Printed and bound in Serbia by Publikum d.o.o.

Head of Zeus Ltd
5–8 Hardwick Street
London EC1R 4RG
WWW.HEADOFZEUS.COM

THE
WILD ISLES

An Anthology
of the Best of
British and Irish
Nature Writing

CONTENTS

INTRODUCTION

I t is autumn and spiders' silk stretches across dewy paths like tape at a finish line. The race to grow, that burgeoning rush of spring and summer, is at an end. The skies have emptied of swifts, the sunlight softens and all is quiet. A mew like a distressed cat falls from the stillness high above the industrial estate next to my home: a young buzzard, fledged and soaring, still asks its parents for food. In the garden, my children and I collect conkers, cool to touch, encased in cream memory foam, and decorated with whorls that resemble a chestnut map of the world. On the walk to school a giant puffball, bridal white and pregnant with possibility, lies on the first fallen leaves, kicked loose by a passing teenager.

We live in a busy, suburban place in lowland Britain, one of the most nature-depleted countries on the planet, in a geological era defined by the destructive dominance of human beings. And yet other species continue to make their lives all around us – and to change our own. We still reside alongside plants, animals and fungi which keep us alive and well – helping us breathe and providing us with food, or pollinating and fertilizing what we grow. If we look up, or down, or pause and take notice with any of our senses, these living things give us a sense of companionship and wonder.

Writing about natural landscapes and wild species is flourishing like never before. Nature writing has been given pleasing green space in many bookshops. The lives of plants and animals intrude more visibly into novels, children's books, poetry, screenplays, blogs, social media and films. Nature seems to be moving through the work of visual artists, sculptures and musicians with a new dynamism. This is no coincidence.

As we live in a world that is more technological than ever, with more of us collected in cities than ever before, we have been liberated from the back-breaking physical labour required to work the land that defined thousands of years of our evolution. But we also find our-selves alienated from the non-human world, and craving connection with it. We find solace and succour, and mental and physical good health from time in nature. An increasing number of us seek to bond with nature vicariously too, via culture and reading about the wild world. The best writing nourishes us in many different ways: it may soothe us, entertain us, inspire us, anger us or encourage us to spend more time among non-human life, as admirers or custodians.

I hope you, like me, will find pleasure, wonder, refreshment, motiv-ation and perhaps a new way of looking at the world from the British and Irish nature writing I have collected in this volume. Nature writing is a complicated term and I should explain how I have chosen to define it. I also want to briefly summarize its history in Britain. Finally, I'll reveal how I chose this selection. Dear reader, I don't want to give too much away yet but it involved many a genuinely exciting hour in the British Library.

Writers today mostly don't particularly like the term 'nature writing'. We are nature, so all writing is nature writing. Like most of my 'nature writing' peers, I also say I'm just a writer. Some of my work is about our relationship with other species or landscapes where other species live. Nature writing is undoubtedly a piece of marketing shorthand, a publishing genre that helps books find a home in a bookshop. How-ever, I think it is a valid concept; a useful banner to march under, as its leading proponent today, Robert Macfarlane, put it back in 2003 when he began to map this flourishing. I define nature writing as any writing that considers other species or non-human places and our relationship with them. Unlike a field-guide, for instance, which pro-vides in plain text some facts about the appearance or habits of a flower or a bird, nature writing usually possesses a lyrical or poetic quality, romance as well as science.

For the purposes of this one modest volume, I've had to tighten that definition. I take the birth of British nature writing to be 1789, when Gilbert White's *The Natural History of Selborne* was published. Never out of print, the Hampshire curate's close observations of the chang-ing seasons and secret lives of plants and animals was an early kind of ecology. White has inspired and informed subsequent generations in many different ways. His work reached scientists, modernists and artists, from Charles Darwin to Virginia Woolf. I decided I could not offer an exhaustive encyclopedia of historic works, and so Gilbert White feels like a good place to begin what is a brief introductory tour of modern British and Irish nature writing.

Of course there is plenty of writing about nature before 1789. When I interviewed the writer and poet Kathleen Jamie, she said that all writing before 1900 was nature writing. When we lived more closely with the land, it seeped into our culture rather more. There is a wealth of poetical observation about the natural world to be found everywhere from Anglo-Saxon poetry to William Shakespeare. Many earlier non-fiction works about nature were by sportsmen-authors, who wrote with varying degrees of accuracy and flair about the species they hunted. George Turberville's *The Noble Art of Venerie or Hunting*, first published in 1575, features a panoply of creatures that lived, and died, solely for our gratification. These hunter-naturalists share with nature writers the quality of taking notice. Plenty of lyrical nature writers from more recent times have been predators too. Gavin Maxwell's first book was a brutal account of hunting basking sharks off the west coast of Scotland.

I see modern nature writing in Britain and Ireland rising from three groups of people: from these sportsmen authors who closely observed the natural world to understand their quarry; from the first scientific naturalists who wanted to explore how the natural world functioned and how it could best be classified; and from the Romantics who defined a radically new relationship with nature – as a place for self-discovery, personal growth, awe, appreciation and wonder. The Romantic poets, particularly William Wordsworth and Samuel Taylor Coleridge, and later Romantics writing in response to fears about the direction of the agricultural and industrial revolutions, are the most significant shapers of modern nature writing. I haven't included poetry in this volume because that would make it an unreadably epic enterprise (and I am *totally* unqualified to assess the merits of poetry) but I have included the prose of Dorothy Wordsworth and John Clare, whose reappraisal in the twentieth century inspired new British nature writing.

There was a boom in nature writing in both novels and non-fiction in the early years of the twentieth century as artists, writers and readers responded to anxieties over industrialism, pollution, urban sprawl and the rise of the machine. The natural world was an escape, and a new literate, urban-dwelling mass audience lapped up magazines such as *Country Life* and the 'country diary' columns in popular newspapers. The first conservation organizations were formed in these decades, popularizing the idea of creating spaces for nature – nature 'reserves' – and saving species, particularly birds, from industrial-scale exploitation. Then nature writing seemed to quietly expire.

The genre did not really flower again until this century. Writing in 2003, Robert Macfarlane dated its disappearance to November 1932, when Stella Gibbons' *Cold Comfort Farm* was published, a satirical novel (by a suburban writer) which lampooned popular rustic novels with their tragic heroines and stereotypical depictions of rural life. Through the middle years of the twentieth century, our finest writers, poets and philosophical thinkers did not, in general, turn their gaze upon the wild world. Nature writing existed in culture mostly in a rather mundane rabbit hole of children's fiction featuring anthropomorphic characters and the occasional adult non-fiction narrative about the nature close to an individual's home. (While researching my book *Badgerlands*, I discovered an intriguing wealth of writing from the mid-twentieth century about people who befriended badgers, watching wild ones or bringing them up as part of the family. Frances Pitt, Eileen Soper and Norah Burke write rather beautifully at times about watching badgers, although I haven't included this trio to avoid a massive badger bias in this selection.)

The fact that British and Irish nature writing was so insignificant in this era is a puzzle when it was steadily gaining significance in North America. Founded upon the writing of Ralph Waldo Emerson, Henry David Thoreau and (Scottish-born) John Muir, and the movement to protect wilderness within national parks, American nature writing has been producing both bestselling and critically acclaimed works for many more decades. Annie Dillard's *Pilgrim at Tinker Creek* won the Pulitzer Prize in 1975 and is still in print. Barry Lopez's *Arctic Dreams* (1986) was a *New York Times* bestseller. Other writers who put the natural world in the centre of their writing, from Gary Snyder to Annie Proulx, have enjoyed huge success in recent decades. American nature writing has numerous sub-genres and university courses devoted to it. Today in North America, many huge literary names and ambitious, prize-winning novels explore explicitly environmental themes, from Margaret Atwood to Richard Powers' *The Overstory*.

British nature writing has been catching up. During the 1970s and 1980s, Richard Mabey was a lone voice in a literary wilderness, virtually the only contemporary writer at the time who was both a serious and popular nature writer. His work, including his biography of Gilbert White and the epic cultural history of plants *Flora Britannica*, helped revive British nature writing. Robert Macfarlane, more than any other individual this century, has shaped the genre – through his justly celebrated books, his academic studies and his championing of writers old and new: J. A. Baker and Nan Shepherd from the lost years of British nature writing, and a whole host of new writers up to 2020 with the brilliant young Irish writer Dara McAnulty.

But the genre has also been criticized for its male character, and the apparently colonialist enterprise of cloaking a landscape, or other species, in fine writing. As Kathleen Jamie wrote in a review of Macfarlane's *The Wild Places* in 2008: 'What's that coming over the hill? A white, middle-class Englishman! A Lone Enraptured Male! From Cambridge! Here to boldly go, "discovering", then quelling our harsh and lovely and sometimes difficult land with his civilized lyrical words.' In the last decade, however, publishers have produced much more nature writing by women. Many of the most successful and critically acclaimed works of recent years have been by women: Helen Macdonald's *H is for Hawk* won the Samuel Johnson Prize after its publication in 2014; *The Outrun* by Amy Liptrot won the Wainwright Prize in 2016. Other recent bestsellers include *Wilding*, Isabella Tree's account of rewilding her West Sussex farm, and *The Salt Path*, Raynor Winn's memoir of homelessness and walking the South West Coast Path.

British nature writing certainly enjoys a higher profile than ever in our cultural life, even though it may not yet be central to it. Nature writing is in more robust health than ever at a moment of awakening to the global extinction crisis and the plummeting diversity of life on our own archipelago. Whether nature writing is – or should be – an escape from this bleak reality or an engagement with it has been the subject of much debate in recent years. The nature writer Mark Cocker believes that it is difficult to produce great nature writing if you live in a landscape where nature has been trashed, and he considers this to explain the invisibility of nature writing in twentieth-century Britain compared with North America, where almost pristine wilderness endures. In 2015, Cocker also criticized British books branded as nature writing for failing to engage with the destruction and exploitation of the natural world or question who controls and shapes the wild health (or lack of health) of our land. Robert Macfarlane responded with an essay appealing for a more inclusive interpretation of nature writing. Nevertheless, as with Jamie's criticism, so Cocker's critical intervention has been followed by a shifting of the terrain. Even the most lyrical nature writers engage with the extinction crisis today. That doesn't necessarily make their writing more creative or original but it certainly makes it more urgent.

I want to tell the story of how I chose this collection. If this introduction has sounded academic, I apologize for misleading you. If you are seeking a rigorous critical assessment of nature writing, you might want to look elsewhere. I am not an academic; I am a reader who is also a writer.

I have read a lot of nature writing in recent years but, and I admit this without pride, when I wrote my first book, *The Butterfly Isles*, in 2009, I had read hardly any non-fiction nature writing apart from Roger Deakin's *Waterlog* and *Wildwood*. During my early adulthood, I read fiction voraciously. This is what inspired me to write. When I researched *The Butterfly Isles*, I began reading Robert Macfarlane's *The Wild Places* but I soon put it down because it was so beautifully written. I feared if I continued imbibing it, my first book would become a very poor imitation. By accident then, or perhaps because we are so shaped by the wider time and culture in which we live and write, *The Butterfly Isles*, a personal quest in which I travelled through Britain trying to find all fifty-nine species of native butterfly in one summer, came to fit rather neatly into this burgeoning genre. Since it was published, I've educated myself by reading much more nature writing, particularly the library-load of books published in the last decade or so.

Since being given this rather wonderful task of editing a collection of British and Irish nature writing, I've read more extensively. The nature writing I love is that which, to my mind, displays some originality. The best books help us see the world in a different way. We emerge from their pages bequeathed with altered vision.

Judgements of what is good are hugely subjective. There will be some books where you and I simply disagree. Some maverick works are a matter of taste. But I still cling to a belief that good and bad writing exists. The nature writing in this volume, like any good writing, eschews the easy phrase or hackneyed observation. It is not overwrought but nor is it dull; it possesses a rhythm and energy; it is tight, like a good band or a nicely fitting pair of trousers. It also holds some kind of moral core or philosophical depth. The digital age, of which I am part, has enabled a great democratization of writing, which is liberating but means there is probably too much writing, created too quickly, without a time-consuming edit. I'm not taking aim at bloggers or self-published authors; mainstream publishers also appear to skip lightly through once-draconian editing processes. No genius's words aren't improved by a second, third or fourth pair of attentive eyes.

Great nature writing is attentive. It draws our attention to minute details and the particularity of things and in so doing tells a bigger story about our relationship with nature, and our short time on this miraculous planet. The poet Patrick Kavanagh put it brilliantly when arguing that parochialism was not to be dismissed as myopic but rather that it dealt with the fundamentals of existence. 'All great civilizations are based on parochialism,' he wrote. 'To know fully even one field or one land is a lifetime's experience. In the world of poetic experience it is depth that counts, not width. A gap in a hedge, a smooth rock surfacing a narrow lane, a view of a woody meadow, the stream at the junction of four small fields – these are as much as a man can fully experience.'

This anthology is arranged in fields of vision – in themes, and I particularly relished pairing up very different works about similar subjects. I hope you enjoy my marriages of corncrakes, childhood, Scolt Head Island, swimming and John Clare.

How did I choose this selection? The first stage was easy. I rifled through my bookshelves and stacked up the books that I really loved for their originality, poetry and big ideas. Works such as *Waterlog* by Roger Deakin, *Being a Beast* by Charles Foster, *H is for Hawk* by Helen Macdonald, *Underland* by Robert Macfarlane. Unlike much nature writing, all four have a narrative that grips the reader. I also returned to old favourites from when I was young, such as *The Wind in the Willows* and *Brendon Chase* by BB. They moved me as a boy, and they move me still, in their delicate evocation of the English countryside and childhood.

You may detect a few personal biases in this book: I am an English lowlander with a particular fondness for butterflies, badgers, marshlands and islands. But I was determined that this anthology should be representative in a multitude of important ways – representing the range of landscapes we have in Britain and Ireland, representing different epochs and representing a fair range of species as well. The latter is possibly the hardest kind of representation because the largest and most significant collections of living things – plants, insects and fungi – are drastically overlooked in our culture. I've tried to devote pages to a few underdogs, although I fear the fine tradition of writing about fish and fishing will feel neglected. Finally, obviously, it was vital that I also think hard about how much this collection could and should fairly represent writers who may be working class, women or from black, Asian and minority ethnic backgrounds. British nature writing, if you haven't already noticed, has historically been overwhelmingly male, white and middle or upper class. I'll return to this thorny issue.

After rediscovering my favourites, I made a list of what might be widely considered an essential library of British nature writing and read more of classics such as Richard Jefferies, W. H. Hudson, J. A. Baker, Nan Shepherd, Richard Mabey and Kathleen Jamie. With the latter quartet, I realized that I could include almost any page of their writing in an anthology. Their writing sang. Then I travelled further. I wandered into libraries wherever I happened to be (Shrewsbury, I discovered, has a particularly magnificent library) and lost myself in their local sections. I checked other people's bookshelves and lists of favourite nature writing books. Reading one book led to another. Mysteriously, on occasion a book found me. I was researching an *Observer* article about the Dafynogg yew, a miraculous tree that may be two thousand years old and grows in a churchyard in Wales. In the musty church porch was a shelf of second-hand books. I was on a deadline and nearly sped past but then felt called to take a look. There I found a compendium of *Guardian* country diaries by women and discovered the marvellous writing of Enid Wilson. (Her inclusion is a bit of a cheat: I haven't otherwise included newspapers' country diaries because the billions of words of journalistic nature writing is too heavy a haul for the net I'm casting.)

I believe novelists are usually the best writers. I first realized the genius of Vladimir Nabokov after I had been ploughing through the protean prose of various guidebooks and naturalists' musings about butterflies, and then read Nabokov's shimmering account of a boy-hood encounter with a swallowtail. (Sadly, it doesn't qualify for this collection because it occurred in Russia.) I doubt any naturalist writer could capture wildlife's takeover of an abandoned house as vividly as Virginia Woolf in an extract from *To the Lighthouse* that I include in this anthology.

I expected to select lots of fiction for this anthology but I struggled to find many that fit the demands of this collection. Novels are mostly about us, not other species, and when they include land-scapes these can rarely be captured by one simple extract. When I considered what I might choose to represent the East Anglian Fens, *Waterland* by Graham Swift was my first choice. I remembered it fondly for its evocation of the spirit of this strange, bleak, watery place. But there was no passage which worked as a short extract. (Swift later confessed that he barely visited the Fens before writing his masterpiece.) I read Emily Brontë, remembering the moorland she so vividly described, and found the same; and again with many twentieth- and twenty-first-century novelists whose writing hums with a sense of place, from D. H. Lawrence to Melissa Harrison and Natasha Carthew.

I saw that good novelists sow a sense of place deeply and yet lightly into their prose, without crowbarring great chunks of description into a narrative. The physical landscape is constructed by each reader's imagination, expertly steered by a deftly chosen word here or there. This makes novels, to use an ugly and ungrammatical phrase, not easily anthologizable. Thomas Hardy made it into this selection because he wrote in an era where a writer would serve up a three-page description of a place in their opening chapters. Where novelists really soared, in this anthology at least, was when they turned their imaginations towards the future of nature. So I include here a passage from Richard Jefferies' prescient early example of apocalyptic fiction, *After London*. Closer to our times, Sarah Hall's *The Wolf Border* convincingly portrays a near-future where rewilding has been unleashed upon the Lake District.

Of Irish nature writing, I confess I knew almost nothing, except that as a teenager I read and adored Patrick Kavanagh's memoir *The Green Fool*. 'I wasn't really a writer,' Kavanagh demurred. 'I had seen a strange beautiful light on the hills and that was all.' To travel beyond him, I obtained expert advice on a large number of writers who were new to me. Exploring this terrain, largely from the crepuscular hush of the British Library, was thrilling. I already knew about the great flowering of Gaelic memoir springing from the last years of the Irish-speaking communities in the far west. For personal stories told without self-pity but with enough emotion to chime with today's readers, it is hard to beat the Blasket Islanders. How about this, from the start of Tomás O'Crohan's memoir?

> I was born on St. Thomas's day in the year 1856. I can recall being at my mother's breast, for I was four years old before I was weaned. I am 'the scrapings of the pot', the last of the litter. That's why I was left so long at the breasts. I was a spoilt child, too.
>
> Four sisters I had, and every one of them putting her own titbit into my mouth. They treated me like a young bird in the nest.

This superb opening reminds me of Kathleen Jamie's point that all earlier writing was nature writing, when people inhabited their natural environment in a way we do not today. But sadly I concluded that O'Crohan's deep connection with his surroundings did not constitute nature writing, for other species only intruded when his kin needed to eat – on one memorable occasion, they drive porpoises into bays, like the Faroese still do today. Another Blasket writer, Peig Sayers, does qualify for this anthology because I found a more reflective tone in her work, as she considered more explicitly her relationship with the land and animals around her. For all my cramming, my knowledge of Irish nature writing will be found wanting by scholars but I share with you here a modest portion of what I've most enjoyed, including the novels of Sara Baume, the wisdom of Michael Kirby – who spent all but three of his ninety-nine years on Ireland's west coast – and the intense prose of John Moriarty, whose two-volume autobiography baffled and entranced me.

Other residents of Britain may argue their place is underrepresented here. Forgive me: I was unable to repel the torrent of great nature writing springing from south-west England. The Highlands and the Western Isles, particularly the Hebrides and St Kilda, and the Lake District also loom similarly large in the annals of nature writing. I found it harder to find nature writing from the Midlands and Wales, where I was unable to accommodate the magnificent place poetry of R. S. Thomas. But I have included modern Welsh writers such as Cynan Jones and I swapped one member of the twentieth-century canon, Ronald Lockley, for a lovely, understated depiction of Skomer by Rosanne Alexander in her memoir *Waterfalls of Stars*. Brenda Chamberlain on Ynys Enlli, or Bardsey, is touched by island genius.

As my shortlist grew longer, I realized my greatest challenge was to offer you a selection that wasn't overwhelmingly white, male and middle class. Of fifty-eight works of 'classic' British and Irish nature writing compiled by *Guardian* readers in 2005, just 15.5 per cent were by women. Of a list of 267 nominations to an Arts and Humanities Research Council project to find Britain's favourite nature writing book in 2017, 18 per cent were by women (and three of these were American works). Clearly, there are published books by women that are overlooked by narrow interpretations of the 'canon' of nature writing. But the brutal fact is that over the past two centuries, far more male nature writers have been published than women.

More women nature writers from the past are now being celebrated. My own extremely belated discovery of Dorothy Wordsworth left me ecstatic. She wrote so finely that it seems astonishing, and damning, that she wasn't feted in her own time like her brother. In what was only her humble diary, and not intended for publication or posterity, she wrote with gorgeous clarity: 'The fern of the mountains now spreads yellow veins among the trees; the coppice wood turns brown.' Her writing stands the test of time much better than most famous male nature writers who coloured the world purple with their prose in subsequent centuries.

I've wrestled with representation and positive discrimination and I hope I've found a reasonable balance. I wanted to get close to having an equal number of men and women writers (my final tally is 31 women and 35 men) but I didn't want to be enslaved by this target. Ultimately, there is no extract here that I do not wholeheartedly love. I could've included a fine piece about badger-watching by several (previously mentioned) women but I chose the one that most moved me, by Horatio Clare. Even so, I've genuinely agonized over some works, by men, that I've omitted. Classics by the likes of John Stewart Collis and David Lack have fallen victim to my cull of the (male) canon. I can think of at least five contemporary male writers whose work I love and could happily grace this anthology but who in the end I've not been able to include. Should they be here on merit? I consider their writing to equal some of this collection, but if I included all this writing that I related to, then I would be perpetuating a male club and structures of power that have marginalized women writers for two centuries. I hope my peers won't take it personally. Like any writer, I know how it feels to be excluded from accolades and shortlists. If it's any consolation, I've excluded my own writing from this anthology. If I presume to place myself in the nature writing tradition, I consider myself a craftsperson who can create an attractive dwelling in the woods. Other genius-dipped pens build shape-shifting time-machines that whizz skywards.

There's another problem that no amount of retrieving obscure published works from the British Library's stores at Boston Spa can solve. Until now, British and Irish nature writing has been almost exclusively white. Writing in 2020, I know of only two published books of what would widely be considered nature writing by writers of a black, Asian or ethnic minority background. I'm delighted to include an extract from one of them, *The Grassling* by Elizabeth-Jane Burnett, which fizzes with joy, poetry and originality.

The whiteness of British and Irish nature writing is stark and it is shared by the whiteness of professional conservationists, with studies showing conservation to be one of the whitest industries in the country. Belatedly, the sector is taking steps to change this. Nature writing must critically examine itself too, and be alive to the conservatism of the genre and how intertwined it has been with those who control our land. Concepts of home soil, 'native' species and the belonging we identify in 'our' landscape are hazardous in the wrong hands and historically fascism has appeared in nature writing. Henry Williamson, whose illuminating and imaginative writing in *Tarka the Otter* is included, became a pacifist after experiencing the horrors of the First World War. His determination that Britain and Germany must never fight again later mutated into an admiration for Nazi Germany and abhorrent support for Oswald Mosley's British Union of Fascists.

Some readers might wonder what barn owls or stag beetles care about the colour of the skin of the person writing about them. Creatively, why is it relevant?

An ecosystem is healthy when it is diverse. Nature-lovers mourn the loss of species and the simplification of our wild places. When we lose one species, others are sure to follow. And for us humans, by shedding species we lose understandings, meanings and words. We are all poorer if forced to live in a monoculture. So it is with nature writing. If British and Irish nature writing is to grow and endure, to survive the whims of fashion, publishing and parody, it must be diverse, complex, multi-faceted and dynamic, and relevant to everyone who lives on this land. In the coming decades, I think nature writing will evolve again, and blossom as it belatedly becomes more diverse and more radical.

I'm sure we all grasp the value of diversity in theory but I'm convinced it becomes instantly real in the six contemporary essays in this volume that I have sought out – some of them specially commissioned – from writers who do not simply spring from a white-British background. The innate power and creativity of diversity is proven when we read Bulgarian-born poet Kapka Kassabova's take on the contemporary Highlands, or Shamshad Khan's eye-opening memoir of her family's exploration of the Yorkshire Dales. Here is diversity in action – prose that revitalizes, widens, deepens and enriches our bond with the natural world. Like all the best writing, it offers a new vision of familiar surroundings. It bequeaths a deeper understanding of life on Earth. And it helps us develop an intimate and necessary appreciation for all the species with whom we share these beautiful wild isles.

PATRICK BARKHAM
Norfolk, 2021

Birds

Illustration overleaf: *Peregrine Falcon*

from THE NATURAL HISTORY OF SELBORNE

Gilbert White

Widely seen as Britain's first ecologist and the country's father of nature writing, the **Reverend Gilbert White** (1720–93) was also a pioneering gardener, particularly regarding the growing of potatoes. Educated at Oriel College, Oxford, he followed his grandfather and uncle into the church, becoming curate of Selborne in Hampshire. *The Natural History and Antiquities of Selborne* – never out of print since its publication four years before his death – began as shared observations of wild birds, plants and animals in letters between himself and two like-minded friends. Most naturalists of the day chose to study dead specimens in their study but White closely observed live species in the wild. He hailed the importance of the earthworm, became the first to distinguish between the chiffchaff, willow warbler and wood warbler on the basis of their song; he was also the first to precisely describe the harvest mouse and noctule bat. He influenced Charles Darwin and was celebrated in a biography by Richard Mabey, the pre-eminent nature writer of the late twentieth century.

LETTER 21, TO THE HONOURABLE DAINES BARRINGTON

Selborne, Sept. 28, 1774

Dear Sir,

As the swift or black-martin is the largest of the British hirundines, so is it undoubtedly the latest comer. For I remember but one instance of its appearing before the last week in April: and in some of our late frosty, harsh springs, it has not been seen till the beginning of May. This species usually arrives in pairs.

The swift, like the sand-martin, is very defective in architecture, making no crust, or shell, for its nest; but forming it of dry grasses and feathers, very rudely and inartificially put together. With all my attention to these birds, I have never been able once to discover one in the act of collecting or carrying in materials: so that I have suspected (since their nests are exactly the same) that they sometimes usurp upon the house-sparrows, and expel them, as sparrows do the house and sand-martin; well remembering that I have seen them squabbling together at the entrance of their holes; and the sparrows up in arms, and much-disconcerted at these intruders. And yet I am assured, by a nice observer in such matters, that they do collect feathers for their nests in Andalusia; and that he has shot them with such materials in their mouths.

Swifts, like sand-martins, carry on the business of nidification quite in the dark, in crannies of castles, and towers, and steeples, and upon the tops of the walls of churches under the roof; and therefore cannot be so narrowly watched as those species that build more openly: but, from what I could ever observe, they begin nesting about the middle of May; and I have remarked, from eggs taken, that they have sat hard by the ninth of June. In general they haunt tall buildings, churches, and steeples, and breed only in such: yet in this village some pairs frequent the lowest and meanest cottages, and educate their young under those thatched roofs. We remember but one instance where they breed out of buildings; and that is in the sides of a deep chalkpit near the town of Odiham, in this county, where we have seen many pairs entering the crevices, and skimming and squeaking round the precipices.

As I have regarded these amusive birds with no small attention, if I should advance something new and peculiar with respect to them, and different from all other birds, I might perhaps be credited; especially as my assertion is the result of many years exact observation. The fact that I would advance is, that swifts tread, or copulate, on the wing: and I would wish any nice observer, that is startled at this supposition, to use his own eyes, and I think he will soon be convinced. In another class of animals, *viz.* the insect, nothing is so common as to see the different species of many genera in conjunction as they fly. The swift is almost continually on the wing; and as it never settles on the ground, on trees, or roofs, would seldom find opportunity for amorous rites, was it not enabled to indulge them in the air. If any person would watch these birds of a fine morning in May, as they are sailing round at a great height from the ground, he would see, every now and then, one drop on the back of another, and both of them sink down together for many fathoms with a loud piercing shriek. This I take to be the juncture when the business of generation is carrying on.

As the swift eats, drinks, collects materials for its nest, and, as it seems, propagates on the wing; it appears to live more in the air than any other bird, and to perform all functions there save those of sleeping and incubation.

This *hirundo* differs widely from its congeners in laying invariably but two eggs at a time, which are milk-white, long, and peaked at the small end; whereas the other species lay at each brood from four to six. It is a most alert bird, rising very early, and retiring to roost very late; and is on the wing in the height of summer at least sixteen hours. In the longest days it does not withdraw to rest till a quarter before nine in the evening, being the latest of all day birds. Just before they retire whole groups of them assemble high in the air, and squeak, and shoot about with wonderful rapidity. But this bird is never so much alive as in sultry thundry weather, when it expresses great alacrity, and calls forth all its powers. In hot mornings several, getting together in little parties, dash round the steeples and churches, squeaking as they go in a very clamorous manner: these, by nice observers, are supposed to be males serenading their sitting hens; and not without reason, since they seldom squeak till they come close to the walls or eaves, and since those within utter at the same time a little inward note of complacency.

When the hen has sat hard all day, she rushes forth just as it is almost dark, and stretches and relieves her weary limbs, and snatches a scanty meal for a few minutes, and then returns to her duty of incubation. Swifts, when wantonly and cruelly shot while they have young, discover a little lump of insects in their mouths, which they pouch and hold under their tongue. In general they feed in a much higher district than the other species; a proof that gnats and other insects do also abound to a considerable height in the air: they also range to vast distances; since loco-motion is no labour to them, who are endowed with such wonderful powers of wing. Their powers seem to be in proportion to their levers; and their wings are longer in proportion than those of almost any other bird. When they mute, or ease themselves in flight, they raise their wings, and make them meet over their backs.

At some certain times in the summer I had remarked that swifts were hawking very low for hours together over pools and streams; and could not help inquiring into the object of their pursuit that induced them to descend so much below their usual range. After some trouble, I found that they were taking *phryganeae, ephemerae*, and *libellulae* (cadew-flies, may-flies, and dragon-flies) that were just emerged out of their aurelia state. I then no longer wondered that they should be so willing to stoop for a prey that afforded them such plentiful and succulent nourishment.

They bring out their young about the middle or latter end of July: but as these never become perchers, nor, that ever I could discern, are fed on the wing by their dams, the coming forth of the young is not so notorious as in the other species.

On the thirtieth of last June I untiled the eaves of an house where many pairs build, and found in each nest only two squab, naked pulli: on the eighth of July I repeated the same inquiry, and found they had made very little progress towards a fledged state, but were still naked and helpless. From whence we may conclude that birds whose way of life keeps them perpetually on the wing would not be able to quit their nest till the end of the month. Swallows and martins, that have numerous families, are continually feeding them every two or three minutes; while swifts, that have but two young to maintain, are much at their leisure, and do not attend on their nests for hours together.

Sometimes they pursue and strike at hawks that come in their way; but not with that vehemence and fury that swallows express on the same occasion. They are out all day long in wet days, feeding about, and disregarding still rain: from whence two things may be gathered; first, that many insects abide high in the air, even in rain; and next, that the feathers of these birds must be well preened to resist so much wet. Windy, and particularly windy weather with heavy showers, they dislike; and on such days withdraw, and are scarce ever seen.

There is a circumstance respecting the colour of swifts, which seems not to be unworthy of our attention. When they arrive in the spring they are all over of a glossy, dark soot-colour, except their chins, which are white; but, by being all day long in the sun and air, they become quite weather-beaten and bleached before they depart, and yet they return glossy again in the spring. Now, if they pursue the sun into lower latitudes, as some suppose, in order to enjoy a perpetual summer, why do they not return bleached? Do they not rather perhaps retire to rest for a season, and at that juncture moult and change their feathers, since all other birds are known to moult soon after the season of breeding?

Swifts are very anomalous in many particulars, dissenting from all their congeners not only in the number of their young, but in breeding but once in a summer; whereas all the other British hirundines breed invariably twice. It is past all doubt that swifts can breed but once, since they withdraw in a short time after the flight of their young, and some time before their congeners bring out their second broods. We may here remark, that, as swifts breed but once in a summer, and only two at a time, and the other hirundines twice, the latter, who lay from four to six eggs, increase at an average five times as fast as the former.

But in nothing are swifts more singular than in their early retreat. They retire, as to the main body of them, by the tenth of August, and sometimes a few days sooner: and every straggler invariably withdraws by the twentieth, while their congeners, all of them, stay till the beginning of October; many of them all through that month, and some occasionally to the beginning of November. This early retreat is mysterious and wonderful, since that time is often the sweetest season in the year. But, what is more extraordinary, they begin to retire still earlier in the most southerly parts of Andalusia, where they can be no ways influenced by any defect of heat; or, as one might suppose, defect of food. Are they regulated in their motions with us by a failure of food, or by a propensity to moulting, or by a disposition to rest after so rapid a life, or by what? This is one of those incidents in natural history that not only baffles our searches, but almost eludes our guesses!

These hirundines never perch on trees or roofs, and so never congregate with their congeners. They are fearless while haunting their nesting places, and are not to be scared with a gun; and are often beaten down with poles and cudgels as they stoop to go under the eaves. Swifts are much infested with those pests to the genus called *hippoboscae hirundinis*; and often wriggle and scratch themselves, in their flight, to get rid of that clinging annoyance.

Swifts are no songsters, and have only one harsh screaming note; yet there are ears to which it is not displeasing, from an agreeable association of ideas, since that note never occurs but in the most lovely summer weather.

They never settle on the ground but through accident; and when down can hardly rise, on account of the shortness of their legs and the length of their wings: neither can they walk, but only crawl; but they have a strong grasp with their feet, by which they cling to walls. Their bodies being flat they can enter a very narrow crevice; and where they cannot pass on their bellies they will turn up edgewise.

The particular formation of the foot discriminates the swift from all the British hirundines; and indeed from all other known birds, the *hirundo melba*, or great white-bellied swift of Gibraltar, excepted; for it is so disposed as to carry 'omnes quatuor digitos anticos' all its four toes forward; besides the least toe, which should be the back-toe, consists of one bone alone, and the other three only of two apiece. A construction most rare and peculiar, but nicely adapted to the purposes in which their feet are employed. This, and some peculiarities attending the nostrils and under mandible, have induced a discerning naturalist to suppose that this species might constitute a genus *per se*.

In London a party of swifts frequents the Tower, playing and feeding over the river just below the bridge: others haunt some of the churches of the Borough next the fields; but do not venture, like the house-martin, into the close crowded part of the town.

The Swedes have bestowed a very pertinent name on this swallow, calling it *ring swala*, from the perpetual rings or circles that it takes round the scene of its nidification.

Swifts feed on coleoptera, or small beetles with hard cases over their wings, as well as on the softer insects; but it does not appear how they can procure gravel to grind their food, as swallows do, since they never settle on the ground. Young ones, over-run with *hippoboscae*, are sometimes found, under their nests, fallen to the ground; the number of vermin rendering their abode insupportable any longer. They frequent in this village several abject cottages; yet a succession still haunts the same unlikely roofs: a good proof this that the same birds return to the same spots. As they must stoop very low to get up under these humble eaves, cats lie in wait, and sometimes catch them on the wing.

On the fifth of July, 1775, I again untiled part of a roof over the nest of a swift. The dam sat in the nest; but so strongly was she affected by natural στοργή [affection] for her brood, which she supposed to be in danger, that, regardless of her own safety, she would not stir, but lay sullenly by them, permitting herself to be taken in hand. The squab young we brought down and placed on the grass-plot, where they tumbled about, and were as helpless as a new-born child. While we contemplated their naked bodies, their unwieldy disproportioned abdomina, and their heads, too heavy for their necks to support, we could not but wonder when we reflected that these shiftless beings in a little more than a fortnight would be able to dash through the air almost with the inconceivable swiftness of a meteor; and perhaps, in their emigration, must traverse vast continents and oceans as distant as the equator. So soon does Nature advance small birds to their ἡλικία [prime of life], or state of perfection; while the progressive growth of men and large quadrupeds is slow and tedious!

I am, &c.

from FINDINGS

Kathleen Jamie

Kathleen Jamie (b. 1962) was born in Renfrewshire and grew up in Currie, outside Edinburgh. Her first poetry collection, *Black Spiders*, was published in 1982 when she was a student and deposited a sheaf of poems on a publisher's doorstep. She is the author of numerous poetry collections including *The Tree House* (2004), which won the Forward Prize for best poetry collection of the year and a Scottish Arts Council Book of the Year Award. Jamie has also won the Somerset Maugham Award, a Forward Poetry Prize for her poem 'The Graduates', a Paul Hamlyn Award and a Creative Scotland Award. Jamie has twice won the Geoffrey Faber Memorial Prize. Her first genre-stretching collection of essays, *Findings*, was published in 2005, followed by *Sightlines* (2012) and *Surfacing* (2019). Her travel writing includes *The Golden Peak: Travels in North Pakistan* (1992) and *Among Muslims* (2002). She is the editor of a collection of Scottish nature writing, *Antlers of Water* (2020). Of her poetry, she has said: 'It's not about voice, it's about listening and the art of listening, listening with attention. I don't just mean with the ear; bringing the quality of attention to the world. The writers I like best are those who attend.'

CREX-CREX

On the wall of my room in the B&B is a print of Constable's *Haywain*. The room's pleasant, with floral curtains and bedspread, a vase of silk flowers and a few prints on the walls. *The Haywain*'s only small, hardly the six-foot original, but you'd know that painting anywhere – grand trees in summer leaf, Constable's piled-up clouds, his black horses pulling their wooden cart through the ford; a never-ending summer's day in southern England, in 1821.

The farmhouse where the print hangs is not in England, but on the Hebridean island of Coll. The window looks over a ragged little bay of rock and seaweed, where a red boat is drawn up. A wire fence, repaired with driftwood, keeps the sheep from the shore. In a boggy place where a thin burn wanders down to the shore there is a stand of yellow flag iris, and a single willow bush, where a sedge warbler is singing.

Coll and its twin island Tiree lie at a northeast-southwest axis, off the west coast of Mull. Between them like a hyphen is the tiny island of Gunna. Coll is a low, sandy affair with no hills and few trees. Only a few miles wide, its heights are rough moor knuckled with bedrock, with lochans in the dips. The island is ringed with beaches of flawless sand, backed by huge dunes. Atlantic squalls pass over rapidly and the air smells of seaweed. The sea and its surf is never far away, a constant Atlantic soughing, a sense that the land is an interruption in a long conversation between water and sky.

The point is, when Constable packed up his easel at the end of that summer's day, what he would have heard as he walked home through the fields – indeed, what we could hear if we could step into his painting – would be the call of the corncrake. A corncrake is a brown bird, a kind of rail, not ten inches tall, which prefers to remain unseen in tall damp grass. Its call – you'd hardly call it a song – is two joined notes, like a rasping telephone. *Crex Crex* is the bird's Latin name, a perfect piece of onomatopoeia. *Crex-crex*, it goes, *crex-crex*.

Perhaps, as he strolled home, Constable had a bit of fun trying to pinpoint the sound in the long grass. Perhaps he thought nothing of it, the corncrake being such a commonplace. 'Heard in every vale,' as John Clare said in his poem. The vales of Northamptonshire, the New Town of Edinburgh, in Robert Burns's Ayrshire, it was recorded in every county in the land from Cornwall to Shetland. In the last century, though, it has been utterly eliminated from the mainland, and if you'd like to hear or even see this skulking little bird of the meadow you must sail to the Hebrides.

Saturday night on Coll. Nowadays the human population is about 160, incomers mostly – much the same as the number of corncrakes.

I don't know how many of them turned up for the disco; that was last night. Monday is the African drumming group, but there are other diversions. It's eleven at night. Elsewhere people are doubtless getting ready to go out clubbing, but I'm pulling on wellies and a jacket. It's not quite dark and a Land-Rover has pulled up at the side of the guesthouse.

The Land-Rover, a smart new example of corporate sponsorship, is driven by Sarah Money, warden of the RSPB reserve on Coll. Her reserve is managed especially for corncrakes, and Sarah's work, late on this Saturday night, is to go out into the fields to census – that is, count – these little brown birds. 'Medium-sized brown birds, please,' Sarah says.

When we're ready, Sarah, a fit woman in her thirties, jolts the vehicle down onto the beach and drives hard across the sand for a mile and a half. There is no road to the guesthouse. Above the engine she's saying that you have to keep a good speed. Too slow, you'll sink into the sand. She's telling a yarn of a man who did just that – got his Land-Rover stuck and went to fetch a tractor to pull it out. That got stuck as well, and then the tide came in and he lost both. Then we're bouncing off the beach again, and wind on a track through the dunes until Sarah stops the Land-Rover and winds down the window to listen. Satisfied, she cuts the engine. We jump down, and in the dark and the breeze open a gate and, by torchlight, enter a field.

Corncrake. Landrail. King of the Quail, the croaking one of the cornsheaf, the nutty noisemaker, the quailie, the weet-my-fit.

'Hear them?' she whispers, and I nod.

What does it sound like? Like someone grating a nutmeg, perhaps. Or a prisoner working toward his escape with a nailfile. *Crex-crex, crex-crex.* We move forward a few paces at a time. Now and again Sarah stops and tilts her head. She wears her hair back in a ponytail and sports two or three small earrings, and when she stops to listen she reminds me of a thrush on a lawn. She cups her hands behind her ears, because it's almost impossble to tell where exactly the sound is coming from. It's obviously on the ground – you'd swear it was right under your feet, but it seems to jump and flit ahead. We walk on carefully, speaking in whispers until we've crossed the whole field, but the sound heard so clearly from the gate is still, somehow, ahead of us.

It's unchancy. Fairy music is said to do this; to lead a man on in his confusion and drunkenness, to start, then stop, then begin again from another place, ever luring him on. This was not a beautiful music, it has to be said; hardly the art of the fairies. Mind you, it could be a goblin carpenter, sawing away at his little workbench, if you'd had a few too many at the island disco and were of fanciful mind.

Again Sarah stops and listens; she explains she's trying to tell whether we're hearing two different corncrakes, or just one who's using a rocky outcrop as a sounding board to give his call a bit of reverb and so steal a march on his rivals. Only males call like this; nocturnal lovers, they're trying to attract a mate. He keeps it up all night, every second or so. Now we're definitely close to the bird, the sound's coming from a patch of cow parsley at our feet, and at such close quarters it's a much lower, slower sound, a real smoky bar room rasp. *Crex-crex, crex-crex*, he goes, more Tom Waits than Tom Jones, but hugely sexy to female corncrakes. Then we're too close, he cuts to silence, and there's only the breeze and seals singing from the shore. We look at one another, trying not to laugh.

We hear it in the weeding time
When knee deep waves the corn.
We hear it in the summer's prime
Through meadows night and morn:

And now I hear it in the grass
That grows as sweet again
And let a minute's notice pass
And now tis in the grain.

Tis like a fancy everywhere
A sort of living doubt;
We know tis something but it ne'er
Will blab the secret out…

So wrote John Clare.

The grim reaper came for the corncrake in the form of the mechanised mower. In the days of the scythe, when hay was long and cut later in the year, then heaped on slow-moving wains, the corncrake had long grasses to hide and breed in. The chicks would be fledged before the meadow was mown, and had plenty of time to escape the swinging blade. With mechanisation, however, and a shift toward earlier cutting for silage, corncrakes, eggs, fledglings and all have been slaughtered wholesale.

The corncrake has long been in relationship with humans, its fortunes have waxed and waned as our own farm practices changed. When prehistoric people cleared woodland and developed agriculture, the bird's range extended: corncrake bones have been discovered in Stone Age middens. Indeed, Mrs Beeton gives a recipe for roasted corncrake. You need four, and should serve them, if liked, with a nice bread sauce. But since Clare's 'mowers on the meadow lea' were likewise banished before the machine, the corncrakes' range has been reduced to a few boggy meadows on the islands. They are the same islands, ironically, whose human populations suffered such decline as ideas on farming changed. But old mowing practices lingered longer in the Hebrides, the fields being too small for machines, so this is where the bird is making its last stand, and where conservation efforts are taking effect.

So Sarah and I are standing in a damp, dark field, listening to corncrakes on the pull. The females' job is to respond to this sound, choose a mate, inspect the several nests the male, in a fit of high optimism, has already prepared on the ground, select one and get laying. You don't see the females much – they keep purdah, hiding deep in the nettles or iris patches, raising one or maybe two broods of jet-black chicks. Once a male has mated a female, he'll stick around for only a short time, until she lays eggs, then he starts rasping again to secure another. The mother duly hatches the chicks, but less than a fortnight later she abandons the little brood to fend for themselves. At that age, they can't even fly and are easy prey to otters or buzzards, but their mother is off choosing a second mate, to raise another brood.

To our minds, this strategy has an air of desperation, of profligacy – raise lots of young against the onslaught. It's one we, as a species, are leaving behind. But Sarah says the corncrake's life is so perilous that the male we're hearing now may not be the one she counted here last year. He has doubtless perished. This may be his son, returned to the place of his birth, to fulfil his imperative and breed. So there he is, a tiny, urgent male rasping at our feet, and it gives Sarah and me the giggles.

At about two o'clock in the morning Sarah's satisfied and ready to go home to bed. By the light of the Land-Rover's lamp, she makes notes on a clipboard. The night's sally has brought her total of calling males to 73, which is on track to beat last year's record. Ten years ago, before this reserve was established with enclaves of long grasses and considerate mowing, there were but twenty, so 73 counts as success. The night is mild, a soft breeze blows from the sea. A mile inland a single light is shining in the window of a house. Maybe someone's sleepless, what with this incessant scratchy chorus all night long.

The next morning I stroll along the beach; the tide has washed away the Land-Rover's tracks. There's an oil drum, an oystercatcher's nest and a long-dead dolphin. Behind the beach, on the huge sand dunes wild flowers are coming into bloom, bloody cranesbill, orchids like pink thumbs. From the end of the beach I follow a track inland until it passes the field where Sarah and I stood last night. Last night it seemed an unsettling place; now it's green and benign. Crouched in the grass like intelligent stones are half a dozen brown hares, and in the middle stands a scarecrow with a bucket for a head. But there, from deep in the growth at the field's far edge, comes that noise again: *crex-crex, crex-crex, crex-crex.*

By her house at the reserve, Sarah's flattening the grass with a strimmer; she's splattered with green gunk. She cuts the motor, invites me into the kitchen for coffee, and at a table piled with guides to flowers and bird reports she tells me she acquired her considerable knowledge of birds quickly, in only eight years, as an adult rather than as an obsessive adolescent. It was an extended visit to St Kilda which turned her interest. Knowing birds is like being fluent in a foreign language, or adept with a musical instrument. Though managing a bird reserve appears more like gardening or housewifery than the call of the wild, what with its careful planting and egg-counting, it still attracts few women. The postings can be hard on a family and a partner's needs, if indeed you have a family. If not, finding a partner in an out-of-the-way place can be difficult.

'Will you stay here?' I ask.

'Not forever. It would drive me mad.'

Coll would be a heavenly place to be a child. There are beaches and boats, everyone knows you, it's the kind of place you leave your door open. If you're on the island, it's known. If you catch the ferry to the mainland, well, that's known about too. Should you have a mishap and require the air ambulance, a helicopter will have you in a Glasgow hospital in twenty minutes, by which time the island will have learned of your fate. A mere thirteen miles of single-track road separates 'the unspoiled end' from 'God's own country'. There are local land feuds, a limited supply of fresh water, and no high school. In effect, the children leave home when they are an unfledged eleven, to travel as boarders to the secondary school in Oban. Higher educa- tion and jobs take them yet farther afield. It seems a price to pay for an apparently idyllic island life, to lose your children so young.

Corncrakes migrate. They arrive in April or May, by night. They fly reluctantly, by all accounts, low, with hunched wings. 'Embarrassed', one field guide says, of their flying style. Sometimes they collide with powerlines and lighthouses. Then in September they leave again. From the Hebrides to southern Africa – it seems unbelievable. But then, folk believed unlikely things of the corncrake: that it vanished underground in winter, or changed into a moorhen or, if it flew at all, it hitched a ride on other birds. Or that it lies on its back when making its call, otherwise the sky would fall in. Where the birds winter is not exactly known – only one corncrake ringed in Scotland has ever been recovered, and that was in the Congo. They endure this epic migration, then lose themselves again in the long grass.

'It's good that we don't quite know,' says Sarah. 'Good that there is still some mystery in the world. And if we don't know, it suggests they go where there are no people, and that's better for the birds.'

'And what do you do then, in the winter, on the reserve?' I ask, and Sarah says, with genuine enthusiasm, 'Oh, we have the geese to look forward to. You know that day in October when you sense the year's turned? Then the geese come.'

Not content with having heard several corncrakes by night, I want to see one. It's a species thing. As humans, we privilege sight; it confirms the other senses. I'd been told, 'You don't see corncrakes if you're looking for them', but still, I'd feel shortchanged if I didn't. The RSPB has established a 'corncrake viewing bench' which is a grand name for a few slats of wood on the edge of a field. Sarah takes me there. Her task today is to survey lapwings' nests, because lapwings too are in decline, and she wants to find out why. 'Might be otters – there's a nice conservation dilemma.' She pulls on jacket and wellies, takes her clipboard and we set out for the fields.

The bench gives a view over the gentle downward slope of two lush meadows, which are divided by a wire fence and a row of telegraph poles carrying wires to a cottage three-quarters of a mile away. Wide borders at the fields' edges have been left to grow long, and cow parsley and grasses sway in the wind. The long grasses provide cover for corncrakes. In the marshy middle of the fields, waders nest. The fields are swathes of muted yellows and creams – buttercups, yellow rattle, cow parsley. The land dips, then rises. In the dip is a little open water, where reeds and flag iris grow, and a couple of greylag geese are idling there. It's not ideal weather for corncrake viewing. The sky's overcast and threatens squalls, the breeze is too fresh. A wind above three knots, and corncrakes don't like to come out. They don't like flying, don't much care for wind and rain, don't want to be seen in public – the kind of bird who'd want to be excused games. Not like these lapwings, hurling themselves down through the air trying to divert Sarah, who's investigating their nests.

I watch her stooping in the field like a gleaner. It looks like a life, a good job to hold, to be counting corncrakes by night, and checking lapwings' nests in a boggy field by day – beats being stuck in an office. She will tell you, however, that most of a warden's work is negotiating and compromising with people, rather than birds. Given the conditions, the birds will look after themselves. It's the tenant farmers and neighbours and visitors that take the management. To be eccentric landlord to some, and charming host to others; to keep smiling, even to those people whom you believe are fouling up the planet. She says there are people hostile to the very idea of conservation; who believe it's somehow anti-human and therefore unacceptable to devote a corner of a faraway field to the endangered corncrake, to let them raise a few chicks and then go.

I want to see a corncrake. So I sit on the bench and watch the lacy heads of cow parsley waft in the breeze. I'm thinking about corncrakes, as though thinking about them could summon one up. A glimpse is all I'll be granted – maybe a female darting from one patch of cover to another, or rival males so forgetting themselves as to have a quick squabble in public view. The corncrake has become a Hebridean bird, part of the Hebridean summer along with the blue windswept skies, the surf and rain, the wild flowers on the machair, the skylarks and the empty, cream-pale beaches. Its decline is doubtless bad for the corncrake, but there's an interesting side effect. In this age of supposed homogeneity and sameness where, as naturalist Richard Mabey put it, 'the differences between native and stranger are fading', we have driven the birds away. Once-common species, like the corncrake, are becoming more localised, more specialised. But, as they do, it seems that people are learning a new identification with the birds of their patch. Mull makes much of its sea eagle, a species that was hunted to extinction, then reintroduced.

On Coll everyone knows about corncrakes – they're adopting them as their own, like the totems of Neolithic tribes. On Coll, it's corncrakes that are good for business. Summer visitors themselves, they beget others. Birdwatchers come especially – Sarah tells of an old lady who sat quiet and demure on this very viewing bench for an hour, two hours… then there was a whoop, and Sarah turned to see the old lady leaping around, punching the air like a footballer, just for a glimpse of an elusive brown bird. I sit on the bench, looking at the long grass, but it's beginning to rain, and though there are geese and lapwings and redshanks, a flock of noisy starlings, and a laverock rising, I see no corncrake. Maybe it's just as well. In Shetland they held it was very bad luck, actually to clap eyes on the thing.

When, later that day, I do see one, it's scuttering away from the wheels of the car. Like a miniature road-runner, a slender upright hen with hunched shoulders and strong, long pinkish legs, it squeezes under a wire fence, and with relief vanishes among the irises, even as I brake. It's the colour of slipware and looks, in that glimpse, like an elegant ceramic water jug suddenly come to life. That's that. I do not punch the air.

Corncrakes don't feature on Christmas cards, or sing after the rain. Their migration has none of the romance of swallows', though they cover the distance. They arrive in spring, but we've forgotten they are spring's heralds. They skulk in the grass like guilty things, hardly encouraging us to look to the skies. They offer us no metaphors about fidelity, or maternal dedication; they are just medium-sized brown birds. Nonetheless, I feel robbed – denied one of the sounds of summer, which all our forebears would have known, that irksome little *crex-crex*. Why conserve them, other than it being our moral duty to another life form on this earth? If there is no 'clam'rin craik', no 'noisy one of the rushes', it betokens something out of kilter with the larger ecosystem on which ultimately, in mysterious as-yet-undiscovered ways, we all depend.

That's what the ecologists and scientists will tell you. But there are things which cannot be said – not by scientists, anyway. Another person arrives at the viewing bench, not an old lady but a man in young middle age, a holiday-maker. We fall into conversation – he obviously knows his stuff about birds. He has a young family with him on the island and, while they're on the beach, he has slunk off for an hour in the hope of spotting a corncrake. So here he is, an Englishman of higher education with a professional job, a family, a cagoule and good binoculars.

'Can I ask why you like them? Corncrakes I mean.'

'Well,' he said. 'They're like… little gods of the field, aren't they?'

I could have punched the air. If corncrakes are rare, animism is rarer still. Anyone can clear his throat and talk about biodiversity, but 'Corncrakes… little gods of the field' will not get you published in ornithologists' journals. That's how I picture them now, however: standing chins up, open-beaked, like votive statues hidden in the grass.

When I nip in to thank Sarah before heading for the ferry she's in her customary work-gear, Barbour and wellies, and is on her way out to replace the battery in an electric fence. A farmer at the other end of the island has just phoned to report corncrakes on his land, thereby bringing her total of calling males on the island to 75, breaking last year's record, so Sarah's pleased – though their future, to paraphrase John Clare, is still 'a sort of living doubt'.

At Arinagour, where the ferry docks, are a few white cottages, a shop, a hotel. There is also a pottery where you can buy a souvenir ceramic corncrake to take back to the mainland. There's talk of re-introducing real corncrakes to England, so it might again *crex* through Constable's Dedham Vale. Till then the mainland's a diminished place; a thousand miles of country without one little god in its fields.

from THE PEREGRINE

J. A. Baker

John Alec Baker (1926–87) grew up in Chelmsford, Essex. Although his first book, *The Peregrine*, won the Duff Cooper Prize soon after its publication in 1967, little was known about Baker until after his death, when Robert Macfarlane and other international nature writers including Barry Lopez did much to bring more attention upon Baker's extraordinary prose. Very short-sighted, suffering chronic arthritis since childhood and unable to drive (despite working for the Automobile Association), Baker was an unlikely birdwatcher. He cycled around the Essex country-side obsessively tracking overwintering peregrines for a decade for his book. His second, *The Hill of Summer* (1969), an account of the passage of summer, has been similarly acclaimed for its beautiful writing. He was scrupulous about his prose, recording the syllables, verbs, adjectives, metaphors and similes he used on every page of his drafts. 'Beginnings', the first chapter of *The Peregrine*, although only six pages long, contains 136 metaphors and twenty-three similes.

BEGINNINGS

East of my home, the long ridge lies across the skyline like the low hull of a submarine. Above it, the eastern sky is bright with reflections of distant water, and there is a feeling of sails beyond land. Hill trees mass together in a dark-spired forest, but when I move towards them they slowly fan apart, the sky descends between, and they are solitary oaks and elms, each with its own wide territory of winter shadow. The calmness, the solitude of horizons lures me towards them, through them, and on to others. They layer the memory like strata.

From the town, the river flows north-east, bends east round the north side of the ridge, turns south to the estuary. The upper valley is a flat open plain, lower down it is narrow and steep-sided, near the estuary it is again flat and open. The plain is like an estuary of land, scattered with island farms. The river flows slowly, meanders; it is too small for the long, wide estuary, which was once the mouth of a much larger river that drained most of middle England.

Detailed descriptions of landscape are tedious. One part of England is superficially so much like another. The differences are subtle, coloured by love. The soil here is clay: boulder clay to the north of the river, London clay to the south. There is gravel on the river terraces, and on the higher ground of the ridge. Once forest, then pasture, the land is now mainly arable. Woods are small, with few large trees; chiefly oak standards with hornbeam or hazel coppice. Many hedges have been cut down. Those that still stand are of hawthorn, blackthorn, and elm. Elms grow tall in the clay; their varying shapes contour the winter sky. Cricket-bat willows mark the river's course, alders line the brook. Hawthorn grows well. It is a country of elm and oak and thorn. People native to the clay are surly and slow to burn, morose and smouldering as alder wood, laconic, heavy as the land itself.

There are four hundred miles of tidal coast, if all the creeks and islands are included; it is the longest and most irregular county coast-line. It is the driest county, yet watery-edged, flaking down to marsh and salting and mud-flat. The drying sandy mud of the ebb-tide makes the sky clear above; clouds reflect water and shine it back inland.

Farms are well ordered, prosperous, but a fragrance of neglect still lingers, like a ghost of fallen grass. There is always a sense of loss, a feeling of being forgotten. There is nothing else here; no castles, no ancient monuments, no hills like green clouds. It is just a curve of the earth, a rawness of winter fields. Dim, flat, desolate lands that cauterise all sorrow.

I have always longed to be a part of the outward life, to be out there at the edge of things, to let the human taint wash away in emptiness and silence as the fox sloughs his smell into the cold unworldliness of water; to return to the town as a stranger. Wandering flushes a glory that fades with arrival.

I came late to the love of birds. For years I saw them only as a tremor at the edge of vision. They know suffering and joy in simple states not possible for us. Their lives quicken and warm to a pulse our hearts can never reach. They race to oblivion. They are old before we have finished growing.

The first bird I searched for was the nightjar, which used to nest in the valley. Its song is like the sound of a stream of wine spilling from a height into a deep and booming cask. It is an odorous sound, with a bouquet that rises to the quiet sky. In the glare of day it would seem thinner and drier, but dusk mellows it and gives it vintage. If a song could smell, this song would smell of crushed grapes and almonds and dark wood. The sound spills out, and none of it is lost. The whole wood brims with it. Then it stops. Suddenly, unexpectedly. But the ear hears it still, a prolonged and fading echo, draining and winding out among the surrounding trees. Into the deep stillness, between the early stars and the long afterglow, the nightjar leaps up joyfully. It glides and flutters, dances and bounces, lightly, silently away. In pictures it seems to have a frog-like despondency, a mournful aura, as though it were sepulchred in twilight, ghostly and disturbing. It is never like that in life. Through the dusk, one sees only its shape and its flight, intangibly light and gay, graceful and nimble as a swallow.

Sparrowhawks were always near me in the dusk, like something I meant to say but could never quite remember. Their narrow heads glared blindly through my sleep. I pursued them for many summers, but they were hard to find and harder to see, being so few and so wary. They lived a fugitive, guerrilla life. In all the overgrown neglected places the frail bones of generations of sparrowhawks are sifting down now into the deep humus of the woods. They were a banished race of beautiful barbarians, and when they died they could not be replaced.

I have turned away from the musky opulence of the summer woods, where so many birds are dying. Autumn begins my season of hawk-hunting, spring ends it, winter glitters between like the arch of Orion.

I saw my first peregrine on a December day at the estuary ten years ago. The sun reddened out of the white river mist, fields glittered with rime, boats were encrusted with it; only the gently lapping water moved freely and shone. I went along the high river-wall towards the sea. The stiff crackling white grass became limp and wet as the sun rose through a clear sky into dazzling mist. Frost stayed all day in shaded places, the sun was warm, there was no wind.

I rested at the foot of the wall and watched dunlin feeding at the tide-line. Suddenly they flew upstream, and hundreds of finches fluttered overhead, whirling away with a 'hurr' of desperate wings. Too slowly it came to me that something was happening which I ought not to miss. I scrambled up, and saw that the stunted hawthorns on the inland slope of the wall were full of fieldfares. Their sharp bills pointed to the north-east, and they clacked and spluttered in alarm. I followed their point, and saw a falcon flying towards me. It veered to the right, and passed inland. It was like a kestrel, but bigger and yellower, with a more bullet-shaped head, longer wings, and greater zest and buoyancy of flight. It did not glide till it saw starlings feeding in stubble, then it swept down and was hidden among them as they rose. A minute later it rushed overhead and was gone in a breath into the sunlit mist. It was flying much higher than before, flinging and darting forwards, with its sharp wings angled back and flicking like a snipe's.

This was my first peregrine. I have seen many since then, but none has excelled it for speed and fire of spirit. For ten years I spent all my winters searching for that restless brilliance, for the sudden passion and violence that peregrines flush from the sky. For ten years I have been looking upward for that cloud-biting anchor shape, that crossbow flinging through the air. The eye becomes insatiable for hawks. It clicks towards them with ecstatic fury, just as the hawk's eye swings and dilates to the luring food-shapes of gull and pigeons.

To be recognised and accepted by a peregrine you must wear the same clothes, travel by the same way, perform actions in the same order. Like all birds, it fears the unpredictable. Enter and leave the same fields at the same time each day, soothe the hawk from its wild-ness by a ritual of behaviour as invariable as its own. Hood the glare of the eyes, hide the white tremor of the hands, shade the stark reflect-ing face, assume the stillness of a tree. A peregrine fears nothing he can see clearly and far off. Approach him across open ground with a steady unfaltering movement. Let your shape grow in size but do not alter its outline. Never hide yourself unless concealment is complete.

Be alone. Shun the furtive oddity of man, cringe from the hostile eyes of farms. Learn to fear. To share fear is the greatest bond of all. The hunter must become the thing he hunts. What is, is now, must have the quivering intensity of an arrow thudding into a tree. Yesterday is dim and monochrome. A week ago you were not born. Persist, endure, follow, watch.

Hawk-hunting sharpens vision. Pouring away behind the moving bird, the land flows out from the eye in deltas of piercing colour. The angled eye strikes through the surface dross as the obliqued axe cuts to the heart of the tree. A vivid sense of place glows like another limb. Direction has colour and meaning. South is a bright, blocked place, opaque and stifling; West is a thickening of the earth into trees, a drawing together, the great beef side of England, the heavenly haunch; North is open, bleak, a way to nothing; East is a quickening in the sky, a beckoning of light, a storming suddenness of sea. Time is measured by a clock of blood. When one is active, close to the hawk, pursuing, the pulse races, time goes faster; when one is still, waiting, the pulse quietens, time is slow. Always, as one hunts for the hawk, one has an oppressive sense of time contracting inwards like a tightening spring. One hates the movement of the sun, the steady alteration of the light, the increase of hunger, the maddening metronome of the heart-beat. When one says 'ten o'clock' or 'three o'clock,' this is not the grey and shrunken time of towns; it is the memory of a certain fulmination or declension of light that was unique to that time and that place on that day, a memory as vivid to the hunter as burning magnesium. As soon as the hawk-hunter steps from his door he knows the way of the wind, he feels the weight of the air. Far within himself he seems to see the hawk's day growing steadily towards the light of their first encounter. Time and the weather hold both hawk and watcher between their turning poles. When the hawk is found, the hunter can look lovingly back at all the tedium and misery of searching and waiting that went before. All is transfigured, as though the broken columns of a ruined temple had suddenly resumed their ancient splendour.

I shall try to make plain the bloodiness of killing. Too often this has been slurred over by those who defend hawks. Flesh-eating man is in no way superior. It is so easy to love the dead. The word 'predator' is baggy with misuse. All birds eat living flesh at some time in their lives. Consider the cold-eyed thrush, that springy carnivore of lawns, worm stabber, basher to death of snails. We should not sentimentalise his song, and forget the killing that sustains it.

In my diary of a single winter I have tried to preserve a unity, binding together the bird, the watcher, and the place that holds them both. Everything I describe took place while I was watching it, but I do not believe that honest observation is enough. The emotions and behaviour of the watcher are also facts, and they must be truthfully recorded.

For ten years I followed the peregrine. I was possessed by it. It was a grail to me. Now it has gone. The long pursuit is over. Few peregrines are left, there will be fewer, they may not survive. Many die on their backs, clutching insanely at the sky in their last convulsions, withered and burnt away by the filthy, insidious pollen of farm chemicals. Before it is too late, I have tried to recapture the extraordinary beauty of this bird and to convey the wonder of the land he lived in, a land to me as profuse and glorious as Africa. It is a dying world, like Mars, but glowing still.

CRAW SUNDAY

Amanda Thomson

Amanda Thomson is a visual artist and writer who is also a lecturer at the Glasgow School of Art. Her first book, *A Scots Dictionary of Nature*, is published by Saraband Books (2018). Originally trained as a printmaker, her interdisciplinary work is often about notions of home, movements, migrations, landscapes, the natural world and how places come to be made. She has exhibited nationally and internationally, and her writing has appeared in *The Willowherb Review*, *Gutter* and *Antlers of Water: Writing on the Nature and Environment of Scotland*, edited by Kathleen Jamie. She earned her doctorate in interdisciplinary arts practice, based around the landscapes and the forests of the north of Scotland, in 2013. She lives and works in Glasgow and in Strathspey in the Scottish Highlands. A collaboration with Elizabeth Reeder, *microbursts: a collection of lyric and intermedial essays*, will be published by Proto-type Publishing in spring 2021.

corvid (*genus*) a bird of the crow family (*Corvidae*)
corbie, *corby* the raven. This like the pyat or magpie, as well
    as the harmless crow, is, in the estimation of the vulgar and
    superstitious, a bird of evil omen.

Driving just outside Glasgow, I'm on the road that cuts north around the west side of the Campsie Fells between the towns of Lennoxtown and Fintry. It is the B822 and is known as the Crow Road, and yes, five or six rooks fly over. The phrase 'to take the Crow Road' comes into my head, and I've heard some use the phrase to mean take the most direct route, and others use it to mean die.

Another day and further north, I'm on the A9, the main artery from the Central Belt into the Highlands of Scotland, and around me rooks and carrion crows in particular seem the most ubiquitous of birds. They insinuate themselves into the landscape, gathering in the fields, perching on and flying above the trees, sitting on the lines between telephone poles and sometimes sweeping down onto the road to pick at roadkill – rabbits, pheasants, an occasional deer. They play chicken with the traffic, taking off at the very last moment as cars speed towards them at sixty miles an hour.

Crows abound in Scotland. There are rooks, carrion crows and jackdaws in our woods and fields; magpies in our cities; ravens on our mountains and cliffs; jays in our woodlands; and choughs, black with red, curved bills, on the islands of Islay and Colonsay. In the north of Scotland, the carrion crow makes way for the hooded crow, with its grey body and black hood, wings and tail. There's a space somewhere between south and north where the ranges of carrion crows and hoodies overlap – and it's proven that hoodies occasionally hybridise with the carrion crow. And all summer here there's been a carrion crow with just a hint of a grey shoulder and I wonder at its provenance. When I'm travelling north, I always wonder when I'll see my first hoodie, though I know that the further west I am, the further south they are likely to be. By the time I get to Sutherland, it's the hoodie that prevails, although in the future this may change. It's thought that since the mid-nineteenth century, climate change has benefited carrion crows and their range has extended north. Some speculate the biggest threat to the survival of the hoodie is this cousin, and if we look at the numbers of these birds, we can see why.

The numbers of crows in Scotland are astonishing. Hoodies exist in the tens of thousands, but carrion crows, and the smaller, grey-naped jackdaws, number in the hundreds of thousands. According to the Scottish Ornithologists' Club's epic two-volume *Birds of Scotland*, Scotland has some of the highest breeding densities for rooks in Europe, with up to half a million breeding birds, rising to a winter population of between 1 million and 1.75 million with the annual influx of European visitors. That's a wintering population of upwards of 2 million crows.

glouk (n., v.) the sound made by crows over carrion

Once, up in Morayshire, I saw some rooks rise from a field and begin to gather with others – enough to catch my attention, but nothing exceptional. Still, something made me follow them, guessing at which unfamiliar side roads to take, not knowing where I was going. They landed on the tops of a stand of trees beside a sports centre. It was towards dusk, and I watched, then filmed, their restless movements from stillness to flight, stillness to flight. As it grew dark, they took off, and when I turned to watch them go, I saw them join hundreds, perhaps thousands of other crows over distant fields, forming a kettling mass of black specks, their wingbeats unhurried, like slo-mo, looser versions of flocks of starlings or the flights of knot that swarm over the water just beyond the shoreline.

If I had not filmed them I would not think that I had seen that many. Now, even with the video of these rooks and jackdaws reeling lazily in the darkening sky, they exist as one of those moments that rest just beyond my peripheral gaze, and though I've been back to that place at the same time, in another year, I have seen nothing like it again, although for two winters now, close to the Spey in the hinterlands of Abernethy Forest, I've found the same phenomenon and watched thousands of rooks and jackdaws fly in in waves for a noisy night-time roost on a pylon. They populate every horizontal girder and line the adjoining wires for a hundred metres, causing them to sag. If something startles them and several of them take off, the reverberation quivers along the wire like a Mexican wave, causing a mass exodus into the night sky before they alight on the cables once more.

Unlike carrion and hooded crows, who tend to stay in pairs or in family groups, rooks and jackdaws are known for their gregariousness and tendency to flock, and that's what I saw and heard that gloaming. During the day, many of these birds can be found on the fringes of woodlands. What I saw that dusk in Morayshire were rooks and jack-daws gathering together before they poured into nearby woodlands to roost overnight in the trees, and what I heard was the lower, guttural calls of the rooks mingling with the higher-pitched sounds of the jackdaws in outrageous cacophony.

Actually, words mostly fail to describe the insistent penetration of their calls, though bird books have to try. The *Collins Bird Guide* describes the call of the rook as being 'hoarse, nasal, noisy croaks without open rolling r-sound of carrion crows, more grinding and irascible "geaah", "geeeh", "gra gra grah"'. The Mitchell Beazley *Birdwatcher's Pocket Guide* states the rook's 'prolonged "kaak" call is higher pitched than Crow' and describes the jackdaw as having 'ringing "keeack" and "kyaw" calls in its wide vocabulary'. The Collins guide further describes the jackdaw as having 'a jolting "kya", readily repeated in energetic series, harder "kyack!", drawn out "kyaar" and slightly harsher "tschreh",' though it goes on to note that 'details and volume vary with mood'. The mood, to me, seems to always hover between irascibility and tetchiness and there's a perpetual restlessness to the air, in movement and in sound.

> *rook* (n., v.) a disturbance, uproar; a noisy company; a set of boisterous companions; a house swarming with inmates; to cry like a raven or crow

The eighteen-volume *Edinburgh Encyclopaedia*, published in the 1830s, contains a more lyrical description of a chorus of rooks: 'The rook has but two or three notes, and makes no great figure in a solo; but when he performs in concert, which is his chief delight, these notes, though rough in themselves, being intermixed with those of the multitude, have, as it were, their ragged edges worn off, and become harmonious when softened in the distant air.'

Still, there's more to what draws me to these birds. Perhaps it is their very blackness, and their other(ed)-yet-connectedness. Crows have always spoken to, and had a close relationship with, us humans. They speak to our humanity and our connections to nature. When I look at them, I see their intelligence, their co-operation and their power. How they control the air and wind currents above a stand of trees. But I'm also aware of their association with domains more disquieting and unnerving. It is, after all, an *unkindness of ravens*; *a murder of crows*. The language of crows pulls us into a myriad of different eras, frames of reference, attitudes and realms both everyday and preternatural; to the facts and fictions of them and how they continue to speak, and to crow, to us.

—m—

A *craw's nest* means a robber's den in old Scots; to sit *like a craw in the mist* is 'to sit in the dark'. To have *a craw* (*in one's throat*) means 'to have a strong craving for drink, especially that induced by a night's debauch'. In the *Edinburgh Encyclopaedia*, the birds are described as follows: 'For the most part they are sagacious, active, and faithful to one another, living in pairs, and forming a sort of society, in which there appears something like a regular government and concert in the warding off threatened danger.' And though the word 'rookery' now refers to their night-time roosts, in the eighteenth and nineteenth centuries a rookery was also a slang term used for a slum. Thus Thomas Beames wrote in *The Rookeries of London: Past, Present, and Prospective* (1852), 'Doubtless there is some analogy between these pauper colonies and the nests of the birds from whom they take their name; the houses for the most part high and narrow, the largest possible number crowded together in a given space.'

The anthropologist Claude Lévi-Strauss suggested that the raven is a mediator between life and death. Max Porter's recent and beautiful *Grief Is the Thing with Feathers* brings Crow to a father and two sons suddenly bereaved of a mother. Says his Crow, 'I find humans dull except in grief. There are very few in health, disaster, famine, atrocity, splendour or normality that interest me (interest ME!) but motherless children do. Motherless children are pure crow. For a sentimental bird it is ripe, rich and delicious to raid such a nest.' Liz Lochhead has a corbie commentator in her play *Mary Queen of Scots Got Her Head Chopped Off*. 'National bird: the crow, the corbie, le corbeau, moi! How me? Eh? Eh? Eh? Voice like a choked laugh. Ragbag o' a burd in ma black duds, aw angles and elbows and broken oxter feathers, black beady een in ma executioner's hood. No braw, but ah think ah ha'e some sort of black glamour?'

Research has found that crows can remember faces, and they have been shown to hold grudges. Other work has found that American crows have 'funerals' – or at least, will stay close to their dead for a time, perhaps to see if they can learn what constituted the threat.

>*hoodie* (n.) a hooded crow; a hired mourner

Rooks apparently pair for life. Research on rooks seems to show that they remain in the sites where they breed – some rookeries are many decades old – and they often nest in the colony where they were born. Such reliability and loyalty to place may explain why in auld Scots the first Sunday in March used to be referred to as *Craw Sunday*, the date 'on which crows were traditionally supposed to start to build nests', or, as D. Gilmour wrote in 1873, 'that day when crows commenced housekeeping for the year'.

> Old Scottish phrases speak of crow collectivity:
> *a craw's bridal*
> *a craw's court*
> *a waddin o' craws*
> *a jet-tribe*

A more ambiguous relationship or perhaps distrust of them can further be seen in the older Scots tongue: a *corbie-messenger* was 'a messenger who returns either not at all or too late', and the adjective *hoodock* meant 'foul and greedy, like a hoody or carrion crow', or 'miserly'. Their presence and symbolism, and sometimes their nuisance, have been noted over hundreds of years. P. Hume Brown, in *A Short History of Scotland*, writes that during the reign of James I (1406–37),

> There must also have been great numbers of crows in Scotland in those days, as a very curious law shows us. Every landlord was commanded to kill the young crows every year, as, when they grew up they did so much damage to the crops. If the landlord did not obey this law, then the tree in which the crows had built their nests was to be taken from him by the king. If the landlord liked, however, he could fell the tree and pay a fine of five shillings.

Crows are still considered a 'pest species' today, and, with a licence, they can be trapped or shot. For all the gregariousness and sociability we see in rooks and jackdaws, it's hard to shift the malevolence often associated with the bigger crows in particular. Even now, the *Collins Bird Guide* describes rooks' nests as looking like 'large witches' brooms'. But it's the crows' relationship with carrion that defines most of our perceptions of their appetites and character: an old Scots word for a carrion crow is *gore-craw*, and the old folk song 'Twa Corbies', or another version, 'Three Ravens', describes the birds wondering where they will eat, before they espy, then feed on the body of a newly dead knight they see lying in a field.

Back to the nineteenth century and the *Edinburgh Encyclopedia* describes crow predation and their eating habits in florid detail:

> In spring, they greedily devour the eggs of quails and partridges, and are so dexterous as to pierce them and carry them on the point of their bill to their young. Even fish and fruits are not unsuitable to their palate. They often attack the eyes of dying animals, destroy weakly lambs, and, when pressed with hunger, will even pursue birds on the wing.

Rooks, it warns, 'not only attack the eyes of lambs and diseased sheep, but of horses that have got entangled in bogs'. Seton Gordon, writing in the early twentieth century, describes the voraciousness of a hooded crow:

> ... a newly-dropped lamb or a sickly ewe may be set upon by a number of Grey Crows and the unlucky victim's eyes pulled out while the breath is still in the body. To the shepherds of the western coasts he is the embodiment of evil. To them he is *An t-eun Acarachd* – 'the bird without compassion' – and they name him truly indeed.

And yet, although crows have long been accused of such heinous acts, the reality is that mostly, their diet is relatively benign, jackdaws eating mainly invertebrates and occasionally seeds and carrion, though they can also prey on the nests of hedgerow and garden birds. The hooded crow has been blamed for killing game birds and lambs, though more recent research has disputed this. Rooks, though they do eat carrion, also feed on invertebrates and, in the winter in particular, cereal grains. It's noted in *The Birds of Scotland (Vol 2)* that some carrion crows, in winter, 'use intertidal areas to feed on shellfish'. These are smart, opportunistic birds.

gore-crow (n.) the carrion crow

More mystically perhaps, according to a nineteenth-century Scots dictionary, *a craw's-court* is described as 'A court of judgment held by crows'. The entry goes on to describe such a thing:

> Numbers [of crows] are seen to assemble on a particular hill or field, from many different points. On some occasions the meeting does not appear to be complete before the expiration of a day or two. As soon as all the deputies have arrived, a very general noise and croaking ensue, and shortly after, the whole fall upon one or two individuals, whom they persecute and beat until they kill them. When this has been accomplished, they quietly disperse.

In another version, Seton Gordon describes how a 'craas' court' of hoodies 'convened' every springtime in the Shetland Islands: 'A large flock of Hoodies appear from all directions. Apparently the court is held for the purpose of dealing out sentences to certain Crows who have been guilty of some offence, for after an hour or so of deliberation the whole assembly turn fiercely on certain individuals and peck them to death.'

The Reverend Dr W. Forsyth relates this story in his book, *In the Shadow of Cairngorm*, published in 1900:

> There was at one time a large rookery in the alders at Coulnakyle. Captain Macdonald, then holding the farm (1826), vowed its destruction. He hired a squad of men and boys, and set them to work. The boys tore down the nests, and the men kept up a

constant fusilade, so as to prevent the rooks from settling. The war went on for some days. Now and again a bird came too near and fell a prey to the marksmen, but most were wary, and kept a safe distance.

At last the rooks seemed to recognise that they were beaten. They held a gathering in a neighbouring field. There was much cawing and conferring, but no reporter to give their speeches. The question was in due time settled. The rooks, as if acting under orders, arose and flew towards the alders, but instead of settling on the trees, they mounted up high above, so as to be safe from all the harm. Then they went through a kind of march, sailing calmly to and fro, and doubtless casting many a longing glance on their old home. By and by they altered their tune. The march became a quickstep, merging into a wild, whirling, commingling dance. It was, as a spectator described it, for all the world like a 'Reel of Tulloch':

> The dancers quick and quicker flew,
> They reel'd, they set, they cross'd, they cleekit.

Then suddenly there was a stop – with a great caw-cawing. Then utter quietness. Out from the rest flew a leader, took his place in front, and like an arrow from a bow, started off. The others fell in line and followed. Suddenly the whole body winged their flight straight for the Boat of Cromdale, where, in the fir-wood over the Spey, they established their new home, and where, unmolested, they have dwelt from generation to generation ever since.

The Highlanders hold that it is unlucky to disturb a rookery; and it was noted that Captain Macdonald, some years later, had reluctantly to flit from Coulnakyle, and to make his home at Clury, which he never loved so well.

There are times when I've been out at dusk and I first hear, then when I look up, see, restless flights of crows – rooks and jackdaws – rising above fields and deuking above and in between trees. Their insistence makes me seek out where they land, sometimes walking through woods to find the source of the racket, before I turn and make my way home before night falls.

A version of 'Craw Sunday' was first published in Gutter, *no. 21, March 2020.*

SOURCES

The impetus for this essay, and the Scots words and definitions for crows, are taken from various nineteenth- and early twentieth-century Scots-language dictionaries, including an abridged version of Jamieson's *A Dictionary of the Scottish Language* and Warrack's *The Scots Dialect Dictionary*.

Other Books

Beames, T., *The Rookeries of London: Past, Present, and Prospective* (London: Thomas Bosworth, 1852).

Brewster, D., *The Edinburgh Encyclopedia* (Philadelphia: J & E Parker, 1832).

Forrester, R. & I. Andrews (eds), *The Birds of Scotland, Vols 1 & 2* (Scottish Ornithologists' Club, 2007).

Forsyth, Rev. W., *In the Shadow of Cairngorm* (The Northern Counties Publishing Company Ltd., 1900).

Gilmour, D., *Reminiscences of the Pen Folk* (Paisley, Alex Gardner, 1873). Referenced in www.dsl.ac.uk.

Gordon, S., *The Hill Birds of Scotland* (London: Edward Arnold, 1915).

Hayman, P., *The Mitchell Beazley Birdwatcher's Pocket Guide* (London: Mitchell Beazley, 1979).

Holmes, B., 'If you think that crow is giving you the evil eye', *New Scientist*, issue 2745, 2010.

Hume Brown, P., *A Short History of Scotland* (Edinburgh: Oliver and Boyd, 1908).

Jamieson, J., *A Dictionary of the Scottish Language* (Edinburgh: William P Nimmo, 1867).

Lochhead, L., *Mary Queen of Scots Got Her Head Chopped Off* (London: Nick Hern Books, 2014).

Mullarney, K., L. Svensson, D. Zetterström, P. J. Grant, *Collins Bird Guide* (London: HarperCollins, 1999).

Nethersole-Thompson, D., *Highland Birds* (Highlands and Islands Development Board, 1978).

Porter, M., *Grief Is the Thing with Feathers* (London: Faber & Faber, 2015).

Swift, K. N. and J. M. Marzluff, 'Wild American crows gather around their dead to learn about danger', *Animal Behaviour*, vol. 109., 2015.

Warrack, A., *The Scots Dialect Dictionary* (Edinburgh: W & R Chambers, 1911).

Music

Malinky (2002), 'Three Ravens', *3 Ravens*, Greentrax Recordings Ltd.

Tannara (2016), 'Three Ravens', *Trig*, Braw Sailing Records.

Mavericks and
Underdogs

Illustration overleaf: *Ragwort*

from A KESTREL FOR A KNAVE

Barry Hines

Melvin Barry Hines (1939–2016) is best known for his second novel, *A Kestrel for a Knave* (1968), which he also helped adapt for Ken Loach's film *Kes* (1969). He was born in the mining village of Hoyland Common, near Barnsley, attended grammar school and left with five O-levels. He was a talented footballer who played for England Grammar Schools and Barnsley reserves, and was invited to a trial at Manchester United but took a job as an apprentice mining surveyor at a colliery. He later returned to school for A-levels and became a PE teacher in London and later in Barnsley. He wrote novels in the library after his pupils had gone home. His first, *The Blinder*, about a young footballer, was published in 1966. He later became a full-time writer, collaborating with Loach to turn his novels *The Gamekeeper* and *Looks and Smiles* into films. He wrote the script for the BAFTA award-winning TV film *Threads* (1984), about the impact of a nuclear war on Sheffield.

The moon was almost complete, its outline well defined, except for the blur on the waxing curve. The sky was cloudless, the air still warm, but when he reached the fields it cooled slightly, taking on a fresher, sharper quality. The moon made it light in the fields, and lent the grass a silver sheen, and the piebald hides of the cows were clearly visible in this silvery light. The wood was a narrow black band beyond the fields, growing taller and taller as Billy approached, until it formed a curtain stretched out before him, and the top of the curtain appeared to touch the stars directly above.

He climbed on to the stile and looked into the trees. It was dark on both sides of the path, but above the path the foliage was thinner, and the light from the moon penetrated and lit the way. Billy stepped down off the stile and entered the wood. The trunks and branches lining the path formed pillars and lintels, terraced doorways leading into dark interiors. He hurried by them, glancing in, right and left. A scuffle to his left. He side-stepped to the right and began to run, the pad of his feet and the rasp of his breath filtering far into the trees, WO-HU-WO-HOOOO. WO-HU-WO-HOOOO. He stopped and listened, trying to control his breathing, WO-HU-WO-HOOO. Somewhere ahead; the long falter radiating back through the trees. Billy linked his fingers, placed his thumbs together and blew into the split between them. The only sound he produced was that of rushing air. He licked his lips and tried again, producing a wheeze, which he swiftly worked up into a single hoot and developed into a strident imitation of the tawny owl's call. He listened. There was no response, so he repeated it, this time working for the softer, more wavering sound, by stuttering his breath into the sound chamber. And out it came, as clear and as clean as a blowing of bubbles. His call was immediately answered. Billy grinned and answered back. He started to walk again, and maintained contact with the owl for the rest of the distance through the wood.

The farmhouse was in darkness. Billy carefully climbed over the wall into the orchard and ran crouching across to the ruins. He stood back from the wall and looked up at it. The moon illuminated the face of the wall, picking out the jut of individual stones, and shading in the cracks and hollows between them. Billy selected his route, found a foothold, a handhold, and began to climb. Very slowly and very carefully, testing each hold thoroughly before trusting it with his weight. His fingers finding the spaces, then tugging at the surrounding stones as though testing loose teeth. If any stones moved he felt again, remaining still until he was satisfied. Slowly. Hand. Foot. Hand. Foot. Never stretching, never jerking. Always compact, always balanced. Sometimes crabbing to by-pass gaps in the stonework, sometimes back-tracking several moves to explore a new line; but steadily meandering upwards, making for the highest window.

As he climbed, his feet and hands dislodged a trickle of plaster and stone dust, and birds brushed his knuckles as they flashed out of their nest holes. Occasionally he dislodged a small stone or a lump of plaster, and when he felt this happen he paused during the time of its fall, and for a time after it had landed.

But there were no alarms, and he reached the window and hooked his left arm over the stone sill. He slapped the stone and sh sh'd at the hole at the other end of the sill. Nothing happened so he climbed astride and hutched across to the nest hole. He peered in, but there was nothing to see, so he stretched belly flop along the sill and felt into the hole, wriggling further along as his arm went further in. He felt around, then withdrew his hand grasping a struggling eyas kestrel. He sat up, caged the bird in his hands, then placed it carefully into the big pocket inside his jacket. Five times he felt into the hole and each time fetched out a young hawk. Some were slightly larger than others, some more fully feathered, with less down on their backs and heads, but each one came out gasping, beaks open, legs pedalling the air.

When he had emptied the nest he reversed the procedure, dipping into his pocket for an eyas and holding it in one hand while he compared it with another. By a process of elimination, he placed them back into the nest until he was left with only one; the one with most feathers and only a little down on its head. He lowered it back into the pocket, then held his hand up to catch the light of the moon. Both back and palm were bleeding and scratched, as though he had been nesting in a hawthorn hedge.

When he reached the bottom of the wall he opened his jacket and clucked down into the pocket. The weight at the bottom stirred. He placed one hand underneath it for support, and set off back across the orchard. Once over the wall, he started to whistle, and he whistled and hummed to himself all the way home…

from WILDING

Isabella Tree

Isabella Tree (b. 1964) is a travel writer now best known for *Wilding* (2018), the story of her pioneering transformation of a failing 3,500-acre dairy and arable farm in West Sussex with her husband, Charlie Burrell. She published her first book, *The Bird Man: A Biography of John Gould*, when she was twenty-five, followed by *Islands in the Clouds*, *Sliced Iguana* and *The Living Goddess* about travels in New Guinea, Mexico and Nepal. Her award-winning travel writing has appeared in publications including *National Geographic*, *Granta*, *The Sunday Times* and the *Observer*. She and Burrell have become hugely influential conservationists since abandoning conventional farming and rewilding their Knepp estate in 2000. They introduced free-roaming wild cattle, pigs, deer and horses, which drive the creation of new habitats which have proved conducive to rare and declining species such as turtle doves and nightingales. Knepp has inspired many other British landowners and conservation NGOs – as well as readers – to rewild their fields, woods and gardens.

LIVING WITH THE YELLOW PERIL

Ragwort, thou humble flower with tattered leaves
I love to see thee come and litter gold.
What time the summer binds her russet sheaves;
Decking rude spots in beauties manifold…

John Clare, 'The Ragwort', *Poems of the Middle Period*
vol. IV, 1832

Many of our neighbours' concerns were allayed over the first few years. No one was gored by fallow bucks during the rut. The Exmoor ponies, with Duncan removed from the herd, were giving no bother to riders on the bridleways. We heard no more from the woman who insisted children should walk with escorts on the footpaths because of attacks from free-roaming animals. Longhorn cows with their calves – once a 'disaster waiting to happen' – were even welcomed by some, glad to see these handsome cattle back in an area where dairy farming was continuing to decline. We were mindful of potential flashpoints. On the footpaths and green lanes we did our best to roll areas that had been churned up by the pigs or badly 'poached', or trampled, by the traffic of animals in wet weather. Neighbouring landowners told us that on their lands, too, complaints about mud, uneven ground and the potential for twisted ankles were on the rise – an indication, it seemed, of an increasingly urban attitude to the countryside.

But one particular aspect of the project refused – and continues to refuse – to lie down. The furore was so intense that at one point it threatened to derail the project altogether. To many people, the most offensive aspect of the Knepp project, epitomizing our neglectful ways and ranging in locals' minds from a 'great disappointment' to an 'unmitigated disaster', is the appearance of 'injurious' weeds. 'Sir Charles has turned a well-farmed estate into a wasteland of thistles, docks and ragwort,' wrote an observer to the *County Times*. Of these three offending species, by far the worst seems to have been – and continues to be – common ragwort. One *County Times* reader was so incensed he was stirred to poetry:

Knepp Castle, ragwort shame
Spread like a plague, and who's to blame?
A sea of yellow, such a disgrace
This poisonous weed takes over the place.
They leave it growing for the 'ground-nesting birds'
But where are they? Never seen nor heard.
Meantime it spreads onto neighbours' land.
Stop this pollution! This we demand.

'Conservation', they cry – a convenient excuse.
Not in my book – it's neglect and abuse.
Readers write letters to the *County Times*
But what about DEFRA – shouldn't there be fines?
This year worst of all, they've had a bad press
But will Knepp Castle tackle this mess?
Mr Burrell take action, this I implore
Or next year we'll be on to you, like never before.

Common ragwort (*Senecio jacobaea*) is native to the Eurasian continent. In Europe it is widely spread from Scandinavia to the Mediterranean, and is naturally abundant in Britain and Ireland. Standing generally around three feet tall, it produces dense, flat-topped clusters of bright yellow flowers from June onwards, and is commonly found on wasteland, waysides and in grazing pastures, where even a rabbit scrape provides enough bare ground for it to germinate. With rootling pigs and the disturbing hooves of herbivores, not to mention thousands of burrowing rabbits, the opportunities for it to flourish on our post-agricultural land are manifold. But in 2008 it was particularly virulent. Being a biennial and responding vigorously to stress, it abounds two years on from a drought summer, like the one we had in 2006. The dry April of 2007 had facilitated germination even further and, in the words of another *County Times* reader, we were seeing 'field after field of ragwort blowing in the breeze'.

The moral outrage ragwort engenders in Britain is usually aimed at alien invasives like Japanese knotweed. Hostility to a plant that has been part of our environment since the last ice age is a peculiar new phenomenon. Less than two centuries ago the poet John Clare was extolling its 'shining blossoms… of rich sunshine'. The Isle of Man knows it as 'cushag' – its national flower. Yet to the rest of Britain ragwort is an evil to be expunged from the world. Its sulphur-yellow flowers are rags to irascible bulls. Feelings run so high that recent attempts by DEFRA and the Wildlife & Countryside Link – a coalition of forty-six conservation organizations – to encourage a sensible approach have failed to dent anti-ragwort propaganda.

The loudest accusation of all is that it is a killer of livestock.

Ragwort is, indeed, a poisonous plant. It contains pyrrolizidine alkaloids – toxins that, when eaten in large quantities by mammals, cause liver-failure and death. But grazing animals have lived with it for tens of thousands of years. Our own longhorns, Exmoors, Tamworths, roe, fallow (and subsequently red) deer graze amongst ragwort with no adverse effects whatsoever. They know to avoid it. The plant itself warns them away with its bitter taste and a smell so bad it has been immortalized in British history. After the Battle of Culloden in 1746, when the victorious English are said to have renamed the garden flower 'Sweet William' in honour of William, Duke of Cumberland, the defeated Scots retaliated by naming ragwort 'Stinking Willy'. In Shropshire and Cheshire its name is 'Mare's Fart'.

The problem of poisoning arises not in the wild but where fields and paddocks are overgrazed and the animals have no choice but to eat it, or when ragwort is cut into silage or hay and the animals are unable to detect and avoid it. Even then, the animal has to eat an excessive amount – an estimated 5–25 per cent of body weight for horses and cattle and 125–400 per cent for goats – for it to be fatal.

The source of the most recent wave of ragwort hysteria can be laid at the door of the British Equine Veterinary Association and the British Horse Society. In 2002 they published the results of a survey claiming that as many as 6,500 of the UK population of around 600,000 horses die every year from ingesting ragwort. It was an astonishing leap from the average of ten ragwort-associated horse deaths per year estimated by the Ministry of Agriculture, Fisheries and Food in 1990. The BEVA's claim – it emerged – was based on bad science. 4 per cent of BEVA members had responded to the survey, reporting that they had seen, on average, three 'suspected' (note, not 'confirmed') cases of ragwort poisoning (note – not deaths) that year. The BEVA had then simply multiplied this average by the full BEVA membership of 1,945 to produce a total of 6,553 cases for that year. No one at the BEVA seems to have considered the most likely reason that the majority of vets failed to respond to their survey was that they had no cases to report. Despite the fallibility of their reasoning and their having subsequently removed the misinformation from their website the BEVA-based myth has developed a life of its own, particularly in the folklore of horsiculture. As the old adage goes, a lie can get halfway round the world before truth has got its boots on.

But then British antagonism towards John Clare's 'humble flower' has stubborn roots – as difficult to grub out, it seems, as the roots of ragwort itself. The ground in which the prejudice first germinated was opened up by the Weeds Act back in 1959. The Weeds Act singled out ragwort and four other species – broad-leaved dock, curled dock, creeping thistle and spear thistle – and labelled them 'injurious'. Back then, the Act had, specifically, agricultural interests in mind. These are weeds that, if uncontrolled, can have a significant impact on arable production in terms of lost revenue from lower crop yields. Creeping thistle, for example, exudes pheromones which inhibit the germination of most grain crops. In the case of ragwort, the cost is in eradicating it from fields and paddocks so it is not processed into animal fodder.

But 'injurious' is a provocative word, a fluttering skull and cross-bones that has waved a welcome to all sorts of scare-mongering over 'pernicious' plants ever since. A common misconception is that ragwort is poisonous to human touch even though the plant's pyrrolizidine alkaloids (which occur naturally in 3 per cent of all flowering plants) cannot be absorbed through the skin. Breathing in ragwort pollen, it is claimed, can give you liver damage, though this, too, is a physical impossibility. Honey from bees feeding on ragwort was recently head-lined in the *Daily Mail* as poisonous to humans, though DEFRA has described this risk as both 'highly unlikely' and 'negligible'. Bees invariably take nectar and pollen from numerous other poisonous flowers including foxgloves and daffodils. Yet none of these have ever been accused of poisoning honey.

Opponents of ragwort, pointing the finger at the offensive weed on other people's land, routinely claim the moral high ground. Land-owners and local councils, they insist, are obliged by law to eradicate it wherever it occurs. But this is categorically not the case. Neither are the five weed species listed under the Weed Act 'notifiable' – there is no such concept in UK law.

The Ragwort Control Act of 2003 – an amendment to the Weeds Act of 1959 – has done little to clarify the situation and allay public fears despite publishing a Code of Practice, under pressure from the Wildlife and Countryside Link, which clearly states that 'common ragwort and other ragwort species are native to the British Isles and are therefore an inherent part of our flora and fauna, along with invertebrate and other wildlife they support. The Code does not propose the eradication of common ragwort but promotes a strategic approach to control the spread of common ragwort where it poses a threat to the health and welfare of grazing animals and the production of feed or forage.'

The government's own guidelines still appear somewhat conflicted and inflammatory about ragwort and other 'injurious' weeds. 'It's not an offence to have these weeds growing on your land', it states in 2014 Land Management advice, but 'you must... prevent harmful weeds on your land from spreading onto a neighbour's property'. While stating it will only take action if these weeds are threatening land used for livestock, forage or agriculture, at the same time it encourages people to 'complain about harmful weeds' on their neighbours' land, and provides an 'injurious weeds complaint form' with which to do so.

It seems that the damage is done. Few people in the countryside nowadays are able to accept common ragwort's place in nature, let alone celebrate it as John Clare did. No one sees it as a beautiful, dazzling explosion of sunshine and – perhaps more importantly – no one values its ecological contribution to our lives. Though we protest that we love nature it seems that this is only on our own terms. We have become a nation of gardeners, more interested in exotic flowers than natives. Plantlife, the environmental organization that seeks to safeguard our wild vegetation, has a membership of 10,500. The Royal Horticultural Society has 434,000. Even Prince Charles, champion of wildflower meadows, patron of Plantlife, in 2015 petitioned Natural England to change its stance on ragwort and 'tackle the problem more proactively'.

Yet the very fact that ragwort is not grazed, leaving it standing when other flowering plants have been nibbled away (and therefore glaringly conspicuous to its critics), should be cause for celebration. Ragwort is one of the most sustaining hosts to insects we have. Seven species of beetle, twelve species of flies, one macromoth – the cinnabar, with its distinctive black-and-yellow rugby jersey caterpillars – and seven micromoths feed exclusively on common ragwort. It is a major source of nectar for at least thirty species of solitary bees, eighteen species of solitary wasps and fifty insect parasites. In all, 177 species of insects use common ragwort as a source of nectar or pollen. When most of the other flowers have died, ragwort continues on into late summer, providing a vital source of nectar. We have it at Knepp sometimes as late as November. Even at night its bursts of luminous yellow attract nocturnal moths – forty species of them. The effect of this boost to insect life is colossal. Natural England, itself, describes the number of predators and parasites dependent on the invertebrate resource supported by common ragwort as 'incalculable'; while its attractiveness to carrion-associated insects plays a key role in supporting the decomposition cycle.

Despite these benefits to our wildlife, anti-ragwort propaganda has, in recent years, inspired eradication programmes anywhere that ragwort appears, including on roadsides and in wildflower meadows, and – incredibly – in areas designated for conservation as Sites of Special Scientific Interest. Broad-spectrum herbicides are often the chosen agent of destruction, causing – inevitably – collateral damage. But even when uprooted by hand there can be losses to other flora. Other native yellow flowering plants – like hoary ragwort, marsh ragwort, tansy, St John's wort and hawkweed – are commonly mistaken for it. Weeds, as the saying goes, are plants in the wrong place – only now, it seems, everywhere is the wrong place for ragwort.

To put ragwort in context, it is only one of a considerable number of plants that can be fatal if eaten by horses and other livestock. In Southern England common species that can kill grazing animals include foxglove, cuckoo pint, ivy, black bryony, white bryony, bracken, elder, spindle and yew. In March our woods in the Northern Block are carpeted with native wild daffodils – a rare sight since nineteenth- and twentieth-century plant collectors dug most of them up elsewhere in the country. The daffodil – both wild and domesticated versions – is one of our most poisonous plants. A few years ago they almost killed a local vicar, who ate a bunch of daffodils to enliven his Easter sermon and had to be rushed to hospital to have his stomach pumped. Yet no one thinks to denigrate them.

The negative reputation of the ragwort derives partly, perhaps, from its method of reproduction. It is not a bulb like the daffodil, and so is thought to be profligate and unpredictable. The number of seeds it can produce varies widely but most reliable sources cite up to 30,000 seeds per plant. They are commonly thought to be carried huge distances by the wind. The explosion of ragwort around Shipley in the summer of 2008 was identified by numerous locals as being a result of seed drifting from Knepp.

A letter Charlie received from the owner of a local stud farm on 8 September 2008, when the ragwort was in full bloom, was one of many:

Sir,

The weed season is here again and may I congratulate you on another bumper crop.

It seems that everyone else is doing their hardest to eliminate ragwort, thistle and dock while you and yours are doing nothing.

I am sure that as part of a Stewardship Scheme you are entitled to do what you are doing but please spare a thought for the people and land all around you to where these seeds are blowing.

I had friends down for the weekend who farm on a large scale near Cambridge and they were appalled at the neglect of the land in the area.

I am sure this letter will have little or no affect but I will of course be finding out from DEFRA how you are able to neglect in this fashion.

Once again, prejudice and alarm outpace science. It was virtually impossible, according to the government's own guidelines, for ragwort to be colonizing the countryside from Knepp. Research has shown that 60 per cent of ragwort seeds fall around the base of the plant, and it is the seed source in the soil, rather than the source from windblown seed, that generally germinates. The seed being blown on the wind is lighter and likely to be infertile. It is estimated that, for a plant producing 30,000 healthy seeds, 18,000 of them land at the base of the plant, 11,700 at 4.5 metres (15 feet) away, and so on, decreasing with distance, until 36 metres (120 feet) away only 1.5 seeds land. In accordance with the code of practice published by DEFRA we had created a 50 metre buffer zone inside our boundary that we keep regularly topped, allowing no weed seed sources to develop, and to further reassure our neighbours we voluntarily pull up ragwort by hand in a further 50 metres. In areas of particular sensitivity where, for example, our land abutted a llama farm, we cut a 100 metre strip – twice the area recommended by DEFRA. Our ragwort seed, viable or not, was – and still is – highly unlikely to be travelling beyond our boundary. According to Professor Mick Crawley, Emeritus Professor of Plant Ecology at Imperial College London, whose ragwort research project, begun in 1981, still continues, 'In our experience, ragwort comes from seed more often from the soil seed bank than from last year's seed production.' The seed can survive for at least ten years in the soil. All it takes is a tiny bit of soil disturbance, which could be no more than the scratchings of a rabbit, and the seed can germinate and recruit to the rosette stage. 'Recruitment in ragwort', he says, 'is usually microsite limited and there are usually plenty of seeds in the soil seed bank to fill up all of the available microsites.'

In the Repton park, where opinions of how a cultural landscape should look are even more acute, and the appearance of ragwort in the closely cropped sward even more conspicuous, we have had to adopt a more Draconian approach. We simply cannot risk jeopardizing the whole project because of the public reaction to a single plant. To this day, across the estate, in a prolific ragwort year, we can spend around £10,000 pulling up a native flower that has countless benefits for wildlife, and is doing no harm to us, our neighbours or our livestock.

We tried our best to explain all this to those who wrote to us but our efforts to allay their anxieties fell, more often than not, on deaf ears. It seemed that there was something more fundamental driving the complaints. Ragwort, like concerns about free-roaming animals, other injurious weeds, unevenness of the ground, even lack of food production, seemed to be symptomatic of some greater sense of unease.

What seemed to exercise our neighbours most about the new regime of management – or lack of it – at Knepp was more nebulous, though perhaps even more disquieting for those living alongside it. It was a question of aesthetics, of what people wanted or were prepared to live with. We were, it seemed to many of our detractors, destroying the native character of our countryside – something they considered to be beautiful, balanced and harmonious; qualities integral to our very existence. 'To my mind,' a local wrote candidly to Charlie in 2007, 'your ex-arable land hurt my sensibilities.'

Aesthetic sensibilities are deeply subjective, and hard to acknowledge and analyse clearly. They take root in us from the moment we're born. They bind us to a particular view of the landscape, something we begin to think of as 'natural' or, at least, benign. What we see as children, particularly where we grow up, becomes what we want to continue to see, and what we want our children to see. Nostalgia, and the sense of security that nostalgia brings, binds us to the familiar. We are persuaded, too, by our own absorption in this aesthetic that what we are seeing has been here for ever. We believe the countryside around us, or something very similar to it, has persisted for centuries and the wildlife within it, if not exactly the same, is at least a fair representation of what has been here for centuries. But the ecological processes of the past are hard for the layman – and often even conservation professionals – to grasp. We are blinded by the immediacy of the present. We look at the landscape and see what is there, not what is missing. And if we do appreciate some sort of ecological loss and change, we tend to go only as far back as our childhood memories, or the memories of our parents or grandparents who tell us 'there used to be hundreds of lapwings in my day', 'skylarks and song thrushes were ten-a-penny', 'the fields round here used to be red with poppies and blue with cornflowers', 'cod was the poor man's fish when I was a nipper'. We are blind to the fact that in our grandparents' grandparents' day there would have been species-rich wildflower meadows in every parish and coppice woods teeming with butterflies. They would have heard corncrakes and bitterns, seen clouds of turtle doves, thousands of lapwings and hundreds more skylarks. A mere four generations ago they knew rivers swimming with burbot – now extinct in Britain – and eels, and their summer nights were peppered with bats and moths and glow-worms. Their grandparents, in turn, saw nightjars settling on dusty country lanes and even hawking for moths around the street lamps in towns, and spotted flycatchers in every orchard, and meadow pipits everywhere from salt-flats to the crowns of mountains. They saw banks of giant cod and migrating tuna in British waters. They saw our muddy North Sea clear as gin, filtered by oyster beds as large as Wales. And their grandparents, in turn, living at the time of the last beaver in Britain, would have known great bustards, and watched shoals of herring five miles long and three miles broad migrating within sight of the shore, chased by schools of dolphins and sperm whales and the occasional great white shark. We don't have to look too deeply into the history books, into contemporary accounts, for scenes dramatically different to our own to be normal. Yet we live in denial of these catastrophic losses.

This continuous lowering of standards and the acceptance of degraded natural ecosystems is known as 'shifting baseline syndrome' – a term coined in 1995 by fisheries scientist Daniel Pauly, who noticed that experts who were charged with evaluating radically depleted fish stocks took as their baseline the state of the fishery at the start of their careers, rather than fish populations in their original state. Hundreds of years ago an area of sea may have been heaving with fish. But scientists' reference point for 'natural' population levels is invariably pinned to levels dating back no more than a few decades from the present. Each generation, Pauly realized, redefines what is 'natural'. Each time the baseline drops it is considered the new normal. Something similar has happened with the British Trust for Ornithology setting 1970 as its baseline year for monitoring British bird populations. Of course, a baseline has to be set somewhere – and the declines since then, meticulously recorded, have been dramatic – but the baseline itself begins to encourage pre-baseline amnesia. We forget that there was once more. Much, much more.

Evidence of shifting baselines was apparent on our first tractor-and-trailer tours of Knepp in the early 2000s, when we began to take mixed generational groups from NGOs like the National Farmers' Union and the Country Landowners' Association around the project.

We were familiar with the usual reaction from our own generation, the forty-to-sixty-somethings. Children of the agricultural revolution were aghast at what we were doing. The twenty-somethings were often more responsive. For them the idea of national food security, of digging for victory, was an anxiety from a bygone age. They had grown up in a time of plenty – an era of globalization, cheap clothes and cheap food, their supermarket shelves stocked with Spanish tomatoes in winter, asparagus from Peru, lamb from New Zealand, tiger prawns from Thailand and beef from Argentina. But they had never heard a turtle dove, and rarely a cuckoo. Most had never seen a living hedgehog. The emptiness of British skies, the absence of birds and butterflies, was their normal. Yet they had also been educated, at school at least, to worry about the environment. Knepp was something new and we watched their confused delight as they waded through insect-filled air, picked up grass snakes and slow-worms, and raised their voices above surround-sound birdsong.

But the real surprise came from the oldest generation. Those in their eighties could remember the agricultural depression between the wars, when marginal land across the country had been abandoned – the era of Charlie's great-grandfather, when most of Knepp had been allowed to revert to scrub. To them, clumps of dog rose and hawthorn, thickets of hazel and sallow – even swathes of ragwort – were not offensive at all. The landscape recalled them, instead, to their childhood ramblings in a countryside heaving with insects and birds, to the days when there was a covey of grey partridges in every field. There was nothing threatening or alarming about what they were seeing. Quite the reverse. To some, it was positively beautiful. 'You don't know what you're talking about,' one old boy berated his son – a baby during the war – who insisted what they were seeing was 'unnatural'. 'This is how the countryside always used to look!'

from CORVUS

Esther Woolfson

The writer and novelist **Esther Woolfson** was brought up in Glasgow and studied Chinese at the Hebrew University of Jerusalem and Edinburgh University. Her award-winning short stories have appeared in many anthologies including *New Writing Scotland*. Her first book, *Corvus: A Life with Birds* (2008), describes learning about the capabilities of other creatures from the birds and animals – rook, magpie, starling, doves, parrots and rats – with whom she and her family lived. *Field Notes from a Hidden City* (2013) examines our relationship with frequently neglected urban species including gulls, slugs and snails. Her latest book, *Between Light and Storm: How We Live with Other Species* (2020), traces the historic origins of our attitudes towards other animals. She lives in Aberdeen.

MADAME CHICKEBOUMSKAYA

The years of keeping doves and other birds laid a foundation, encouraged a kind of enquiring acceptance of whatever, or whoever, might transpire or arrive, and so I was prepared. We all were. The evening the doorbell rang, we were ready, Chicken too, it seemed, smiling from her box, as infant rooks do, with their tragi-comic look, their corvid gravitas wholly at odds with the wide, frilled, amiable look of all small birds. This one, the offspring of the rooks that have lived for a long time in the woods near Crathes Castle, flying through and over its beautiful gardens, its yew hedges and its rose borders, peered from her box, her blue eyes interested, observing us as we were observing her. At once I was fascinated by her black, banded feet and legs, the fineness of her toenails, her pink skin erupting with dark feathers. The inside of her beak was bright, attention-grasping red, opening readily for food. Naturally, I took the advice of Kenton C. Lint. On the subject of feeding members of the crow family, his dietary recommendations were both reassuring and daunting: on the one hand, corvids would eat, it appeared, anything; on the other, part of their daily diet should include

Rodents: 40g

Chicks: 51g

Choice of insects: 14g grasshopper, locusts, crickets, beetles, grubs, moths or mealworms.

In feeding Chicken, I avoided the freshly killed or caught and gave her minced meat and eggs and chopped-up nuts instead. I had had no dealings with an infant corvid but from her learnt that healthy corvid chicks are vigorous, greedy, their beaks sturdy enough for a little finger, food-laden, to be thrust down the waiting throat to the accompaniment of the sounds of strangled gargling. She fed and slept and watched and I carried her around with me everywhere in her box. She sat beside my desk in daytime, on the kitchen floor as I cooked, beside the fire in the evenings. When I greeted her, she greeted me. I was entranced. After some weeks, she began to leap on to the side of her box to stand, clearly anticipating flight. Then, one day, she flew. I picked her up from the table where she had landed and put her back in her box. I realised that this could be only a temporary measure. We looked at one another, this small corvid and myself. *Well,* we seemed to say, at this moment of mutual, inter-species questioning, *what now?* What indeed.

By now it seems at best disingenuous to say that I didn't know enough of birds to consider reintroducing her to the wild. I wouldn't have known how to. Even now I'm not sure that I would know. Her home was fifteen miles away and there were no rooks nearby. The matter seemed simple. She had been brought to us and was, therefore, our responsibility.

We constructed a house for Chicken from wood and wire, forerunner of her present abode, and placed it in the rat room, where the rats houses once stood. Left alone for the brief periods she was, she began the first of her building projects, excavating the wall beside her house, picking determinedly at the plaster until she had removed the top layer. I didn't know then why she did it but there seemed to be no good reason to stop her. Holes can always be filled in.

I can't remember how much attention she got – less, certainly than she does now although she was always with us, always around us, playing with the toys we gave her, the rubber mice she liked to carry in her beak or to punish by shaking, pecking, bashing against the floor, for crimes unknown. She hid under tables, chairs, explored and began to take her place easily in the household. She was small, fluffy-feathered, and ever underfoot. We had to be careful not to stand on her as she pulled at the hems of our jeans or played with our bootlaces. She would fly on to the tops of cupboards and not know how to find her way down. We had to climb up to rescue her. She began to respond to each of us in an individual way, with a different voice, different mannerisms, seeming to know from each of us what she might expect: a certain, limited degree of parental discipline from David and me, teasing fraternal playfulness from Bee and Han. Wisely enough, from the beginning, she understood that I was the one who fed her and although now I like to think that it was a bond of a different sort, I accept reluctantly that this might have provided the basis for our future relationship.

We progressed together, rook and human, and the knowledge, for the humans at least, was revelatory, mind-expanding, world-expanding. Chicken was clearly different from the other birds. I tried to examine the ways in which she was, to analyse what made her so. She seemed more inquisitive, more considered, as if her expectations of the world were broader. The doves' expectations and desires seemed confined – entirely reasonably – to the single-minded pursuit of the affairs of doves. Whilst the parrots too were intelligent and responsive to humans, they seemed simply to have a different world-view, one that extended less far than Chicken's. Chicken had an insatiable desire to find out. She wanted to know about the qualities of the small stones glittering with mica that she'd pick up in the garden, the purpose of the passing butterfly, what paper sounded like when it was torn. She wanted too to communicate, to be spoken to, to be heard.

Everywhere there were corvids and now I began to notice them, to appreciate them suddenly in another way. Driving, I'd see rooks as I had before, but with a new eye, a new acuity, the endless desultory pairs feeding, perhaps in the company of assorted crows, a few starlings, a handful of sparrows, in the grass of roadside verges, scattered as black flickers around every stand or thicket of trees, dusting, drifting, picking over the tilled surfaces of fields. They were all, as Chicken would grow in time to be, of sober mien, elegant of dress in well-tended black (except in summer when moulting renders them grey-edged and unkempt) with neat polished feet like tight, shining boots, somewhere between eighteenth-century Scottish minister (Henry Raeburn's 'Skating Minister' perhaps) and wealthy, black-clad, fashionable 1930s Parisian lady of distinguished years. I watched their walk, their gestures, what seemed to pass between them, in an infinity of behaviour I still had to learn.

There was more to know than I could have imagined; there was place and history and time. We knew corvids only in their wary, distant presence, in the sound of their voices. Corvids of one sort or another are found in many places in the north, as they are in most of Britain, among other birds, the lapwings and curlews whose calls are part of the sound of Scotland, the oystercatchers, gulls, herons, eagles, buzzards, hawks. Recently, I saw a map of rook distribution, which looked like a red scarf flung across the northern world. In urban settings, crows and jackdaws seem ubiquitous, pottering a few steps away, cautiously aware of us as we walk through the park, through the town gardens, black shapes in stark branches above us, silhouetted against pale clouds and sky. They're there on every stretch of roadway, every supermarket car park. Over farmland rooks fly, nest, feed and roost. One of the constants of many northern European cities is the presence of corvids; the crows I pass in a Warsaw park, the rooks on the spires and in the trees of Vilnius. In some cities, because of changes in farming practices and the greater availability of food in towns, their presence is fairly recent. Most corvid populations are settled, although rooks migrate from Russia, Sweden and the southern Baltic south to Britain and other north European countries for winter. Worldwide, too, they're found in most places except Antarctica; in South America there are no crows, only jays and magpies. Populations differ in number and vulnerability, a few highly adapted species declining now to the point where they face extinction, the Flores, the Hawaiian and the Mariana crows among them, the latter two tree foragers, their habitats reduced by logging, as others' are by farming, industrial development or any of the other dangers humans introduce when their interests coincide with, and ultimately overwhelm, those of native bird populations.

Of the corvids found in Britain the ravens, *Corvus corax*, are the largest of all, with their neck ruffs of feathers and big, strong beaks. Rooks, *Corvus frugilegus*, have grey faces, long slender beaks and full leg feathers, whilst carrion crows, *Corvus corone*, are all black, neat-feathered, with shorter beaks than rooks. Hooded crows, *Corvus corone commix*, look like crows wearing shaggy grey body-warmers. The jackdaws, *Corvus monedula*, have unmistakable silver eyes, short, pointed beaks and flattened panels of feathers at the sides of their heads. The other British corvids are not black: the magpie, *Pica pica*, is unmistakably, dazzlingly black and white; the chough, *Pyrrhocorax pyrrhocorax*, the rarest of the corvids, is red-legged and red-beaked. Jays, *Garrulus gladarius*, are colourful, light brown and blue and black and white.

Colonial nesters, rooks group in tight-knit, extended families, in rookeries of many nests, some containing many hundreds or thousands of birds. Some rookeries have been established for centuries, like ancestral homes with history behind them as rich and as long as any nobility. No coat of arms, no heraldry resonates as loudly, as profoundly as the sight and sound of rooks in their historic territory. In the vast rookery at Hatton Castle, a few miles to the north of here, there are thousands of nests where, every February, the rooks return to rebuild and repair their former homes. They choose to build nests in tall trees, in high, open situations, protected from predation by other birds probably by the proximity of other corvids and from the malign attention of humans by height. Rooks have occasionally adopted the dubious, unrookish and probably insecure practice of nesting on buildings as other birds do. E. M. Nicholson writes in *Birds and Men* that after the Napoleonic Wars, London rooks were seen to nest on the weathervanes on the turrets of the White Tower in the

Tower of London and on the wings of the dragon on the vane of Bow Church. They can't have enjoyed the sophisticated life of inner-city London, even at these well-chosen sites, because the experiment was never seen to be repeated.

As with us all, human or bird, history has formed what corvids are, their behaviour the product of their long evolution, of lives often lived in close proximity to humans, subject to the demands made on us all to learn, adapt, survive. Their social organisation is complex, highly developed and whilst there are differences in the social lives of different corvid species, most are broadly similar. Ravens seem to live in the least social way, rooks and jackdaws the most.

The basis for most corvid existence is the monogamous pair. Many live in flocks, move in flocks, roost in flocks, separating to mate, nest and rear young. Most corvids live in 'nuclear' families, parents and offspring, for the length of the breeding season, the raising and grow-ing season at least, until the offspring are fledged. Some young will leave their parents, some will remain, sometimes for as long as a year, 'helping' to rear the next generation. Among the ones who leave, it has been shown that the females often travel further, putting more distance between themselves and their homes than males.

Certain niceties of interaction smooth the ways of crowded roosts, allowing corvids to live together without conflict in the numbers they do. There are necessary foundations to their relationships: mutual recognition, the ability to learn quickly, the skills of negotiation. To us they all look the same. Chicken (individual though she is to us) is in appearance as all rooks appear to be. I see many every day and whilst I've tried to see differences, apart from size or feather con-dition, a slight difference in the face, I can't. They do not, however, encounter such problems. Corvids' recognition of one another is a prerequisite for the kind of organised, highly social existence they lead, for recognising family members, accepting and reintroducing ones who have gone away and returned. They may even be rather better at both mutual and inter-species recognition than we are. Not only do they recognise one another, corvids can recognise individual humans, and there are countless stories of people involved in crow research of one sort or another being singled out from among large, busy crowds to be personally, individually subjected to harassment, a kind of revenge, no doubt, for what crows appear to regard as unwarranted scientific attention. (Chicken certainly recognises many people, apart from the members of her immediate family. Some she greets with particular enthusiasm and what may or may not be expressions of welcome and pleasure.)

If corvid distribution is uneven, it's because each species has its preferences, or imperatives, dictated by the physical, evolutionary, climatic and social factors that have made it what it is. Ravens are birds of high, quiet places, of mountains; rooks, birds of farming country, in Scotland predominantly easterners; whilst 'hoodies', hooded crows, are the opposite. Choughs like rocky coasts, and jays woodlands. Jackdaws and magpies, like rooks, prefer the east. (Of all of them, the only ones that appear to like the north-west of Scotland are hooded crows and ravens. It may be that, in order to choose to live there, you simply have to like rain.)

From the first, I realised how little I had really observed the birds around me. It may be that the very ubiquity of corvids makes them all but invisible, beyond or beneath the interest of those who see them every day. Paradoxically, this may be why they appear to be noticed less, because they're just there, part of an accepted background, because their beauty is subtle, or unrecognised as such, their forms appearing at first glance to be clothed in unvarying blacks and greys, revealed only when close to as complex, shimmering, gilded with iridescent purple, blue, green. Their voices are perceived as harsh, unvarying, and except in rare cases, denying humanity the opportunity to hear reflections of themselves.

Perhaps, if the corvids we see around us were rare – had they, as others, already set their neat, black feet on the increasingly swift pathway to extinction – voices would be raised, and money, and campaigns set up, but since they are neither they require no such attention.

In time, Chicken developed her full adult plumage and became as she is now, beautiful, as are all crows, rooks, ravens, magpies. She is in every aspect, as they all are, in every movement, a sharp, tenebrous grace in her stillness, in her wings and feet and head. Corvids' beaks are balanced, proportionate, burnished and striated like the metal of a Damascene sword. The Japanese word '*shibui*' most encapsulates for me what they are and how they look, a word defined as 'austere, simple, quietly beautiful'. (It is no surprise to me that they are portrayed at their most exquisite in the art of Hiroshige, Hokusai and others, the art of a culture that sees crows so differently from our own.)

Because we seldom have the opportunity to be close enough to see the colour of their eyes, we may not know the depth and expression of the chestnut irises, the black pupils of the rook, the darker, fulvous plum and brown of crows and magpies.

Corvids, by being in the main black, are seen as representations of darkness, sources or conduits of evil, possibly messengers of dark forces. In fact, black feathers are protective, the strongest of all feathers, offering both camouflage and metabolic advantages over white feathers in their greater absorption of solar energy, which allows corvids to live more easily in the wide span of geographical territory they do, protected from the sun's rays and insulated against the Arctic cold.

As Chicken's feathers grew to thick, piled black, the irises of her eyes too changed from blue to grey-blue, then to deep, rich brown. She began to show the characteristic grey cere of the rook, a mysterious, ever-changing landscape. It's one of the aspects of her I could know only by closeness, by watching over time; that the grey portion of her face is not static. The texture of the skin, which reminds me of lizards (and makes me think of her distant dinosaur relatives), is of a strange and wondrous beauty, like lava or pumice, porous rock which erupts, melts back, is smooth then pocked, in an ever-altering pattern beneath the folds of grey skin under her eyes.

In summer, when she was small, we would take her into the garden. We began to clip her wings after the occasion when a sudden sound – I don't know what, a door opening, a voice from the next garden, a siren, another bird calling from a tree – sent her into panicked flight into a neighbour's garden. A child was dispatched over the wall and

Chicken retrieved. Clipping involves the careful removal of secondary feathers, watching for their regrowth. When recently I omitted to do it, I realised only when, to my shock (and Chicken's), startled by something outside, she took off and flew round the high ceiling of the study in two stunned and fearful circuits. Her relief on landing was clear. The possibilities of danger for her, of becoming tangled in lights, colliding with walls, was too great. Again, I wielded the clippers.

For the first years, when there were fewer cats in vicinity, we'd let her peck in the grass, investigate the flowerbeds under the bushes. Most of the time though she'd sit with us, on the back of the garden bench eating the aphids from the overhanging roses, their fine green legs waving helplessly from the sides of her beak, or 'sunning' – spreading her wings to the warmth and light (neither particularly abundant entities in north-east Scotland). The first time I saw her do it, I was transfixed by horror and panic – Chicken in sunshine, sitting on the edge of the garden bench, beak hanging open, head to the side, wings held wide and drooping (a posture we now call 'dying rook'), eyes veiled, apparently in the throes of a trance or coma. I didn't know what had befallen the unfortunate bird while my back was momentarily turned. A tentative calling of her name appeared to summon her back from this unknown realm, from her innocent pursuit of sunbathing.

No one knows the true purpose of birds' sunning. They may do it to help regulate their temperature, to increase their exposure to vitamin D, or to reduce feather parasites, but whatever it is, pleasure too appears to be involved. Since first seeing it, I notice birds everywhere spreading their wings in the sun, beaks gaping – blackbirds in the hedges of Union Street gardens, a thrush on the grass, the tiny robin on the garden table – all of them looking to the uninitiated as if they're in the last, painful throes of some alarming, rapid, fatal avian malady.

Adjusting to life with a rook was gradual, mutual, for us all, a process of interpretation, supposition, trial, learning the gestures of another's culture, the avoidance of the causes of fear or offence, matters of etiquette, slowly stepping one cautious step over the sacrosanct boundary into an unknown country.

Chicken seemed to enjoy being with us, perching under the table while we ate, hopping speculatively, carefully, on to someone's foot and, in time, their knee. We learnt not to extend our hands too quickly towards her, or indeed towards any bird. Her wariness of hands, maintained until today, is entirely reasonable. One doesn't know what hands, or their owners, intend to do. But then, if Chicken is wary of fingers, we are equally so of beaks.

Corvid fears seem cultural, innate, rational as well as irrational. The Nobel Prize-winning naturalist Konrad Lorenz, in his book about animal behaviour *King Solomon's Ring*, describes his jackdaws' responses to seeing him holding a black, fluttering object (in his case, what he refers to as his 'bathing drawers') and being immediately surrounded by a crowd of angry jackdaws, trying to peck his hand, for they interpreted the object as one of their own, a dead jackdaw; other black objects, such as his camera, were regarded with equanimity. Chicken is used to most black objects by now, obliged to be perhaps by living in a household inhabited by inveterate and unregenerate wearers of black. She will though occasionally still complain loudly at the sight of a black dustbin bag.

The parrots we have kept, by comparison, have always seemed less afraid, more rational, less flighty in their fears, disliking cats and sparrow-hawks but regarding everything else with either calm or a degree of interest. It may be their different experience and history, being reared in aviaries, distant from their places of origin and from the circumstances of life in the wild, that allows them a greater ease, but it may just be the way parrots are. (Bardie is afraid of chessboards. It may be that the bold pattern of black and white looks too much like the pattern of a snake's skin for relaxation in its presence but he may just dislike the game of chess.)

I don't know what she thought of ours, but we began to discover the grace of Chicken's demeanour. She made, and makes, me think of the fastidious conventions of courtly love, the way in which, with such refinement, she initiates and responds: each movement is careful. Not only rooks but even birds with reprobate reputations like magpies could shame humanity by their exquisite attention to manners, effusive displays of gratitude. Nothing, we discovered, is gracious like a corvid. Nothing displays such old-world, mannerly attention to others, such elaborate *politesse*, such greetings and such partings. Never, before meeting Chicken, could I have imagined the rituals, worthy of Japanese life at its most effulgently ritualistic, of coming in and going out, of waking in the morning and retiring at night, in acceptance and rejection, in speech and gesture, in meeting and making acquaintance, in the presentation of gifts; the bowings and callings, circlings and head-bendings, the solemn placing, as a morning gesture, of one cool black foot on the bare skin of my own.

At the beginning it had seemed simple, a question of responsibility. Then it started to seem less so, as I began to think of what it meant to keep a wild bird, one whose life in its natural setting would be so apparently alien, so dissimilar from our own. Dogs and cats are different. They have been bred for centuries for the lives they are to lead, for the small circuit, the delineated future. They live as they do, in a close relationship with humans, for the most part dependent on them because in the universe they have nowhere else to go. Birds, except for those bred in captivity, have plenty of other places to go. I am always aware that rooks are sociable, and that Chicken is without other rooks. But she isn't, as a member of the family, on her own. She's always with one or other of us, always within the sound of other birds, and if they're not the ones she might have expected, I hope it's consolation of a sort.

For years now, I've reflected on the facts of our coming by the wild birds we have, considered their prospects and their alternatives, what would have been their fate had they been anywhere but here. For each, Chicken and later Spike the magpie, the alternatives, I believe, would have been limited. Both birds were small when they first came here, too unfeathered for flight. Why they fell or were dislodged from their nests is impossible to know. Larger nestlings dislodge smaller ones while spreading their wings, practising for flight. Or, active creatures, they fall of their own accord. The trees from which they came are far too high for them to be restored to their nests by any practicable means. Reintroducing them to the wild might have been possible, but at best, in amateur hands, with individual birds, success is limited (everything I've read confirms it). Where would I have done it? How? Around us are urban gardens, busy streets, traffic.

Scattered by every roadside, the black corpses of corvids lie, feathers ruffled slowly by the wind. I don't regard their lives as cheap; the opposite, only infinitely fragile. The birds who have lived and live here have done so for much longer than they would have lived in the wild, although I am always aware of the ways in which they haven't lived, what they have been denied, either by my actions or by what might loosely be described as fate.

People have, I tell myself, for as far back as one knows, kept birds but there is no consolation in the telling because, for as far back as one knows people have similarly done things that are wrong. If I believe, or hope, that what I did was the best I could and can for them, I have to be ready always to answer to my sternest critic.

As we began to look at all corvids with new interest, we saw Chicken do as the corvids around us did. In time, we could recognise the complex series of movements of body, wings and feathers that told of mood and inclination. It may be the apparently sober colours, the lack of sexual dimorphism in corvids that obliges them to a subtlety of behaviour required less by birds that have more to show, more to flash, males with more brilliantly coloured feathers, sets of magnificent head plumes, vast, apparently bejewelled tails, elaborate songs with which to woo and win. We began to discern her state of mind from her stance, her walk, her feathers, to know that, when going about her day-to-day business, untroubled and busy, her head feathers would be smoothed to her skull, her auricular feathers (the panels of feathers by the sides of her head that cover the openings that are her ears) flattened, with no 'eyebrows' or 'ears' visible – the raised head feathers that indicate alterations of mood – no raised, irritated crown of Dennis the Menace feathers round the top of her head, a posture that indicates surprise, alarm, anger. Annoyance or some other stimulus, we saw, could bring this about instantly; when teased, or crossed in any way, she'd fluff her feathers, lower her head, adopt an aggressive stance, her leg feathers bagged out and full. When teased, as she often was (and still is) by Bee, she'd lower her head and spread her feathers, bow, fan her tail and lunge herself towards Bee in full, rookish fury. (Theirs, like Han's with Chicken, has always remained what appears to be a sibling relationship.)

'Crow!' Bee will say to Chicken, who becomes angry, begins to strut and spread her feathers. 'CROW!' This is clearly offensive, a crime against taxonomy. In our midst, a shape-shifter, a smallish, smooth-feathered, glossy rook one moment, a strutting, baggy-feathered, almost large, self-important, angry one the next. When, years later, we had an opportunity to observe a magpie, we'd know that the appearance of 'ears' on Spike's perfect, shining black head was a warning signal. *I'm getting angry*, it said, in preparation for violence and attack, the controlled fury of the probably dangerous; *why did you have to annoy me?* Get ready for the vengeance of one small and angry magpie, it said. One did. Their raised 'ears' always remind me of Batman's ears and are perhaps similarly indicative of righteous indignation or the highest moral intent.

We'd watch amazed as Chicken did what Bernd Heinrich (in his book *Ravens in Winter)* describes in ravens as 'jumping jack', when birds will leap up and down, hopping and calling, behaviour that occurs in the presence of an unfamiliar food source, a carcass perhaps, in a process of investigation. She does it still, leaping into the air, both feet off the ground, wings wide and flapping, tail raised, uttering quick, high yelps, 'Wup! Wup! Wup!', continuing for a half a minute before she stops and stands, slightly out of breath. In the absence of carcasses it's difficult to know why, what inspires her, what initiates it, and although I have tried to see a pattern or a cause, I never have.

I began to read books about corvids and to appreciate that what is known of their lives, the patterns of their behaviour and social organisation, has most often been learnt by careful, painstaking and sometimes dangerous research, undertaken among the most obser-vant, the most wary, quick and communicative of birds. I often read the accounts with awe, admiration and gratitude, knowing that if people who carry out research into corvids and other bird beha-viour didn't climb trees, the very high ones that are the first choice of most corvids, didn't spend long, freezing winters in cold, wild places, watching, tagging, measuring, didn't set up experiments that, because of corvid wariness, fail after lengthy preparation, we would know considerably less than we do and people like me would not be able to exclaim from their armchairs in revelatory recognition at a piece of corvid (or other avian) behaviour they read about in one of these astonishingly detailed accounts. Bernd Heinrich describes climbing high trees, precariously, dangerously, in storms in order to reach a raven's nest; he writes too of those who have sustained injuries while carrying out research, of Thomas Grunkorn who fell out of a tree and broke his back, of Gustav Kramer who was killed falling from a cliff while studying wild pigeons.

In their book *In the Company of Crows and Ravens*, researchers John Marzluff and Tony Angell describe being picked out from among forty thousand others on the campus of the University of Washington by crows who, while happily walking among other people, fly away from them. Kevin McGowan of Cornell University was routinely identified among crowds, followed and shouted at by crows he had studied (and some he had not). Bernd Heinrich, attempting to discover what it is that allows ravens to identify each other, describes experiments with his own ravens, who happily accept him but no one else. Using a variety of techniques – swapping clothes with other people before approaching the ravens, changing his outfits or elements of his out-fits, wearing masks, wigs, sunglasses, making grotesque faces, limping, hopping, carrying a broom – he proves that if it's him they're not fooled for long by any subterfuge, that, just as the visual clues the birds use in recognition of humans are diverse, so probably are those they use in identification of other birds. (Included in the account is the unforgettable sentence 'After my thirteenth approach in the kimono, they again allowed me to get next to them.')

Interestingly, the broom was the one thing the ravens never accepted, as Chicken will not. Even after years of close, daily acquain-tance, Chicken still runs away at the sight, hides under the table until it's put away. Corvids must know something I don't about brooms.

Gradually I began to realise how much more there was to know, that what I had learnt, what I had observed from Chicken, was just a beginning. I read in the introduction to Kenton C. Lint's feeding instruction for corvids that crows and ravens can live for twenty to twenty-five years in well-planted aviaries. While this isn't a well-planted aviary, I wondered if it might do instead. It seemed that with good fortune, or whatever else it might take to look after this bird properly, we could well have some time to spend together. I hoped it would be so.

from LIFE ON LIMESTONE

Anna Adams

The poet and artist **Anna Adams** (1926–2011) was born in Surrey and grew up in Northwood in north-west London. She won a scholarship to Harrow School of Art, where she met her husband, the painter Norman Adams, whom she married in 1947. She taught art in Manchester and later at Settle College secondary school but poured her creative energy into poetry. Her first poem was published in 1969 and her prize-winning work subsequently appeared in *Poetry Review*, *The Countryman* and *The Spectator*. She was poetry editor of *The Green Book* (1989–92) and a member of the Poetry Society. She published more than twenty collections of poetry and two collections of prose, poetry and art, *Island Chapters* (1991) and *Life on Limestone* (1994). The former was inspired by the decade that she and her husband and their two small children spent on the island of Scarp in the Outer Hebrides. The latter draws from thirty years living in a converted farmhouse in the Yorkshire Dales. The poet Anne Stevenson hailed Adams' 'virtues of immediacy and intelligence and keen sense of humour which make [her] popular among many readers'.

THE PAPER CITY

At about midsummer I noticed what I at first thought was a swallows' nest clinging to the underside of our high studio-door lintel. A second look told me that the cement-coloured protuberance was a wasps' nest, but this was more or less a guess, as I had never seen one before. I remembered having seen a queen wasp, in April, going snipper-snapper among last year's raspberry canes. She had sounded like a certain much-advertised breakfast cereal, or the kindling of a twig fire. I soon traced the sound to the large wasp which, in the very breakfast-time of the year, was gathering wood fibre for her paper-making operation. She was about to lay the foundations of her summer palace. Later, the first-born workers would continue the building to house her thousand children.

As June turned into July, and July to August, the neat whorl of the nest became a greyish inverted turban, a bandaged head, a very dead cabbage, a tumour on the beam. Visitors cried out with horror at it and said we would be stung to death, but we lived in perfect peace with our lodgers who went about their daily business outside while we went about ours within. Wasps are not like houseflies; they take little interest in humanity unless we are making jam, and they are clean and wholesome in their habits. They are not gratuitously aggressive towards people, and sting us only in self-defence.

Humans who flap newspapers at wasps, or go berserk with fly-sprays all over the picnic food, are much more of a menace than this urbane and elegant insect, with its glittering wings, scissoring mandibles, armoured thorax, and middle waisted away to a mere isthmus between jacket and tiger-striped bustle. Wasps are less destructive of human substance than cabbage-white butterflies, rabbits, or plagues of pigeons encouraged by old ladies in towns. Live and let live, said I in this case.

In early September, after several wet weeks and one or two slight frosts, all activity in the cement-grey excrescence seemed to have ceased. No more dead wasps were to be found on the doorstep, there were no more comings and goings at the round hole that pierced the multiple paper walls, and it was some time since any wasps had been at work along the edges of the paper cabbage's outside leaves, adding their fee for life to the wrappings of the mysterious gift within. So I thought it was high time to harvest this summer's growth. I fetched a ladder and a paint-scraper and, supporting the soft and flimsy udder with my left hand, I scraped at its attachment to the underside of the stone lintel with my right. Soon the whole bundle was detached, without being too much dented, and I climbed down the ladder with it.

Looked at closely, the stone-grey paper was a lovely composite of grey, silver and greenish stripes, each one being made of different sorts of wood, some of it mossy, so each wasp's contribution had dried out a different colour. The paper had a faint silkiness, but it was very absorbent, like the softest of soft toilet-rolls, of almost the goose-neck texture that Rabelais extolled.

I bore away this floppy parcel, reflecting that I held a defunct civilisation in my hands. I intended to dissect it, for I had to know what it contained, though I suppose I might have lit the fire with it. I imagined a mass of papery leaves right through to its papery heart, and expected to find that the dead wasps and grubs had lived between its layers. So I scissored carefully into it, as though cutting a quarter out of a cabbage, and I anticipated the discovery of corpses at every snip. But, having gone through about twelve layers of paper, I discovered that the inverted dome was hollow, and I was in the heart of the wasps' collective womb.

Within its shadowy cave was a tree-like structure in four hexagonal layers, rather like a simplified cedar, but this tree would have grown downwards from its root. The suspended storeys were linked by a trunk of papier mâché, and were composed of empty hexagonal cells where infant wasps had matured. Crouched at the edge of the latest and smallest floor, still brooding over her countless cradles, and still poised to lay yet another egg, was the venerable queen. She had died on the job. Round the rim of this newest area, many of the close-packed egg-boxes were still sealed with paper blisters covering the unhatched dead. They had set out too late to catch the summer and had missed the bus of life forever. So cradles became coffins.

The whole tableau made me feel that I and my scissors had intruded upon a holy mystery wherein the gods were still at their work of creating the everlasting future: yet it was also a necropolis. Summer's city had met disaster: the neutron bomb of frost.

from MEHALAH

Sabine Baring-Gould

Born to parents who owned a 3,000-acre estate in Devon, **Sabine Baring-Gould** (1834–1924) was a sensitive and sickly child who was taken on Grand Tours by his father when young. He was fluent in five languages before he went to school, aged fifteen, where he was bullied. He remained an individualist and maverick all his life. After training as a vicar, he fell in love with Grace Taylor, a millworker's daughter half his age who may have been the inspiration for George Bernard Shaw's *Pygmalion*. Taylor was trained in upper-class mores before marrying Baring-Gould. For ten years, Baring-Gould was vicar of East Mersea on the Essex island. Although he disliked the place and its people, it inspired him to write *Mehalah*, perhaps the most enduring of his 130 books and hundreds of articles, stories, poems and letters. He was most proud of collecting folk songs but was also a hagiographer, historian, archaeologist and author of *The Book of Werewolves*. He also found the time to father fifteen children.

THE RAY

Between the mouths of the Blackwater and the Colne, on the east coast of Essex, lies an extensively marshy tract veined and freckled in every part with water. It is a wide waste of debatable ground contested by sea and land, subject to incessant incursions from the former, but stubbornly maintained by the latter. At high tide the appearance is that of a vast surface of moss or Sargasso weed floating on the sea, with rents and patches of shining water traversing and dappling it in all directions. The creeks, some of considerable length and breadth, extend many miles inland, and are arteries whence branches out a fibrous tissue of smaller channels, flushed with water twice in the twenty-four hours. At noon-tides, and especially at the equinoxes, the sea asserts its royalty over this vast region, and overflows the whole, leaving standing out of the flood only the long island of Mersea, and the lesser islet, called the Ray. This latter is a hill of gravel rising from the heart of the Marshes, crowned with ancient thorntrees, and possessing, what is denied the mainland, an unfailing spring of purest water. At ebb, the Ray can only be reached from the old Roman causeway, called the Strood, over which runs the road from Colchester to Mersea Isle, connecting formerly the city of the Trinobantes with the station of the Count of the Saxon shore. But even at ebb, the Ray is not approachable by land unless the sun or east wind has parched the ooze into brick; and then the way is long, tedious and tortuous, among bitter pools and over shining creeks. It was perhaps because this ridge of high ground was so inaccessible, so well protected by nature, that the ancient inhabitants had erected on it a *rath*, or fortified camp of wooden logs, which left its name to the place long after the timber defences had rotted away.

A more desolate region can scarce be conceived, and yet it is not without beauty. In summer, the thrift mantles the marshes with shot satin, passing through all gradations of tint from maiden's blush to lily white. Thereafter a purple glow steals over the waste, as the sea lavender bursts into flower, and simultaneously every creek and pool is royally fringed with sea aster. A little later the glass-wort, that shot up green and transparent as emerald glass in the early spring, turns to every tinge of carmine.

When all vegetation ceases to live, and goes to sleep, the marshes are alive and wakeful with countless wild fowl. At all times they are haunted with sea mews and roysten crows, in winter they teem with wild duck and grey geese. The stately heron loves to wade in the pools, occasionally the whooper swan sounds his loud trumpet, and flashes a white reflection in the still blue waters of the fleets. The plaintive pipe of the curlew is familiar to those who frequent these marshes, and the barking of the brent geese as they return from their northern breeding places is heard in November.

At the close of last century there stood on the Ray a small farm-house built of tarred wreckage timber, and roofed with red pan-tiles.

The twisted thorntrees about it afforded some, but slight, shelter. Under the little cliff of gravel was a good beach, termed a "hard."

On an evening towards the close of September, a man stood in this farmhouse by the hearth, on which burnt a piece of wreckwood, opposite an old woman, who crouched shivering with ague in a chair on the other side. He was a strongly built man of about thirty-five, wearing fisherman's boots, a brown coat and a red plush waistcoat. His hair was black, raked over his brow. His cheekbones were high; his eyes dark, eager, intelligent, but fierce in expression. His nose was aquiline, and would have given a certain nobility to his countenance, had not his huge jaws and heavy chin contributed an animal cast to his face.

He leaned on his duck-gun, and glared from under his pent-house brows and thatch of black hair over the head of the old woman at a girl who stood behind, leaning on the back of her mother's chair, and who returned his stare with a look of defiance from her brown eyes.

The girl might have been taken for a sailor boy, as she leaned over the chairback, but for the profusion of her black hair. She wore a blue knitted guernsey covering body and arms, and across the breast, woven in red wool, was the name of the vessel, *Gloriana*. The guernsey had been knitted for one of the crew of a ship of this name, but had come into the girl's possession. On her head she wore the scarlet woven cap of a boatman.

The one-pane window at the side of the fireplace faced the west, and the evening sun lit her brown gipsy face, burnt in her large eyes, and made coppery lights in her dark hair.

The old woman was shivering with the ague, and shook the chair on which her daughter leaned; a cold sweat ran off her brow, and every now and then she raised a white faltering hand to wipe the drops away that hung on her eyebrows like rain on thatching.

"I did not catch the chill here," she said. "I ketched it more than thirty years ago when I was on Mersea Isle, and it has stuck in my marrow ever since. But there is no ague on the Ray. This is the healthiest place in the world, Mehalah has never caught the ague on it. I do not wish ever to leave it, and to lay my bones elsewhere."

"Then you will have to pay your rent punctually," said the man in a dry tone, not looking at her, but at her daughter.

"Please the Lord so we shall, as we ever have done," answered the woman; "but when the chill comes on me—"

"Oh, curse the chill," interrupted the man; "who cares for that except perhaps Glory yonder, who has to work for both of you. Is it so, Glory?"

The girl thus addressed did not answer, but folded her arms on the chairback, and leaned her chin upon them. She seemed at that moment like a wary cat watching a threatening dog, and ready at a moment to show her claws and show desperate battle, not out of malice, but in self-defence.

"Why, but for you sitting there, sweating and jabbering, Glory would not be bound to this lone islet, but would go out and see the world, and taste life. She grows here like a mushroom, she does not live. Is it not so, Glory?"

The girl's face was no longer lit by the declining sun, which had glided further north-west, but the flames of the driftwood flickered in her large eyes that met those of the man, and the cap was still illumined by the evening glow, a scarlet blaze against the indigo gloom.

"Have you lost your tongue, Glory?" asked the man, impatiently striking the bricks with the butt end of his gun.

"Why do you not speak, Mehalah?" said the mother, turning her wan wet face aside, to catch a glimpse of her daughter.

"I've answered him fifty times," said the girl.

"No," protested the old woman feebly, "you have not spoken a word to Master Rebow."

"By God, she is right," broke in the man. "The little devil has a tongue in each eye, and she has been telling me with each a thousand times that she hates me. Eh, Glory?"

The girl rose erect, set her teeth, and turned her face aside, and looked out at the little window on the decaying light.

Rebow laughed aloud.

"She hated me before, and now she hates me worse, because I have become her landlord. I have bought the Ray for eight hundred pounds. The Ray is mine, I tell you. Mistress Sharland, you will henceforth have to pay *me* the rent, to me and to none other. I am your landlord, and Michaelmas is next week."

"The rent shall be paid, Elijah!" said the widow.

"The Ray is mine," pursued Rebow, swelling with pride. "I have bought it with my own money—eight hundred pounds. I could stubb up the trees if I would. I could cart muck into the well and choke it if I would. I could pull down the stables and break them up for firewood if I chose. All here is mine, the Ray, the marshes, and the saltings, the creeks, the fleets, the farm. That is mine," said he, striking the wall with his gun, "and that is mine," dashing the butt end against the hearth; "and you are mine, and Glory is mine."

"That never," said the girl, stepping forward, and confronting him with dauntless eye and firm lips and folded arms.

"Eh! Gloriana! have I roused you?" exclaimed Elijah Rebow, with a flash of exultation in his fierce eyes. "I said that the house and the marshes, and the saltings are mine, I have bought them. And your mother and you are mine."

"Never," repeated the girl.

FIELDS AND FARMING

Illustration overleaf: *Making Hay*

from A SHEPHERD'S LIFE

W. H. Hudson

William Henry Hudson (1841–1922) is now regarded as a classic English nature writer but was born near Buenos Aires and grew up speaking Spanish and roaming the Pampas where his New Englander parents were sheep farmers. After his parents died, he travelled widely and didn't settle in Britain until he was in his thirties, when he moved to Bayswater, West London, and married. He produced ornithological studies of Argentine and British birds but first became widely known as a writer of popular romances, often set in South America, such as *Green Mansions* (1904) and *The Purple Land that England Lost* (1885). Later, his books about the English countryside, including *A Shepherd's Life* (1910) and *A Hind in Richmond Park* (1922), chimed with the popular appetite for getting back to nature.

SHEPHERD ISAAC BAWCOMBE

To me the most interesting of Caleb's old memories were those relating to his father, partly on account of the man's fine character, and partly because they went so far back, beginning in the early years of the last century.

Altogether he must have been a very fine specimen of a man, both physically and morally. In Caleb's mind he was undoubtedly the first among men morally, but there were two other men supposed to be his equals in bodily strength: one a native of the village, the other a periodical visitor. The first was Jarvis the blacksmith, a man of an immense chest and big arms, one of Isaac's greatest friends, and very good-tempered except when in his cups, for he did occasionally get drunk, and then he quarrelled with anyone and everyone.

One afternoon he had made himself quite tipsy at the inn, and when going home, swaying about and walking all over the road, he all at once caught sight of the big shepherd coming soberly on behind. No sooner did he see him than it occurred to his wild and muddled mind that he had a quarrel with this very man, Shepherd Isaac, a quarrel of so pressing a nature that there was nothing to do but to fight it out there and then. He planted himself before the shepherd and challenged him to fight. Isaac smiled and said nothing.

'I'll fight thee about this,' he repeated, and began tugging at his coat, and after getting it off again made up to Isaac, who still smiled and said no word. Then he pulled his waistcoat off, and finally his shirt, and with nothing but his boots and breeches on once more squared up to Isaac and threw himself into his best fighting attitude.

'I doan't want to fight thee,' said Isaac at length, 'but I be thinking 'twould be best to take thee home.' And suddenly dashing in he seized Jarvis round the waist with one arm, grasped him round the legs with the other, and flung the big man across his shoulder, and carried him off struggling and shouting, to his cottage. There at the door, pale and distressed, stood the poor wife waiting for her lord, when Isaac arrived, and going straight in dropped the smith down on his own floor, and with the remark, 'Here be your man,' walked off to his cottage and his tea.

The other powerful man was Old Joe the collier, who flourished and was known in every village in the Salisbury Plain district during the first thirty-five years of the last century. I first heard of this once famous man from Caleb, whose boyish imagination had been affected by his gigantic figure, mighty voice, and his wandering life over all that wide world of Salisbury Plain. Afterwards when I became acquainted with a good many old men, aged from 75 to 90 and upwards, I found that Old Joe's memory is still green in a good many villages of the district, from the upper waters of the Avon to the borders of Dorset. But it is only these ancients who knew him that keep it green; by and by when they are gone Old Joe and his neddies will be remembered no more.

Down to about 1840 it was customary to burn peat in the cottages, the first cost of which was about four and sixpence the wagonload – enough to keep me warm for a month in winter. But the cost of its conveyance to the villages of the Plain was about five to six shillings per load, as it came from a considerable distance, mostly from the New Forest. How the labourers at that time, when they were paid seven or eight shillings a week, could afford to buy fuel at such prices to bake their rye bread and keep the frost out of their bones is a marvel to us. Isaac was a good deal better off than most of the villagers in this respect, as his master – for he never had but one – allowed him the use of a wagon and the driver's services for the conveyance of one load of peat each year. The wagonload of peat and another of faggots lasted him the year with the furze obtained from his 'liberty' on the down. Coal at that time was only used by the blacksmiths in the villages, and was conveyed in sacks on ponies or donkeys, and of those who were engaged in this business the best known was Old Joe. He appeared periodically in the villages with his eight donkeys, or neddies as he called them, with jingling bells on their headstalls and their burdens of two sacks of small coal on each. In stature he was a giant of about six feet three, very broad-chested, and invariably wore a broad-brimmed hat, a slate coloured smock-frock, and blue worsted stockings to his knees. He walked behind the donkeys, a very long staff in his hand, shouting at them from time to time, and occasionally swinging his long staff and bringing it down on the back of a donkey who was not keeping up the pace. In this way he wandered from village to village from end to end of the Plain, getting rid of his small coal and loading his animals with scrap iron which the blacksmiths would keep for him, and as he continued his rounds for nearly forty years he was a familiar figure to every inhabitant throughout the district.

There are some stories still told of his great strength, one of which is worth giving. He was a man of iron constitution and gave himself a hard life, and he was hard on his neddies, but he had to feed them well, and this he often contrived to do at someone else's expense. One night at a village on the Wylye it was discovered that he had put his eight donkeys in a meadow in which the grass was just ripe for mowing. The enraged farmer took them to the village pound and locked them up, but in the morning the donkeys and Joe with them had vanished and the whole village wondered how he had done it.

The stone wall of the pound was four feet and a half high and the iron gate was locked, yet he had lifted the donkeys up and put them over and had loaded them and gone before anyone was up.

Once Joe met with a very great misfortune. He arrived late at a village, and finding there was good feed in the churchyard and that everybody was in bed, he put his donkeys in and stretched himself out among the gravestones to sleep. He had no nerves and no imagination; and was tired, and slept very soundly until it was light and time to put his neddies out before any person came by and discovered that he had been making free with the rector's grass. Glancing round he could see no donkeys, and only when he stood up he found they had not made their escape but were there all about him, lying among the gravestones, stone dead every one! He had forgotten that a churchyard was a dangerous place to put hungry animals in. They had browsed on the luxuriant yew that grew there, and this was the result. In time he recovered from his loss and replaced his dead neddies with others, and continued for many years longer on his rounds.

To return to Isaac Bawcombe. He was born, we have seen, in 1800, and began following a flock as a boy and continued as shepherd on the same farm for a period of fifty-five years. The care of sheep was the one all-absorbing occupation of his life, and how much it was to him appears in this anecdote of his state of mind when he was deprived of it for a time. The flock was sold and Isaac was left without sheep, and with little to do except to wait from Michaelmas to Candlemas, when there would be sheep again at the farm. It was a long time to Isaac, and he found his enforced holiday so tedious that he made himself a nuisance to his wife in the house. Forty times a day he would throw off his hat and sit down, resolved to be happy at his own fireside, but after a few minutes the desire to be up and doing would return, and up he would get and out he would go again. One dark cloudy evening a man from the farm put his head in at the door. 'Isaac,' he said, 'there be sheep for 'ee up't the farm – two hunderd ewes and a hunderd more to come in dree days. Master, he sent I to say you be wanted.' And away the man went.

Isaac jumped up and hurried forth without taking his crook from the corner and actually without putting on his hat! His wife called out after him, and getting no response sent the boy with his hat to overtake him. But the little fellow soon returned with the hat – he could not overtake his father!

He was away three or four hours at the farm, then returned, his hair very wet, his face beaming, and sat down with a great sigh of pleasure. 'Two hunderd ewes,' he said, 'and a hunderd more to come – what d'you think of that?'

'Well, Isaac,' said she, 'I hope thee'll be happy now and let I alone.'

After all that had been told to me about the elder Bawcombe's life and character, it came somewhat as a shock to learn that at one period during his early manhood he had indulged in one form of poaching – a sport which had a marvellous fascination for the people of England in former times, but was pretty well extinguished during the first quarter of the last century. Deer he had taken; and the whole tale of the deer stealing, which was a common offence in that part of Wiltshire down to about 1834, sounds strange at the present day.

Large herds of deer were kept at that time at an estate a few miles from Winterbourne Bishop, and it often happened that many of the animals broke bounds and roamed singly and in small bands over the hills. When deer were observed in the open, certain of the villagers would settle on some plan of action: watchers would be sent out not only to keep an eye on the deer but on the keepers too. Much depended on the state of the weather and the moon, as some light was necessary; then, when the conditions were favourable and the keepers had been watched to their cottages, the gang would go out for a night's hunting. But it was a dangerous sport, as the keepers also knew that deer were out of bounds, and they would form some counterplan, and one peculiarly nasty plan they had was to go out about three or four o'clock in the morning and secrete themselves somewhere close to the village to intercept the poachers on their return.

Bawcombe, who never in his life associated with the village idlers and frequenters of the alehouse, had no connection with these men. His expeditions were made alone on some dark, unpromising night, when the regular poachers were in bed and asleep. He would steal away after bedtime, or would go out ostensibly to look after the sheep, and, if fortunate, would return in the small hours with a deer on his back. Then, helped by his mother, with whom he lived (for this was when he was a young unmarried man, about 1820), he would quickly skin and cut up the carcass, stow the meat away in some secret place, and bury the head, hide, and offal deep in the earth; and when morning came it would find Isaac out following his flock as usual, with no trace of guilt or fatigue in his rosy cheeks and clear, honest eyes.

This was a very astonishing story to hear from Caleb, but to suspect him of inventing or of exaggerating was impossible to anyone who knew him. And we have seen that Isaac Bawcombe was an exceptional man – physically a kind of Alexander Selkirk of the Wiltshire Downs. And he, moreover, had a dog to help him – one as superior in speed and strength to the ordinary sheepdog as he himself was to the ruck of his fellow men.

It was only after much questioning on my part that Caleb brought himself to tell me of these ancient adventures, and finally to give a detailed account of how his father came to take his first deer. It was in the depth of winter – bitterly cold, with a strong north wind blowing on the snow covered downs – when one evening Isaac caught sight of two deer out on his sheepwalk. In that part of Wiltshire there is a famous monument of antiquity, a vast mound-like wall, with a deep depression or fosse running at its side. Now it happened that on the highest part of the down, where the wall or mound was most exposed to the blast, the snow had been blown clean off the top, and the deer were feeding here on the short turf, keeping to the ridge, so that, outlined against the sky, they had become visible to Isaac at a great distance.

He saw and pondered. These deer, just now, while out of bounds, were no man's property, and it would be no sin to kill and eat one – if he could catch it! – and it was a season of bitter want. For many many days he had eaten his barley bread, and on some days barley flour dumplings, and had been content with this poor fare; but now the sight of these animals made him crave for meat with an intolerable craving, and he determined to do something to satisfy it.

He went home and had his poor supper, and when it was dark set forth again with his dog. He found the deer still feeding on the mound. Stealing softly along among the furze bushes, he got the black line of the mound against the starry sky, and by and by, as he moved along, the black figures of the deer, with their heads down, came into view. He then doubled back and, proceeding some distance, got down into the fosse and stole forward to them again under the wall. His idea was that on taking alarm they would immediately make for the forest which was their home, and would probably pass near him. They did not hear him until he was within sixty yards, and then bounded down from the wall, over the dyke, and away, but in almost opposite directions – one alone making for the forest; and on this one the dog was set. Out he shot like an arrow from the bow, and after him ran Isaac 'as he had never runned afore in all his life'. For a short space deer and dog in hot pursuit were visible on the snow, then the darkness swallowed them up as they rushed down the slope; but in less than half a minute a sound came back to Isaac, flying, too, down the incline – the long, wailing cry of a deer in distress. The dog had seized his quarry by one of the front legs, a little above the hoof, and held it fast, and they were struggling on the snow when Isaac came up and flung himself upon his victim, then thrust his knife through its windpipe 'to stop its noise'. Having killed it, he threw it on his back and went home, not by the turnpike, nor by any road or path, but over fields and through copses until he got to the back of his mother's cottage. There was no door on that side, but there was a window and when he had rapped at it and his mother opened it, without speaking a word he thrust the dead deer through, then made his way round to the front.

That was how he killed his first deer. How the others were taken I do not know; I wish I did, since this one exploit of a Wiltshire shepherd has more interest for me than I find in fifty narratives of elephants slaughtered wholesale with explosive bullets, written for the delight and astonishment of the reading public by our most glorious Nimrods.

from AKENFIELD

Ronald Blythe

Ronald Blythe (b. 1922) is an essayist and novelist best known for *Akenfield* (1969), his study of a (fictionalized) Suffolk village through intimate interviews with its residents. He was born in Suffolk and spent ten years working as a librarian in Colchester where he first met Christine Nash, wife of the artist John Nash. Christine encouraged Blythe's writing. For three years in the late 1950s, Blythe worked for Benjamin Britten at the Aldeburgh Festival, befriending E. M. Forster among others, a period remembered in his memoir *The Time by the Sea* (2013). Blythe's first novel, *A Treasonable Growth* (1960), was followed by *The Age of Illusion* (1963), a social history of the inter-war years. He edited the Penguin Classics series and later cared for the Nashes, writing presciently about old age in *The View in Winter* (1979). He continued to write prolifically in his later years, revealing his remarkable memory and panoramic knowledge of country life in a long-running *Church Times* column, collected in various books including *Word from Wormingford* (1997). Living in the old farm he inherited from the Nashes on the border of Essex and Suffolk, he has influenced many recent nature writers including his friends Richard Mabey and Roger Deakin.

JOHN GROUT – AGED EIGHTY-EIGHT – FARMER

Mr Grout has been recently widowed after sixty-seven years of marriage. He was married at eighteen – 'I was a pretty lad' – but had begun work on his father's farm when he was eleven. Both his father and his grandfather had worked this farm of some 150 acres and had lived to a great age, so Mr Grout had often talked with men who knew the Suffolk farmers of the eighteenth century. He is short and sturdy, with a shining brown face and the strange new-looking wide blue eyes of the very old countryman. Day by day he sits in his hilltop house, dressed in thick rough clean clothes and polished buskins, sometimes listening to the clock, sometimes to the radio. [Where is Vietnam, Mr Grout? – 'Far away…']

The rooms in the house, once the Akenfield miller's home, are sedately brown: brown paint, pale oatmeal brown wallpaper, snuff-brown tablecloth, oily brown lampshade, creamy brown curtains. There are sash windows at a right angle and nothing passes on the road which doesn't offer the chance of a second complete glimpse if one happens to have missed the first. Just outside, and casting a livid reflection on to the ceiling, is the harsh green circle of the miller's pond. At the side of the house rest the millstones, with nettles and honeysuckle sprouting through the shaft-holes.

I have farmed in Akenfield since 1926. I had 135 acres and didn't use a tractor until 1952, and then I never got on with the thing. I have been a man without machinery, as you might say. I was born near Campsey Ash and worked for my father as a child. I did the cows. He was a man who didn't like cows, so I did them. Then I went to school. My father had five labourers who got 9s. a week but he always gave them a shilling extra when they got wed.

Nobody really saw money then, though that didn't mean that they didn't want to see it. I wanted to see it so much that I applied for a job on the railway. A 'situation', they called it, and they weren't so far wrong – it was a situation all right. Whatever could I have been thinking about! A relation of mine spoke for me and soon I was working at Broad Street Station near Liverpool Street. There were lots of Suffolk men working there and hardly any mortal one of them ever got home again. They all wanted to get home, they were that sad in London. And their big wages were little there. Some ran away to Canada and were never heard of again. They couldn't write, you see; that is how they got lost. There was a place in Broad Street Station where you can stare through the arches and see the stars, and they were the only things I can remember seeing in London. That is the truth.

I stayed ten months and then I got home. I wouldn't go back to my father's farm, I got a job with Lord Rendlesham. He was a rare big gentleman in the neighbourhood and was famous for his horses. Why, he kept three men who did nothing else but see after the stallions. There were scores of horses – mostly shires and punches. The greatest of these was a punch stallion called Big Boy who had won so many brass medals he couldn't carry them all on his harness. Men came from all over to see these horses but they hardly ever saw Big Boy. He was hid up and not to be looked at.

The head horseman was called the 'lord' – and that's what he was, lord of all the horses. That was me one day, I was the lord of the horses. The place ran like clockwork. All the harnessing was done in strict order, first this, then that. The ploughing teams left and returned to the stable yards according to the rank of the ploughman. If you happened to get back before someone senior to you, you just had to wait in the lane until he had arrived. *Then* you could go, but not before.

The horses were friends and loved like men. Some men would do more for a horse than they would for a wife. The ploughmen talked softly to their teams all day long and you could see the horses listening. Although the teams ploughed twenty yards apart, the men didn't talk much to each other, except sometimes they sang. Each man ploughed in his own fashion and with his own mark. It looked all the same if you didn't know about ploughing, but a farmer could walk on a field ploughed by ten different teams and tell which bit was ploughed by which. Sometimes he would pay a penny an acre extra for perfect ploughing. Or he would make a deal with the ploughman – 'free rent for good work'. That could mean £5 a year. The men worked perfectly to get this, but they also worked perfectly because it was *their* work. It belonged to them. It was theirs.

The plough-teams left for the field at seven sharp in the morning and finished at three in the afternoon. They reckoned a ploughman would walk eleven miles a day on average. It wasn't hard walking in the dirt, not like the rough roads. The horsemen were the big men on the farm. They kept in with each other and had secrets. They were a whispering lot. If someone who wasn't a ploughman came upon them and they happened to be talking, they'd soon change the conversation!

And if you disturbed them in a room where the horse medicine was, it was covered up double quick. They made the horses obey with a sniff from a rag which they kept in their pockets. Caraway seeds had something to do with it, I believe, although others say different.

A lot of farmers hid their horses during the Great War, when the officers came round. The officers always gave good money for a horse but sometimes the horses were like brothers and the men couldn't let them go, so they hid them. I wasn't called up. Nothing happened to me and I didn't remind them. We didn't really miss the men who didn't come back. The village stayed the same. If there were changes, I never felt them, so I can't remark on them. There was still no money about. People seemed to live without it. They also lived without the Church. I'm sorry about this but it is true. I hardly ever went when I was young. The holy time was the harvest. Just before it began, the farmer would call his men together and say, 'Tell me your harvest bargain'. So the men chose a harvest lord who told the farmer how much they wanted to get the harvest in, and then master and lord shook hands on the bargain.

We reaped by hand. You could count thirty mowers in the same field, each followed by his partner, who did the sheaving. The mowers used their own scythes and were very particular about them. They cost 7*s*. 6*d*. in Wickham Market, but it wasn't the buying of them, it was the keeping them sharp. You would get a man who could never learn to sharpen, no matter how he tried. A mate might help him, but then he might not. Some men mowed so quick they just fled through the corn all the day long. Each mower took eleven rows of corn on his blade, no more and no less. We were allowed seventeen pints of beer a day each and none of this beer might leave the field once it had been brought. What was left each day had to be kept and drunk before eight on a Saturday night. It was all home-brewed beer and was made like this:

You boiled five or six pails of water in a copper. Then you took one pail of the boiling water and one pail of cold water and added them together in a tub big enough to hold eighteen gallons. You then added a bushel of malt to the water in the tub. You then added boiling water from the copper until there was eighteen gallons in all in the tub.

Cover up and keep warm and leave standing for at least seven hours, although the longer the better. When it has stood, fill the copper three parts full from the tub, boil for an hour and add half a pound of hops. Then empty into a second tub. Repeat with the rest. All the beer should now be in one tub and covered with a sack and allowed to cool. But before this, take a little of the warm beer in a basin, add two ounces of yeast and let it stand for the night. Add this to the main tub in the morning, then cask the beer. You can drink it after a week. And it won't be like anything you can taste at the Crown, either.

The lord sat atop of the last load to leave the field and then the women and children came to glean the stubble. Master would then kill a couple of sheep for the Horkey supper and afterwards we all went shouting home. Shouting in the empty old fields – I don't know why. But that's what we did. We'd shout so loud that the boys in the next village would shout back.

Stacking was the next job, all very handsome they had to be – handsome as a building. Then thrashing. It was always reckoned you had to thrash a stack in a day. There wasn't any rest after the harvest. The year had begun again, you see.

from IN THE COUNTRY

Kenneth Allsop

Kenneth Allsop (1920–73) was the first of a new breed of writers and environmentalists who came to the public eye as broadcasters and journalists. He served in the RAF during the Second World War and was in constant pain from the amputation of his leg after an accident on an assault course. He became a familiar face on television in the 1960s as a reporter on the BBC's innovative *Tonight* programme, and then as an anchorman on other current affairs shows *24 Hours* and *Midweek*. He was a prolific journalist, writing for *Picture Post*, the London *Evening Standard*, *The Spectator*, *Punch* and others. He estimated he wrote one and a half million words during twenty years in journalism. He left London and moved to the Dorset countryside, writing about wildlife and presciently warning about its destruction by modern industrial farming. Among his novels is *Adventure Lit Their Star* (1949), inspired by Allsop's love of birds and the natural world. He also wrote a history of prohibition in America, *The Bootleggers* (1961), and *The Angry Decade* (1958), an account of new British writing in the 1950s. He took his own life in 1973.

Kale is all right in its place. That is inside the tubby bellies of those sumptuous beige sheep grazing the stonewalled uplands with their lambs.

What is not its place is growing along Eggardon's arched spine, above the tumuli and hut circles, and eight hundred feet above the blue dazzle of sea.

This rooftop of turfed limestone is a place for kestrels and orchids, for butterflies like flecks of the sky itself, the chalkhill blue and the Adonis blue. They waver among the scabious and harebells, vast as angels against the miniaturized woods and barns on the unfolding tracts below.

This is the grand soaring finale to the westward drive of chalk, the furthermost tip of the arrowhead plateau which narrows across half England from its widely-splayed base points, one in north Norfolk and the others on the High Weald of Kent.

On this last great limb, a dominion of wind, cloud and turf, there is a sense of pure form and power of rock-formation which I have felt nowhere else. Ahead, the Marshwood Vale dissolves into the Devon border.

Sitting quietly here you can see a fallow deer in the rough dell far beneath. Buzzards idle over the oaks of King John's hunting preserve. The wind which planes the flesh from your cheek-bones blows meadow pipits down into the gorse scrub.

This is the great inland promontory about which Andrew Young wrote:

… there on the hill-crest
Where only larks or stars look down,
Earthworks exposed a vaster nest,
Its race of men long flown.

A newer race can now roar in high-powered tractors brilliantly marked as Formula One machines and capable of surmounting one-in-two slopes. They slice up those majestic flanks. The kale looks as daft here as would hollyhocks in a window box. The best bit of news from Whitehall recently has been the revocation of government grants for ploughing virgin land – but there is still encouragement to get at high ground.

It is painful to contemplate the damage done in just this part of Wessex by non-selective cash handouts luring ploughshares into old sward, the 'living garment' as W. H. Hudson called it.

Since the 1952 Ploughing Grants Enabling Act, seventy local downs, headlands and hilltops have been done over – and, in the process, irreplaceable ancient green lanes, ridgeways and sheep droves wiped out.

It is no good, I suppose, setting one's face against the post-war agricultural mechanical revolution which has boosted food production.

But the strip-and-exploit policy, gone at with such zest, went too far – and not with the stupendous benefits forecast. Some farmers, uneasy at dustbowl scouring on East Anglian prairies, are now resowing quickthorn where were the hedges they grubbed out. 'Intensive methods', 'maximized production' and so on may mean intensive and maximized trouble – and in the meantime so much irrecoverable beauty gone for good.

I can still descend Eggardon's steep snout on a track probably used by prehistoric settlers, but the footprints of the past are fainter.

from THE SHEPHERD'S LIFE

James Rebanks

The descendant of generations of Cumbrian hill farmers, **James Rebanks** (b. 1974) told the story of his life from schoolboy dropout to obtaining a first-class degree at Oxford University before returning to run the family farm in *The Shepherd's Life* (2015), an echo of W. H. Hudson's *A Shepherd's Life*. It became a bestseller and has been translated into sixteen languages. Rebanks obtained his book deal after coming to public attention as @herdyshepherd1 on Twitter, writing sharply and intimately about his working life and his scenic workplace in the Lake District. His follow-up, *English Pastoral: An Inheritance* (2020), documents the agricultural revolution since his grandfather's day, and his own determination to farm with sympathy for the soil, landscape and wildlife. He has worked as a consultant to UNESCO, which designated the Lake District as a World Heritage Site, and is an advocate for wildlife-friendly farming while remaining a staunch critic of rewilding.

Some of my earliest memories are of summers in the hay fields following my grandfather around. I would be sitting or sleeping behind the forever-bouncing seat of a tractor whilst someone else baled or turned the hay. Once I was mobile, it was a time for running and leaping over rows of hay, building dens in the bales, fishing in the streams that cut through our meadows. As long as the sun shone, it always felt like a special time of the year – as if all was well with the world because the cattle and sheep could look after themselves, for the most part, for a few weeks in summer, and we were going to have the crop to feed them over the next winter.

Hay times were like chapter markers in my life, each one showing me to be a little stronger and more useful and my grandfather a little older and weaker. I literally grew into his shoes. In the good summers, or perhaps just in my memory, there was an air of joy about it, and my grandmother would come to the field at regular intervals with meals or afternoon tea, cakes she'd baked and a large tin jug of tea. We'd sit around on makeshift chairs made of bales, and the old men would tell stories and joke about summers past. I loved those stories about working horses, the heroic labours of men in the past, and the German and Italian POWs who had come to work on the farm during the Second World War.

Granddad didn't reckon much of the Italian officers, their claims of aristocratic pedigrees, or their somewhat different work ethic. 'They were all Count-bloody-this… and Count-bloody-that.' And they wolf-whistled at girls passing by in the train carriages. Some of those POWs were still living on the farms they'd chosen to stay at after the war, rather than return to a home that didn't exist anymore. They lived in little bedrooms in farmhouses all over our area, like strange living ghosts of the war that had ended before my father was even born.

The wind would catch wisps of hay in little tornadoes and whizz it off across the field. Swallows would hawk around the field catching insects. High atop bale-laden trailers, I rode home, dodging branches and telephone wires. Once, the trailer caught a gate post as we turned into the yard. I tumbled down on an avalanche of bales, landing at my grandmother's feet. She clucked and fussed. The men denied, perhaps truthfully, any knowledge of me being up there. I just shrugged.

The hay meadows were criss-crossed with shadowy little streams, flanked with foxgloves, havens from the heat of the day for sheepdogs and children. These meadows were not mown until late summer, so that the flowers and plants could drop their seeds. Traditional upland hay meadows are a thing of beauty. Rich multicoloured waves of grasses dancing in the light summer winds. Mosaics of brown, green and purple grasses and flowers are home to a multitude of insects, birds and occasional roe deer calves. Lush, green, thistle-scattered pastures flank the hay fields, with the twin-rearing ewes watching the commotion with interest. Grasshoppers call to each other from the ribbons of green that are the field boundaries, and magpies chatter from the crab apple trees.

In an ideal world, hay timing would be easy. Three or four days of perfect drying weather after the grass is mown, two or three sessions of turning it to ensure it is uniformly dried by the wind and sun. The hay, dry and sweet-smelling, would be baled and then led into the barn, never so much as touched by a drop of rain. But it is not like that very often in English summers. Timing the mowing to hit the gaps between rains is a calculated gamble at best and a bad summer can ruin a winter's fodder, and often did in the Lake District. So hay time is often a battle between the farmer and the weather.

Cutting the meadows leaves the mower covered with a thick carpet of grass seeds, pollen and insects. It also opens up a hidden world where voles had lived in peace, but now scurry off to the dykes. In one of our meadows, the sun-bleached skeletons of two elm trees stood, from where a kestrel would watch us work, occasionally hovering above the field and swooping down on a vole and carrying it off in a fistful of talons.

Following the mower, perhaps a day later, would come the haybob, which fans the grass out of the rows in which it lies and helps it to wilt evenly in the sun and wind. For the next few days, sand martins sweep past us as we turn the hay each day, scattering insects to the breeze.

When the greenness and sap have wilted out of the grass after a few days, it is rowed up ready for the baler. And at last the baler starts thumping out its dusty clunking rhythm. The men work under the keen eyes of greedy lice-tormented rooks, which wander the fields searching for worms and grubs under the cleared rows. From time to time a 'sheer-bolt' might snap on the baler and you would hear frenzied hammering and a few 'fucking hells'.

Today, hay time is increasingly mechanized (in the 1980s new machinery came in which meant that crop can be wrapped in plastic even in damp summers and some nutritional value is saved by pickling it as 'silage'), but throughout my childhood and youth it was a full-on physical effort with everyone expected to pitch in.

Once the bales were made, they had to be taken to the barns and eventually manhandled into the 'mews'. Stacking bales was one of the jobs we dreamt of being strong enough to do when we were boys. Each slow year of growing up was filled with the hope that, next year

maybe, we would stack bales with the men. Our family had a shortage of young men, so we looked enviously across the fence to our
neighbours who could muster a full gang. As each bale was hand-
lifted several times before it was put in the barn – and we made
thousands – strength mattered.

Each year I found myself a little stronger, and able to lift the bales
higher, while my grandfather grew weaker. His sense of his own
decline was only eased by the pride he had in me, his grandson, growing up to take his place. As a child, I had rolled bales to his knees,
thinking I was helping, and carried his bottle of cold tea from heap
to heap, wishing I was as strong as him. And each year the balance
between us altered in my favour. Then we reached a curious halfway
point where we worked as equals, when I was about thirteen years
old, but I quickly agreed each time he suggested that 'us two old men'
ought to stop 'for our pipe' (neither of us smoked). The next year I
was much stronger than him and pretended I needed to stop, every
now and then, so he could rest. A couple of years after that, he was
following me around the field, rolling bales to my knees for me to lift,
and lifting the odd one when he could.

Making hay in daydreams tends to be idyllic and sunny, but in real life
it can be a bitch of a thing. I can remember 1986, the worst summer,
when we burnt all our hay. A disaster. You need nearly a week of dry
and sunny weather to make hay. And you need to be able to travel
on the meadows with a tractor and mower to mow the grass at the
start of that week. What could possibly go wrong in one of the wettest
places in England?

In 1986 it just never stopped raining. Black clouds. Miry fields. Endless
rain. Sometimes summer never quite happens. It must have offered
brief moments of respite, though, because somehow we got the hay
baled, but then the heavens opened and it rained for days and days.
If you understand the importance of good hay, there is something
irretrievably sad, pitiful and pathetic about ruined hay. What should

be a lovely sun-bleached green slowly becomes grey, rotten and dead. What should have been our harvest for the winter rotting into something worse than useless, a time-consuming liability. We tried stacking the bales against each other, on days when the wind blew and rain eased. But the bales now sagged deadweight beneath the baler twine in your stinging hands. More rain. Fat splashing drops. The heaviest I've ever seen. The hay was ruined. It had started to sprout green on the tops of the bales. It would never dry out. Everyone knew it. Even if we got it into the barns, it would 'heat'. It might even combust and burn the barn down as sometimes happened on farms. Or it might simply rot. There was no point in bringing it in. Rooks skulked in the ash trees, waiting for worms under the heaps.

The fields were now green with 'fog' (the sweet regrowth after cropping that we use for the lambs that are weaned off their mothers in August and September), the bales sulking and leaving rotten dead marks where the grass should now have been cleared. However bad it was, the hay needed to go somewhere. Clearing the fields of this sodden junk was like moving corpses. Cruel work. Sickening for men. Pointless. Rotten smelling. We took thousands of bales to the ruins of an old stone barn, created a fire beneath one corner of the pile. Stood back and watched. But the cursed stuff couldn't even burn properly. It smouldered sulkily for weeks. I can still smell the hay burning in a stupid, pointless, charred heap. We brought bales to the heap for days until the fields were cleared, sweating, with rain dribbling down our necks. When we were finished, we had nothing to show for weeks of work or a year's growth on the meadows. No hay in the barns. Fields now boot-deep in grass except for coffin-shaped dead yellow stains where the bales had lain. My father turned away and said, 'Never mention this to me ever again, I don't want to remember it.' Grey smudgy clouds anchored to the fells and it rained on for weeks.

from THE GRASSLING

Elizabeth-Jane Burnett

Elizabeth-Jane Burnett (b. 1980) is a poet, a writer and an academic, currently associate professor in creative writing at Northumbria University. Educated at Oxford University, with a PhD in contemporary poetics from the University of London, her poetry collections include *Swims* (2017) and *Of Sea* (2021). Her innovative memoir, *The Grassling* (2019), is an exploration of her deep connection with her father and their landscape of rural Devon. The writer Bernardine Evaristo highlighted the uniqueness of Burnett's book in the deeply white ecosystem of British nature writing. 'Burnett is breaking new ground as a mixed-heritage English/Kenyan woman connecting so deeply to the historic land of her father's family in the West Country,' said Evaristo.

ELK-SEDGE

*itcomesitcomesitreallycomestousitsstemfoldsitscurvestouchourcurve-
itstrokespullsitsfingersthroughhourhairfeelsthebristlesofourbladesfur-
offlowersitfillswithuswemoveintoitsmouthitstoestenseitspillsitswords-
intoourswedouseitinlightbutonlyitseyesseeandtheymissmostofitbutthe-
lightithasfindsitswayintoitsmouthandwhatcomesoutisachurningbutter-
inglanguagetonguingdandelungingfromthegrasslingitnamesitswimming-
thispullingofitselfoverthisflatteningtensings/wallowingitfeelsourwateron-
itsskininitsthroatalongitswindpipeittinglesitsmouthopenswiderwepour-
initexpandswhatisinitbesideswaterandbreathandwordsandlightitdoes-
notseemtohaverootsyetthisfeelslikeonlythetipofititisheavy*

As I move through the grass with her, it is strange to be talking to someone other than the land, or those living inside it. Blackthorn bursts in the Drewshill hedges as Rebecca, an artist, sketches. She talks about Cézanne. 'He was also interested in the depth of things, the extension beneath the ground,' she says. 'Are you concerned with the sky?' It's a startling question, and with the shamefacedness of someone realizing they've only been looking at half the picture, I reply that I am not. It's the ground level and deeper, beyond that, I say. Rebecca nods, as though this is a satisfactory answer, though I feel that it is not. After some time spent silently with the grass, I start making exploratory moves with my fingertips. I press into the earth, slowly increasing the pressure. Is anyone in? Deeper fingers, then palms, rocking, kneading the ground. I take my socks off and the wet, soft grass – dandelion and clover – is delicious. I go through the same motions with my feet: first the toes, then the balls, then the rocking back and forth. This is the start, the sounding out, the seeing if the other is open to conversation.

'I'm about to roll,' I announce to Rebecca, who nods, securing our cameras. But the ground is full of water and I'm already starting to shiver, just from the contact of hands and feet. 'I'll wait for that cloud to pass,' I pronounce, as though it's of vital importance to the project, that I'm awaiting the perfect alignment of celestial and earthly bodies, but it is really just the small, all-too human need for warmth. As I hover between stillness and movement, nestling into wet grass, sedge, purple dead nettles, I hear the elk-sedge: a rune, depicting an 'x' sound in the Old English *Rune Poem*. Its flowering body calls from the ground, in amongst the grass it chinks and chimes, whispering its wetness. The light and water held on the grass-tips reminds me of my blade of grass, and home. Before I spin, I feel afraid of the wetness, of being out of control; of falling and not being able to stop. I feel fear of becoming field, of being swept into its contours. And what will I be when I roll over? A plough? That flattens the earth in order to mine it. But I won't take from it – only words. I won't penetrate – only soften. I let go.

Rebecca makes swift movements, dabbing and scratching the sur-face of the paper. And depth seems important to the paper too, to our movements over the recording material. I turn and turn into wetness. The plunge of it. The thud on the spine and the speed of it. Weightless. Unable to stop. Plummeting, grass on face, in ears, in throat. The hit of the spine. Were it not for that, I could go on forever.

It is hard to stop. At the end I lie prostrate, face down, arms straight out in front. I must flatten in order to stop. Lying there, stretched and wet, I wonder if any of my ancestors lowered in this spot, this Druid's Hill, kneeling to this earth, in prayer. And I think of my father as I lie there: all body, all slippage. In the tissue of the land and skin and bone and sky, I think of him, across the fields. *He is still here*, I think, and I rise.

As I warm up from the wetness, things with wings visit. As if they see me more as one of them now, as a part of the field, or a type of tall grass. A cricket sits on the bottom of my jeans; a black beetle on my hand. A peacock butterfly brushes over my arm for the lightest of seconds. My arms glow. I start to think of my actions as a sort of poem:

FIELD SWIMMING
FIELD BATHING
FIELD STROKING

And just as with the water, I want to get back in. But I must be gentler on the spine that is already carrying an injury. So this time I roll sideways, a horizontal, rather than vertical turn. Arms and legs stretched, as long as I get, I come to the top of the hill and tip. At the start, the eye is a camera. Blades of grass in the foreground, landscape correcting itself in the back, to form a picture. I try to keep my eyes open, though they keep wanting to close. I want to record everything. Be fully in the moment, yet also to store it. I let go. The same phrase from my earlier action. What is it that I am letting go, when I fling or slip along a landscape? The responsibility of standing up? It is a casual disappearance, this exit from gravity. An absence that can be readily achieved, that I can fit into dailyness.

As I move, I find I am rotating into the direction of the hedge, instead of straight down the hill. Once more, it is difficult to stop. I pause on all fours and wait for the world to stop spinning, and when it seems to, jump up. But no sooner am I standing than I plummet three, four, five steps down again. The hill is still in me – its incline, its roll. Finally, I come back up and try again. I will myself to remain in a straight line but this requires so much tension in the body that I give up and allow myself to roll where I want to – back towards the hedge. My angle is taking me parallel to the church below, in the valley. I wonder about the possibility of some sort of spiritual ley line.

And here, in land, the body regulates your possibilities, just as in the sea. When the coldness of the water dictates the duration of the movement, here it is the coldness of the wetness of the grass. And if you lived beyond that? In the soil? Are you still subject to the body's limits? I wonder about the temperature of the soil, and how the worms weather it. In cold spells, they burrow down more deeply. They can even freeze entirely, then be thawed back to life. I think about the tiny resurrections that may be taking place under me, in the warming soil.

A fly moves along a blade, close by. It has legs *and* wings, which seems greedy. Though it walks along the grass, at any moment it could lift itself off and into air. It edges along the edge of things – all leg. I try it for a while, taking a long, slow stalk through the grass. As I walk into the hill's incline, I approach its brow. Where does the field become a hill? Where does the head become the spine? Where is the neck of the hill? Flat becomes curved, spine ricochets into ribs, erupts into breast. I stroke the field, pulling fingers through grass like hair: the soft clover, spider, beetles; the small button mushrooms, the open dandelions. Breast. Stroke. I start field swimming. Again, words come as poems:

BREAST STROKING
NETTLING
DANDELUNGING
GRASSLING

Pulling my fingers through, my mouth fills with grass, my toes dig in to propel me. I feel my internal circuitry change: I am plant as well as animal. My blood transports oxygen; my chlorophyll produces it. Oxygen, carbon, hydrogen, nitrogen, phosphorus surge along tissue, torso, culm, to my blades. Blood blends magnesium as well as iron. I am grass made flesh. Grassling.

With no malleable water to move through, only fixed ground, I have to use my body more. The push comes from the toes, which are rooted, along my culm to the knees, which repeat the movement, only larger and deeper. Leaved arms sweep out, gathering and spreading wetness and sweetness; the words get tangled: swetness and spreetness; weading and sweeting; all knotting and breathing in and over the tongue.

Once more, I knead the earth, wondering about its energies. How churches were dowsed and located on ley lines of supposedly beneficial energies. If the land, like the body, can hold a trauma (I think of where he lies, across the fields), it can also, perhaps, hold a healing. I always feel better here, always. When I pull up from the field, it is as if from a spa. Skin tingles with life. I breathe it all in, the moment, and the capture of the moment. The moment where I am closer to my father through being in a space that he has been in. A space where his father has been, and his father too. And I will tell him about the field, though not the rolling and spinning and swimming, but I needed all that to get in. To get close enough to what is here; to what it feels and means to be here. By being here, I become part of his story. Through a shared space and shared narrative, I write myself into him.

from FOUR FIELDS

Tim Dee

A lifelong birdwatcher, **Tim Dee** (b. 1961) was a radio producer for the BBC for thirty years. His first book, *The Running Sky* (2009), described his first five decades watching birds. In the same year he collaborated with the poet Simon Armitage on the anthology *The Poetry of Birds*. Since then he has written and edited several critically acclaimed books: *Four Fields* (2013), a study of modern pastoral; *Ground Work* (as editor, 2017), a collection of new commissioned writing on place by contemporary writers; and *Landfill* (2018), a modern nature-junk monograph on gulls and rubbish. *Greenery: Journeys in the Springtime* (2020) describes the movement of spring over the planet. Dee divides his time between the Cambridgeshire fens, Bristol and the Cape of Good Hope in south-west Africa.

HOME FIELD

I was driving home in the dark. The stop-start charms of the A14. Lorries heaving into the night and boxy with containers, metal bergs not long off the sea struggling over the land, Stonehenge and Easter Island heads to be delivered to the interior. Body shunts and heart attacks on every incline. The Midlands up in front. Dusk had taken the fields next to the hurrying road out of sight. The lit trench was all. I was thinking of nothing, as you must to survive, when stems of grass suddenly glanced in my beams and crowded at my windscreen, their straight thin bars of strobing light tinkling against the glass. Somewhere in front of me a hay lorry was travelling and throwing behind it this green storm. The traffic slowed. As I braked, the hectic sprinkle fell away and I could see in my headlights and then feel beneath my tyres that the whole of the road's surface was covered in the thinnest spread of hay. A cigar butt or two of the stuff must have bounced from the back of the lorry and split on the road. We were all driving on grass. It brought a smile to my face. I might have strayed into some nativity scene of straw carried into a church and spread across a stone floor to make a point. I might have drifted into the story of the Princess and the Pea. The road had been transported or turned over into a kind of field and the grass was announcing itself in our ungreen and ungrowing world. My car and all the cars and lorries around me inched forward over the strange luxury beneath our tyres and, though the hay blades were thin and crushed thinner, I could still feel the new field under me with its tiny ridges and furrows briefly repossessing the road.

Throughout my life much of my happiness has come from being outside. That brief smile on the A14 was declaring it. I became a serious birdwatcher at the age of seven in 1968. I've grown less serious with time but, ever since my childhood, going out *into the field* has been part and parcel of what I do. The *field* might mean the fields of a farm but it can also mean anywhere that birds live and especially places where you deliberately look for them. Mostly this has been away from towns and cities, but not always: a back garden would do on a good day, or a park. My wanting to see birds simplified the world: if you didn't go out, you didn't see anything; if you did go out, regardless of what you saw, you seemed to have been somewhere and to have done something. Thoreau used the same phrase having spent a day kneeling to the earth to collect fallen sweet chestnuts in October 1857. Any day out for me, any day in the field, was better than a day indoors – I think that is what Thoreau meant too. Being outside was never a waste of time: even a day in July in a wood in the middle of England at the year's green midnight, when no birds sing; even an expedition in February with a grumpy girlfriend to an urban sewage farm; even a day with only a pitiful species list or wet feet to show for your efforts. Without any fieldwork of this kind, life inside stalled. Long before I read it, I knew the damp grey constriction – in my chest and between my eyes – of the first page of *Jane Eyre*: 'There was no possibility of taking a walk that day.'

Indoors, looked at from the field, seemed at best to be talk about life instead of life itself. Rather than living under the sun it fizzed – if it fizzed at all – parasitically or secondarily, with batteries, on printed pages, and in flickering images. I realised this around 1968 in my seven-year-old way. At the same time, however, I learned that I needed the indoor world to make the outdoors be something more than simply everything I wasn't. I saw it was true that indoor talk helped the outdoor world come alive and could of itself be living and lovely, too. Words about birds made birds live as more than words. Jane Eyre, held inside by bad weather, takes Thomas Bewick's *History of British Birds* to the window and reads looking out into the wind and rain.

A yellowhammer on a flaming gorse a mile from my childhood home, my first ring ouzels on spring migration on the grassed bank of a slurry pit – these birds, once found and named (real, flighty, not interested), started something off like a shock into living. The world leaned on me, as it were, and the green gears of outside became part of the machinery of my mind, and 'a language of my whole life', as Ted Hughes described animals in his. Ever since, being in the field, following the field's seasons and its birds, and, at the same time, moving words from indoors out, and outdoors in, has more or less dominated my years.

Without fields – no us. Without us – no fields. So it has come to seem to me. 'This green plot shall be our stage,' says Peter Quince in *A Midsummer Night's Dream*. Fields were there at our beginning and they are growing still. *Earth* half-rhymes with *life* and half-rhymes with *death*. Every day, countless incarnations of our oldest history are played out in a field down any road from wherever we are. Yet these acres of shaped growing earth, telling our shared story over and over, are so ordinary, ubiquitous and banal that we have – mostly – stopped noticing them as anything other than substrate or backdrop, the green crayon-line across the bottom of every child's drawing. For Walt Whitman, prairie-dreamer of the great lawn of men, grass fitted us and suited; it was a 'uniform hieroglyphic'. It grew and stood for us and, because it goes where we are, we tread where it grows.

Yet because it meant everything it could easily mean nothing. It is in the nature of all commonplaces that they are overlooked, in both senses of the word: fields are everywhere but we don't see them for they are too familiar and homely; being the stage and not the show, they are trodden underfoot, and no one seeks them out, no one gives a sod.

Might it be possible to look again and to see the grass and the fields afresh? Our making of fields, first of all from that grass, has tied us to nature more than any other human activity. The relationship is rooted yet simple, ancient yet living. Fields offer the most articulate description and vivid enactment of our life here *on earth*, of how we live both within the grain of the world and against it. We break ground to lay foundations, sow seeds and begin life; we break ground to harvest life, bury our dead and end things. Every field is at once totally functional and the expression of an enormous idea. Fields live as proverbs as well as fodder and we reap what we sow.

'The fields!' urged John Ruskin, early conjuror of cultural landscapes, 'follow but forth for a little time the thoughts of all that we ought to recognize in those words.' What follows here is an attempt to say some more about the fields in my life; to understand why these four fields mean as much to me as they do and how they have given me the sentimental education, the heart's journey, that they have; to explore what they have meant to others; to discover the common ground they make, the *midfield*; to walk and work them in the only way I know, to name their birds and to read their words; to remember their other workers, their makers, mappers, gleaners, fighters; to count their flowers and to smell them; to link wild fields to factory fields; to argue that the most meaningful green squares might be the most banal, the most beautiful meadows the most ruined; to learn how they all work and how they all fail; to find the future of some in their past and, in others, their present enduring through change; to dive into their grass and sneeze alive, to lie in their grass and feel it a grave; to enlist every acre.

My beginning is the simple discovery of a simple truth. The outside places that I like are the places that I know. And being born in the 1960s and growing up in southern England, the places I know best, apart from the A-roads and the paved and heaped-up world of towns and cities, are the man-made fields close to home in between them. A *terra cognita*.

I hardly know a single wild place. There is none left in England. 'Natural England' is a government department. I am not actually sure that you can know a wild place. Not knowing how to be in a rainforest, I couldn't wait to get out of the only one I have ever been in. I am equally frightened of the open sea. In 1972, I thought I was going to drown when the father of a schoolfriend lost his nerve as we sailed a little dinghy off the Isle of Sheppey and the sea slopped over the side of the boat. The nearest I have come to divorcing my wife was just last year when she scampered on ahead and left me frozen in terror on a (humiliatingly) small cliff on Table Mountain above Cape Town.

For Claire the mountain isn't wild – it is her outside place, a mountain as it happens, and which begins at the end of the street where she grew up. I would say the same for most of the fields in this book. They are places where I find myself. My plots and theirs overlap. I am not a farmer but like almost all of us I am a fieldworker. Jane Eyre peers at Thomas Bewick's Arctic vignette of 'forlorn regions of dreary space' and makes the English weather outside her window speak. Seamus Heaney digs with his pen as outside his window his father lifts potatoes with a spade. The plough was the first constellation in the night sky that I learned. It remains the only one I can point to reliably.

In what follows I want a field to mean most often a man-made outside place, but my definitions will run wild at times and be close-cropped at others, my facts and my metaphors (those carried into and out of the fields) will change with every ground. Come with me, then, as I plough my own furrow, but forgive me, knowing that we all must.

The word *field* is almost as big and elusive as its neighbour *nature*. And fields are talk of nature as well as ways of talking to nature. One of our oldest words, speaking of one of the first things we made and one of our oldest concepts, is alive and growing still. Fields are ordinary, universal, tamed and practical, but they are also none of those things or their opposite; they are strange, particular, wild, and as far beyond money as human-inflected things can be. The hedged allotment and the open prairie coax different poems as well as different meals. Kept places keep us in all sorts of ways. Fields are pay dirt but also the greatest land art on the globe. There is a story that John Ruskin once took a plough into an art lecture at Oxford to ensure his students – who, like me, might have known the plough of the night sky better – would recognise what one of the most effective sculptural tools ever invented by man looked like.

What is predictable in a field is never quite understood and what is extraordinary about them often seems familiar. 'Visionary dreariness', Wordsworth reported in *The Prelude*, and fields mist with the same negative capability or paradoxical potential. A fallow field is life in waiting. But so are all fields. In their ubiquity and in their endless difference, they are places of continuity and of security but also of risk and of transformation. In a dream scene in the Taviani brothers' film *The Night of San Lorenzo*, a troop of Italian partisans in World War Two hides below the ripe wheat of a field and then, moments later, stands up armoured as Virgilian heroes to fight the Black Shirts with pitchforks. A bread field becomes a battlefield. In a ballad sung by Nic Jones, a smart lady is tempted and lies outdoors all night with seven yellow gypsies. A green field becomes a seamy bed of grass. Who wouldn't smile?

For a year or so around my tenth birthday I was perhaps the only subscriber in Croydon to *Farmers Weekly*. Before I fell in fully with birds, I had wanted to be a zookeeper or a farmer. But I have never had a field of my own nor worked in one. I have never cut hay nor driven a tractor. Once I rode on a horse. It tried to throw me into a puddle. More recently, I abandoned a walk across a fen field because a herd of cows was gathered at its gate and I was frightened to cross into their bulky company. I don't like milk, fatty meat, gravy, thick butter, or runny eggs.

For a few months in my twenties I had a girlfriend who was a farmer's daughter. We ended in a mess, strung out in different cities in different countries, but the beginning of our end happened I think near our very beginning, in her bed in her old childhood bedroom down the farmhouse corridor from her parents' room. Not that anyone was asleep, except for me; not that anyone was even in their bedrooms, except for me. Me – the visitor who knew about the early whitethroat singing in the hawthorns along the farm hedge but who wasn't expected or even invited to join the rest of the family out in the lambing barn in the middle of the night. Shifts had been allocated: my girlfriend's visit, even with a new boy, didn't excuse her, and when they weren't pulling lambs from ewes, or forking bloody straw from the cobbles, or cutting the fleece off dead lambs to wrap others that had been orphaned at birth so they might be fostered by the mothers of the dead, she and her family were behind the lines at the big range in the farmhouse kitchen on tea-making duty (the slab-tongue of milk into a mug), or cutting crumbling ham slices for midnight sandwiches (a brick of butter oiling its own dish). Eventually the farmer's daughter came back to bed and she smelled of the ewes and the lambs, of birth and afterbirth, of grass and wool, of everything that I wasn't, and I smelled of nothing at all, and we were never to work.

I had though, aged six, loved my little silvery-grey rubber milk churns that were part of my Britains toy farm set. I also loved how I could have a Ford tractor (blue) and a Massey Ferguson one (red) and could fix on the back of either my Lely Snipe Rotary Tedder (four words I have never written in that order until now nor uttered to anyone ever but which I know to be as indelibly true as anything in this world). When you steered the tractor with your finger the tines on the tedder spun round. And at the same time, in the next field, made with plastic drystone walls that clicked together, you could have a one-inch tall shepherd carrying a crook in one hand and a lamb in the other, and put next to him a shire horse with great feathered feet, some tiny saddleback piglets, and a blonde girl wearing wellingtons and a short 1960s sky-blue dress who spooned maize for chickens or ducks forever. And I loved it, and her for getting it for me, when my mother persuaded a greengrocer to part with some of his plastic display grass so that I might lay out on the proper ground my whole farm, barns, fences, tractors, farmers, animals, and so be installed in heaven, irked only by a problem of scale that meant that the blades of greengrocer grass came too high up the sides of my livestock and they tended to fall over in it.

I did the falling over, on a family holiday to Skye in Scotland, when I was ten. My sister and I were encouraged to feed two orphaned lambs with bottles of fresh milk from the farm cow. The lambs were small and stood only to our knees, but they butted us with surprising force, knocking me over in their haste and my nervousness. I got up and patted them, and their fleece was thick and my fingers came away greased with lanolin. The next time I knew that same strange ointment was holding for a quick minute in my surprised arms the oily purple body of my first son, just after he was born and before he was dried and delivered to his mother's breast. On Skye, my sister and I were dragged around the sheepfold by the amazing suck of the lambs on their teated bottles which they pulled at as if everything they needed was in the milk. I next knew that sensation when after his first feed I slipped my finger into the warm wet pucker of my baby's mouth and felt concentrated there all of his world.

The farmer's wife did the milking on Skye. She was a farmer too, though we have no word for her despite her centuries of toil. 'The farmer wants a wife', was the end of the round we sang at school of cattle and chattels. The wife followed 'the farmer wants a sheep' and 'the farmer wants a pig'. One morning she invited me into the byre to watch her milking. The Old English *byre* is related to *bower*, which is related to the German *Bauer* or birdcage. Sure enough, as I followed her muddy boots, swallows flew in and out above us, cutting into the dark, twittering one quick tune as they arrived and another slightly amended one as they left. The cowshed was heavy with the catching smell of sweet-grass-made-shit, a half-dirt-half-dream smell, rising up out of an old world that you find, even aged ten, you know already. I stood against the stone doorway and watched.

The farmer's wife pulled the pail of new milk towards me from between the cow's dirty legs. She had leaned in there on a little low stool, her cheek pressed against the cow's flank, a great black furry wall, while her hands moved on the swaying full moon of udder. The jet of milk rattled like peas at first in the empty bucket and then, as it frothed and filled, like nothing so much as the sound of my own desperate peeing after a run home from school. And, like my pee accidentally touched, it was surprising for being warm, almost hot.

In the dark of the byre, the brightest things were all the same washed creamy colour: the farmer's hands, her cow's udder, and the rising disc of milk. 'Try it,' she said, and I knew I should even though I already knew that it wasn't for me. I drew her enamel cup through the bubbles and they burst into tiny flecks of curd that fell back on to the skin of the milk. I wanted to pour it direct to my throat but it covered the inside of my mouth in a warm chalky paint. As it went down it pulled just below my ears, at the place where my jaw was joined to my head. One mouthful was enough. I gave up on *Farmers Weekly* not long after.

Two grass truths I have learned anyway. Like anyone in the temperate world I lived these without knowing them. If you cut grass it doesn't die. If you eat its tops it doesn't mind, because it grows from near its base at what is called an intercalary meristem. This is the joint-like node on the stalk, the bump you feel beneath your fingers when you pluck a stem from the side of a path. Grasses and intercalary meristems are inseparable. In the growth tissue at the meristem, rapid cell division occurs and pushes the grass upwards. A simple and beautiful adaptation has brought us to where we are: hay can be cut, lawns mown, plains grazed. Herbivores – grass-croppers – drove this evolution. Grazing by buffalo maintained the prairie. A savannah is a wildebeest.

The second unknown known: our bodies are grass. We are grass 'carnified' as Thomas Browne said: 'all those creatures we behold, are but the hearbs of the field, digested into flesh in them, or more remotely carnified in our selves'. A cow eats grass and makes milk; a steer eats grass and becomes beef. We toast our cheese and barbecue our burgers and wrap the ensemble in a bread roll made of grass. The three great food crops of the north (now of the whole world) are grasses: rice, corn and wheat. They made us but we made them, as well. We have more than grown up together. Our domestication of the wild has drawn the wild after us. The transubstantiation of the earth works on.

Grass, like us, is young, fresh and green across many time zones. Our bodies are grass, and our days, as the Psalmist said, are 'as' grass. Grass has been a metaphor for our short life as long as we have known it. Land plants have been around for more than 400 million years but grasses evolved only 50 or 60 million years ago. The world's grasslands are young landscapes. Grass has dominated the temperate northern hemisphere only in the last 10,000 to 12,000 years. We appeared in these places about the time they became grasslands. And grass itself seems endlessly young while endlessly dying. Nowhere do its blades grow older than any autumn makes them. A meadow is a year.

Fields are not often famous for what they are. But begin to make a list of those you recall and it is hard to stop. South of the High Atlas Mountains of Morocco there is pitifully little grass. In this rock-desert the soil is thin. The last fields before the Sahara are here. Some giant has unpacked, tearing impatiently at a parcel, and the surface of the Earth is littered like a new planet with the debris of its making, with black shattered stones that might have fallen from above or sliced their way up from beneath. They are hot from the sun or with the smoulder of the core. In the hills east of N'kob, a Berber family was making a field near a dry riverbed, clearing stones and raising low walls from them, twisting thorns into shrunken hedges. Seeing my friend Mark and me looking for scrub warblers, they said hello and invited us for tea. The young mother, forever pulling her headscarf across her shy smiling face, bent to a pile of thorn twigs and made a fire from them under a soot-blackened kettle. Her two teenage boys brought more kindling. Their father stooped lightly to their field, with a familiarity that made the stones at his feet seem like his crop. He collected an armful as he walked through the cleared place he was making and dropped the stones at the field edge, then crouched to the kettle and leaned in to his wife. I smiled and bent too. We had no language in common. The boys were picking at a thorn; in the next bush along I could see a scrub warbler, my first ever, carrying smaller twigs for its own purposes. The new field beyond the little fire of sticks and its three hearthstones ran for no more than fifty feet in one direction and thirty in the other. There were still many stones to clear. The soil without the stones was as dry and as hard as the stones. The mother shook green tea leaves from a box into their blue enamelled teapot and took a rough block of sugar from the folds of her clothes and passed it to her husband. He hit it with a stone and dropped shattered angular chunks into four blue tea glasses. The boys had to wait while Mark and I drank. The warbler came closer and scolded us with a call as dry as the grey thorn it hid among. The family would try to grow a few lines of wheat here, for couscous. When the kettle had finished a small cooking pot replaced it on the tiny flames; in the pot were a few slices of potato in dilute harissa, their lunch.

Two days later we came down from the mountains into Marrakesh, descending through white storks and cattle egrets planing to their roosts, and arriving as the high violet dusk gave way to a night of blue velvet above the Djemaa el-Fna, the teeming square at the heart of the old medina. There was drumming and singing and a thousand mopeds. Wood smoke from the grills thickened the air and the lanterns of the cafes floated in it like so many full moons. We ate and then walked into the souk, losing ourselves within moments between the beetling cliffs of goods bursting from the fronts of crowded stalls that deepened giddily beyond like tunnels without end. There were reclining torsos of pungent leather bags, star clusters of verdigris-stained copper lamps, forests of rusty carpets. The vendors were packing up, getting everything that had been laid out in front of their stalls back into the narrow spaces beyond. We were chased down alleys by the judder of metal roller-blinds and we stumbled out of the maze to stop in front of the smallest unit of any that we had passed: a lit green cave, fluorescent bright and deeply scented, a mint stall. The mint-man in a khaki greatcoat was tiny-faced and old and he stood (there was only standing room) framed or wrapped by bunch after bunch of countless serrated green leaves in a sweet and clean-smelling cloud. For the female customer ahead of us, he selected eight or so handfuls from beneath a freshening wet sack at the front of his stall. We spoke briefly (me in halting French) and she said that the carrier bag of mint she had bought was all for tea, would keep in the fridge, and would last about a week. We smiled at the green man in his green cave, the smallest, freshest and greenest field in the world, and walked on out into the riot of the dusty old city.

—m—

At the other end of Europe, a few months later, I slept in the final field before the Atlantic.

After the last of the mainland fell away behind us, there was an hour and a half of open water. The sea rolled and slapped the boat. The engines churned, roaring when the propellers rose out through the swell. The seabirds thinned. I tried not to be sick. More slapping, the sea's leer and its bully lean. Then the auks came again, flying ahead of us now, towards where we were going. Slowly out of the marine-blue rose a low grey whaleback. It calmed my guts, grew up, and turned island-green. The engines were cut and we sunk down in the boat, finding our level in the sea at the base of a cliff. We landed in a tender, clambering down to the sea's surface, touching it as we gripped the dinghy, then scrambled up again, wet rocks, then dry, then grass. We dragged barrels of fresh water up the rough slope, its green rising in front of me to fill my sweating eyes, as the salt sea had done minutes before. At the top, I threw my bags from my back and found myself sitting in a field – fifty miles out into the ocean west of Cape Wrath, and the only field on North Rona.

I pitched my tent in a grassed ditch at what looked like the field edge. Away from its cliffs most of the top of the island is grass; on its gentlest slope looking back towards the mainland is the remains of its one field. My friend Kathleen had a bunk in the hut where seal scientists stay. No one has lived on North Rona since 1844; no one could live there now. It and its neighbour, Sula Sgeir, twelve miles off to the south-west, are like accidental islands, crumbs brushed from the table of the mainland and lodged in the sea. Even huddling into the bank there is no real shelter to be had from the wind. But once, under the same oceanic barrage, the island was farmed. The ditch was dug to raise an adjacent bed of soil in order to grow things to eat. Dug and re-dug between the eighth century and the nineteenth, the lazy bed (a mean name far removed from the effort needed to make it) marks the land still, just as it did on the day it was cut from the turf and soil. It is part of a beautiful sinuous geometry, a delta of green corduroy, which drains furrows and ridges, runs and rigs, down the island's sloping southern flank to the sea. It is as human a mark as we have made anywhere before or since.

There is an unmanned lighthouse on Rona now, and the hut is used by the seal people for a few weeks of the year. Both buildings are too recent to look anything other than garish and temporary, ludicrously – and vulnerably – square-angled and blocky in this place of rounded and winded things. The grass blows into a permanent wave along the lazy beds; the ruined houses and chapel in the old village with their turf roofs and drystone walls curve out of and back into the land as if they have grown from it. Storm petrels and Leach's petrels now breed in burrows they dig between the stones of the village.

The ditches, like the ruins, are an imposition on Rona; they mark a clearance, an enclosure, something made in our scale, and yet the space they create has found some natural equivalence in the scale of the island and so of the Earth. The human space has become a landscape that endures even in its ruin. A centre, somehow, even on the edge. The ripples of green man-made lines spilling down the grass-topped island seem good. If marks have to be made, they seem to be the best marks to make. Thus fields anywhere and everywhere: old but apt; imposed but giving; made in proportions that fit the Earth and us, which bring us together, that allow us to belong, that take the oldest and most searching human measurement – how much land does a man need? – and say, this can be yours, these acres, this plot, your field, man's not nature's, but the best thing of man, and the thing of his that is nearest to becoming nature.

After a midsummer night of the snag and fret of half-light and sea wind, I lay in my sleeping bag with my head out of the tent looking up at the sky. A migrant swallow flew above me along the shelter of the ditch, seeking – as I had – the calmed air made by people shifting earth hundreds of years ago. It fed, as it flew, on the insects that gathered in the windless lee. The sea had stilled to the south and tracks and furrows had stretched to meander across its surface, oiled smooth in places, more choppy in others, marking deeper currents beneath, and the way the sea, even in its continuousness, drifts and ripples variously under the wind and around the land. It looked like a field of grass.

If you were not a commoner or a parishioner in early-modern England and you wanted to rent part of a common field or hire rights to pasture, you might seek someone called a *fieldsearcher*, who would act as an agent on your behalf. Without fields of my own, these chapters are *my fieldsearches*. The field to which I return most often is currently rough grazing land at Burwell in the Cambridgeshire fens, one mile from where I live. This field was once a fen and the intention of its current owners is that it will be fen again, one day. The other three are foreign plots that I have known (in part) across some years: far afield, but not. The first of these is in Zambia on an old colonial farm. This particular field once grew tobacco but is at present overgrown with grasses and scrub. I have already written a little about these Zambian fields. Since those first words the farmer has died (he is buried near his old crops) and I have married Claire, the woman who showed me the field, the farm and the farmer. The second foreign field is a battlefield, and the remnant shortgrass prairie and adjacent croplands, in Montana in the USA where Sioux and Cheyenne warriors killed George Custer and his party in June 1876, in a battle which as much as anything was a fight over grass. The last field is in the abandoned village of Vesniane in the Exclusion Zone near the exploded nuclear reactor at Chernobyl in Ukraine. Until April 1986 it was a meadow grazed by cows. When I went there, the last thing I saw was an empty aluminium milk churn lying on its side, in the open doorway of a ruined byre at the field edge.

Each of these four fields has been turned over in one way or another for as long as they have been fields – it's in their nature. But now each is at a more angled point in its life. Fields cut from cleared scrub are abandoned back to thorns and thickets. Wild grasslands have become battlefields and then the holding place for the dead of those battles. Pasture is poisoned. A plot will be unplumbed. Territory, ownership, the exploitation of land, its meaning and value, the grass itself – all has been and is being argued over. There are tangled human voices in each field but there is also the sound of the grass. Just as fields aren't famous, grass isn't heroic of itself. It works anonymously. But I am trying to hear that as well. In John Clare's great poem 'The Lament of Swordy Well' a put-upon, enclosed field talks back. It's worth listening.

—⁂—

I'll begin by taking us once again to the worst so we might get it behind us. The road, encore. The anti-field. A place that is not even a place, which is the opposite of where you want to be, but where you find yourself again and again. I grow old even thinking about it, even as I tell you. This time we will walk up to it, in order to best catch the sting of its slap, but so that we might also have a means of escape. Stand at the last field edge before the asphalt. In front of you is a main road, the A14 once more, sunk into the ditch of a cutting. You don't see it until you arrive at the lip of its wound but you have heard it already, forever, the crenellated din of combustion and hardware passing without end. If you are lucky it sounds like a sea heard from the top of a cliff; more likely it puts a boxed fever into the brain, a swarfed headache driving between your ears. You have been here many times before; indeed, part of you lives here, though you are never at home. Your car will dip below the earth's surface, angle down the slipway, and latch on. But today, on foot, turn your back on the road and walk west down the green path through the wheat fields.

The dual carriageway of the A14 marks the eastern edge of the English fields of this book. The road forms the county border between Suffolk and Cambridgeshire and also the upland end of the parish of Swaffham Prior where Claire and I live. From the house it takes half an hour to walk to the main road, up a farm lane or along a footpath on the top of a chalk dyke (the Anglo-Saxon Devil's Dyke or Ditch). Depending on the wind's quarter I hear the road between five and fifteen minutes after leaving the front door. Once, when I was near, a crash had stopped the traffic on both sides and I could hear skylarks singing in Suffolk, otherwise I have never heard it quiet. Every day it fights its fight, dug into its trench.

Halfway into the last field before the traffic, a lesser whitethroat rattling from the final hedge stole into my ears. After that the road silenced all apart from itself. I flushed a skylark and it rose nervously and banked to avoid having to fly over the cars. I saw its beak open but couldn't hear its call. In the last wide fields of Cambridgeshire that run to the road there were forty hares spread through the young wheat in twos and threes. The sun streamed through their long black ears flushing them blood-pink. Such ears for such noise. At the road, parallel with it, is a hedged bridleway, just twenty feet from the metal run of traffic. I have never seen any person or horse there. A dead mole was on the path, lying with its head pointing towards the road, *unsoiled* – encumbered by being above the earth and to be buried in the air. It looked, as D. H. Lawrence said of a mole in his story 'Second Best', 'like a very ghost of joie de vivre'. It was earless and its eyes were lost into its soft fur, giving its front a blank and incomplete look. Its mouth grinned half open and showed two tiny canines, ivory needles against its sooted snout. Its fleshy hands and feet hung at its four corners like pink flags.

I turned from the mole and the road and headed west. If you look from the Suffolk hills to the Cambridgeshire fens, the sky leaps up above you and doubles in height. In the spring on days of silvery cloudless sheen it seems higher still and able to further flatten the fields beneath it. The country before me opened but it also disappeared, thinning at the horizon about ten miles away to a level green line. This is a fen effect. Shining green ground hurries like dark water spilled across a tabletop to fill the flat space. The width of the view tugs at the corners of your eyes, its shallowness makes you frown. There is a lot of light to take in and not much else.

I heard a bee flying past my ear. The chalk hills behind me (though they would barely count as hills anywhere but here) made a bony barn of stone and they shouldered the dyke back towards the main road. Ahead, where the bee had gone, the fens were a soft and glistening skin, streaming from beneath me, cambered at either edge, an offering of earth, thin and damp but vividly alive. The green squares of the farms of Burwell, Reach and Swaffham Prior were chopped and trimmed by their hedges and ditches and, rolled hard under the silver-blue noon, they receded like Euclid's geometry or Alice's chessboard. Descending towards them and the fen beyond from the last few feet of altitude on the dyke was like watching from the windows of a landing aeroplane, when distance and spread shrink and narrow until you arrive on the ground as if buried by the near edge of things. But there were consolations: new weather came and conversation. A skylark got up from the path ahead, climbing over a field, its wings and throat rippling in one continuous action of flight and song. A lapwing shadowed a buzzard. Cowslips on the bank shook in the wind like smeared butter. There were swallows laying their slates, one over the other, up above my head. They sang as they worked.

The village of Reach marks the fen end of the dyke. It finishes on the village green but the dyke line continues beyond the cluster of houses and joins another man-made pathway running across the flat fen: Reach Lode, a cut waterway draining west. Though my feet remained dry I had crossed into a world of wet. I felt it beneath me. The calcified spine of the dyke was replaced by stoneless earth banks held together by the lush green grass and the soft dampness of the soil itself. Back on the dyke the molehills had been pale and powdery and lumpy with nubs of chalk and blades of flint. A hundred steps away on the banks of the lode they were soft and peaty, smooth and sticky, and as black as mole fur.

My fen field begins here, the first of the four in this book. From here, there is not much to look at. It is the same closer up. But the field, once a stretch of fenland, has worked its way into my life, as have the three others. All four are grassed at the moment. They are real fields: a few hundred acres standing for the world. They could be walked, mapped, mown and known. Each has lived, at least for some time, as an apparently flat and plain place but also as a living sheet on which people sketched or screened various dreams for a while. Yet regardless of their fieldworkers' attentions, each also holds on to its own life, and remains itself even as it is harvested or grazed, preserved or abandoned. All fields are places of outlasting transience. They reset time. Each has a past but each lives in the present; each has a biography but is still a work in progress.

It happens that the same species of bird, the swallow (known internationally these days as the barn swallow), flies and feeds over all my four fields, and I love the bird and our world for that, though that doesn't make the grass beneath the swallows the same. The fields have some things in common but much that is particular. They are site-specific, idiomatic and accented; they are shaped by what they are near and speak of where they are. We made them and we were made by them. 'The land has been humanised, through and through', D. H. Lawrence wrote of rural Italy as he might have of all fields, 'and we in our own tissued consciousness bear the results of this humanisation.' I wonder if there are any two fields in Britain that are identical? I doubt it. I've been keeping watch. I know there are no ways into a field, no field-gateways in the world, that are the same. But I also know in no field anywhere do you feel properly lost.

And yes, as well as being a book of four fields, I want this to be a book *for* fields, a work of advocacy as much as of observation. My field love is different from my swallow love. Swallows I love for not being us, for not knowing they are swallows, for quickening the air while flying so closely and so swallowishly about our lives. I love fields for what they are, parcels of the earth we have gathered to us (almost always beautifully, could there be an *ugly* field?), but also for the picture they give us of ourselves (not always beautiful), the way all fields tell of how we have orphaned ourselves from the world – how hard we must work for even a whisper of Eden – but also how best we can be at home in it.

FOUR SEASONS

Illustration overleaf: *Blackberries*

from THE SOUTH COUNTRY

Edward Thomas

Perhaps unusually, **Philip Edward Thomas** (1878–1917) was a literary critic, biographer and nature writer before he became best known for his poetry. He was born in Lambeth, London, and married while he was still studying at Oxford. Determined to live by his writing, he reviewed up to fifteen books each week, becoming the *Daily Chronicle*'s literary critic and later residing on his wife's family farm near Sevenoaks, Kent. He wrote prolifically about wildlife, the countryside and earlier 'nature writers' including Richard Jefferies and John Clare, but also suffered from depression and attempted suicide on numerous occasions. Widely acclaimed by critics and writers from Aldous Huxley to Seamus Heaney, Thomas wrote all his poems over the final three years of his life after meeting American poet Robert Frost in 1913. Often considered a war poet, in fact few of his poems directly document his experiences fighting in the First World War. He was killed in the battle of Arras in 1917.

HAMPSHIRE

The beeches on the beech-covered hills roar and strain as if they would fly off with the hill, and anon they are as meek as a great horse leaning his head over a gate. If there is a misty day there is one willow in a coombe lifting up a thousand silver catkins like a thousand lamps, when there is no light elsewhere. Another day, a wide and windy day, is the jackdaw's, and he goes straight and swift and high like a joyous rider crying aloud on an endless savannah, and, underneath, the rippled pond is as bright as a peacock, and millions of beech leaves drive across the open glades of the woods, rushing to their Acheron. The bush harrow stripes the moist and shining grass; the plough changes the pale stubble into a ridgy chocolate; they are peeling the young ash sticks for hop poles and dipping them in tar. At the dying of that windy day the wind is still; there is a bright pale half-moon tangled in the pink whirl of after-sunset cloud, a sound of blackbirds from pollard oaks against the silver sky, a sound of bells from hamlets hidden among beeches.

Towards the end of March there are six nights of frost giving birth to still mornings of weak sunlight, of an opaque yet not definitely misty air. The sky is of a milky, uncertain pale blue without one cloud. Eastward the hooded sun is warming the slope fields and melting the sparkling frost. In many trees the woodpeckers laugh so often that their cry is a song. A grassy ancient orchard has taken possession of the visible sunbeams, and the green and gold of the mistletoe glows on the silvered and mossy branches of apple trees. The pale stubble is yellow and tenderly lit, and gives the low hills a hollow light appearance as if they might presently dissolve. In a hundred tiers on the steep hill, the uncounted perpendicular straight stems of beech, and yet not all quite perpendicular or quite straight, are silver-grey in the midst of a haze, here brown, there rosy, of branches and swelling buds. Though but a quarter of a mile away in this faintly clouded air they are very small, aerial in substance, infinitely remote from the road on which I stand, and more like reflections in calm water than real things.

At the lower margin of the wood the overhanging branches form blue caves, and out of these emerge the songs of many hidden birds. I know that there are bland melodious blackbirds of easy musing voices, robins whose earnest song, though full of passion, is but a fragment that has burst through a more passionate silence, hedge-sparrows of liquid confiding monotone, brisk acid wrens, chaffinches and yellowhammers saying always the same thing (a dear but courtly praise of the coming season), larks building spires above spires into the sky, thrushes of infinite variety that talk and talk of a thousand things, never thinking, always talking of the moment, exclaiming, scolding, cheering, flattering, coaxing, challenging, with merry-hearted, bold voices that must have been the same in the morning of the world when the forest trees lay, or leaned, or hung, where they fell. Yet I can distinguish neither blackbird, nor robin, nor hedge-sparrow, nor any one voice. All are blent into one seething stream of song. It is one song, not many. It is one spirit that sings. Mixed with them is the myriad stir of unborn things, of leaf and blade and flower, many silences at heart and root of tree, voices of hope and growth, of love that will be satisfied though it leap upon the swords of life. Yet not during all the day does the earth truly awaken. Even in town and city the dream prevails, and only dimly lighted their chalky towers and spires rise out of the sweet mist and sing together beside the waters.

The earth lies blinking, turning over languidly and talking like a half-wakened child that now and then lies still and sleeps though with eyes wide open. The air is still full of the dreams of a night which this mild sun cannot dispel. The dreams are prophetic as well as reminiscent, and are visiting the woods, and that is why they will not cast aside the veil. Who would rise if he could continue to dream?

It is not spring yet. Spring is being dreamed, and the dream is more wonderful and more blessed than ever was spring. What the hour of waking will bring forth is not known. Catch at the dreams as they hover in the warm thick air. Up against the grey tiers of beech stems and the mist of the buds and fallen leaves rise two columns of blue smoke from two white cottages among trees; they rise perfectly straight and then expand into a balanced cloud, and thus make and unmake continually two trees of smoke. No sound comes from the cottages. The dreams are over them, over the brows of the children and the babes, of the men and the women, bringing great gifts, suggestions, shadowy satisfactions, consolations, hopes. With inward voices of persuasion those dreams hover and say that all is to be made new, that all is yet before us, and the lots are not yet drawn out of the urn.

We shall presently set out and sail into the undiscovered seas and find new islands of the free, the beautiful, the young. As is the dimly glimmering changeless brook twittering over the pebbles, so is life. It is but just leaving the fount. All things are possible in the windings between fount and sea.

Never again shall we demand the cuckoo's song from the August silence. Never will July nip the spring and lengthen the lambs' faces and take away their piquancy, or June shut a gate between us and the nightingale, or May deny the promise of April. Hark! before the end of afternoon the owls hoot in their sleep in the ivied beeches. A dream has flitted past them, more silent of wing than themselves. Now it is between the wings of the first white butterfly, and it plants a smile in the face of the infant that cannot speak: and again it is with the brimstone butterfly, and the child who is gathering celandine and cuckoo flower and violet starts back almost in fear at the dream.

The grandmother sitting in her daughter's house, left all alone in silence, her hands clasped upon her knees, forgets the courage without hope that has carried her through eighty years, opens her eyes, unclasps her hands from the knot as of stiff rope, distends them and feels the air, and the dream is between her fingers and she too smiles, she knows not why. A girl of sixteen, ill-dressed, not pretty, has seen it also. She has tied up her black hair in a new crimson ribbon. She laughs aloud with a companion at something they know in common and in secret, and as she does so lifts her neck and is glad from the sole of her foot to the crown of her head. She is lost in her laughter and oblivious of its cause. She walks away, and her step is as firm as that of a ewe defending her lamb. She was a poor and misused child, and I can see her as a woman of fifty, sitting on a London bench grey-complexioned, in old black hat, black clothes, crouching over a paper bag of fragments, in the beautiful August rain after heat. But this is her hour. That future is not among the dreams in the air to-day. She is at one with the world, and a deep music grows between her and the stars. Her smile is one of those magical things, great and small and all divine, that have the power to wield universal harmonies. At sight or sound of them the infinite variety of appearances in the world is made fairer than before, because it is shown to be a many-coloured raiment of the one.

The raiment trembles, and under leaf and cloud and air a window is thrown open upon the unfathomable deep, and at the window we are sitting, watching the flight of our souls away, away to where they must be gathered into the music that is being built. Often upon the vast and silent twilight, as now, is the soul poured out as a rivulet into the sea and lost, not able even to stain the boundless crystal of the air; and the body stands empty, waiting for its return, and, poor thing, knows not what it receives back into itself when the night is dark and it moves away. For we stand ever at the edge of Eternity and fall in many times before we die. Yet even such thoughts live not long this day. All shall be healed, says the dream. All shall be made new. The day is a fairy birth, a foundling not fathered nor mothered by any grey yesterdays. It has inherited nothing. It makes of winter and of the old springs that wrought nothing fair a stale creed, a senseless tale: they are naught: I do not wonder any longer if the lark's song has grown old with the ears that hear it or if it still be unchanged.

from CIDER WITH ROSIE

Laurie Lee

Laurie Lee (1914–97) grew up in the small Cotswold village of Slad, which provided the material for the first of his autobiographical trilogy, *Cider with Rosie* (1959). He left school at fifteen to become an accountant's errand-boy in Stroud and his next volume, *As I Walked Out One Midsummer Morning* (1969), told of his escape from rural England for London and then Spain, where in December 1937 he voluntarily joined the International Brigades during the Spanish Civil War. He later worked as a journalist and screenwriter. During the Second World War, he made films for the government and from 1950 to 1951 was caption-writer-in-chief for the Festival of Britain. He became a full-time writer after the success of *Cider with Rosie*, which depicts the pleasures and hardships of rural life just before it was irrevocably changed by the motor car.

Summer, June summer, with the green back on earth and the whole world unlocked and seething – like winter, it came suddenly and one knew it in bed, almost before waking up; with cuckoos and pigeons hollowing the woods since daylight and the chipping of tits in the pear-blossom.

On the bedroom ceiling, seen first through sleep, was a pool of expanding sunlight – the lake's reflection thrown up through the trees by the rapidly climbing sun. Still drowsy, I watched on the ceiling above me its glittering image reversed, saw every motion of its somnambulant waves and projections of the life upon it. Arrows ran across it from time to time, followed by the far call of a moorhen; I saw ripples of light around each root of the bulrushes, every detail of the lake seemed there. Then suddenly the whole picture would break into pieces, would be smashed like a molten mirror and run amok in tiny globules of gold, frantic and shivering; and I would hear the great slapping of wings on water, building up a steady crescendo, while across the ceiling passed the shadows of swans taking off into the heavy morning. I would hear their cries pass over the house and watch the chaos of light above me, till it slowly settled and re-collected its stars and resumed the lake's still image.

Watching swans take off from my bedroom ceiling was a regular summer wakening. So I woke and looked out through the open window to a morning of cows and cockerels. The beech trees framing the lake and valley seemed to call for a Royal Hunt; but they served equally well for climbing into, and even in June you could still eat their leaves, a tight-folded salad of juices.

Outdoors, one scarcely knew what had happened or remembered any other time. There had never been rain, or frost, or cloud; it had always been like this. The heat from the ground climbed up one's legs and smote one under the chin. The garden, dizzy with scent and bees, burned all over with hot white flowers, each one so blinding an incandescence that it hurt the eyes to look at them.

The villagers took summer like a kind of punishment. The women never got used to it. Buckets of water were being sluiced down paths, the dust was being laid with grumbles, blankets and mattresses hung like tongues from the windows, panting dogs crouched under the rain-tubs. A man went by and asked 'Hot enough for 'ee?' and was answered by a worn-out shriek.

In the builder's stable, well out of the sun, we helped to groom Brown's horse. We smelt the burning of his coat, the horn of his hooves, his hot leather harness, and dung. We fed him on bran, dry as a desert wind, till both we and the horse half-choked. Mr Brown and his family were going for a drive, so we wheeled the trap into the road, backed the blinkered horse between the shafts, and buckled his jingling straps. The road lay deserted in its layer of dust and not a thing seemed to move in the valley. Mr Brown and his best-dressed wife and daughter, followed by his bowler-hatted son-in-law, climbed one by one into the high sprung trap and sat there with ritual stiffness.

'Where we goin' then, Father?'

'Up the hill, for some air.'

'Up the hill? He'll drop down dead.'

'Bide quiet,' said Mr Brown, already dripping with sweat, 'Another word, and you'll go back 'ome.'

He jerked the reins and gave a flick of the whip and the horse broke into a saunter. The women clutched their hats at the unexpected movement, and we watched them till they were out of sight.

When they were gone there was nothing else to look at, the village slipped back into silence. The untarred road wound away up the valley, innocent as yet of motor-cars, wound empty away to other villages, which lay empty too, the hot day long, waiting for the sight of a stranger.

We sat by the roadside and scooped the dust with our hands and made little piles in the gutters. Then we slid through the grass and lay on our backs and just stared at the empty sky. There was nothing to do. Nothing moved or happened, nothing happened at all except summer. Small heated winds blew over our faces, dandelion seeds floated by, burnt sap and roast nettles tingled our nostrils together with the dull rust smell of dry ground. The grass was June high and had come up with a rush, a massed entanglement of species, crested with flowers and spears of wild wheat, and coiled with clambering vetches, the whole of it humming with blundering bees and flickering with scarlet butterflies. Chewing grass on our backs, the grass scaffolding the sky, the summer was all we heard; cuckoos crossed distances on chains of cries, flies buzzed and choked in the ears, and the saw-toothed chatter of mowing-machines drifted on waves of air from the fields.

We moved. We went to the shop and bought sherbet and sucked it through sticks of liquorice. Sucked gently, the sherbet merely dusted the tongue; too hard, and you choked with sweet powders; or if you blew back through the tube the sherbet-bag burst and you disappeared in a blizzard of sugar. Sucking and blowing, coughing and weeping, we scuffled our way down the lane. We drank at the spring to clean our mouths, then threw water at each other and made rainbows. Mr Jones's pond was bubbling with life, and covered with great white lilies – they poured from their leaves like candle-fat, ran molten, then cooled on the water. Moorhens plopped, and dabchicks scooted, insects rowed and skated. New-hatched frogs hopped about like flies, lizards gulped in the grass. The lane itself was crusted with cow-dung, hard baked and smelling good.

We met Sixpence Robinson among the bulrushes, and he said, 'Come and have some fun.' He lived along the lane just past the sheep-wash in a farm cottage near a bog. There were five in his family, two girls and three boys, and their names all began with S. There was Sis and Sloppy, Stosher and Sammy, and our good friend Sixpence the Tanner. Sis and Sloppy were both beautiful girls and used to hide from us boys in the gooseberries. It was the brothers we played with: and Sammy, though a cripple, was one of the most agile lads in the village.

Theirs was a good place to be at any time, and they were good to be with. (Like us, they had no father; unlike ours, he was dead.) So today, in the spicy heat of their bog, we sat round on logs and whistled, peeled sticks, played mouth-organs, dammed up the stream, and cut harbours in the cool clay banks. Then we took all the pigeons out of their dovecots and ducked them in the water-butt, held them under till their beaks started bubbling then threw them up in the air. Splashing spray from their wings they flew round the house, then came back to roost like fools. (Sixpence had a one-eyed pigeon called Spike who he boasted could stay under longest, but one day the poor bird, having broken all records, crashed for ever among the cabbages.)

When all this was over, we retired to the paddock and played cricket under the trees. Sammy, in his leg-irons, charged up and down. Hens and guinea-fowl took to the trees. Sammy hopped and bowled like murder at us, and we defended our stumps with our lives. The cracked bat clouting; the cries in the reeds; the smells of fowls and water; the long afternoon with the steep hills around us watched by Sloppy still hid in the gooseberries – it seemed down here that no disasters could happen, that nothing could ever touch us. This was Sammy's and Sixpence's; the place past the sheepwash, the hide-out unspoiled by authority, where drowned pigeons flew and cripples ran free; where it was summer, in some ways, always.

Summer was also the time of these: of sudden plenty, of slow hours and actions, of diamond haze and dust on the eyes, of the valley in post-vernal slumber; of burying birds out of seething corruption; of Mother sleeping heavily at noon; of jazzing wasps and dragonflies, hay-stooks and thistle-seeds, snows of white butterflies, skylarks' eggs, bee-orchids, and frantic ants; of wolf-cub parades, and boy scouts' bugles; of sweat running down the legs; of boiling potatoes on bramble fires, of flames glass-blue in the sun; of lying naked in the hill-cold stream; begging pennies for bottles of pop; of girls' bare arms and unripe cherries, green apples and liquid walnuts; of fights and falls and new-scabbed knees, sobbing pursuits and flights; of picnics high up in the crumbling quarries, of butter running like oil, of sunstroke, fever, and cucumber peel stuck cool to one's burning brow. All this, and the feeling that it would never end, that such days had come for ever, with the pump drying up and the water-butt crawling, and the chalk ground hard as the moon. All sights twice-brilliant and smells twice-sharp, all game-days twice as long. Double charged as we were, like the meadow ants, with the frenzy of the sun, we used up the light to its last violet drop, and even then couldn't go to bed.

When darkness fell, and the huge moon rose, we stirred to a second life. Then boys went calling along the roads, wild slit-eyed animal calls, Walt Kerry's naked nasal yodel, Boney's jackal scream. As soon as we heard them we crept outdoors, out of our stifling bedrooms, stepped out into moonlight warm as the sun to join our chalk-white, moon-masked gang.

Games in the moon. Games of pursuit and capture. Games that the night demanded. Best of all, Fox and Hounds – go where you like, and the whole of the valley to hunt through. Two chosen boys loped away through the trees and were immediately swallowed in shadow. We gave them five minutes, then set off after them. They had churchyard, farmyard, barns, quarries, hilltops, and woods to run to. They had all night, and the whole of the moon, and five miles of country to hide in...

Padding softly, we ran under the melting stars, through sharp garlic woods, through blue blazed fields, following the scent by the game's one rule, the question and answer cry. Every so often, panting for breath, we paused to check on our quarry. Bullet heads lifted, teeth shone in the moon. 'Whistle-or-'OLLER! Or-we-shall-not-FOLLER!' It was a cry on two notes, prolonged. From the other side of the hill, above white fields of mist, the faint fox-cry came back. We were off again then, through the waking night, among sleepless owls and badgers, while our quarry slipped off into another parish and would not be found for hours.

Round about midnight we ran them to earth, exhausted under a haystack. Until then we had chased them through all the world, through jungles, swamps, and tundras, across pampas plains and steppes of wheat and plateaux of shooting stars, while hares made love in the silver grasses, and the large hot moon climbed over us, raising tides in my head of night and summer that move there even yet.

from THE GREEN FOOL

Patrick Kavanagh

A poet and novelist, **Patrick Kavanagh** (1904–67) was raised in rural Ireland, the fourth of ten children and son of a farmer and cobbler. He left school at thirteen to work on his farm and as an apprentice to his father. As Kavanagh later depicted in his memoir, *The Green Fool* (1938), he was a dreamer who preferred to read. His first poems were published in newspapers in 1928. Encouraged by George William Russell, the editor of the *Irish Statesman*, Kavanagh walked to meet him in Dublin and was given books by Fyodor Dostoyevsky, Victor Hugo, Walt Whitman, Ralph Waldo Emerson and Robert Browning. Kavanagh's first poetry collection, *Ploughman and Other Poems* (1936), was feted for its realistic and unsentimental portrayal of Irish country life. Kavanagh was sued for libel by the Irish poet Oliver St John Gogarty for a self-deprecating description of Kavanagh visiting the great poet's home and mistaking his maid for a wife or mistress, with Kavanagh assuming that every poet had multiple wives. Kavanagh later worked as a journalist and bartender, and became known for his heavy drinking. After winning his own libel case in 1954 – a newspaper had portrayed him as an alcoholic sponger – and after losing a lung to cancer, his writing career revived and he was championed by fellow poets and publishers and lectured in Dublin and the United States.

During the Great War Rocksavage farm was let in con-acre* on the eleven months' system. The letting was a godsend to the neighbourhood. Small farmers who before had only one old horse or a jennet now kept a pair of horses.

* Con-acre: land let to farmers by the year.

The letting was held in December. There would be a barrel of porter for the customers. The porter and the soaring prices of farm-produce combined to set the bidders merry.

I went with father to the letting. It was a bitterly cold day. In the cobbled yard behind the Big House a large crowd were gathered. The porter was being handed round in tin porringers by a hunchback. There weren't enough porringers. I saw one old man with a bucketful of frothy porter on his head. Tinkers, chimney-sweeps, professional porter-drinkers, they were all there. The auctioneer was waiting in the Big House till the porter would have time to work. Father had come to take an acre for potatoes. The auctioneer came out at last. He was a big, fat man with a glass eye. He mounted the stone steps of an old loft. He cracked a few dry jokes to test the temper of his audience. The laugh-replies were satisfactory. The porter was beginning to barm in bellies.

All the bidding was done by a nod of the head. There was an old fellow who suffered from head-shakes. The auctioneer accepted this fellow's reflex-action as an authentic bid. Everybody laughed.

When all the land in the vicinity of the Big House had been let, we trailed through the muddy fields. Puddles of yellow water filled the cattle tracks. There was only the ghost of the sun low in the sky. I shivered.

The auctioneer stood on a knoll in a stubble field. Those men who were hungriest for land gathered in close. Only one woman was among the crowd. There was no chivalry. She had to out-bid the field.

The stubble field was put up for potatoes or turnips. Father bid fifteen pounds an acre. There was a lull. I thought the crowd were giving him a chance. I was mistaken. A near-neighbour nodded his head.

Sixteen pounds bid, seventeen, eighteen, twenty, twenty-five.

Father was the highest bidder. He took one acre. If his rival had been the highest he would have taken the whole field, he was buying for profit and not out of necessity.

I worked in all the fields of Rocksavage and developed a home-lover's sentiment for them. I knew every corner of those fields, and every well and stream.

Some of the fields possessed aristocratic names such as the Sundial, but others, like Eden Bawn, which means 'the bright face', told of the days when there was poetry in the land.

Rocksavage filled a great place in our lives. Before the War there were thousands of beautiful trees on the farm. Close to our school these trees leaned over the wall and dropped us nuts – monkey-nuts for making toy-pipes, horse-chestnuts of which we made whistles and hazel-nuts which we ate.

Then came the timber-hunger and the trees began to fall.

'O what will we do for timber
The last of the woods are down?'

No wonder the old Gaelic poet, lamenting the destruction of the woods of Kilcash, sang so sadly.

Rocksavage trees were sold by auction. The man who bought one cut down five as there was nobody to stop him. Father didn't buy any of the trees. There were no young, strong men in our house to help. There was no love for beauty. We were barbarians just emerged from the Penal days. The hunger had killed our poetry and we were mere animals grabbing at the leavings of the dogs of war. Money was pouring in every front door and pouring out the back door. Our house had no back door.

At school we wrote compositions on the War. I got a home exercise to write. Father wrote it for me – 'On Submarine Warfare'. A very profound essay, it quite flabbergasted Miss Cassidy.

On the classroom wall was hung a map of Europe, coloured red for the Allied nations, green for the Germans, and white for the neutral nations.

An inspector came in one day. He examined us on our war-knowledge. I knew every general on both sides. The inspector said I should be a colonel. Miss Cassidy was very pleased.

The money was coming into our house in a steady stream. Our hens were good layers – Black Minorcas and Brown Leghorns. Our parents paid more attention to the fowls than they paid to us children. The hens were laying golden eggs.

Father and a constable of the Royal Irish Constabulary joined in sending to Kent, in England, for a pair of prize cocks. The constable was a fanatical hen-fancier. The pair of prize cocks arrived at the Inniskeen railway station. Through the crate father and the constable surveyed the birds. One of the cocks was a real prize bird, a fellow with a fine curving tail and a rose-red comb. The second bird looked like a starved chicken that had been out in the rain. His comb was pale, and his tail-plumes would not be decorative in a woman's hat.

The constable suggested drawing lots and father agreed. Father won and the constable had to take the poor scraggy bird. Even though father won he declared that that would be the last time he'd have anything to do with a pig-in-a-poke business.

During the War money grew on the tops of the bushes. Blackberries were five shillings a stone. Rocksavage farm was the home of briars, rich fruit-bearing briars ignored by all the money-grubbers. Very few people ate blackberries, the one man who did we thought a bit touched on that account. Myself and two sisters were sent out each morning with cans and porringers.

'Go out and push your tenants,' our mother told us. 'Whoever has the most in a dinner-time will get something.'

Very few children were gathering the berries, it was considered a mean business and there was a lot of pride among the people. So we had nearly all the berries to ourselves. We could each of us pick two stones per day and more if we chanced upon a real good spot. Before setting out we arranged our different routes.

One day I had the fox-covert plantation; it was on top of a high hill looking across to Cavan and Meath. Up here the blackberries grew in wonderful abundance, good ones the size of big plums. I filled my can full to the brim in a short time. I was raking in the money. All I had to do was pull the berries off in fistfuls.

Harvest men were working in the same field and when I had my can filled I went down among the golden sheaves and the sunny music of the reaping machine. My bare legs were raw with briar-scratches, and the stubbles when I sat down stung me. My hands were blue with berry-dye and my face as well – we used to stain our faces with the first blackberry.

Blackberrying was a great way of seeing the secrecies of the good earth, the rabbit-holes and the fox-dens that seemed to open into a fairyland, and the strange untrodden places in briary corners where a child could explore.

Rocksavage was a fine place for a dream-wanderer. There was no caretaker, or at least, no one to trim the hedges and whins where the fairy folk hide. The whins on the Forth Hill grew ten feet high, and in between them were magical countries where cowslips and banshees' thimbles grew. The banshee's thimble was a wild foxglove. I once put the thimbles on my fingers and was told that the Banshee would call for me before a year.

We lived long and happy days in that blackberry time. The world that was Rocksavage was boundless and uncharted as the broad places of the imagination. Time had no say in that place, a day could be as long as a dream. We were in the Beginning, before common men had driven the fairies underground.

On top of the Forth Hill was the Forth with its three royal rings and its cave in the middle. The cave I often heard ran to join another Forth five miles away. No one had ever been able to get to the end of it till Ned Gilligan backed into it with a flashlamp and declared when he came out that it was only ten or twelve feet long. I would have been disappointed but I didn't believe him, I knew there must be a secret door which the flashlight of science couldn't find, a door which led far away, far away.

We had ways of adding to the weight of our blackberries, we added water or sand. I thought of the people who would be using bramble jam and swore I'd never taste bramble jam the longest day I'd be alive.

Once we met a crowd of blackberry gatherers advancing towards our preserves. We advised them to go to another place where we said there were a terrible lot of blackberries and crab-apples. This crowd were also gathering crab-apples which were ten shillings a stone. The crab-apple business was a chancy one, like digging for gold, you might come upon a tree and make a small fortune, but the chance was greatest that you'd have all your walk for nothing. We wanted these people to chase the elusive crabs so that we might have the certain blackberries for ourselves. Selfish, of course! They turned at our advice and we were glad. I can still remember that it took ten porringers full to fill a can.

'How are you off?' I could often hear my sisters call to one another.

'Oh bad, only the bottom of the porringer covered.'

'I have three porringers full.'

'Give me a lock, you'll make a show of us.' We would shake up the berries in our cans on our way home so as to make them look fuller. I once saw a man giving oats to a strange horse, he twirled a small quantity round in the bucket so that the grain stood high round the edge. So did we with the blackberries. We put the berries in a forty-gallon barrel which when full had a few buckets of water added to... make the fruit more juicy, I suppose.

from A COUNTRY DWELLER'S YEARS

Jessie Kesson

Jessie Kesson (1916–94) was a Scottish playwright, novelist and radio producer. She was born in an Inverness workhouse, the illegitimate daughter of Elizabeth MacDonald, a domestic servant who had turned to prostitution. Aged eight, Kesson was placed in an orphanage because of her mother's neglect. Although Kesson shone academically, the orphanage board decided an education would be wasted on her and sent her into domestic service. She suffered a breakdown and spent a year in hospital in Aberdeen before being 'boarded out' to a croft near Loch Ness. There she met and married Johnnie Kesson in 1937, taking farm labouring jobs in the Highlands. Kesson began to write in 1941 and was encouraged by encounters with Nan Shepherd and Neil Gunn. She began writing radio plays for the BBC in Aberdeen and *The Childhood* (1949) stimulated a government review of policies for 'problem' children. She moved to London with her husband and two children in 1951, supporting her writing with jobs in radio (helping to produce *Women's Hour*). Her novel *The White Bird Passes* was made into a TV drama, while *Another Time, Another Place* was turned into a film.

OCTOBER

The strange charm of October is something that has come up the years with me. October was birthday month and it held Hallowe'en. Now, of course, I'm too old to have a birthday, but I can still find witchery in the gloom of any October night.

Day itself is furnace-coloured. Trees have the brooding aspect of doomed things. It is uncanny – almost as if they sensed instinctively that their resilience has left them till a distant spring. Sometimes, when the wind sweeps through the wood, "false" resilience returns to the beech trees. Their remaining leaves rustle dryly and sway stiffly before making their first – and last – contact with the loam that reared them. The sensitive onlooker has the curious feeling that he is watching a graceful, poignant moment in a ballet scene.

But day passes, and with its passing this elusive grace disappears from the wood. October nights are stark, intense, and every night is a Hallowe'en. Darkness is heralded by grotesquely-shaped shadows; the wind sombre in sound, reckless in attack, cackles at its own devilry, the leaves go to earth almost soundlessly;

> The dusk is full of sounds, that all along
> The muttering boughs repeat.
> So far, so faint, we lift our heads in doubt;
> Wind, or the blood that beats within our ears,
> Has feigned a dubious and delusive note
> Such as a dreamer hears.[1]

That is the wood. And, although we live in the "ilka day" familiarity of our cottages, the wood is the background of our lives. We welcomed its spring, rejoiced in its summer, replenished our fires in its autumn; and now, though we become remoter from it in person, it still figures largely in our minds and in our conversations. The glow from our firesides transforms our conceptions of the wood.

It becomes the legends we tell on a winter's night. It is the breeding-place of all our remembered ghosts and recollected adventures. It even becomes the threat that settles our disgruntled bairns: "If ye dinna gang till yer beds this very meenit, ye'll gang oot tae the wud for the nicht!" For, apart from unknown terrors like ghosts, the wood has become the winter abode of those "eternal squatters" – the tinkers. For the next few months the wood is something that we glance at furtively in the passing, or view from the security of our scullery window, but with which we have no intimacy after dusk; not when the tinkers' voices rise from its depths in drunken song and drunken anger. Civilisation – in the form of ourselves – is aye embarrassed at contact with the primitive.

The farm labourers' brief respite, after the ardours o' leadin' the hairst, is over; the "tattie hairst" is near. The end of this month catches the lilt of an old song in the voices of the bairns forming the tattie squads:

Fa saw the tattie-lifters.
Fa saw them gaun awa'?
Fa saw the tattie-lifters
Mairchin' doon bi Balahaugh?
Some hiv sheen an some hiv stockin's,
Some hiv nane ava.
So fa saw the tattie-lifters
Mairchin' doon bi Balahaugh?[2]

The song was maybe appropriate twenty years ago. The young tattie-lifters who sing it now sing wi' their tongues in their cheeks. They've a' got baith "sheen an' stockin's," and they earn as much in one day as the bairns who first sang the song earned in a week. "Tattie-holidays" and tattie-lifting has become an institution like queueing; it is more an adventure now than dire need to earn a supplementary copper – and it never was a task for those whose bones hinna haen time tae "set" yet. They supply cheer and laughter for their adult fellow-workers, and anxiety for the "grieve," who, according to his nature, either shouts loudly or wheedles so that the bairns "lift their stages betimes."

This is the last insistent task on the farm before winter settles itself firmly in its groove. The last "stage" o'tatties lifted, and syne the hale landscape sinks intae placidity – the queer, uncertain placidity o'an October nicht.

NOTES

1. Edward Shanks (1892–1953) "A Night-Piece", *Georgian Poetry 1918–19*.
2. Adaptation of popular song: cf. Crimean War – "Wha'saw the Forty-Second?"

from WHAT THE CURLEW SAID

John Moriarty

John Moriarty (1938–2007) was an Irish philosopher, writer and mystic. He grew up in County Kerry and trained to be a primary school teacher in Dublin. After teaching at a boarding school, he left to travel through Greece. A chance meeting led to his appointment as a lecturer in philosophy at Leeds University. Later, he taught English literature at the University of Manitoba in Canada where he immersed himself in learning about native Americans. After six years, he decided he needed a more contemplative life and settled on Inishbofin, an island off the coast of Connemara. He worked as a gardener before visions directed him to a Carmelite monastery in Oxford, where he also gardened. He returned to Connemara and gave talks, which led to more discussions on radio and TV and the publication of his critically acclaimed and notoriously 'difficult' writings including *Dreamtime* (1994), *Turtle Was Gone a Long Time: Volume One, Crossing the Kedron* (1996), *Volume Two, Horsehead Nebula Neighing* (1997) and his autobiography, *Nostos* (2001).

Cycling home after work on a summer's evening to Lisnabrucka was very different from cycling home after work on a winter's evening to Leitirdyfe. As well as knowing it by sight, I knew this eight and a half mile stretch of Connemara road in my muscles and in my bones. Streams along the way I knew. Trees I knew. Woodcock getting up from the edge of the spruce woods I knew. Herons I knew. And sheep. And the river. And ponies on Derradda Hill. And cows lying down for the night on dry ground on the sides of the road. And all the houses and everyone in them I knew. And, from Cushatrower on, I knew the long inlet of sea, all its loose stones and its rocks and the shores of its little islands yellow with seaweed when the tide was out. And it always did strange things to me, not because I was reaching home, to hear a curlew calling in the mudflats beyond Leitirdyfe's seaward trees. Quite ordinary by comparison would be my response to the screeches of oystercatchers coming over water from Inishnee. What it was about the call of a curlew I could never say. The first two vowels a few times repeated and then the thrill – surely these sounds should be totemic to all human speech. Or, rather, when we see things as Manannán sees them, surely then they will be the phonetic Principia of all that we say. Had he called as the curlew below on the mudflats under Leitirdyfe calls, surely God would have called a far finer world into existence, but I could never persuade myself that this would be a good thing, because the world He did call into existence is tremendous and as between tremendousness and fineness I would choose tremendousness any day. But, as it is in the call of a curlew, the world is tremendous in its fine things too, in the geometry of a snowflake or, to use the old word, in the ars metric of a daisy, not that any metric, even when it is an ars, as it is in Chartres Cathedral, can fully figure things in their fineness, in their tremendousness. Unfigurable also of course, and not measurable by ordinary metrics, is the terror of the lugworms and the ragworms that the curlew gobbles down into its crushing gizzard. But as I approach the gate to Leitirdyfe, there it is again, the call, probably the last for the day, and hearing it, I know why Keats so yearned to rise up out of dis-eased mundanity and merge immortally with the immortal song of the nightingale:

Thou wast not born for death, immortal Bird!
   No hungry generations tread thee down;
The voice I hear this passing night was heard
   In ancient days by emperor and clown:
Perhaps the self-same song that found a path
   Through the sad heart of Ruth, when, sick for home,
     She stood in tears amid the alien corn;
      The same that oftimes hath
   Charmed magic casements, opening on the foam
     Of perilous seas, in faery lands forlorn.

The call of the curlew, I often felt, is such an opening in the world, but it is an opening not into somewhere beyond the world, rather is it an opening into a mode or mood, mostly unvisited, of the world itself. Sitting silently over long hours in the oak wood in Ballinafad, I had come to know that all elsewheres, supernatural and natural, are where we are. Sitting there, I had come to know what Keats didn't seem to know, that our mortality is a sometimes wonderful, sometimes dreadful way of experiencing our immortality. If there are days when I am so busy that I do not consciously know this, I only have to hear the call of a curlew and now, in the opening again, I know that Time is Eternity living tremendously, living dangerously.

Blake knew as much:

> The roaring of lions, the howling of wolves, the raging of the stormy sea, and the destructive sword, are portions of eternity too great for the eye of man.

I hear unwritten, because unspeakable, because unthinkable, gospels in the curlew's call, he calling alone below on the shore under the house where I live. I hear unwritten, because unspeakable, because unthinkable, Upanishads and Sutras in it. In it, I sense, are further enlightenments for Aruni and the Buddha.

> He who knows does not speak.
> He who speaks does not know.

Even so, I am glad that our local curlew does speak. And yet more glad would I be if his talk was totemic to all talk, immortal and mortal.

As Mallarmé saw it, a chief task of the poet is to purify the dialect of the tribe. As, inordinately, Wallace Stevens did:

> Deer walk upon our mountains, and the quail
> Whistle about us their spontaneous cries;
> Sweet berries ripen in the wilderness;
> And, in the isolation of the sky,
> At evening, casual flocks of pigeons make

Ambiguous undulations as they sink,
Downward to darkness, on extended wings.

In these seven lines the quail's spontaneities of talk and the curlew's spontaneities of talk are totemic to human talk, hence their perfection.

I would imagine it: going to Him in the cool of the day in Paradise, Adam and Eve said to God, We yearn to be mortally immortal, and with that the gates opened and with God's blessing they walked out and, the same blessing descending upon them as they did so, the animals in like need came out after them, and knowledge and remembrance of this I hear in the curlew's unbiblical call.

Entering by the gate in the dying light was a real transition. I was crossing from day to night, from the public road to a private drive, from the likelihood of meeting someone to the likelihood of not meeting anyone. Especially when you live through it in a wood, and that a kind of Birnam Wood, a weirdness in it, there is all of forever in a dark December night and that now is what I was walking into.

Coming to the near half of the heavy iron gate, I would lift the latch and push it open and when I had passed through it with my bike I would gently give it impetus and, leaving it to gravity, it would fall back and click shut with a small shudder. Facing me now on a high bank under the trees on my left would be a run of water breaking to crystal over a shallow rock face. Momentarily, I would be reduced to two sensations, a sound and a sight, the click and the pouring, breaking to crystal. Compared to the on and on and on of thinking, they gave me clarity and precision of being, a welcome reprieve from philosophical much ado about this, that and the other thing, a kind of redemption.

Already, having come back for the night from seashore and lakeshore, and their cantankerous rituals of reassembly insecurely at an end, the herons would have settled down to roost on their nests, many of which at this time of year would be ghostly wickerworks of sticks hanging on till the next storm.

A heronry gone silent but, dug into a bank farther along on the floor of the wood, a badger village coming to nocturnal life. By now, no doubt, most of those badgers whether sows or boars who were minded to come out tonight would have already come up more than once to sniff the air in the mouths of their earths. More daringly perhaps, a few would have already emerged and they would now be giving themselves a good scratch or they'd be exercising their claws on fallen tree trunks or, having a mind to play, they'd be scampering about the place, chasing each other, before they would then shuffle gruntingly off, smelling their way in a wood multitudinous in its scents. By now also, it being their mating season, the dog foxes and vixens would be intently out and about and, exquisitely alert to scent and sound, soon a vixen will screech and a dog fox will yap and, on fire for it, out in the bogs maybe, there will be conception and, Nature having had its way in this too, she will come home at first light to her lie in furze or to her den in the wood, five intuitions of further fox-life germinating within her.

And tonight or some night in this wood a pine marten will pick up the scent of a mate and no other scent, even of easy prey, distracting him, he will follow it to a bout of vastly virtuous copulation. I had never either seen or heard pine martens at it, but the first time I saw a nest of pine marten kittens, evidence of murder near by, I had to believe that theirs was an immaculate conception.

Given its roar after a day's rain, the stream I would cross two-thirds of the way up the drive could be Alph, the sacred but doomed river of Coleridge's opium dream:

In Xanadu did Kubla Khan
    A stately pleasure-dome decree:
Where Alph, the sacred river, ran
Through caverns measureless to man
    Down to a sunless sea…

The immaculate screech of a vixen in immaculate heat.
A woman wailing for her demon lover.
Demon and Beast.
It is only in human beings always in consequence of repression that the Beast emerges. Properly and exclusively, Beast is an anthropo-logical category.

It is only human beings and beings ontologically superior to human beings who can become demonic, to begin with in behaviour, then more or less in essence.

And bad dreams.

Bad dreams in a house in a wood.

Bad dreams under a roof down on to which a pine marten leaps, she that very morning maybe having committed fantastic infanticide.

Now o'er the one half-world
Nature seems dead, and wicked dreams abuse
The curtain'd sleep…

And no redress. No point in going to the Court of Human Rights in the Hague, there to charge our own nature with abusing us, serially, night after night. And what does this mean for our eighteenth-century ambitions for ourselves? How perfectible in its oldest phylogenetic roots is the leafless cauliflower? Ascending this drive on a December night the best outcome I could imagine was

Apophis Anthropus.

Leitirdyfe Wood and Birnam Wood.

Ever since I first heard about it in *Macbeth* I would return again and again in my mind to Birnam Wood. In it, given a cue in the play, I felt free to estimate things in a Hindu way. Typically I would think, here guise is disguise, here instead of making it manifest appearances mask reality. Being an epitome of the whole, this wood suggests that what we naively think of as an objectively real world is as illusory as the snake we might mistakenly see in a coil of rope left behind on the side of the road. Instead therefore of talking about the world we should talk about the world-illusion and if we should wish to know how complicit with it we can be we only have to look at *Macbeth*.

Our Birnam Wood world.

Our Birnam Wood mind.

The Birnam Wood mind with which we seek to know our Birnam Wood world.

Moors, Heaths
and Mountains

Illustration overleaf: *Coire an Lochain, Cairngorms*

from THE LIVING MOUNTAIN

Nan Shepherd

Anna 'Nan' Shepherd (1893–1981) was a Scottish writer and poet who was born and lived near Aberdeen for most of her life. Her career was predominantly as a lecturer at the Aberdeen Training Centre for Teachers but her literary reputation was made by her modernist novels, *The Quarry Wood* (1928), *The Weatherhouse* (1930) and *A Pass in the Grampians* (1933), all set in north-east Scotland. In recent times she has been championed by contemporary nature writers who have helped new readers rediscover *The Living Mountain*, a beautifully written account of walking in the Cairngorms. She wrote it during the Second World War, drawing on her memories of an earlier time, but did not publish it until 1977. 'Shepherd came to know the Cairngorms "deeply" rather than "widely",' wrote Robert Macfarlane in his book *Landmarks*. 'They are to her what Selborne was to Gilbert White, the Sierra Nevada were to John Muir, and the Aran Islands are to Tim Robinson.'

THE RECESSES

At first, mad to recover the tang of height, I made always for the summits, and would not take time to explore the recesses. But late one September I went on Braeriach with a man who knew the hill better than I did then, and he took me aside into Coire an Lochain. One could not have asked a fitter day for the first vision of this rare loch. The equinoctial storms had been severe; snow, that hardly ever fails to powder the plateau about the third week of September, had fallen close and thick, but now the storms had passed, the air was keen and buoyant, with a brilliancy as of ice, the waters of the loch were frost-cold to the fingers. And how still, how incredibly withdrawn and tranquil. Climb as often as you will, Loch Coire an Lochain remains incredible. It cannot be seen until one stands almost on its lip, but only height hides it. Unlike Avon and Etchachan, it is not shut into the mountain but lies on an outer flank, its hollow ranged daily by all the eyes that look at the Cairngorms from the Spey. Yet, without knowing, one would not guess its presence and certainly not its size. Two cataracts, the one that feeds it, falling from the brim of the plateau over rock, and the one that drains it, show as white threads on the mountain. Having scrambled up the bed of the latter (not, as I knew later, the simple way, but my companion was a rabid naturalist who had business with every leaf, stalk and root in the rocky bed), one expects to be near the corrie, but no, it is still a long way off. And on one toils, into the hill. Black scatter of rock, pieces large as a house, pieces edged like a grater. A tough bit of going. And there at last is the loch, held tight back against the precipice. Yet as I turned, that September day, and looked back through the clear air, I could see straight out to ranges of distant hills. And that astonished me. To be so open and yet so secret! Its anonymity – Loch of the Corrie of the Loch, that is all – seems to guard this surprising secrecy. Other lochs, Avon, Morlich and the rest, have their distinctive names. One expects of them an idiosyncrasy. But Loch of the Corrie of the Loch, what could there be there? A tarn like any other. And then to find this distillation of loveliness!

I put my fingers in the water and found it cold. I listened to the waterfall until I no longer heard it. I let my eyes travel from shore to shore very slowly and was amazed at the width of the water. How could I have foreseen so large a loch, 3000-odd feet up, slipped away into this corrie which was only one of three upon one face of a mountain that was itself only a broken bit of the plateau? And a second time I let my eyes travel over the surface, slowly, from shore to shore, beginning at my feet and ending against the precipice. There is no way like that for savouring the extent of a water surface.

This changing of focus in the eye, moving the eye itself when look-ing at things that do not move, deepens one's sense of outer reality.

Then static things may be caught in the very act of becoming. By so simple a matter, too, as altering the position of one's head, a different kind of world may be made to appear. Lay the head down, or better still, face away from what you look at, and bend with straddled legs till you see your world upside down. How new it has become! From the close-by sprigs of heather to the most distant fold of the land, each detail stands erect in its own validity. In no other way have I seen of my own unaided sight that the earth is round. As I watch, it arches its back, and each layer of landscape bristles – though *bristles* is a word of too much commotion for it. Details are no longer part of a grouping in a picture of which I am the focal point, the focal point is everywhere. Nothing has reference to me, the looker. This is how the earth must see itself.

So I looked slowly across the Coire Loch, and began to understand that haste can do nothing with these hills. I knew when I had looked for a long time that I had hardly begun to see. So with Loch Avon. My first encounter was sharp and astringent, and has crystallised for ever for me some innermost inaccessibility. I had climbed all six of the major summits, some of them twice over, before clambering down into the mountain trough that holds Loch Avon. This loch lies at an altitude of some 2300 feet, but its banks soar up for another fifteen hundred. Indeed farther, for Cairn Gorm and Ben MacDhui may be said to be its banks. From the lower end of this mile and a half gash in the rock, exit is easy but very long. One may go down by the Avon itself, through ten miles as lonely and unvisited as anything in the Cairngorms, to Inchrory; or by easy enough watersheds pass into Strathnethy or Glen Derry, or under the Barns of Bynack to the Caiplich Water. But higher up the loch there is no way out, save by scrambling up one or other of the burns that tumble from the heights: except that, above the Shelter Stone, a gap opens between the hills to Loch Etchachan, and here the scramble up is shorter.

The inner end of this gash has been howked straight from the granite. As one looks up from below, the agents would appear mere splashes of water, whose force might be turned aside by a pair of hands. Yet above the precipices we have found in one of these burns pools deep enough to bathe in. The water that pours over these grim bastions carries no sediment of any kind in its precipitate fall, which seems indeed to distil and aerate the water so that the loch far below is sparkling clear. This narrow loch has never, I believe, been sounded. I know its depth, though not in feet.

I first saw it on a cloudless day of early July. We had started at dawn, crossed Cairn Gorm about nine o'clock, and made our way by the Saddle to the lower end of the loch. Then we idled up the side, facing the gaunt corrie, and at last, when the noonday sun penetrated directly into the water, we stripped and bathed. The clear water was at our knees, then at our thighs. How clear it was only this walking into it could reveal. To look through it was to discover its own properties. What we saw under water had a sharper clarity than what we saw through air. We waded on into the brightness, and the width of the water increased, as it always does when one is on or in it, so that the loch no longer seemed narrow, but the far side was a long way off. Then I looked down; and at my feet there opened a gulf of brightness so profound that the mind stopped. We were standing on the edge of a shelf that ran some yards into the loch before plunging down to the pit that is the true bottom. And through that inordinate clearness we saw to the depth of the pit. So limpid was it that every stone was clear.

I motioned to my companion, who was a step behind, and she came, and glanced as I had down the submerged precipice. Then we looked into each other's eyes, and again into the pit. I waded slowly back into shallower water. There was nothing that seemed worth saying. My spirit was as naked as my body. It was one of the most defenceless moments of my life.

I do not think it was the imminence of personal bodily danger that shook me. I had not then, and have not in retrospect, any sense of having just escaped a deadly peril. I might of course have overbalanced and been drowned; but I do not think I would have stepped down unawares. Eye and foot acquire in rough walking a co-ordination that makes one distinctly aware of where the next step is to fall, even while watching sky and land. This watching, it is true, is of a general nature only; for attentive observation the body must be still. But in a general way, in country that is rough, but not difficult, one sees where one is and where one is going at the same time. I proved this sharply to myself one hot June day in Glen Quoich, when bounding down a slope of long heather towards the stream. With hardly a slackening of pace, eye detected and foot avoided a coiled adder on which the next spring would have landed me; detected and avoided also his mate, at full length in the line of my side spring; and I pulled up a short way past, to consider with amused surprise the speed and sureness of my own feet. Conscious thought had had small part in directing them.

So, although they say of the River Avon that men have walked into it and been drowned, supposing it shallow because they could see its depth, I do not think I was in much danger just then of drowning, nor was fear the emotion with which I stared into the pool. That first glance down had shocked me to a heightened power of myself, in which even fear became a rare exhilaration: not that it ceased to be fear, but fear itself, so impersonal, so keenly apprehended, enlarged rather than constricted the spirit.

The inaccessibility of this loch is part of its power. Silence belongs to it. If jeeps find it out, or a funicular railway disfigures it, part of its meaning will be gone. The good of the greatest number is not here relevant. It is necessary to be sometimes exclusive, not on behalf of rank or wealth, but of those human qualities that can apprehend loneliness.

The presence of another person does not detract from, but enhances, the silence, if the other is the right sort of hill companion. The perfect hill companion is the one whose identity is for the time being merged in that of the mountains, as you feel your own to be. Then such speech as arises is part of a common life and cannot be alien. To 'make conversation', however, is ruinous, to speak may be superfluous. I have it from a gaunt elderly man, a 'lang tangle o' a chiel', with high cheek bones and hollow cheeks, product of a hill farm though himself a civil servant, that when he goes on the hill with chatterers, he 'could see them to an ill place'. I have walked myself with brilliant young people whose talk, entertaining, witty and incessant, yet left me weary and dispirited, because the hill did not speak. This does not imply that the only good talk on a hill is about the hill. All sorts of themes may be lit up from within by contact with it, as they are by contact with another mind, and so discussion may be salted. Yet to listen is better than to speak.

The talking tribe, I find, want sensation from the mountain – not in Keats's sense. Beginners, not unnaturally, do the same – I did myself. They want the startling view, the horrid pinnacle – sips of beer and tea instead of milk. Yet often the mountain gives itself most completely when I have no destination, when I reach nowhere in particular, but have gone out merely to be with the mountain as one visits a friend with no intention but to be with him.

from THE RETURN OF THE NATIVE

Thomas Hardy

Thomas Hardy (1840–1928) was the eldest of four children of Jemima and Thomas Hardy, the latter a stonemason and builder. Growing up in rural Dorset, he was relatively well educated in Latin and maths at school in Dorchester and apprenticed to a local architect. Lack of money and a declining faith saw him abandon his ambition of university and ordination in the Church of England, and he devoted his time to private study and poetry instead. His first novel, *The Poor Man and the Lady* (written in 1867–8), was rejected by three London publishers, but Hardy persevered, combining his architectural work with writing *Desperate Remedies* (1871) and *Under the Greenwood Tree* (1872), which were published anonymously. *Far from the Madding Crowd* (1874) saw the arrival of Hardy's 'Wessex' and its wit, drama and realistic pastoral setting made him famous. His later novels, *Tess of the d'Urbervilles* (1891) and *Jude the Obscure* (1895), are notable for their fine writing and tragic, deeply sympathetic working-class heroes. In 1898, Hardy published his first collection of poetry and in his latter years, during the twentieth century, he only published poems.

A FACE ON WHICH TIME MAKES BUT LITTLE IMPRESSION

A Saturday afternoon in November was approaching the time of twilight, and the vast tract of unenclosed wild known as Egdon Heath embrowned itself moment by moment. Overhead the hollow stretch of whitish cloud shutting out the sky was as a tent which had the whole heath for its floor.

The heaven being spread with this pallid screen and the earth with the darkest vegetation, their meeting-line at the horizon was clearly marked. In such contrast the heath wore the appearance of an instalment of night which had taken up its place before its astronomical hour was come: darkness had to a great extent arrived hereon, while day stood distinct in the sky. Looking upwards, a furze-cutter would have been inclined to continue work, looking down, he would have decided to finish his faggot and go home. The distant rims of the world and of the firmament seemed to be a division in time no less than a division in matter. The face of the heath by its mere complexion added half an hour to evening; it could in like manner retard the dawn, sadden noon, anticipate the frowning of storms scarcely generated, and intensify the opacity of a moonless midnight to a cause of shaking and dread.

In fact, precisely at this transitional point of its nightly roll into darkness the great and particular glory of the Egdon waste began, and nobody could be said to understand the heath who had not been there at such a time. It could best be felt when it could not clearly be seen, its complete effect and explanation lying in this and the succeeding hours before the next dawn: then, and only then, did it tell its true tale. The spot was, indeed, a near relation of night, and when night showed itself an apparent tendency to gravitate together could be perceived in its shades and the scene. The sombre stretch of rounds and hollows seemed to rise and meet the evening gloom in pure sympathy, the heath exhaling darkness as rapidly as the heavens precipitated it. And so the obscurity in the air and the obscurity in the land closed together in a black fraternisation towards which each advanced half-way.

The place became full of a watchful intentness now; for when other things sank brooding to sleep the heath appeared slowly to awake and listen. Every night its Titanic form seemed to await something; but it had waited thus, unmoved, during so many centuries, through the crises of so many things, that it could only be imagined to await one last crisis – the final overthrow.

It was a spot which returned upon the memory of those who loved it with an aspect of peculiar and kindly congruity. Smiling champaigns of flowers and fruit hardly do this, for they are permanently harmonious only with an existence of better reputation as to its issues than the present. Twilight combined with the scenery of Egdon Heath to evolve a thing majestic without severity, impressive without showiness, emphatic in its admonitions, grand in its simplicity. The qualifications which frequently invest the façade of a prison with far more dignity than is found in the façade of a palace double its size lent to this heath a sublimity in which spots renowned for beauty of the accepted kind are utterly wanting. Fair prospects wed happily with fair times; but alas, if times be not fair! Men have oftener suffered from the mockery of a place too smiling for their reason than from the oppression of surroundings oversadly tinged. Haggard Egdon appealed to a subtler and scarcer instinct, to a more recently learnt emotion, than that which responds to the sort of beauty called charming and fair.

Indeed, it is a question if the exclusive reign of this orthodox beauty is not approaching its last quarter. The new Vale of Tempe may be a gaunt waste in Thule: human souls may find themselves in closer and closer harmony with external things wearing a sombreness distasteful to our race when it was young. The time seems near, if it has not actually arrived, when the chastened sublimity of a moor, a sea, or a mountain will be all of nature that is absolutely in keeping with the moods of the more thinking among mankind. And ultimately, to the commonest tourist, spots like Iceland may become what the vineyards and myrtle-gardens of South Europe are to him now; and Heidelberg and Baden be passed unheeded as he hastens from the Alps to the sand-dunes of Scheveningen.

The most thorough-going ascetic could feel that he had a natural right to wander on Egdon: he was keeping within the line of legitimate indulgence when he laid himself open to influences such as these. Colours and beauties so far subdued were, at least, the birthright of all. Only in summer days of highest feather did its mood touch the level of gaiety. Intensity was more usually reached by way of the solemn than by way of the brilliant, and such a sort of intensity was often arrived at during winter darkness, tempests, and mists. Then Egdon was aroused to reciprocity; for the storm was its lover, and the wind its friend. Then it became the home of strange phantoms; and it was found to be the hitherto unrecognised original of those wild regions of obscurity which are vaguely felt to be compassing us about in midnight dreams of flight and disaster, and are never thought of after the dream till revived by scenes like this.

It was at present a place perfectly accordant with man's nature – neither ghastly, hateful, nor ugly: neither commonplace, unmeaning, nor tame; but, like man, slighted and enduring; and withal singularly colossal and mysterious in its swarthy monotony. As with some persons who have long lived apart, solitude seemed to look out of its countenance. It had a lonely face, suggesting tragical possibilities.

This obscure, obsolete, superseded country figures in Domesday. Its condition is recorded therein as that of heathy, furzy, briary wilderness – 'Bruaria.' Then follows the length and breadth in leagues; and, though some uncertainty exists as to the exact extent of this ancient lineal measure, it appears from the figures that the area of Egdon down to the present day has but little diminished. 'Turbaria Bruaria' – the right of cutting heath-turf – occurs in charters relating to the district. 'Overgrown with heth and mosse,' says Leland of the same dark sweep of country.

Here at least were intelligible facts regarding landscape – far-reaching proofs productive of genuine satisfaction. The untameable, Ishmaelitish thing that Egdon now was it always had been. Civilisation was its enemy; and ever since the beginning of vegetation its soil had worn the same antique brown dress, the natural and invariable garment of the particular formation. In its venerable one coat lay a certain vein of satire on human vanity in clothes. A person on a heath in raiment of modern cut and colours has more or less an anomalous look. We seem to want the oldest and simplest human clothing where the clothing of the earth is so primitive.

To recline on a stump of thorn in the central valley of Egdon, between afternoon and night, as now, where the eye could reach nothing of the world outside the summits and shoulders of heathland which filled the whole circumference of its glance, and to know that everything around and underneath had been from prehistoric times as unaltered as the stars overhead, gave ballast to the mind adrift on change, and harassed by the irrepressible New. The great inviolate place had an ancient permanence which the sea cannot claim. Who can say of a particular sea that it is old? Distilled by the sun, kneaded by the moon, it is renewed in a year, in a day, or in an hour. The sea changed, the fields changed, the rivers, the villages, and the people changed, yet Egdon remained. Those surfaces were neither so steep as to be destructible by weather, nor so flat as to be the victims of floods and deposits. With the exception of an aged highway, and a still more aged barrow presently to be referred to – themselves almost crystallised to natural products by long continuance – even the trifling irregularities were not caused by pickaxe, plough, or spade, but remained as the very finger-touches of the last geological change.

The above-mentioned highway traversed the lower levels of the heath from one horizon to another. In many portions of its course it overlaid an old vicinal way, which branched from the great Western road of the Romans, the Via Iceniana, or Ikenild Street, hard by. On the evening under consideration it would have been noticed that, though the gloom had increased sufficiently to confuse the minor features of the heath, the white surface of the road remained almost as clear as ever.

SELECTED EXTRACTS *from* THE GRASMERE JOURNAL

Dorothy Wordsworth

Dorothy Wordsworth (1771–1855) was an English author, poet and diarist with a rather famous brother. She was born in Cockermouth, Cumberland, and after her father's death in 1783 was sent alone to live with an aunt in Halifax, West Yorkshire. She was reunited with William in 1795 and lived with him – in some poverty – at Alfoxton House in Somerset, and later in Dove Cottage on the edge of Grasmere in the Lake District. She kept beautifully written diaries and wrote poetry but declared she had no desire for the fame her brother enjoyed. 'I should detest the idea of setting myself up as an author,' she once wrote, 'give Wm. the Pleasure of it.' She did not marry and continued to live with William after he married Mary Hutchinson in 1802. In 1829 she fell ill and was incapacitated for much of her remaining long life. Her *Grasmere Journal* was first published in 1897. Her writing revealed how much William borrowed from her journals, particularly relying on his sister's detailed accounts of the natural landscapes they both so enjoyed. Of his sister, he wrote: 'She gave me ears, she gave me eyes.'

Sunday Mor. 26th [*27th July 1800*]. Very warm—Molly ill—John bathed in the lake. I wrote out Ruth in the afternoon, in the morning I read Mr Knight's Landscape. After tea we rowed down to Loughrigg Fell, visited the white foxglove, gathered wild strawberries, & walked up to view Rydale we lay a long time looking at the lake, the shores all embrowned with the scorching sun. The Ferns were turning yellow, that is here & there one was quite turned. We walked round by

Benson's wood home. The lake was now most still & reflected the beautiful yellow & blue & purple & grey colours of the sky. We heard a strange sound in the Bainriggs wood as we were floating on the water it *seemed* in the wood, but it must have been above it, for presently we saw a raven very high above us—it called out & the Dome of the sky seemed to echoe the sound—it called again & again as it flew onwards, & the mountains gave back the sound, seeming as if from their center a musical bell-like answering to the birds hoarse voice. We heard both the call of the bird & the echoe after we could see him no longer.

Thursday 2nd October [1800]. A very rainy morning—We walked after dinner to observe the torrents—I followed Wm to Rydale, he afterwards went to Butterlip How. I came home to receive the Lloyds. They walked with us to see Churnmilk force & the Black quarter. The black quarter looked marshy, & the general prospect was cold, but the Force was very grand. The Lychens are now coming out afresh, I carried home a collection in the afternoon. We had a pleasant conversation about the manners of the rich—Avarice, inordinate desires, & the effeminacy unnaturalness & the unworthy objects of education. After the Lloyds were gone we walked—a showery evening. The moonlight lay upon the hills like snow.

Tuesday 24th [*November 1801*]. […] It was very windy & we heard the wind everywhere about us as we went along the Lane but the walls sheltered us—John Greens house looked pretty under Silver How— as we were going along we were stopped at once, at the distance perhaps of 50 yards from our favorite Birch tree it was yielding to the gusty wind with all its tender twigs, the sun shone upon it & it glanced in the wind like a flying sunshiny shower—it was a tree in shape with stem & branches but it was like a Spirit of water—The sun went in & it resumed its purplish appearance the twigs still yielding to the wind but not so visibly to us. The other Birch trees that were near it looked bright & chearful—but it was a Creature by its own self among them.

We could not get into Mr Gells grounds—the old tree fallen from its undue exaltation above the Gate. A shower came on when we were at Bensons. We went through the wood—it became fair, there was a rainbow which spanned the lake from the Island house to the foot of Bainriggs. The village looked populous & beautiful. Catkins are coming out palm trees budding—the alder with its plumb coloured buds. We came home over the stepping stones the Lake was foamy with white waves. I saw a solitary butter flower in the wood. *I found it not easy to get over the stepping stones*—reached home at dinner time. Sent Peggy Ashburner some goose. She sent me some honey—with a thousand thanks […]

Thursday 10th December [1801]. […] we walked into Easedale to gather mosses, & then we went past to Aggy Fleming's & up the gill, beyond that little waterfall—it was a wild scene of crag & mountain. One craggy point rose above the rest irregular & ragged & very impressive it was. We called at Aggy Fleming's she told us about her miserable house she looked shockingly with her head tyed up. Her mother was there—the children looked healthy. We were very unsuccessful in our search after mosses. Just when the evening was closing in Mr Clarkson came to the door—it was a fine frosty Evening. We played at cards.

Saturday 12th [*December 1801*]. A fine frosty morning—snow upon the ground—I made bread & pies. We walked with Mrs Luff to Rydale, & came home on the other side of the Lake. Met Townley with his dogs—all looked chearful & bright—Helm Crag rose very bold & craggy, a being by itself, & behind it was the large Ridge of mountain smooth as marble & snow white—all the mountains looked like solid stone on our left going from Grasmere i.e. White Moss & Nab scar. The snow hid all the grass & all signs of vegetation & the Rocks shewed themselves boldly everywhere & seemed more stony than Rock or stone. The Birches on the Crags beautiful, Red brown & glittering—the ashes glittering spears with their upright stems—the hips very beautiful, & so good!! & dear Coleridge—I ate twenty for thee when I was by myself. I came home first—they walked too slow for me. William went to look at Langdale Pikes. We had a sweet invigorating walk. Mr Clarkson came in before tea. We played at Cards—sate up late. The moon shone upon the water below Silverhow, & above it hung, combining with Silver how on one side, a Bowl-shaped moon the curve downwards—the white fields, glittering Roof of Thomas Ashburner's house, the dark yew tree, the white fields—gay & beautiful. Wm lay with his curtains open that he might see it.

[*23 January 1802*] On Saturday January 23rd we left Eusemere at 10 o clock in the morning, I behind Wm Mr C on his Galloway. The morning not very promising the wind cold. The mountains large & dark but only thinly streaked with snow—a strong wind. We dined in Grisdale on ham bread & milk. We parted from Mr C at one o clock—it rained all the way home. We struggled with the wind & often rested as we went along—A hail-shower met us before we reached the Tarn & the way often was difficult over the snow but at the Tarn the view closed in—we saw nothing but mists & snow & at first the ice on the Tarn below us, cracked & split yet without water, a dull grey white: we lost our path & could see the Tarn no longer. We made our way out with difficulty guided by a heap of stones which we well remembered—we were afraid of being bewildered in the mists till the Darkness should overtake us—we were long before we knew that we were in the right track but thanks to William's skill we knew it long before we could see our way before us. There was no footmark upon the snow either of man or beast. We saw 4 sheep before we had left the snow region. The Vale of Grasmere when the mists broke away looked soft & grave, of a yellow hue—it was dark before we reached home. We were not very much tired. My inside was sore with the cold. We had both of us been much heated upon the mountains but we caught no cold———O how comfortable & happy we felt ourselves sitting by our own fire when we had got off our wet clothes & had dressed ourselves fresh & clean. We found 5£ from Montague & 20£ from Chris.ʳ We talked about the Lake of Como, read in the descriptive Sketches, looked about us, & felt that we were happy.

—*m*—

Sunday 31st [January 1802]. William had slept very ill, he was tired & had a bad headache. We walked round the two lakes—Grasmere was very soft & Rydale was extremely beautiful from the pasture side. Nab Scar was just topped by a cloud which cutting it off as high as it could be cut off made the mountain look uncommonly lofty. We sate down a long time in different places. I always love to walk that way because it is the way I first came to Rydale & Grasmere, & because our dear Coleridge did also. When I came with Wm 6½ years ago it was just at sunset. There was a rich yellow light on the waters & the Islands were reflected there. Today it was grave & soft but not perfectly calm. William says it was much such a day as when Coleridge came with him. The sun shone out before we reached Grasmere. We sate by the roadside at the foot of the Lake close to Mary's dear name which she had cut herself upon the stone. William employed cut at it with his knife to make it plainer. We amused ourselves for a long time in watching the Breezes some as if they came from the bottom of the lake spread in a circle, brushing along the surface of the water, & growing more delicate, as it were thinner & of a *paler* colour till they died away—others spread out like a peacocks tail, & some went right forward this way & that in all directions. The lake was still where these breezes were not, but they made it all alive. I found a strawberry blossom in a rock, the little slender flower had more courage than the green leaves, for *they* were but half expanded & half grown, but the blossom was spread full out. I uprooted it rashly, & I felt as if I had been committing an outrage, so I planted it again—it will have but a stormy life of it, but let it live if it can. We found Calvert here. I brought a handkerchief full of mosses which I placed on the chimneypiece when C was gone—he dined with us & carried away the Encyclopaedias. After they were gone I spent some time in trying to reconcile myself to the change, & in rummaging out & arranging some other books in their places. One good thing is this—there is a nice Elbow place for William, & he may sit for the picture of John Bunyan any day. Mr Simpson drank tea with us. We payed our rent to Benson.

———

Thursday [*18th March 1802*]. [...] Rydale vale was full of life & motion. The wind blew briskly & the lake was covered all over with Bright silver waves that were there each the twinkling of an eye, then others rose up & took their place as fast as they went away. The Rocks glittered in the sunshine, the crows & the Ravens were busy, & the thrushes & little Birds sang—I went through the fields, & sate ½ an hour afraid to pass a Cow. The Cow looked at me & I looked at the cow & whenever I stirred the cow gave over eating. I was not very much tired when I reached Lloyds, I walked in the garden. Charles is all for Agriculture. Mrs Ll in her kindest way. A parcel came in from Birmingham, with Lamb's play for us & for C. They came with me as far as Rydale. As we came along Ambleside vale in the twilight—it was a grave evening—there was something in the air that compelled me to serious thought—the hills were large, closed in by the sky. It was nearly dark when I parted from the Lloyds that is, night was come on & the moon was overcast. But as I climbed Moss the moon came out from behind a Mountain Mass of Black Clouds—O the unutterable darkness of the sky & the Earth below the Moon! & the glorious brightness of the moon itself! There was a vivid sparkling streak of light at this end of Rydale water but the rest was very dark & Loughrigg fell & Silver How were white & bright as if they were covered with hoar frost. The moon retired again & appeared & disappeared several times before I reached home. Once there was no moonlight to be seen but upon the Island house & the promontory of the Island where it stands, 'That needs must be a holy place' &c—&c. I had many many exquisite feelings when I saw this lowly Building in the waters among the dark & lofty hills, with that bright soft light upon it—it made me more than half a poet. I was tired when I reached home I could not sit down to reading & tried to write verses but alas! I gave up expecting William & went soon to bed.

from THE GUARDIAN COUNTRY DIARY

Enid J. Wilson

Enid Wilson (1905–88) died a week after writing her last Country Diary for the *Guardian* from her home in Keswick, a column she wrote with distinction for thirty-eight years. Her mother was a trained botanist and her father was a mountain climber and photographer. Wilson had to sit as 'ballast' in a car in which her father made the first day-return journey by motor vehicle over the vertiginous Hardknott and Wrynose passes in the Lake District. Wilson grew up with a deep knowledge of the wildlife of the Lake District but also listened closely to the dialect and people of the Lakes, such as the smiley man who lived on the other side of Skiddaw who was a 'cheerful laal beggar, he shines like a closet door on a frosty morning'. The broadcaster David Bean once wrote of Wilson: 'Like many of the creatures she writes about, she is not often spotted tending to move around early in the morning or late at night. 4.30am is a good time to catch her – if you know where to look.'

ICE AND THE OTTERS
January 1963

There is no doubt that the otters enjoy snow and ice. It is possible to find slides they have used to play on the river banks where the slope is steep enough to take them down-bank towards the water, but I have never seen them in action. My young cat treats the snow in much the same way and is otter-like in looks – short, sleek coat and over-long tail. He has a variety of snow games. He follows a thrown snowball, which skims the surface of the frozen lawn, at a fast gallop that often ends in a four-pawed skid or on his side sweeping the ice clear of its snow-covering.

The otters have snug homes in the river bank and the cat his fireside but the hares who live on these upland meadows can find little comfort in this bitter weather. I met one last night near midnight in the moonlight and deep snow near the Castle Rigg stone circle. It was searching for food and it looked thin and seemed much slower than hares usually do until it found an opening in the wall where a beck runs out of the field and then it was off over the hill. It looked very big and dark, however, against the moon-shining snow and its shadow ran with it as it went. The ground inside and round the stone circle is criss-crossed with hare tracks and the moonlight showed, too, where the snow was plastered against the stones and cast long blue shadows on the hard ground. It touched the flanks of the encircling hills, Saddleback, Helvellyn and the Derwentwater fells and, far to the east, the long line of the Pennines, as substantial as a silver cloud.

NIGHTWALKING
July 1983

It seems foolish these nights to waste time by coming home to bed – so many lost and unreturning hours while the summer half-light and the moonlight, together, fade towards dawn. The day's heat often draws moisture from the land and, after sunset, it lies along the high narrow valley and its beck, softening every contour and filling every hollow. The white May blossom on the isolated fellside thorns floats like snow above the mist and the muted green of the fields. There were, last night, few sounds by the beck – only the run of the water, the crying of a curlew disturbed at its nest and the champ and snort of grazing cattle. They walk out into midstream to eat the water dropwort, a plant highly poisonous to man. There is probably a new badger home on the sloping river bank, half-hidden in nettles; for nettles mark badger occupation just as surely as they do old human use. The sett is, however, as well-guarded as any royal residence, not by the police, nor the military nor even a menacing landowner but by a large herd of inquisitive and gieversome (playful) cows. They are only too happy to join in whatever is going on but while I like cows (who does not, within reason?) they are no help at all in badger-watching. So that sett is written off. The next valley on the way home, edged with pale elderflowers and wild roses, seemed more promising, it had no mist and no cows – not even sheep – and only trout, jumping clear of the small pools to fall back with a gentle plop, broke the silence.

A WILD CHILDHOOD

Illustration overleaf: *Tadpoles*

UNTAMED

Shamshad Khan

Shamshad Khan is a poet and resilience coach. She works with individuals and organizations using writing and coaching techniques to engage and empower. She was first published in 1990 by Manchester-based Commonword and her short stories have been published by Virago and Comma Press. Khan's poetry collection *Megalomaniac* (Salt, 2007) was studied on the Lancaster University English Literature degree course. Her work has featured on BBC Radio 3 and 4. She has collaborated with dancers, musicians and with theatres, including The Horse and Bamboo as co-writer/director of the multi-media show *The Moonwatcher* (2018). 'Untamed' is original to this anthology.

We can't wait to get out of the car. The cattle grid is a threshold. A forced slowing down of our white Cortina saloon. We are out of the city, waves of stone walls climbing and falling into the horizon, shouldering seas of greens and tinted mauves.

Back in Leeds the sycamore is holding its shade for us for a few days. It filled our red-brick world with more than we could dream of. It will wait for us to come twizzling back from heights, finding ground wherever we land. This is more than a day trip to Scarborough, this is the real wild west of the North Yorkshire Moors. Second World War army training meant our dad has taught us map reading and route planning. We have made the drive well before it is dark. The car is economically packed tight with five kids, razai quilts, pans, cooked food and provisions to feed the family army.

Three of us get out as we leave the last hamlet of houses behind us. It's a mile's walk to the hostel. The acrid smell of peat bogs loosens our breath as we climb the hill.

This is where following a map stops making sense. Where we feel inclined to ignore the helpful guidance and tips and all the notes provided to make our stay safe and comfortable.

Me and my younger brother, born-and-bred Yorkshire, feel excitedly free. Who doesn't feel going into nature is a kind of homecoming? We spread ourselves out on the heather, light enough to balance like clothes stretched out to dry. We semi-float with a wobble on the haze of dryish purple flowers. Eyes close to cobwebs; spying on a busy team of ants finding their way through the dark forest of wonky wooden stems below. We wriggle over to face up into the seamless blue, the stripes of my Bay City Rollers socks protecting my legs from scratches. Interrupted by frantic search calls from distant family, we scramble off our perches and disappear deeper into bracken.

Countryside feels like the closest thing to arriving nowhere. It is going to be easy to lose ourselves here, and where a heart is lost, there is no getting it back. Brown spores furled in on the naked backs of fractals. Our twinned spirits caught like wool fluff or long strands of hair on brambles.

These were *our* broad Yorkshire moors. Convinced of our seven- and eight-year-old quintessential Englishness. Not understanding until we visited Punjab for ourselves that what we had seen on our parents' faces was not just holiday ease, it was familiarity. A recognition as between old friends being welcomed home. Land markings like creases on the face of a childhood sweetheart. Grain and cattle fodder heaped in bundles in the entrance of their village homes. The moors were more like home to our parents than they could ever be to us city-born kids. We stamped our shoes and left them in the muddy porch.

We never tried to retrieve what we lost, neither in Scugdale nor Kot Sarang. Both places were blood roots, coursing an iron belonging into us forever. The Bronze Age landscape shaping our emotions, the dales and khayt farmlands holding our voices; our feelings giving co-ordinates to the crags, fields and heath walks that framed us. Boring a tube into the depths of ourselves, overlaid experiences revealed like in soil pollen analysis. Generations of depletion and enrichment.

We foray into the village once, but mostly walk the miles of iso-lated hills around our Yorkshire homestead. Our big sisters setting the pace. Us two fascinated by shining clusters of rolled tarmac balls that turn out to be fresh sheep droppings. The onyx-striped eye of a sheep as cool as playground marbles. We fall behind but catch the others up easily.

We think it might have picked up our mother's weightless steps, the decibeled walk of our father, definitely the rapid tabla drumming of the rest of us. Its lithe intelligence remembering every reverberation of our footfall in its endless body.

Thick coiled markings curled close under a drystone wall. Surprise is enlivening. We startle as much as it startles us, trilingual snake that took all words away. The snake does not move. We do not move. The gaps between the stones widen, citadel of spore turrets, shaggy green chenille on the rocks.

When a snake doesn't know what to make of you, when a snake is surprised to see you, when a snake glides away without saying a word, longer than an unwound copper sari.

Adder or grass snake. Poisonous or not poisonous. Cross-hatched markings. Cool or warm, we do not touch it. We accept our dad knows how to unspeak snake. A friendly salute, and that's it. Breathing deepened breaths that ease unbelonging away.

For twenty years our dad has been giving himself back to a hillside in Leeds. We are locked down and unlocking. We ache for green space more than ever. Bubbling and unbubbling care, plaiting and unplaiting black diamonds into my mother's silvering hair.

I'm writing to you from inner-city Manchester, breaking out every day that I can for something untamed.

from THE AUTOBIOGRAPHY

John Clare

John Clare (1793–1864) was a poet who wrote little prose but depicted the natural world with such vivid, intimate brilliance that he continues to be a major influence on prose writers today. He remains a relatively rare example of a truly working-class writer who could never – for better and for worse – escape his roots. He was born in Helpston, a village between the Northamptonshire wolds and the fens, the son of a farm labourer. Clare left school at twelve and worked as a gardener, camped with Gypsies, and began to write poems and sonnets. When his parents were faced with eviction Clare took his poems to a local bookseller, who sent them to his cousin, John Taylor, who had published John Keats. Clare's *Poems Descriptive of Rural Life and Scenery* (1820) was highly praised; so was *Village Minstrel, and Other Poems* (1821). Clare became torn between his Northamptonshire heartland – which was being transformed by the Enclosures – and the glamour of literary London. He suffered severe depression, drank heavily; his poetry sold less well and he struggled to support his wife, Patty, and seven children. Between 1837 and 1841 he was treated in a private asylum in Epping Forest, where he suffered delusions and claimed to have once been Byron and Shakespeare. In 1841, he absconded and walked nearly 100 miles home, believing he was married to his first love, Mary Joyce, as well as Patty. After five months living at home, he returned to an asylum in Northampton where he was encouraged and continued to write poetry, including 'I Am'. An appreciation of Clare's poetry was revived in the later twentieth century. His biographer, Jonathan Bate, judged Clare to be England's greatest working-class poet. 'No one has ever written more powerfully of nature, of a rural childhood, and of the alienated and unstable self,' he wrote. The following extract is taken from Clare's autobiography.

I know not what made me write poetry but these journeys & my toiling in the fields by myself gave me such a habit for thinking that I never forgot it & always mutterd & talkd to myself afterwards I have often felt ashamed at being overheard by people that overtook me it made my thoughts so active that they became troublesome to me in company & I felt the most happy to be alone

with such merry company I heard the black & brown beetle sing their evening song with rapture & lovd to see the black snail steal out upon the dewy baulks I saw the nimble horse bee at noon spinning on wanton wing I lovd to meet the woodman whistling away to his toils & to see the shepherd bending over his hook on the thistly greens chattering love storys to the listening milkmaid while she milkd her brindld cow

The first primrose in spring was as delightful as if seen for the first time & how the copper colord clouds of the morning was watchd

On Sundays I usd to feel a pleasure to hide in the woods instead of going to Church to nestle among the leaves & lye upon a mossy bank where the fir-like fern its under forest keeps

In a strange stillness

watching for hours the little insects climb up & down the tall stems of the wood grass o'er the smooth plantain leaf a spacious plain or reading the often-thumbd books which I possessd till fancy 'made them living things' I lovd the lonely nooks in the fields & woods & my favourite spots had lasting places in my memory that bough that when a schoolboy screened my head before enclosure destroyed them

I lovd to employ leisure when a boy wandering about the fields watching the habits of birds to see the woodpecker sweeing away in its ups & downs & the jaybird chattering by the woodside its restless warnings to passing clowns & the travels of insects were the black beetle mumbld along & the opening of field flowers such amusements gave me the greatest of pleasures but I coud not account for the reason they did so a lonely book a rude bridge or woodland style with ivy growing round the posts delighted me & made lasting impressions on my feelings but I knew nothing of poetry then yet I noticd everything as anxious as I do now & everything pleasd me as much I thought the gipseys camp by the green wood side a picturesque & an adoring object of nature & I lovd the gipseys for the beautys which they added to the landscape I heard the cuckoos wandering voice & the restless song of the Nightingale & was delighted while I paused & [it] utterd its sweet jug-jug as I passd its blackthorn bower I often pulld my hat over my eyes to watch the rising of the lark or to see the hawk hang in the summer sky & the kite take its circles round the wood I often lingered a minute on the woodland stile to hear the woodpigeons clapping their wings among the dark oaks I hunted curious flowers in rapture & muttered thoughts in their praise I lovd the pasture with its rushes & thistles & sheep tracks I adored the wild marshy fen with its solitary hernshaw sweeing along in its mellancholy sky I wandered the heath in raptures among the rabbit burrows & golden blossomd furze I dropt down on the thymy molehill or mossy eminence to survey the summer landscape as full of rapture as now I markd the varied colors in flat spreading fields checkerd with closes of different tinted grain like the colors in a map the copper tinted colors of clover in blossom the sun-tannd green of the ripening hay the lighter hues of wheat & barley intermixd with the sunny glare of the yellow car-lock & the sunset imitation of the scarlet headaches with the blue cornbottles crowding their splendid colors in large sheets over the land & troubling the cornfields with destroying beauty the different greens of the woodland trees the dark oak the paler ash the mellow lime the white poplar peeping above the rest like leafy steeples the grey willow shining chilly in the sun as if the morning mist still lingered on its cool green I felt the beauty of these with eager delight the gadflys noonday hum the fainter murmur of the beefly 'spinning in the evening ray' the dragonflys in spangled coats darting like winged arrows down the thin stream the swallow darting through its one archd brig the shepherd hiding from the thunder shower in a hollow dotterel the wild geese skudding along & making all the letters of the alphabet as they flew the motley clouds the whispering wind that muttered to the leaves & summer grasses as it flitted among them like things at play I observd all this with the same raptures as I have done since but I knew nothing of poetry it was felt & not uttered Most of my Sundays was spent in this manner about the fields

I noticd the cracking of the stubbs in the increasing sun while I gazed among them I lovd to see the heaving grasshopper in his coat of delicate green bounce from stub to stub I listend the hedgecricket with raptures

the evening call of the partridge the misterious spring sound of the landrail that cometh with the green corn.

I lovd the meadow lake with its flags & long purples crowding the waters edge I listend with delight to hear the wind whisper among the feather-topt reeds & to see the taper bulrush nodding in gentle curves to the rippling water & I watchd with delight on haymaking evenings the setting sun drop behind the brigs & peep agen through the half circle of the arches as if he longd to stay

from KITH

Jay Griffiths

Jay Griffiths grew up in England and now lives in Wales. She is the author of *Anarchipelago*, a story about the British anti-roads protests, *Pip Pip: A Sideways Look at Time* (1999), *Wild: An Elemental Journey* (2006) and *A Love Letter from a Stray Moon* (2011), a novella about the life of Frida Kahlo. *Wild* won the Orion Book Award and was also shortlisted for the Orwell Prize and a World Book Day award. Of *Wild*, the critic John Berger wrote: 'If bravery itself could write (by definition it can't), it would write, I believe, like she does.' Griffiths has also won the Barnes & Noble Discover Award for the best new non-fiction writer to be published in the United States.

THE PATRON SAINT OF CHILDHOOD

Reading the poetry of John Clare is like reading the autobiography of a robin. Perched on a spade, tucked into a hedgerow or gleaning seed-syllables in a field, England's 'peasant poet' sang the songlines of his native Northamptonshire.

Like a bird, he made nests for himself in particular trees including one called Lee Close Oak. When the robin sings 'A music that lives on and ever lives,' Clare could be writing of himself. The nightingale sang 'As though she lived on song' and in Clare's own life there were times when he lived on little more. Both boy and bird were 'Lost in a wilderness of listening leaves,' and his fledgling childhood was spent 'Roaming about on rapture's easy wing' in the circle of land around Helpston in the wheel of the year, as time turned in its agricultural cycles and reeled in its festivals.

It is hard today to imagine what children's lives were like before the Enclosures and it is impossible to overstate the terrible, lasting alteration which those Acts made to childhood in Britain. Although it is not, in the great scheme of things, so very long ago, we today are effectively fenced off from even its memory. My grandfather's grandfather would have known what it was like to make himself a nest on the commons of mud, moss, roots and grass but neither the experience nor a record of it is my inheritance and, for that, I hold a candle for John Clare, patron saint of childhood, through whose work we can see what childhood has lost: the enormity of the theft.

The commons was home for boy or bird but the Enclosures stole the nests of both, reaved children of the site of their childhood, robbed them of animal-tutors and river-mentors and stole their deep dream-shelters. The great outdoors was fenced off and marked 'TRESPASSERS WILL BE PROSECUTED.' Over the generations, as the outdoors shrank, the indoor world enlarged in importance.

PRIVATE: KEEP OUT

You see that sign in two places: on the bounds of the landowner's domain and on a child's bedroom door; and they are wholly related for, when children were banished from the commons, they lost their nests on the land. Over the years, as they came to be given their own bedrooms, a perfect and poignant mimicry evolved. Wanting some privacy but deprived of their myriad dens in the woods and on the commons, children have retaliated against the theft by sticking up signs on scraps of paper in wobbly writing: their last – unconscious – protest against the Enclosures which robbed them of all their secluded nests in the denning world, while giving them in return a prefab den, one small cage of a room. It was not, as children say, a good swap.

Born in 1793 to a sense of freedom as unenclosed as 'nature's wide and common sky', John Clare knew that the open air was his to breathe, the open water his to drink and the open land, as far as his knowledge of it extended, his to wander, and he began to write poetry of such lucid openness that it can best be described as light: his poems are translucent to nature, which shines through his work like May sunlight through beech leaves. Clare writes of the land as if he were a belonging of the land, as if it owned him, which is an idea one hears often in indigenous communities. His childhood belonged to that land and to its creatures; he knew them all and felt known in turn. One day, Clare writes, he wandered and rambled 'till I got out of my knowledge when the very wild flowers and birds seemed to forget me'.

And then, to his utter anguish, came the Enclosures, the acts of cruelty by which the common land was fenced off by the wealthy and privatized for the profit of the few. The Enclosures threw the peasantry into that acute poverty which would scar Clare's own life and mind so deeply. His griefstricken madness, alcoholism and exile as a result of this land-loss encapsulates in one indigenous life the experience of so many indigenous cultures.

In 1809, there was a parliamentary act to enclose his home territory, Helpston, and Clare saw the bitter effects at first hand as the Enclosers fenced off site after site of his memory. 'The axe of the spoiler and self interest' felled his beloved Lee Close Oak, and felled something inside himself. He lost one of his actual childhood nests but he also lost the metaphoric nest which is childhood itself where the young adult can, in a vulnerable moment, flit. Trying to console Clare for his loss, a local carpenter who had bought the timber gave Clare two rulers made from the tree. It is a poignant image for, despite the good intentions of the carpenter, the rulers represented the linear remodelling of Clare's world, wrenching the cyclical qualities of the commons (the rotation of crops and the slow cycles of time, the rounds of nests) into the strict fence-lines of Enclosure. 'Rulers' also suggests the ruling class of the Enclosers who invaded the land of the poor like an imperial army: Enclosure came 'like a Bonaparte,' wrote Clare.

One of the greatest poets of childhood, Clare is without rival as the poet of Enclosure in part because of his identification with his homeland. The Acts of Enclosure signified the enclosure and destruction of his spirit as well as his land. Winged for the simplest of raptures, he now limped at the fences erected by the 'little minds' of the wealthy. His own psyche had been as open as the footpaths of his childhood, paths which wend their way 'As sweet as morning leading night astray' but with sudden brutality 'These paths are stopt – and

Each little tyrant with his little sign
Shows, where man claims, earth glows no more divine.

It is winter. It is always winter. In one of Clare's poems, the over-arching metaphor is that the Enclosures have brought a bleak, cold, unseasonable season, 'strange and chill'. Partly, this was a direct description of the physical cold which children experienced when commoners lost their right to collect firewood for warmth; it was only because of common rights that people could 'maintain themselves and their Families in the Depth of Winter'. The Enclosures also brought a coldness of spirit, a winter of the heart. It was as if the wheel of the year had stopped turning, frozen at midwinter all year, and summer childhood would never roll round again.

Eastwell fountain never froze in winter and Clare describes how, every Whit Sunday from time immemorial, the young people of Helpston had gathered at that particular spring to drink sugar-water for good luck. He recalls tying branches together to make a swing and fishing with crooked pins, not catching anything. It's easy to picture the giggles, flirting and games. But after Enclosure, Eastwell fountain was made private property and the children were fenced out. Later, unchilded and unsung, the site had become 'nothing but a little naked spring', he writes, and it makes me wonder why he says 'naked'. I imagine that they literally clothed the spring with ribbons as children have so often garlanded wishing wells and lucky fountains, on the Well-Dressing Days which used to be a part of a child's calendar but, further, I imagine that their custom clothed the spring with meaning and memory. Not only are the children bereaved but the land too, once possessed by children's voices, is now owned, as it were, by silence. Bereft of its children, the land is 'all alone'. The sense that a site may be lonely without its children recalls the beliefs of Indigenous Australians, the Emu waterhole grieving.

So the children of Helpston lost Eastwell fountain, site of their festival, and the festival itself died. This was one example of a wide-spread effect of the Enclosures, for carnivals typically had been held outdoors on the commons but when Enclosure stole those commons both the sites of carnival and the customs themselves disappeared.

When the rights to the commons were abolished, the rites of the commons were lost: Enclosure made carnival homeless and it affected children badly because carnivals were once an enormous part of the glee of childhood. Today's few festivals are the shreds, the tattered remains, of the rites which once ribboned a child's year with dozens of carnival days and festooned it with Mischief Nights. There were Feasts of Fools, Apple-Tree Wassailings, Blessing-of-the-Mead Days, Hare-Pie-Scrambling Days, Hobby-Horse Days and Horn-Dance Days, the Well-Dressing Days which John Clare recalls, and Cock-Squoiling Days, Doling Days, Hallooing Largess led by the Lord of the Harvest, and all the variations of Hallowe'en (the Celtic festival of Samhain which archaeologists say has been celebrated for at least five thousand years), including Somerset's Punkie Night, when lanterns were made of mangel-wurzels. Mangel-wurzels. Give me mangel-wurzels, for the love of all that is good: mangel-wurzels.

It is not only a matter of the quantity of festivals but of their quality too. Carnival used to be a very public affair, sited outdoors with children playing a crucial role in this open, flamboyant theatre of exuberance. Carnival was public play but the Enclosures privatized it and over the years play moved indoors, so children today, enclosed in their bedrooms alone in an Xbox-fest with their PRIVATE: KEEP OUT signs on the door, cannot even know what used to lie on the other side of the fence, the public, excessive, inebriated, unbridled efferves-cence seizing a whole community.

When children were robbed of their carnivals, they lost a particular aspect of their relationship with nature, something at once intimate and political. For carnival renders political facts in personal ways, it plays its public roles in individual masks. Carnivals were part of children's political education in, for example, the joint-stock merrymakings which celebrated rights of grazing, gathering and gleaning on the commons, or in the 'beating of the bounds' by which a parish mapped its territories. In one case, at Scopwick in Lincolnshire, boys were made to stand on their heads in holes to make them remember the extent of their land.

Children lost the festivals, but they also lost something of the spirit of carnival, that ancient principle of reversal which subverts the *status quo*, which turns things upside down, as topsy-turvy as boys standing on their heads in holes. Carnival, rooted in the land, sends up its shoots, of play, of rudeness and licentiousness, and sends up the authorities, too, with its days of misrule. But with the Enclosures, the authorities had a field day. Children suffered, not only from a loss of freedom and of carnival but because they were prosecuted under other laws passed to protect newly enclosed lands.

There was a small common near my childhood home, called Cow Common, one tiny patch which had escaped the historical Enclosures. My first memories include the cow parsley there, which was taller than me, a parasol between me and the sun. In my memory, Cow Common was all commonness. It was the scruffy-normal from which all else diverged. It was what happened when things were left alone. It had no manners, no wealth, no restriction and no clocks. On the common, everything breathed easy and wild.

Particularly children. They are born commoners on the common ground of earth. Children, whatever their parents' class, are commoners; they come from beyond the ha-ha, beyond horticulture, decorum and dedicated grapefruit spoons. In landscape terms, they belong on the heath. They don't like the spirit of the Enclosures which mows its lawns and minds its manners, which strictly fences neatness in and untidiness out, and speaks of it all in clipped language. Nature under control. Paved patios. Miniature golf. Children prefer the spirit of the commons. Dirty. Open. The Unoccupied Territories.

And today? Does Cow Common still exist? I don't know. I don't want to go back. I don't want to see how, as an Internet search has just told me, 'most of Cow Common has gone.' I would feel robbed of a bit of my childhood if I met its absence. I would cry if I saw how the Cow Common of my very common childhood has been fenced off and privatized for the profit of the wealthy. The developers think it is valuable: we children knew it was priceless. Our wreck is long gone; developers nabbed it years ago. The Enclosures of the commons are still happening, from the profiteering bank which has seized the bank of the river in Jericho, Oxford, for luxury flats, to developers across America eyeing up worlds of childhood in disused plots of land.

The *Cow* Common of my childhood recalls the way that a peasant family could keep a cow (and perhaps geese) on the common, maybe tilling a little land. The commons had given people independence, but Enclosure threw the peasantry into pauperism. Prices rose. Wages fell. People starved. While the Enclosures drove people to starvation, they were forbidden from leaving their parish by the 'Settlement Acts', which from 1662 had prevented poor people's freedom of movement. Corralled within their parish, people turned to poaching and smuggling in huge numbers.

'All our family were smugglers,' one of my grandmothers once told me proudly, and they had to be to survive. Smugglers saw their work as legitimate trade and considered that the excise men were acting illegitimately in seizing profit from it. I have seen the man-traps used to catch smugglers in the town which my grandmother and all her ancestors were from, and a shiver runs through my genetic memory at the iron jaws, shattering bones and crippling someone for life. It could have been me.

By 1816, poachers, including children of nine or ten, were given punishments of imprisonment or transportation for offences against the Game Laws, enacted to protect the hunting rights of the wealthy. Transportation often meant a death sentence through abuse, cruelty and disease on the prison ships. Meanwhile, so widespread was the practice of poaching that, by 1830, one in three criminal convictions was for a crime against the Game Laws.

Pause a moment on this. In the 'Game' Laws, the clue is in the title. The games of the gentry – hunting for fun – were fiercely protected, while hunting for sheer starving necessity, engaged in by children and adults, was outlawed. The wealthy, engaged in sports and game shooting, were made wholly exempt from the Malicious Trespass Act of 1820, while a commoner's child, playing and breaking a branch, could be thrown in jail. Together, these acts amounted to a privatization of play. Common play – child's play – was privatized for profit.

Poaching, incidentally, something Wordsworth did as a child, has never died. Scottish artist Matthew Dalziel, from the age of seven in the 1970s, went out poaching with his dad and dog in rural Ayrshire. His mother did not always approve, tight-lipped as she cleaned the boy's clothes and berated her husband for stewing ram's horns in her jelly pan. As a boy it seemed 'a sort of human right to be able to take a fish from the river or a hare from the hill', says Dalziel. It was an adventure of the senses for a child. Chasing hares by moonlight, he recalls the rhythm of their paws 'quickening like a drumming across the earth's surface', with the grasses hissing as they ran. After the kill, the dog's heavy breath would be full of blood and sweat and would mingle with the oily woollen smell of his father's damp jumper, a madeleine of poaching.

Poachers are the hunters and the hunted. The boy feared the game-keepers who regarded them as trespassers. 'Like the animals you hunted, your senses would get highly tuned to seeing a shape behind a hedge-row that didn't quite look right, the sound of a gate squeaking, a steel wire fence lightly ringing, birds suddenly flying off, crows circling: all became voices saying someone was coming, something was not as it should be.' It was – and has always been – a nocturnal class war, where children could get a bit of their own back, their own commons, their own unenclosed freedom, trespassing a little against those who had so maliciously trespassed against them.

John Clare fears being told that his walking is 'trespass', saying that he 'dreaded walking where there was no path'. As a child, I shared that dread of the word 'trespass' and I still feel a fear which is wholly disproportionate to any punishment meted out today. Generations of children forced to recite the Lord's Prayer which uses the word 'trespass' instead of the Biblical 'sin' or 'debt' were further frightened off their own land. I learned my fear from my mother who learned it from hers: it would only need some six such transfers of fear, mother to child, to span the decades from the Malicious Trespass Act to my own wide-eyed fear at the fences. As a result of this act, children were sent to prison in large numbers. Mothers would have wanted to instil fear of trespass into their children as deeply as they would fear of poisonous snakes. As a girl, my mother misread the sign as 'TRESPASSERS WILL BE EXECUTED', and she was not alone. Another friend also mistook the word but not the threat, for, nailed next to the sign to frighten the children, a gamekeeper had hung a dead, executed, fox.

The figure of the Gamekeeper stalks children's fiction, acknowledging their persistent fear, so 'Giant Grum' in *The Little Grey Men* kills the animals in the woods; meanwhile TRESPASSERS WILL hangs over all the landscapes of childhood, from Winnie-the-Pooh to today's woodland privatizations, denying children their role as part of the wildlife.

The ideology of the Enclosures was driven by some of the less likeable attitudes of the Enlightenment: a loathing of wildness, a will to control nature, a love of hierarchies and subordination. Children suffered from these ideologies and childhood was to be enclosed as surely as land. This is not only a matter of shutting children off the land but also a matter of enclosing the playful spirit of childhood and prohibiting its carnival-heart and, further, subjecting it to domination, harsh discipline and punishment.

The experience of children was mirrored in the treatment of land. Although some early Enclosures had taken place in the thirteenth century, it was the fifteenth and sixteenth centuries that saw a wave of Enclosures, with an extreme peak in the eighteenth century, falling off by 1830. Map this with the history of childhood and something fascinating emerges: children were subjected to increasing discipline from the very end of the fourteenth century to the fifteenth and sixteenth centuries, reaching its height in the eighteenth century, until the tide began to turn by about, yes, 1830. The nature of the land and the nature of the child were both to be controlled, fenced in. Enclosure, both literal and metaphoric, was enacted against land and childhood.

Clare associated the commons with an everyday arcadia, so 'Nature's wild Eden' is found 'In common blades of grass'. Eden is here and how green is that valley, how evergreen, Eden, common as chaffinches, Eden-at-large, Eden-at-will, Eden belonging to everyone who will not wall others out. Clare welcomes everything; his Eden blesses thistles and embraces weeds, knowing that Eden is only truly Eden when the nettles are as welcome as the honeysuckle, when there is hard graft as well as moonlight, frozen well-water in winter as well as the zest of love in the zenith of summer.

His Eden is 'ruled' by nothing except 'Unbounded freedom' and, like all children given half a chance, Clare's sense of freedom included a quintessential freedom of time. He was a loafer, a dawdler, a *flâneur* of the fields, describing himself sauntering, roaming, lost in another time which existed before Enclosure:

Jumping time away
on old Crossberry Way.

Children today, peeping through the strict fences of their over-scheduled and clockworked lives, can only guess at his unenclosed sense of time. Steeped in, saturated with, drunk on the wine of time as if he had drunk it to the lees, the leavings, *laissez-boire*, the child Clare is rich on the leazings of life, the gleanings, the gatherings of memory, 'When I in pathless woods did idly roam.'

Ah, idleness, those long and lazy days when the clock is drowsy, the hours hazy and minutes erased, idleness is a friend to childhood and an enemy of the state. The 1794 Report on Enclosure in Shropshire states with nasty approval that a result of Enclosures would be that 'the labourers will work every day in the year, their children will be put out to labour early.' Children's hard labour would become necessary for survival, as families lost one right after another, including gleaners' rights to leaze after the harvest. 'Leazing' is a rich word which, like 'gleaning', means picking up what lies scattered after a harvest. Clare literally leazed in the fields but was also the poet-as-gleaner.

I found the poems in the fields
I only wrote them down.

He weaves together leaves and leazings, reading both language and nature; the birds and the words are interwoven as the yellowhammer weaves its nest of real sticks in the inspired air. 'And hang on little twigs and start again,' he writes, as if the infinite circle of a nest was a part-song sung by every bird.

Clare's was a nesting mind, delicate as tiny twigs, feathered with fellow-feeling and warm with tufts of grass tucked round the circle of his land in the cycle of the year. 'I've nestled down and watched her while she sang,' wrote Clare of the nightingale: the psyche which is well nested may sing the truest and when, as an adult, he writes about his childhood it is as if his childhood were a nest for his spirit. Nests within nests, his whole work is a nesting-place.

As a child, Clare nested in the lands which were his home and, charmed by nests, he wrote of the martin's nest, and a magpie's nest, the nests of linnet, blackbird, nightingale, pettichap or chiffchaff, skylark, landrail, yellowhammer, moorhen, thrush and robin. He includes the nests of hedgehogs and children's burrows, their little 'playhouse rings of sticks and stone'. His work seems to suggest that as a child he could feel safely nested only when the land around him was a safe nesting-place for every other kind of creature, knowing that the human mind can nest or make a home only when the ecology provides a home for all species. (The word 'ecology' comes from *oikos*, home.) Many children are disturbed by the idea that any animal, from a tiger to a snail, could lose its home, in a kind of instinctive ecological empathy.

It was the destruction of all the forms of home which unnested Clare's mind. He was evicted from his land by forces of undwelling and his madness and misery were written into his poems. I have been with Amazonian people when they have seen the searing brutality of their lands being ripped apart for gold in today's acts of corporate enclosure, and I have watched men weep while they say, aghast, 'We are the land,' a truth which John Clare would have effortlessly understood.

The Enclosures spiked the nest of Clare's psyche. Where moss and feathers had been, there was now a torque of barbed wire. When Clare writes of flowers or butterflies or birds being made homeless, he notes how they lose their depth of association so the landscape of the mind is pauperized by Enclosure.

> But, take these several beings from their homes.
> Each beauteous thing a withered thought becomes;
> Association fades and like a dream

They are but shadows of the things they seem.

Torn from their homes and happiness they stand

The poor dull captives of a foreign land.

Language and meaning need to be nested in nature, and the immensity of the destruction Clare perceives is enormous. Enclosure, he tells us in various places, fenced off rapture and play, joy, customs, games, carnival and the past; it obliterated the glow of divinity, of generosity and kindness; it silenced songs and poetry; it prohibited lingering, lazing, roaming and straying; it closed the pathways; it brought the chill of winter into every season; it caged freedom, time and wildness; it ruined dwelling, refuge and shelter; it denied belonging and so stripped the psyche of every protection. It evicted childhood from its immemorial nest on the land and it exiled his adulthood from its nest of childhood memory.

Enclosure threatens the homes of all, whether a squirrel's dray, a mouse's nest or a badger's sett. Out on the heath, after Enclosure, the rabbits had nowhere to make a warren and were left to 'nibble on the road' while the moles became 'little homeless miners' and even the birds are ordered out of their homes in the woods by forbidding signs, so they must keep flying, from felled tree to felled tree, storm-driven and nestless.

Clare, in the sympathetic magic of poetry, gives a home to everything in the only commons he still had access to: the commons of imagination. If, as a result of Enclosures, creatures no longer had their nests on the common land, he would build nests for them in that other commons: language. One creature after another is given a home and shelter in Clare's writing and each of Clare's poems is a nest. The littlest twigs are caught, laid lightly, woven of thought and love; each gentle green adjective is like moss, each soft felt word a sheltering leaf, each verb a feather for a reverie of home. All poetry is dwelling, but Clare's are daydream dwellings for both creature and human, and when each nest-song is complete the bird of poetry alights there.

But in all these nested images – nests within nests – there is one more. John Clare, building his nests of land-poetry, has in fact made a nest for us all, a home and a flitting-place for every one of us to dwell in a while, in order to know what an unenclosed childhood was like and how the child's heart can find its nestness on the land.

ON CLASS AND THE COUNTRYSIDE

Anita Sethi

Anita Sethi was born in Manchester, UK, and is an award-winning writer, journalist and critic. She is the author of *I Belong Here: A Journey Along the Backbone of Britain* (Spring 2021), the first in her nature writing trilogy, to be followed by *Nocturne* (2022) and *Forces* (2024), all published by Bloomsbury.

She is forthcoming in *Women on Nature* edited by Katharine Norbury, and has been published in the *Seasons* nature writing anthology edited by Melissa Harrison, *Common People* (in which 'On Class and the Countryside' first appeared), *Seaside Special: Postcards from the Edge*, *We Mark Your Memory* and *Solstice Shorts* among others.

She has written for national and international newspapers and magazines including the *Guardian* and *Observer*, the *i* newspaper, the *Independent*, *The Sunday Times*, the *Telegraph*, the *Sydney Morning Herald*, BBC *Wildlife*, *Vogue*, *Harper's Bazaar*, the *New Statesman*, *Granta*, the *Times Literary Supplement* and BBC *Travel* among others. In broadcasting she has appeared as a guest critic and commentator, panellist and co-presenter on several channels including BBC Radio 4, BBC Radio 5 Live, the World Service and ABC Australia. She has been a judge of the British Book Awards, Society of Authors Awards and Costa Book Awards among others.

The huge grey road wound its way up through the hills, further and further up. Out of the M6, the heavy greyness, the cluttered-up world gradually spaced itself out, lifted itself up. Up and up and up we drove, into the high regions of the earth, where the space dived straight into my belly, leaving me winded. The world grew softer, wider, dragged me out of myself and into something larger, layering into the mountains. Suddenly, everything was slightly warmer. Everything was slightly lighter. The world seemed to open itself up, lift itself, lighten up, shrug a weight off its shoulders.

Those roads were taking us to the highest mountain in England, and to the deepest bodies of water.

We were on a journey to the Lake District with Mum. Mum had got a weekend stay in a bungalow in a place called Barbon, subsidised through the nursing association, and for ages beforehand I'd sing about soon going to the Lake District, although technically the Barbon bungalow was in the nearby district of South Lakeland, Cumbria. The nurses at her work had to sign up if they wanted to go, and finally, Mum's turn had come up.

I wonder if I would even have had this early experience of the countryside had it not been for that nurses' subsidy. My earliest memories of nature were visiting the local park in my hometown of Manchester, which had felt like a safe space before I heard about the guns. After hearing that guns belonging to gangs were rumoured to be buried beneath the trees, I could not walk through the park in quite the same way. My childhood home was just two miles from the city centre in the M16 postcode, which criss-crosses Old Trafford, Moss Side and Whalley Range, and at the time my hometown had acquired the nickname 'Gunchester'. It seemed a world away from the Lake District.

There were some trips to parks further afield than our local park, to Lyme Park and Dunham Massey Park. I found a colour photo with my mother, siblings and two cousins, all gazing at a deer, which must have been taken in Lyme Park. This is the closest I came to nature, beyond a school trip to Chester Zoo. For the most part, though, growing up in a single-parent family with a mother who worked multiple jobs, there was not much time or money for many trips away. I rarely ventured out of my home city in early childhood.

But one day we did leave the city behind and venture beyond it; we ventured higher up in the world than I'd ever been before. I don't have a photo of it, but now it's coming out of the dark and into full colour. Before leaving, Mum stuffed all valuables into black bin liners and hid them in the cubbyhole, scared, we all were, of burglars.

We drove away from the city and up through the hills, up and up and up, the roads growing thin and steep and windy and I looked out of the car window and gasped as the grey fell away into an astonishment of green and blue and gold. Then the car swooped down and we were heading towards a lake, a pinprick of blue in the distance that grew larger and larger until it swamped the whole vision. I fixed my eyes on the blue water glinting with jewels on its surface cast by the sunlight, and it seemed as if I was flying towards the lake, flying into the blue.

It was as if a surface had been stripped off the world to reveal its colours beneath.

It was a shock to step out into the world and breathe in, for the air was so much clearer, the light so lucid, the sky vast and blue, reflected in the lakes. I breathed more deeply than I ever had done before and for the first time I could remember, it was a joy to breathe and the oxygen was flowing through the lungs, around the body, lifting the heart, clearing the head. I walked through the grass, which tickled my bare brown legs.

We stayed in a couple of rooms in the bungalow. A strange conception, to have the whole of life spread out on one floor, so sleeping and waking were all on the same level. It was the first time I had slept under the same roof as Mum that wasn't our house curving around a corner of Manchester.

I played outside, picking the flowers, and watching the old couple who pruned the vegetables in the garden next door, not really saying much at all, yet seeming to listen and watch us.

'You don't see many brown folks out here in the countryside,' mumbled the elderly man as he paused from pruning to gaze towards me, squinting his eyes, his face contorting in a frown, then going back to his gardening.

It would be true to say that there were not many brown people to be seen in the countryside, and not many 'common people', either. Over the course of my life I've experienced not only a north–south divide, but class divides within the same region too. When I told someone from Bramhall, Cheshire, whereabouts I lived, nearby the Manchester United football ground in Old Trafford, he shuddered and commented that it was 'not very nice around there'.

One morning I went for a walk with Mum through the mountains, watching how the great expanse of green gave way to the water and watching the wide-open spaces. Mum held my hand as we walked and walked through this new world, stopping to inspect flowers and plants that grew and watch as birds and butterflies fluttered past. We walked through a place filled with so many species I had never known existed. We stopped near a huge tree and I stretched out all my limbs so I was standing firm and proud like the bark of that tree. For the first time I remember, it felt right to be. I felt strong, as if, like that tree, I would be able to withstand any fierce gale that may come battering. The heart was opening; somewhere a tulip that had been trapped in darkness was unfurling itself in the daylight. The heart was growing, becoming as vast and deep as those lakes, as wide as those woods. I walked and walked through the world and the grass brushed my skin and the sweet scents of the flowers filled the lungs and a bright purple butterfly fluttered by so quickly that the heart leapt, and I walked and walked and forgot about myself entirely as the world flooded in and all the bad feelings drained away into the hills, which absorbed them, and Mum's rage seeped away into the lakes, which swallowed it up and washed it away, and I walked and walked and walked, and the skin was renewing itself, each cell was opening up and welcoming in the light, and the skin was shedding itself, the bruised skin, the hurt skin, the thickened, sore skin, shed as the self renewed and strengthened and healed and new skin began to grow. The hard shell that had built up around the self began to melt away amidst all this beauty. Love came flooding in. The world came flooding in, pouring into the emptiness.

I walked through the world and the air filled my lungs until the heart was beating in the ears so I knew that I was alive alive alive and I was no longer just a girl from home but a girl of the lakes, a girl of the hills, a girl of the flowers, spilling filling thrilling the lungs with their scents, a girl from the world I was becoming.

I fell in love with the lakes.

After the bank holiday, we loaded back into the Peugeot and drove back down the mountains, the softness fading away, the car splattered in grey rain.

We got lost on the way back, stuck out in the middle of the mountains. We asked a farmer who was passing by for directions, pointing to Manchester on our map, but it fell between the creases of two pages, between the dark groove in the middle of the faulty road atlas, so that the city was swallowed up, eluding all directions.

The roads swerved through the hills, round bends and past lakes flashing and flickering in the sunlight, and we drove through them for a while, lost, before getting back on the right track and finding the road that took us back down through the mountains and towards Manchester.

It felt strange thinking about our house in Old Trafford without being in it, thinking about it while being so high up, having a distance from it and from everything that had gone on inside it. From up there, near what seemed like the top of the world, I gained a new perspective.

Down down down we drove, away from that place where the light is clear, where the fresh air is abundant, down down down until soon it seemed we were driving into the very heart of a thick blanket of grey clouds. I looked out of the window and the world had vanished beneath the cotton-wool grey as if it had been snuffed out, and even the car headlights made only a thin orange gleam through the fogginess. Back down we drove, back towards our city until soon it had grown dark and the street lights appeared, and we got stuck in a traffic jam, for it was match day and I knew we were close to home again. I felt a lurch of something like excitement mixed with dread to be back in our city for, despite all the goings-on in our house, I must have loved our city, still.

One day soon after our trip, Mum brought the world home for us. It was wrapped in a see-through plastic bag and I saw it before she took it out. It was a bulge in the bag, huge as a pumpkin, though blue, not orange.

'Close your eyes,' she said. She switched off the lights and when we opened our eyes the world was glowing in the corner of the room, spilling its blues into the room, the colours of the land masses bright green or yellow or pink. Then she switched the lights back on again and switched the world off – it was only to be put on on special occasions.

She brought another world back with her too, a flatter, rectangular world. She stuck it up in the living room with Blu Tack and drew some circles around it in blue biro, lines of significant places, as if to remember them even though we were far away from them. Every now and then the world's edges curled precariously, defying their flatness, and it slipped on to the floor.

After the trip to the Lake District, Mum was more gentle, parcelling out her love for us in just the right quantities, not stifling us with it, or starving us of it when it was buried so far down inside her depression that she had none to give.

So full of promise they were, but those days shone in the light precariously.

Those days started to stiffen and gloss over; they moved from being fluid, something we lived in, and froze over. We were trapped in the house once more. I can't remember going to the lakes after that; Mum mustn't have got another subsidised place through the nursing association. I can't remember going to the countryside after that. I think of the world pressed onto the wall, and consider how we move through the world; social mobility and class – how certain places are inaccessible to certain classes, and how important it is to break down such barriers of place. It's vital that children of all classes and cultural backgrounds have ready access to nature and the countryside.

Even from my one trip to the mountains and the lakes, that landscape lived inside. The heart had opened huge enough to be filled with those deep lakes and high mountains; the heart had opened up and fallen in love with the world all over again.

Nothing could take away the great lakes from me; when I closed my eyes, there they swam. There was another world out there, beyond these walls, and another world too, within the mind.

When I had to go swimming in Stretford Leisure Centre and felt the burning shame of self-consciousness, I would imagine that I was wild swimming in a lake, practising my butterfly stroke, and as the cold water crashed against my skin I was a wild thing, I was alive and I was swimming through the world, pressing ahead through the water, and I swam until the heart was beating in the ears, the heart was beating so I knew that I was alive, and I learnt to hold my head beneath the surface for seconds and see beneath the surface and survive and carry what I had seen up to the outer world, and I was no longer just a girl from home but a girl of the lakes, a girl of the hills, a girl of the flowers, spilling filling thrilling the lungs with their scents, a girl from the world I was becoming.

Mum sat on a chair by the window in her darkened bedroom, curtains parted, cheeks pressed against the glass. I stood and watched her. The radio clock by her bedside glared out 02:34 in green ghoulish numbers. She stared out into the street. I couldn't see from here where she was looking. When her breath fogged up the window she wiped it away with her face, stroking her cheek against the glass until it was clear again. She did this over and over again, but one time the window fogged up and she didn't wipe it away, so soon a window of white breath rose up in front of her. I thought she must have fallen asleep, so I crept towards her with the irrational intention of trying to lift her into the bed and cover her up so she didn't catch cold. But her eyes were wide open, glazed over, moving.

I touched her arm and she jumped and I instinctively flinched away, expecting a huge thwack across the face, but she lifted me up on to her knee and she held me close to her, tightly, and she rocked me back and forth, back and forth, and started to sing.

The notes floated into the air, clear and bright, bubbles, and I wanted to touch them and keep them safe; something palpable, instead of this fogginess in front of us. She stroked my hair and kissed my cheek.

'What are you looking at in the foggy window, Mum?'

'Oh, I wasn't looking at the fog, I was thinking, just thinking…'

I wiped away the fog, hoping the bad pictures would also be wiped away. It came off clean and cold and squeaky in my hands.

We looked through the window together at the rainy night, empty of all but the dirty gold of the street lights, making the black puddles shine more blackly, glistening. I gazed down at the black puddles and searched their reaches and soon I could see the great lakes inside them; the black water was parting to reveal that glorious blue.

I would draw pictures and paintings for Mum – little bits of inarticulate love – and leave them in places where I knew she'd find them: pictures of houses, when I had just learnt the magic of 3D; houses with paths stretching from their doors away over the hills and towards the lakes and off the page into a future we could dream about, if there was space left in the head for dreams; paths stretching into a space off the picture, off the edges of the page, where hope might live.

from FINGERS IN THE SPARKLE JAR

Chris Packham

Chris Packham (b. 1961) grew up in suburban Southampton and trained as a wildlife cameraman after a zoology degree. He began presenting *The Really Wild Show* in 1986 and has been on television ever since, most seen as a presenter on the BBC's BAFTA award-winning *Springwatch*, *Autumnwatch* and *Winterwatch* series. As well as broadcasting, he is a wildlife photographer, writer, designer, painter and has become an increasingly influential environmental campaigner in recent years, leading opposition to the badger cull and the persecution of hen harriers. He is the co-founder of Wild Justice, which uses court challenges to change government policy on wildlife. His memoir, *Fingers in the Sparkle Jar* (2016), was voted Britain's favourite nature-writing book in a 2018 poll organized by the Arts and Humanities Research Council (AHRC). Packham's awards include a CBE for services to wildlife and nature conservation, and the Dilys Breese BTO Medal for 'his outstanding work in promoting science to new audiences'. He lives in the New Forest.

THE POND
April 1967

Better than my birthday, much better than Christmas, *Crackerjack* or the Supermarine Spitfire Mk. V, or even going to the zoo three days in a row, was 'Tadpole Time'.

In spring we made a special trip to the ornamental lake on Southampton Common, a large park just north of the city centre, where common toads gathered in enormous numbers. We went on a school night, after dinner, in the dark, parked the Ford Anglia and then walked silently with the torch switched off carrying jam jars and a bucket, the orange pin light of my dad's cigarette glowing as we picked our way between the trees towards the pale tray of water where ducks murmured and a few surly fishermen hunched in the cold. I quietly begged my dad to ask them if I could see in their nets, which stretched out across the gravel and into the silt, presumably holding invisible riches. But he wouldn't, he just shushed my whispers and ignored my short sulk as we slipped past them and squelched out on the slushy path that led to the marshy side of the lake, ducking under willows, him out front in charge of the torch and the big net, me tripping over stumps trying to see the ground between the shadows of his legs, listening to him swear as his work trousers got snagged by brambles. And we heard an owl.

In the lea of an island covered in thick pines the shallows churned with rafts of amorous amphibians, splashing from the surface and diving into the amber water where we spied on them with our weak beam, and in my excitement I scooped up a load of silt and weed so heavy it bent the net we'd got from the newsagents at the weekend, green plastic, white wire, bamboo cane.

Eventually we got a few in the bucket and I crouched over it with the lamp, my dad leaning on a stump smoking, the toads paddling in circles, the big fat females carrying one or more males on their backs. Their heads craned down, pushing obliviously round, the single males were blinded in torch-tortured confusion in the orange bucket orgy, their skin soft, slippery and knobbly, their bodies bony beneath my probing, stroking finger. In the big jam jar, crystal lit and cold, held up to my face, I saw their throats undulating, their rough marbled bellies, their chubby fingers pressed against the glass and their enamelled eyes and pinhole nostrils all mixed in a minestrone of colours from khaki to cinnamon to olive, splodged and splattered with chocolaty spots, with no symmetry but lovely all the same.

I wasn't allowed to take any home, the bucket was just for looking and to carry the 'spawn water', the spawn itself wound into the jars, a milky jelly suspending blue-black beads, slopping in the battery-flattening flashes over my damp thighs, my clammy long trousers stuck to the red vinyl seats and in the mix some curly shrimps and a boatman were struggling amid the viscous phlegm. In through the back door, the prizes lined up and dried on the kitchen sink, wet sock prints on the lino, into my pyjamas and one last look before the light went out, I heard the theme to *Softly, Softly* and the windowsill aquaria seeded dreams of thousands of wriggling tadpoles, ink spots in sparkling water with bright green weed.

Tadpoles were brilliant. Better than mice, otters, bats, seahorses and even things like pythons and cobras. They were free, came every year, lived in jam jars, weren't dangerous or poisonous and if they died I just went to get some more. But I didn't want them to die, I wanted them to turn into toads. Or frogs. Of course they did die, by accident, or if my mum put a finger-sized chunk of liver in with them as food or if I left them on the outside of the curtains when it was sunny. Or if my stupid sister kicked the jar over whilst we were pretending to endure a violent storm whilst playing shipwrecked on a make-believe life-raft bed. Even if I rushed to get a spoon I couldn't get their squashy bodies off the bedcovers in time.

And when it came to tadpoles a teaspoon was, after the net, the most important tool so I had a special 'tadpole spoon'. To the uninformed it would have looked like any other battered piece of Sheffield steel, it was after all only one of several old spoons that were part of a mass of cutlery my parents kept amongst a tangle of other scrap in a sticky uncompartmentalised kitchen drawer.

Every breakfast, lunch, tea, dinner or suppertime this crate would be yanked open causing the multitude of metal things to slide violently back and forth, mixing the forks with sugar tongs, knives with nutcrackers and spoons with centuries of battered silver, nickel-plate, stainless and chromium. Trying to find enough matching items to make up four complete place settings was a tiresome daily puzzle. To achieve the minimum of twelve pieces needed, the luckless table-layer would have to rattle the grinding junk of metal round, peering into its jigsaw to recognise any visible fragments of a telltale handle. I learned to start two patterns going from the outset and mulled over the mathematics as I laid each out neatly on the grey Formica top whilst repeatedly re-enforcing my ambition to have a kitchen, a house, a life with separate sections for everything.

Once a year I'd pull the sagging drawer out onto the floor and kneel over it, flicking through the grimy, gooey items that had gradually gravitated to the back. It was from here that I'd retrieve the sacred 'tadpole spoon'. I'd wash it and rinse it in cold water and place it in plain, simple, clean and neat isolation on my windowsill, lined up nicely with equal space all around it, as befitted any valued tool. It was slightly modified, I'd bent its neck through about forty degrees to facilitate more efficient removal of those tricky tadpoles which clustered like berries just under the neck of the jam jar, a place that normal spoons just couldn't reach.

As a toddler I probably ate tadpoles, especially as I was given bowls to collect them in and spoons to fish for them, but such consumption wasn't deliberate and contributed little to my habit of tadpolephagy. And whilst terminal for the amphibians it obviously did no harm to me. Considered ingestion came later, between five and nine with a peak between six and seven and a half. By this age I was very actively curious, not only about the taste of tadpoles but also about their potential ill effects; having by then experienced stomach ache, flatulence and bouts of diarrhoea, I wondered what would happen if I ate a few. Having returned from school, watched Captain Scarlet improbably survive another absurdly explosive scenario without even the severance of a single strand of the puppeteer's string, jabbed rubberised fish fingers back and forth across a plate until the banana-flavoured Angel Delight arrived with slices of cut banana set in it and a generous blob of strawberry jam dropped vaguely centrally, been allowed to get down and retreated to my bedroom to unnecessarily decant several hundred tadpoles from jar to jar, I found before me, glistening in the early evening light, a spoon full of small, soft, benign, stingless fruits of nature of which there was no shortage. So what could be the harm? And critically when my world was constantly erupting with novel experiences, what, I wondered, did tadpoles taste of?

Muddy water, slightly gritty, strange when one wriggled beneath my tongue and quite tricky to bite or chew. Not like jelly, or sweets of any kind, or like rice pudding or tapioca. Maybe similar to very watery semolina in terms of texture. But beads of softened wheat didn't thrash about in my mouth, unlike… half-matured toad larvae. And they were quite 'moreish' simply because they were so difficult to taste, easier when I scooped ten to fifteen big ones all into the spoon at once.

The result of my possibly excessive appetite for juvenile amphibians wasn't diagnosed through any medical examination so I can't prove anything scientifically. But these harmless inoculations probably positively contributed to the ignition of a spark that fuelled a lifelong interest in living things, an enduring curiosity in everything that creeps, climbs, bites, stings, slithers, scuttles or slimes; and in entirely romantic terms, I imagined, the molecules of the tadpoles I digested were fused into the fabric of my eyes to facilitate a heightened awareness of life and instilled a profound love for it, the likes of which could never have arisen from my sterile school studies, from the disconnected or imagined experiences that I gleaned from my books and television, but only from that heart that fluttered, as my throat was tickled, softly, by simple beauty at that essential point in my own metamorphosis.

Woods

Illustration overleaf: *Wistman's Wood, Devon*

from THE WIND IN THE WILLOWS

Kenneth Grahame

In 1908, the Secretary of the Bank of England retired because of ill health and also to devote his life to writing. That year saw the publication of **Kenneth Grahame**'s (1859–1932) enduring novel, *The Wind in the Willows*. Early reviews were mystified by the anthropomorphic tale of Mole, Ratty, Badger and Toad but readers of all ages loved it and it became an international bestseller. Grahame was born in Edinburgh but his mother died when he was young and his father was an alcoholic, so Grahame and his three siblings were raised by their grandmother in Cookham Dean, Berkshire. The nearby River Thames helped inspire *The Wind in the Willows*. As a young man, Grahame mixed with ideal- istic Fabians and wrote essays and stories – published in *Pagan Papers* (1893), *The Golden Age* (1895) and *Dream Days* (1898) – which revealed his sensitive perception of childhood. *The Wind in the Willows* was based on bedtime stories he told Alastair, his only child. Toad's exasperating, rebellious behaviour was in part modelled on his son, who took his own life aged nineteen while he was an undergraduate at Oxford University.

THE WILD WOOD

The Mole had long wanted to make the acquaintance of the Badger. He seemed, by all accounts, to be such an important personage and, though rarely visible, to make his unseen influence felt by everybody about the place. But whenever the Mole mentioned his wish to the Water Rat he always found himself put off. "It's all right," the Rat would say. "Badger'll turn up some day or other – he's always turning up – and then I'll introduce you. The best of fellows! But you must not only take him *as* you find him, but *when* you find him."

"Couldn't you ask him here – dinner or something?" said the Mole.

"He wouldn't come," replied the Rat simply. "Badger hates Society, and invitations, and dinner, and all that sort of thing."

"Well, then, supposing we go and call on *him*," suggested the Mole.

"O, I'm sure he wouldn't like that at *all*," said the Rat, quite alarmed. "He's so very shy, he'd be sure to be offended. I've never even ventured to call on him at his own home myself, though I know him so well. Besides, we can't. It's quite out of the question, because he lives in the very middle of the Wild Wood."

"Well, supposing he does," said the Mole. "You told me the Wild Wood was all right, you know."

"O, I know, I know, so it is," replied the Rat evasively. "But I think we won't go there just now. Not *just* yet. It's a long way, and he wouldn't be at home at this time of year anyhow, and he'll be coming along some day, if you'll wait quietly."

The Mole had to be content with this. But the Badger never came along, and every day brought its amusements, and it was not till summer was long over, and cold and frost and miry ways kept them much indoors, and the swollen river raced past outside their windows with a speed that mocked at boating of any sort or kind, that he found his thoughts dwelling again with much persistence on the solitary grey Badger, who lived his own life by himself, in his hole in the middle of the Wild Wood.

In the winter time the Rat slept a great deal, retiring early and rising late. During his short day he sometimes scribbled poetry or did other small domestic jobs about the house; and, of course there were always animals dropping in for a chat, and consequently there was a good deal of story-telling and comparing notes on the past summer and all its doings.

Such a rich chapter it had been, when one came to look back on it all! With illustrations so numerous and so very highly coloured! The pageant of the river bank had marched steadily along, unfolding itself in scene-pictures that succeeded each other in stately procession. Purple loose-strife arrived early, shaking luxuriant tangled locks along the edge of the mirror whence its own face laughed back at it. Willow-herb, tender and wistful, like a pink sunset cloud, was not slow to follow. Comfrey, the purple hand-in-hand with the white, crept forth to take its place in the line; and at last one morning the diffident and delaying dog-rose stepped delicately on the stage, and one knew, as if string-music had announced it in stately chords that strayed into a gavotte, that June at last was here. One member of the company was still awaited; the shepherd-boy for the nymphs to woo, the knight for whom the ladies waited at the window, the prince that was to kiss the sleeping summer back to life and love. But when meadow-sweet, debonair and odorous in amber jerkin, moved graciously to his place in the group, then the play was ready to begin.

And what a play it had been! Drowsy animals, snug in their holes while wind and rain were battering at their doors, recalled still keen mornings, an hour before sunrise, when the white mist, as yet undispersed, clung closely along the surface of the water; then the shock of the early plunge, the scamper along the bank, and the radiant transformation of earth, air, and water, when suddenly the sun was with them again, and grey was gold and colour was born and sprang out of the earth once more. They recalled the languorous siesta of hot mid-day, deep in green undergrowth, the sun striking through in tiny golden shafts and spots; the boating and bathing of the afternoon, the rambles along dusty lanes and through yellow cornfields; and the long, cool evening at last, when so many threads were gathered up, so many friendships rounded, and so many adventures planned for the morrow. There was plenty to talk about on those short winter days when the animals found themselves round the fire; still, the Mole had a good deal of spare time on his hands, and so one afternoon, when the Rat in his arm-chair before the blaze was alternately dozing and trying over rhymes that wouldn't fit, he formed the resolution to go out by himself and explore the Wild Wood, and perhaps strike up an acquaintance with Mr Badger.

It was a cold still afternoon with a hard steely sky overhead, when he slipped out of the warm parlour into the open air. The country lay bare and entirely leafless around him, and he thought that he had never seen so far and so intimately into the inside of things as on that winter day when Nature was deep in her annual slumber and seemed to have kicked the clothes off. Copses, dells, quarries and all hidden places, which had been mysterious mines for exploration in leafy summer, now exposed themselves and their secrets pathetically, and seemed to ask him to overlook their shabby poverty for a while, till they could riot in rich masquerade as before, and trick and entice him with the old deceptions. It was pitiful in a way, and yet cheering – even exhilarating. He was glad that he liked the country undecorated, hard, and stripped of its finery. He had got down to the bare bones of it, and they were fine and strong and simple. He did not want the warm clover and the play of seeding grasses; the screens of quickset, the billowy drapery of beech and elm seemed best away; and with great cheerfulness of spirit he pushed on towards the Wild Wood, which lay before him low and threatening, like a black reef in some still southern sea.

There was nothing to alarm him at first entry. Twigs crackled under his feet, logs tripped him, funguses on stumps resembled caricatures, and startled him for the moment by their likeness to something familiar and far away; but that was all fun, and exciting. It led him on, and he penetrated to where the light was less, and trees crouched nearer and nearer, and holes made ugly mouths at him on either side.

Everything was very still now. The dusk advanced on him steadily, rapidly, gathering in behind and before; and the light seemed to be draining away like floodwater.

Then the faces began.

It was over his shoulder, and indistinctly, that he first thought he saw a face: a little evil wedge-shaped face, looking out at him from a hole. When he turned and confronted it, the thing had vanished.

He quickened his pace, telling himself cheerfully not to begin imagining things, or there would be simply no end to it. He passed another hole, and another, and another; and then – yes! – no! – yes! certainly a little narrow face, with hard eyes, had flashed up for an instant from a hole, and was gone. He hesitated – braced himself up for an effort and strode on. Then suddenly, as if it had been so all the time, every hole, far and near, and there were hundreds of them, seemed to possess its face, coming and going rapidly, all fixing on him glances of malice and hatred: all hard-eyed and evil and sharp.

If he could only get away from the holes in the banks, he thought, there would be no more faces. He swung off the path and plunged into the untrodden places of the wood.

Then the whistling began.

Very faint and shrill it was, and far behind him, when first he heard it; but somehow it made him hurry forward. Then, still very faint and shrill, it sounded far ahead of him, and made him hesitate and want to go back. As he halted in indecision it broke out on either side, and seemed to be caught up and passed on throughout the whole length of the wood to its farthest limit. They were up and alert and ready, evidently, whoever they were! And he – he was alone, and unarmed, and far from any help; and the night was closing in.

Then the pattering began.

He thought it was only falling leaves at first, so slight and delicate was the sound of it. Then as it grew it took a regular rhythm, and he knew it for nothing else but the pat-pat-pat of little feet, still a very long way off. Was it in front or behind? It seemed to be first one, then the other, then both. It grew and it multiplied, till from every quarter as he listened anxiously, leaning this way and that, it seemed to be closing in on him. As he stood still to hearken, a rabbit came running hard towards him through the trees. He waited, expecting it to slacken pace, or to swerve from him into a different course. Instead, the animal almost brushed him as it dashed past, his face set and hard, his eyes staring. "Get out of this, you fool, get out!" the Mole heard him mutter as he swung round a stump and disappeared down a friendly burrow.

The pattering increased till it sounded like sudden hail on the dry-leaf carpet spread around him. The whole wood seemed running now, running hard, hunting, chasing, closing in round something or – somebody? In panic, he began to run too, aimlessly, he knew not whither. He ran up against things, he fell over things and into things, he darted under things and dodged round things. At last he took refuge in the deep dark hollow of an old beech tree, which offered shelter, concealment – perhaps even safety, but who could tell? Anyhow, he was too tired to run any further and could only snuggle down into the dry leaves which had drifted into the hollow and hope he was safe for the time. And as he lay there panting and trembling, and listened to the whistlings and the patterings outside, he knew it at last, in all its fullness, that dread thing which other little dwellers in field and hedgerow had encountered here, and known as their darkest moment – that thing, which the Rat had vainly tried to shield him from – the Terror of the Wild Wood!

from GOSSIP FROM THE FOREST

Sara Maitland

Sara Maitland (b. 1950) grew up in London and south-west Scotland, studied English at Oxford University and had her first short stories published by Faber in 1972. Maitland wrote *Tales I Tell My Mother* with a feminist writing group including Michele Roberts and Zoe Fairbairns. Her first novel, *Daughter of Jerusalem*, won the Somerset Maugham Award in 1978. 'I write about women and the entangled emotions of terror and beauty,' she says. 'I use a lot of old stories from diverse traditions – fairy stories, myths and folk tales. I am a deeply committed (Roman Catholic) Christian, and that also informs my work.' Her non-fiction includes *A Book of Silence* (2008), *Gossip from the Forest* (2012) and *How to Be Alone* (2014). She lives with Zoe – 'a sort of border terrier' – in a house she built on a moor in northern Galloway.

MARCH – AIRYOLLAND WOOD

It is dark, a soft, rustling night and not too cold. Adam, my son, and I are sitting on a moss-covered rock eating baked beans. He has pitched the small tent with the grace that goes with experience; I have heated the baked beans on the camping stove with the clumsiness that comes from lack of practice. It is dark now, and above us the branches of the trees are darker still, patterning themselves against the clouds. There is not much wind, but enough to make the branches a little restless. We can hear the burn and the branches and some other unidentifiable night noises, but it is quiet and calm. Airyolland Wood is a magical place for us and we are enjoying ourselves.

Airyolland is a tiny triangle of ancient oak wood that clings to the side of a steep valley in Galloway. It is a little fragment of what was once a far more extensive forest and we are lucky to have it still. A small stream, crystal clear and fast, rushes down towards the river in a series of sharp little falls; each sudden drop has a miniature deep pool at the bottom of it and the sides of the pool are rich with ferns, even this early in the year. The oak trees are old and tangled, many multi-trunked from long-ago coppicing, and they are festooned with epiphyte ferns, with moss, and with epicormic twigs sprouting whiskery from the rough bark. Their buds are fattening now, but there are no leaves, and the moon, slipping out from the filigreed clouds, occasionally breaks through the bare branches. The ground is both steeply sloped and complexly humped and carved; it is scattered apparently casually with erratic boulders – some as large as garden sheds and some much smaller – pushed here by a glacier and left when the ice retreated. Immediately to the south, abutting this wood, just across the stream, is a fairly typical patch of forestry plantation, huddling up against the little wood; above it is a well-greened field with a farmhouse just out of sight. The Southern Upland Way runs through here, and – totally incongruously – the single-track railway line from Glasgow to Stranraer cuts through the bottom edge of the wood. And still Airyolland is a magical place for both of us and we are enjoying ourselves.

As we came down from the high moor where I live earlier this afternoon, I could sense the spring pushing up the valley to meet us. There were daffodils out in the village and new lambs in the fields along the river. The hawthorn in the hedges is showing bright, pale green buttons of buds, and a wych elm on the edge of the wood is covered in tiny red-gold balls which will flower before the end of the month. In the grass on the slope as we enter the oak wood itself there are the first primroses, and underfoot the darker green shoots of what will be ramson – wild garlic – later on.

But the trees themselves show fewer conspicuous signs: oak leafs out later than most trees, except ash,[1] and the moss here is so thick and the rock so near the surface that there is surprisingly little under-growth. The spring is coming nonetheless. Although it is still nearly ten days before we move the clocks forward, the evenings are getting longer and there are hard, pale little nubs down by the burn which will push up into fresh fern fronds over the coming month. Some of them are visibly beginning to do that exquisite fern thing: pushing up straight, sturdy stems and then uncoiling the tight spiral at the very top, so that briefly they look like Gothic bishops' crosiers. Earlier, while it was still light, there was a new twitter of birds, and there has been no frost for over two weeks.

We are here to catch the early sun tomorrow morning as it rises over the moor. The sun will spill light, colour and long shadows through the branches and across the green moss. That is what Adam wants to photograph. We are also here trying to learn how to work together as adults. So far so good, except that I demanded that we brought a cafetière with us, and he can hardly be expected to approve of such foppish ways, especially as he does almost all the portering.

'So,' I say, into the dark, 'which fairy stories do you know? Do you remember?'

'Goldilocks, Red Riding Hood, Cinderella, Snow-white. Jack and the Beanstalk.' There's a short pause, and then, 'The one with the swans and the shirts, Rumplestiltskin… the princess with that long hair…'

I am quite impressed. But it is somehow easier to remember these stories in this wood, as though the wood itself was reminding us. 'Where did you learn them? Who told them to you?' I ask.

'You,' he says. Then, 'School perhaps. I don't know really, I just know them.'

We expand our list of stories, dig for the details, re-run the plots and laugh a bit at some of them – for some reason, 'The Mouse, the Bird and the Sausage' pleases us immensely, and we chant together, giggling, a suddenly mutually recalled snippet:

> The bird encountered a dog and learned that this dog had con-sidered the sausage free game and swallowed him down. The bird was furious and accused the dog of highway robbery, but it was of no use, for the dog maintained he had found forged letters on the sausage and therefore the sausage had to pay for this with his life.[2]

This is a totally absurd little tale from the Grimms' collection about some improbable housemates who fall out over the division of the domestic chores, and it has nothing to do with forests or magic. God knows what the psychoanalysts, or the universal folklorists, or the academic textual deconstructers, or anyone else for that matter, would make of it. It is important to remember how many of the fairy stories we do not remember; and it is worth thinking about which ones. A large number of them are funny and silly, but these do not tend to feature in the modern canon.

Later he says, 'OK. Tell me about the book.'

I say, 'Once upon a time it was all forest...'

It was all forest before the last Ice Age.

'Don't call it the Ice Age,' he says, 'call it...'

It was all forest before the last *glaciations*, which is why we have coal mines – every coal seam is a dead forest, but we aren't going there now. We're going to begin about 10,000 years ago, when the ice began to retreat. For tens of thousands of years, in places up to 3,000 metres thick, it had pressed heavily on northern Europe and America; the sea level had dropped as more and more water was frozen up in the Arctic Circle and high in the mountain ranges; glaciers had pushed down from the mountains, carving new valleys with flat bottoms and steep sides. Now, gradually, it began to retreat, leaving behind a stripped land, ground down and naked.

As the ice retreated, living things moved in from the south, opportunist as always, and greedy for space. First lichens, those great pioneers that break up land, build soils, prepare the way; and then, gradually, mosses, fungi, ferns, and, last but not least, seed-bearing plants – low scrub, flowers, and eventually, trees. It takes thousands of years to make a good forest – but they did well in this wet northern land, and flourished and spread out. And so, once upon a time it was all forest. Forest enough to be lost in it for ever.

To be honest, this itself is a fairy story. It was never 'all forest'. Once upon a time, before people knew how much of it had been forest, the wide open down lands of southern England and the bare hills of Scotland and the wide flat fens and the rich green shires were all thought to be 'how it was' – natural, timeless and somehow pure.

People tended to like it, rather in the way they liked the idea that the statuary of the classical world or the interiors of the great medieval cathedrals came in pure stone, pristine and restrained, and on the whole were rather sorry to learn that originally they had been gaudily painted. More recently we realised that these open spaces had once been forested, and we took that story on board instead. Our forests grew deeper and denser – fertilised by Arthurian romances and the Wild Wood in *The Wind in the Willows* and tales of Robin Hood – until we knew that once it had indeed been 'all forest'. And forest became the pure place of primal innocence, where children could escape from their adults, get away from the order and discipline of straight roads and good governance, and revert to their animal origins.

But it is more complicated than that really. There was more forest than there is now, but not as much as we like to think. Oliver Rackham, the leading academic of woodland history, believes that less than 7% of Scotland was ever ancient forest and that the great Caledonian Forest is as much a story as the Merlin who ran mad in it. More importantly perhaps, large swathes of this 'forest' were never the untrodden tanglewood of the imagination, but were inhabited, worked, used. Much of the so-called forest was what is more properly called 'wood pasture' – trees more widely spaced out, standing independently in grass, like savannah, cropped not just by deer and wild boar and aurochs, but later by cows and sheep and pigs. The wild animals followed the trees and grasses northwards from Europe easily enough, because Britain was still joined to the continent by a broad band of dry land until about 7000 BCE; and by the same route, Neolithic people followed the animals. There had in fact been people in Britain before the last glaciation, but they seem to have retreated southwards, fleeing the ice and the bitter cold. Now they returned, and almost as soon as they were established they started to manage and exploit the forest – for hunting, for grazing, for fuel, for food.

The same pattern was repeated across much of northern Europe, and indeed the people were much the same, too. The ice shrank back towards the polar regions, the forests chased it northwards as far as they could, and *homo sapiens* followed the forest. Right from the very beginning, the relationship between people and forest was not primarily antagonistic and competitive, but symbiotic. Until recently people could not survive without woodland, but perhaps more sur-prisingly, woodland flourishes under good human management – coppicing, for example, increases the amount of light that reaches into the depths of the forest, and so encourages germination and new growth and increases biodiversity. This was not wild wood that had to be 'tamed', but an infinite resource, rich, generous and often mysterious. The forests were protective too. Of course you can get lost in the forest, but you can also hide in the forest, and for exactly the same reason: in forests you cannot get a long view. In his history of the Gallic Wars, Julius Caesar comments that the Gauls defended themselves in forts within 'impassable woods', although they were clearly not impassable to the Britons, whatever the Roman military made of them.[3]

Forests to these northern European peoples were dangerous and generous, domestic and wild, beautiful and terrible. And the forests were the terrain out of which fairy stories (or, as they are perhaps better called in German, the *Märchen*), one of our earliest and most vital cultural forms, evolved. The mysterious secrets and silences, gifts and perils of the forest are both the background to and the source of these tales.

Modern scholarship has taken a number of approaches to this material, which presents a delightfully insubstantial and tricky body of work. Two approaches that I will mention here have been a Jungian psychoanalytic approach (arguing that the tales resonate for children, and adults too, because they deal in archetypes, in universal experi-ences, usually sexual ones), and a global ethnographic approach, which finds tropes from the tales in every culture everywhere; both these and other ways of looking at the stories are illuminating, but tend to lose the specificity of place. What is interesting to me is not the ways in which the tales of the Arabian Nights or of the Indian sub-continent or of the indigenous Americans of the Great Plains are the *same* as the stories collected and redacted by Jacob and Wilhelm Grimm and published initially in 1812, but the ways they are *different*.

The fairy stories from, for instance, the Arabian Nights do demon-strably have many of the same themes and narrative sequences as those in the Grimm brothers' collections, but they are not the same stories. One of the great services that the great Grimm expert Jack Zipes[4] has done is to show how 'site specific' fairy stories are. To put it at its most basic, in the Arabian Nights the heroes do not go out and get lost in the forest, or escape into the forest; this is because, very simply, there aren't any forests. But it goes deeper than this – they do not get lost at all; the heroes either set off freely seeking adventure – often by boat, like Sinbad the Sailor – or they are exiled, escape murder (rather than poverty), or are abducted. Children do not get lost in deserts; if they wander off, which they are unlikely to do because of the almost certain fatal consequences of being lost alone in deserts, they can be seen for as far as they can roam. Children get lost in cities and in forests. As I will discuss later, forests are places where a person can get lost and can also hide – losing and hiding, of things and people, are central to European fairy stories in ways that are not true of similar stories in different geographies.

Landscape informs the collective imagination as much as or more than it forms the individual psyche and its imagination, but this dimension is not something to which we always pay enough attention.

It cannot be by chance that the three great monotheist religions – the Abrahamic faiths – have their roots in the desert, in the vast empty spaces under those enormous stars, where life is always provisional, always at risk. Human beings are tiny and vulnerable and necessarily on the move: local gods of place, small titular deities, are not going to be adequate in the desert – you need a big god to fill the vast spaces and speak into the huge silence; you need a god who will travel with you.

It cannot be simply accidental that Tibetan Buddhism emerges from high places, where the everlasting silence of the snows invites a kind of concentration, a loss of ego in the enormity of the mountains.

It cannot be totally coincidental that the joyful, humanistic polytheism of the classical Mediterranean – where the gods behave like humans (which means badly), and humans may become gods, and heroes (god-human hybrids) link the two inextricably, and metamorphosis destabilises expectation – arose in a terrain where there was infinite variety, where you can move in a matter of hours from mountain to sea shore, where islands are scattered casually, and where one place is very precisely not like another.

Less certainly, but still suggestively, the gods of the Vikings, far north in the land of the midnight sun and its dreadful corollary, the six months night, are unique in being vulnerable. Most myths and legends look forward to a final triumphant consummation at the end of time; but Viking gods and heroes cannot offer much reassurance for all the noise they make, and they will march out to Ragnarok with only a slim chance of victory and a tragic certainty of loss.

I am not comparing the forms of religious myth, legend and folk tale (although sometimes, as in Ovid's *Metamorphosis* or some parts of Genesis, we can see all three merging together). I am just trying to give some better-known examples of how the land, the scenery and the climate shape and inform the imaginations of the people.

I believe that the great stretches of forest in northern Europe, with their constant seasonal changes, their restricted views, their astonishing biological diversity, their secret gifts and perils and the knowledge that you have to go through them to get to anywhere else, created the themes and ethics of the fairytales we know best. There are secrets, hidden identities, cunning disguises; there are rhythms of change like the changes of the seasons; there are characters, both human and animal, whose assistance can be earned or spurned; and there is – over and over again – the journey or quest, which leads first to knowledge and then to happiness. The forest is the place of trial in fairy stories, both dangerous and exciting. Coming to terms with the forest, surviving its terrors, utilising its gifts and gaining its help is the way to 'happy ever after'.

These themes informed the stories and still inform European sensibility, sometimes in unexpected ways. For example, concepts of freedom and rights, and particularly the idea of meritocracy – that everyone, regardless of their material circumstances, has an inner self which is truer than their social persona, and which deserves recognition – are profoundly embedded in the fairy story. You may be a beggar, but truly you are a princess; you may be seen to be a queen, but truly you are a wicked witch; you may have been born a younger son, but your real identity is as a king. Intellectually, these are modern radical ideas of the Enlightenment, but imaginatively they are already there at the core of the fairy stories. With them, growing out of the same root, I think, goes the ideal, so baffling to many other cultures, that romantic love, as opposed to parental good sense and a dowry system, is the best basis for marriage. Or at a less high-flown level, even up to the present day, stepmothers, despite so many people growing up with them, are still *always* wicked: culturally, to be a birth mother is good and to be a stepmother is at best highly problematic.

In Britain we often like to see ourselves as Sea People, island dwellers, buccaneers and Empire Builders; most British people like to emphasise their Celtic or Viking origins – and this self-image is probably enhanced by the new Britons who have more recently come across the oceans and settled. We tend to obscure the fact that, essentially, most of us are predominantly Germanic. This denial is made easier for us by the fact that until the modern period there was no Germany; but the waves of settlers who pushed the Celts westward were all Germanic – among them, the Angles and Saxons whose language is the basis of English. We share deep roots and cultural similarities with the people of northern Europe, as politically we are beginning to acknowledge. To help with this, I tend to use the word 'Teutonic', a wider, less nationalised term than 'Germanic', to describe those cultural phenomena we draw from this tradition. This includes our fairy stories. At our deep Teutonic roots we are forest people, and our stories and social networks are forest born.

Now the forests themselves are at risk. About 5,000 years ago the process of deforestation began. With the discovery of iron working, the process speeded up because wood in its raw state does not burn hot enough to smelt; charcoal, however, does. To produce sufficient charcoal, as well as to meet the other human needs like grazing, hunting and timber production, forest management began. Overall, the earlier phases of such management reduced the area covered by the forests but extended their biodiversity. Over the following centuries the forests came under increasing pressure. The growing population and its needs required ever-increasing quantities of both arable land and fuel. The agricultural revolution of the eighteenth century increased the value of ploughed land, and through enclosure, agriculture encroached further on the forest and radically changed the psychological experience of space and view. The Industrial Revolution destroyed forests to create cities, transport systems, mines and factories – and the development of coal mining did not relieve this latter need because so much timber was needed for pit props and subsequently for railway tracks. In the UK, deforestation reached its limits immediately after the 1914–18 war. There is now very little ancient woodland still flourishing.

Nonetheless, the forests that remain are strange and wonderful places with a rich natural history, long narratives of complex relationships – between humans and the wild, and between various groups of human beings – and a sense of enchantment and magic, which is at the same time fraught with fear.

One problem about forests, especially ancient ones, is that they are chaotic from even a fairly short distance away. Their inhabitants knew intimately both the value and beauty of their woods, as well as the real dangers that lurked there. But from the point of view of an absentee landlord, ancient woodlands are non-economic; grubbing out patches of useless old trees and bringing the area under the plough was an obvious way of increasing rental income. The Industrial Revolution needed the wood but not the forests: well-managed plantation was an obvious way of increasing productivity. An unexpected development was the introduction of two opposing forms of 'fake' forest – the supposedly economically viable monoculture of mass forestry tracts on land that was never going to prove sufficiently profitable agriculturally; and the beauty of ornamental woodland – the parks, large gardens and arboreta of the rural upper classes. But forests, like fairy stories, need to be chaotic – beautiful and savage, useful and wasteful, dangerous and free.

Somewhere I picked up some of that horror about forests. When I was writing *A Book of Silence* I discovered that I was avoiding forests and their silences because I was frightened. Startled, I took myself off to Glen Affric – one of the remaining fragments of ancient pine forest in Scotland – to challenge and examine my fear. The forest was very beautiful, in a weird and ancient-feeling way. I discovered that, in reality, it was not 'fear' that I experienced, but something rather stranger. Glen Affric is famous for its lichens; they trailed from the birch and rowan trees like witches' tresses, long, tangled and grey. Perhaps initially it was that image which triggered an unexpected response: the forest gave me the same set of feelings and emotions that I get when I first encounter a true fairy story. For me, this is a visceral response and hard to articulate – a strange brew of excitement, recognition and peril, with more anticipation or even childlike glee than simple 'terror of the wild' because of the other sense that this is somewhere I know and have known all my life. The hairs on the back of my neck do not actually rise as the cliché would have it, but I know exactly what the phrase is trying to express.

I have always had a strong imaginative reaction to fairy stories. As an adult, I have read a lot of them and a lot about them. It was not hard to recognise the almost identical feeling that the Glen Affric forest gave me, but it was surprising. Naturally, then, I was intrigued by my so similar responses. I started to think about this, and have come to realise that these feelings do have a real connection, lying buried in the imagination and in our childhoods, as well as in the more regulated historical and biological accounts.

I grew up on fairy stories. Luckily for me, from early childhood my parents read to us widely and they also told us stories. Although, like all oral storytellers, they moulded and edited the stories to their own ends, they did not – as I remember it – make up new stories for us, but gave us a wide range of traditional ones – history stories,[5] Bible stories, and, particularly in my father's case, classical myths. But fairy stories have some big advantages for parents with six children because they are age appropriate for nearly everyone; they can be shifted and altered to match the moment's need; there is a fairly even balance of male and female characters; they are mercifully short; and they are memorable.

'Once upon a time,' the stories would begin… no particular time, fictional time, fairy-story time. This is a doorway; if you are lucky, you go through it as a child, aurally, before you can read, and if you are very lucky, you become a free citizen of an ancient republic and can come and go as you please.

These stories are deeply embedded in my imagination. As I grew up and became a writer, I found myself going back to them and using them, retelling them ever since, working partly on the principle that a tale which has been around for centuries is highly likely to be a better story than one I just made up yesterday; and partly on the deep sense that they can tell more truth, more economically, than slices of contemporary social realism. The stories are so tough and shrewd formally that I can use them for anything I want – feminist revisioning, psychological exploration, malicious humour, magical realism, nature writing. They are generous, true and enchanted.

My parents also gave us an unusual degree of physical freedom and space. We were allowed to go out into the big bad world and have adventures, both rural ones and – more surprisingly for middle-class children in the 1950s – London ones. I have not fully worked out the connection here, but it feels important to make a note of it.

I honestly do not remember when I became aware that there were mediators of these parental gifts – printed fixed versions of these stories. At some point I must have learned that they were different sorts of stories from Joseph's coat of many colours, from Helen's great beauty, and from Drake's game of bowls. By the time I reached that recognition I had also begun to separate out the different strands. Well into early adulthood I thought of the Classical Myths as being somehow superior to the fairy stories, more important and more dignified; more grown-up indeed, because adults around me read Greek mythology, admired and encouraged references to it, and thought the acquisition of Latin a necessary part of education, but to the best of my knowledge then, fairy stories were for the children. I suspect that this was both a learned response to my adults' preference for high over popular culture, but also, with the best will in the world, it is impossible to tell Greek mythological stories without at least hinting at sexual shenanigans of a pretty exotic kind, while this element can be much more efficiently repressed in fairy stories. Sex seemed highly grown-up and sophisticated to me then. It probably was not until 1979, when Angela Carter's *The Bloody Chamber* taught me a thing or two, that I realised just how sexy the bog-standard fairy story could really be.

And as I learned these distinctions about genre, I also learned to distinguish between different sorts of fairy stories and different ways of telling them. Quite early I discovered that I did not like Hans Andersen's stories. I knew they were fakes: they were too pious, too complicated and often too sad as well – all traditional fairy stories, I knew, have happy endings, it is one of the central codes of the genre. Oscar Wilde's got nearer to the real thing, but they only worked when they were read, not told; Tolkien was like that too, and also he wanted you to care about, rather than identify with, particular characters in longer sagas, and there was always an inexplicable sense that he was up to something else, even when he touched some deep roots.

Gradually I came to recognise that the best fairy stories are very ancient and originally oral and that you are allowed to retell them at whim and in your own way. Eventually, probably not until my teens, I became conscious that a large number of the most popular fairy stories had been recorded from verbal narrators by two German linguists, brothers called Jacob and Wilhelm Grimm: 'Rumplestiltskin', 'Snow White', 'Sleeping Beauty', 'Hansel and Gretel' and, of course, 'Cinderella'. They published a first collection of 86 tales, *Kinder- und Hausmärchen*, in 1812 and went on adding stories until the seventh and final edition, in 1857, contained 210 stories.

The Grimm brothers have come in for a good deal of criticism more recently, and much of it is justified. Specifically, while they inferred that these stories were collected verbatim from oral storytellers, simple local peasants, particularly old women, we know now that their sources were more often second hand, the stories gleaned from their middle-class social circle, although usually with a claim that they had first heard them from a servant or old nurse. Jacob and Wilhelm themselves, despite their linguistic and 'scientific' ethnographic intentions, edited the stories heavily, shifting their focus and making them more Christian, more family orientated, less explicitly sexual, more nationalistic and more sexist. One nice little example of this tendency is the fact that in the 1812 version of 'Rapunzel', the witch learns about the girl's princely visitor when Rapunzel wonders why she is growing fat, not having been taught about pregnancy. In the later editions, Rapunzel gives the game away by a slip of the tongue – she asks the witch why the witch is not as heavy as the prince to haul up on her long plait – thus becoming more innocent but more stupid to make the plot better suited to the nursery.[6]

Another criticism is of their 'nationalism'. They believed there was a distinct 'German' tradition, rather than a wider European one. They had a debate, for example, as to whether Sleeping Beauty was properly German, rather than 'too French' (the story had already been retold in a more literary form by Charles Perrault in 1697). Drawing on more ancient Germanic myths, they concluded that the trope was entirely Teutonic, and included the tale. Perhaps the reason why we imagine all those princesses being blonde (golden haired) is because their Teutonic character is so well embedded in the Grimm versions. Oddly enough, in the stories themselves blondness is very seldom mentioned – and many a princess (like Snow White) is explicitly dark haired. Certainly both brothers saw all the aspects of their work as a contribution to a common culture and shared historical understanding in the political cause of the unification of Germany; however they were deeply democratic and, indeed, lost jobs because of the radical tendency of their politics. We all know why individuals working at a similar period for the unification of Italy tend to be seen as heroes while their German equivalents are vilified, but we need to be careful with such a post-Nazi viewpoint.

The brothers also had various more personal agendas which surfaced in their editing: they emphasised the good but absent father (theirs died, and this changed their lives from idyllic to penurious overnight) and the cruel, malignant stepmother, who seemed, under the pressure of poverty and bereavement, to have banished the sweet, warm mother of their infancy. The editing work continued throughout the brothers' lifetimes, partly in response to direct requests from readers to eliminate material that was perceived as being inappropriate for children, and partly because Wilhelm, who became increasingly responsible for the work, wanted to add a wash of Christian piety to it.

I acknowledge the basic facts behind these criticisms, but, for me, these do not outweigh the extraordinary potency of the collection. The timing was good – I suspect that within decades it would have been impossible to have collected the stories even as indirectly as they did; the capacity for such easy telling was already diminishing. There is no British collection with this sort of authority. However much the supposedly pure stream of rural peasant culture was diverted and canalised, it was not allowed to get totally lost or desiccated. As Jack Zipes shows in his powerful contemporary translation and annotation of the *Complete Works* (Vintage, 1987 and 2002) (from which all the Grimm quotations in this book are drawn) they captured a language so unscholarly and vigorous, as well as an authentic narrative form, that the oral origins of the stories are made transparent without fuss. One of the major claims for an oral tradition, as opposed to a literary (printed) text, is that it is amenable to change, to an editing process that makes it accessible to new listeners, over and over again: told stories are impregnable against copyright law – no one can own or claim them. Every teller may, and does, change the story in reaction to individual understanding and a particular audience. Jacob and Wilhelm started their work on the *Märchen* as an academic and linguistic sideline to their serious study of German etymology, but their audience wanted something more domestic, and more child orientated – and they provided it, just as many doctoral students have edited their theses to make a publishable book. This reactive process has gone on freely ever since. Even when writers acknowledge the Grimm brothers as their source, they do not feel constrained by them. In the Grimm version, Cinderella's stepsisters were not 'ugly'; they were 'fair of face, but vile and black of heart' and there was no fairy godmother, but a little white bird in a hazel tree.

In relation to my book, the Grimm stories have a singular and important advantage: precisely because of their much-criticised nationalistic agenda, they stand a good distance away from the universalising global approach not only of modern scholarship, but of many important collections of fairy stories: Andrew Lang's 'colour' (Red, Blue, Lilac, etc) series is proudly drawn from any and all traditions, stirring up a rich brew of Arabic, Indian and European tales without distinction, a notable and proper project at the height of Empire, but one which nonetheless disguises and even edits out local specificity. Because the Grimm brothers were deliberately and determinedly seeking out a *Teutonic* folk culture, they emphasise Germanic aspects. And one of the central aspects of the northern European fairy story is that it takes place in the forest.

It is surprising how seldom this is noticed. When I have discussed my book with other people, even experts, they have expressed surprise at my claim that the forest is of primary importance in these tales. But in fact, over half the stories (116 out of 210) in the 1857 edition[7] explicitly mention forests as the location of some part of the story, and at least another 26 have very clear forest themes or images. For example, a story about a woodcutter or huntsman who, during the story, does not actually leave his house, or about a central animal (a wolf) or a tree (often a hazel), suggests to me that a forest is implicitly the location of the story. (The others are set in a wide variety of locations – often other agricultural settings, like farms, fields or mills; a few in towns; several in castles, palaces or other houses; some in clearly imaginary non-realistic places; and a couple in heaven. There is also a substantial number of usually shorter tales where there is no clue at all about the 'scenery'.)

Now fairy stories are at risk too, like the forests. Padraic Colum has suggested[8] that artificial lighting dealt them a mortal wound: when people could read and be productive after dark, something very fundamental changed, and there was no longer need or space for the ancient oral tradition. The stories were often confined to books, which makes the text static, and they were handed over to children. In this century, our projected tenderness or sentimentality towards children, as well as our somewhat literalistic addiction to scientific realism, has made us more and more unwilling to expose the young to the violence and irrationality of the forest and its stories. If we are honest, we know very well that children do not actually wish or need to be protected from this: at the physical level, one of the things that children like best is to be allowed to wander off, alone or with each other, into the woods and have adventures; and at the imaginative level, they are delighted when Hansel and Gretel push the witch into her own oven or the wicked stepmother is forced to dance in red hot iron slippers until she is dead. I suspect it is our own sense of refinement and culture, our pride (and our own self-protective fear because we do not want our children standing in

judgement over or even laughing too much at us), that we are protecting, perhaps dishonestly.

The whole tradition of storytelling is endangered by modern technology. Although telling stories is a very fundamental human attribute,
to the extent that psychiatry now often treats 'narrative loss' – the
inability to construct a story of one's own life – as a loss of identity
or 'personhood', it is not natural but an art form – you have to learn
how to tell stories. The well-meaning mother is constantly frustrated
by the inability of her child to answer questions like 'What did you do
today?' (to which the answer is usually a muttered 'nothing' – but the
'nothing' is a cover for 'I don't know how to tell a good story about it,
how to impose a story shape on the events'). To tell stories, you have
to hear stories and you have to have an audience to hear the stories
you tell. Storytelling is economically unproductive – there is no
marketable product; it is out with the laws of patents and copyright;
it cannot easily be commodified; it is a skill without monetary value.
And above all, it is an activity requiring leisure – the oral tradition
stands squarely against a modern work ethic. One of the unexpected
things we have learned from anthropology is the extraordinary quantity of 'down time' that hunter-gatherer societies enjoy – the hours
and days they spend just sitting around and talking, singing, chilling
out. Even in medieval Europe, the most humble worker laboured for
shorter hours and on far fewer days of the year than we – despite all
our 'labour-saving devices' and regulated maximum hours – can easily
imagine. Traditional fairy stories, like all oral traditions, need that sort
of time – the sort of time that *isn't* money. This is probably one reason
at least why they were so readily handed over to children – socially,
we can accept that children have 'free' time. Unfortunately, they do
not have many of the other attributes that good storytelling requires,
like accurate memory, audience sensitivity, critical but affectionate
listeners and good role models; the social separation of generations
and age groups has added to this problem. (It is all in the telling: there
is no event so thrilling that it can't be made dull by bad narrative,
and no event so trivial, senseless or petty that cannot rivet attention
when narrated by a good teller.)[9]

The deep connection between the forests and the core stories has been lost; fairy stories and forests have been moved into different categories and, isolated, both are at risk of disappearing, misunderstood and culturally undervalued, 'useless' in the sense of 'financially unprofitable'.

So that is what this book is about: it is an attempt to bring them back together, so that they can illuminate and draw renewed strength from each other.

'Hang on,' said Adam, after hearing an edited version of all this. 'You talk about British woods, British history and being specific and all that. But the Grimms were German, not British, and these are all German stories. How are you going to plonk them down in British woods?'

This was pretty smart of him and I was not unimpressed, but I argued stoutly, 'No, they are not German stories; they are Germanic stories. The British are Germanic people from the northern European forests, and I believe we had the same stories. Well, not just the same stories, because we also have Celtic fairy stories and some Viking fairy stories, but they are really different.'

'You're just guessing.'

I admitted that I was a bit. And I told him that it will always be hard to tell with oral stories, because they are always changing and shifting and we just cannot know. But there is some evidence. The oldest printed fairytale we have in English is 'Tom Thumb', from 1621. It is nearly identical to the Grimms' version – not simply the same type of story (there are midget hero stories in all sorts of cultures), many of the episodes and details are the same too. It must have been widely known because Phineas Taylor Barnum (1810–1891), the American circus impresario, gave Charles Stratton, his famous performing dwarf, the stage name of 'General Tom Thumb' in the early 1840s – only twenty years after the Grimms' stories were first translated. There are lots of little clues like that. And the Grimms' stories became popular in English very quickly. Even during the Second World War, W. H. Auden praised the collection 'as one of the founding works of *Western* culture'. But I told Adam he was right in a way – I *am* guessing. It is a deep guess though, from how the stories fit into our forests and how our forests fit into the stories. It is a guess that works.

By this point in our conversation, Adam and I had long finished with the baked beans and had crawled into our sleeping bags in the tent. I last slept in a tent forty years ago, and Adam slept in this one a few months ago high up above the snow line of the southern Andes. It was cosy but a little strange to be snuggled up so close together, although the dog thought it was heaven and wriggled around our feet ecstatically. Occasionally she jumped up, rigid, attentive, aware of something outside in the wood even though we could not hear it, and then turned round and round, stirring herself into the sleeping bags as her ancestors must have stirred themselves into grassy nests in long-vanished forests.

'So, how do we go about it?' he asked.

'We walk in some woods,' I said.

We would walk and talk about fairy stories and forests. We would talk to contemporary forest people – people who still live or work in the forest. I want the forests in the book to be real – real walks, real people, and real 'nature'. I want the book to be specific, not general. And then I want to match up what is in the forests with fairy stories, see how the themes of the fairy stories grow out of the reality of the forest, and the other way round too – show how people see the forests in a particular way because of the fairy stories. So then I hope I can retell some of the Grimms' stories so that the connection gets made again and maybe both fairy stories and ancient woodland get protected, valued, seen for what they are: our roots, our origins. And it will be fun.

It felt adventurous. I snuggled down with some satisfaction. Then he said, 'Mum, do you know about mycorrhiza?'

'What?'

'Well, trees need their own fungi. They've only worked this out quite recently; but it turns out that trees – well, most plants actually – have a sort of double or twin life. They are partnered with fungi called mycorrhiza, and they cannot live without them – or even germinate. I don't mean aggressive, parasite fungi; I mean they make a team, you can't have one without the other.'

(The next day, back at home, I looked up *mycorrhiza*:

Most land plants are dual organisms. Attached to their roots is a fungus whose hyphae are thinner and more richly branched than the root itself; they invade more soil than is directly accessible to the roots. The host plant supplies the fungus with the carbon needed to make its hyphae. The fungus does much of the job that schoolchildren used to be taught was done by the root hairs. It supplies the plant with nitrogen, phosphorus and other nutrients, and sometimes water too; it can even defend its host against competition from non-mycorrhizal neighbours. Neither functions well without the other; seedlings use their seed reserves to make contact with the fungus, and die if they fail to find a partner.)[10]

'So maybe that's what the book is: forests and fairy stories are like trees and their mycorrhiza.' After a pause, he added, 'Well, I suppose the forests don't need the fairy stories.'

But I love this image and wanted to run with it. 'Yes they do,' I said firmly.

The fairy stories teach us how to see the forests, and how to love them too. They are spooky but special in our imaginations. Woods are part of our fantasy of childhood because of the fairy stories. That love protects our woodlands. An astonishing number of people who had voted Conservative and seemed happy to cut benefits for the disabled, make students pay for their degrees, risk massive unemployment, and all the other cuts, were suddenly up in arms about a perceived threat to the forests – and that was only a consultation document. Our almost hidden and often bizarrely ignorant love for wildwood comes from the fairy stories and keeps the forests safe. If you have got a decent chunk of ancient woodland near you, you will be safe from development or wind farms or whatever. People do not love fen or moor or arable farm-land or even mountains in that way; the people who live in them may love them, but the protest about making the forests more commercially viable came from a far wider constituency. I believe the relationship between forests and fairytales is mutual, symbiotic.

In this book I want to see forests and fairy stories like this – partners necessary to one another and at risk if *either* fails or cannot find and connect with the other. The relationship is specific; there are different mycorrhiza for different species of plant, so the forests of this book are not generalised. In each chapter I will go and seek out a different and particular forest. Luckily, there are lots of different kinds of forest in Britain – very distinct both as to the species that flourish there and as to the history that has led to their survival (or in some cases introduction). Between them, I sense that they can give access and depth to the central themes of the northern European fairy stories. Simultaneously, the stories can make us see and know the forests afresh.

I turned over, almost ready to sleep, pleased with things so far.

Then Adam said, 'OK, then. Tell me a story.'

'I don't tell them, I write them. I'm a *writer*. Telling-aloud storytelling is something special; I don't have those skills. I fake them.'

'Well, give it a go now to get me in the mood and then you can write it up properly later.'

I searched for a story that would make all these points, and could not find one. Then I looked for a story that is about mothers and sons. Oddly, there are not that many of these – mostly the fairy stories are about fathers-and-sons or mothers-and-daughters. (Not that this should matter too much: when he was eight and I read him *The Lord of the Rings*, Adam was – to this feminist mother's great pride – so offended by the masculinity of all the characters in the Fellowship that I had to read the whole text re-grammaring one of the hobbits – we chose Merry because it seemed the easiest name to do it with – as female throughout.) Then I thought about being frightened of imaginary forests and snug in this real one.

'OK,' I said into the dark.

NOTES

1. The old proverb says of tree leafing: 'If the oak before the ash, we will only have a splash; if the ash before the oak, we will surely have a soak.' Each spring I try to notice if this is true, but have not come to any definite conclusions.
2. Jack Zipes, *The Brothers Grimm: From Enchanted Forests to the Modern World* (Palgrave, 2002).
3. Julius Caesar, *De Bello Gallico*, verse 21.
4. Zipes, *Brothers Grimm*.
5. I note with considerable joy that *Our Island's Story* by H. E. Marshall

(Galore Park Publishing, 2005), first published in 1905, is back in print. That is what I mean by 'history stories'.

6. Not much more suitable really, because Rapunzel still manages to have twins without ever getting married – but hopefully the mid-nineteenth-century child would not put two and two together here.

7. The first collection was published in 1812, and added to with a second volume in 1815. These contained 87 tales. The brothers (but increasingly Wilhelm) continued both to edit and to add to their collection. The final edition was published in 1857, and contained 210 stories (which include 10 that were called 'legends' and are more explicitly pious than the 200 tales). Zipes (and others) have expanded this to 268 stories, by including some that were so heavily edited as to constitute new or different tales and others that for one reason or another were not included in any of the editions that the Grimm brothers edited (although some were published elsewhere). In his 2002 edition, Zipes also includes 11 tales which were found in letters in the Grimm archive but that were never edited by them.

8. Padraic Colum, *The Complete Grimm's Fairy Tales* (RKP, 1975), Introduction.

9. *Cod: A Biography of the Fish That Changed the World*, by Mark Kurlansky (Vintage, 1999), always seems to me to be a perfect example of this latter phenomenon.

10. Oliver Rackham, *Woodlands* (Collins, New Naturalist Library No. 100, 2006), p. 34.

from THE TREE

John Fowles

John Fowles (1926–2005) grew up in Leigh-on-Sea, Essex, and studied French and German at Oxford University before rebelling against the 'establishment' man he was becoming. He became a teacher at a school on a Greek island, the setting for his hugely successful second novel, *The Magus* (1966). Influenced by Jean-Paul Sartre and Albert Camus, Fowles' postmodernism chimed with the Sixties and *The Magus* became a critically acclaimed international bestseller, as did his follow-up, *The French Lieutenant's Woman* (1969). Later fiction included *The Ebony Tower*, *Daniel Martin* and *A Maggot*. Natural history was a lifelong interest for Fowles, and wild landscapes and species play important roles in his fiction. Fowles has fallen out of fashion and the sexual politics of his novels are dated but many of his essays, particularly *The Tree* (1979), explore environmental issues in a farsighted way.

We park by a solitary row of granite buildings. To the east and behind it is a small half-hidden valley with two tall silent chimneys and a dozen or so ruined stone sheds, scattered about a long meadow through which a stream runs. The valley is bowered, strangely in this most desolate of Southern English landscapes, by beech trees. Its ruins are now almost classical in their simplicity and seeming antiquity – and one is truly old, a medieval clapper bridge, huge slabs of rock spanning the little stream. But the rest were not designed, nor the beeches planted, to be picturesque. In Victorian times gunpowder for quarry-blasting was made and stored here. The stone sheds and chimneys were scattered, the trees introduced, the remote site itself picked, for purely safety reasons. Most contemporary visitors to Powder Mill Farm, on the southern fringe of the barren, treeless wastes of northern Dartmoor, are industrial archaeologists, summoned by this absurdly – in regard to its former use – Arcadian and bosky little valley behind. But we are here for something far more ancient and less usual still.

We set off north-west across an endless fen and up towards a distant line of tors, grotesque outcrops of weather-worn granite. Though it is mid-June, the tired grass is still not fully emerged from its winter sleep; and the sky is also tired, a high grey canopy, with no wind to shift or break it. What flowers there are, yellow stars of tormentil, blue and dove-grey sprays of milkwort, the delicate lilac of the marsh violet in the bogs, are tiny and sparse. Somewhere in the dark and uninhabited uplands to the north a raven snores. I search the sky, but it is too far off to be seen.

We cross a mile of this dour wasteland, then up a steep hillside, through a gap in an ancient sheep-wall, and still more slope to climb; and come finally to a rounded ridge that leads north to an elephantine tower, a vast turd of primary rock, Longford Tor. At our feet another bleak valley, then a succession, as far as the eye can see, of even bleaker tor-studded skylines and treeless moorland desert. My wife tells me I must have the wrong place, and nothing in the landscape denies her. I do, but not with total conviction. It is at least thirty years since I was last in this part of the Moor.

We walk down the convex slope before us, into the bleak valley, and I begin to think that it must indeed be the wrong place. But then suddenly, like a line of hitherto concealed infantry, huddled under the steepest downward fall of the slope near the bottom, what we have come for emerges from the low grass and ling: a thin, broken streak of tree-tops, a pale arboreal surf. For me this secret wood, perhaps the strangest in all Britain, does not really rise like a line of infantry. It rises like a ghost.

I can't now remember the exact circumstances of the only other time I saw it, except that it must have been late in 1946, when I was a lieutenant of marines in a camp on the edge of Dartmoor. This was not part of our training area, and I can't have been on duty. It was winter, there was ice in the air and a clinging mist, and I was alone. I think I had been walking somewhere else, trying to shoot snipe, and had merely made a last-minute detour to see the place, perhaps to orient myself.

At least it lived up to the reputation that I had once heard a moorland farmer give it: some tale of an escaped prisoner from Princetown a few miles away, found frozen to death there – or self-hanged, I forget. But it had no need of that kind of black embroidery. It was forlorn, skeletal, almost malevolent – distinctly eerie, even though I am not a superstitious person and solitude in nature has never frightened me one-tenth as much as solitude in cities and houses. It simply felt a bad place, not one to linger in, and I did not go into the trees; and I had never gone back to it, though often enough on Dartmoor, till this day. In truth I had forgotten about it, in all those intervening years, until I began writing this text and was recalling my father's suspicion of the wild. One day then its memory mysteriously surged, as it surges itself from the moorland slope, out of nowhere. Its name is Wistman's Wood.

I do not know who Wistman was – whether he was some ancient owner or whether the word derives from the old Devonshire dialect word *wisht*, which means melancholy and uncanny, wraithlike; and which lies behind one of Conan Doyle's most famous tales. There would never have been a hound of the Baskervilles, were it not for the much older Wisht Hounds of Dartmoor legend.

Wistman's Wood may be obscurely sited, but it is no longer, as it was in the 1940s, obscurely known. The rise of ecology has seen to that. In scientific terms it is an infinitely rare fragment of primeval forest, from some warmer phase of world climate, that has managed to cling on – though not without some remarkable adaptations – in this inhospitable place; and even more miraculously managed to survive the many centuries of human depredation of anything burnable on the Moor. Culturally it is comparable with a great Neolithic site: a sort of Avebury of the tree, an *Ur*-wood. Physically it is a half-mile chain of copses splashed, green drops in a tachist painting, along what on Dartmoor they call a clitter, a broken debris of granite boulders – though not at all on true tachist principle, by chance. These boulders provide the essential protection for seedlings against bitter winter winds and grazing sheep. But the real ecological miracle of Wistman's Wood is botanical. Its dominant species, an essentially lowland one, should not really be here at all, and is found at this altitude in only one other, and Irish, site in the British Isles. Here and there in the wood are a scatter of mountain ashes, a few hollies. But the reigning tree is the ancient king of all our trees: *Quercus robur*, the Common, or English, Oak.

We go down, to the uppermost brink. Names, science, history… not even the most adamantly down-to-earth botanist thinks of species and ecologies when he or she first stands at Wistman's Wood. It is too strange for that. The normal full-grown height of the common oak is thirty to forty metres. Here the very largest, and even though they are centuries old, rarely top five metres. They are just coming into leaf, long after their lowland kin, in every shade from yellow-green to bronze. Their dark branches grow to an extraordinary extent laterally; are endlessly angled, twisted, raked, interlocked, and reach quite as much downward as upwards. These trees are inconceivably different from the normal habit of their species, far more like specimens from a natural bonsai nursery. They seem, even though the day is windless, to be writhing, convulsed, each its own Laocoön, caught and frozen in some fanatically private struggle for existence.

The next thing one notices is even more extraordinary, in this Ice Age environment. It is a paradoxically tropical quality, for every lateral branch, fork, saddle of these aged dwarfs is densely clothed in other plants – not just the tough little polypodies of most deciduous woodlands, but large, elegantly pluming male ferns; whortleberry beds, grasses, huge cushions of moss and festoons of lichen. The clitter of granite boulders, bare on the windswept moors, here provides a tumbling and chaotic floor of moss-covered mounds and humps, which add both to the impression of frozen movement and to that of an astounding internal fertility, since they seem to stain the upward air with their vivid green. This floor like a tilted emerald sea, the contorted trunks, the interlacing branches with their luxuriant secondary aerial gardens… there is only one true epithet to convey the first sight of Wistman's Wood, even today. It is fairy-like. It corresponds uncannily with the kind of setting artists like Richard Dadd imagined for that world in Victorian times and have now indelibly given it: teeming, jewel-like, self-involved, rich in secrets just below the threshold of our adult human senses.

We enter. The place has an intense stillness, as if here the plant side of creation rules and even birds are banned; below, through the intricate green gladelets and branch-gardens, comes the rush of water in a moorland stream, one day to join the sea far to the south. This water-noise, like the snore of the raven again, the breeding-trill of a distant curlew, seems to come from another world, once one is inside the wood. There are birds, of course… an invisible hedgesparrow, its song not lost here, as it usually is, among all the sounds of other common garden birds, nor lost in its own ubiquity in Britain; but piercing and peremptory, individual, irretrievable; even though, a minute later, we hear its *prestissimo* bulbul shrill burst out again. My wood, my wood, it never shall be yours.

Parts of all the older trees are dead and decayed, crumbling into humus, which is why, together with the high annual humidity, they carry their huge sleeves of ferns and other plants. Some are like loose brassards and can be lifted free and replaced. The only colour not green or bronze or russet, not grey trunk or rich brown of the decaying wood, are tiny rose-pink stem-beads, future apples where some gall-wasp has laid its eggs on a new shoot. But it is the silence, the waitingness of the place, that is so haunting; a quality all woods will have on occasion, but which is overwhelming here – a drama, but of a time-span humanity cannot conceive. A pastness, a presentness, a skill with tenses the writer in me knows he will never know; partly out of his own inadequacies, partly because there are tenses human language has yet to invent.

We drift from copse to copse. One to the south is now fenced off by the Nature Conservancy to see what effect keeping moorland sheep, bullocks and wild ponies from grazing will have. It has a much denser growth at ground level, far more thickety, and is perhaps what the wood would have looked like centuries ago, before stock was widely run on the Moor; and yet now seems artificial – scientifically necessary, aesthetically less pleasing, less surreal, historically less honest beside the still open wood, 'gardened' by what man has intro-duced. There is talk now of wiring off the whole wood like this, reserving it from the public, as at Stonehenge. Returning, we come on two hikers, rucksacks beside them, lying on their backs inside the trees, like two young men in a trance. They do not speak to us, nor we to them. It is the place, wanting it to oneself, and I am prey to their same feeling. I persuade my wife to start the long climb back. I will catch up.

I go alone to the most detached and isolated of the copses, the last and highest, to the north. It grows in a small natural amphitheatre, and proves to be the most luxuriant, intricate and greenly beautiful of the chain. I sit in its silence, beneath one of its most contorted trees, a patriarchal gnome-oak. The botanist in me notices a colony of woodrush, like a dark green wheat among the emerald clitter; then the delicate climbing fumitory *Corydalis claviculata*, with its maidenhair-fern leaves and greenish-white flowers. A not uncommon plant where I live in Dorset; yet now it seems like the hedgesparrow's song, hyperdistinct, and also an epitome, a quintessence of all my past findings and knowledge of it; as with the oaks it grows beneath, subsuming all other oaks. I remember another corydalis, *bulbosa*, that they still grow in the garden at Uppsala in honour of the great man, who named the genus.

From somewhere outside, far above, on top of Longford Tor, I hear human voices. Then silence again. The wood waits, as if its most precious sap were stillness. I ask why I, of a species so incapable of stillness, am here.

I think of a recent afternoon spent in discussion with a famous photographer, and how eminently French and lucid his philosophy of art seemed, compared to mine. I envied him a little, from the maze of my own constantly shifting and confused feelings. I may pretend in public that they are theories, but in reality they are as dense and ravelled as this wood, always beyond my articulation or rational comprehension, perhaps because I know I came to writing through nature, or exile from it, far more than by innate gift. I think of my father and, wrily, of why I should for so many years have carried such a bad, unconsciously repressing mental image of Wistman's Wood – some part or branch of him I had never managed to prune out. It is incomprehensible now, before such inturned peace, such profound harmlessness, otherness, selflessness, such unusing… all words miss, I know I cannot describe it. A poet once went near, though in another context: *the strange phosphorus of life, nameless under an old misappellation.*

So I sit in the namelessness, the green phosphorus of the tree, surrounded by impenetrable misappellations. I came here really only to be sure; not to describe it, since I cannot, or only by the misappellations; to be sure that what I have written is not all lucubration, study dream, *in vitro*, as epiphytic upon reality as the ferns on the branches above my head.

It, this namelessness, is beyond our science and our arts because its secret is being, not saying. Its greatest value to us is that it cannot be reproduced, that this being can be apprehended only by other present being, only by the living senses and consciousness. All experience of it through surrogate and replica, through selected image, gardened word, through other eyes and minds, betrays or banishes its reality. But this is nature's consolation, its message, and well beyond the Wistman's Wood of its own strict world. It can be known and entered only by each, and in its now; not by you through me, by any you through any me; only by you through yourself, or me through myself. We still have this to learn: the inalienable otherness of each, human and non-human, which may seem the prison of each, but is at heart, in the deepest of those countless million metaphorical trees for which we cannot see the wood, both the justification and the redemption.

I turned to look back, near the top of the slope. Already Wistman's Wood was gone, sunk beneath the ground again; already no more than another memory trace, already becoming an artefact, a thing to use. An end to this, dead retting of its living leaves.

from UNDERLAND

Robert Macfarlane

Robert Macfarlane (b. 1976) is the most influential British nature
writer of the twenty-first century. He grew up in Nottinghamshire
and studied English at Cambridge, where he continues to teach
as a fellow of Emmanuel College. His debut, *Mountains of the
Mind* (2003), won the Somerset Maugham Award, the *Guardian*
First Book Award and the *Sunday Times* Young Writer of the
Year Award. His subsequent books *Wild Places* (2007), *The Old
Ways* (2012), *Landmarks* (2014) and *Underland* (2019) have won
multiple awards, including the Wainwright Prize. Macfarlane's
thinking and writing about the genre has widened nature writing's
scope in Britain, both historically and in the present day, with
Macfarlane proving an influential mentor to many young writers
from more diverse backgrounds. He has collaborated with artists,
musicians and filmmakers and is also an increasingly active public
intellectual and environmental campaigner. He highlighted the
disappearing vocabulary of nature with *The Lost Words* (2017), a
picture book illustrated by the artist Jackie Morris, which grass-
roots campaigns delivered free to every school in Scotland and
hundreds of schools in England and Wales. Their follow-up, *The
Lost Spells*, was published in 2020.

Merlin and I stand side by side in a beech coppice – the biggest I have ever seen, let alone entered. The stool is ten
yards from one end to another, the tree perhaps 400 or
500 years old.

'I'd guess this hasn't been coppiced for at least half a century,' I say
to Merlin.

Coppice shoots have grown, unlopped, into upright trunks, raying
up around the edge of the coppice's base and leaving a space in the
centre easily big enough to hold us both. We stay there for a while,

enjoying being inside this ancient tree, looking out at Epping Forest from between the grey-barked bars of our cage.

Two of the beech's lower limbs have melted into one another, their bark conjoining into a single continuous skin, their vascular systems growing and uniting. Living wood, left long enough, behaves as a slow-moving fluid. Like the halite down in the darkness of Boulby mine, like the calcite I had seen beneath the Mendips, like glacial ice drawing itself on over topsoil and bedrock, living wood seems to *flow*, given time.

'I've heard this called "pleaching",' I say to Merlin, patting the fused branches. 'The artist David Nash planted a circle of ash trees in a clearing in North Wales, then bent and wove the trees so that they grew not just next to one another but *into* one another, a dancing "Ash Dome", made of a meld of boughs and limbs.'

'Actually,' says Merlin, 'plant scientists have a technical term for this. We call it "snogging", or to give it its full name, "tree snogging".' He smiles: 'Well, not quite. The technical term is actually "inosculation", from the Latin *osculare*, meaning "to kiss". Inosculation means "to en-kiss". It can happen across trees and between species too.'

Though I know the word 'inosculation', I had not known its etymology; what seemed a chilly specialist term gains a passionate warmth, and feels true to this arboreal 'en-kissing', which makes it hard to say where one being ends and another begins. I think of Ovid's version of the 'Baucis and Philemon' myth, in which an elderly couple are transformed into an intertwining oak and linden, each supporting the other in terms of both structure and sustenance, drawing strength for each other from the ground through their roots – and tenderly sharing that strength through their en-kissing.

'This kind of merging happens below ground too,' says Merlin, 'but probably more intensely between the roots of the trees than between branches, because space is more limited below ground and the criss-crossing will be denser. And it happens *vastly* more profusely in the fungal networks, often between quite different species.' He follows the pleaching of the two branches with a finger.

'From being two hyphal tubes, two fungi are suddenly one, and things can start flowing between them, including genetic material and nuclei. This is why it's so hard to deal with species concepts in fungi, or even the question of what an organism is – because while fungi do the sex thing, they also have this *wildly* promiscuous horizontal transfer of genetic material that is unpredictable in a still ill-understood way.'

Merlin Sheldrake, as the oldest joke in mycology goes, is a fun guy to be around. During the days in which he conjures open the underland of Epping Forest for me, I ask more questions than I have of anyone for what feels like years. What he tells and shows me in that modest peri-urban forest reshapes my sense of the world in ways I am still processing.

The night of Merlin's birth was that of the Great Storm, 15 October 1987, when hurricane-force winds, gusting to strengths of 120 mph, capsized carriers, drove ferries ashore, and felled some 15 million trees – ripping up the forest floor across southern England and northern France and tilting it skywards in the form of root plates. The first full day of Merlin's life was Black Friday, when the Dow Jones suffered a record fall, wiping trillions off global wealth and triggering a crash in financial markets worldwide.

No, the omens of Merlin Sheldrake's arrival into the world were not auspicious. In Greek myth he would surely have been fated to be a force for destruction and ruin. But he was given a magical name and he grew into a magical person. He is tall, slim, and very upright in his bearing. He has tight curls of dark hair, intense eyes with full circles of white visible around each iris, and a wide, warm grin. He is also a formidable scientist, with a doctorate in Plant Science from Cambridge. There is something faintly antiquarian to him – a disinterest in disciplinary boundaries, a boundless curiosity – and something of the heroic-age plant hunter too. He puts me in mind of a cross between Sir Thomas Browne and Frank Kingdon Ward, collector of *Meconopsis betonicifolia*, the legendary blue poppy of the Himalayas.

It is typical of Merlin that he became fascinated from a young age not with the charismatic megafauna of the world, but instead with the undersung, underseen inhabitants of the biota: lichens, mosses and fungi. He studied them as an amateur teenage scientist, counting lichen species on gravestones and granite boulders, and trying to com-prehend the subterranean architecture of fungal life – above-ground mushrooms as fruiting bodies that stand as mere fleeting allusions to immense underland structures.

'My childhood superheroes weren't Marvel characters,' Merlin once said to me, 'they were lichens and fungi. Fungi and lichen annihilate our categories of gender. They reshape our ideas of community and cooperation. They screw up our hereditary model of evolutionary descent. They utterly *liquidate* our notions of time. Lichens can crumble rocks into dust with terrifying acids. Fungi can exude massively powerful enzymes *outside* their bodies that dissolve soil. They're the biggest organisms in the world and among the oldest. They're world-makers and world-breakers. What's more superhero than *that?*'

Merlin and I set off on foot into Epping Forest one morning from a high clearing, heading roughly north, keeping the sun to the right of our line.

Epping extends to the north-east of London, and it is very far from a wildwood. It was first designated as a royal hunting forest in the twelfth century by Henry II, with penalties for poaching that included imprisonment and mutilation. Presently it is managed by the City of London Corporation, and has more than fifty bye-laws governing behaviour within its bounds – though the punishments are now fiscal rather than corporal. It is fully contained within the M25, the orbital motorway that encircles outer London. Minor roads traverse it, and it is never more than two and a half miles wide. Despite its small extent, Epping is easy to get lost in – a forest of forking paths to which, for a thousand years, the people of London and its surrounds have gone for shelter, sex, escape and a relic greenwood magic.

Growl of roads. Whirr of a low-flying bumblebee, stirring the leaf litter with its downdraught. Buzzard overhead, turning, mewing. Old coppice trees left uncut, hydra-headed pollards. A fallen log, thick with moss; small orange fungi sprouting from wet breaks in its grain. Where trees thin out and light falls, hundreds of green beech seedlings are pushing up through the litter, none more than an inch high. Five fallow deer appear between hollies ahead of us, the dapple of leaf-light flicking off the dapple of their flanks as they move through the understorey.

In the language of forestry and forest ecology, the 'understorey' is the name given to the life that exists between the forest floor and the tree canopy: the fungi, mosses, lichens, bushes and saplings that thrive and compete in this mid-zone. Metaphorically, though, the 'understorey' is also the sum of the entangled, ever-growing narratives, histories, ideas and words that interweave to give a wood or forest its diverse life in culture.

'What interests me most,' says Merlin, 'is the understorey's understory.' He points around at the beech, the hornbeam, the chestnut. 'All of these trees and bushes,' he says, 'are connected with one another below ground in ways we not only cannot see, but ways we have scarcely begun to understand.'

While studying Natural Sciences at Cambridge, Merlin read Simard's groundbreaking research into the wood wide web. He also read E. I. Newman's classic 1988 paper, 'Mycorrhizal Links between Plants: Their Functioning and Ecological Significance'. There Newman argued against the assumption that 'plants are physiologically separate from each other', proposing instead the existence of a 'mycelial network' that might link plants together. 'If this phenomenon is widespread,' wrote Newman, 'it could have profound implications for the functioning of ecosystems.'

Those 'implications' were indeed profound, and they fascinated Merlin. He already loved the alien realm of fungi. He knew that fungi could turn rocks to rubble, could move with swiftness both overground and underground, could reproduce horizontally, and digest food outside their bodies by means of metabolically ingenious excreted acids. He knew that their toxins could kill us, and their psychoactive chemicals could induce hallucinogenic states. The work of Simard and Newman, however, revealed to him that fungi could also allow plants to communicate with one another.

Merlin was taught as an undergraduate by Oliver Rackham, the legendary botanist whose research transformed our understanding of both the cultural and botanical history of the English landscape. Working with Rackham, Merlin found himself most intellectually attracted to places where orthodox evolutionary theory felt thinnest – and for him the thinnest places were where mutualisms were at work. Mutualism is a subset of symbiosis in which there exists between organisms a prolonged relationship that is interdependent and reciprocally beneficial.

'What fascinates me about mutualisms,' says Merlin, 'is that one would predict from basic evolutionary theory that they would be massively unstable, and collapse quickly into parasitism. But it turns out that there are very ancient mutualisms, which have remained stable for puzzlingly long times: between the yucca plant and yucca moths, for example, or of course between the bacteria that illuminate the bioluminescent headlamp of the bobtail squid, and the squid itself.'

'Of course,' I reply. 'The ancient glowing-bobtail-squid-and-bacteria mutualism.'

'The ultimate mutualism, though,' says Merlin, 'is between plants and mycorrhizal fungi.'

The term 'mycorrhiza' is made from the Greek words for 'fungus' and 'root'. It is itself a collaboration or entanglement; and as such a reminder of how language has its own sunken system of roots and hyphae, through which meaning is shared and traded.

The relationship between mycorrhizal fungi and the plants they connect is ancient – around 450 million years old – and largely one of mutualism. In the case of the tree-fungi mutualism, the fungi siphon off carbon that has been produced in the form of glucose by the trees during photosynthesis, by means of chlorophyll that the fungi do not possess. In turn, the trees obtain nutrients such as phosphorus and nitrogen that the fungi have acquired from the soil through which they grow, by means of enzymes that the trees lack.

The possibilities of the wood wide web far exceed this basic exchange of goods between plant and fungi, though. For the fungal network also allows plants to distribute resources between one another. Sugars, nitrogen and phosphorus can be shared between trees in a forest: a dying tree might divest its resources into the network to the benefit of the community, for example, or a struggling tree might be supported with extra resources by its neighbours.

Even more remarkably, the network also allows plants to send immune-signalling compounds to one another. A plant under attack from aphids can indicate to a nearby plant via the network that it should up-regulate its defensive response before the aphids reach it. It has been known for some time that plants communicate above ground in comparable ways, by means of diffusible hormones. But such airborne warnings are imprecise in their destinations. When the compounds travel by fungal networks, both the source and recipient can be specified. Our growing comprehension of the forest network asks profound questions: about where species begin and end, about whether a forest might best be imagined as a super-organism, and about what 'trading', 'sharing' or even 'friendship' might mean between plants and, indeed, between humans.

The anthropologist Anna Tsing likens the below-ground of a forest to 'a busy social space', where the interaction of millions of organisms 'forms a cross-species world underground'. 'Next time you walk through a forest,' she writes memorably in an essay called 'Arts of Inclusion, or How to Love a Mushroom', 'look down. A city lies under your feet.'

Merlin and I have been walking the forest for two hours or so when we reach one of Epping's great pollard beech groves. Pollarding – the pruning of the upper branches of a tree to promote dense growth – keeps trees alive for longer, indeed can enter them into an almost indefinite fairy-tale time of longevity. Here in the grove, long waving trunks yearn up to the sun. Through their leaves falls a green sub-sea light. It feels as if we are swimming through a kelp forest.

We stop and lie down for a while on the woodland floor, on our backs, not speaking, watching the trees' gentle movements in the breeze, and the light lacing and lancing from fifty feet or more above us. Where the pollards spread out to form the canopies, I realize I can trace patterns of space running along the edges of each tree's canopy: the beautiful phenomenon known as 'crown shyness', whereby individual forest trees respect each other's space, leaving slender running gaps between the end of one tree's outermost leaves and the start of another's.

Lying there among the trees, despite a learned wariness towards anthropomorphism, I find it hard not to imagine these arboreal relations in terms of tenderness, generosity and even love: the respectful distance of their shy crowns, the kissing branches that have pleached with one another, the unseen connections forged by root and hyphae between seemingly distant trees. I remember something Louis de Bernières has written about a relationship that endured into old age: 'we had roots that grew towards each other underground, and when all the pretty blossom had fallen from our branches we found that we were one tree and not two.' As someone lucky to live in a long love, I recognize that gradual growing-towards and subterranean intertwining; the things that do not need to be said between us, the unspoken communication which can sometimes tilt troublingly towards silence, and the sharing of both happiness and pain. I think of good love as something that roots, not rots, over time, and of the hyphae that are weaving through the ground below me, reaching out through the soil in search of mergings. Theirs, too, seems to me then a version of love's work.

Merlin gets up, walks towards the centre of the grove as if looking for something, then bends down and brushes away leaf litter and beech mast, to clear a patch of soil the size of a saucer. I get up and follow him. He pinches some of the earth and rubs it between his fingers. It smears rather than crumbling: a rich, dark humus, made of composted leaves.

'This is our problem when it comes to studying the fungal network,' he says. 'Soil is fantastically impenetrable to experiments, and the fungal hyphae are on the whole too thin to see with the naked eye. That's the main reason it's taken us so long to work out the wood wide web's existence, and to discern what it's doing.'

Rivers of sap flow in the trees around us. If we were right now to lay a stethoscope to the bark of a birch or beech, we would hear the sap bubbling and crackling as it moves through the trunk.

'You can put rhizotrons into the ground to look at root growth,' Merlin says, 'but those don't really give you the fungi because they're too fine. You can do below-ground laser scanning but, again, that's too crude for the fungal networks.'

I am reminded once more of how resistant the underland remains to our usual forms of seeing; how it still hides so much from us, even in our age of hyper-visibility and ultra-scrutiny. Just a few inches of soil is enough to keep startling secrets, hold astonishing cargo: an eighth of the world's total biomass comprises bacteria that live below ground, and a further quarter is of fungal origin.

'We know the network is there,' Merlin says, 'but it's so effortful to track it. So we have to look for clues to the labyrinth – find clever means of following its paths.'

I kneel beside him. I can see dozens of insects just in this small area, the names of most of which I do not know: gleaming spiders and red-bronze beetles battling over the leaves, a woodlouse curled up into a sphere, a green threadworm writhing through the humus.

'It's *roiling* with life,' I say to Merlin.

'That's just the visible life. Hyphae will be growing into the decomposing matter of this half-rotting leaf,' says Merlin, 'into those rotting logs and those rotting twigs, and then you'll have the mycorrhizal fungi whose hyphae grow into hot spots – all of them frothing and tangling and fusing, making a network that's connecting holly to holly but also to this beech, and to a seedling of something else over there, layering and layering and *layering* – until, well, it blows your computational brain!'

As Merlin speaks I feel a quick, eerie sense of the world shifting irreversibly around me. Ground shivering beneath feet, knees, skin. *If only your mind were a slightly greener thing, we'd drown you in meaning…* I glance down, try to trance the soil into transparency such that I can see its hidden infrastructure: millions of fungal skeins suspended between tapering tree roots, their prolific liaisons creating a gossamer web at least as intricate as the cables and fibres that hang beneath our cities. What's the haunting phrase I've heard used to describe the realm of fungi? *The kingdom of the grey.* It speaks of fungi's utter otherness – the challenges they issue to our usual models of time, space and species.

'You look at the network,' says Merlin, 'and then it starts to look at you.'

In the underland of the hardwood forests of Oregon's Blue Mountains there exists a honey fungus, *Armillaria solidipes*, that is two and a half miles in extent at its widest point, and covers a total lateral area of almost four square miles. The blue whale is to this honey fungus as an ant is to us. It is a deeply mysterious organism: the largest in the world that we know of, and one of the oldest. The best guess that US Forest Service scientists have been able to offer for the honey fungus's age is between 1,900 and 8,650 years old. The fungus expresses itself above ground as mushrooms with white-flecked stems rising to tawny, gill-frilled cups. Below ground, where its true extent lies, *Armillaria solidipes* moves as rhizomorphs resembling black bootlaces, out of which reach the hyphal fingers of its mycelium, spreading in search both of new hosts which they might kill, and the mycelia of other parts of the colony with which they might fuse.

All taxonomies crumble, but fungi leave many of our fundamental categories in ruin. Fungi thwart our usual senses of what is whole and singular, of what defines an organism, and of what descent or inheritance means. They do strange things to time, because it is not easy to say where a fungus ends or begins, when it is born or when it dies. To fungi, our world of light and air is their underland, into which they tentatively ascend here and there, now and then.

Fungi were among the first organisms to return to the blast zone around the impact point in Hiroshima, the point from which the mushroom cloud had risen. After Hiroshima, too, images of the mushroom cloud began to appear ubiquitously in media and culture – the fruiting bodies of a new global anxiety. Scientists working in Chernobyl after the disaster there were surprised to discover fine threads of melanized fungi lacing the distressed concrete of the reactor itself, where radiation levels were over 500 times higher than in the normal environment. They were even more surprised to work out that the fungi were actively thriving due to the high levels of ionizing radiation: that they benefited from this usually lethal gale, increasing their biomass by processing it in some way. Ecologists in the US seeking to understand how American trees will respond to the stress of climate change have begun to focus on the presence of soil fungi as a key indicator of future forest resilience. Recent studies suggest that well-developed fungal networks will enable forests to adapt faster at larger scales to the changing conditions of the Anthropocene.

'Learning to see mosses is more like listening than looking,' writes the ethnobotanist Robin Wall Kimmerer; 'mosses… issue an invitation to dwell for a time right at the limits of ordinary perception.' Learning to see fungi seems even harder – requiring senses and technologies that we have yet to develop. Even to try and think with or as fungi is valuable, though, drawing us as it does towards lifeways that are instructively beyond our ken.

Certainly, orthodox 'Western' understandings of nature feel inadequate to the kinds of world-making that fungi perform. As our historical narratives of progress have come to be questioned, so the notion of history itself has become remodelled. History no longer feels figurable as a forwards-flighting arrow or a self-intersecting spiral; better, perhaps, seen as a network branching and conjoining in many directions. Nature, too, seems increasingly better understood in fungal terms: not as a single gleaming snow-peak or tumbling river in which we might find redemption, nor as a diorama that we deplore or adore from a distance – but rather as an assemblage of entanglements of which we are messily part. We are coming to understand our bodies as habitats for hundreds of species of which *Homo sapiens* is only one, our guts as jungles of bacterial flora, our skins as blooming fantastically with fungi.

Yes, we are beginning to encounter ourselves – not always comfortably or pleasantly – as multi-species beings already partaking in timescales that are fabulously more complex than the onwards-driving version of history many of us still imagine ourselves to inhabit. The work of the radical biologist Lynn Margulis and others has shown humans to be not solitary beings, but what Margulis memorably calls 'holobionts' – collaborative compound organisms, ecological units 'consisting of trillions of bacteria, viruses and fungi that coordinate the task of living together and sharing a common life', in the philosopher Glenn Albrecht's phrase.

Little of this thinking is new, however, when viewed from the perspective of animist traditions of indigenous peoples. The fungal forest that science had revealed to Merlin and that Merlin was revealing to me – a forest of arborescent connections and profuse intercommunication – seemed merely to provide a materialist evidence-base for what the cultures of forest-dwelling peoples have known for thousands of years. Again and again within such societies, the jungle or woodland is figured as aware, conjoined and conversational. 'To dwellers in a wood almost every species of tree has its voice as well as its feature,' wrote Thomas Hardy in *Under the Greenwood Tree*. The anthropologist Richard Nelson describes how the Koyukon people of the forested interior of what we now call Alaska 'live in a world that watches, in a forest of eyes. A person moving through nature – however wild, remote... is never truly alone. The surroundings are aware, sensate, personified. They feel.' In such a vibrant environment, loneliness is placed in solitary confinement.

There in the grove with Merlin, I recall Kimmerer, Hardy and Nelson, and feel a sudden, angry impatience with modern science for presenting as revelation what indigenous societies take to be self-evident. I remember Ursula Le Guin's angrily political novel, set on a forest planet in which woodland beings known as the Athsheans are able to transmit messages remotely between one another, signalling through the medium of trees. On Athshe – until the arrival of colonists committed to the planet's exploitation – the realm of mind is integrated into the community of the trees, and 'the word for world is forest'.

AN ELEGY FOR LIGNUM VITAE

Zakiya McKenzie

Zakiya McKenzie (b. 1988) was born in South London, raised in Kingston, Jamaica, and now lives in Bristol in the south-west. She is a researcher who loves translating what she's learned through storytelling. McKenzie was 2019 'writer in the forest' for Forestry England, producing *Forest Collection* at the end of the year. She has always been interested in cultural history and its relationship to rural and urban environments heard in her 2020 BBC Radio 4 podcast, *Nightvisions: The Forest*, about the Blue Mountains in Jamaica and the Forest of Dean in England. McKenzie has contributed to *BBC Wildlife Magazine*, *Smallwoods* magazine and *The Willowherb Review*. She is a PhD candidate in English at the University of Exeter with the Caribbean Literary Heritage project, writing about the Black British alternative press in post-war Britain. Her creative home will always be at Bristol community radio station, Ujima 98FM. 'An Elegy for Lignum Vitae' is original to this anthology.

Indigenous to the Caribbean and South America, the wood from the lignum vitae tree (genus Guaiacum) was once most sought after in England. Much of the British West Indies was deforested to extract the wood back to Britain for a plethora of uses. Today, the remnants of this shared legacy are found in the national tree of the Bahamas, the national flower of Jamaica, in British museums and on the Convention on International Trade in Endangered Species of Wild Fauna and Flora (CITES) list of potentially endangered species. This is an elegy for lignum vitae trees.

I hesitate to mourn the loss of my dear friend Lignum Vitae because he is not gone. We tend to think of the dead as those to be planted in the dirt, buried to start a new type of existence as roots grow underground. This was the opposite for my dear old friend. It was when they took him from the ground that he began his death. It has continued since. But Lignum Vitae is here, even as just a ghost, a dark shadow in an even darker forest, suffering a perpetual, centuries-long death. I will continue to invoke dear old Lignum Vitae for his legacy is in this land.

I remember meeting him centuries ago on a special voyage to the Americas. He was alive and thriving in a place where everything was there for the taking. It was Crown land, after all, and we had our allegiance. But I got to know him more than anyone else from the Old World, and I appreciated his stance. He stood lumbering over me as an imposing being because of his majestic nature, but still subtle, like a person who felt himself a quiet, watchful tree. As a tree, Lignum Vitae was not the tallest, but what he had, he wore well. His stout body, trunk-like, leapt up with appendages of crooked branches reaching to beyond. Here he opened into a rounded crown of glossy, deep green leaflet clusters, a welcoming canopy for weary visitors. How beautiful was Lignum Vitae when he bloomed! You wouldn't think the muted man could be so flawlessly dramatic – blues so deep they were purple midnight and purples so blue they hinted at the tropical sea when it reflects the sky. Fleshy orange fruit after flower was him offering up even more of himself but we did not care for his showing off.

All year round Lignum Vitae was a sight to behold. I remember him like that, evergreen, nothing like the dead wood I encountered back on the docks in London, Bristol and Liverpool. Nothing like the man I saw in the stately homes and castles he was put to work in. Nothing like the subdued remnants to be found in the museums of our empire. The truth is, my fellow men in England never knew the Lignum Vitae I did; he was stripped of stem, stalk and flower before being shipped to this land. Logs. Our dear friend travelled like deadweight logs. But this is not to say that his death did not influence the landscape. Quite the contrary, he needed to be dead for us to build our commerce.

Thus, our dear friend Lignum Vitae endured a long and tough dead-living. He helped build the world we know but is now no more than a mere murmur, forgotten on this side of the Atlantic Sea. I know it is true that we only speak of the great things people do after their glorious prime, but Lignum Vitae was abused and overlooked, more dead than alive, for to acknowledge that he was unjustly treated would be to admit that everything else was wrong too.

I will tell you of his qualities now, instead of his pain, but the irony is that it was these same qualities that made him the favourite of plunderers.

Our dear friend Lignum Vitae was heavier than water as no one had ever seen. Despite this, he was present on many of our empire's greatest ships – chosen for this task due to his extreme density and ability to stay well-oiled, always ready to work. He made the shaft and rudder bearings and these did not weather or jam. He was an essential part of the shipbuilding industry. Yes, the basis of England's expansion was bolstered by him. Once he was found in the New World, he would never stay in one place again. No doubt when Blackbeard and Henry Morgan sang sea shanties with their crews, Lignum Vitae heard them so many times that he knew all the words. He never told me the truth, too ashamed of his browbeaten history, too scared that maybe he was complicit, but our dear friend probably sailed back to Europe with Columbus on that first voyage. He went on to sail the Seven Seas. Lignum Vitae was known everywhere because of his prowess on the waters.

Sadly, he went around bringing people and product in a way he never consented to. Still, he was the strongest of them all, the most dedicated and reliable. So hard that he would blunt saws and axes, so sharp he was employed to cut diamonds. Lignum Vitae made the deadeyes and bullseyes, the sheaves and the wheels of pulleys, the belaying pins, bushings and ballast for some of the greatest slaving ships of centuries past. Many times he travelled back and forth between Britain and its colonies bringing sugar, coffee, bananas, tobacco and blood. Every other slaving nation hired him out from the English to make their ships, the living dead carrying the living dead. Every part of the Americas was hunted for the will and wood of Lignum Vitae. He too was forced to work from field to great house. Our dear friend had no mouth to say no.

When he made it to England, our dear friend was salvaged from dockyards where he was discarded with ballast wood. He was then beaten into police billy clubs used to beat other beings. Lignum Vitae was also beaten and sculpted into place for our leisure undertakings. Traditional crown green bowls were handmade by Lignum Vitae. This is a quintessentially English game that our dear friend made possible. He went on to specialise in making the tools and trinkets of our fancy – lawn bowls, croquet, skittles, even bowling balls developed around what our dear friend provided, what he would whittle. On windy days, special balls made by Lignum Vitae kept play going in cricket matches where regular balls would blow away. To this day, Lignum Vitae cricket knocking mallets are very rare, expensive and coveted. Though popular at a time, golf club heads made by our dear friend have long disappeared. Lignum Vitae was once on the run from Oliver Cromwell (even though the two had been friends once) after Cromwell's puritanical heavy hand ruled the games sinful. Our whole culture of lawn games owes itself to Lignum Vitae.

Lignum Vitae always laughed at how they thought him some magical bush doctor, using him to treat syphilis as early as the 1500s in that wild European epidemic. He earnt the name Pockwood for this because they thought he would cure the pox. Speaking of venereal disease, our dear friend met Charles Dickens too. So taken aback was the writer by the fortitude of our forgotten friend that he created a character called Lignum Vitae (or Matthew Bagnet) in *Bleak House* in 1852, 'in compliment to the extreme hardness and toughness of his physiognomy'.

Lignum Vitae became world-renowned for his fortitude. To this day he is called the 'wood of life' and it is he who birthed much of modern Britain.

Our dear friend Lignum Vitae survived for more than four hundred years being overused like this. He must have felt felled and broken a thousand times over as he was made to do task after task under duress. Lignum Vitae is slow-growing and took a long time to heal. He hasn't fully recovered and maybe he never will. Where he once lived in thick, full forests, now all that remains is a vast, empty field of overuse. But he never really died. The landscape of England has little pieces of him all over, tiny fragments that hardly warrant a record, but without which everything would fall apart.

When I want to think of him in happier times, I look at the work of natural historians like Hans Sloane who visited him in his native home before he was made to leave. They painted portraits that captured this budding stalwart. He did not know that they were recording him whole because soon he would be broken. How much of him, like the forest, was there before we recognised his face? How much of him has been long lost? His sturdiness fuelled a New World, yet he was rarely seen with lustre like Ebony and Mahogany who sit fat with praise and gleaming from polish by people who pamper them and revere them for their beauty. Our Lignum Vitae was to be worked, not sat on display to show the stolen brilliance of someone else's back-breaking labour (it was his back). Now he is hardly spoken of – find his seed in banks and his shards in the back of museums, find him as a faint whisper in a bare wood.

Our dear friend Lignum Vitae has gone from dust to dust
Yet I still find it hard to mourn a loss
For he was always the living dead when he travelled this land
From full forest patches to ashes
To dirt in England.

SWIMMING

Illustration overleaf: *Otter*

from WATERLOG

Roger Deakin

Roger Deakin (1943–2006) grew up on the edge of London, studied English at Cambridge University and became an advertising executive in the 1960s. He quit his well-paid job to move to the Suffolk countryside in 1970, where he restored an old farmhouse, taught at a local school, and became an environmental activist, music impresario and filmmaker. He co-founded the charity Common Ground and worked on campaigns for Friends of the Earth and Greenpeace. His documentaries examined diverse subjects including allotments, the Southend rock music scene and horse racing. His first book, *Waterlog* (1999), was a critical and commercial success and frog-kicked the 'wild swimming' movement into existence. His subsequent books *Wildwood* (2007) and *Notes from Walnut Tree Farm* (2008) were published posthumously.

THE WASH
Norfolk, 11 August

At five o'clock in the morning I set out for the north, via the Norfolk Breckland, the northern fens, and the Wash. The sun was still rising when I swam at Santon Downham, a hamlet of squat single-storey foresters' cottages in yellow-grey Cambridge brick encrusted with lichens. The place was dwarfed by the tree canopy that surrounded it in a sudden clearing in Thetford Forest, down avenues of lime, Scots fir and oak. Everything seemed little; the post office, the pretty white criss-cross iron bridge, and the Little Ouse. I bathed from a bay of sand so fine and clean it could have been the seaside. I have known it as a swimming hole most of my life, since coming here as a miserable little army cadet on a school field camp when I was about fourteen. It was high summer and the rough, woollen, khaki uniforms were prickling us all crazy in the heat. So were the thick socks and heavy boots. Someone must have taken pity on us because we were piled into the back of a truck and bumped along endless sandy tracks until we reached this mirage of a river, stripped off, and felt its welcome embrace like all our mothers soothing and kissing us cool. I felt then, as now, the caress of long tresses of viridian water crowfoot swaying and trembling in the current. The water was crystalline and sparkling, with the sun's brightness reflected back off the fine, chalky, gravelly bed and fish skidding in and out of the weed sheafs. The river here is thigh deep and its silky waters suspend you almost stationary as you swim upstream, like the countless minnows that nibbled shyly at my feet as I sat in the shallows, glad of the early-morning solitude.

The Little Ouse is a wadi running through the Breckland desert. It comes as a surprise to find a river of such beauty in this arid, sandy place, like coming over a barren ridge and seeing the lush palm groves of the Draa Valley south of Marrakesh. In the neolithic days when the whole area was a populous centre of industrial flint-mining, the river must have been a busy place.

I left my clothes near the bridge and walked barefoot on the warm sand along the river bank upstream for a mile and drifted back down, swimming gently with the current, pushing between the sensual weed, past more sandy bathing bays and sun-hollows in the miniature reedy dunes along the banks. The river was covered in a fine orange dusting of poplar pollen only visible at surface level, and rainbows played in the spray curtains of water-jets hosing a potato field with pumped river water. Dark chubb dodged under the banks amongst the roots of crack willows, and every river stone I turned over had a whole caddis-larva housing estate hidden beneath it.

The Little Ouse is the reflection of the Waveney, rising out of the peat pools of Redgrave Fen to flow in the opposite direction and join the Great Ouse in the Fens at Brandon Creek. I dawdled and splashed back to the bridge between banks full of the lush rankness of willowherb, reed and loosestrife, reaching it just as the post van crossed, and the first bathing party of children arrived.

Driving on through Santon Warren past Grime's Graves towards

Ickburgh, I turned off and parked, and set off on foot down a wood-land ride and across a meadow. I heard the brimming river before I saw it, pouring and dancing more like mountain water beside a grassy path that bordered a marshy wood. This was the Wissey, a river so secret that even its name sounds like a whisper; a river of intoxicating beauty that appears somehow to have avoided the late twentieth century altogether and to know nothing of drought or over-abstraction, let alone pollution. It was full of fish and wild flowers, and, for all I knew, crayfish and naiads, wonderfully remote from any sort of civilisation. The banks were thick with purple water-mint, forget-me-not, hawkbit, and clouds of yellow brimstones and cabbage whites browsing on the purple loosestrife along the banks. The water was polished deep green and gold, shining from its velvet bed of crowfoot and fine gravel; it seemed quite out of time, flowing as sweetly as the river in Millais' painting of the drowned Ophelia decked in wild flowers. (He actually painted it near Ewell in Surrey.)

The Wissey rises in a moated fish pond at a farm in Shipdham near East Dereham in Norfolk and quite soon runs through the never-never land of an army training ground, forbidden to most of us for over fifty years, left undisturbed for months on end, and, crucially, unfarmed. Thus insulated from modern agricultural pollution, the Wissey is one of the purest lowland streams in East Anglia.

Feeling like a philanderer of rivers, with the water of the Little Ouse still in my hair, I went in respectfully through some reeds and began breaststroking tentatively downstream, in water that kept changing tempo, through chalky shallows and deeper pools under the intermittent shade of alders. At times it was so shallow I hauled myself along through nine-inch riffles, cushioned on lush beds of water buttercup. Then I would round a curve and be tilted and rushed downhill almost as I had been on Dartmoor, emerging into waist-deep water full of the fleeting shadows of trout or chubb.

The Wissey probably derives its name from an Old English word, 'wise', meaning simply 'river' and an early East Anglian tribe, the Wissa, may originally have been the People of the Wissey. But how did Wisbech, further west in the Fens, come to derive its name from a river that goes nowhere near it? It is interesting evidence of the dramatic extent to which rivers have changed course over the ages in the Fens. The Wissey, which once ran all the way west to Wisbech, has been intercepted on its way by the Ouse at Denver, and thus finds its way to the Wash at King's Lynn. Many of these changes have been caused by successive drainings of the Fens, beginning with the Romans. Fenland rivers build up silt in their beds and rise up above the surrounding land. Eventually, one may burst its banks somewhere and set off across country on a new course. The rich, silted beds of the extinct rivers and dykes are called roddons, and the twisting roads that cross the Fens follow the earlier meanderings of the rivers. Lines of old willows are also signs of ancient watercourses. At Cottenham, north of Cambridge, you can walk in the course of the old Carr Dyke, and the black, silt roddon of the prehistoric River Cam is clearly visible at Welney.

A series of wooden breakwaters set diagonally into the Wissey caught my eye as I swept along in a green tunnel. They were like paddles dug in to steer a canoe, and created similar eddies in the stream. These were croyes, constructed by the Environment Agency to deflect the current and enliven the river. They would have the same effect as rocks in the course of a Cumbrian river. By forcing the current through a narrowed gap they cause turbulence, which will gradually gouge out a pool downstream, flushing away the sandy bottom to reveal gravel. Different kinds of creatures live on gravel, so this enriches the diversity of the river's life. When the river is in flood, eddy pools develop as havens for fish and other creatures to hole up; shelter from the storm. In relatively straight rivers you can offset alternate croyes and help recreate the lost meanders. It seems odd that the same people who ironed out the meanders in the first place are now busy spending more of our money putting them back in.

There wasn't a soul about, and the insect hum of a really hot day was already building up. A kingfisher streaked right over me in a searing afterburn of blue. You always hear them first, piping a shrill little whistle as they fly, as if to clear the airspace, like Mr Toad at the wheel. Iridescent, black-barred demoiselle courting couples flew in and out of the rushes or rested on them in clinches. These graceful insects are aptly christened *Agrion splendens*. Blue was the fashionable colour in this river. Delicate blue damselflies and big blue aeschna dragonflies hung in the air just above the surface, taking no notice of me at all. I felt like Gulliver, moving through the Lilliputian fleet. Stones concealed caddis larvae like pearly kings and queens, and lively water shrimps scuttled for cover.

At Didlington bridge, a mile downriver, I found myself in a natural swimming hole complete with the regulation rope dangling from a branch. The river was deep and free of weed and I swam in a shaded bower formed by a curious miniature grove of stunted oaks planted close together and never thinned. The ornamental cast-iron bridge was wreathed in wild hops, but the Breckland around Didlington felt abandoned; I had hardly seen a living soul all morning, except hundreds of miserable-looking white ducks standing about in a distant stubble field in the shade of green awnings like disconsolate wedding guests. At the Water Board's Gauging Station by Didlington weir, swimmers were put firmly in their place by an attractive red proclamation from the Environment Agency:

WARNING

IT IS AN OFFENCE: TO JUMP INTO THE RIVER FROM A BRIDGE, LOCK

OR ANY OTHER STRUCTURE. TO SWIM WITHIN 36M OF ANY LOCK

SLUICE, WEIR OR WATER

INTAKE OR IN ANY LOCK PEN.

MAXIMUM FINE £50. WE CARE ABOUT YOUR SAFETY.

After a picnic lunch by the little river, I drove on to Hilgay, to the south of King's Lynn, where I swam by mistake in what turned out to be the poetical-sounding Cut-off Channel, one of the main arteries of the fenland system of drains. It runs west in a big arc from Mildenhall to Denver Sluice. I realised afterwards that I had misread the map, and was under the impression I was swimming the lower reaches of the self-same Wissey, when in fact it runs parallel through the same village half a mile away. Such is the confusion of interlacing water courses in the Fens. I crossed the somnolent water by Snore Hall, an ancient pile snoozing through the centuries, half sunk in the peat, that could have been a model for Toad Hall. The channel was forty yards wide, deep, and stretched away for ever in both directions. A pair of anglers watched me as I swam over, rescuing a roach en route. It had jumped and landed on a patch of tangled, floating weed. The puzzling experience contrasted wildly with my bathe in the upper Wissey. It was like swimming in warm minestrone. Much of the surface was choked with floating islands of half-rotten weed and I staggered out gratefully through black water into a silty reed-bed, wondering what on earth had become of the pristine river of half an hour ago. I felt profoundly disillusioned, and it wasn't until later that I realised my mistake.

Just downstream from Denver Sluice, a gigantic arrangement of lock gates that controls the main outlet of the Fen river system, I swam the Great Ouse, which runs out to the sea at King's Lynn. The river here is a hundred yards wide, and I crossed its deep, thick, brown waters glancing nervously at an armada of swans bearing down on me from the massive green, steel hulk of Denver Sluice. I felt the depth and power of the river under me, and imagined it must feel something like this to swim the Ganges. The water was grained with silt, like an old photograph. Along the far bank was a gypsy scrapyard full of dead lorries and cranes and two piebald ponies trotting about amongst alarming quantities of ragwort. (It is very poisonous to animals, but the food plant of the beautiful crimson-winged Burnet moth.)

I swam towards the chimneys of a coypu's dream: the biggest sugar beet factory in Europe. On the verge near the roundabout leading to the giant factory I had passed a miniature encampment of chrome caravan, lorry, dog kennel and a small cabin cruiser up on chocks. I had entered gypsy country here, and it continued all the way to Wisbech. Horses are still grazed by gypsies along the river banks, but their numbers have declined since the days when fenland farmers like Coley Ambrose at Stuntney kept and bred over 200 working horses. The gypsies used to go beet-hoeing, and pea-, onion- or potato-picking all over the Fens. There was fruit-picking too, alongside the village women. I had met a woman in Wilburton a few weeks earlier who described how they followed the seasons' rhythms in their free-lancing: 'We would start beet singling, then gooseberries, then plums, then apples, then potato-picking, then more apples, then we would be packing them in the sheds.' The days were often full of fen mists:

'We once went potato-picking and it was so foggy we thought we were alone, but when it cleared, the field was full of people.'

With one eye on the living swans, I almost swam into a dead one on a last journey to the sea, and when I hoisted myself to the bank, I couldn't avoid coming out like the Green Man, covered in duckweed. It was hard to accept, rowing myself through this turbid cocktail of dilute fenland, that the Great Ouse at this point included the sparkling Little Ouse and Wissey, the limpid Granta, the sacred Lark, and the sweet springwater of the Wicken Lode, all converging into the Great Ouse to run down to the Wash at King's Lynn. The Great Ouse. It sounded and felt like the origins of life itself, when we all began, where we all end, the Alpha and Omega of the Fens, the gateway of all the eels in thirteen counties, a port of call both ways on the Sargasso run. The swim and its setting were so bizarre that only the duckweed on my towel reminded me, days later, that it wasn't all a dream.

I drove on west, pressing deeper into the Fens, past houses tossed this way and that on sinking raft foundations, through Salters Lode and Nordelph to Well Creek, where I bathed in the Middle Level Drain in the evening sunshine. Well Creek is a narrow canal that follows the course of the original River Wissey, and forms a navigation link with the Old River Nene, the Twenty Foot River, and the Old Bedford River. It crosses over the Middle Level Drain at this point in an aqueduct, which I swam through for the perfectly good reason that I had never swum an aqueduct before, or at two different levels in the same place. There were some big sluice gates here controlling the Middle Level Drain, and water gushed into the canal, pumped up from the drain below.

A gang of boys was busy clocking up hundreds of pounds in Environment Agency fines, climbing up the sluice gates and leaping twenty feet into the Middle Level Drain. The canal narrowed to not much more than boat width where it passed through the aqueduct, and the boys further amused themselves by leaping aboard each narrowboat that chugged through, swaggering its full length in their swimming trunks, then leaping off the other side, to the dismay of its crew and much shouting on both sides. This, they explained to me, was traditional; a fenland pirate game since time immemorial.

At first disposed to regard me with suspicion, even hostility, as an oldie trespassing on their territory, the Well Creek Gang perceptibly mellowed when I executed quite a respectable, if furtive, dive into the Middle Level Drain then swam along it for a quarter-mile, past a charming waterside cottage with an old wooden landing-stage, orchard and vegetable garden. The scent of several thousand cultivated roses drifted across the water from the surrounding fields. The river was about thirty yards wide, surprisingly clear and warm, and as I swam due west up the middle, deep gold in the sun. It was the most beautiful drain I had ever seen.

All this was really a rehearsal for the grand swim I had in mind for later, by way of crowning the day, in the Wash itself. Returning to the aqueduct and sluice, I swam under them both to the far side with less than six inches' headroom above the surface. I blame Enid Blyton for such laddish behaviour; the Famous Five were always swimming in and out of smugglers' caves or in forbidden canals, usually at night, signalling to one another with torches. Everyone in Enid Blyton books always carried a torch, and the batteries never went flat. The improbable adventures were amongst my earliest stories, so I have only to see a sluice, or an aqueduct, and I am six years old again. There were no fines for the Famous Five; only a stern 'Now then children, what *is* the meaning of this?'

In the dusty sunset glow, I motored over towards the Wash to swim at last in the wake of King John, whose treasure has been lost in the quicksands since 1216. From the map, I had chosen Gedney Drove End as the most likely-looking starting point, on the grounds that it sounded remote and romantic. It was certainly remote. I parked outside the pub, then walked through a cornfield on a lonely footpath, almost obliterated by the plough, so that it constantly threatened to edge me off into the dyke. (De Quincey says this is what Wordsworth did to all his walking companions. He would start off on your left and edge you inexorably over to the right until you were nearly in the ditch, at which point you would move round to his left, and he would veer off the other way.)

I eventually reached the sea wall, a thirty-foot grassy bank with steep wooden steps and a rickety handrail. There were notices about the dangers of the tides and creeks, and another depicting a swimmer with an ominous red line through him. He looked remarkably like me. In spite of all this there was a stark beauty about the minimal landscape in the failing light. The creeks and marshes stretched away to oblivion and a watchtower for the RAF shooting range here was silhouetted against the sky. There was nothing but the last gurgling trickles of the departing tide.

Out on the horizon were three or four hulks, small *Belgranos* for the planes to strafe and bomb on weekdays. The watchtower door was heavily padlocked, yet someone had been unable to resist the opportunity to put up a notice: NO UNAUTHORISED PERSON BEYOND THIS POINT. There was a picture of an unauthorised person with a diagonal line through him. I fancied he, too, looked uncannily like me, and realised that the same compulsive urge that makes a great graffiti artist is also at work amongst the bureaucrats. I ventured gingerly out on to the marsh, a desert of cracked mud and little meandering creeks that suddenly came to life with dozens of crabs, running for their lives into the craters whilst gesturing at me defiantly, not to say rudely, with their front claws.

I had tiptoed past yet another sign: DANGER, UNEXPLODED BOMBS AND MISSILES. IT IS ILLEGAL AND HIGHLY DANGEROUS TO EXCAVATE ANY OBJECTS FOUND ON THE MARSH. THEY MAY EXPLODE AND KILL YOU. Now that was more like it. No piddling £50 fines for would-be paddlers, samphire-gatherers, or King John's treasure-hunters in the Wash. Just death. I glanced guiltily at the loudspeakers on the watch-tower, half expecting a ticking-off. Peering into the middle distance I made out more targets planted in the mud like unauthorised persons stuck fast in their wellingtons.

I had been naive in imagining I might swim in the Wash. Even if it hadn't had the plug pulled out of it, I would probably have appeared on someone's radar screen and been strafed. I retired to the New Inn at Gedney Drove End, noted for its collection of several hundred china pigs, where I got my head in the trough, then zig-zagged back down the footpath, after the manner of Wordsworth, to camp for the night, an unauthorised person, on the lonely rim of the unswimmable Wash.

from TARKA THE OTTER

Henry Williamson

Henry Williamson (1895–1977) grew up in Ladywell, south-east London, and developed a love of nature through his forays into the Kent countryside. He saw lengthy service and was wounded in the First World War. Inspired by Richard Jefferies' *The Story of My Heart*, he moved to Devon and began writing. *Tarka the Otter* (1927) won the Hawthornden Prize, was praised by Thomas Hardy and made Williamson a household name. He wrote more than fifty published books about rural life, farming (Williamson bought a farm in Norfolk) and wildlife as well as a fifteen-volume series of autobiographical novels. Williamson had been horrified by war and was a pacifist in the 1920s but his determination that Britain and Germany must never fight again morphed into fascist views and an admiration of Nazi Germany in the 1930s. He visited a Nazi congress in 1935, joined Oswald Mosley's British Union of Fascists in 1937 and continued to write for the Mosley-sponsored journal, *The European*, after the war. He died on the day filmmakers completed the death scene for the film of *Tarka the Otter*.

When he went into the water the next night and tried to walk towards his mother, he floated. He was so pleased that he set out across the river by himself, finding that he could turn easily towards his mother by swinging his hindquarters and rudder. He turned and turned many times in his happiness; east towards Willow Island and the water-song, west towards the kingfisher's nest, and Peal Rock below Canal Bridge, and the otter-path crossing the big bend. North again and then south-west, where the gales came from, up and down, backwards and forwards, sometimes swallowing water, at other times sniffing it up his nose, sneezing, spitting, coughing, but always swimming. He learned to hold his nose above the ream, or ripple, pushed in front of it.

While swimming in this happy way, he noticed the moon. It danced on the water just before his nose. Often he had seen the moon, just outside the hollow tree, and had tried to touch it with a paw. Now he tried to bite it, but it swam away from him. He chased it. It wriggled like a silver fish and he followed to the sedges on the far bank of the river, but it no longer wriggled. It was waiting to play with him. Across the river Tarka could hear the mewing of his sisters, but he set off after the moon over the meadow. He ran among buttercups and cuckooflowers and grasses bending with bright points. Farther and farther from the river he ran, the moonlight gleaming on his coat. Really it was brown like the dust in an October puff-ball, but the water sleeked the hair.

As he stopped to listen to the bleat of lambs, a moth whirred by his head and tickled him. While he was scratching, a bird flying with irregular wingbeats and sudden hawk-like glidings took the moth in its wide gape and flew out of his sight. Tarka forgot the moon-play. He crouched in the grasses, which rose above his head like the trees of a forest, some with tops like his rudder, others like his whiskers, and all whispering as they swayed. The nightjar returned, clapping its wings over its head with the noise of a dry stick cracking. Tarka was glad to hear his mother calling him. He mewed. He listened and her whistle was nearer, so he ran away in the wet grasses. The cub did not know how alarmed his mother was nor did he know that less than fifty flaps away a bird with great eyes and wings spanning a yard was flying upon him. The nightjar had seen the bird, too, and had clapped its wings as a danger signal to its mate whose two eggs were laid among ferns in the woods.

The nightjar twirled and planed away; Tarka scampered on. The great bird, who had raised two tufts of feathers on its head, dropped with taloned feet spread for a clutch. The otter saw it drop and ran forwards so swiftly that the sound of her going through the grasses was like the first wind which uncoils as it runs before the south-westerly gale. The bird, which was a short-eared owl, thought that Tarka was a small rabbit, and fanned above him while it considered whether or not he was small enough to be attacked. It did not hesitate longer than the time of six flaps, but stopped, while screaking to terrify and subdue its prey. But Tarka came of a family fiercer and quicker in movement than the owl. Tissing with rage, he jumped and bit his assailant as a foot grasped his back and four talons pierced his skin. The other foot of the bird grasped grasses and it had turned with clacking beak to peck the base of the cub's skull when the paw-stroke of the bitch tore half the feathers from its breast. She stood on it, bit once, twice, thrice, in a second of time, and so the owl died.

Tarka was nipped in the neck, shaken, picked up, bumped all the way back to the bank, scraped over the stones, and dropped into the water. Obediently he followed his mother across the river, to where the dog was lying on his back and gravely watching two cubs playing with the tip of his rudder.

Fish were brought alive to the cubs when they had been swimming about a fortnight and dropped in the shallowest water. And when they were nearly three months old their mother took them downstream, past Leaning Willow Island, and across the bend, to where the banks were glidden into mud smothered by the sea. The tide had lapsed from the mud, leaving fresh water to tear the rocky bed below.

Tarka galloped through the tall green reeds to the river, stopping by a gut to sniff at the tracks of a curlew, which had been feeding there during the ebb-tide. Near the water he found another track, of five toes well spread, and the prick of five claws. The dog had walked there. Just above Halfpenny Bridge they saw him, half out of the water, and chewing a fish which he did not trouble to hold in his paws. He crunched it from the head downwards, gulping his bites quickly, and as soon as the tail was swallowed, he turned and went underwater for more.

The bitch took her cubs to a pool below the bridge and walked with them across a shallow tail of water. She stared at the stones, brown and slippery with seaweed, and the cubs stared also. They watched the glimmers in the claws of water, sometimes trying to bite them. While they were watching the mother ran along the bank to the top of the pool and slid into the water. More often than usual her head looked up as she swam from bank to bank, for she was not hunting, but driving the fish down to the cubs. Tarka became excited and, seeing a fish, he swam after it and went underwater to get it. In order to travel faster, he struck out with all four webs together, and lo! Tarka was swimming like an otter near a fish. It was the biggest fish he had seen, and although he kicked after it at the rate of nearly two hundred kicks a minute, he lost it after a yard. He yikkered in his anger, and oh! Tarka was no longer swimming like an otter, but gasping and coughing on the surface, a poor little sick-feeling cub mewing for his mother.

He felt better when he had eaten a mullet caught by his mother. The fish had come up with the tide and remained in the still pool. Later in the night Tarka caught a pollywiggle, or tadpole, in a watery hoof-hole and thought himself a real hunter as he played with it, passing it from paw to paw and rolling on his back in the mud. He was quite selfish over his prey when his mother went to see what he was doing, and cried, *Iss-iss-ic-yang!* an old weasel threat, which being interpreted, means, Go away, or I will drink your blood!

Old Nog, the heron, beating his loose grey wings over Leaning Willow Island as the sun was making yellow the top of the tall tree, saw five brown heads in the salmon-pool. Three small heads and a larger head turned to the left by the fallen tree, and the largest head went on upriver alone. The cubs were tired and did not like being washed when they were in the holt. Afterwards Tarka pushed his sister from his mother's neck, the most comfortable place in the holt, and immediately fell asleep. Sometimes his hindlegs kicked, gently. He was trying to catch a shining fish that wriggled just before his nose, when he was abruptly flung awake. He yawned, but his mother, tissing through her teeth, frightened him into silence. The day was bright outside the hole.

Halcyon the kingfisher sped down the river, crying a short, shrill *peet!* as it passed the holt. The otter got on her forelegs and started towards the opening. Soon after the kingfisher had gone, a turtle dove alighted on the ash tree above the holt and looked about her; she had just flown off her two eggs, nearly dropping through a loose raft-like nest in a hawthorn by the weir. The bird held out a wing and began to straighten the filaments of a flight-quill which had struck a twig during her sudden flight out of the bush-top. She drew the feather through her beak thrice, shook her wings, listened, and went on preening.

Tarka closed his eyes again, breathed deeply and settled to sleep on the youngest cub's neck. He looked up when his mother ran to the opening. The otter was listening to a sound like the high, thin twang of a mosquito. Hair bristled on her neck. From far away there came a deep rolling sound, and a screaming cheer. The otter instantly returned to her cubs and stood over them in a protective attitude, for she knew that hounds were hunting the water.

Tarka crouched down, listening to the cries. They became more distinct. Always a deeper, gruffer note was heard among them. The sounds, almost continuous, became louder and louder. Nearer came another sound – the wings of the dove striking against twigs as it flew away.

A minute later the pair of cole-tits that had a nest in a hole of the ash tree began to make their small, wheezy notes of alarm. The white owl had flown from the bridge and was perched against the ivy of the trunk, turning its head from side to side and blinking. One cole-tit, about as long as a man's finger, flittered with rage on the twigs a few inches from the gold-grey head. The owl blinked slowly; the baying swelled under the bridge; it swung its head round without moving its body and stared straight behind it. *Chizzy-chizzy-chizzy-te!* wheezed the cole-tit as the owl floated away. Tarka was used to this sound, for usually it greeted him whenever he looked out of the holt in daylight.

Chizzy-chizzy-chizzy-te! the bird wheezed again, and then Tarka saw the big head of the dog-otter by the opening, and his wet paws on the bark. The bitch tissed at him, her teeth snapped at his head, and the dog was gone.

The cries were now very loud. Tarka heard thuds in the wood all around him. The cubs crouched in the darkest corner. Nearer came the shouts of men, until the thuds of running feet ceased on the bank. The water began to wash against and lap the half-drowned trunk, claws scraped the wood, the opening grew dark and the tongue he had heard above the others boomed in the hollow. The otter crouched back, larger than usual, for her body was rigid and all the hair of her back stood straight. Swish, swish swept her rudder. She recognized another sound and tissed every time it cried the names of hounds, in a voice thin and high as though it were trying to become as the horn which so often took its rightful breath. The voice ceased. The horn sang its plain note. Whips cracked.

By their big feet hounds pulled themselves out of the water, except the one who threw his deep tongue at the holt opening. He was all black-and-white, with great flews, and the biggest stallion-hound in the pack. He was black from nose to neck except for the pallid nicks of old quarrel scars on his muzzle and head. No hound quarrelled with him now, for Deadlock was master of all. In his veins ran the blood of the Talbots, and one of his bloodhound ancestors had eaten man. He had mastiff in him. His dam and sire had pulled down many a deer at bay in the waters of the moor, and died fireside deaths after faithful service to red coats. A pink weal ran down his belly, for in his second stag-hunting season the great pied hound had been ripped open by the brow-point of a stag; and his pace had gone from him afterwards. The otter-hunters bought him for a guinea, liking his long legs, and now Deadlock was the truest marking hound in the country of the Two Rivers.

He held by his paws, and his teeth tore at the sodden tinderwood. He could thrust in only his head. While he was kicking the water for a foothold, the otter ran forward and bit him through the ear, piercing the ear-mark where the blue initial letters of his original pack were tattooed. Deadlock yarred through his bared teeth. Three small mouths at the other end of the holt opened and tissed in immense fright.

Then Tarka heard a cry which he was to hear often in his wanderings; a cry which to many otters of the Two Rivers had meant that the longest swimmings, the fastest land-looping, the quietest slipping from drain or holt were unavailing.

Tally Ho!

The cry came from down the river, just above Leaning Willow Island, from the throat of an old man in a blue coat and white breeches, who had been leaning his bearded chin on hands clasping a ground-ash pole nearly as long and as old as himself. From his lookout place he had seen something moving down like brown thongweed just under the clear and shallow water. Off came the hat, grey as lichen, to be held while he cried again.

Tally Ho!

The horn of the huntsman sang short and urgent notes; the air by the holt was scored by the names of hounds as he ran with them to where, amidst purple-streaked stems of hemlock, the old man was standing on the shillets.

Soon afterwards the horn sounded again near the holt and the baying of hounds grew louder. Footfalls banged the wood above Tarka's head, as a man climbed along the trunk. The water began to lap: hound-taint from a high-yelping throat came into the holt: the bitch grew larger along her back when, above her head, a man's voice cried snarlingly, *Go'rn leave it, Captain! Go'rn leave it!* A thong swished, a lash cracked. *Go'rn leave it, Captain!*

The high yelping lessened with the taint of breath. The cries went up the river. The rudder of the bitch twitched. The hair on her back fell slanting; but it rose when something scratched above. Her nose pointed, she breathed through her mouth. She moved away uneasily. Tarka sneezed. Tobacco smoke. A man was sitting in the branches over them.

After half an hour the cries came down to the holt again. They passed, and then Tarka heard a new and terrible noise – the noise as of mammoth iron-toed centipedes crossing on the stones, or shillets, at the tail of the pool.

Tally Ho! Look out, he's coming down!

Iron toes scraped the shillets faster. Here, across the shallow, a dozen men and women stood almost leg-to-leg in the water, stirring the stream with their ironshod poles to stop the dog-otter passing down to the next pool.

Tarka and the cubs breathed fast again. Deadlock's great bellow swam nearer, with the high yelping of Captain. Many wavelets slapped against the tree. A dozen hounds were giving tongue between Canal Bridge and the stickle above Leaning Willow Island. A shaggy face looked into the holt and a voice cried just over Tarka's head, *Go'rn leave it, Dewdrop! Go'rn leave it!* Boots knocked on the trunk. *Is-isss-iss! Go'rn leave it!* And Dewdrop left it, bitten in the nose.

Unable to break the stickle, the dog-otter went back under the bridge. Baying became fainter. The notes of the cole-tits in the ash tree were heard again.

In the quiet hollow the otter unstiffened and scratched for ticks as though the hunt had never come there. Hounds and men were above the bridge, where another stickle was standing. The water flowed – with small murmurs. She heard the rustling clicks of dragon-flies' wings over the sun-splashy ripples. Silence, the tranquil *chee-chee* of a cole-tit seeking a grub in an oak-apple, and the sunbeam through the woodpecker hole roving over the damp wood dust on the floor. The otter lay down, she dozed, she jumped up when sudden cries of *Tally Ho!* and a confused clamour arose beyond the bridge. Now all the sounds of the past hours were increasing together, of tongues, and horns, and cheers; and very soon they were overborne by a deep new noise like the rumbling of the mill when the water-wheel was turning. Then with the deep rumbling came the prolonged thin rattle of the horn, and the triumphant whooping of whips and hunts-men. The sounds slowed and ceased, except for the lone baying of a hound; they broke out again, and slowed away into silence; but long afterwards the strange blowing noises made by their mother frightened the huddled cubs.

from RING OF BRIGHT WATER

Gavin Maxwell

Gavin Maxwell (1914–69) was born into a wealthy family and grew up in Wigtownshire, south-west Scotland. He studied estate management at Oxford University and served as an instructor with the secret Special Operations Executive during the Second World War. After the war, he bought the island of Soay in the Inner Hebrides and attempted to establish a basking shark fishery – his brutal killing of sharks is described in his first book, *Harpoon at a Venture* (1952). In 1956, he toured the marshes of southern Iraq with explorer Wilfred Thesiger, who gave him a smooth-coated otter called Mijbil. Maxwell raised Mijbil at his new home in Sandaig, Scotland, telling the otter's story in *Ring of Bright Water* (1960). The title was taken from a poem by his friend Kathleen Raine – Maxwell, who was privately gay, had been the love of her life. The book was a huge success but Maxwell's subsequent life was troubled, despite the support of friends and young mentees including the broadcaster Terry Nutkins and nature writer John Lister-Kaye. After Maxwell's home was destroyed by fire in 1968, he moved to the lighthouse keepers' cottages on Eilean Bàn, and died of lung cancer in 1969.

In the sea, Mij discovered his true, breath-taking aquabatic powers; until he came to Scotland he had never swum in deep waters, for the lakes and lagoons of his native marshes are rarely more than a fathom or two deep. He would swim beside me as I rowed in the little dinghy, and in the glass-clear waters of Camusfeàrna bay, where the white shell sand alternates with sea tangle and outcrops of rock, I could watch him as he dived down, down, down through fathom after fathom to explore the gaudy sea forests at the bottom with their flowered shell glades and mysterious, shadowed caverns.

He was able, as are all otters and seals, to walk on the bottom without buoyancy, for an otter swims habitually underwater and does not dive with full lungs, depending for oxygen—we must presume in the absence of knowledge—upon a special adaptation of the venous system. The longest that I ever timed Mij below the surface was almost six minutes, but I had the impression that he was in no way taxing his powers, and could greatly have exceeded that time in emergency. Normally, however, if he was not engrossed, he would return to the surface every minute or so, breaking it for only a second, with a forward diving roll like that of a porpoise. Swimming at the surface, as he did if he wanted to keep some floating object in view, he was neither very fast nor graceful, a labouring dog-paddle in amazing contrast to his smooth darting grace below water. For hours he would keep pace with the boat, appearing now on this side and now on that, sometimes mischievously seizing an oar with both arms and dragging on it, and from time to time bouncing inboard with a flurry of water, momentarily recalled to his mission of drying people.

Only when I was fishing did I have to leave Mij shut up in the house, for he was a creature who must test everything with his mouth, and my worst nightmare was the vision of a mackerel hook in his jaw. At first I fished little, having no great liking for the lythe and coal fish that are all one may depend upon in early summer round the Camusfeàrna skerries. Though by mid-June there are all the signs of summer, the teeming, clangorous bird life of the islands established for many weeks and the samphire and goose-grass alive with downy chicks, it is not until July that with the coming of the mackerel the sea appears to burst into life; for following them come all the greater creatures that prey upon them, and the mackerel in their turn force up to the surface the lesser fishes upon which they feed, the small, glittering, multitudinous fry of many species, including their own. When far out on the blank face of the summer sea there are screaming patches of gulls that dip and swoop, half running, half flying, alighting with wings still open to grab and to swallow, one may guess that somewhere beneath them lies a great shoal of mackerel, who are pushing up to the surface and the waiting gulls the little fish fleeing in panic from, perhaps, their own parents. Sometimes there are curiously local patches of fry at the surface, and at sunset when the sea is really as smooth as glass—a much misused simile, for it rarely is—I have seen, miles from shore, little dancing foot-wide fountains of blue and silver mackerel no longer than a man's thumb, and have found no predator below them.

After the mackerel had arrived I fished for a few minutes in the cool of every evening; for them Mij, though he never caught one himself, so far as I knew, had an insatiable passion, as had Jonnie before him; and I too welcomed them, perhaps because of childhood associations. When I was a child in Galloway we used to fish for mackerel by trolling from a sailing-boat a single hook baited with bright metal, or with a sliver of flesh and skin sliced from a mackerel's flank (how well I recall the horror of seeing for the first time this operation performed upon the living fish; the tears, the reassurance, all among the blue waves and the spindrift and the flapping brown sail). We caught our fish singly and re-baited the hook each time, and if we caught twenty or thirty fish in an afternoon we chattered about it for weeks. It was not, I think, until shortly before the war that the murderous darrow came into general use in the West Highlands, and at Camusfeàrna, where there is no means of disposing of surplus fish but dumping them, it has the disadvantage of limiting fishing time to a few minutes. A darrow consists of a twelve-foot cast carrying up to twenty-two flies of crudely-dyed hen's feathers, weighted at the bottom with a two-pound sinker. The boat is stationary in anything from six to twenty fathoms of water, and the darrow and line are allowed to run out until the sinker bumps the bottom. By that time, as often as not in Camusfeàrna bay, there are half a dozen or so mackerel on the hooks. If there are not, it is simply a question of hauling in two fathoms of line and letting it run out again, and repeating this process until either the boat drifts over a shoal or a moving shoal happens to pass beneath the boat. Sometimes the mackerel are in shallower water, clear water where one can see fathoms down to pale sand and dark sea-tangle and rushing shoals of aquamarine fish as they dart at the bright feathers. Quite often every single fly is taken at once; then at one moment the line is lead-heavy, tugging and jerking, and at the next light as floating string as the mackerel swim upward carrying the sinker with them. There is a great art in dealing with a full darrow, for twenty-two large fishhooks flipping wildly about the hold of a small boat catch more than fish. In the days of the Soay Shark Fishery I saw many barbs sunk deep in hands and legs of mackerel fishers; there was only one way of extraction, and a very painful one it was—to push the hook clean through, as opposed to pulling on it, then to snip off the barb with wire cutters and work the hook all the way back again.

It is not always mackerel that take the darrow flies; there are saith and lythe and the strangely heraldic gurnards, so fantastically armoured with spikes and thorns as to make their capture by anything but man seem nothing short of impossible, yet I have watched, with the same sensations as a man might view a big snake swallowing an ox whole, a shag swallow a large gurnard tail first—against the grain, as it were. This extraordinary and surely gratuitously painful feat took the shag just over half an hour of grotesque convulsion, and when the stunt was at last completed the bird had entirely changed its shape. From being a slim, graceful, snake-like creature with a neck like an ebony cane, it had become an amorphous and neck-less lump—its crop so gigantically distended as to force the head far back down the spine and flush with it—unable to rise or even to swim without danger of ridicule.

Mij himself caught a number of fish on his daily outings; and week by week, as his skill and speed grew, their size and variety increased. In the burn he learned to feel under stones for eels, reaching in with one paw and averted head; and I in turn learned to turn over the larger stones for him, so that after a time he would stand in front of some boulder too heavy for him to move, and chitter at me to come and lift it for him. Often, as I did this, an eel would streak out from it into deeper water and he would fire himself after it like a brown torpedo beneath the surface. Near the edge of the tide he would search out the perfectly camouflaged flounders until they shot off with a wake of rising sand-grains like smoke from an express train—and farther out in the bay he would kill an occasional sea trout; these he never brought ashore, but ate them treading water as he did so, while I thought a little wistfully of the Chinese who are said to employ trained otters to fish for them. Mij, I thought, with all his delightful camaraderies, would never offer me a fish; I was wrong, but when at last he did so it was not a sea trout but a flounder. One day he emerged from the sea on to the rock ledge where I was standing and slapped down in front of me a flounder a foot across. I took it that he had brought this for congratulation, for he would often bring his choicer catches for inspection before consuming them, so I said something encouraging and began to walk on. He hurried after me and slammed it down again with a wet smack at my feet. Even then I did not understand, assuming only that he wished to eat in company, but he just sat there looking up and chittering at me. I was in no hurry to take the gesture at its face value, for, as I have said, one of the most aggressive actions one can perform to a wild animal is to deprive it of its prey, but after perhaps half a minute of doubt, while Mij redoubled his invitation, I reached down slowly and cautiously for the fish, knowing that Mij would give me vocal warning if I had misinterpreted him. He watched me with the plainest approval while I picked it up and began a mime of eating it; then he plunged off the rock into the sea and sped away a fathom down in the clear water.

Watching Mij in a rough sea—and the equinoctial gales at Camusfeàrna produce very rough seas indeed—I was at first sick with apprehension, then awed and fascinated, for his powers seemed little less than miraculous. During the first of the gales, I remember, I tried to keep him to the rock pools and the more sheltered corners, but one day his pursuit of some unseen prey had taken him to the seaward side of a high dry reef at the very tide's edge. As the long undertow sucked outward he was in no more than an inch or two of marbled water with the rock at his back, crunching the small fish he had caught; then, some forty yards to seaward of him I saw a great snarling comber piling up higher and higher, surging in fifteen feet tall and as yet unbreaking. I yelled to Mij as the wave towered darkly towards him, but he went on eating and paid no heed to me. It curled over and broke just before it reached him; all those tons of water just smashed down and obliterated him, enveloping the whole rock behind in a booming tumult of sea. Somewhere under it I visualized Mij's smashed body swirling round the foot of the black rock. But as the sea drew back in a long hissing undertow I saw, incredulously, that nothing had changed; there was Mij still lying in the shallow marbled water, still eating his fish.

He rejoiced in the waves; he would hurl himself straight as an arrow right into the great roaring grey wall of an oncoming breaker and go clean through it as if it had neither weight nor momentum; he would swim far out to sea through wave after wave until the black dot of his head was lost among the distant white manes, and more than once I thought that some wild urge to seek new lands had seized him and that he would go on swimming west into the Sea of the Hebrides and that I should not see him again.

As the weeks went by his absences did grow longer, and I spent many anxious hours searching for him, though as yet he had never stayed away for a night. When I had drawn blank at the falls and at all his favourite pools in the burn or among the rock ledges by the sea, I would begin to worry and to roam more widely, calling his name all the while. His answering note of recognition was so like the call of some small dowdy bird that inhabits the trees by the waterside that my heart would leap a hundred times before I knew with certainty that I had heard his voice, and then my relief was so unbounded that I would allow him to dry me without protest.

The first time that I found him in distress was in the dark ravine above the waterfall. The waterfall divides, in some sense, the desert from the sown; the habitable world from the strange, beautiful, but inhospitable world of the dark gorge through which the burn flows above it. In summer, when the water is low, one may pick one's way precariously along the rock at the stream's edge, the almost sheer but wooded sides rising a hundred feet at either hand. Here it is always twilight, for the sun never reaches the bed of the stream, and in summer the sky's light comes down thin and diffused by a stipple of oak and birch leaves whose branches lean out far overhead. Here and there a fallen tree-trunk spans the narrow gorge, its surface worn smooth by the passage of the wildcats' feet. The air is cool, moist, and pungent with the smell of wild garlic and watery things such as ferns and mosses that grow in the damp and the dark. Sometimes the bed of the stream widens to deep pools whose rock flanks afford no foothold, and where it looks as though the black water must be bottomless.

Once Morag asked me, in an offhand way behind which I sensed a tentative probing, whether I felt at ease in that place. It was a question that held a tacit confession, and I replied frankly. I have never been at ease in it; it evokes in me an unpleasant sensation that I associate only with the unfurnished top floor of a certain house, a sensation which makes me want to glance constantly over my shoulder, as though, despite the physical impossibility, I were being followed. I catch myself trying to step silently from stone to stone, as though it were important to my safety that my presence should remain undetected. I should have been abashed to tell Morag of this had she not given me the lead, but she told me then that she had had a horror of the place ever since she was a child, and could offer no explanation.

To conform to the spirit of my confession the gorge ought, of course, to be shunned by bird and animal alike, but it has, in fact, more of both than one might expect. There are foxes' and badgers' and wildcats' dens in the treacherous, near-vertical walls of the ravine; the buzzards and hooded crows nest every year in the branches that lean out over the dark water; below them there are the dippers and grey wagtails (a crass ornithological misnomer for this canary-yellow creature), and, for some reason, an unusual number of wrens that skulk and twitter among the fern. Whatever makes the gorge an unpleasant place to some people does not extend its influence beyond human beings.

The deep pools spill in unbroken falls a few feet high, and after two hundred yards or so there is the second real waterfall, dropping fifty feet interrupted by a ledge pool half-way down. That is the upper limit of the 'haunting', though the physical details of the gorge above the second falls differ little from those of the stretch below it; then, a further hundred yards up the burn's course, the way is blocked by the tall cataract, eighty feet of foaming white water falling sheer.

Mij, certainly, found nothing distasteful in the reach where my ghosts walked, and he had early used his strength and resource to scale the Camusfeàrna waterfall and find out what lay beyond. Thereafter this inaccessible region had become his especial haunt, and one from which his extraction presented, even when he was not in difficulties, almost insuperable problems. The clamour of the falling water effectively drowned the calling human voice, and even if he did hear it there was little chance of the caller perceiving his faint, bird-like response. On this occasion there was more water in the burn than is usual in summer, and there had been, too, a recent landslide, temporarily destroying the only practicable access from above. I lowered myself into the ravine on a rope belayed to the trunk of a tree, and I was wet to the waist after the first few yards of the burn's bed. I called and called, but my voice was diminished and lost in the sound of rushing water, and the little mocking birds answered me with Mij's own note of greeting. At length one of these birds, it seemed, called so repeatedly and insistently as to germinate in me a seed of doubt, but the sound came from far above me, and I was looking for Mij in the floor of the burn. Then I saw him; high up on the cliff, occupying so small a ledge that he could not even turn to make his way back, and with a fifty-foot sheer drop below him; he was looking at me, and, according to his lights, yelling his head off. I had to make a long detour to get above him with the rope and all the while I was terrified that the sight of me would have spurred him to some effort that would bring tragedy; terrified, too, that I myself might dislodge him as I tried to lift him from his eyrie. Then I found that the trees at the cliff-top were all rotten, and I had to make the rope fast to a stump on the hill above, a stump that grew in soft peat and that gave out from its roots an ominous squelching sound when I tugged hard on it. I went down that rock with the rope knotted round my waist and the feeling that Mij would probably survive somehow, but that I should most certainly die. He tried to stand on his hind legs when he saw me coming down above him, and more than once I thought he had gone. I had put the loop of his lead through the rope at my waist, and I clipped the other end to his harness as soon as my arm could reach him, but the harnesses, with their constant immersion, never lasted long, and I trusted this one about as much as I trusted the stump to which my rope was tied. I went up the rope with Mij dangling and bumping at my side like a cow being loaded on to a ship by crane, and in my mind's eye were two jostling, urgent images—the slow, sucking emergence of the tree roots above me, and the gradual parting of the rivets that held Mij's harness together. All in all it was one of the nastiest five minutes of my life; and when I reached the top the roots of the stump were indeed showing—it took just one tug with all my strength to pull them clean out.

But the harness had held, though, mercifully, it broke the next time it was put to strain. Mij had been missing, that day in the ravine, for nine hours, and had perhaps passed most of them on that ledge, for he was ravenously hungry, and ate until I thought he must choke.

There were other absences, other hours of anxiety and search, but one in particular stands out in my mind, for it was the first time that he had been away for a whole night, the first time that I despaired of him. I had left him in the early morning at the burn side eating his eels, and began to be uneasy when he had not returned by mid-afternoon. I had been working hard at my book; it was one of those rare days of authorship when everything seemed to go right; the words flowed unbidden from my pen, and the time had passed unheeded, so that it was a shock to realize that I had been writing for some six hours. I went out and called for Mij down the burn and along the beach, and when I did not find him I went again to the ravine above the falls. But there was no trace of him anywhere, though I explored the whole dark length of it right to the high falls, which I knew that even Mij could not pass. Just how short a distance my voice carried I realized when, above the second falls, I came upon two wildcat kittens at play on the steep bank; they saw me and were gone in a flash, but they had never heard my voice above the sound of the water. I left the burn then and went out to the nearer islands; it was low tide, and there were exposed stretches and bars of soft white sand. Here I found otter footprints leading towards the lighthouse island, but I could not be certain that they were Mij's. Later that summer his claws became worn so that his pad-marks no longer showed the nails, but at that stage I was still unsure of distinguishing his tracks from those of a wild otter, unless the imprints were very precise. All that evening I searched and called, and when dusk came and he still did not return I began to despair, for his domestic life had led him to strictly diurnal habits, and by sundown he was always asleep in front of the fire.

It was a cloudy night with a freshening wind and a big moon that swam muzzily through black rags of vapour. By eleven o'clock it was blowing strong to gale from the south, and on the windward side of the islands there was a heavy sea beginning to pile up; enough, I thought, for him to lose his bearings if he were trying to make his way homeward through it. I put a light in each window of the house, left the doors open, and dozed fitfully in front of the kitchen fire. By three o'clock in the morning there was the first faint paling of dawn, and I went out to get the boat, for by now I had somehow convinced myself that Mij was on the lighthouse island. That little cockleshell was in difficulties from the moment I launched her; I had open water and a beam sea to cross before I could reach the lee of the islands, and she was taking a slosh of water over her gunwale all the way. If I shipped oars to bale I made so much leeway that I was nearly ashore again before I had done, and after half an hour I was both wet and scared. The bigger islands gave some shelter from the south wind, but in the passages between them the north-running sea was about as much as the little boat would stand, and over the many rocks and skerries the water was foaming white and wicked-looking in the half light. A moment to bale and I would have been swept on to these black cusps and molars; the boat would have been crunched on them like a squashed matchbox, and I, who cannot swim a stroke, would have been feeding the lobsters. To complete my discomfort, I met a Killer whale. In order to keep clear of the reefs I had rowed well north of the small islands that lie to landward of the lighthouse; the water was calmer here, and I did not have to fight to keep the nose of the boat into the waves. The Killer broke the surface no more than twenty yards to the north of me, a big bull whose sabre fin seemed to tower a man's height out of the water; and, probably by chance, he turned straight for me. My nerves were strung and tensed, and I was in no frame of mind to assess the true likelihood of danger; I swung and rowed for the nearest island as though man were a Killer's only prey. I grounded on a reef a hundred yards from the tern island, and I was not going to wait for the tide to lift me. Slithering and floundering in thigh-deep water over a rock ledge I struggled until I had lifted the flat keel clear of the tooth on which it had grated; the Killer, possibly intent upon his own business and with no thought for me, cruised round a stone's throw away, I reached the tern island, and the birds rose screaming around me in a dancing canopy of ghostly wings, and I sat down on the rock in the dim windy dawn and felt as desolate as an abandoned child.

The lighthouse island was smothered in its jungle-growth of summer briars that grip the clothing with octopus arms and leave trails of blood-drops across hands and face; on it I felt like a dream walker who never moves, and my calling voice was swept away northwards on gusts of cold, wet wind. I got back to the house at nine in the morning, with a dead-weight boat more than half full of water and a sick emptiness in my mind and body. By now part of me was sure that Mij too had met the Killer, and that he was at this moment half digested in the whale's belly.

All that day until four o'clock in the afternoon I wandered and called, and with every hour grew the realization of how much that strange animal companion had come to signify to me. I resented it, resented my dependence upon this subhuman presence and companionship, resented the void that his absence was going to leave at Camusfeàrna. It was in this mood, one of reassertion of human independence, that about five in the evening I began to remove the remaining evidence of his past existence. I had taken from beneath the kitchen table his drinking bowl, had returned for the half-full bowl of rice and egg, had carried this to the scullery, what the Scots call the back kitchen, and was about to empty it into the slop pail, when I thought I heard Mij's voice from the kitchen behind me. I was, however, very tired, and distrustful of my own reactions; what I thought I had heard was the harshly whispered 'Hah?' with which he was accustomed to interrogate a seemingly empty room. The impression was strong enough for me to set down the bowl and hurry back into the kitchen. There was nothing there. I walked to the door and called his name, but all was as it had been before. I was on my way back to the scullery when I stopped dead. There on the kitchen floor, where I had been about to step, was a large, wet footprint. I looked at it, and I thought: I am very tired and very overwrought; and I went down on my hands and knees to inspect it. It was certainly wet, and it smelled of otter. I was still in a quadrupedal attitude when from the doorway behind me I heard the sound again, this time past mistaking— 'Hah?' Then Mij was all over me, drenched and wildly demonstrative, squeaking, bouncing round me like an excitable puppy, clambering on my shoulders, squirming on his back, leaping, dancing. I had been reassuring myself and him for some minutes before I realized that his harness was burst apart, and that for many hours, perhaps a day or more, he must have been caught like Absalom, struggling, desperate, waiting for a rescue that never came.

I am aware that this scene of reunion, and the hours that for me had preceded it, must appear to many a reader little short of nauseous. I might write of it and subsequent events with a wry dishonesty, a negation of my feeling for that creature, which might disarm criticism, might forestall the accusation of sentimentality and slushiness to which I now lay myself open. There is, however, a certain obligation of honesty upon a writer, without which his words are worthless, and beyond that my feeling for animals that I adopt would, despite any dissimulation that I might essay, reveal itself as intense, even crucial. I knew by that time that Mij meant more to me than most human beings of my acquaintance, that I should miss his physical presence more than theirs, and I was not ashamed of it. In the penultimate analysis, perhaps, I knew that Mij trusted me more utterly than did any of my own kind, and so supplied a need that we are slow to admit.

from OTTER COUNTRY

Miriam Darlington

Miriam Darlington (b. 1966) was brought up in Lewes and educated at Sussex University. She has lived in France, and the Isles
of Scilly, and is now settled in Devon as there may be more otters
there than anywhere else in the UK. She taught French and
English in secondary school for twelve years while writing poetry
and prose. A poetry collection, *Windfall* (2008), was followed
by her first narrative non-fiction book, *Otter Country* (2012),
and a PhD in nature writing from Exeter University. As well as
obsessively tracking wildlife and gaining several certificates in
field ecology, her second book, *Owl Sense*, was published in 2018.
She writes the Nature Notebook column for *The Times* and teaches
creative writing at Plymouth University, leading the MA course
and supervising several PhDs. She continues to write poetry and
can usually be found creeping along a riverbank watching birds or
sneaking up on otters.

The meadow comes to an end where the stream crosses the
farm track. If I want to continue, I must cross where the water
dips into the dark under a low bridge and heads into the
tidal marsh. It's too low for me to swim through, but an otter might.
I scramble down to the water on the other side of the bridge and find
spraint just where it should be, on a rock where the otter must have
left the water. There is also a rubbing place with a lot of stray hair, the
sort a moulting feline would leave on a favoured cushion. But what
cat would sleep in the wet, mossy armpit of a stream?

The wet pathway is only a few centimetres deep as it riffles away
and disappears into the marsh. I make my way through into the overgrown reeds and my feet begin to sink through the surface. This is
treacherous ground, unmapped swamp-territory. Strange drowned
trees poke out of the mud, their bleached limbs catch the light like

ivory bones. The reeds and sallow are soon taller than my head, and I am dwarfed, sinking lower and lower into the silt. It's easier to walk along the gravelly bed of a sister stream where the water has fanned into an unidentifiable number of trickles; the sound kaleidoscopes all around. This is moorhen and coot land. Their wide toe marks balance easily in the shifting wet. It's no good for heavy-footed intruders. This tangle has no path unless you are in the water at nose-level, and the marsh begins to unnerve me. An uncanny squealing makes the hairs on my neck prickle. It is not otter, and badger would not be out at this hour; listening to the scintillating array of voices, I press on into a world of waterbird language and alarm calls.

Where the reeds end the stream has collected into a vast, swirling pool behind an old dam wall and it is being sucked unnaturally down as if into a plughole, bursting through a submerged pipe and out of the marsh. At the point where the stream meets the banks of the wide, glittering river Dart, mud is everywhere. It glares and shines and dazzles. I crouch down to hear a thousand tiny mouths creaking with mud-sound. This is the view an otter might have as it came out of the marsh. At the edges, water and mud lose themselves together. Higher up, oak trees and rock are moored to the bank, and there are dry places between trunks to curl up. I place myself in the crook of a rock and a woody root, and my nostrils fur with earth-odours. If I were a hungry otter I would follow the rim of the crumbling wall and bank, blending myself with the contours, and later drop down a level onto the rocks to search for crayfish and eels as they emerge on the rising tide. I can smell otter in a tangle of fishy grass that lies pungently right beneath my feet. I move to the cover of an oak trunk and lean back. Right beside my seat the otter track comes out of the wide tidal stretch, just where the river curls in an elegant meander around the farmland and vineyards of the estate on the opposite bank. In the silt I can clearly see where the tracks begin on the tide line. The tracks move in a straight line up to the mouth of the tributary. For the first time, I notice there are two sets of tracks, and on closer inspection I decide it might be three. Some of the pad-marks are smaller. A mother and cubs!

The tracks move so closely together they mingle and cross one another, as if they were moving symbiotically. I can see the fusion of their mud-coloured forms moving together in my mind's eye, as they scurry back to the sheltering labyrinth of the marsh, the cubs following their mother's every move. The otters stopped to spraint here on the low wall, and disappeared into the reed beds in the valley bottom. Close to the tracks are those even smaller, scratchier marks that the light-fingered mink make. This is not the first time I have found mink and otter tracks so close together, and it intrigues me. It is as if the mink has been following in the track of the otter, maybe just out of sight, and perhaps by some clever trick disguising its own scent.

As the tide rises I wait. Time blurs, the water darkens and the day softens into something other than itself. Just as the light fades they come, on the threshold of dusk, out of the reeds, mud-coloured, so close to the ground in colour and shape they are barely distinguishable. My heart flips and my eyes struggle to focus. They do not sense me, but undulate over to the edge of the river, sleeking into the water as one. Whether they sense my presence or not, they are cat-footed and stealthy, with the bodily knowledge that danger could be anywhere.

I meld myself into the bank, trying not to breathe. A family of otters, so close to my home! I stretch up to peer as their heads resurface and the two cubs, three-quarters the size of their mother, move alongside her as shadows. Perhaps they know I'm here, the hint of my human scent drifting toward them.

A little while later, I decide to go in after them. I came prepared for this: out of my bag I pull a wetsuit, a hood and some water shoes. In a sheltered spot I shed my clothes and pull these on, stashing my dry things by the cliffs, and walk down to the water. I take the otter's way in, and slide in down the shallows in a slick of silt, head first into the water, into the brackish stench. Weed and mud waft into my face as the cold ripple of the incoming tide comes up to meet me. It lifts me into the cold, salty flow and seeps into my wetsuit, down my neck and all over my skin. For a moment fear freezes my limbs and air dislocates itself from my lungs.

The tide is drifting gently upriver. I relax a little as I feel the water carrying me. The suit makes me unnaturally buoyant, and I realise I can swim easily. Heading around the meander in front of me, nose at water level, I adjust to the temperature and move my legs. Otters learn to swim on the surface as cubs, and it takes them a while to learn the knack of tipping the nose slightly skyward, so the nostrils can still breathe. In this way, they make a ream of water in two lines that fan out behind them, like the wake of a subtle boat. Swimming like this, nose up on the current, takes hardly any effort at all, and below me, in this green-brown world, lie glutinous depths of eel-soft mud. I try not to touch its octopus-tentacle slime; mud and oil patterns slide over one another in dark slicks. I can't look at it, and when I feel things brush against me, whether it's the brown sides of fish, eels or evil-fingered drowned trees, I feel vertigo and cannot think. All the memory of the river is here, hidden, concealing time, stories, lives; old sunlight, life and earth rubbing up against one another in a rich, vibrant, dynamic muddle. I wonder if the otter can read all these layers, or if they are significantly different from place to place as it moves over the water-scape of the river in all its phases.

In patches the river is the colour of dark amber, moving constantly with reflections of geese, a cormorant drying its wings in a tree, flurries of starlings. I swim until I can swim no further, and haul out a short distance upriver, close to some woods on the edge of town. The otters are nowhere, but I can still smell them; the otter and cubs must enter and exit the water frequently on this stretch, to eat, spraint and aerate their fur.

from SWIMMING WITH SEALS

Victoria Whitworth

Victoria Whitworth (b. 1966) is a novelist and historian who specializes in Britain in the early Middle Ages. She studied English at Oxford and later lectured at the Centre for Nordic Studies on the Orkney campus of the University of the Highlands and Islands. Her academic research has primarily focused on Pictish, Scottish and Anglo-Saxon stone sculpture and as Victoria Thompson she is the author of *Dying and Death in Later Anglo-Saxon England* (2004). She has also published three historical novels (as V. M. Whitworth), *The Bone Thief* (2012), *The Traitors' Pit* (2014) and *Daughter of the Wolf* (2016) set in England's Dark Ages. *Swimming with Seals* (2017) is a memoir of swimming and the history and archaeology of Orkney.

When I first started swimming in the sea it was always a shock to hear that deep-lunged snort, sometimes only a few feet away; to see the dark head of a seal rise from the water: the huge eyes, alert nostrils, water dripping from whiskers and beading on sleek spotted fur. Seals gaze in a way that suggests intense curiosity. They are predators, with sharp teeth and strong jaws. But I rapidly grow comfortable being with them in the water. They're in their element, and I'm their guest. I never swim towards them, and although friends who are scuba divers report the seals coming close, mouthing the swimmers' flippers, allowing – even enjoying – physical contact, my seals are warier. Seals are confident when fully immersed, more cautious when bobbing on the surface, shy and easily spooked when hauled out on the rocks. I've never felt any threat, though if one comes too close for its own comfort and dives with a sudden, shocked thrust of its body, the thud of the displaced water is a visceral reminder of their strength and mass. And sometimes, when there are five or six of them, and they're feeling self-assured, diving and surfacing ever closer, I have to remind myself that they don't hunt in packs.

The seals are everywhere along the Orkney coast, sunning themselves on the rocks, or sleeping nose up in the shallows, or swimming along, following you as you walk by the shore. The best way to summon them is to take a dog down to the beach: the German word for common seal is *Seehund*, sea-hound, and the seals seem to recognize the affinity, popping up from the water, coming into the shallows, their eyes wide and fascinated. The two indigenous species are the common or harbour seals, and the grey seals, although occasionally exotic visitors like bearded seals come down from the Arctic. The grey and common seals haul out on the rocks together: from a distance it is hard to tell one from the other, and it's often said that *grey seals are common and common seals are grey*. But the more time you spend with them, the easier it is to tell them apart, even from a glimpse. The common seals are cuter, smaller, snub-nosed. Their nostrils converge, in a heart shape. When they lie on the rocks in the sun they lift their heads and tails at the same time, as though doing V-sits in the gym, working on their formidable abdominals.

The grey seals are much larger and more dignified. They have ponderous Roman profiles and haunted eyes. It is the grey seals who give rise to the selkie stories. It is they who are the *haaf fish*, creatures of the deep sea. They have souls. The common seals are 'only' animals, the *tang fish*, creatures without souls, named for the shallow-water weed among which they hunt crabs. Common seals can dive down as far as fifty metres, and keep under for ten minutes at a time. They stay in the sunlit zone, which extends to about 180 metres, but grey seals have been recorded diving to 400 metres, well into the gloom, cold and pressure of the twilight zone. They can remain submerged for an hour. Common seals forage up to sixty kilometres from the beaches on which they haul out; grey seals have been recorded 145 kilometres away from the shore.

Common seals are impressive enough. Grey seals are hard-core.

Seals are not the apex predators in these waters, not by a long way. That honour goes to the orca, and orcas, unlike seals, definitely hunt in packs. No matter how often we Polar Bears reassure each other that *no wild orca has ever attacked a human being*, if I were to spot a dorsal fin in the distance I'd be leaving the water as fast as I could flounder. An orca's open mouth is a metre across, its teeth up to five centimetres long.

A Shetland sea-swimmer shared a story recently; she'd been swimming in her usual patch when she noticed a crowd of people on the shore, pointing at her, waving. *I swim here every day*, she thought, *what are they fussing about?* They'd spotted what she had somehow missed: the dorsal fin of a male orca – as high as a tall man – speeding fast in her direction. He dived, only a stone's throw from her, and the onlookers were convinced that she would be eaten. She didn't realize what was going on until a pulse of energy in the water made her look down. The orca was only a few feet below her, sussing her out. Before she could react, he swam away.

Still, despite the heart-race, the throat-lump, the adrenalin-rush, I can't help thinking, even here and now wading into their territory, that there are many worse ways to die than in an orca's jaws. No doctor, no drugs, no long slow decline of power or personality. Observers of big cats hunting down gazelle in the Kenyan savannah have noted how, despite the fury of the chase, in the last moments the prey animal appears resigned, calm, just as a kitten stops fighting when its mother picks it up by the scruff, or a sheep enters a quasi-catatonic state when the shearer pulls her into a sitting position, or a shark turned over on its back goes into tonic immobility. Human survivors of attacks by wild animals have reported something similar: in the jaws of the beast there is no panic, no struggle, only an eerie calm. Shock, perhaps. But I imagine also that Freudian Thanatos, the death wish, comes into play. All our lives we fear the thing under the bed, the shape behind the door, the spider that scuttles out from the skirting board, the creature that lurks in deep water, the vengeful god.

Thanatos, the joy of consummation: *Here it is at last.*

As a very small child, before we moved to Kenya, when we still lived in the tall narrow house in North London, I was dreadfully afraid of wolves. My terrors were the wolves of fairy tale, skulking and devious, monsters of teeth and red wet tongue, whose only thought was to devour children. But they were real wolves, too. My father used to take us to Regent's Park to see the bits of London Zoo which could be viewed from the park without paying. He wasn't really a cheapskate, he had his moments of flamboyant generosity, but he was always looking for an advantage, some way of beating the system. The wolf enclosure was one of the most accessible: those leggy grey creatures through the wire fence, running among the trees. When I expressed my terror, my mother would ask in frustration whether I really thought the wolves were capable of escaping from the zoo? Would they *really* make their way to Islington, more specifically into my bedroom, and eat me? Out of all the little girls in the world? To which the only possible answers were *yes*, *yes*, and *yes*. The knowledge was self-evident to me, embedded in some deep part of the hominid brain. My mother thought it was 1970 and London N1, but I might as well have been an Australopithecine child, four million years ago, on the Plio-Pleistocene grasslands of East Africa, knowing full well that the noises in the dark were made by what the palaeontologists call the *hypercarnivores*: giant lions, leopards and hyenas. This is where the nightmares are born.

Once we'd settled in Nairobi my fear of wolves ebbed in the face of a developing passion for wildlife. I got used to a suburban garden in which the pepper tree by the back door was full of caterpillars with poisonous bristles, the Cape gooseberry bush harboured a boomslang, baboon spiders lurked in tunnels on the lawn, *siafu* – army ants – marched through the grass in Napoleonic columns. I ignored the caterpillars, and backed cautiously away from the boomslang; my father rushed me to hospital once with a nasty spider-bite, and the mighty-jawed *siafu* got into my little sister's hair when she lay down on the lawn, though I was more distressed by their devouring a whole litter of our rabbits' babies. At school, we were taught two alarm drills: the fire bell, for which we went outside; and the lion bell, for which we came in. We never had a fire, but there were lions on the rounders field once, and the wardens from Nairobi National Park came in a green Land-Rover with a cage on the back to retrieve them. The nightmare that the wolves had once embodied retreated in the face of the waking world and these manageable dangers.

But being eaten by an orca would be to meet that nightmare face to face, to look it in the eye and name it, to say, *I know you.* Surely there's virtue in this. I talked it through once with Yvonne, another Polar Bear, a poet, while we were at the Sands of Evie, swimming at a summer-leisurely pace out to the buoys that mark the lobster creels. We further speculated that there would be other advantages to this death. No funeral expenses. The satisfaction of providing a good meal for a species that is threatened, if not yet endangered. We'd make the front page of *The Orcadian.* A worthwhile contribution to scientific understanding of orca behaviour. Nonetheless, as we rounded the buoy and started our way back, we agreed that we would rather the orcas held off at least until our children had left secondary school. And we were both swimming rather faster, and looking over our shoulders more often.

I knew nothing about orcas when we first moved here. It's an obsession which has moved in on me gradually, fuelled by that occasional glimpse of a dorsal fin, the arcing back, the flick of flukes, and by the realization that globally we are coming to a better understanding of these extraordinary beings. I track the different communities through the Facebook pages of the scientists studying them – rejoicing to learn that Granny of the Southern Residents J pod is still going strong aged 105 (and grieving to hear of her death, just as this book went to press), swimming up and down the western coasts of North America; delighted when I see that Mousa, one of our local matriarchs, has a new baby; sorrowful to hear that for yet another year the little Hebridean community is calfless. I am beyond intrigued to learn that orcas are not only matriarchal, they are menopausal. The females lose the ability to reproduce aged around fifty, just as we do; but they go on being the power in the nuclear family and the wider pod. Both sons and daughters stay with their mother for life, and young male orcas work as nannies for their younger siblings and cousins.

But – let's be honest – they are also really, *really* scary. Writing in the first century AD Pliny describes orcas in the Mediterranean attacking other whales when they are calving. His usually precise language breaks down under the strain: 'its image cannot be properly represented or described other than as an immense mass of flesh with fierce teeth'. 'Carnis inmensae dentibus truculentae' – all hiss and click and the tap of tongue on palate, as though anticipating the monster breaking the surface. Olaus Magnus's map from the 1530s shows the *orcha* (*sic*), looking like a marine triceratops with fangs, attacking a whale, a *balena* (which also has teeth), just to the west of Orkney.

They will pursue a grey whale and her newborn at such a pace that the calf cannot stop to feed, and finally eat the baby when it is starving and exhausted. In Argentina they intentionally strand themselves to pluck sea lion pups from beaches. Off San Francisco a solo female orca took down a great white shark: rammed it in the gills to stun it, flipped it over into tonic immobility, ate its liver, left the rest for the swarming gulls. They'll kill a sperm whale, and only eat its tongue. Do I really want to enter these creatures' realm?

This is not a book about *overcoming* fear of predators, or cold water, or the dark – or death, which is the shapeless thing that lurks behind all these masks. The word with which I am grappling is *reclaiming*, as land is reclaimed from the sea. Awareness of death cannot and should not be overcome, and I am learning as I voyage on through middle age that I don't want to overcome it. What I want to do is map it, colonize it, rename it, make it my own. That dark thread, the panic, the sense of the scree slipping beneath my feet, the lurch, the visceral tug, the undertow; these are utterly woven into the fabric of self. I do not want a map that is all rich pasture and well-watered uplands, bright expanses of sand and sunlit shallows. I need access to the shady side of the valley, the crevasse, the depths where light never reaches, where monsters lurk. Reciting the names of the levels of the sea reclaims them for me, makes them into a meditative technique for taking consciousness down into the depths:

Sunlit zone.

Twilight zone.

Midnight zone.

Abyss.

And, underlying the abyss, there are the deep-sea trenches, the *hadal zone*, named for Hades, lord of the underworld, the god who stole Persephone/Proserpine and conned her into giving up her freedom in return for six seeds of pomegranate, until her mother the earth goddess Demeter came and haggled successfully for Persephone to live half her year in the sun, half in the darkness. Our technical, scientific language has potent myth lurking just under the skin, like the fine fan of facial muscles that underpins and gives power to human expression.

Reclaiming. Giving myself something to stand on. Gaining an understanding of why, every time a loving friend tells me I am *strong, clever, confident, beautiful,* I lurch and stagger internally. Over the years the pressure of trying to achieve the expected standards – both external and (much more dangerous) the hopelessly high ones I set myself – has become impossible. I am never aware of what I manage to do, only of the yawning gap between vision and reality, and I live in permanent terror that someone will notice. The strain of maintaining the façade: scaffolding and pit props holding the stucco and sash windows in place while behind all is rubble, fly-tipping and fireweed. My relationship with reality has become ever more tenuous: going into cold water shocks me back into myself and what really exists, here and now. What really matters.

This is not a book about overcoming the fear of the dark. This is a book about meeting that nightmare face to face in the waking world, looking it in the eye and naming it, saying, *I know you.*

Islands and
Coastlines

Illustration overleaf: *The Isthmus, Skomer*

from BIRD WATCHING ON SCOLT HEAD

E. L. Turner

Emma Turner (1867–1940) was a pioneering writer, photographer, ornithologist and conservationist who grew up in Kent. A chance encounter with Richard Kearton, one of the most notable early wildlife photographers, encouraged her to capture wildlife on camera. This led her to spend summers living on *The Water Rail*, a houseboat that she designed on a tiny island that now bears her name on the Norfolk Broads. Working with local gamekeeper Jim Vincent, she rediscovered the bittern as a breeding bird in England and obtained photographic proof. She wrote eight books including *Broadland Birds* (1924) and *Birdwatching on Scolt Head* (1928), where she worked as a warden for two summers. She lived alone on this remote tidal island, protecting the tern colonies from foxes, day-trippers and egg-collectors. Her photographs and writing appeared in numerous publications from *Country Life* to *British Birds*.

SCOLT HEAD

After a meeting of the Norfolk and Norwich Naturalists' Society in December, 1923, the Secretary, Dr. Sidney Long, said to me: 'I cannot find a watcher for Scolt Head.' In a fit of recklessness I replied, 'Why not have me?' In a half-joking way we began to discuss the matter, and after a prolonged chat while the museum officials were evidently getting impatient and beginning to turn out the lights, the conversation had assumed such serious proportions that a definite answer, yes or no, was to be placed before the next committee meeting. The post was to be entirely a voluntary one, my only stipulation being that instead of paying me, a man should be paid to come to and fro daily with letters and supplies. It was never suggested that the appointment should be a permanent one. I was only a stop-gap until a suitable man could be found. My decision was made in three days. The committee appointed me as their official watcher on February 15th, and my duties began on April 1st, 1924. Most of my friends thought this a very suitable day! The committee was very generous to me. I cannot lay too much stress on this point, because of misunderstandings which arose in some quarters when visitors saw that it was too big a task for one person to carry out satisfactorily. It was essentially a pioneer job, and its diffi-culties could be tackled only as they cropped up. It is one thing to acquire these beauty spots, such as Scolt Head, Blakeney Point, and many others; it is another thing to maintain them for the nation. The public for whose benefit they are acquired, does not grasp this fact. Money, and yet more money, is needed. But for the indefati-gable work of the honorary secretary, Dr. Long, many of these nature reserves would not be laid at the feet of the public to-day. They would have shared the fate of all the one-time lovely coastal villages of Norfolk. But now, if any one wishes 'to stand and stare,' there is a glorious stretch of isolated seashore where you can lie in the bosom of the great Earth Mother and absorb her vitality as Antaeus of old did every time he came in contact with her. And, thank Heaven, there are still numbers of people who have not given the sordid boon of their hearts away. Go to Scolt Head, Blakeney Point, and Cley, and you can still

'Have sight of Proteus rising from the sea
Or hear old Triton blow his wreathed horn.'

But do not disturb the birds in their sanctuaries. There should be no need of sanctuaries for birds in this land of bird and animal lovers. The places which these summer residents seek for their nurseries should need no protection. But they do. The acquisitive collector who must adorn his cabinet with their spoils, the stupid yokel who stamps on eggs and young for the mere pleasure of destroying them, even the thoughtless lover of nature who elects to picnic amongst the nesting birds—all these tiresome people have to be eliminated or moved on, and money is needed to do it.

I, as the first watcher on Scolt Head, was given a free hand with the furnishing. On February 27th some of us met and unpacked the big cases of household plenishing. Snow lay on the hills and marshes, an unusual sight on saltings and one which gave a touch of even greater isolation to the island and accentuated the bastion-like end of the actual Head.

My position as watcher was after all nothing to make a fuss about, and certainly did not warrant the misguided enthusiasm of the press. I was never lonely and seldom alone. Ten days was the longest consecutive period of solitude. From the beginning it was obvious to me that I could not look after twelve hundred acres and do all I undertook to do unaided. What really gave rise to the myth of 'The Loneliest Woman in England' was due entirely to the vivid imagination of the first newspaper man who came hot on my trail from crowded Fleet Street to the solitude of Hickling Broad. He arrived somewhere about 11 p.m. on Saturday night (March 31st, 1924) and insisted on interviewing me in my cabin boat. It was a rough night and this intrepid reporter had a wet and windy crossing and a very morose reception from me and my dogs. The stormy night and the darkness probably fired his imagination and by adding a hundred per cent to the circumstances under which he found me, he painted the first picture of the lonely watcher. Others followed in a bewildering stream till in desperation I said to the ferry-man, 'Drown the next.' He smiled and said, 'All right, Miss.' Anyway the stream ceased for the time being. One who seemed vexed at finding others of his craft with me, besides several personal friends who came to help with my packing, only stayed five minutes. He exclaimed crossly, 'Call yourself lonely, you're one of a crowd, there's many a woman in London lonelier than you.' To whom I replied, 'I have never said I was lonely, it's the invention of your trade.' When the motor-lorry conveying me and my mate, my two terriers and three nine-day-old puppies reached Brancaster, we found three more reporters awaiting us. By that time I was hardened and told them how I hated them, but they were forgiving and willing to be made use of as carriers. We missed the high tide, so all the heavy stuff had to be carried nearly a quarter of a mile across the saltings. They were cheerful and willing helpers and entered into the fun of the journey. It was a beautiful April day and everything wore its most becoming smile.

The next day my mate had to return home, so I was alone and busy 'assembling' the oil cooking stove and finding places for my luggage. The crockery failed to greet me and did not turn up for nearly a month. We borrowed a few plates and mugs and collected oyster shells which were used as extra plates and soap-dishes. One of those oyster shells is in use as a soap-dish to this day. It is wonderful what a stretch of seashore can produce in the way of necessities—even to smoke-pearl buttons. That first day of solitude has bitten deep into my memory; it filled me with wild joy to think that for months I should possess the island with all its mystery and loveliness. Every isolated spot has its own presiding spirit, and, however much one might at times kick against the pricks, the spirit which brooded over Scolt Head was essentially one of rest and peace. Not an indolent peace, but rather that of rest in motion.

I should indeed have been very lonely without my dogs. When I first landed I carried in my haversack three nine-day-old black-and-tan terrier puppies, while two of the newspaper men brought over the parents in their kennel. There were a few heart-burnings over my dogs, but after all we needed something to play with and there was ample room for them, and later on plenty of work. All five were taught to scour the marrams and hunt the acres and acres of *suaeda* bushes where migrants skulked. But for them we should never have flushed certain birds. The two older dogs always accompanied me to the Ternery and kept watch if I slept. They soon learnt that commotion amongst the birds might mean unlawful disturbance, and they often spotted a stray prowling dog or distant visitor before I did. The foolish restlessness of the Terns annoyed them. They would spring up from their sun-baked hollow, erect, alert, and if there was no apparent cause for the disturbance flopped down again with a grunt, as much as to say, 'What fools these birds are, making all that fuss about nothing.' One dog I lost for nine days; presumably he was down a rabbit-hole. He ultimately returned at dawn, thin and weak, with a bit nicked off the cornea of one eye and consequently blind for a time. He completely recovered eventually.

The island with its long backbone of sand-hills flanked by the sea on the north, and wide salt marshes on the south, possesses beauty both of form and colour. One never tired of watching the wind tossing the tawny manes of the marram grass, and driving the great galleon-like clouds across the sky, or chasing their shadows over the wet sand. The gradual changes which almost imperceptibly crept over the mud flats were a revelation to me. In early April they looked uniformly dun coloured unless touched up by sunset or sunrise. But as the stately pageant of summer passed by, each month brought its own flowers and revealed new beauties. October decked them in a riot of colour as sea purslane (*Obione*), samphire (*Salicornia*), the sea lavenders and rabbit-bitten *suaeda*, changed to grey and gold, orange and scarlet, copper and brown, while the tide filled the runnels with blue and silver. The great salt marsh below the hut was like a vast oriental carpet spread at one's feet. We called this marsh the great jig-saw puzzle because of the interminable turnings and twistings of the innumerable tiny channels intersecting it. In the hey-day of summer it was the most perfectly planned landscape garden imaginable, with its overhanging banks, massed borders of sea lavender and meandering streams. We loved to paddle about in it when it was half covered at the spring tides, taking care not to slip into the deeper channels. There was a wonderful fascination too in watching the tide crawling over the marsh and trickling lazily along the tiny runnels; so quiet at times, so relentless in its oncoming. When the spring tides reach their limit nothing is left exposed but the sand-hills. This occurs about 9 a.m. and 9 p.m. twice a month, but as the water recedes very quickly from the saltings, some portion is soon left clear. During the fortnight of neap tides the whole area between Norton Creek on the south, and the coast line on the north is dry enough to walk over. It is Norton Creek that makes Scolt Head an island. Midway between Burnham Overy and Deepdale the tides in Norton Creek meet, one arm of the creek empties itself at Burnham Overy, and the other runs out by Brancaster. During the high tides the creek seems just to spill itself over the saltings. This impressed me very much the first time I saw it.

I was lying on the Head watching a rather rough sea beating its way up all along the coast, when, turning to look over the mud flats, I found the whole area covered right up to the sand-hills. It was as if while one arm of an invading army fought its way desperately towards its goal, the other had crept up insidiously from the rear and completed the enveloping movement. As this was my first experience of a high tide I naturally wondered how long this splendid isolation would last.

We of course made the best use we could of the spring tides, and tried to arrange for all heavy luggage to coincide with the fortnightly high tide, because then a boat could sail right up to the steps leading to the hut on the south, deliver its cargo and get away before the water receded.

If gales accompany the spring tides they cause considerable coast erosion by under-cutting the hills and loosening huge masses of sand. There is however a certain amount of compensation for this waste, when blown sand drifts back into the hills with suitable winds. There is constant movement one way or the other, but in some vulnerable places a good deal of artificial work is necessary in order to prevent waste.

The duties I undertook were fairly onerous. First and foremost there was the finding of nests and eggs and looking after these. That alone in the breeding season is one person's job. Then there was the housework and cooking. A man watcher always has someone to cook for him, in fact what sensible man ever does *any* work that a woman will do for him? Visitors had to be looked after and catered for. The catering alone sometimes was difficult to cope with, especially during spells of warm weather. There was no cool larder, and consequently in summer food would not keep more than a day. Sometimes, in the midst of cooking an evening meal, a boatload of trippers would be seen rounding the far beach and making for the Ternery. By running hard and making a bee-line for the Ternery (given a low tide), the distance could be covered in seventeen minutes and the visitors intercepted as they landed. Ultimately someone was always on the spot during the hours when boats could land there. We took it in turns to watch all day and put up a little tent which afforded shade and some shelter.

At first all firewood had to be collected from the shore. Originally there was a big baronial open fireplace in the hut. The fire always smoked, except with an east wind and with the door wide open. The bringing in of logs was severe labour, because we had to wander two or three miles in order to find any after the first week or two. The improvised stretcher made out of a canvas bath (a useless adjunct owing to lack of water) and two broom handles would not bear a great weight, nor could we carry many heavy logs at a time. We made dumps of wood all along the shore and expected every man visitor to do his bit in carrying them home. But after a morning's struggle getting a load up to the hut, if the fire was in a good mood, it licked up all the pile in less than an hour. One member of the committee undertook to saw up some logs for us on Easter Monday. He came, he sawed (or tried to) and gave it up, saying, 'Here, this must stop, it's impossible.' Sea-soaked wood simply turns and blunts the best of saws. As a matter of fact it was impossible to keep that fire fed, and a terrible waste of time and energy. Things reached a climax one night. Almost a full gale was raging and it rained as it only can rain on Scolt Head. I had to go out and lace down the awning over my kennel as it was loosened. Empty boxes and tubs were hurtled along the hill and on to the shore. Almost as soon as I had closed the door my mate cried out. Looking through the window I saw that the whole of the fire had blown across our living-room, and hot embers were careering round one of the little sleeping cabins. I dashed back, and, after our combined efforts had closed and locked the door, we hastily swept up the burning wood and extinguished what remained of the fire. And that was the end of the baronial fireplace! By the end of June a small cooking range was put in and the terribly draughty chimney filled up. All our cooking was done on the very efficient oil cooker, but heat which starts half a yard from the floor does not warm one's feet. Spring on the east coast can be arctic, whilst the autumn is often balmy and mild. Our greatest trial was the shortage of water. Theoretically there should be fresh water in the sand-hills, lying on top of the salt water. Practically there was none where the shaft was sunk below the hut. After a high tide there was some salt water which we used at first for cooking vegetables. Ultimately this fell into disuse. The big open concrete shaft was a great attraction to small boys and various things were thrown down it.

The water from the oak shingled roof of the hut was thick and brown to start with owing to the tannin in the new oak. When soap or soda was added it took on that dirty greenish tinge that was characteristic of mid-Victorian unrefined treacle. This was all the water we had for domestic purposes. Even that was limited, especially during a dry spell. It should at least have had the redeeming qualities of soft water, but during the first two months it cracked the skin and even the flesh round our finger nails. All drinking water had to be brought from the mainland until August 1925. By drinking water I mean all that was required for cooking purposes. We tried to make two nine-gallon barrels last a fortnight, that is, between the spring tides. Often this was impossible, and consequently our henchman had to carry a barrel across from the Far Beach or from Butcher's Beach—the two principal landing-places, a distance of a mile in one instance and nearly half a mile in the other. If any visitor dared to leave any water in his or her tumbler, it was either saved over for the next meal or the visitor was taken by the scruff of the neck and made to swallow it. People living in towns and using twenty or thirty gallons to a bath cannot realize what it means to conserve every drop. We were always short of water. A basin of roof water was used repeatedly by several of us for hand-washing, until it was fairly stiff! Minor tragedies sometimes occurred. One June day my mate and I had to go ashore for the day. An unexpected visitor came for the night just as we were starting to walk across the sands. This lady said she could fend for herself; we told her that water was sure to come soon but that there was not a drop in the hut. But when we returned at 6 p.m. supplies had not come, and she had nothing to drink till 9 p.m. The committee then supplied me with a case of bottled water for emergencies, but soon afterwards Mr. Douglas Carruthers put up sloping sheets of corrugated iron on the hill-side, these were linked up with big cisterns, and from that time onwards there was always a plentiful supply of good drinking water. These little trials are amusing if you are merely a week-end visitor, but for those of us who were resident for weeks on end the joke quickly palled.

The publicity given by the press to Scolt Head brought many visitors; these we classified under three headings—the merely curious, bird lovers, and those who were really interested in the work of the Watcher. The first merely gaped and went away, and the second were shown enough to satisfy them. Of those belonging to the third order I have happy memories. There were pleasant talks and merry scratch meals in the hollow by my tiny look-out hut near the Ternery. They were of all sorts and conditions. One enthusiastic mechanic suddenly appeared in next to nothing, having somehow waded up to his arm-pits from the Brancaster golf links side. He retired behind a blade of grass, re-arranged himself, and stayed for hours regaling us with tales of his boyhood's escapades in search of bird lore; hard-won knowledge gained before school hours or, in later life, during scanty hours of leisure.

Throughout the breeding season of 1925 there was always some-one watching the Ternery early and late. Often there were two of us, and if, as occasionally happened, a suspicious looking party landed, a sign to my mate would bring her lounging casually in my wake, able thus to keep an eye on the tail end of the party.

A bird-reserve under the National Trust is not ideal. The watcher's powers are limited. Unfortunately for the birds, as soon as an area is preserved all and sundry want to visit it. This is quite natural. Subscribers want to see that they are getting their money's worth, and bird lovers like to see the birds. Both types of visitors call up all their conductor's reserves of patience and tact. It is heart-breaking sometimes to look round an egg-strewn shore after a party has been conducted over the breeding grounds. Visitors, with the best inten-tions possible, cannot help doing damage, especially to newly hatched and perfectly camouflaged young. One day a man badly wanted to see the eggs and young of lesser terns. I took him to one of their colonies and pointed out the nests. The poor man was suddenly seized with fright and remained for a considerable time with one leg suspended in the air, not daring to set foot anywhere.

The inhabitants of Deepdale and Brancaster were unswervingly loyal to the Trust. During the first weeks of my residence numbers of village women came to inspect the hut. They were far more interested in *my* domestic arrangements than in those of the birds. Most of them left me with a pitying smile or an openly expressed 'Rather you than me,' so that I was surprised and gratified when a quiet looking dreamy-eyed young woman murmured 'You can never be lonely near the water.' Children, too, came over on Saturdays and told me about their little lives, and what 'teacher' said about this and that, and how they had seen lots of marked eggs but 'never touched them.' I missed no eggs till Whit-Sunday 1925, when I was left alone with a party of fifteen, some of whom were markedly inimical to the whole scheme of local bird protection.

There was much controversy at Blakeney just then over the food of the terns. The Brancaster men seemed rather amused about all these heart-burnings. While their brethren along the shore were complaining that the birds destroyed too much fish, Deepdale men were manuring their gardens with the coveted 'whitebait,' pailfuls of which they dredged out of the harbour and channel.

During my time at Scolt Head daily supplies were brought or sent by Harry Loose. He did his best for us but seldom came himself, except on Sundays or at high tides. The daily service was a bit irregular but it never failed. The committee thought I should have some method of signalling, and suggested various devices such as Verey lights and pistols. Finally it was decided that a flag should be hoisted daily from the Head just to show that I was alive. In addition I had the code flags N.C. in case of distress. In the beginning I told Loose that if ever he saw *two* flags hoisted he was to come post-haste with the doctor and coroner. The second summer I had quite forgotten my instructions and thoughtlessly hauled up a tea-cloth above the Union Jack. This was a pre-arranged signal to inform a friend at Overy that I was coming to tea. Being Sunday, Loose came himself in his beautiful white thigh boots and his hair of Scandinavian gold. His bronzed face and his hair were streaming with perspiration, as he had run most of the way from the far beach, remembering my injunctions with regard to two flags. Naturally he was annoyed at finding me quietly writing in the hut. I grovelled.

There was only one occasion when I was unable to climb up the Head and hoist the flag. Nothing happened; Loose was away at sea and his subordinate failed to notice the blank. About mid-day two kindly strangers happened to come along and one stayed with me till medical aid arrived. I had been bitten the day before by a specially vindictive fly and was unable to walk for a week. Happily two able-bodied visitors came for the week-end, and they did most of the work till I could hop about.

There was one day when about 10 a.m. the flag flew at half-mast. It had been hoisted at dawn on a lovely misty October morning before we set off on our migration round. As we returned I called attention to the drooping flag and ran up the hill to tighten the halliards, which having dried since dawn, had caused the flag to drop. At the top I suddenly came face to face with my henchman, Pells, who had approached from the opposite side. His look of horror soon gave place to relief. Evidently he thought that I had lowered the flag with my last breath and that my corpse would be found at the foot of the flagstaff.

The second year 'Mabel' brought our supplies and in many ways added to our comfort. She could handle a boat and carry heavy weights, and of her own freewill cleared up the hut and wrestled with that bugbear of daily life—the washing-up. Being a woman she saw what had to be done and did it.

There was always something of interest or amusement to be seen. One day, as I was walking along the shore towards Smuggler's Gap, I came upon the largest and most venerable crab I have ever seen, dead or alive. The tide was ebbing and this ancient crustacean was left high and dry. It had lost one big claw and only waved its antennae feebly. On either side of it stood a great black-backed gull apparently waiting for its demise. I spied the gulls from afar as they stood erect and motionless. Now and again they seemed to cast furtive and jealous glances at each other. They did not move until I was close up to them. I gingerly picked up the crab and, walking into the sea up to my knees, flung it as far out as I could. On my return an hour later the crab was again left stranded with the gulls in attendance. Curiosity urged me to sit down and see what happened, but pity gained the day. Again I took it into the sea, but what its ultimate fate was I cannot tell. There was no sign of it on the shore the next day.

Small crabs and sea trout were our great delicacies, and sometimes when food was short I could get several yard-long fish for three half-pence. They were quite good eating, but their veins turned emerald green in the cooking, which rather put off some of my guests. Samphire (*Salicornia*) we considered a great delicacy when it was in its prime. The natives like it pickled, but we preferred it fresh.

There were of course leisure hours between the strenuous walks. These were frequently spent in some sheltered spot on the Head where rest and observations could be indulged in simultaneously. There is a great fascination about the fringes of the world, and the fringe of coast forming my horizon landwards was full of beauty. The gently undulating hills had charm of colour and outline. During my first season I watched the first faint pale green of the springing corn through all its colour changes till the uplands were a blaze of gold and the ripe harvest was gathered in. The woodlands chanted the epic of the seasons from April to October There was one great rectangular field of blood-red poppies on the slope of the hill-side which was a joy to us though probably a grief to the farmer. There was also, to me, a mystic road winding over the uplands and passing out of view between two tall sentinel trees. It seemed to be the one link with the big world beyond. Roads, next to birds, are my ruling passion. Often I fell to musing over the great network of green roads which intersect all that coastal area and run far inland—not only the well-known and Romanized Peddars Way but many others, the origin of which is forgotten. One's mind would often turn to the Count of the Saxon Shore and to the fort of Branodunum commanding the entrance to the Wash, the site of which was visible to me.

> 'Trackway and camp and city lost.
> Salt marsh where now is corn.'

The regiment of Dalmatian Horse stationed at that then desolate outpost must often have scoured the uplands both inland and along the coast. Swift communication was very necessary in those days, and some of these old green roads may have been in more direct communi-cation with Brancaster than the Peddars Way, which is four miles west of the fort. A lost road once connected Brancaster with Caister.

Then there was the sea, and on rare occasions one saw the whole outline of the coast from the Wash to Skegness, thirty-five miles away. Once I saw this in a mirage upside down. Ordinarily it was only visible from the hills, but on that occasion I was lying by my tent on the Ternery. It was an extraordinary and beautiful sight. All the trees along that part of the Lincolnshire coast and the houses in Skegness were plainly visible. The mirage lasted about fifteen minutes.

Only once was I seized with panic. I was alone walking towards the harbour bar. The tide was far out, everything was still and a thin white mist enshrouded land and sea. The thin vapour seemed to add to the immensity. Nothing moved or uttered a sound. Suddenly a single Jack snipe got up at my feet and flew silently away as is its wont. The tiny bird and I seemed 'Alone, on a wide, wide sea.' I do not know why, but terror seized me and I fled back to the warmth of the hut.

When there was nothing doing in the way of birds we amused ourselves picking up the innumerable carnelians which may be found on the beach, especially after a gale.

The flowers too were a joy; many of them were new to me. The most beautiful were the sea holly and sea convolvulus (*Calystegia soldanella*). I had never seen so much sea holly anywhere. One could not be dull during the long hours spent on the Ternery while its delicate and indescribable 'powder blue' stretched across the marrams like a faint mist. Certain hillocks of sand too were covered with the great white pink-striped trumpets of sea convolvulus. Then there were the sea lavenders. I never found more than three out of the four, but they sufficed. In many places the shingle was carpeted with the delicate *Statice reticulata*, a rare variety elsewhere. The sea heath (*Frankenia laevis*) was new to me. It covered the shingle ridges in places with its delicate pink blooms. The marshes east of House Hills were ablaze with thrift. The great masses of golden ragwort, *Senecio jacobæa*, were always ruined by the larvae of the Cinnabar Moth. The only plant we each and all disliked and cursed was hounds-tongue (*Cynoglossum officinale*). It grew everywhere. The flower is dull, and the seeds are a nuisance. They clung to our clothes till at times we could not move and had to clear each other of these rough spiky pests. They even walked up our sleeves and down our necks, causing much discomfort.

There were many other flowers of course, a detailed account of which has been already published.*

Time softens everything. In the strange warp and woof of life it is the bright threads which retain their colours. So looking back on the Scolt Head episode I remember best the sunlit sea and sands, the wind in the marrams, the white blur of shimmering wings, the faint glimpses behind the veil enshrouding the great mystery of migration; and last, but not least, the constant kindly remembrances from friends and also from utter strangers.

My appointment as official watcher came to an end on November 9th, 1925. The committee had before that found a good successor to me in Robert Chesney, who is in every way the man for the task.

---

* 'Vegetation of Scolt Head Island' by F.G. Deighton and A.M. Clapham. *Transactions of Norfolk and Norwich Naturalists' Society*, vol. XII, part I.

HYPNAGOGIA

Caspar Henderson

Educated at Cambridge University, **Caspar Henderson** is the author of *The Book of Barely Imagined Beings* (2013) and *A New Map of Wonders* (2017). He has written about the environment, science, energy and human rights for many years, and has been a regular reviewer of books about science and nature. He has also worked as a senior editor at OpenDemocracy, for BBC Radio 4's *Costing the Earth* programme and for Oxford University. His next books, *A Book of Noises* and *The Green Ways*, will be published in 2022. He likes running and singing. He was born on Midsummer's Day, 1963.

Seen from space, northern Norfolk domes like a skull against the sea, a clean edge between land and water. But Google-Earth it and zoom in, and the top of the crown bursts into fractal complexity. West of Blakeney, which lies a little forward of where the parietal and frontal bones would meet, the smooth clean curve of the coast all the way from Yarmouth on the back of the skull to the east yields to marshes, creeks, mud flats, shingle banks and sand dunes: an intricately reticulated shoreline that contrasts with both the sweeping coastline to the east and the rectangles and polygons of human farming and settlement inland.

Running east–west overall, the northern coast may look higgledy-piggledy in its fine detail, but there is something like a pattern or process at the medium scale, at least in the stretch from Blakeney to Brancaster about sixteen miles further west. Between these two, a form, or the ghost of it, occurs three times as Blakeney Point, Bob Hall's Sand, and Scolt Head Island. Each one, seen from high above, increases in size from east to west and then curls over, like a standing wave curving over on its crest. Taken in a row they resemble what fluid dynamicists call a Kelvin-Helmholtz instability, which arises when two fluids slide past each other at different speeds. The form is common in nature. It is visible in the atmosphere of the planet Jupiter and has recently been discovered in slow-breaking waves on the Atlantic sea floor.

Each of these 'waves' of the Norfolk coast is different. Blakeney Point is a long shingle rampart enclosing dunes and areas of marsh. Bob Hall's Sand is a broad sand terrace that only fully emerges at low water. Scolt Head is a true island and, indeed, one of very few islands on the east coast of England between Mersea in Essex and the Farne Islands in Northumbria. Separated by tidal creeks, topped with sand dunes and sheltering intensely-curved and profusely-branching channels in the marshes on its landward side, Scolt Head Island is, according to English Nature, which manages it as a National Nature Reserve, 'the prime example of an offshore barrier island in the UK… situated on a very dynamic coastline and steadily growing westward.' It is about four miles long and three-quarters of a mile wide at its broadest point. There is nowhere else in the British archipelago quite like it, although several of the Frisian islands on the Dutch and German coasts are strikingly similar. Complex and subtly shaded patterning of many kinds is visible even in fairly crude satellite images, enticing the brain to see shapes that transform into others even before they are fully formed. Viewed in aerial and satellite photos, Scolt Head Island looks like the leaping cat depicted in the Jaguar car marque or like a stomatopod (a mantis shrimp), with the hooked sand-and-shingle forms laid down as the island has moved westward as its legs. At all times the island looks wildly alive.

I woke early on the morning of the spring equinox. It was a bright day at the place where I was staying a few miles inland. An ebb tide low enough to allow one to wade safely across the narrow channel to Scolt (for no boats were available so early in the year) would not occur until later in the day so I went for a run. It had been a cold spring and snowdrops still carpeted a spinney. I saw several hares lolloping in the quiet fields. In the hedgerows, the thick trunks of singleton oaks twisted and attenuated to narrow branches snaking up, down and sideways. Silhouetted against the sky, the branching looked like channels in sea marsh when seen from the air.

Later, as I drove north over the whaleback hills, the pitch of the light changed as it began to reflect the not-yet-visible sea. 'In a direct and Meridian Travell', wrote Sir Thomas Browne in an epistle prefacing *Urn Burial* addressed to his friend Thomas Le Gros, who lived in Crostwick about 15 miles south of this coast, 'there are but few miles of known Earth between your self and the Pole.' And I felt the vastness of sea beyond the edge of the land, which does indeed stretch all the way to the high Arctic, before I could see it. Then, like a door opening, there it was: the edge of the sea, an horizon aglow; and Scolt Head Island – a wide, low, irregular dike or levee the colour of African savannah – just inside it, about a mile away.

Crossing the coast road, I walked along a grass track past the Saxon round tower of St Mary's Church in Burnham Deepdale and into the salt marsh. The island and the marshes are well known for their bird life. Geese dotted a mosaic of bathtub-size ponds amidst the vegetation. Dark, slim-bodied, and erect, almost amphora-shaped with elegant necks, they were strikingly different to the squat teapot forms of domestic breeds. Greylag or Bean Geese, probably, soon to migrate to the far north. (In the summer months, terns nest on Scolt in large numbers and waders such as shelduck, wigeon, teal and curlew are plentiful, but in March the dominant birds are wildfowl that have overwintered here.) As I passed each gaggle they shifted nervously, opened their wings and lifted into the slight breeze as easily as children's kites.

Within quarter of an hour or so I reached the main channel separating the island from the mainland. Now, at low tide, it was a rolling expanse of mud and sand with a shallow silver-yellow braid of water at its lowest point. Unnecessarily, I checked my tide tables again, wanting to make double sure I would have plenty of time to cross, explore the island and return. With a flood tide that rose ten or twenty feet and strong currents, I did not want to make a mistake.

Landscape is sometimes treated as metaphor, imbued with meaning because it is a code for something else. When parts of the cliff at Happisburgh (pronounced: Haze-bruh) on the skull coastline of Norfolk crumbled into the sea in 2006, taking away back gardens and threatening houses, some people saw this as emblematic of climate change, or a nation under siege, or something. But metaphor can easily get out of hand. (Recall *The Onion*'s headline for the sinking of the Titanic: WORLD'S LARGEST METAPHOR HITS ICEBERG.) Better, perhaps – better for the ecology of the planet and the ecology of the human mind – to see landscape as synecdoche: place can be simply, wonderfully itself and nothing but itself, but it can also speak for something larger or, indeed, smaller than itself. And so it goes for the smell of the land and the sea. A smell, notes the computer scientist and musician Jaron Lanier, is quite literally, a synecdoche: a few molecules of an actual something sensed directly on tendrils of the brain outcropping in a cave inside the front of the skull.

I crossed the bed of the creek, treading warily at first through sticky mud and then with lighter step over sand before wading across the final boundary to the island, a seawater stream that barely reached my knees. This water, I had read, has ebbed and flowed for perhaps four thousand years. As Islands go, Scolt Head is a recent creation. It may have existed when Avebury and Stonehenge were built, or it may be younger even than the Saxon tower at Burnham Deepdale.

The British isles have formed and reformed over recent geological time. Around two and a half million years ago Britain was an island surrounded by shallow seas much as it is today, but by one million eight hundred thousand years ago – at the time *Homo ergaster* was foraging in river valleys of eastern and southern Africa – it was fused to the rest of Europe by a wide bridge of land between what is now south-eastern England and France. The size and shape of this bridge changed as sea levels fluctuated over a succession of ice ages that began around seven hundred thousand years ago. During some interglacials, major rivers flowed along courses that are invisible today or reached the sea at different points. Around a million years ago, for example, the Thames reached the sea at Happisburgh on the north Norfolk coast, while half a million years ago a great river called the Bytham of which there is now no trace flowed from what are now the West Midlands across the middle of East Anglia to reach what is now the North Sea on the latitude of the Norfolk/Suffolk border. Around two hundred thousand years ago the Thames continued to flow far beyond its present day estuary east and then north across flatlands between what are now East Anglia and Holland, but a hundred and fifty thousand years later (fifty thousand years before the present day), the Thames, the Meuse and the Rhine joined into a common channel that flowed west before emptying into a bay between what are now Sussex and Normandy.

At some point, and probably more than once, a huge flood burst through the land bridge where now lie the straits of Dover. To the north-east, rivers and melting ice had filled a great lake behind a wall of ice to bursting point. When the water topped over in a giant water-fall it caused what some geologists believe to have been the largest flood in Earth history, carving a channel that dwarfs even the valleys gouged by the Missoula floods in the Columbia river valley in North America fifteen to thirteen thousand years ago. Such monumental features are more commonly found on the surface of Mars, where the last floods took place billions of years ago.

During warmer periods between ice ages Britain was abundant in life that seems impossibly exotic today: savannahs, forests and marshes supported rhinos, straight-tusked elephants, hyenas, macaques, hippos. In cooler periods mammoths, reindeer and muskox grazed on tundra to the south of an ice sheet that covered most of the north. The first humans may have arrived in Britain as long as a million years ago. (As it happens, the earliest evidence for human presence is also at Happisburgh.) Bands of *Homo antecessor* and, later, *heidelbergensis*, related to or resembling the common ancestor of both Neanderthals and ourselves, they found plenty to hunt and gather, at least in the more benign climatic periods. At least eight times, reckons the paleoanthropologist Chris Stringer, all human presence was erased by rapid and large-scale climatic change. Massive walls of ice scoured much of the land of virtually all life. But every time the ice retreated and the climate tempered humans returned, following their prey. Every time except once: the evidence suggests that from about one hundred and eighty thousand to seventy thousand years ago Britain was ice-free and supported rich forests and animal life but had no human population even though Neanderthals were present throughout much of Europe at the time. Thinking of this period of abundant life without humans – more than a hundred thousand springs and summers of forests filled with the rustle and raindrop on leaves, rippling streams, birdsong and animal noises but no human voices – fills me with a deep sense of calm and happiness.

On the far side of the creek the mud bank rose steeply to the flat edge of marsh. I started to climb. The mud was like the thickest double cream, and each step made a delicious glooping and shlocking sound. Reaching the top, a little above eye level from the creek, the grey-brown marshland vegetation stretched for about a third of a mile towards the wheat-coloured dunes of the island, which curved like the edge of an amphitheater descending irregularly in height from left to right. Between me and dunes were, I knew, scores of channels in the marsh whose forms, when seen in aerial and satellite photos, had fascinated me because of their resemblance to stunted and contorted tree branches or the vasculature of a human brain. Viewed from high above, the channels appear 'squashed' in the direction of flow: more baobab than poplar, they widen very rapidly in a manner characteristic of low velocity flow. (Marshlands on the coast of Georgia in North America such as Green Island Sound, St Catherine's Sound and Sapelo Sound look much the same, at least in satellite photographs.) But from ground level I couldn't see them at all. Only as I began to cross the marsh and came upon each turn did I see them: the smallest easily jumpable at their higher end but each quickly widening to the main channels as much as thirty meters across – miniature Grand Canyons with buttes and gorges sculpted from mud. Bob Chestney, who was warden of Scolt Head for many decades, wrote 'often, when standing among these creeks or channels at dusk, waiting for ducks to fly in to feed, I have heard what sounds like thousands of little sea animals talking to one another. In actual fact the noise is the top and bottom of shells of cockle-like creatures scraping together as they open and close.'

After I had walked and scrabbled for twenty minutes the marsh-land shaded abruptly into the shingle and sand backbone of the island. I climbed a little way up the dune to a grassy ledge topped by a small hut, paused to drink from my water bottle and then continued upwards. All the way, the ground was firm and dry underfoot, and the sound of the sea became louder and louder. And then, at last, for the first time since descending from the hills inland, I could see out to sea. The summit was only thirty or forty feet high but because of the extreme flatness of the surroundings and the clear air it seemed much higher. The view was grand, almost epic: a clear line of sight along the dunes, with the marshes sheltering on the inland side and seaward the great sweep of the beach – a broad and benign sunlit terrace lapped by blue-grey ripples – stretching for miles in each direction.

Once, I took a night flight from Lima to Houston. It was a clear night and the moon, just about full, was bright as we ascended to cruising altitude above the Andes. Huayhuash, Huascarán and then, yes, Alpamayo, where only a few days before we had been hiking – all the snowy peaks cut clearly through the moonlight. Far to the east was the Amazon basin: vast, illuminated both by moonlight and by distant flashes of lightning now here now there. It may seem bathetic that standing on a thirty-foot dune in Norfolk I saw a similarity – the dunes, an Andes, enclosing the marshland, an Amazon basin and its winding rivers – but the similarity in form, the repeated proportions in big and small, seemed quite evident to me. Landform not as synecdoche exactly, but as echo; landscape as miniature; topography as scale-free network. It was in landscape as miniature that, as a child, the great evolutionary biologist W. D. Hamilton first found beauty.

All small islands – separate little worlds – have their own magic, and there is something especially paradoxical about islands made of sand, an extraordinary substance, as Michael Welland shows in his extensive writings, with the properties of both a solid and a liquid. Not least, sand-made bars and barrier islands are always shaping and reforming. Exactly how they grow and dissolve is not completely pre-dictable, but grow and dissolve they surely do, as surely as the grains of which they are formed endlessly fuse into rocks and separate again. The largest island made of sand in the world is Fraser Island off the coast of Queensland in Australia. Its indigenous name, K'gari, means paradise. According to legend, when humans needed a place to live the primal god Beiral sent the goddess K'gari from heaven to create the world. K'gari so fell in love with what she had made that she wanted to stay. So the messenger god Yendingie changed her into a heavenly island that bears her name. Scolt Head, windswept for much of the year beneath lowering northern skies, may be few people's idea of paradise, but it was, I found, a good place to dream.

Do we dream in order to remember? Nicholas Humphrey, who helped discover the phenomenon of blindsight, compares what he calls the 'thick moment' of consciousness to the experience of being on a ship: deep, unknown water extends far behind and in front of us, but we find ourselves in a penumbra of awareness that surrounds us in a little loop. One could, I think, substitute a small island for the ship in Humphrey's simile. In great seas, an island – like a ship – can mean life itself. And if the island-ship is moving, well is consciousness in the flow of water or the island? 'History is a child building a sandcastle by the sea,' said Heraclitus, 'and that child is the whole majesty of man's power in the world.'

I began the final part of my outward journey, leaving the highest dunes for the beach and the edge of the sea. Descending first into a bowl between dunes, the breeze and the sound of the sea were suddenly baffled as if I had come into a room. The bowl was a sun trap, even this early in the year; still, and thick with grass and bushes like a walled country garden. The sea was only a far echo. But then, climbing over the far lip of the bowl, breeze and sound hit me full face again, and I tumbled down a small sandy cliff to crunch on wet shells.

The beaches of northern Norfolk are like enormous stages. Swept and cambered by tide and wind, light and colour, they are mottled with pools and ridges that seem like forgotten symbols hinting at a something momentous. But what? 'Underlying the beauty of the spectacle there is meaning and significance,' wrote Rachel Carson in her 1955 book *The Edge of the Sea*; 'it is the elusiveness of that meaning that haunts us…'

'For as long as there has been an earth and sea', wrote Carson, 'there has been this meeting place of land and water. Yet it is a world that keeps alive the sense of continuing creation and of the relentless drive of life.' And much of that life exists, invisible to the casual walker, in the apparently sterile and abstract sands beneath one's feet. Walking across the great flats of a beach in Georgia, Carson saw herself treading on the 'thin rooftops of an underground city':

In the intertidal zone, this minuscule world of the sand grains is also the world of inconceivably minute beings, which swim through the liquid film around a grain of sand as a fish would swim through the ocean covering the sphere of the earth. Among this fauna and flora of the capillary water are single-celled animals and plants, water mites, shrimplike crustacea, insects and the larvae of certain infinitely small worms – all living, dying, swimming, feeding, breathing, reproducing in a world so small that our human senses cannot grasp its scale, a world in which the micro-droplet of water separating one grain of sand from another is like a vast, dark sea.

There are thirty-six or so phyla on Earth. Arthropods, which include insects, spiders and crabs, are one. Chordates, which include all animals with backbones from coelacanth to Lady Gaga, are another. Tropical rainforests, the 'flagships of biodiversity', contain sixteen phyla. But the spaces between grains of sand hold twenty-two, each with countless different species. Among the most astonishing of those studied so far are certain kinds of foraminifera, single-celled organisms which select grains of sand of consistent shape and size, glue them together to form a tight sphere and then add a single larger red stone to their newly completely structure. Scientists from Charles Darwin to Lynn Margulis have marveled at the subtlety, and the capacity for discrimination in something so tiny. Is there something like awareness at work here?

I crossed the wide beach and reached the sea at last. The water lapped on the edge of sand as gently as ripples on the edge of a pond. I took off my boots and stood with my feet in the liquid, watching wet sand fill and ebb between my toes. Then I turned around, put on my boots again and started for the mainland. The tide would not wait.

Earlier in this piece I described Scolt Head as a place to dream. But I'm not satisfied with the word 'dream' because in our culture it often refers to something trivial, childish; day dreaming is often considered idleness. Yes, I had spent the day mucking about in the mud and sand like a kid, but I have in mind 'dream' more in the sense of W. B. Yeats's over-quoted line, supposedly from an old play, 'in dreams begins responsibility'. Perhaps we could say the island was, rather, a place for hypnagogia – the transitional state between sleep and waking where both obtain. Psychologists suggest that this state of mind is typical of very young children, who have little sense of the past and future but live intensely in the present and thereby experience it in a way that adults seldom do. But hypnagogia, or something like it, can be important for adults too, allowing us to differently imagine the past and future as well the dimensions of the present moment. 'Hypnagogic states', writes Pascal Boyer, 'often include associations that are extraordinarily difficult to express once the mind is fully conscious again.' And in *The Other Side of Eden*, a study of hunter-gatherer societies, Hugh Brody notes that such states of mind are treasured by these eminently practical and resourceful people as ways of 'combining and using more information than the conscious mind can hold... [allowing] memory and intuition and facts to intermingle'.

Scolt Head, a landform that shifts and grows like a living thing and is almost untouched by human hand even in an archipelago as intensively managed as the British Isles, is good to think on. 'O thou who dwellest not in temples made with hands...', begins a prayer in the church at Burnham Deepdale. Scolt, my island-boat glimpsed between two tides. 'I sleep and my heart stays awake,' wrote George Seferis, 'it gazes at the stars, the sky and the helm, and at how the water blossoms on the rudder.'

from WATERFALLS OF STARS

Rosanne Alexander

Rosanne Alexander is an environmentalist, writer and illustrator. *Waterfalls of Stars* (2017) describes her ten years, from 1976, living on the Welsh island of Skomer, an uninhabited Wildlife Trusts nature reserve which she moved to when she was twenty. Her novel, *Selkie*, about the life of a young grey seal, was published in 1992.

The sea that surrounded Skomer that summer was as gorgeous as a desert island fantasy. The weather was so persistently calm that the water was permanently a glisteningly translucent turquoise. There were no waves, just a pale, fizzing trail of bubbles at the very edge of the water where it touched against the shingle. I had always thought of British seas as dense and opaque, with an undertone of grey even on the bluest of days, and the surface forever broken by fractious little waves. These pellucid waters reminded me of something I had only seen in pictures of far-off places. It was breathtaking looking down from the cliff top into the bays below; the sand and the rocks and the seaweed, seen through the clear water, shimmered in a stunning kaleidoscope of patterns and colours, with everything stained faintly blue-green. In the stillness, we could see fish swimming and spider crabs, with their enormously long legs and spiky bodies, wandering idly across the seabed.

In the absence of any bath water, regular dips in the sea seemed almost as much of an obligation as a recreation, despite the fact that I felt much more sticky and unclean after a plunge in salt water. I could never quite believe how unpleasant the cold water actually felt. All day, as the sun scorched the back of my neck, and the soles of my feet felt as though they were melting into the ground, I stared longingly at the cool water, waiting for the quiet of the evening when I could plunge below the surface and wash away the clinging heat. It was difficult to bring myself to accept that the reality of that longed-for sensation was almost unbearable.

The sea around Skomer was more achingly cold than anything I had experienced before. As a little blip in the ocean, surrounded by restless currents, there was none of the warming effect of the land that I would have enjoyed on my childhood dips at the seaside. It was impossible to enter the water there without feeling the breath snag in back of my throat and thinking 'never again', but its appearance was so limpidly enticing that I fell victim to its temptations over and over again. Then, as the first sensation of shock subsided, I was won over. I became lost in the fascination of that different world, following my ghostly pale hands as they parted a trail through the shuddering fronds of seaweed. Wearing a mask and snorkel I could swim down to where the fish flitted among the weed. And if I moved slowly, without causing too much disturbance, I could become an object of interest to the occasional curious puffin as they swum towards me for a closer look. The birds looked astoundingly beautiful under water. When they dived below the surface, air trapped against their dark feathers formed a silvery skin. Just for a moment, we would be held together as I watched them watching me through the flickering undersea light.

Back in those early years, the summer boat service had a gloriously random feel to it. With the boatman and his son doubling up as farmers, we might not see the boat for days when more pressing matters, like the harvest, intervened. It must have been frustrating for anyone trying to visit the island, but I cherished that element of uncertainty, the reminder that, however good the weather, we were still isolated.

It was essential that we met every visitor as they arrived, to help them understand the island's wildlife and, above all, to explain the extreme fragility of some of the more vulnerable areas. A single person wandering at random among the burrows or venturing too close to the cliff nesting colonies could cause damage. Since we had no way of knowing whether the boat would run, we spent many hours sitting on the cliffs above North Haven, watching for it to come into view around the distant headland of Wooltack Point. When she did appear, the *Sharron* was an impressive sight: an old lifeboat, painted royal blue and white, glinting in the hard sunlight. She was a sturdy wooden boat with remarkably graceful lines, built long before the First World War and originally designed to be powered mainly by oars. Even now that she had been fitted with a relatively modern engine she maintained a dignified serenity as she cut across the sea leaving a slowly unfolding trail of ripples in her wake.

Our niche for boat watching, set back into the slopes above North Haven, seemed to draw in every scrap of heat, sucking it up like blotting paper. I half expected to see the air around me shimmer with the sheer intensity of it. It was hot enough to bring the secretive lizards out of their hiding places to stretch out and bathe in the downpour of sun. Often, it was only the noise of desiccated grasses swaying and rustling as the lizards darted out that drew our attention to them. If we took care not to disturb them, they would remain sitting companionably alongside us, blending almost invisibly into the sun-baked rocks, as we all kept vigil for the boat.

Butterflies wandered aimlessly, as if dizzied by the heat, meandering with the same random motion as blossom scattering from a cherry tree. They came to rest on our arms and legs, brushing our skin with their powdery wings. All around us crickets and grasshoppers – some brilliant green, some splashed with orange – were springing with such beguiling speed that they seemed to materialize and vanish again like part of a conjuring trick. The air was misted by their gently abrasive rasping sound, which mingled sleepily with the faint graze of water against the shingle. The combination of sights and sounds made me feel that I had been transported not just a short stretch across the sea but far, far away from a British summer. It had an exotic strangeness that was beyond my experience.

Nothing could cut more sharply through this soporific atmosphere than the arrival of the choughs. First came the clear, exultant notes, rebounding against the rocks with a sound of brash self-confidence. We always had to look up; it was an irresistible sound that couldn't be ignored. And there they would be, a cluster of sleek, black birds pirouetting and somersaulting through the sky, eclipsing everything.

Of all the birds I ever saw, they were the ones that really made flying look fun. Some made it look easy, but none showed the fluid grace of such effortless acrobatic skills. Choughs were unmistakable, even in silhouette, with their up-flicked wing feathers splayed like outstretched fingers, but their most striking features were the bright red legs and curved beak. For a few seconds they filled the bay with their presence and then, as their calls slipped echoing into the distance, they left behind an empty space that nothing else could fill.

from SEA ROOM

Adam Nicolson

Adam Nicolson (b. 1957), the grandson of the writers Vita Sackville-West and Sir Harold Nicolson, is a writer, broadcaster and environmentalist who was educated at Eton and Cambridge. He is the author of more than twenty books including travel writing, biographies and nature writing. *Frontiers* won the Somerset Maugham Award in 1986 and *The Seabird's Cry* (2017) won the Richard Jefferies Society Award for nature writing and the Wainwright Prize. *Sea Room* (2001) tells the story of the Shiants, an uninhabited trio of Hebridean islands he inherited from his father. He has made television series and radio programmes on subjects as varied as the King James Bible and the untold story of Britain's twentieth-century whalers.

T he Barnacle geese are on their way to Greenland. They follow the spring north, catching the wave of new grass as it sprouts under the sunshine. The birds are tuned to the world, to the planetary fact of the northern hemisphere tipping towards the sun and their journey is an elegant and perfectly measured surfing on the breaking wave of greenness that ripples towards the Arctic with the spring. From a satellite you could see them, long skeins of the goose bodies, sewn like stitches into the air, travelling in family and in island groups, flogging north with the lengthening of the days. From offshore islands along the entire length of the west coast of Ireland, clouds of them from the coast of County Clare and the Arans, a huge concentration leaving from the Inishkeas at the tip of County Mayo, others in Sligo Bay, a scattering all along the coast of Donegal, up to Malin Head, over to Islay and Tiree, from one island after another the flocks have lifted away.

The Shiant birds have joined them. Day and night they are making their way to the Faeroes and then on to the valleys of north-west

Iceland, concentrating in the spring-time in their tens of thousands, descending en masse to the wet river pastures of Húnavatnssýsla and Skagafjarðarsýsla before heading off again, across the Denmark Strait to the breeding grounds in north-east Greenland, between Kangertittivaq and Orleans Land. There, at last, in a savage stretch of country, whose hinterland is one enormous glacier, sliced with deep fjords and glacial valleys, and on the islands that lie offshore, they arrive for the nightless summer months to breed. The Shiant geese, it is thought, will remain together there, recognising each other, a flock within a flock, and will return together in the autumn with their young.

The geese are en route for a few weeks each spring and again each autumn. If you could watch the North Atlantic over the centuries, you would see their passage flashing on and off twice a year. From the west coast of Ireland, across to the Inner Hebrides, up past the Shiants to Rona and Sula Sgeir, on to the Faeroes, Iceland and Greenland, this is a line creased into the palm of the world's hand. It is also a map of something else. These were the paths taken by the Celtic hermits between the sixth and the tenth centuries. Is it possible that they, in search of 'a desert in the ocean', followed the track the geese had blazed for them? It is often said that the wild goose became a symbol in the early Celtic church of the Holy Spirit. There is no evidence for that. But this is a separate question. Did these wonderful birds lead the churchmen, by example, to the north?

Whether in the wake of the geese or not, the idea of holiness clings to the Shiants, as to other islands. Remoteness from the world looks like a closeness to God and intriguingly, it turns out that the association of islands and holiness predates anything Christian. There was an important Christian moment on these small Hebridean islands but it was part of a much longer continuum. There is some evidence that, in Britain in particular, islands were thought of as holy places long before the Christian idea of the hermit arrived here from Egypt in the sixth century. Three pieces of evidence coalesce. In Plutarch's essay 'On Oracles that have ceased to function', the Athenian scholar and philosopher reports a conversation that occurred in Delphi in about AD 83. A traveller called Demetrius of Tarsus, a *grammatikos*, a literature teacher, had just returned from Britain. The traveller told the priests at Delphi what was happening at the far end of the world:

> Demetrius said that many of the islands off Britain were uninhabited and widely scattered, some of them being named after deities and demigods. He himself had sailed, for the sake of learning and observation, to the island nearest to the uninhabited ones, on an official mission. This island had a few inhabitants, who were holy men, and all held exempt from raiding by the Britons.

At just this period, another man called Demetrius (or perhaps the same one: there are few Greeks mentioned on Roman inscriptions in Britain) left two small bronze votary tablets at a temple in the Roman city of York. One was dedicated to the 'Gods of the Governor's Praetorium'. The other 'to Ocean and Tethys', the male and female deities presiding over the wildness of the outer sea. And again, at this same period, the last years of the first century AD, Agricola was conducting large-scale sea-borne explorations of the west coast of Britain, sending a fleet around Cape Wrath and through the Minches. It is at least a possibility that Demetrius was describing the situation in the Outer Hebrides and the Shiants may well have been holy for millennia. And were these islands once, I wonder, named after a Pictish deity, as Demetrius described?

What can only be called a pagan sense of the holiness of islands lasted well into the historical period. When Martin Martin in the 1690s asked a man of Lewis

> if he pray'd at home as often, and as fervently as he did when in the Flannan Islands [a group to the west of Lewis], he plainly confess'd to me that he did not: adding further, that these remote Islands were places of inherent Sanctity; and that there was none ever yet landed in them but found himself more dispos'd to Devotion there, than anywhere else.

Because of this sense of 'inherent sanctity', a whole set of superstitious rules applied to the language people could use on the Flannans and to the way they could behave.

Customs of this kind are not recorded for the Shiants but the same conditions apply. They, too, are never given their true name in Gaelic but are called 'the Big Islands' or even simply 'The Islands'. What is it about islands that summons this tiptoeing around them? This is difficult and speculative territory, but it is worth considering why, outside any Christian framework, islands have for so long felt holy. The Christian experience is centrally shaped by the experience of Christ in the desert, and by the idea that Satan and the flesh can be overcome by exposure to the dangers of a desert place. That idea is important in the history of hermits in the Hebrides, but leave it aside for a moment and other aspects of islandness move to the foreground.

For want of a better word, the holiness of the Shiants, their numen, the inherent spirit which the Lewisman described to Martin, is tangible enough. Only once in my life have I felt it strongly enough to be disturbed by it, but that single experience has entered my own private understanding of the place and it remains an underlayer which shapes everything I know and feel about the Shiants. The first time I was there on my own, I was nineteen and an undergraduate at Cambridge. Donald MacSween had dropped me on the beach and I had with me no more than my one or two boxes of supplies, books and candles, a small canoe and a dog. I had waved goodbye to Donald's boat, the *Favour*, as it disappeared around the rocks on its way back to Scalpay and I spent the day of my arrival arranging everything I needed. I collected wood from the beach and water from the well, I unpacked my stores into the house's cupboard and laid out my sleeping bag. I was there alone with a dog. I had three weeks' literal isolation in front of me.

Even then, before I had learned what I know now, I knew the islands had a reputation. Their name in Gaelic could mean 'haunted' as well as 'holy'. And there was a more recent story. In about 1911, a man was said to have gone to live in the house which had been finally deserted by the Campbells only a few years earlier. He had his furniture delivered by boat and his stock of sheep. He set everything up in the two simple rooms, one for living and cooking, the other a bedroom.

He lay down to sleep and in the middle of the night woke to find an old man at his bedside. 'Do you realise,' the figure said in a straight-forward and conversational tone, 'that you are sleeping on my grave?'

As soon as he could draw the attention of a passing fishing boat – he was said to have set fire to the heather on the top of one of the islands so that its whole upper surface sprouted a blazing head of flame – he left again, taking with him his furniture and his pots and pans. Except for visiting shepherds and lobstermen, the islands had been deserted ever since.

I knew the story but I didn't want to pay attention to it. I did not want to be alarmed at the prospect of being alone on this big, remote and empty place. I had been here before with others and loved its many uncompromised beauties. The idea that it was haunted lay somewhere in the background, in the basement of my feelings. More, I was filled with a deep underswell of excitement and pleasure at being out there, exposed and unfettered, at the feeling of being dangled in a solution of such richness, so uninvadable. But perhaps, now, looking back on it, these twenty years later, I can recognise that those are the pre-conditions for an awareness of the metaphysical.

I know I was frightened because I moved the bed from one room to the other. I moved it in other words away from the grave and went to sleep there, deeply ensconced in the red, downy sleeping bag. The dog, a terrier, was curled up on the mattress beside me and the fire was well stoked, flaming and then glowing.

Nights are not long in northern Scotland in mid-summer. Real dark only lasts for three or four hours, but when it comes it is as black as night ever is. There is no sodium haze. There is no electricity on these islands, but I had a torch with me. Right in the middle of this dark darkness I suddenly woke up. The dog, a terrier, keen to dig any rat out of any hole, not a fearful creature by any account, was stand-ing on the bed next to me, shaking, utterly alert, staring at the far side of the room. I shone the torch over there. Nothing to see beyond my own pots and pans, the washing up bowl, my own coat hung on the back of the door.

His fear infected me. I felt at that moment colonised by terror. There was nothing to see, but my torch made the places where it wasn't shining even darker. The dog would neither move nor relax. There was no sound beyond the swell on the shore fifty yards away. I began to shake, dragged the dog down into the sleeping bag with me and then pulled its hood over the two of us, the torch still in my hand, cocooned from that fear. I couldn't sleep. The dog and I shook together. From time to time I would make a little eyehole of an opening at the top of the bag where I was holding its rim gripped in two fists, waiting for the light to come, for colour to drain back into the shapes and blackness of this room.

The length of short nights! Again and again that eye, opened on to the world beyond the downy warmth of the dog and the cotton of the sleeping bag, revealed only blackness. It became a matter of patience, of out-waiting the night. At three or four o'clock, the world started to grey. I could put my head out into air. It felt as though the room and I had been through something deep and long together, that used-up sensation of exhaustion and a world clarified because some of its deeper possibilities had been seen.

I realised, as I cooked breakfast over the fire, that I was exhilarated. Perhaps this was some physiological effect, a drained, post-adrenaline high, but it felt more than that, a new intimacy with a place that went beyond the purely aesthetic. I had somehow met its soul. But at the same time I knew I didn't want to go through it again. It was too frightening. That day, after the sleepless night, I did everything I could to exhaust myself, walking from end to end of the islands, rowing from one to the other, setting pots, collecting firewood from the shore. By the time the evening came, my whole body was slack with tiredness, my limbs drooping like eyelids. The dog had come with me here and there, to and fro, and by early evening it was asleep.

I drank beer in front of the dropping sun. I knew I would sleep and I did, straight through, waking to find a beam of sun pointing its finger through the window and across the room in a diagonal on to the floor. From my bed I could reach out and put my hand into its light, which felt warm, like sun in a greenhouse. The morning was calm and the sea slick in its stillness. I spent the whole day out in the boat, the dog curled up on a rope in the bow, and the sun plunging through the green water, lighting the guillemots diving there for fish. That was a morning not to be forgotten. Whatever had frightened me that first night now seemed to embrace me. I lay adrift in the boat and felt the arms of the islands around me. They could never frighten me again. If there was a tutelary spirit here, I could live with it, I could love every aspect of it, however bitter its moods, or harsh its treatment of me and that love would, in a way that I cannot properly describe, be returned and sustain me. From that moment I can date my love and affection for this place, an attachment to it beyond the touristic. In the course of those nights and days, the Shiants became a kind of home, a place which would never desert me wherever I might be, the touchstone of reality.

Years afterwards, I read a remark by Jung to the effect that if ghosts are said to be 'nothing but projections of your own unconscious thoughts and fears on to the outside world, no intellectual acrobatics are needed to turn that sentence around and describe your own fears as ghosts that have taken up residence in you.' That permeability of the skin, the flippability of inner and outer, seems to me now like a true description of that experience and perhaps of island experience more generally.

Islands, because of their isolation, are revelatory, places where the boundaries are wafer-thin. My sons tell me that night after night, asleep in their tent on the island, they have heard footsteps beside them in the grass. Not the pattering of rats, nor the sheep but something else. And although I have never heard anything like that, I am inclined to believe them. These remote islands are 'places of inherent Sanctity' and the footsteps are perhaps some of the last modern echoes of an ancient presence.

Everyone who comes here responds to it. This is not the preserve of outsiders or holiday-makers. The shepherds acknowledge it conversationally enough. For them all it is a kind of dream country, a place over which the mind can roam, to which your thoughts always turn at a spare moment, walking with your mind's eye across the loved contours of the place. Both Hugh MacSween and John Murdo Matheson, the young shepherd from Gravir, who since 1996 has had the sheep on the Shiants, have talked to me about the Shiants with an intensity outsiders would never credit. We can have entire conversations about hollows in rocks and pools in streams. It is a bond for anyone who comes here, or at least for anyone that allows the islands to envelop them, to be the encompassing limit of their world, even for a while.

That is a strange but perfectly real effect: after a few days here, the place seems to expand. The Shiants no longer seem, as Compton Mackenzie described them, like 'three specks of black pepper in the middle of that uncomfortable stretch of sea called the Minch' but a world in themselves. To walk the mile or so from one end of Garbh Eilean to another becomes a day-long expedition. Eilean Mhnire is another continent. The details of rocks and plants, of the little alders growing in the rock clefts, the honeysuckle twined around them, the acre after acre of dwarf willow growing on the marsh, the wrinkles in the turf which might or might not hint at previous lives: all of this becomes as varied as America. The Shiants have no wood but they have hidden places, tucked among the rocks. They have no rivers, but they have streams in which the watermint and the forget-me-nots grow. They have no lakes, but pools around whose margins the turf luxuriates into neon green and across whose still, dark surface the water boatmen paddle like Polynesians between their archipelagos. And they have of course the richness of the sea.

Something of the sense of holiness on islands comes, I think, from this strange, elastic geography. Islands are made larger, paradoxically, by the scale of the sea that surrounds them. The element which might reduce them, which might be thought to besiege them, has the opposite effect. The sea elevates these few acres into something they would never be if hidden in the mass of the mainland. The sea makes islands significant. They are defined by it, both wedded to it and implacably set against it, both a creation and a rejection of the element which makes them what they are. They are the not-sea within the sea, standing against the sea's chaos and erosive power, but framed by it, enshrined by it. In that way, every island is an assertion in an ocean of denials, the one positive gesture against an almost overwhelming bleakness. They would not be what they are without the bleakness. The state of siege is creative and an island, in short, is life set against death, a life defined by the death that surrounds it. Like the peak of a mountain, or perhaps more like your own presence on the peak of a mountain, it is an image of salvation and of eternity.

from TIDE-RACE

Brenda Chamberlain

The artist, poet and novelist **Brenda Chamberlain** (1912–71) was born in Bangor and studied art at the Royal Cambrian Academy in Conwy and at the Royal Academy in London. She married a fellow artist, John Petts, in 1935 but divorced in 1944 and moved to Bardsey, or Ynys Enlli, in 1947. She lived on this small Welsh island for fifteen years, painting, and writing and illustrating *Tide-Race*, her account of life there. Bardsey Island and its islanders were the subjects of much of her art, which was exhibited in London. She also painted murals on the walls of the island houses. She was awarded the gold medal for fine art at the National Eisteddfod in 1951 and 1953. After Bardsey, she moved to the Greek island of Ydra, where she wrote her only novel, *The Water Castle* (1964). She returned to Wales but, suffering bouts of depression, took her own life in 1971.

Here I am, here I am, wrested, reeling.
Can I dare? Can I plunge?

R. M. Rilke

1

Listen: I have found the home of my heart. I could not eat: I could not think straight any more; so I came to this solitary place and lay in the sun.

Six miles across the Sound from the white village lies the sea-crag to which three pilgrimages equal one to Rome. At the ruined abbey of Saint Mary I will pray for the souls of my friends. The treasures of Britain are to be found in the fertile earth of the fields or in the bays of the south-west or in the seal-cave to the east; for Merlin buried or planted here in some secret place certain mystical properties. If they can be found, you shall learn from them.

The question was, could I dare plunge into the hermit-life, into the fisherman-farmer's? Alone; most certainly not. With a man, perhaps. Could I take the outward leap into the great depths of the living sea? I was eager and yet mortally afraid of giving myself to this sort of adventurous Robinson Crusoe-type of existence.

The beach stretched its curving arms towards two green islets in the bay, with the inhabited island away to the westward out of sight. The sands were poor and colourless; there were no splendid cliffs, no fishermen to be seen, no craft on the water.

Walking up and down at the tide-edge, Friedrich offered me a drink from a silver flask, and asked:

'Do you not find this place full of atmosphere?'

Behind us at the top of the strand rose a strong wall to keep back the sea from the graveyard and the grey church with its twin transepts. The headstones standing erect on the rising ground were like so many birds on nesting ledges.

There was no sign of a boat coming for us. Friedrich began to grow anxious, because it was already long past the time at which he had been told to be on the beach.

'Perhaps,' said Friedrich unhappily; 'Perhaps a cow has calved or the boatman is ill.'

A black dot appeared off the furthest headland, and soon we were able to make out a motor boat close-in under the land.

They were coming for us!

There were two men in the boat: from their appearance, they might have been father and son. Nodding briefly to us, they began to remove boxes of lobsters from the scuppers of the boat, and walked away towards the village.

A little later, the elder of the two, a short man in thigh waders, carried us in turn, like sacks from the sand of the steeply-shelving beach into the motor boat.

Ah, chapel by the sea, with blue and white headstones erect as birds on nesting ledges; white of razorbills' breasts, blue of black-backed gulls, I was leaving you and the mainland traffic and highways; with its green and yellow gilded trees, the hyacinth-carpeted undergrowth, the fine-drawn shoulders of mountains withdrawn from primitive foothills.

The sea was almost dead calm, a summer calm already in May. The inner side of an oyster shell, or silk shaken out in shallow folds.

Over the face of the elder man whose name we discovered was Twm Huws Pantannas, reflections from the oyster-blue waves ran clear with light, and the bronze of his skin proclaimed him fisherman-farmer. He had a suave, untroubled, crafty face; and a sort of radiance lent by the sun striking sparks from the sea, streamed from him. His face was covered with a fine trellis-work of wrinkles, and there was a fox-cunning smile about his mouth; but the brightness of the day and the glamour of the salt air gave to him a deceptive calm and simplicity.

The suave, secretive faces of sea-farers! You may know them by the radiance that streams from their cheeks and brows. Their lips are cunning as they smile with mouths of men who have almost mastered fear.

The sea took us, and it became immaterial whether we made landfall or not. We began to live in the present moment and, Miracle! time did stand still on the waters between here and there.

The inhospitable island had seduced mystics since the sixth century. There is less wonder in the number of men buried in its earth than in the enigma of why it first became a magnet to the long-thighed ones travelling the sacred roads following the sun towards the west. And the inhabitants have been free since the earliest times from nearly all diseases, and live to extreme old age.

The finger of the Stone Mother points to it, and it is in the far west, but this cold hill descending into the sea has gulfs about her sides, through which grinning dogfish move in twenty fathoms of water. So old are her enchantments, so subtle, that we who cling to the vestiges of the legendary past, sink unknowingly into the moulds of our race, becoming upon her shores Mankind in search of a sign from heaven.

Who can distinguish between the dust of the saint and the lecher?

Like bell-sounds, their spoken names: Lleuddad, Dafydd, Deiniol, Beuno, Dyfrig Beneurog.

Birds flew low over the surface of the dreaming waves.

There were five of us aboard; the two islanders, Twm Huws and Dai Penmon, Friedrich and me, and the man who had followed us down the beach, the vagabond Ancient Mariner. He was an Englishman, his face weathered by sea and wind; and he wore clothes so shapeless and stained that he might have been a shipwrecked sailor just rescued from a coral island; but judging from the familiar way in which he lounged in the stern I guessed that he too was an inhabitant of the island. The young man Dai Penmon stood at the tiller, his face inscrutable.

Our boat softly breasted an indigo, green, and violet sea; we were rocked absurdly like toys, up and down, momentarily fixed, as if the event of being brought together held enough significance to make time stand still.

Clear as glass in the blue and gold day the rock Leviathan lying to the westward sent out an unending cry.

The islets to the south, the sheltered coves fell away from us. The headland was splashed with flowers over which gulls stood preening their feathers.

The cockle-shell in which we sat began to nose its way through the treacherous currents of the Sound. Friedrich sat beside me, his kindly round face at peace, his mind far away in romantic dreams. In the stem the three men were gossiping about dogs, cattle and sheep.

Friedrich broke his reverie to ask Twm if there would be accommodation for us when we landed. With obvious malice, Twm answered: 'No, nothing, but there are plenty of empty houses.'

Friedrich was horrified.

'But it was all arranged months ago,' he stammered. 'The postmaster arranged everything; the boat, the house where we were to stay, everything.'

Twm continued to smile, and to repeat that there were plenty of empty houses.

The land fell away; the world became two elements, water and air. The cockle-shell in which we sat, how brave and gay it was, nosing for home through the Sound.

From the sea, the hump of rock looked idyllic, a place of pilgrimage to the neophyte. It was so calm that we seemed not to be moving;

it was the island that swung slowly round to meet us out of the blue ocean. On her eastward side her five hundred foot mountain stood sheer behind salty vapours that gave her an austerity, an aloofness.

The Ancient Mariner glared forth, one eye focused, the other unfixed as if he saw either nothing or everything too blindingly.

Twm seemed possessed of an ancient virility in the strong thrust of his thighs, and in his smile that told nothing. Fisherman, farmer, boatbuilder, he was probably of all those living at that time on the island, the most close in spirit to the original islanders who some twenty years before, had become disgusted at the invasion of the mainlanders, and had left their homes and gone forth to live on the peninsula.

Friedrich sat unmoving, lost in visions of the past. O let the past sleep on. The bones of the faithful make for a fertile earth. The past is too much with us.

Those lamenting sea-birds are the present, the wings of the bright today. The sea is too salt, too alive to admit of ghosts. Friedrich can see them though: processions of saints lighting beacon fires in the cave near the sacred well; beacons speaking a fire-code: 'We have come, we are holy men and seers. Put out your boats for us.'

In his mind he was watching an answering flame rise up from the brow of the island. A watcher in the rocks, a forerunner of Twm, another man with a twist in his soul, could see the pilgrims' pyre, but would send out no answering signal; instead, he quietly retreated down the mountain, feeling a kingliness in his blood at the thought of his power over men, a power that lay in voluntary isolation. He drew power to himself and thought, 'On the third day after tomorrow (if it is clear weather) I shall suddenly appear to them on the waves majestically, a sea creature battling with the current in open combat.'

Maen Bugail, in her blackness and savagery resembling a wrecked coaster, lay in the distance of the Sound. She is full in the track of the tide which, forking at Pen Dinmor the south-easternmost tip of the island, runs north-westward, and setting round the north headland, runs between her and the sea-rock. The other tongue of the tide sets outside Craig y Llanw to meet the first stream over a mile from the island. From their mingling, a convulsion of water sets back against the sides of the island.

We passed close under black and lichen-encrusted cliffs; nearer, nearer, close, close, until the fangs of wet rock were snapping at us; but in this proximity there was safety, for we were in slack water, in a sullen backwash. Rock rose in galleries and on every shelf stood solemn congregations of sea-birds. We slowly crept past the ramparts of this world of birds.

And still there was no sign of any place where a man might build himself a shelter.

At last, the high land fell away and we were in the anchorage.

Seated four-square on the middle of the beach was an ancient man with a neptune beard and flowing hair. He had a light metal crown chased with a design of seahorses and shells, worn slightly sideways on his head, and in his crablike fingers he held a plug of twist from which he was cutting thin wafers of tobacco. By his side lay an empty rum bottle. He was gross with majesty, and must have been a good trencherman and an heroic drinker. He reeked of fish and salt and tarry ropes.

Behind the old King lay the boats with one many times bigger than the rest; a great black cattle-boat nearly a hundred years old, of giant proportions. She looked as if she had been built for the use of trolls, but the planks of her bottom were now broken and weakened from the lashing of hoofs and the weight of furniture, for she had been in constant use for carrying stock and possessions to and from the island.

Twm said, 'You might try at each farm for a lodging. It's no use asking at our house. We are full up. There are plenty of empty houses.'

Empty houses. We were by now very hungry, and had no food with us; no blankets, no tents.

We followed the cart track that ran from the lighthouse in the south to the abbey ruins in the north. Before us lay the western side; sweet-smelling, level, and fertile. We turned in at the first farm and asked a dark-haired woman with a pouter-pigeon breast whether she could provide us with food and shelter. From the open doorway came a smell of freshly baked bread and cakes.

'No,' said the woman, 'I cannot take you in. My house is full of children.'

'No,' said the stout blonde woman barring the door of the second house. 'There's no room here.'

She was openly hostile.

The third house was empty, dark, and locked.

The fourth house lay away from the path at the bottom of a steep field. A thread of smoke was rising from its chimneys. Out in the meadow, a foxy-looking dog barked at us, and a tall man came out, but quickly went inside again.

I knocked at the door. A Scots voice called:

'Come in.'

A thin man was standing in the middle of the room, staring at us in amazement. On a table in the window was a loaf of bread, a half bottle of whisky and an empty tumbler.

The man hesitated, searching for words. At last he said:

'Come in, make yourselves at home.' He added: 'My wife is away on the mainland,' as he cleared chairs for us.

'You see,' he went on to explain, 'This isn't my house. It belongs to friends, to the Levens's. They are coming here to start farming in a few weeks' time, and I am going into partnership with them. When my wife comes back from her holiday, we shall be moving up to Garthwen, the empty house you passed down the road.'

After a little persuasion, because he was a charitable and a lonely man, he gave in to our request for a night's lodging.

The kitchen was furnished in suburban style; there were horse brasses over the fireplace, a cheap dresser covered in orange and biscuit coloured pottery, and chintz-covered easy chairs. Gripping the frame of a Victorian picture of a snowy landscape was a small bird, a baby Little Owl. It clicked its beak at us in rage, opened its eyes until they seemed to be starting from its head, then swooped down on to one of the chairs where it lay on its back with curled talons in an act of juvenile aggression.

The man picked the bird up and nestled it against him, saying: 'I took him from the nest; he's great company and most affectionate. He's called Doom.'

2

There was a twilight gloom about the house that put me in mind of the sea-floor. The living-room faced east, and the westering sun shining full on the steep field rising from this back part of the house, threw a diffused light over walls and ceiling.

Hens and ducks scratched in the tiled hall, shaking out their feathers which sent up little clouds of fluff. Blinking their eyelids and moving their heads rapidly from side to side, they hovered in the doorway, hoping for crumbs.

A sun-radiant sheep lifted its head from grazing the mountain and wailed into the clear chasm between it and the house. Moved by its piercing cry, the three of us looked up from where we sat at table.

Stewart Hopkinson, the man of the house, invited us to remain a few days and to share his solitude.

'My wife is away,' he said briefly; walking about the room with the air of a lost being.

3

'Let us look at the abbey,' said Friedrich after tea.

It is a very meagre ruin, but the remaining walls are beautiful in age and atmosphere. The greyish green and bitter wormwood, a plant that grows by the gate at home and is picked by the mountain people as a remedy, here enriches the weathered stone. A narrow fissure cunningly built with a twist in the setting of the arch, squints in a slit-eyed vision of the sea.

A farmer and his son, both bearing heavy loads like sacks of sin, were passing in and out of the arched yard nearby. The wife was watching us intently, her head stuck out of an upstairs window, reminding me of when tramping through a crofting village in the Western Highlands, we saw the skylight of every cottage open and a head poke out to watch us. Up there, the women laughed and shouted to us in friendly greeting; the children sang out cheerfully. It was such a delicate humour, to stare like jack-in-the-boxes from their roofs instead of watching like common mortals from their doors. Here on the island the woman was silent as she peered from under the broken cardboard-mended panes. Cadwaladr's wife must have little cause for laughter in her life.

We looked in at the windows of the minister's recently vacated house. The furniture was still there, heavy brown leather chairs and sofa; there were books and papers spread over the table. We half expected to see the traces of a meal, so casually did the house seem to have been left. The minister having cleaned his neighbours' windows for the last time as a hint that they should not throw stones at glass houses, had walked out of his front door, padlocked the chapel, and with knobkerry in hand, had set sail for Africa and the saving of more tractable souls.

The island children had screamed their heads off for joy.

'By Christ and the Devil, the dog-collar has gone to the blacks!'

The men were delighted too; the minister had often accompanied them on the sea where because of his presence they were forced to curb their language. Above all, they were weighed down by the superstitious dread that his presence would bring disaster to the boat; for clergymen, corpses, and rabbits bring bad luck to seamen.

From the north, one could see the whole island; a handful of farms, a lighthouse, a ruined monastery, an earth made fertile with the bones of men. The farm buildings, solidly made to withstand all weathers, had yards walled like fortresses. In the arch of a cart-shed at Pant was a stone bearing an incised sword or cross. The block had been built in lengthwise and had presumably come from the holy house.

The monastery stones had since the sixth century stood as a symbol of the human spirit, not only of religious faith but of escape as well. Men had fled here to live and to die, to begin a new life or to kiss the soil with the last touch of their withered mouths. It had always stood for freedom; now, in the modern sense, it stood for escapism too.

A rock shore; cliffs of mussel-blue shell. Wine-red, icy pink, pure white, yellow and green. The surf creamed at the foot of the coloured walls. Colours evoked images, images evoked words. Wall of jasper, tower of quartzite. How can a common seacliff be a wall of jasper? I would, knowing this salt channel and these bastions, make a new hymn to the virgin; say she was a wall of jasper with eyes clear as the running tide.

There was the solid wall, and round it ever-widening circles of association. For example, the south end of the island was linked with the memory of the Wild Cats. When the 'old people' moved off the island they left behind them all their cats. Having to fend for themselves, they became quite savage and grew to the size of small dogs from the success of their hunting. They would not go near the new inhabitants, except to raid their larders. They became such a menace to rabbit-trapping that they had to be exterminated, for unlike tame cats they did not kill one rabbit and eat it until they were satisfied, but went from body to body in the gins, eating only those succulent parts they particularly fancied.

At the bottom of Clogwyn land we discovered a blood-red cave, full of sea-anemones and egg-smooth pebbles, where years later I found the vari-coloured stone that became the 'wave-worn pebble burnt with sealight' dedicated to the feast day of Saint Rose of Lima.

In the late evening, as we sat on the grassy parapet that rims along the northern coast; among flowers, sea-pinks and vernal squills, we saw the young man we had watched earlier in the day near the monastery, disappearing round the mountain with a bucket for gulls' eggs.

At this northern end are black sea caverns. Above the caves the rock is white and worked over in raised veins, polished and fine as ivory. Some of these rock-veins were thin as spider web, others were thick as human arteries. The stone would seem to be composed of petrified tissues, skin, muscle, delicate bones. We ran our fingers over the filigree patterns. Falling to our knees, we touched the remains of our ancestors. Or their sculptured memorials in stone; their ivory-bright bird-bone perfection, the metamorphosed flesh. A valley of sun-whitened skeletons seen through a reducing mirror.

Why this preoccupation with stone, the framework of the earth? While turning over the soil here, a man might philosophise like the gravediggers in Hamlet. The second clown asks a riddle: 'Who builds stronger than a mason, a shipwright or a carpenter?'

And the first clown answers: 'A grave-maker; the houses that he makes last till doomsday.'

In every part of the island which is free of stone, the spade strikes against human thigh and breast-bone. In an island of only four hundred and forty-four acres, with half of that mountain and with reputedly twenty thousand saints buried there, it is understandable that certain areas of the earth should be thick with bones.

Under the eastern height men turn the remains of their ancestors when they dig; forking them over happily under the wide sky-benediction; for these are the bones of men who fulfilled themselves, who found realisation of visions in a fragment of land left miraculously to the air when other portions of this mountain range were submerged in the Pleistocene Age.

We turned southwards, walking to Ogof Lladron, where in a cirque of rock that on one side rises to a saddle, on the other to overhanging cliff, lies a snug and secret anchorage. I could imagine the French smugglers putting in here, swart men in stocking-caps and ear-rings, carrying their cargo of liquor up the precipice. Delightedly, the welcoming islanders used to guide them up to their farms, with talk of roast goose and duck; their eyes on the wine flagons.

A rough grassy track runs the whole way along the west side. While we walked there I mused over the lonely man we had left behind us in the house. He was like someone uprooted too violently, a man out of his place; highly strung and too unstable for this mode of life.

Friedrich began to tell me of his own loneliness, partly from over-burdened emotions, partly because for a few days he was to be out of the world, simplicity and peace loosening his tongue.

In the south, on the black rock of Pen Dinmor, Arthur of the Round Table is said to have been shipwrecked. The boat was lost but the king was saved. The legend has it that the king with torn breast, his royal garments salt-caked and stained, was dragged from the hungry sea by unknown hands and carried inland to the holy fathers, who tended his ragged wounds.

We caught sight for a moment of a tawny cat, one of those domestic animals left behind by families that had moved out. At this time, many homeless cats lived in the gullies of the south end. Island cats quickly revert to the wild, with many rabbits and birds for the hunting, and with much space in which to move freely, except for the danger of gins and snares.

This is a land that hoards its past and merges all of time in the present. The cargo boat that was salvaged last year off Maen Bugail, whose coal cargo will keep the island in fuel for the next twenty years; the illicit sweet wine of France; the shipwreck of Arthur; are of equal importance and freshness. It might be said that what happened here yesterday has taken on the colour of a long-past event, so timeless do happenings appear to be; as if the drama had been written long ago, and we who come by chance to the island play our parts that were designed for us, walking on to the stage at the twitch of a string held in the firm hand of the master.

Puppet strings took me by the hair-roots, drawing me back to the house in the quiet dusk; I had a sense of being forcibly drawn into the life of this elusive world.

It was almost dark by this time. A man in a peaked cap was sitting behind the door, his chair drawn back against the wall. The man had pale ginger hair and a white exhausted face.

'This is Merfyn, one of the lighthouse keepers,' said our host.

An hysterical, high-pitched laugh came from the mask behind the door. It was just possible to see his hands falling limply between his knees, from which hung a cloth bag holding full milk bottles.

After supper, when the two of us were alone, Hopkinson told me something of himself.

'I was brought up by foster-parents. Then I studied the law; while preparing for my examinations, I began to drink a lot of whisky and absinthe. I married Alice, and persuaded her to come here, overlooking that she has an Irish temper, and that she needs to go to a palais de dance every Saturday night. How she hates the sea! But real blind hatred. Now, she's gone off to the mainland to stay with her mother. I'm riding her on a loose rein in the hope that some day she will become resigned to this place.'

He paused to brood, with hunched shoulders.

'Last year, I threw up my law studies, and took this farm with the Levens's. We arrived in December, after a terrible crossing in which Alice lay flat on her back in the bottom of the boat. The house was no comfort; the bedrooms and living-room walls were running with moisture. The sheets and blankets felt like snails' beds. We were cut off from the mainland for four weeks after the day we arrived, and had to live on corned beef and potatoes. By the end of that time, Alice would not eat any more tinned meat. The islanders were not particularly friendly, either.'

4

Those first irradiant nights were like nothing I had ever experienced. Before getting into bed, I crouched at the window. There were no sash cords, so the frames were held open by pieces of stick. Across the slope of the mountain the lighthouse beam flashed like a scythe with stronger radiance than moonlight. Illuminating night: such innocence was in the cool winds and mooncast shadow. There was no nightmare, no dream. The house being in the middle of fields, took the full flash of the beams, the uninquisitive arcs passing over with a scythe's movements or like ground-lightning.

How different it was from those nights in Galloway, in the dark house above the Firth of Solway. That bedroom's leaf-heavy, tree-haunted gloom, where on entering, my heart felt the midnight shiver of massed foliage breathing and growing.

And the sea makes clean our hearts.

With the coming of full darkness, shearwaters began to shriek with the ghostly cries of dead men.

What had Stewart said during our long conversation? 'When I am out in the dark looking to my rabbit-snares, the shearwaters cry like banshees from their winding passages among the rocks.'

With the coming of first light, I would wash all over from a basin on the floor. Bending down in front of the small square of window I could feel the salt wind making me whole. The cows passed up the field into the main track on their way to be milked, with the timid hang-dog white bull limping slowly after them, hobbled and wretchedly impeded as he painfully dragged along his great bulk.

During the day, I walked from end to end of the island, Stewart's dog following me, moving foxlike through the high bracken of the eastern slopes. From the mountain-top the low land was small to the eye. In the simple unfoliated landscape where tawny stems break the horizontal lines of the low land, the fields were parcelled neatly into small squares of cultivation about an acre in extent; each field was surrounded by an earthen, grass-covered dyke, along the top of which it was pleasant to travel.

Every farm has its own withy bed for the making of lobster creels, but the beds have become so neglected in the past few years that withies have to be brought over from the mainland in the winter months.

Never had I seen ground so overrun by rabbits. They were a small variety, both grey and black and crosses of both, the black having been introduced by a lighthouse keeper. The fur of the black variety was long and of a silken fineness. Stewart, who had decided to experiment with the two breeds, had taken young rabbits out of his snares, tied string to the leg of each and pegged them down in the hope that they would breed.

5

I sat at Stewart's feet on top of a tall slab rearing from the sea. The cave, a narrow fissure always dark except at early morning when the sun shines in, was glutted through its narrow-necked entrance by the incoming tide.

Below us, a seal cow lay on her back in the bottle-green gloom of the cavern. With head out of water and flippers waving us to come down, down, to the depths of the sea, her brown eyes besought: Come to me, come to me. Her arms extended, folded again to her creamy underside. So great was the human mermaid attraction that I could have leapt to my death by drowning.

A woman on land and a silkie in the sea.

We had come with infinite caution down the precipitous holdless grass of the mountainside. Never before on any hill have I known such sheer grass. To slip a few inches, to lose the slightest control, would be enough to set a body rolling and bouncing over the cliffs into the waves. The wind was piercingly cold, so I had borrowed two of Stewart's sweaters and a pair of his old army trousers turned up in many folds, and a raincoat. By going barefoot, it was possible to move comfortably, digging heels and fingers into the turf. Below the awful expanse of grassy precipice came the ledges of firm and honest rock giving sound hold.

Our minds grew dazed by the thunder of the conflicting tides. As we let ourselves down the last yards where a few tussocks of thrift wait to crumble from the slope under unwary fingers, we came face to face with the Ancient Mariner. With bent knees and one hand against the rock he moved along a narrow lip made greasy with the droppings of birds. On his arm he carried a basket full of gulls' and razorbills' eggs bedded in fleece. Calmly plundering the hatcheries, with nothing but the assurance of balance to keep him from death, he moved warily and sinuously as a weasel. Swinging round with an extravagant gesture of alarm at sight of us above him, he nearly pitched forward over the rocks. He had been walking with his glass eye towards us. He was unshaven and his finger-nails were long, black, and hooked as talons.

Stewart called out harshly to him:

'This is a sanctuary for birds; you have no right to take so many eggs!'

For answer, he blew him a kiss, and touched an egg with his foot so that it rolled away over the edge of the precipice.

Deeply hurt, Stewart moved on, his cheeks and neck a deep red with mortification.

A hen and cock bird stood side by side, the mother bird sheltering her green egg between prehistoric feet. Having no nest in which to lay it, she guarded it against the soft wall of her belly. She cooed, nodded, danced, bowed, in reply to her mate. The cliffs murmured with their warm and mysterious communication. She was maternal and careless all at the same time. Feeling the need for a silver fish, she shuffled off the ledge, taking the egg with her.

'This stench is unbearable,' shouted Stewart. 'My God, how these birds do stink.'

Feeling like a pigmy, I climbed up and down among the crags. The sea was emerald, frothed with white. In lee of the land, submerged rocks of the reef showed as soft purple stains under the water.

We began to collect a few eggs while birds circled wildly round us. Herring gulls lay their eggs in shallow, primitive nests made of dead grass, feathers, sheeps' wool, or seaweed, along the rocky shore; or simply drop their eggs in depressions on the grass slopes. We found razorbills' eggs hidden in deep crannies. They were of a chalky white splashed with brown blotches the colour of old blood, and were more beautiful than the mottled dun-green eggs of the herring gull. Against the stones whitened with bird-droppings, they were perfectly camouflaged. Whenever we found a gull's nest with three eggs in it, Stewart broke one to test whether it was addled, for usually if the full clutch was there, it meant that the chicks had begun to form. When we had gathered about two dozen eggs for the making of omelettes, we hid them under a fleece ready to put into our bag on the way back to the west side.

After the chill currents of the sea-way, the breast of the island gave off an intense heat. Everywhere, birth was taking place; chicks were breaking from speckled shells under the burning-glass of the sun. On every shelving ledge, on hard-baked pockets of earth, whole eggs and green fragments of shell lay beside blind creatures beating the dust with embryonic wings. The gull king, his head hawklike between his shoulder blades, was watchful from eyes of cold amber. He alighted on the cliff, sea-water dripped from his beak of lemon bone. Around him squatted his clumsy off-spring.

The chipping of shells grew more insistent as the breeding sun gained its zenith. We trod with a sort of fear over the bald surface, stepping around new-born creatures and their shards.

There was an area rank with purple henbane, hollow-stalked flowers scarcely visible above shielding husks. The flowers, springing one above another on the stalk, were of a deadish yellow. The tough covering of the fruit of this soulless plant was like the husk of assara-bacca, and in it was contained much small seed like poppy semen but with the colour of house-dust. Not only the root but the whole plant gave off a heavy smell that filled the surrounding air. This herb under Saturn draws melancholy humours from the region of the heart.

Sea parrots stood stiffly to attention at the mouths of abandoned rabbit-burrows, and as we approached, either drew back into the shelter of the holes or launched themselves with fiercely whirring wings down into the sea.

A pigeon with a shot-silk breast of bronze and green crouched on a limestone bluff and disregarded us. From the tilted stone platform, from the nesting ledges, there fell a constant shower of liquid excreta. The confused sound of love-making, scolding, and gossip, came from row upon row of bottle-shaped guillemots standing upright along the terraced walls. The cliff-face was spattered with the broken eggs that careless webbed feet had set rolling. Close to the water, shags were drying out their wings.

What fate overtakes each wave as it breaks against the land? I began to count, waiting for the seventh wave. How are we to know which is the first and which the seventh? How can we rationalise and set to numbers pulsations of water that have been world without end? A green wall of water advanced, only to spend itself and become diffused. Another and another followed it.

From clumps of bladder-campion we heard the cheeping of young birds and came upon a deep niche high in the cliff where chicks clamoured for food. I inserted myself in the entrance and wormed up into the darkness of the narrow cleft. When it became so constricting that I could push in no further, and when head was bent to the breast by the roof, I cautiously put out my arm into the dank air, to find that at full stretch I could feel inside the deep nest made of grass stems and wool; three, four, five pulsating heads. Their beaks gaped wide in a clamour for food. Carefully, I passed one chick down for Stewart to touch. It was a naked grey thing, with skeleton head and unfeathered wing-elements; pink-legged, pink-throated. After it had been returned to the nest, we retreated to the rocks below. Soon the parent birds returned; glossy, blue-black, bright-legged choughs. They fluttered with rustling wings on to the face of the cliff over the crevice, and after talking to their young and mobbing other birds that flew too near, flashed in to their chicks with loudly echoing cries.

In the height of the vault, black-backed gulls screamed at us, dropping close to our eyes with splayed talons. Wingless, grounded, our feet stumbled over pebbles, our faces burned in the oven-heat given off by dry rock. The air quivered, shaken as wind-disturbed water, making insubstantial the green headlands.

A bird power-dived. Alas, humankind; featherless, wingless, crawling the earth.

The whole east side resounded with the harsh anger of seafowl.

6

The waves were green, greenly came they, waves came ever-green out of Ireland, to fall upon the cliffs of Wales and glut her caverns with salt and broken things.

'There, quickly,' he said. 'Porpoise!'

A group of slug-backs rolled, curved up, disappeared, each behind the other as if there undulated a loch monster.

A little more faith O Lord, and I could walk on the water, or roll brightly gleaming like the basking shark.

'What really brought you here?' I asked Stewart.

'This seemed a wild place, and I needed wildness. The King is old and without a son so, who knows, I may be the next King or at the least, president of the island. Alice says she hates the life but summer is on the way, when things will be easier for her. She must learn to like it. Out in the world, what was I? But here, I stand a good chance of leadership.'

'Leadership: strange word.' A fanatic, an uncomfortable kind of man, burning himself out.

He was looking straight before him, his face severely secret. Did he ever, I wondered, peel away the protective covering when he was safe behind a locked door at the end of a corridor in the halls of loneliness? To a man perhaps; no woman would ever see his naked face.

After a little reflection he went on, 'Possibly I shall become a whole man in time, after my life and love have been simplified. If we lived in a tent, we could burn it down each spring and begin again.'

The sea was emerald, frothed with white. In lee of the island, the rocks of a submerged reef showed as purple stains under the water. Below us was the seal cave. Through a narrow fissure we saw the slimy ledges on which seals lie up, and the deep pool fed from the sea through a narrow-necked entrance. A seal cow was lying on her back in the gloom of the cavern. Her head was out of water. She waved her flippers, bidding us to come down to her. They were like fronds of weed floating loose from the heavy root of body. Something barked with a deep voice. It was the bull seal. Ah, there he went, smooth and black as oil, nine feet of solid flesh, twisting and rolling without a ripple to disturb the depths of the pool.

'He is almost twice as long as you are,' laughed Stewart.

Look, look, now he comes out, his black bull head dripping. One moment, he is in the stillness of the cavern; the next, he is in that boiling emerald sea. His nose is nobly aquiline, his heavy lids droop, hooding the eyes. He does not look directly at us, this bull seal, Leviathan. He will leave that to the cows of his harem. In the emerald, jewel-coloured sea, from the white foam-lace rise gentle stone-grey heads. Whiskered, human-eyed, they are the heads of his cows. They are dappled, white-breasted, their undersides seemingly vulnerable, gleaming as those of mackerel.

Ho there! beautiful beast. Moon-dappled silkie!

She twists to dive into the under-water tunnel leading to the pool, and where her back of mottled fur touches the surface, is iridescent as mother of pearl. Rainbow, mother of pearl, sheen of the sleek and mottled skin.

And the seal that wanted me to leap down into her arms—

'Look,' said Stewart. 'She is calling you again.'

'Come to me, come to me.'

From the deep pit, from the roof of whose galleries giant spiders hung spinning their white cocoons, in waning light, she sent messages of desire, that I should give myself to the sea and plumb the cold stillness of water under the rock. I leaned far over into darkening air; and her mild eyes spoke of human feelings. She took me down to my deepest roots nurtured on legend and fantasy. She told me that once I was a lonely woman living on a desert beach, without husband, without children; and if in the spring I was crowned it was with sea-tangle of my own wreathing. One day, she said, so great had been my desire to be a mother that I stole a baby seal silken-haired and innocent, from a rock that spray blew over. What a temper it had! It bit and scratched and tore its own face furiously when it could not get at mine. It screamed with the voice of any human child. The bereft cow roared and came up from the surf to beat my door and windows with her flippers. She blew like a whale through the keyhole; she moaned and whimpered for her little bull. At last, she was forced by lack of success to go back to the cold wastes of the sea; and I was left in peace. After a time, my adopted child grew listless, the fight went out of it, and at last it pined away, dwindling inside its long fur. It died; then, because I feared the vengeance of its real mother, I went to live far away from the seals' breeding ground.

O seal cow in the cavern; your mournful eyes.

Was it your baby I stole sometime in a former life? Rooted deeper still in legend, I once married a stranger with whom I lived in great contentment above the tidal ledge. I was happy enough until he began to leave me for whole weeks with only turnstones and green-shanks for company. But one night, when he had been away for a long while, I went to the shore to gather driftwood by the moon's light. A bull seal had risen from the sea and lay resting on a rock. He was singing with a human voice, an old song, 'I am a man upon the land, I am a silkie in the sea.'

The shock of it made me scream; and hearing me, he gave a great bellow of disgust because I had seen him as he really was, and flapped away into his true element away from me for ever.

In truth, and quite apart from the weaving of legends, a bull seal sometimes shows sexual interest in women when they are swimming near him; particularly in fearless young virgins. For instance, I have when bathing at night in the company of young people among a herd of seals, and a girl has stood upright in the water, seen a bull seal swim rapidly to her with powerful interest, stare into her face and at the last moment dive between her legs. There is often so strong a link between woman and seal that it would seem almost normal for them to co-habit.

Stewart left me, to go back along the shore in search of Friedrich, who had been daunted by the steepness of the grassy precipice, and whom we had not seen for the past hour. He was a long time gone.

Evening has come: it is cold on this sunless rock. Waves toss tumultuously past the shore. The pool grows more and more mysterious, and a stench rises from the sleeping-ledges. The old black bull seal snorts at me from somewhere below. A pale moon rises in the wind-burnished sky. I sit and sit alone with the waves, the creatures and the stones.

The sea pours relentlessly past, the sea is cold: the white moon is cold also, a virginal spring moon. I do not move at all on top of my rock so that birds fly close and show their bellies, trailing feet, and clear eyes. But I do not see the razorbills' eyes; they are too small and black. They would seem to be blind, so small and black are their eyes against the dark plumage.

The bull seal snorts below in the darkness; it is a cold desolate sound, filled with repugnance. He wishes I would go away.

Stewart does not come, and I am surrounded on one side by water, on the other by blocks of stone.

To the left, there is the rock wall a few inches from my head; to the right, I can see a few yards as far as the corner round which birds circle. If Stewart does not come back I shall wait until the moon has gained mastery in the sky, and then climb the cliff and find my own way home to the stone house in the middle of the island.

I am cold; I am happy. Not until the moon is high—there, the signal from the gulls! He is returning, for the birds have risen and gone seaward over the waves. Head and shoulders first, then the whole figure moves among the rocks. He raises an arm in greeting and I smile, being comforted on my cold throne. I smile, going back in memory to an evening in childhood when walking near Gorad, a boat passed in slack water and those aboard her raised hands in benediction.

Salutation to the shores of worlds.

On a shelf above the cave were tunnels dug in curiously powdered grey soil that contained much bird excreta. Stewart opened one of the tunnels with his knife, hoping to find a shearwater in it, but it was empty. One hole went down into the soft crumbly earth. I dropped a stone into it, and heard the faint splash about thirty feet below in the cave pool. We had to tread carefully, as there was a danger of the earth giving way beneath us at any moment.

From the summit ridge we looked westward to where the sunset was falling into grey ash. The lamp suddenly burned in the eye of the lighthouse, its beam beginning to play over the twilit fields.

We could see Friedrich's figure far below, standing at the side gate of Pen Craig, waiting for us. He had been overcome by vertigo on the steepest part of the east side and had with great difficulty on hands and knees dragged himself back up the slope, with a swimming head. He was silent and shaken, and said very little when we rejoined him.

After supper, yawning, stretching, on the hard wooden chair, with night flowing past the window, I had to listen to a continuation of the story of Stewart's life. Friedrich had gone to bed, saying he was a bachelor and unused to late hours.

'It was grim,' said Stewart, 'to live in the shadow of two guardian aunts.' He mused for awhile, then spoke again.

'The great thing in life is desire, or as some prefer to call it, Love,' he pronounced.

'Love, desire, poetry. Women and poetry.' He plucked an imaginary guitar.

Women with thighs the colour of meadowsweet; and maidenhair crisp as fern. Darkness of the navel in the smooth belly. Where the string has been, it is dark, it is empty. All of us, with severed, perished navel strings, desire the mother from whom we were cut by the scissors of a nurse. We desire the breast and the womb even after our beards are grown. In the beginning it is: Mother, carry me; I am tired. In the long middle period: Hold me in your arms, beloved. At the last: Raise me a little on the pillow to see the sun.

Women wash mother's blood from us when we are born, and wash the world's dirt from us after we are dead.

I listened carefully, as if it was important that I should be his confessor; and watched the man's thin, sickly, and unhappy face. There was an awkwardness in his gestures but when speaking in the heat of memory, he lost self-consciousness.

from STONES OF ARAN: PILGRIMAGE

Tim Robinson

Tim Robinson (1935–2020) was an artist, cartographer, mathematician, novelist and non-fiction writer. Born in England, he studied at Cambridge and worked as an artist under the name Timothy Drever in Vienna, Istanbul and London before moving to the Aran Islands in 1972. Here he began his life's work, surveying and writing about the landscape and folklore of the islands, wider Connemara and the geological region known as the Burren. He produced his first map of the Aran Islands in 1975. The Irish writer Michael Viney described his two-volume study of the topography and culture of the Aran Islands, *Stones of Aran: Pilgrimage* (1986) and *Stones of Aran: Labyrinth* (1995), as 'one of the most original, revelatory and exhilarating works of literature ever produced in Ireland'. Robert Macfarlane wrote: 'Many landscape writers have striven to give their prose the characteristics of the terrain they are describing. Few have succeeded as fully as Robinson.' Robinson, who had Parkinson's, died of coronavirus in London two weeks after the death of his wife and collaborator Máiréad Robinson.

WRITING ON THE BEACH

Because the bay of Port Mhuirbhigh curves so deeply into the flank of the island its waters are undisturbed by the currents that sweep along the coast, and so have deposited a beach of fine sand. Onshore winds have carried the sand inland to build dunes, now grassed over. The whole area around the bay is a *muirbheach*, a sea-plain of sandy pasturage; hence the name Port Mhuirbhigh, the bay of the *muirbheach*. There was once a little burial ground or *cill*, perhaps an ancient church site, close to the head of the bay, which in turn has been buried by the dunes so that its only memorial is the name of the nearby village and the surrounding townland, Cill Mhuirbhigh, anglicized as Kilmurvey. The Kilmurvey House farm, which almost monopolizes this *muirbheach*, is the best holding in the three islands.

Sand, then, sets the tone here. A beach the colour of the moon waxes from a poor crescent to a good half and wanes again twice a day. Behind it is another crescent, a pale and ragged area of marram-grass hillocks between a foreshore path and the road going by to the village. Sometimes young visitors set up their tents in the snug hollows of this field, which for some reason is called The Vinegar, and the currachs of the Cill Mhuirbhigh men are kept on their stone stocks in the shelter of its walls. All around are the vivid green and unbroken acres grazed by the cattle of the "Big House"; in contrast, the background of hill-slopes to the south-east and south-west is grey and lined with walls.

All the roads and tracks of this area run to or loiter by the beach. The stony coastline itself seems to holiday here and unwind from its severities. Sunbathers and sandcastle-builders dispel the old equation of the shore with labour and its new one with loneliness, at least for those short and radiant times in which the angle of a gull's white wing against the unstable Atlantic blue defines high summer in Aran. At such hours even the pulse of the breaking waves, the universal constant of all shores, never quite stilled, becomes a whisper, a merely subliminal reminiscence of storm, of winter.

Winter is defined by a bird here too, a solitary great northern diver that comes with falling temperatures from the far north to haunt the bay, and lives for months out there on the heaving waters, rising and falling in time to the crash of waves on the beach, a dark, secretive thing that keeps its distances and refuses one a view, slipping silently under the surface if one approaches the water's edge and reappearing after a long interval farther off, half lost in the poor light. One gives up peering, identifying, and wanders along the heavy ever-repeated landfall of the sea. At this season the resistant depths of colour on land, sea and sky slow down the pace of perception to that of con-templation. If a gleam from the low sun comes across to catch the countless overlapping marks on the sand, then idleness and the absence of humankind can tempt one into the error of thinking: "Signatures of all things I am here to read." Each fallen wave, for instance, rushes up the strand with a million urgently typing fingers, and then at the moment between writing and erasing subscribes itself in a negligent cursive across the whole breadth of the page. Signatures and counter-signatures accumulate, confuse, obliterate. Seabirds put down their names in cuneiform, lugworms excrete their humble marks. And then come my boots to add the stamp of authenticity, not of the endless process of the beach which needs no authentification from anybody, but of my witnessing of it.

Is this an image of the work I have dreamed of, that book—with which the present book has a certain flirtatious but respectful relationship—preliminary to the taking of an all-encompassing stride? A muddled draft of it perhaps, or more usefully a demonstration of its impossibility; for the multitudinous, encyclopaedic inscription of all passing reality upon a yard of ground is ultimately self-effacing. But no; for if the book like the beach lies open to all that befalls it, welcomes whatever heterogeneous material is washed up or blown in, then must begin the magic transubstantiation of all this intractable stuff into the person fit to make the step. A work of many generations, I wonder? Let a few almost frivolous examples of the countless marks that have been impressed temporarily on this particular beach and more lastingly upon myself demonstrate how nearly overwhelming is even my limited and ill-defined project.

In the spring of 1975 almost the entire area of sand between high water mark and the foot of the dunes rather suddenly filled up with low clumps of a silvery-leaved plant never recorded in Árainn before, the frosted orache. This is in general rare on Ireland's western coasts, though commoner on the east, but I heard later that it had turned up at Roundstone in Connemara the previous year, and perhaps a drift of its seeds had come across the channel from there. This insemination has probably not added permanently to the Aran flora, for year by year since then its summer growth has been thinner and thinner, and now it is difficult to find a single specimen. In my capacity as self-appointed resilient scientific busybody I kept the botanical authorities informed, and now I read in D. A. Webb's almost-but-of-course-not-quite definitive "Flora of the Aran Islands," published in 1980:

> *Atriplex Laciniata…* observed in 1975 on Kilmurvey beach,
> where (*fide* Robinson) it has since much decreased.

The Latinism was new to me; I am tempted to adopt it as a motto.

Similarly, on the 27th August 1977, I witnessed the presence of a small bird running to and fro and pecking at the margins of retreating waves, a slim, stilt-legged, long-beaked wader very like a common sandpiper but with a reddish underside. Unlike the other shore-birds that feed in mixed flocks here from the autumn onwards, and which take flight as one approaches, circle round over the sea and re-alight behind one, this elegant little oddity stayed there, busy and preoccupied, until it was almost under my feet. Later the reference books told me it was a buff-breasted sandpiper, a vagrant from America recorded less than a dozen times in Ireland, and well known as an unusually tame bird—though "tame" is hardly the word for a creature to whom human beings are of no more concern than any other solid obstacle in its way. I referred this observation to higher authorities too, and was informed that a body called the Rare Birds Committee was "sitting on it" and might well accept it as an authentic record, but I never heard the outcome of their incubations. In fact I would say to them "*Diffide* Robinson!," for my certainty about the identification is of the sort oddly called a "moral certainty," which seems to be inferior to a factual one. (For instance, Professor Webb once found on Inis Oírr a certain plant, a little stonecrop called *Sedum dasyphyllum*, at least, that is what the specimen he brought away with him turned out to be. The discovery was unusual enough to demand confirmation, but although he, his acolytes and rivals have like myself diligently searched the place, that particular stonecrop has not been refound. And although he is still "morally certain" about it, he has excluded it from his Aran *Flora*.)

What else? The dolphins, forty or fifty of them, did indeed dance in the bay one year, just as I described to the lightkeeper who saw them praying on the beach. I am told that their splashy leapings are more practical than expressive, and that they were probably rounding up a shoal of fish; also that they were of the species known prosaically as the bottle-nosed dolphin, from their elongated snouts. Aran does not distinguish between the various dolphins and the smaller porpoises, lumping them all together as *muca mara*, sea-pigs, a libellous name for such lithe hydrobats. The expanding ring-waves made by that circus troupe can hardly have shifted a grain of sand on the shore, and I can include dolphins in this catalogue of beach-marks only on the strength of those fanciful, prayerful, kneeprints.

A last impression: a stumpy-legged dog, white with brown blotches, mainly gundog but "with a bit of a seal in him" according to his owner; our adopted pet, Oscar, dearly loved and sadly missed as the death-notices put it. I used to throw a ball for him on the strand, a game that almost killed the neglected creature with delight. If I stood forgetful with the ball in my hand, lost in my musings over the riddles propounded by the sea to the sand, he would wait patiently at my feet, looking up, and very delicately place a paw on my toe to recall me. Then I would glance down and catch him saying, "There are just two ways, or perhaps three, in which you can hope to give supreme pleasure to another living being. You can go home and make love to her who loves you, or you can throw that ball for your dog. This is the time for the second alternative, for the third is to go on trying to perfect your book, which I do not believe you have it in you to do."

No, dogs do not speak. The sea does not riddle, dolphins do not pray, the vagrant bird neither trusts nor distrusts Robinson, waves never sign anything; what I myself witness is my own forgery. One should forego these overluxuriant metaphors that covertly impute a desire of communication to non-human reality. We ourselves are the only source of meaning, at least on this little beach of the Universe. These inscriptions that we insist on finding on every stone, every sand-grain, are in our own hand. People who write letters to themselves are generally regarded as pathetic, but such is the human condition. We are writing a work so vast, so multivocal, so driven asunder by its project of becoming coextensive with reality, that when we come across scattered phrases of it we fail to recognize them as our own.

A Nature Cure

Illustration overleaf: *Corncrakes*

RECCOLECTIONS &c OF JOURNEY FROM ESSEX

John Clare

John Clare (1793–1864) was a poet who wrote little prose but depicted the natural world with such vivid, intimate brilliance that he continues to be a major influence on prose writers today. He remains a relatively rare example of a truly working-class writer who could never – for better and for worse – escape his roots. He was born in Helpston, a village between the Northamptonshire wolds and the fens, the son of a farm labourer. Clare left school at twelve and worked as a gardener, camped with Gypsies, and began to write poems and sonnets. When his parents were faced with eviction Clare took his poems to a local bookseller, who sent them to his cousin, John Taylor, who had published John Keats. Clare's *Poems Descriptive of Rural Life and Scenery* (1820) was highly praised; so was *Village Minstrel, and Other Poems* (1821). Clare became torn between his Northamptonshire heartland – which was being transformed by the Enclosures – and the glamour of literary London. He suffered severe depression, drank heavily; his poetry sold less well and he struggled to support his wife, Patty, and seven children. Between 1837 and 1841 he was treated in a private asylum in Epping Forest, where he suffered delusions and claimed to have once been Byron and Shakespeare. In 1841, he absconded and walked nearly 100 miles home, believing he was married to his first love, Mary Joyce, as well as Patty. The following extract is his account of this journey. After five months living at home, he returned to an asylum in Northampton where he was encouraged and continued to write poetry, including 'I Am'. An appreciation of Clare's poetry was revived in the later twentieth century. His biographer, Jonathan Bate, judged Clare to be England's greatest working-class poet. 'No one has ever written more powerfully of nature, of a rural childhood, and of the alienated and unstable self,' he wrote.

July 24 1841. Returned home out of Essex & found no Mary her & her family are nothing to me now—though she herself was once the dearest of all—& how can I forget

July 18 1841. Felt very melancholly went a walk in the forest in the afternoon—fell in with some gipseys one of whom offered to assist in my escape from the madhouse by hiding me in his camp to which I almost agreed but told him I had no money to start with but if he would do so I would promise him fifty pounds & he agreed to do so before Saturday On friday I went again but he did not seem so willing so I said little about it—On Sunday I went & they were all gone—I found an old wide-awake hat & an old straw bonnet of the plum-pudding sort was left behind & I put the hat in my pocket thinking it might be usefull for another oppertunity & as good luck would have it it turned out to be so

July 19. Monday—Did nothing

July 20 Reconnitred the route the Gipsey pointed out & found it a legible one to make a movement & having only honest courage & myself in my army I led the way & my troops soon followed but being careless in mapping down the route as the Gipsey told me I missed the lane to Enfield Town & was going down Enfield Highway till I passed the Labour in vain Public-house where a person I knew coming out of the door told me the way

I walked down the lane gently & was soon in Enfield Town & bye & bye on the great York Road where it was all plain sailing & steering ahead meeting no enemy & fearing none I reached Stevenage where [it] being night I got over a gate [&] crossed over the corner to a green paddock where seeing a pond or hollow in the corner I [was] forced to stay off a respectable distance to keep from falling into it for my legs were nearly knocked up & began to stagger I scaled some old rotten paleings into the yard & then had higher pailings to clamber over to get into the shed or hovel which I did with difficulty being rather weak to my good luck I found some trusses of clover piled up about six or more feet square which I gladly mounted & slept on there were some trays in the hovel on which I would have reposed had I not found a better bed I slept soundly but had a very uneasy dream I thought my first wife lay on my left arm & somebody took her away from my side which made me wake up rather unhappy I thought as I woke somebody said 'Mary' but nobody was near—I lay down with my head towards the north to show myself the steering point in the morning

July 21 Daylight was looking in on every side & fearing my garrison might be taken by storm & myself be made prisoner I left my lodging by the way I got in & thanked God for his kindness in procuring it for anything in a famine is better than nothing & any place that giveth the weary rest is a blessing I gained the north road again & steered due north On the left hand side the road under the bank was like a cave—I saw a man & boy coiled up asleep which I hailed & they woke up to tell me the name of the next village

Somewhere on the London side the 'Plough' public-house a Man passed me on horseback in a slop-frock & said 'here's another of the broken-down haymakers' & threw me a penny to get a half-pint of beer which I picked up & thanked him for & when I got to the Plough I called for a half-pint & drank it & got a rest & escaped a very heavy shower in the bargain by having a shelter till it was over—afterwards I would have begged a penny of two drovers who were very saucy so I begged no more of anybody meet who I would

Having passed a Lodge on the left hand within a mile & a half or less of a town I think it might be St Ives* but I forget the name I sat down on a flint heap where I might rest half an hour or more & while sitting here I saw a tall Gipsey come out of the Lodge gate & make down the road towards where I was sitting when she got up to me on seeing she was a young woman of an honest-looking countenance rather handsome I spoke to her & asked her a few questions which she answered readily & with evident good humour so I got up & went on to the next town with her—she cautioned me on the way to put

* Clare's note: It was St Neots

something in my hat to keep the crown up & said in a lower tone 'You'll be noticed' but not knowing what she hinted I took no notice & made no reply at length she pointed to a tower-church which she called Shefford church & advised me to go on a footway which she said would take me direct to it & should shorten my journey fifteen miles by doing so I would gladly have taken the young woman's advice feeling that it was honest & a nigh guess towards the truth but fearing I might lose my way & not be able to find the north road again I thanked her & told her I should keep to the road when she bade me 'Good-day' & went into a house or shop on the left hand side the road I passed 3 or 4 good built houses on a hill & a public-house on the roadside in the hollow below them I seemed to pass the Milestones very quick in the morning but towards night they seemed to be stretched further asunder I got to a village further on & I forgot the name The road on the left hand was quite overshaded by some trees & quite dry so I sat down half an hour & made a good many wishes for breakfast but wishes were no hearty meal so I got up as hungry as I sat down—I forget here the names of the villages I passed through but recolect at late evening going through Potton in Bedfordshire where I called in a house to light my pipe in which was a civil old woman & a young country wench making lace on a cushion as round as a globe & a young fellow all civil people—I asked them a few questions as to the way & where the clergyman & overseer lived but they scarcely heard me or gave me no answer

I then went through Potton & happened with a kind talking country man who told me the parson lived a good way from where I was or overseer I don't know which so I went on hopping with a crippled foot for the gravel had got into my old shoes one of which had now nearly lost the sole had I found the overseer's house at hand or the parson's I should have gave my name & begged for a shilling to carry me home but I was forced to brush on penniless & be thankful I had a leg to move on I then asked him whether he could tell me of a farmyard anywhere on the road where I could find a shed & some dry straw & he said 'Yes if you will go with me I will show you the place—its a public house on the left hand side the road at the sign of the Ram' but seeing a stone or flint heap I longed to rest as one of my feet was very painfull so I thanked him for his kindness & bid him go on—But the good-natured fellow lingered awhile as if wishing to conduct me & then suddenly recolecting that he had a hamper on his shoulder & a lock-up bag in his hand cramfull to meet the coach which he feared missing—he started hastily & was soon out of sight—I followed looking in vain for the countryman's straw bed & not being able to meet it I lay down by a shed side under some elms between the wall & the trees being a thick row some 5 or 6 feet from the building I lay there & tried to sleep but the wind came in between them so cold that I lay still I quaked like the ague & quitted the lodging for a better at the Ram which I could hardly hope to find—It now began to grow dark apace & the odd houses on the road began to light up & show the inside tenants' lots very comfortable & my outside lot very uncomfortable & very wretched—still I hobbled forward as well as I could but at last came to the Ram the shutters were not closed & the lighted windows looked very cheering but I had no money & did not like to go in there was a sort of shed or gig-house at the end but I did not like to lie there as the people were up—so I still travelled on the road was very lonely & dark in places being over-shaded with trees at length I came to a place where the road branched off into two turnpikes one to the right about & the other straight forward & on going by my eye glanced on a milestone standing under the hedge so I heedlessly turned back to read it to see where the other road led to on doing so I found it led to London & then suddenly I forgot which was north or south & though I narrowly examined both ways I could see no tree or bush or stone heap that I could recolect I had passed so I went on mile after mile almost convinced I was going the same way as I came & these thoughts were so strong upon me that doubt & hopelessness made me turn so feeble that I was scarcely able to walk Yet I could not sit down or give up but shuffled along till I saw a lamp shining as bright as the moon which on nearing I found was suspended over a Toll-gate before I got through the man came out with a candle & eyed me narrowly but having no fear I stopt to ask him whether I was going northward & he said 'when you get through the gate you are' so I thanked him kindly & went through on the other side & gathered my old strength as my doubts vanished I soon cheered up & hummed the air of 'highland Mary' as I went on I at length fell in with an odd house all alone near a wood but I could not see what the sign was though the sign seemed to stand oddly enough in a sort of trough or spout there was a large porch over the door & being weary I crept in & glad enough I was to find I could lye with my legs straight the inmates were all gone to roost for I could hear them turn over in bed so I lay at full length on the stones in the porch—I slept here till daylight & felt very much refreshed as I got up I blest my two wives & both their familys when I lay down & when I got up & when I thought of some former difficultys on a like occasion I could not help blessing the Queen—I have but a slight reccolection of my journey between here & Stilton for I was knocked up & noticed little or nothing—one night I lay in a dyke bottom from the wind & went to sleep half an hour when I suddenly awoke & found my side wet through from the sock in the dyke bottom so I got out & went on—I remember going down a very dark road hung over with trees on both sides very thick which seemed to extend a mile or two I then entered a town & some of the chamber windows had candle lights shining in them—I felt so weary here that I [was] forced to sit down on the ground to rest myself a while & while I sat here a coach that seemed to be heavy laden came rattling up & stopt in the hollow below me & I cannot reccolect its ever passing by me* I then got up & pushed onward seeing little to notice for the road very often looked as stupid as myself & I was very often half asleep as I went on the third day I satisfied my hunger by eating the grass by the road side which seemed to taste something like bread I was hungry & eat heartily till I was satisfied & in fact the meal seemed to do me good the next & last day I reccolected that I had some tobacco & my box of lucifers being exhausted I could not light my pipe so I took to chewing tobacco all day & eat the quids when I

---

* Clare's note: The Coach did pass me as I sat under some trees by a high wall & the lamps flashed in my face & wakened me up from a doze when I knocked the gravel out of my shoes & started.

had done & I was never hungry afterwards—I remember passing through Buckden & going a length of road afterwards but I don't reccolect the name of any place until I came to Stilton where I was compleatly foot-foundered & broken down when I had got about half way through the town a gravel causeway invited me to rest myself so I lay down & nearly went to sleep & a young woman (so I guessed by the voice) came out of a house & said 'poor creature' & another more elderly said 'O he shams' But when I got up the latter said 'O no he don't' as I hobbled along very lame I heard the voices but never looked back to see where they came from— when I got near the Inn at the end of the gravel walk I met two young women & I asked one of them wether the road branching to the right by the end of the Inn did not lead to Peterborough & she said 'yes it did' so as soon as ever I was on it I felt myself in home's way & went on rather more cheerfull though I [was] forced to rest oftener than usual before I got to Peterborough a man & woman passed me in a cart & on hailing me as they passed I found they were neighbours from Helpstone where I used to live— I told them I was knocked up which they could easily see & that I had neither eat nor drunk anything since I left Essex when I told my story they clubbed together & threw me fivepence out of the cart I picked it up & called at a small public house near the bridge where I had two half pints of ale & two pen'orth of bread & cheese when I had done I started quite refreshed only my feet were more crippled than ever & I could scarcely make a walk of it Over the stones & being half ashamed to sit down in the street I [was] forced to keep on the move & got through Peterborough better than I expected when I got on the high road I rested on the stone heaps as I passed till I was able to go on afresh & bye & bye I passed Walton & soon reached Werrington & was making for the Beehive as fast as I could when a cart passed me with a man & a woman & a boy in it when nearing me the woman jumped out & caught fast hold of my hands & wished me to get into the cart but I refused & thought her either drunk or mad but when I was told it was my second wife Patty I got in & was soon at Northborough but Mary was not there neither could I get any information about her further than the old story of her being dead six years ago which might be taken from a bran new old newspaper printed a dozen years ago but I took no notice of the blarney having seen her myself about a twelvemonth ago alive & well & as young as ever—so here I am homeless at home & half gratified to feel I can be happy anywhere

from PEIG

Peig Sayers

Translated from the Irish by Bryan MacMahon

Máiréad 'Peig' Sayers (1873–1958) left school at twelve and never learned to write but became one of Ireland's greatest story-tellers and an embodiment of a Gaelic literary revival, just as an ancient rural culture was vanishing forever. Sayers was born on the Dingle Peninsula in western Ireland and her father was a storyteller. She worked as a domestic servant and moved to the Blasket Islands after marrying Pádraig Ó Guithín, a fisherman, in 1892. They had eleven children, of whom six survived. Robin Flower, an English poet and scholar who worked at the British Museum, visited the Blaskets and recorded Peig's stories, which then reached an academic audience. In the 1930s, a Dublin teacher and regular visitor to the Blaskets encouraged Peig to tell her life story to her son Mícheál. Peig dictated her biography, pub-lished in 1936 and went on to dictate more than 350 folk tales to Seosamh Ó Dálaigh of the Irish Folklore Commission. In 1942, she returned to her birthplace on the mainland, Dunquin. All Peig's surviving children, except for Mícheál, emigrated to the United States. The population of the Blasket Islands dwindled and the last twenty-two residents, all Irish speakers, were evacu-ated by the government in 1953.

While the children were growing up the school wasn't a stone's throw away from them and I was easy in my mind while they were attending school. I was terrified they'd be drowned on the beach because they were obsessed with the notion of going there when they were small. The breed of the sea was in them. Often I'd smash their toy boats. Then again, while they were attending school they could have little recourse to the strand for when they'd come home from school I'd put them drawing turf and at night they'd have their lessons to occupy their minds. Scarcely an evening passed without Cáit O'Brien paying us a visit.

You can well understand that at that time poor people weren't too hot in their skins. Potatoes and fish was their fare with now and again an odd mouthful of meat—good wholesome food—that's what they had at that time. At certain times of the year there was milk but, my word, it's often we had to do with very little of that same. The children grew up and, thanks be to God, they never went to bed hungry. They were cross enough when they were small but then again, sense never comes before age. But alas and alas, death gored us! It swept three of my family in their infancy and then measles took Siobhán, a fine bouncer of a girl eight years old.

But no one in this life is exempt from the law of God and it gives me pleasure to think that they are before me in the Kingdom of Heaven and my prayer is that the God of Glory will grant myself and those of my children still alive never to break His law in this life in such a way as would separate us on Judgement Day, but that my little family will rise up from the dead about me and that we'll all be united in the Kingdom of God.

Well! I had buried four of my children and, worse still, their father's health was broken for he caught a cold out fishing and he was making no headway towards recovery.

One day, I had buried my fourth child and it was no wonder that I was troubled in my mind. As the evening was fine I decided to go out so I took up a stocking from the window in order to be knitting, but to tell you the truth, I hadn't much mind for work that same evening. I drove the cow back before me and let her into the field for I reckoned that I could do no better than sit down for a while herding her.

I sat on the bank above the beach where I had a splendid view all around me. Dead indeed is the heart from which the balmy air of the sea cannot banish sorrow and grief. The passage between the Great Blasket and Beginnis is like a little harbour and it looks most attractive when the weather is calm. As I had no interest in the work I put down my stocking on a tussock and began to look away out to sea at the thousands of seabirds flying here and there in search of a bite to eat. Every bird from the stormy petrel to the cormorant, from the sand-snipe to the gannet was there and each variety of bird had its own peculiar call. There were many thousands of small seagulls; some, hovering lightly, were searching for little sprat or other morsels of food. Whenever one of them found a mouthful she'd utter a call and straightaway thousands of others were down on top of her. Such scuffling and pecking no one ever saw before! They were all entangled in one another trying to snatch the morsel from her.

At last I grew tired of watching the gulls and I turned my gaze to the south—towards Iveragh and Dingle Bay. It was a beautiful view. The whole bay was as calm as new milk, with little silver spray shimmering on its surface under a sunlight that was then brilliant. To the south Slea Head stood boldly in view as if it would stand there for ever—not a stir out of the water at the edge of the rocks nor in the creek itself so that even an old woman need not be troubled if she were sitting in a sheltered nook by the edge of a rock—for there was no fear of her being drowned! Dunmore stood out before me and Liúir too, like its watchdog, its crest covered with seagulls and cormorants resting at their ease; the Seanduine—Old Man Rock himself—was grinning beside them, his skull covered with a fleece of seaweed—though a person might say that it was high time for that same skull to be shaken and stripped by the mighty and insolent ocean waves that were forever crashing down upon it. Maol, or Baldie Bank, looked so peaceful and mild-tempered that you wouldn't think he ever did hurt or harm, though the old people said that it was on that rock the King of Spain's ship was wrecked long ago. And that finished the vessel and all on board—God save those who hear the tale!

Out before me stood Dunquin—the fresh colour of summer on its fields and gardens—this was where I had spent my early days. Many the fine evening I was on top of that hill, Mount Eagle, when I was young and airy and with no responsibility whatsoever to carry. Away to the north stood the headland of Ceann Sratha and there also lay the mouth of Ferriter's Cove and Dún an Óir. Binn Diarmada appeared both triumphant and stately; the sunlight glistened brightly on its sides and on the deep scars the mighty ocean had wrought upon it.

From Fiach to Barra Liath was one great sea harbour; it resembled a single sheet of glass and indeed, an observer might see it as a great city lying under a magic spell.

A sigh welled up from my heart and I said aloud: 'God! isn't it an odd person indeed who would be troubled in mind with so much beauty around him and all of it the work of the Creator's hand?'

I jumped with fright as a voice came from behind me. 'Isn't it time you were going home?' the voice said—it was Seán Eoghain who spoke.

'I daresay it is, Seán,' I told him, 'but to tell the truth I haven't much mind to do so.'

'That's no wonder, my poor woman,' said Seán. 'Everyone feels lonely after a death of a child.'

'Not child, Seán,' I said, 'but children.' I would have preferred any other topic of conversation at that time and so as to change the subject I said. 'Look, Seán! There's Hy-Brasail to the north!'

'You devil you, where?' said Seán for he was a man with curses to burn. He turned on his heel.

'No doubt about it, but it's a lovely view on a summer afternoon,' he said. 'A person would take his oath that it's some enchanted land.'

'Yes, indeed,' I said. 'I often heard Eibhlís Sheáin say that she herself saw Hy-Brasail appearing in that very place one autumn evening while she was cutting furze on the Brow of Coum.'

'The devil sweep yourself and Eibhlís Sheáin,' Seán replied in a humorous way that was meant for my good. 'And when you go to Hy-Brasail that you may never leave it! Get up and go home for yourself. 'Tis time for you to be off now!'

'You're right, I suppose,' I said, and I took up the stocking that lay beside me; indeed I hadn't much work done that afternoon.

It has been said that there is no joy in life without its own sorrow to accompany it. I thought I had finished with the woes of the world for those of my family who lived were now grown men. Muiris and Pádraig were fishing for themselves and Mícheál and Tomás were coming to maturity after them. Even if their father's health had failed they weren't depending on him; their uncle was giving them a hand and well able he was to do so.

from THE OUTRUN

Amy Liptrot

Writer and journalist **Amy Liptrot** (b. 1981) grew up on a sheep
farm in Orkney. Her debut, *The Outrun* (2016), describes her
alcohol addiction while working in London, followed by her re-
habilitation in Orkney, where she worked to help the endangered
corncrake population. It won the Wainwright Prize and the PEN
Ackerley Prize. She has written regularly for *Caught by the River*,
the *Guardian* and the *Observer* and has also worked as an artist's
model, a trampolinist and in a shellfish factory. Liptrot has lived in
Berlin and London and is now based in West Yorkshire, with her
partner and two sons.

THE CORNCRAKE WIFE

It is two a.m. on Friday night and I'm alone down a farm track,
dancing in the glow of my headlights because I heard the call I
know belongs to a medium-sized brown bird. Unexpectedly, I got
the job working for the RSPB on the Corncrake Initiative, a long-
running conservation project and, rather than return to London,
signed a contract for a summer in Orkney.

I spent the summer staying up all night. When everyone else was
asleep, I was out in the gloaming with the livestock and the wildfowl,
searching for a rare, endangered bird: the corncrake.

Corncrakes, sometimes known as landrails, are similar in size and
shape to moorhens, but brown with a ginger wing and pink beak,
inhabiting farmland rather than wetland. At one time they were
common across the whole of the UK. Numbers declined dramatically
in the twentieth century, and now they are found only on the western
isles and Orkney in this country. The birds are on the Red List of
threatened species of the International Union for Conservation of

Nature, and last summer, 2011, just thirty-one calling males were located here.

My job is to locate every calling male – only the males call – in Orkney. I appeal for public reports, asking people to call my 'corncrake hotline' if they hear one. My answerphone message contains a recording of the call so that people can compare it with what they have heard. The sound is like a credit card being scraped over a comb, or a guiro percussion instrument or, like the corncrake's onomatopoeic Latin name, *Crex crex*. The oldest islanders are already familiar with the call, which was once the sound of the countryside on summer nights.

As well as collecting other people's reports, I carry out my own comprehensive survey. It is lucky that I've just got my driving licence back after the ban for drink-driving because my survey is carried out by car between midnight and three a.m. Corncrakes call throughout the night, peaking between these hours when the males are at the centre of their territories. Over seven weeks, following a standardised national methodology, I survey twice every one-kilometre map-grid square in Orkney containing suitable corncrake habitat – hay and silage fields, and tall vegetation such as nettles or iris. Corncrakes are elusive. They hide in the long vegetation and we locate them by ear, rather than sight. I stop every 250–500 metres, wind down the windows and listen for two minutes.

Now that lambing has finished, I've come back to stay at Mum's in Kirkwall and she's already in bed when I leave the house around eleven – nightclub time – having filled my Thermos with coffee rather than wine, dressed in warm layers, made sure I have my maps and phone charged, and drive out into the countryside. I pass homes putting their lights out for the night, then ancient standing stones and modern wind turbines on the dark hillsides.

At this time of year in Orkney – the weeks around midsummer – it barely gets dark overnight: the sky just dims. This time between sunset and sunrise is known as the 'simmer dim' or the 'grimlins', from the Old Norse word *grimla*, which means 'to twinkle or glimmer'. I feel like the only person awake on the island, and am usually the only driver on the road. On a clear night with little cloud, there is a perpetual sunrise or sunset during the hours of my survey.

I am lucky to have an excuse to stop and listen. It takes a few seconds for the car's engine to stop running and quieten, then for my personal velocity to come to a halt, heartbeat to slow, clothes to stop rustling, for the noise in my head to fall away and the sounds of the night to reveal themselves. I become dark-adjusted and alert to noise: chin on the open window, cool wind on my face, occasionally catching my reflection in the wing mirror, ears held forward by my woolly hat into prime listening position. Two minutes can seem a long time when you're concentrating.

Even at one a.m. – the darkest point of the night in British Summer Time – the birds are going bonkers. I hear the 'classic three' Orkney birds – bubbling curlews, piping oystercatchers and lapwings, which sound like a dial-up modem – nearly every time I stop. I note down unfamiliar calls to ask my knowledgeable colleagues back in the RSPB office: 'creaking bedsprings', 'haunted chicken'. They inform me that the 'shivery baby goat' sound I hear is snipe 'drumming', an eerie, memorable wobble made by its tail feathers. There are other noises too: of wind turbines, domestic animals and livestock, a flowing burn, the sea, wind and rain. I learn that, although I can't see much on foggy nights, sound travels further in the mist.

The sun both rises and sets north-ish at this time of year, just dipping below the horizon, so surveying the north coast is particularly special. Speeding home, just getting light, the currents of Eynhallow Sound are churning through the mist. I park at the top of Wideford Hill next to the communications pylons and look down at the lights of Kirkwall.

I can go for nights without hearing a corncrake. The weather gets into the car. On the rare occasions I see another vehicle I wonder what they're doing out in the country at this time of night, and they think the same about me. A few times farmers, and once a police car, ask me what I'm doing but I have a good reason. At times I'm scared, down an unfamiliar country road alone at night, shocked by a scarecrow. I'm connected to the world through my phone, Google Maps helping me navigate in the dark. On Friday and Saturday nights, I think about what my friends are doing back in London, reading their drunk tweets before they delete them in the morning. The survey can become monotonous, but when I'm flagging, the sky does something amazing. I love the mist that hangs below me in Orkney's gentle valleys, as if I've climbed to the top of the beanstalk.

In the bottom right-hand corner of my photograph is a pair of bright flashes – the eyes of a sheep I hadn't even realised was there when I pointed my phone camera into the night. Livestock are close by, dark and quietly chewing. I've caught a goose, a hare and a teenager in my headlights. I caught the full moon in my wing mirror. I drove to the edge of the cliff, trying to get closer to the sky, looking out to smaller islands, with their lighthouses glowing, flashes of colour in the dark, reflected on Scapa Flow. I share the night with cats – their eyes shining in the dykes – voles and hedgehogs.

According to the timestamp on my photograph, it was 1.08 a.m. when I saw noctilucent cloud for the first time, on a back road in the Stenness area. I knew its visibility was limited to more northern latitudes, the weeks around midsummer and late nights, so I had a chance of seeing it when out doing the corncrake surveys. Tonight there it is, at the top of my field of vision, unmistakable. Fifty miles high, in the deep twilight, icy blue wisps hang like lightning crossed with cotton wool. I get out of the car and hold my phone to the sky, smiling like a nutter. At this time of night most clouds are silhouetted but the space cloud – it shines.

I am in perpetual hope. I want to hear corncrakes at each stop and briefly mistake for its call the quack of a duck, the churning of the blades of a wind turbine, the rasping breathing of a cow. But although I have heard quite a few, I have not seen one yet. They are extremely secretive birds, hiding low in the long grass. In his poem 'The Landrail', John Clare describes the phenomenon of birds that can be heard but rarely seen as 'like a fancy everywhere / A sort of living doubt'. I begin to doubt my belief in corncrakes.

When I do find a corncrake – on a still night, they can be heard a kilometre away – it's almost too much to believe. I get out of the car and, keeping to the road so I don't disturb the bird, lit by the grimlins and my headlights, I move slowly towards the call until I can pinpoint its location by ear.

In my confusion I don't know where I am. Dusk blends into dawn and I can't say whether the day is ending or beginning. Then I'm confused by the sight of a cruise ship, all lit up out to sea, like a tower block floating in space.

But the light – by three a.m. I don't need the car light to read my map – reveals where I have been all along. It's just my familiar island. Surveying the West Mainland in particular, each road is full of memories. I stop at the former post office where my birth was registered while Dad was in hospital, at the school bus stop where I often found four-leaf clovers, at the passing place near Yesnaby where the police caught me drink-driving. I've driven thousands of miles within a fifty-mile-diameter island. I have driven all of Orkney's roads and traversed its tracks, grooved its geography into my mind, its contour lines onto my skin, making it more difficult to leave again.

I have had to visit some of the smaller Orkney islands and I travel to them on the roll-on, roll-off – 'ro-ro' – car ferries that run on bacon butties and in nearly all weathers. On Sanday, I see a couple walking their ferrets off the ferry, hear two male corncrakes call in competition from either side of a loch, and a story about a cow that swam a mile. I'm told on Stronsay about a corncrake that got caught in a lobster creel. On Eday, where there are no corncrakes, I hear about how fishermen on the isles didn't want to learn how to swim so that if the boat went down they would drown more quickly. On Burray, the haar comes in but the fog turns pink in the sunrise and I can hear seals, across the fields, down on the shore, howling like ghouls.

As I drive, I try to unpick what happened: all the houses I've lived in, the lost jobs, the treatment centre, my aching heart. At first, I counted the days I had been sober, then the weeks. Now it's just the months and the cravings come less frequently, but they still come. Driving home in a beautiful dawn, the only person on the road, listening to happy hardcore, I feel like the Queen of Orkney. Then, suddenly, all I want is a bottle of wine and it's a good thing the island has no twenty-four-hour off-licences.

—w—

The main reason for the decline in numbers of corncrakes over the twentieth century is increasingly mechanised farming methods, in particular larger and more efficient grass mowers. Most corncrakes live in fields intended for hay or silage and when the mowers come to cut the grass, the birds – particularly the chicks – are usually killed. Corncrakes move away from the mower into the ever-decreasing area of uncut grass, and are eventually caught in the middle of the field and mown to death on the final swathe.

Once I've located the corncrakes, through reports from the public and my night surveys, I visit the landowners. I feel nervous driving down unfamiliar tracks, knocking at farmhouse doors, dogs barking. Older Orcadians tend to refer to women, regardless of marital status, as 'wives' so, arriving at farms to speak to farmers about the endangered birds on their land, I am announced with 'The corncrake wife is here.' The RSPB offers the farmers money to delay cutting or grazing the grass, or to mow in a 'corncrake-friendly' pattern: from the inside of the fields outwards, giving the birds more of a chance to escape. Every farmer is willing to discuss the options with me. I find them knowledgeable about the wildlife on their land and most are able to change the mowing pattern, although delaying the crop until August is often, despite the payment, too drastic a change. No one flat-out refuses: that's not really the Orcadian way. They just say they'll think about it, then I never hear back.

I learn as much as I can about this one species. I read scientific papers and follow research on their migration routes. They're all that people ask me about. I accidentally replace other words with 'corncrake' when I'm typing; I change my ringtone to a corncrake's call; I set a Google alert for corncrake references in the world's media. Somehow this bird has become my thing. I am hallucinating a *Crex crex* call in the background of music on the radio and at night I dream of corncrakes.

In June 2011, fifty adult male corncrakes were caught on the Hebridean island of Coll, lured into nets by a taped call of what they thought was a rival male. Geolocators, weighing less than a gram, were attached to their legs on plastic rings. The following summer, some of the birds were re-caught, and their tags revealed that they had travelled all the way to the Democratic Republic of the Congo in Central Africa. This seems incredible: in Scotland, corncrakes are reluctant to fly at all, which is what makes them so vulnerable to farm machinery. There is even local folklore about them going 'underground' instead of migrating, turning into moorhens or perhaps riding on other birds' backs. But fly they do, although just 30 per cent of adults survive the migration to return to Orkney the following year. Many are trapped in hunters' nets in north Africa. Corncrakes need to rear a lot of chicks just to replenish the population, let alone increase it.

.

Since before I started the job, I've been reading *Moby-Dick*. I've been reading it for so long it feels like I've been on a three-year round-the-world whaling trip, carrying it back and forth every day, hefty in my shoulder bag, like a harpoon. I'm storm-crazed Captain Ahab, but instead of a whale I'm chasing an elusive bird. Although I've heard almost thirty males, I still haven't seen one. The corncrake is always just beyond me.

On tough nights, I start to ask myself questions. Why save this bird, a bird seldom seen, a relic from the crofting times, a bird unable to adapt to modern land use? What difference does it make? And then I learn that, in 1977, corncrake remains were excavated from the Pictish and Viking Age site at Buckquoy, in Orkney's West Mainland. It shocks me to discover that corncrakes had been here for thousands of years, yet in less than a century we have all but wiped them out. Their decline is undoubtedly down to human activity so it seems right that we should take responsibility to conserve the last few.

An isolated male, perhaps the only corncrake on his island, calls for three, four, five hours a night, for months. One was heard calling on Flotta all summer, and I am delighted to learn that chicks were seen at the end of the season – he found a mate, after all.

I reach a total of thirty-two calling male corncrakes heard in Orkney during the season, just one more than last year. Each male that calls from the same spot for more than a few days is assumed to be accompanied by a female. Although numbers still remain low, since the RSPB's Corncrake Initiative has been running, there has been a slight upward trend in Orkney. Unlike the fabled drowning sailors, the corncrakes are struggling against death and somehow it is as if my fate becomes intertwined with that of the bird. I'm trying to cling to a normal life and stay sober. They are clinging to existence.

My friend told me about when her mother died, leaving behind a husband and three young children. The family went on holiday in America, and my friend described her dad as 'just driving'. You might feel that you can't go on, yet you do, just driving to give yourself something to do while things settle, shift and gain form, until the way that life is going to be makes itself clear. I'm driving on, one-kilometre grid square by one-kilometre grid square. Imperceptibly, the churning in my chest is subsiding. Like when I cycled at night in London, I find relief by being in motion. One night, I realise I'm feeling easier and more normal, even lucky to live and work here in Orkney.

This is a different kind of nightlife. The life I had in the city – parties and clubs – is no longer there for me but these never-nights, marking off grid references and following maps in the mist, they are my own. I've found no corncrakes tonight but dawn is coming. I've got a flask of coffee and I can hear seals.

There are wonderful moments. I make eye contact with a short-eared owl, plentiful this year and known locally as 'catty faces'. It's on a fence post next to where I park, and we both turn our heads and see each other. I gasp, the owl flies. One still-pink dawn, just before midsummer, I stop at the Ring of Brodgar on the way home. There's no one around, and I take all my clothes off and run around the Neolithic stone circle.

Then, just after three a.m., when I finish my survey one night towards the end of the seven weeks, I pull away slowly in the car and something unexpected happens: I see a corncrake. It's just a moment but it's in the road right in front of me, running into the grass verge. Its image – the pink beak and ginger wing – keeps darting through my mind: just a second that confirmed the existence I'd spent months searching for. My first and only corncrake. Usually dawn comes slowly but tonight I drive out of a cloud and suddenly it's a new day.

from H IS FOR HAWK

Helen Macdonald

A polymath in the old nature writing tradition, **Helen Macdonald** (b. 1970) is an academic historian of science, an artist and illustrator, falconer, poet and writer. She grew up in Camberley, Surrey, and possessed a keen interest in local wildlife – and birds of prey in particular – as a child. Her memoir, *H is for Hawk* (2014), an international bestseller which won the 2014 Samuel Johnson Prize, Costa Book Award and the Prix du Meilleur Livre Étranger in France, tells the story of her grief over her father's death and recovery through training Mabel, a goshawk. It is also a biography of T. H. White. Macdonald is the author of *Falcon* (2006) and an essay collection, *Vesper Flights* (2020), and writes regularly for *The New York Times*. She has presented radio series and TV documentaries including a *Natural World* programme about training a new goshawk chick and an examination of the hidden nature of motorways.

EXTINCTION

Falconers have a word for hawks in the mood to slay: they call the bird *in yarak*. The books say it comes from the Persian *yaraki*, meaning power, strength and boldness. Much later I was amused to find that in Turkish it means an archaic weapon and is also slang for penis: never doubt that falconry is a boys' game. I'm back in Cambridge now, and as I carry Mabel up the stony track to the hill each day I watch her come into yarak. It is disturbingly like watching her slow possession by a demon. Her crest feathers rise, she leans back, tummy feathers fluffed, shoulders dropped, toes very tight on the glove. Her demeanour switches from *everything scares me* to *I see it all; I own all this and more*.

In this state she's a high-tension wire-strung hawk of murderous anticipation, wound so tight she bates at anything that moves – things she's not a hope of catching: flocks of larks, distant racing pigeons, even a farmyard tomcat – and I hold her jesses tight and don't let her go. But when a hen pheasant rockets up from my feet I do. She chases it fiercely but it has too much of a head start; after fifty yards she slows, turns in mid-air and comes back to me, planing over the top of a hedgerow ash to land gently upon my fist. On another day she bursts downhill in pursuit of a rabbit and is about to grab it when the rabbit stops dead in its tracks. She overshoots and crashes into the ground; the rabbit jinks, doubles back on itself and runs uphill to the safety of a hole. She leaps back into the air to resume her pursuit but the rabbit is gone. She alights, confused and crestfallen, on the grass.

I'm crestfallen too. It's not that I'm baying for blood. But I don't want Mabel to get discouraged. In the wild, young goshawks will sit for hours hidden in trees waiting for an easy opportunity to present itself: a fledgling crow, a baby rabbit. But it is September now: nature's easy pickings are grown. And while most goshawkers have a dog to help them find game, or a ferret to bolt rabbits for their hawk to chase, I do not. All I can do is walk with the hawk and hope we find something to catch. But I am a liability; her senses are far better than mine. We walk past a gully under a hedge where there are rabbits and rats and God knows what, all covered with brambles and briars and robins' pincushions set on briar stems like exotic fruit, their vegetable hairs brushed green and rose and carmine. She dives from my fist towards the undergrowth. I don't know she's seen something – so I don't let her go. Then I curse my pathetic human senses. Something was there. A mouse? A pheasant? A rabbit? With a stick I poke about in the gully but nothing comes out. It is too late; whatever it was has gone. We walk on. Mabel stops looking murderous and assumes an expression of severe truculence. *How the hell*, I imagine her thinking, *am I supposed to catch things with this idiot in tow?*

I return exhausted from our latest attempt: a hellish, traumatic afternoon, fractious, gusty and sour. I'd met Stuart and Mandy out on the hill. 'I'll run the dogs for you,' he said. 'See if we can get a point for her.' But Mabel wasn't having any of it. She bated and twittered and glared. She hated the dogs, she hated it all. I hated it too. I fed her up and drove us home. Then I started pulling clothes from a wardrobe, attempting to transform myself into a cheerful, civilised person who does things like go to art galleries. I brush the burrs from my hair, wash my face, shrug on a skirt, push the sleeves of a cashmere jumper back to my elbows, paint a black line over each eyelid. Foundation. Mascara. A smear of lipsalve to seal my wind-dried mouth, a pair of shiny boots with heels that make me worry that I can't run in them – for running seems essential these days – and I check the result in a mirror. It is a good disguise. I'm pleased with how convincing it seems. But it's getting late, and I'm running against the clock. I have twenty minutes to get to a gallery for the opening of an art exhibition. I'm supposed to give a talk about it in a few weeks' time and I have to see the bloody thing first. I battle with sleep as I drive, and by the time I reach the gallery doors my knees are ready to give way.

I expect a room of paintings and sculpture. But when I open the doors there's something so unexpected inside my brain turns cartwheels. It is a full-sized bird hide built of rough-hewn pine, and it is – I read the sign – an exact copy of a real structure in California. Seeing it in the gallery is as disconcerting as opening a fridge door and finding a house within. The hide is dark inside and packed with people peering through a window in one wall. I look out of it too. *Oh!* I see the trick. It is a neat one. The artist has filmed the view from the real hide, and is projecting it onto a screen beyond the window. It shows a soaring California condor, a huge, dusty-black carrion-eating vulture rendered nearly extinct by persecution, habitat destruction and poisoning from lead-contaminated carcasses. By the late 1980s only twenty-seven birds remained, and in a last-ditch effort to save the species they were trapped and taken into captivity so that their domestic-bred young could be used to repopulate the wild. Some people tried to stop this happening. They believed honestly and sincerely that once all the birds were captive, condors would cease to exist. These birds are made of wildness, they argued. A captive condor is a condor no more.

I watch the condor for a while. It makes me impatient. My head is packed with real skies and real hawks. I'm remembering live condors I'd met at a captive-breeding centre years before: vast, loose-feathered, turkey-necked birds with purpose and curiosity; avian hogs in black feather-boas. Precious, yes, but complicated, real, idiosyncratic, astonishing. The condor on the gallery screen was nothing like them. *Helen, you are an idiot*, I think. *That is the whole point of this exhibition. The whole point of it, right there in front of you.*

I think of what wild animals are in our imaginations. And how they are disappearing – not just from the wild, but from people's everyday lives, replaced by images of themselves in print and on screen. The rarer they get, the fewer meanings animals can have. Eventually rarity is all they are made of. The condor is an icon of extinction. There's little else to it now but being the last of its kind. And in this lies the diminution of the world. How can you love something, how can you fight to protect it, if all it means is loss? There is a vast difference between my visceral, bloody life with Mabel and the reserved, distanced view of modern nature-appreciation. I know that some of my friends see my keeping a hawk as morally suspect, but I couldn't love or understand hawks as much as I do if I'd only ever seen them on screens. I've made a hawk part of a human life, and a human life part of a hawk's, and it has made the hawk a million times more complicated and full of wonder to me. I think of my chastened surprise when Mabel played with a paper telescope. She is real. She can resist the meanings humans give her. But the condor? The condor has no resistance to us at all. I stare at the attenuated, drifting image on the gallery screen. It is a shadow, a figure of loss and hope; it is hardly a bird at all.

The other exhibit is perfectly simple. It is a bird lying on its back in a glass box in an empty room. Seeing it makes all my soapbox musings fade and fall away. It's a parrot, a Spix's macaw. There are none left in the wild now and the last captive birds are the focus of desperate attempts to keep the species alive. This one is long dead. Stuffed with cotton wool, a small paper label tied to one of its clenched dry feet, its feathers are the deep blue of an evening sea. It might be the loneliest thing I have ever seen. But leaning over this spotlit skin in a glass coffin, I don't think of animal extinction at all. I think of

Snow White. I think of Lenin in his ill-lit mausoleum. And I think of the day after my father died, when I was shown into a hospital room where he lay.

But this isn't him, I thought, wildly, after the woman closed the door. *He isn't here.* Someone had dressed a waxwork of my father in hospital pyjamas and a patterned duvet. Why would they do that? It made no sense. It was nonsense. I took a step back. Then I saw on his arm the cut that would not heal and stopped. I knew I had to speak. For ages I could not. Physically could not. Something the size of a fist was in my throat and it was catching the words and not letting them out. I started to panic. Why couldn't I speak? *I have to speak to him.* Then the tears came. They were not like normal tears. Water coursed in sheets down my cheeks and dripped to the hospital floor. And with the water came words. So I leaned over the bed and spoke to my father who was not there. I addressed him seriously and carefully. I told him that I loved him and missed him and would miss him always. And I talked on, explaining things to him, things I cannot now remember but which at the time were of clear and burning importance. Then there was silence. And I waited. I did not know why. Until I realised it was in hope that an answer might come. And then I knew it was over. I took my father's hand in my own for the last time, squeezed it in a brief goodbye and quietly left the room.

The next day out on the hill Mabel learns, I suppose, what she is for. She chases a pheasant. It crashes into the brambles beneath a tall hedge. She lands on top of the hedge, peering down, her plumage bright against the dark earth of the further slope. I start running. I think I remember where the pheasant has gone. I convince myself it was never there at all. I know it is there. Clay sticks to my heels and slows me down. I'm in a world of slowly freezing mud, and even the air seems to be getting harder to run through. Mabel is waiting for me to flush the pheasant, if only I knew where it was. Now I am at the hedge, trying to find it, constructing *what will happen next* scenarios in my head, and at this point they're narrowing fast, towards point zero, when the pheasant will fly. I cannot see Stuart and Mandy any more, though I know they must be there. I'm crashing through brambles and sticks, dimly aware of the catch and rip of thorns in my flesh. Now I cannot see the hawk because I am searching for the pheasant, so I have to work out what she is doing by putting myself in her mind – and so I become both the hawk in the branches above and the human below. The strangeness of this splitting makes me feel I am walking under myself, and sometimes away from myself. Then for a moment everything becomes dotted lines, and the hawk, the pheasant and I merely elements in a trigonometry exercise, each of us labelled with soft italic letters. And now I am so invested in the hawk and the pheasant's relative positions that my consciousness cuts loose entirely, splits into one or the other, first the hawk looking down, second the pheasant in the brambles looking up, and I move over the ground as if I couldn't possibly affect anything in the world. There is no way I can flush this pheasant. I'm not here. Time stretches and slows. There's a sense of panic at this point, a little buffet of fear that's about annihilation and my place in the world. But then the pheasant is flushed, a pale and burring chunk of muscle and feathers, and the hawk crashes from the hedge towards it. And all the lines that connect heart and head and future possibilities, those lines that also connect me with the hawk and the pheasant and with life and death, suddenly become safe, become tied together in a small muddle of feathers and gripping talons that stand in mud in the middle of a small field in the middle of a small county in a small country on the edge of winter.

I stare at the hawk as she grips the dead pheasant, and her mad eyes stare right back at me. I'm amazed. I don't know what I expected to feel. Bloodlust? Brutality? No. Nothing like that. There are thorn-scratches all over me from where I dived through the hedge, and an ache in my heart I can't place. There's a sheeny fog in the air. Dry. Like talc. I look at the hawk, the pheasant, the hawk. And every-thing changes. The hawk stops being a thing of violent death. She becomes a child. It shakes me to the core. She is a child. A baby hawk that's just worked out who she is. What she's for. I reach down and start, unconsciously as a mother helping a child with her dinner, plucking the pheasant with the hawk. For the hawk. And when she starts eating, I sit on my heels and watch, watch her eat. Feathers lift, blow down the hedge, and catch in spiders' webs and thorn branches. The bright blood on her toes coagulates and dries. Time passes. Benison of sunlight. A wind shifts the thistle stalks and is gone. And I start crying, soundlessly. Tears roll down my face. For the pheasant, for the hawk, for Dad and for all his patience, for that little girl who stood by a fence and waited for the hawks to come.

·

Urban Nature

Illustration overleaf: *Fox*

from THE UNOFFICIAL COUNTRYSIDE

Richard Mabey

For several decades, **Richard Mabey** (b. 1941), widely regarded as the father of modern British nature writing, was a lone voice for nature in a publishing wilderness. The genre didn't exist when Mabey published *Food for Free* (1972) followed by *The Unofficial Countryside* (1973), which presciently examined urban nature and 'edgelands' four decades before other writers. A 'hedge kid', Mabey grew up roaming the countryside around Berkhamsted, studied philosophy, politics and economics at Oxford, and worked as a teacher, book editor, and TV producer and presenter before becoming a full-time writer. As well as working in nature conservation, Mabey has written more than thirty critically acclaimed books and hundreds of columns and essays, often drawing attention to flowers and plants, local wildlife and our relationships with other species. His biography of Gilbert White (1986), which won the Whitbread Biography Award, and epic cultural history of plants, *Flora Britannica* (1996), are key texts in the revival of British nature writing. More recently, Mabey's *Nature Cure* (2005), an account of discovering a new landscape in the wake of a breakdown, heralded a new sub-genre of nature memoir that pays attention to the healing power of other species and landscapes.

Rubbish tips, I suppose, are the real untouchables in our caste system of landscapes. They are ugly, smelly, and act like magnifying glasses to the swelling volume of indestructible garbage that we toss over our shoulders. But nature, always more economically efficient than us, does what it can to make use of these places, and what sewage farms are to birds, refuse tips are to plants.

This is not really the place to look into the complex technology and increasingly involved ethics of rubbish disposal. Within the next decade or so the haphazard dumping of refuse on tips is likely to become an indulgence we can afford neither in terms of the ground space it occupies nor the resources it squanders. Already some local authorities are developing techniques for extracting valuable elements (particularly metals) from garbage and incinerating as much as possible of the remainder, using the precious calories generated for community heating schemes. There's no doubt that systems of this sort will become more widespread, and that the old-style rubbish tip will become a museum-piece, a habitat as rare and relict as a fen. (It would be ironic if the last few examples of a land-use that many amenity societies are fighting to eradicate ended up as nature reserves, artificially conserved in all their fertile slumminess!) This is the fate of land in the unofficial countryside. This year's wasteland is next year's wasted land.

But for the time being, most of our household refuse, and a fair amount of non-toxic industrial waste, will continue simply to be dumped on specially assigned plots of ground at the edges of towns. Sometimes the designated area is an abandoned quarry or gravel pit. More often it's a patch of low-lying waste ground with little obvious potential for farming or housing. But whatever the chosen receptacle, the technique of disposal follows much the same pattern. The garbage – kitchen and garden refuse that will eventually decay, plastic containers that won't, ash, glass, a multitude of small solid objects from thrown-out toys to motor car tyres, the waste from tanneries and mills, the whole adding up to nearly 10 cwt. per person per year – is tipped from the carts and strewn in a thin layer across a section of the tip. Some of the paper and more easily combustible materials may be roughly sorted out for burning, and the rest covered by bulldozer with a thin layer of soil. This may come from another part of the dump or be imported from nearby earthworks. This plot is then allowed to settle for a few months before another stratum of refuse is laid over it.

Consider then the geology of the surface of a tip from a plant's point of view. On the top, a thin layer of well-worked soil. Underneath, what amounts to a layer of vegetable manure, slowly rotting as the bacteria and fungi get their teeth into it. The drainage and aeration are good on account of the loose packing of the vegetable refuse and its skeleton of solid debris. There is light, for there's no time for any shade-giving shrubs to become established, and even warmth from the decaying vegetable matter. In short, the dump is like nothing so much as a huge compost heap, and is mightily congenial to plant growth. The snag is the bulldozers and the ominous looming of the next smothering layer of garbage. So it is the fast growing annuals, those opportunist weeds that are so adept at nipping into bare and short-lived plots of ground, that make out best here. The bulk of the flowers are those that you would find in any patch of disturbed ground – groundsel, petty spurge, fat hen, shepherd's purse, docks. There will also be a smattering of those low-lying plants that are tolerant of the constant pounding of the dustcarts: plantains, knotgrass and pine-apple weed. And there are perennial plants that actually thrive from being sliced up by the bulldozers, like the common creeping thistle, which can send up new shoots from strips of chopped-up root.

But if rubbish tips nourished these plants alone, they'd warrant no more special attention than any other type of waste ground. It is the plant material – and seeds in particular – that finds its way into the ground as part of the refuse itself that can turn dumps into such exciting hunting grounds. And it is the unnatural origins of this plant material that is responsible for the excitement.

Even ordinary kitchen refuse can provide the beginnings of a huge range of plants. There may be discarded but still fertile root vegetables, the remains of bottles of oriental spice, the sweepings from the budgie's cage. And it is not just that, cosseted in the well-prepared refuse beds, these can turn into flowers that are an astonishment to find blooming in a down-and-out English field, but that each crop is fascinatingly tied to the social changes in the community that threw out the refuse. A newly settled immigrant group may bring in their native spices with them. A local firm's latest import line can introduce seeds from halfway across the world, caught up in the packaging materials. Even an ephemeral fad for a new vegetable will show up eventually in the tip flora.

It's typical of botanising in the unofficial countryside that your techniques can turn out to be as eccentric as your quarry. It didn't seem incongruous that my first encounter with the flora of refuse dumps was on a charabanc tour of the East London tips on a dull day at the tail-end of September. My travelling companions were for the most part professional botanists – which was lucky for me, for the plants we discovered that day were a stunning and exotic collection that I would have been hard pressed to sort out from my humble collection of field guides.

Most of London's rubbish is dumped on the rough marshes that lie on both sides of the Thames estuary, and it was on one of these in South Essex that we began our forage. It's not an encouraging pros- pect, the first sight of one of these really big dumps. They are wreathed perpetually by hazy smoke and permeated by an unmistakable musty smell of ash mixed with decaying vegetables. Yet they have a rural character – marshland crossed with working farmyard perhaps – that is often quite absent from our pampered city parks.

This particular tip was a showpiece for bird-seed flowers. The oily seeds that are sold as food for cage birds are imported in prodigious quantities from all over the world (together with seeds of the local weeds). Thirteen thousand tons of canary grass seed alone are brought in every year. Much of this is spilled inside the cages and ends up – ready-fertilised with a dressing of bird droppings – on the tips.

Here, the sunflowers, products of the plumpest and most favoured seeds, outshone everything else, awkward though they looked thrust- ing out of this flat and derelict moor. Then there were the deep purple cascades of love-lies-bleeding; countless breeds of millet and canary grass from Australia, Morocco and South America; niger from India; yellow safflowers, blue flaxes, and most curious of all, a shoo-fly plant from Peru, with pale lilac flowers tightly closed in the gloom and Chinese lantern fruit cases.

These were the brightest and most conspicuous flowers on the dump. But a plant doesn't need to have a gaudy blossom to ensure its discovery in these places. Most are growing against a backcloth of bare soil, not a camouflage of thick grass. And grubbing about with your eyes fixed firmly on the ground is not simply a matter of scientific self-discipline but of sheer survival among the broken bottles and wrecked prams.

So we chanced upon many meek and sombre plants, but very few that hadn't a fascinating history to compensate for their drab looks. One of the very first plants I found myself on this ramble was another thorn-apple, perhaps sprung up from drug manufacturer's refuse. This was almost certainly the origin of the deadly nightshade plant growing only a hundred yards away, climbing mangily amongst the clutter, and already bearing its seductive black cherries. In the wild, deadly nightshade grows almost exclusively on chalk and limestone. But it is still cultivated in this country for the drug *belladonna*, which is a valuable local anaesthetic, particularly in eye surgery. It's pleasing that the plant should be used in this way under its Latin name, for it echoes the practice of the old herbalists. By all accounts the plant acquired its name in Italy, where it was called *herba bella donna* (beautiful lady herb), since the juice of the leaves was used as a cosmetic to give an alluring dilation to the pupil of the eye. It must have been a scary business, for the whole plant is so toxic (children have been killed by as few as three berries), that it was not until the nineteenth century that chemists could administer it internally with safety.

A plant with an even more curious pharmacological effect was buckwheat, the source of those splendid pancakes that are served in drug-stores across America. These are made from the nutritious seeds, ground up into flour. But if the green parts of the plant are eaten by animals with pale skins (including man), they are apt to develop 'fagopyrism' – a form of photosensitivity which results in the animals developing allergic rashes if they're exposed to strong light. Buck-wheat probably came to this country from Asia in the fifteenth or sixteenth century, and up until the nineteenth was widely grown for chicken-feed and as a subsistence cereal crop for humans. The early settlers took it to America with them, and it grew readily in the poor soils of New England. It is this tolerance of rough ground and rapid growth that makes buckwheat such a regular denizen of the dumps. Yet it's a shame that it's confined to these waste places. Buckwheat cakes would taste as good over here as they do in America, where the plant is still regarded as a commercially viable crop. But even forgetting its food value, it's a compact and attractive little plant, with its triangular spinach-green leaves and pyramidal seeds. A field of buckwheat in flower must have been a marvellously mottled thing, the spikes of white blossoms against the rich green, shot through with the red-brown of the stalks.

It was a positive witches' garden, this tip. To complete a potent trio there was a single plant of darnel rye-grass, in all probability the 'tares' of the Bible. Darnel was a rampant weed of arable land in Elizabethan times, and not one that farmers could turn a blind eye to, literally: bread containing its seeds as impurities could blur the sight and cause convulsions. Modern grain screening techniques can filter out darnel's fruits, which are only two-thirds the width of wheat ears, and the grass is consequently almost extinct as an agricultural weed. But seeds still find their way into this country as impurities in bird-seed crops.

Virgil mentions darnel in *The Georgics*. Shakespeare moans about the taste of bread containing it. John Donne quotes the legend that slipshod husbandry made wholesome wheat turn into this poisonous weed (called cockle then):

Good seed degenerates, and oft obeys
the soil's disease, and into Cockle strays.

Two thousand years of agricultural and mythological history in this one weed. No wonder the botanists became excited when one of these ancient plants was found. There was a delightful ritual that accompanied these special discoveries. The expedition leader would blow a whistle, and the members of the party leave their private explorations and cluster round the plant. Photos would be taken, and a debate begin about who should 'carry on' the plant. All these flowers would be smothered anyway within the next few weeks, so for once it was excusable to dig them up and carry them back to greenhouses and botanical gardens, to nurse them through to seed-time or next flowering. What astonishing herbaceous beds some of these botanists must have. And what frustrated yearnings to gather bushels of wild flowers too, to judge from the great polythene bag-fuls of cuttings and blossoms that were gleefully humped back to the coach!

Back on board we sifted through our findings. By the time we had reached our next stop – a dump behind the Ford factory at Dagenham – the warmth inside the coach had made those secretive shoo-fly blossoms open wide.

We had moved farther downriver, and passed brackish ditches where giant hogweed and sea aster grew equally side by side. It was private land here, and we poked about the dump watched by a handful of bemused security guards. They needn't have worried. It was not the factory and its encircling acres of unregistered cars that we had our eyes on, but the ash raked out of its furnaces and spread over this waste ground. In this apparently sterile refuse a large colony of Russian thistle had established itself. This native of arid soils in Eurasia has been spreading across the world, homing in, as immigrant plants uncannily will, on patches of ground that resemble its natural habitat. It's not a particularly distinguished plant, looking a little like a low-lying gorse. But we know it better than we think: remember those balls of tumbleweed that roll around the dusty plain in cowboy films? They are Russian thistle. Those mobile, self-uprooted clumps are the plant's specialised technique for distribution in inhospitable terrain. They are blown about until they stick on a patch of ground sufficiently fertile for them to take root. Russian thistle is spreading, and maybe one dust-blown evening, the drinkers in Dagenham saloons will look out into the main street to see the tumbleweeds rolling past their reined-up Cortinas.

Not, perhaps, a particularly useful employment for the refuse of one of our most wasteful industries. But the success of recycling is in the eye of the beholder!

Every tip seemed to have its specialist leanings. Over the river and farther east still, we visited a veritable spice garden. Cummin, fenugreek, coriander, dill, fennel – you could have flavoured a whole Indian meal from this one dump. These could well have been restaurant throw-outs, though the ancient oriental spice ajowan (*Trachyspermum ammi*), that we also discovered, had more likely found its way here in bird-seed. Ajowan is an inconspicuous little umbelliferate and caused some difficulty to the less experienced members of our party. But not to the gang of young totters that latched onto us at this tip. They were spending their Saturday afternoon ferreting for rather more substantial trophies than we were, and were clearly astonished at the spectacle of this gaggle of donnish strangers picking over the weeds on their manor.

They followed us round besieging us with questions, and yanking up plants for identification. After a while they fanned out by themselves, gathering up specimens which they channelled back to us through their gang leader. One of the younger children poked an ajowan under the nose of this burgeoning taxonomist. 'Ammy', he said in best Cockney Latin. 'Nah, they've had that already.' I wish some of our educational cynics could have seen these nine-year-old East End kids getting to grips with one of our most difficult plant families – and some botanical Latin to boot – in thirty minutes flat.

This was the dump, too, where we found the biggest marijuana plant (*Cannabis sativa*), that I have ever seen, five feet tall and nearly as wide. Until the drug scare began, hemp seeds were a regular ingredient of most proprietary bird foods. Now the seed wholesalers will indignantly deny that any smuggle themselves through the new screening techniques. But a few always do, and are liable to spring to life anywhere. If this should happen to be in the garden of a wild bird fancier, he may have a tricky job explaining to a sharp-eyed constable – drilled in identification but not in the mitigating enterprise of alien weed seeds – that he is not farming the stuff.

Eyeing this magnificent, lupin-leaved clump, whose flowering tops would contain only a fraction of the active drug compared to those ripened in hotter climates, but which could still fetch a pound or two on the black market, I wondered how the Greater London Council would get off the hook if they were busted for growing the plant on their property!

It was the last tip that was my personal favourite, tucked under a loop of the Thames about fifteen miles east of St Paul's. Looking across it we could see flocks of brent geese flighting downriver, and the tops of the barges that are used as another way of ferrying refuse out of the City.

It was not until we reached this dump, late in the afternoon, that I discovered the source of the monotonous chirping that had been a constant background to our meanderings that day. It was the crickets that were clustered in dozens underneath the vegetation. The common house cricket was the most abundant, but there were at least two other species, which could well have come here along with the garbage they feed on. Crickets and cockroaches from the tropics are often found in tips which receive refuse from dockside areas.

There were more functional growths here to add to those bulging polythene bags. Water melons, pumpkins, tomatoes that had ripened up in the Indian summer, and gourds knobbly enough to grace any Swedish fruit bowl. It's a measure of just how much the jungle-like luxuriance of these places infects one, that I found myself tweaking plastic chrysanthemums and rubber balls just to make sure they weren't living!

It had been an extraordinary day, and one to whip up the appetite, for all the stifling air. Stopping off for a celebratory curry on the way home, I took pot luck with a dish with the temptingly evocative name of 'green gram'. It was a delightful, but, I felt, wholly suitable coincidence, that it turned out to be none other than mung bean, the last plant we had found on that self-made market garden south of the river.

from THE MOTH SNOWSTORM

Michael McCarthy

Michael McCarthy (b. 1947) is one of Britain's leading writers on the environment and the natural world. He was Environment Correspondent of *The Times* before becoming the long-standing Environment Editor of the *Independent*. Awards for his journalism include Specialist Writer of the Year at the British Press Awards and the RSPB medal for 'outstanding services to conservation'. As an author he has written *Say Goodbye to the Cuckoo* (2009), a study of Britain's summer migrant birds, and *The Moth Snowstorm: Nature and Joy* (2015), which was shortlisted for the Wainwright Prize and the Richard Jefferies Prize. His latest book is *The Consolation of Nature: Spring in the Time of Coronavirus* (2020) written with Jeremy Mynott and Peter Marren.

Moths have long been unloved. There are about a dozen mentions of moths in the Bible and all of them are unfavourable: they are wretched little brown things akin to rust, which eat your clothes, as well as your books and your tapestries, if you believe the Good Book, and nothing more. The prejudice has been persistent: people have for centuries seen moths as haunting the night, like owls and bats, like ghosts and goblins and evil-doers, and thus sinister and shudder-provoking, whereas butterflies, their relatives, eternally symbolise sunshine and have been adored. Yet in my own country of Britain, perceptions are changing. Lovers of the natural world are becoming more and more drawn to moths, many of which are every bit as big and as bold in their colour schemes as butterflies are, such as the black and cream and orange Jersey tiger, or the pink and green elephant hawkmoth, or even the legendary Clifden nonpareil, the outsize and shadowy species which shows on its underwings a sumptuous colour found nowhere else in the moth world: lilac blue. The difficulty of seeing them at night can easily be circumvented with a moth trap, essentially just a powerful light attached to a box, which exists in several designs but is always based on the same principle: moths are attracted to light, moths fall into box, moths settle down and go to sleep, and then can be released perfectly unharmed in the morning – after you've had a close look at them and identified them. This may seem like prime nerd territory, and sure, it may be, but the number of nerds is soaring: according to the charity Butterfly Conservation, there may now be as many as ten thousand enthusiasts in Britain operating moth traps in their gardens on summer nights. I am one of them.

When you do that, you start to realise for the first time a basic wild-life truth: it is moths, not butterflies, which are the senior partners in the order Lepidoptera, the scale-wing insects, even if in our culture, the positions have been reversed. For there are about 200,000 moth species in the world, as a ballpark figure, but only about 20,000 butterflies: butterflies are just a branch, halfway down, on the moth evolutionary tree, a group of moths which split off and evolved to fly by day, and developed bright colours to recognise each other. This disparity in species numbers is even more pronounced in Britain, where there are a mere 58 regularly breeding butterfly species, but about 900 larger moths (all with English common names) and another 1,600 or so smaller or micro-moths (which for the most part have only scientific names in Latin), for a total of about 2,500. Thus, in the world as a whole, there may be ten times as many moth species as butterfly species; but in Britain, it is approaching fifty times as many.

This means, of course, that in the dark there are far, far more moths out and about than ever there are butterflies during the daytime; it's just that we don't see them. Or at least, we didn't, until the invention of the automobile. The headlight beams of a speeding car on a muggy summer's night in the countryside, turning the moths into snowflakes and crowding them together the faster you went, in the manner of a telephoto lens, meant that the true startling scale of their numbers was suddenly apparent, not least as they plastered the headlights and the windscreen until driving became impossible, and you had to stop the car to wipe the glass surfaces clean. (I know there are many other insects active at night as well, but let the moths stand proxy for the rest.) Of all the myriad displays of abundance in the natural world in Britain, the moth snowstorm was the most extraordinary, as it only became perceptible in the age of the internal combustion engine. Yet now, after but a short century of existence, it has gone.

In recent years I have often talked to people about it, and I am surprised, not just at how many of those over fifty (and especially over sixty) remember it, but at how animated they become once the memory is triggered. It's as if it were locked away in a corner of their minds, and in recalling it and realising that it has disappeared, they can recognise what an exceptional phenomenon it was, whereas at the time, it just seemed part of the way things were. For example, I talked about it to one of Britain's best-known environmentalists, Peter Melchett, the former director of Greenpeace UK and now the policy director of the Soil Association, the pressure group for organic farming. As soon as I raised the subject he said: 'I remember being at a meeting with Miriam Rothschild [the celebrated natural scientist], and Chris Baines was there, the TV naturalist, the guy who founded the Birmingham Wildlife Trust, and we were talking about the loss of insects in general and the loss of moths in particular, as Miriam was a great moth expert, and I said I remembered in the fifties driving from Norfolk to London with my dad, and him having to stop to wipe the windscreen and the headlights two or three times during every journey, so he could see.' He laughed. 'And Chris Baines said, it was all very well for you, being driven around in a flash car – for me, you couldn't bicycle with your mouth open, because you would swallow so many insects.'

I looked up Chris Baines, and he laughed in turn, and said it was true. He said: 'Yes, I remember it very well, having to scrape the windscreen and the headlights clear of insects, but I did also experience it on my bike. I used to cycle to Cubs or to church choir practice and you would get them in your eye, or if you had your mouth open, you ended up spitting out bits of moth wing, there were just so many in the air on any evening.' He thought about it for a moment and he said: 'If you drove down any kind of hollow way, like a country lane with hedges on both sides, you would be driving through a terrific mass of insects, and now that never happens. I remember it until my twenties. It's difficult to be precise, but I was a student in Kent, at Wye College, and my recollection is that it was still the case then, in the late 1960s, but not after that, really. It certainly never happens now. We spend a lot of time in rural Wales, driving in north Wales, and there have been evenings when I have commented that we've seen a moth. It's almost literally that – one or two moths in a journey. That's a completely different kind of situation from when I was growing up.'

It was in the millennium year, 2000, that I myself began to realise that the moth snowstorm had disappeared, and I began to write about it as part of the issue of insect decline as a whole, which seemed to me to be wide-ranging and extremely serious – the honeybees and the bumblebees were declining, the beetles were disappearing, the mayflies on the rivers were plunging in numbers – but very under-appreciated: no one was interested in it. Yet every time I wrote about the snowstorm, people would respond. They would say how vividly they remembered it, and how now they never saw it, and a frequent memory was of the long drive to the coast for the summer holiday in July or August (in the fifties, Spanish beaches were still in the future) when the car windscreen would unfailingly be insect-plastered; and then it all stopped. The experts remembered it just like the members of the public. Mark Parsons, the principal moth man at Butterfly Conservation, recalled it vividly from twenty or thirty years earlier, but he said to me: 'I may have seen it once or twice in the last decade.'

All this was just anecdotal, of course. There were no scientific figures for moth decline, as Britain's community of naturalists, enthusiastic though they were, had never got round to creating monitoring surveys for moths like they had done for birds, wild flowers, and butterflies. It was merely memories. Then one day the figures suddenly appeared.

They came from an unexpected source: Rothamsted, the celebrated agricultural research station in Hertfordshire (the oldest agricultural research station in the world, in fact, with experiments on the effects of fertilisers on crops going back to 1843). From 1968 Rothamsted had operated, through volunteers, a nationwide network of moth traps, the data from which had been used, within the station itself, to study various aspects of insect population dynamics. But in 2001 it was perceived that one well-known, widespread and common moth, the strikingly beautiful garden tiger, appeared to be collapsing in numbers. As a result, the Rothamsted scientists began to analyse the long-term population trends of 337 larger moth species regularly caught in the traps over the full thirty-five-year period the network had been running, from 1968 to 2002. The results, made public in conjunction with Butterfly Conservation on 20 February 2006, were astounding: they showed Britain's moth fauna to be in freefall. Wholly unsuspected in its scale, the position was even worse than that of the birds, the wild flowers, and the butterflies. Of the 337 species examined, two-thirds were declining: 80 species had declined by 70 per cent or more, and 20 of these had gone down by over 90 per cent. In southern Britain, three-quarters of moth species were tumbling in numbers; their total cumulative decline since 1968 was estimated at 44 per cent, while in urban areas, the losses were estimated at 50 per cent. The snowflakes which had made up the snowstorm were simply no longer there.

It had been the most powerful of all the manifestations of abundance, this blizzard of insects in the headlights of cars, this curious side effect of technology, this revelatory view of the natural world which was only made possible with the invention of the motor vehicle. It was extraordinary; yet even more extraordinary was the fact that it had ceased to exist. Its disappearance spoke unchallengeably of a completely unregarded but catastrophic crash in Britain of the invertebrate life which is at the basis of so much else. South Korea may have destroyed Saemangeum, and China may have destroyed its dolphin, but my own country has wreaked a destruction which is just as egregious: in my lifetime, in a process that began in the year I was born, in this great and merciless thinning, it has obliterated half its living things, even though the national consciousness does not register it yet. That has been my fate as a baby boomer: not just to belong to the most privileged generation which ever walked the earth, but, as we can at last see now, to have my life parallel the destruction of the wondrous abundance of nature that still persisted in my childhood, the abundance which sang like nothing else of the force and energy of life and could be witnessed in so many ways, but most strikingly of all in the astonishing summer night display in the headlight beams, which is no more.

But if we know full well why half our wildlife has gone – step forward. Farmer Giles, with your miserable panoply of poisons – the reason for the disappearance of one particular part of it, London's sparrows, remains a mystery entirely.

How utterly bizarre that it should happen to him, the Cockney sparrer! The urban survivor par excellence! The bird that has lived alongside humans since human settlements began twelve thousand years ago… the bird which is wholly at home in the city… what is it that, in one of the world's greatest cities where previously it flourished, has destroyed its population? To this day, more than twenty years after the event, nobody knows.

The phenomenon is all the more perplexing in that in major cities ostensibly very similar in infrastructure and atmosphere to London, such as Paris or New York or Washington, sparrows are flourishing still, darting in their flocks around the feet of the tourists in hope of the dropped crumb or the piece of ice-cream cone. Yet in Britain's capital, over the decade of the 1990s, the population collapsed, and the birds vanished almost completely. Within the London sparrow ecosystem, something mysterious, something catastrophic, took place. But even now, no one has worked out what.

The bird we are talking about is the house sparrow, *Passer domesticus*, which has hitherto been one of the world's most successful creatures. It occurs naturally all across Europe, much of Asia and North Africa, and has been introduced to Southern Africa, the Americas and Australasia: Antarctica is the only continent without it. It has been found breeding at 14,000 feet up in the Himalayas and nearly 2,000 feet down in Frickley Colliery near Doncaster (really: in 1979). It is one of the world's commonest birds, and almost certainly the most widespread; but more than that, it is beyond doubt the most familiar. Down the ages, the house sparrow has generated a special affection in us, based on its close association with people and towns, and a perception of its character as humble but hardy; as an urchin, but an urchin that lives on its wits. When Hamlet told Horatio there was a special providence in the fall of a sparrow, he was making it the exemplar of the lowly, but the bird was that already, more than sixteen hundred years earlier in Rome: Catullus' famous and charming poem on the death of Lesbia's sparrow is mock-elegiac, calling all Venuses and Cupids to grieve for his lover's beloved pet. Lowly, yes; but also street smart, like Paris's most celebrated singer, tiny and irrepressible, who called herself after the French slang word for sparrow, *piaf*.

The house sparrow has needed its survival skills. When I asked the world expert on the bird and on sparrows in general, Denis Summers-Smith, what he liked most about them, he took me by surprise; he said: 'I greatly admire their ability to live with an enemy.' 'Who's the enemy?' I said. 'Man,' he said. I said I thought that sparrows and humans had always got along fine, but he disabused me of that; farmers in particular used to hate them for the grain they consumed, he said, yet the birds continued to live on farmhouses. They were often killed, but they managed to get by, from generation to generation, by remaining intensely wary of this primate with whom they had thrown in their lot. Speaking of when he first began observing them closely, from his Hampshire garden in the late 1940s, Denis said: 'If I was gardening, they wouldn't look at me, but if I started to look at them, then they would look at me. They were very conscious of me. If I was going about my normal business, they weren't bothered, but as soon as I started watching them, they would watch me back.'

A Scottish engineering consultant and former senior scientific adviser to ICI, who at the time of writing is ninety-three and still going strong, Denis has been studying the twenty-seven members of the genus *Passer*, and *Passer domesticus* in particular, for nearly seventy years, a lifelong interest which has made him perhaps the most eminent amateur ornithologist in Britain of the second half of the twentieth century, with five books on sparrows to his name, including the standard monograph. *The House Sparrow*, published in the famous Collins New Naturalist series in 1963. In them, he elucidated many aspects of sparrow private life which yet may have a bearing on its mysterious London collapse; two in particular are that sparrows are very sedentary, and sparrows are very social. They are in fact the most sedentary of all songbirds, usually living out their lives within a one-kilometre radius, and foraging if they can within fifty metres of the nest; and their sociability is just as pronounced. Sparrows live in colonies: they deeply need and depend upon each other. This is vividly illustrated by the behaviour Denis has christened 'social singing'. After feeding, with their crops full of seeds which need time to be digested, sparrows gather in cover such as a thick bush, in groups of typically a dozen, and sit back, as it were, and begin cheeping to each other. The call generally sounds like a monosyllabic *cheep*, although if you slow it down, it is clearly a disyllabic *chirrup!* They each take it in turns to give a single sound, with a separated abruptness which is very distinctive:

Hey!
What?
You!
What?
You!
Eh?
Who?
Him.
Him?
Nah.
Her?
Nah.
Me?
Nope.
Him?
Yup.
Really?
Yup.
Me?
Yeah.
Oh.
Yeah.

Why?
What?
Me.
Cos.
What?
You.
Eh?

This was one of the most familiar sounds of my childhood in the suburbs, when sparrows were everywhere; it is almost wholly lost from London now, even though comparable small songbirds, from robins and wrens to blue tits and blackbirds, continue to give full voice in the capital's parks, and the other archetypal bird of the city, the feral pigeon, prospers as ever in London's streets (and makes up most of the diet of the peregrine falcon, several pairs of which now breed in the heart of the capital). What was different about the house sparrow, that it was singled out for disappearance?

Certainly, there had been an extended decline through the length of the twentieth century: the figures are there. In November 1925 a young man of twenty-one went into one of central London's greenest parks, Kensington Gardens, and with the help of his brother counted the house sparrows: there were 2,603 of them. The man was Max Nicholson, a passionate ornithologist and the founding father of Britain's environmental institutions, who as a senior civil servant in 1949 brought into being the world's first statutory conservation body, the Nature Conservancy, and subsequently ran it for fifteen years; he ended up as the Grand Old Man of the natural world in Britain, having been the founding secretary of the British Trust for Ornithology, president of the Royal Society for the Protection of Birds, and having helped to launch, in 1961, the first of the world's great Green pressure groups, the World Wildlife Fund (now the Worldwide Fund for Nature). But for all his prominence in officialdom, Nicholson remained a practical ornithologist at heart, and in December 1948 he repeated his Kensington Gardens sparrow survey: there were then 885 birds. In November 1966 there were 642, and in November 1975 there were 544; but when he took part in the count in February 1995, at the age of ninety-one, there were a mere 46, and on 5 November 2000 I went back with him to Kensington Gardens – he was ninety-six by now – and we watched as members of the Royal Parks Wildlife Group carried out a seventy-fifth anniversary census of his original count: they found 8 birds.

What on earth had happened? The earlier decline apparent in the Nicholson figures, between 1925 and 1948, has been attributed to the disappearance from London's streets of the horse, and the loss of the grain spilled from nosebags and even the undigested grain in horse manure, which was an important source of food for small birds; but then for forty years or more the sparrow population was on what we might call a gently declining slope. However, from about 1990, it fell off a cliff: this is the enigma. In Buckingham Palace gardens, which in the sixties supported up to twenty sparrow pairs, there were none after 1994; and in St James's Park, where once sparrows could be found by the hundred, where squabbling flocks of them would cluster on the shoulders and arms and palms of bird-food-proffering tourists – I can remember that myself – a single pair nested in 1998, and in 1999, for the first time, no birds bred.

Alert observers began to notice. Among the first was Helen Baker, then the secretary of the ornithology research committee of the London Natural History Society, whose morning walk to work at the Ministry of Agriculture in Whitehall took her through St James's Park. In particular she noticed that the sparrows had gone from the shrubbery at the end of the bridge over the lake, where in the past she had counted the birds by the hundred and had had them feeding from her hand; and in 1996 she organised the LNHS house sparrow survey, to try and get a handle on what was happening. News of the decline began to seep out in London's evening paper, the *Evening Standard*; I myself became aware of it in 1999, realising that the sparrows had gone from my commuter terminus, Waterloo Station, where once they had been plentiful. I began to look out for them, and couldn't spot them; but it was not until a trip to Paris with my wife and children in March 2000 that the true scale of the situation dawned on me, for in the French capital *les piafs* were everywhere, in stark contrast to London, where now they seemed to be nowhere. I wrote a piece about it which was featured prominently in my newspaper, the *Independent*; I continued writing about it; and eventually in May 2000 we launched a campaign to Save The Sparrow, the centrepiece of which was a £5,000 prize for the first scientific paper published in a peer-reviewed journal which would explain the vanishing of the house sparrow from London and other urban centres, in the opinion of our referees, who were the Royal Society for the Protection of Birds, the British Trust for Ornithology, and Dr Denis Summers-Smith.

The *Independent*'s campaign, and especially the offer of the £5,000 prize, put the disappearance of London's sparrows firmly on the news agenda nationally and internationally – it was reported around the world – and it elicited a substantial reader response, with nearly two hundred and fifty letters in the first weeks (about twenty of them being emails; this was just on the cusp of the email revolution, and most of the missives were still handwritten or typed). There were two significant aspects to this. One was the surprising passion with which people lamented something so seemingly inconsequential as the disappearance of a small brown bird: it was as if an emotional floodgate had been opened, a commonly expressed feeling being gratitude that someone besides the writer had at last taken note of this development and also considered it important ('I thought it was only me…').

The other prominent aspect to the response, of course, consisted of readers' theories for the disappearance, and two weeks after launching the campaign, we listed ten of them. They were, in order of frequency of expression: predation by magpies; predation by sparrowhawks; predation by cats; the effect of pesticides; the tidying up of houses and gardens, which removes nesting places; loft insulation, ditto; climate change; the effects of radiation from the Chernobyl disaster; the introduction of lead-free petrol to Britain in the 1990s; and finally, peanuts (the suggestion being that the vogue for putting peanuts in bird feeders was perhaps upsetting the sparrows' digestion – fatally). The response reflected the detestation of the British bird-feeding classes for the magpie, the bold black-and-white crow which from the 1970s onwards had moved from its previous rural habitat into suburban and urban gardens – the sparrowhawk effected a similar shift in the 1990s – and was often observed preying, with upsetting relish, on songbirds, their nests and eggs and chicks. Nearly all the letters were deeply felt, although the odd one was a tad presumptuous ('It's cats. Send money to address below…').

But if deeply felt, they did not necessarily reflect expert judgement, so I sought out the experts. I went to see the venerable Max Nicholson in his house in a backwater of Chelsea, and in his curious high-pitched lisp, with an articulacy quite undimmed by the imminent approach of his ninety-sixth birthday, he advanced what at first seemed to me to be a quite startling idea: that, in his words, sparrows as a species had a strong suicidal tendency. What he meant was that if sparrow numbers, in the colonies in which they nested, fell below a certain level – for reasons such as a lack of food – the colony might suddenly cease breeding and dissolve. The problem, he thought, was ultimately a psychological one: the birds, which were so strongly social, felt that life in such low numbers was no longer worth living. The basis of this idea is actually supported by a well-known piece of biological theory, the Allee effect, which states that declines in socially breeding species can become self-reinforcing, but it was the vividness with which Max Nicholson expressed it which initially took me aback. 'I think they suddenly get to a critical point where they say, let's give up,' he said. 'I don't think it's about safety in numbers. I think it's psyche.' He said that this should be correlated absolutely with material factors like food shortage, which was his own suggested trigger for the initial numbers drop which might precipitate a psychological crisis; and he stressed he was speculating, and fully accepted that what he was suggesting would be difficult to verify experimentally. 'I accept it's an element that can't be measured,' he said. 'It's a psychological thing – there's no scientific way of measuring it.'

He smiled.

'But a lot of things that can't be measured, are real.'

I thought then and I think now that Max Nicholson may have been right and that sparrow colonies might well drop in numbers to the point where they suddenly dissolved; but the mystery was, what was causing the drop? And Denis Summers-Smith, when I went to see him at his home in Guisborough in the north-east of England, had a specific view about that. With his intimate knowledge of sparrow biology, he was aware that although sparrows are granivorous birds – they feed on seeds – the sparrow chicks, for the first few days of their lives, need insect food, such as aphids (the greenfly abhorred by gardeners), small grubs, flies, and spiders. He conjectured that insect numbers might have fallen, and to the point where the chicks might starve and the birds' reproductive rate might fall itself, triggering a population decline, since to make up for natural winter mortality and maintain their population levels, sparrows need to rear between two and three broods of chicks every summer.

And Denis had a candidate for what might be killing off the insects in towns and cities like London: motor vehicle pollution, and specifically, the introduction of lead-free petrol into Britain, in 1988; for not only did that represent the major change in the composition of vehicle exhaust fumes in previous years, but there was also a strong temporal correlation between the introduction of unleaded and the sparrow decline itself (as a couple of canny readers had noticed, in our initial trawl of ideas). At first, unleaded sold in only tiny amounts, but sales picked up rapidly during the nineties, leading to the complete phasing out of leaded petrol at the end of 1999, and the uptake clearly paralleled the London sparrows' demise. It was the substitute chemicals added to the petrol to replace the lead and reboost the octane rating, Denis believed, which might be causing the problem, and he focused on two additives in particular: benzene and MTBE (methyl tertiary butyl ether), both of which had health and safety question marks against them. He accepted there was no scientific evidence as yet linking MTBE or benzene directly with house sparrows, but he thought that the circumstantial evidence of a connection was strong. Hence he took the view: 'This is my hypothesis – what's yours?'

It was intriguing, and a potentially devastating example of the law of unintended consequences. Unfortunately, it was a hypothesis that was very hard to test, as although a highly specialised agricultural research station like Rothamsted might be uniquely equipped to measure insect biomass on farmland, nobody at all, as far as I could find out, was measuring insect biomass in towns and cities; it was seen as a near impossible job, and anyway, what would be the reasons to fund it? So you simply couldn't tell if the aphid population of

St James's Park, say, was plummeting. I also felt there was a gaping hole in the theory: New York and Washington had unleaded just as London did, and Paris had *sans plomb* – so why weren't their sparrows disappearing in the same way?

Yet Denis's instinct that the proximate cause of the decline might be starvation of the chicks through lack of insects was eventually borne out by a young postgraduate research student at De Montfort University in Leicester, Kate Vincent. For her doctoral thesis, Kate put up more than six hundred sparrow nest boxes in the Leicester suburbs and the adjoining countryside, and monitored them for three years, closely observing the birds' breeding success. (I visited her and watched her gamely clambering up and down her ladders.) Her finding, in 2005, was remarkable: that in the summer, completely unseen by the outside world, considerable numbers of sparrow chicks were starving to death in the nest, and the closer towards the centre of town the nest was, the higher the mortality. Furthermore, those whose diet had consisted largely of vegetable matter – seeds and scraps of bread – were much more likely to die than those whose diet had contained plenty of invertebrates. (Kate worked out the chicks' diet by analysing their droppings: in an ornithological labour of Hercules, every time she weighed and measured a chick in the nest, she collected the poo it would tend to deposit in her hand, and then, under the microscope, she could identify in it the tiny remains of insects – an aphid leg here, a beetle mandible there – and estimate their abundance.) The chicks that were dying were largely in the sparrows' second brood of the year: Kate found an 80 per cent success rate in the first brood, but only a 65 per cent success rate in the second, and with the birds needing between two and three broods annually to maintain their population levels, this could be enough to precipitate a decline.

Eventually, Kate wrote up her findings in a scientific paper with fellow researchers from the RSPB and English Nature (then the government's wildlife agency), and in November 2008 this was entered for the *Independent*'s £5,000 prize. However, the referees were split. The problem was that Kate's research revealed the starvation but not why the insects were hard for the birds to find: it was half a solution. One referee said, award the prize. One said, do not award the prize. And the third said, award half the prize. In the circumstances, it did not seem possible to award it. And there, to date, the matter rests.

In early 2014 I went to Guisborough again to see Denis Summers-Smith and talk the whole issue over once more, fourteen years after we had first highlighted it. I spent two enjoyable days admiring his wonderful sparrow archive of more than five thousand items, and his collection of sparrow artefacts ranging from Chinese sparrow fans to Japanese sparrow netsuke, and we talked late into the night of such subjects as, what species was Lesbia's sparrow? (Denis thinks it was the Italian sparrow, *Passer italiae*, which replaces *Passer domesticus* in the Italian peninsula, although the Spanish sparrow, *Passer hispaniolensis*, also occurs in southern Italy. My friend, the academic ornithologist, Tim Birkhead, basing his view on the sound it made – 'pipiabat,' says Catullus, 'it used to *pipe*' – thinks it was probably a bullfinch.) And Denis told me of how his involvement with sparrows had begun, which really dated back to 6 August 1944, when he was a twenty-three-year-old captain leading his company of the 9th Cameronians in Normandy, in the race to close the Falaise gap, and a German shell landed by him and almost took off his legs. But not quite: eight operations later he still had them, and lying in hospital in Worcestershire, he became fascinated by the sparrows which came in through the windows of the ward. When he had recovered (although with legs full of shrapnel that set off airport alarms), he began his lifelong study.

He had changed his mind about unleaded petrol and MTBE, although he still believed motor vehicle pollution was to blame for the decline of sparrows in London and other urban centres; now, however, he thought that a major cause of the decline was 'particulate' contamination from diesel engine exhausts (essentially nanoparticles of soot that are not filtered out in the nasal passage). This may have led directly to mortality of juvenile birds, he thought.

For my part, I wanted to discuss with him the question that continued to preoccupy me: how could the house sparrow have been 'singled out', as it were, for disappearance? How could it vanish from St James's Park, say, when similar songbirds such as robins and blue tits, blackbirds and wrens, still seemed to lead satisfactory lives there?

The key fact, Denis said, was that sparrows did not disperse.

I asked him what he meant.

He said: 'They live in a small area, which they get to know very well. They spend their lives within a kilometre. They are completely sedentary, the most sedentary of all passerines. But other small birds, like blue tits or chaffinches, are unable to do this; when they leave the nest, they have to disperse. They have to move considerable distances away, to find food or new partners.'

And how did that relate to the situation in St James's Park?

Denis said: 'If the sparrow population in St James's Park dies out, it will not renew itself, because no new birds will come in. But if the blue tit population dies out, other young birds, which are dispersing, will arrive.'

The implication started to dawn on me.

I said: 'So is it possible, then, that what went wrong in the eco-system… what made the sparrows die out… is actually affecting all species? But the other species, because they are dispersers, are able to renew their populations…'

Denis said: 'Yes.'

'But we can only observe the effect in sparrows, because the sparrows are the ones that can't replace themselves…'

Denis said: 'This is my hypothesis.'

'So what we may actually be looking at is a disguised devastation of all these common species?'

'Yes.'

I was dumbfounded. 'This is completely new, Denis. Nobody's ever said this.'

'Well I've been saying it to a lot of people.'

Was it possible? That *all* the birds of St James's Park died out, or failed to breed successfully, every year? But all, except the house sparrows, could renew their populations from outside?

That we had actually witnessed something far more wide-ranging than the downfall merely of *Passer domesticus*?

I could not say.

Whatever had done it so effectively to the sparrows, and possibly was doing it without our knowledge to all the songbirds of central

London, and possibly even to more organisms than that – including us – remained unknown.

We still had no idea what it was.

I come from the north of England, but I have lived in London for forty years and grown to know it well and love it, and when I first realised the sparrows had gone from its heart, I felt the loss as keenly as other people did. And six months after visiting Denis, while writing this book, I was suddenly seized with a desire to go out into central London and look for them, wondering if, two decades after their disappearance, any trace of them might remain.

I approached Helen Baker, who had spotted the birds' disappearance almost before anyone else. She had risen in the London Natural History Society and was now its president, but was as fascinated as ever by the sparrows' fate; she was a receptacle for all the reports which surfaced from time to time, of the odd colony clinging on here and there, in quiet corners. Helen told me she thought there might be three small colonies still in central London, two of them on the South Bank, and on a hot July day we set out in search of them, meeting in the Guildhall Yard, the very hub of the old City. Helen was attending a lunchtime concert in the Guildhall church and while I waited for it to finish I watched the office workers with their sandwiches being half-heartedly hassled for crumbs by the pigeons. When I first came to London, sparrows would have been the hasslers-in-chief.

We began our South Bank search at Borough Market in the shadow of Southwark Cathedral, whose pinnacled tower Shakespeare would have eyed (the churches on the north bank all being consumed, of course, in the Great Fire of 1666). Borough Market epitomises what we might call the Mediterraneanisation of London which has taken place over recent decades – the introduction into the capital of exhilarating new foods and the enthusiasm of crowds for them and habits of eating in the open air (on a sunny day it could almost be Barcelona) – and if ever there was a place where sparrows would thrive, this was it. The local birds knew it too. But they were pigeons and lesser black-backed gulls and, I was delighted to see, a crowd of starlings; of *Passer domesticus*, there was no sign. There was no sign of him either as we skirted the replica of Francis Drake's *Golden Hind* in St Mary Overie dock and moved up Clink Street past the medieval remains of the Bishop of Winchester's Palace and out on to the riverbank, and the Anchor Pub. In the garden beyond the old pub, said Helen, sparrows had occasionally been seen over the previous year, and we watched and we listened for several minutes, because with sparrows you may well hear them cheeping before you see them. The only sound was the laughter of drinkers. There were no sparrows there that day.

Helen's second potential South Bank sparrow site was another garden, further upstream at Gabriel's Wharf, and as we walked there I was struck by the number of pigeons, especially outside Tate Modern, the power station turned temple of contemporary art on whose soaring art deco brick tower peregrine falcons – notable pigeon consumers – roosted. 'It pleases a lot of people that peregrines eat pigeons,' said Helen, who explained that in the school holidays she was one of the people manning the RSPB telescope trained on the tower so that the public could observe the peregrine pair who had been named Misty and Bert. I wondered how many of the pigeons I was watching would end up as peregrine dinners; they were in the sort of numbers that sparrows would once have exhibited, hundreds and hundreds of them. But there was no sign of the sparrows; not there, not anywhere along the embankment, and not at Gabriel's Wharf either, where we thoroughly explored the garden in which Helen had in the past counted up to forty; now there were merely sixteen pigeons on the lawn. 'Oh, this is disappointing,' said Helen. 'It used to be such a very good colony. It may be that the food supply has gone. They used to nest in the houses and flats nearby. One would hear them and one would see them, going back and forth from these houses.' Not any more.

It seemed to me that London was completely sparrow-free; for the South Bank was such a tourist trap, it had so many eating places with people sitting outside dropping crumbs, that in any other European city it would be a sparrow food resource par excellence. But there were none whatsoever. It was uncanny. It was chilling, almost. The disappearance of the birds seemed complete.

Helen had one remaining site to try, which was on the north side of the river, so we walked over Waterloo Bridge and into the West End; we wound our way into a celebrated and historic area, and Helen said to be on the lookout, for birds had been seen in the street we were in, on the window boxes. 'Look up, keep your eyes open,' she said. I could see nothing. We turned into another street, a famous one, and she repeated her exhortation; I could still see nothing. Then, as we were passing a well-known Italian restaurant, I heard it:

> Hey!
> What?
> You!
> What?
> You!
> Eh?
> Who?
> Him.
> Him?
> Nah.
> Her?
> Nah.
> Me?
> Nope.
> Him?
> Yup.
> Really?
> Yup…

A flood of elation swept through me. I shouted: 'I can hear them! I can hear them!' Helen called out: 'I can see them too!'

'Where?'

'Here they are on the wall…'

'Oh God, yes! Suddenly! Two of them!' – all this from my tape recorder – 'Wow you're right! A third one! On the flats, on the old Victorian flats!'

They might have been the rarest birds in the land, red-backed shrikes or black-winged stilts, they might have been Siberian ruby-throats, such was my delight. I said to Helen: 'I never imagined I would ever feel this way about sparrows.'

The chirping was continuous by now. We were opposite a tiny park, just a garden really, full of bushes: the chirping was coming from inside, and when we went in, we found the birds, hovering around feeders which had been placed deep into cover. It was in a very quiet part of a famous street, almost a backwater in the heart of tourist London; the birds foraged in the garden, and nested in the old flats across the road.

Just a handful of them.

Very shy, hiding in the foliage.

But there they were.

from BEING A BEAST

Charles Foster

Charles Foster (b. 1962) is more than a writer about nature. He is
also a travel writer, a qualified veterinarian, a practising barrister,
a religious and medical philosopher, an Oxford fellow and a taxi-
dermist. After university at Cambridge, he studied the compara-
tive anatomy of the Himalayan Hispid hare and chemotaxis in
leeches and worked in Saudi Arabia studying the immobilization
of goitred and mountain gazelles. He teaches medical law and
ethics at the University of Oxford and practises primarily medical
law. His contributions to numerous books include offerings on
everything from desert travellers to personal injury and clinical
confidentiality. He turned to nature writing in 2016 with *Being
a Beast*, where he tried to live in the wild – with varying degrees
of success – as a badger, an otter, a deer, a fox and a bird. It did
not win a literary award but did win an Ig Nobel prize in biology,
an international award which celebrates scientific research that
makes us laugh and then think.

Foxes trickled up with the Pleistocene ice and then trickled
down railway lines and canal fringes into the inner cities.
They are Tories. Urban fox numbers correlate perfectly with
blue rosettes. They like the gardens that come with affluence. Some
commute – in both directions. Many (though not my East End foxes)
have nice, leafy country houses and come to town, like the men in
suits, for the rich, easy off-scourings of the city. Others choose to live
and raise cubs under a lawyer's shed by the Tube station, and to relax
and get a breath of fresh air in the country.

The East End of London doesn't vote Tory, despite the corporate
laptops and the avocado foam, and the foxes here are hard pressed.
There are shed-owning lawyers whose kids like to feed foxes, but

they're in small ghettos with polished floor-boards, walled in by towering concrete cabinets where the desperate are filed.

The humans here have small brains. Smaller, that is, than those of the wild men from whom they descend. They've shrunk about 10 per cent over the past 10,000 years. Since dogs faithfully follow their masters, their brains have shrunk too. Dog brains are about 25 per cent smaller than those of wolves – their immediate ancestor. Domestication makes everything shrivel.

We don't know what effect inner-city living will have on foxes, but urban foxes have lost no length or weight. It's not surprising. Even in the fat suburbs, where they could live off bird tables, hedgehog food and the interested benevolence of the middle class, they choose to hunt. Like us, they are built to be multivalent. It's how they and we triumphed over heat, ice, drought and monoculturalists. Strenuous though it is for them – demanding a lot more ingenuity and energy than it takes simply to pick up pizza and lap up sweet-and-sour sauce – they've opted to listen, pounce, prospect and innovate. We haven't. In a few generations we've turned into sclerosed super-specialists, each in a niche so tight that our limbs can't stretch and our brains can't turn. I bet foxes' choices will keep their brains throbbingly big and keen and their legs like steel wire when we can't hoist ourselves from the sofa.

It's easy enough to march to the urban fox's beat. They are those most onomatopoeic of creatures: crepuscular. They live, by preference and as befits brilliant physiological generalists, along the mucky tideline where the night washes into the day. Here in the East End, though, there are no proper nights: just dirty days, and nights of scorching twilight. For these foxes the dusk is not the dimming of the light but the thinning of the traffic. Sound and tremble take over from photons. When the taxis have dropped off most of the bankers, out come the foxes. They forage over a big area here (probably getting on for half a square mile) and show the generic fox's caching behaviour. They forage or hunt, then cache (usually burying, in an often rather messy, approximate way), and then continue to forage and hunt and cache before returning to cached food. It's hard to bury under tarmac:

my foxes shove food clumsily under pallets and cardboard boxes used to deliver wide-screen TVs. Then, the territory trawled, they select what they need (going for the most toothsome first) and head home.

The traffic dawn and the sun dawn more or less coincide. Trucks shudder down the Old Ford Road; Porsches purr off to Canary Wharf; buses rumble west to disgorge people into open-plan, air-conditioned comfort, with cooled-water dispensers. The foxes lick last night's aloo gobi off their lips and curl up under the shed.

The more respectably dressed you are, the harder it is to be a fox. No one has ever accused me of being respectably dressed, but even so I soon realised that I should be even more shabbily shambolic than usual. Someone in unstained trousers and an unripped jumper looks criminal if he's raking through a herniated bin bag, but if you're dirty, tired and slumped, no one minds. You're translucent. People look through you. The grubbier you are, the more translucent you are. If you're on all fours, sniffing at a sack, you're invisible. Except to the authorities. And even there, sleeping is more offensive than doing.

I was shaken awake under the rhododendrons.

'Afternoon, sir.'

'Good afternoon.'

'Can I help, at all, sir?'

'No thanks. All's fine.'

'Can I ask what you're doing, sir?'

'Just having a little sleep, officer.'

'I'm afraid you can't sleep here, sir. You sure you're OK, sir?'

'Fine, thank you. And what's the problem with sleeping here?'

'It's forbidden, as I'm sure you know. Trespassing. The owners can't have people just sleeping.'

(Just sleeping?)

'I can't see that I'm interfering materially with the enjoyment of its title of a property management company registered in Panama.'

'Are you trying to be clever, sir?'

I could think of no palatable answer to this. The policeman didn't press me for one. He moved to another topic.

'Why do you have to sleep here, may I ask?'

'You may indeed ask, but I don't suppose you'll like the answer. I'm trying to be a fox, and' – I rushed on, trying to avert my eyes from the torrential haemorrhage of the officer's residual goodwill – 'I want to know what it's like to listen all day to traffic and to look at ankles and calves rather than at whole people.'

This last observation was a bad, bad mistake. I knew it as soon as it was out. For him, calves, ankles and concealment in an evergreen shrub meant perversion so deep that it should be measured in years inside. But I could see him struggling to identify the right pigeonhole for my depravity, and imagining the paperwork. Uncertainty and workload trumped his instincts, and he told me to 'bugger off home, *sir* – the italics were powerful on his lips – 'and get a life.'

'That', I said, 'is exactly what I'm trying to do.'

He looked paternalistically at me as I brushed the leaves off my jersey and walked home.

After that I cravenly slept under a groundsheet in my backyard.

Foxes sometimes sleep on the central reservation of motorways. Three thousand vehicles an hour shriek past in oily vortices of dust, rubber, deodorant, vomit, electric muttering and what we've absurdly come to call power. I've slept on the verge of an A road myself, beneath a canopy of cow parsley and dock, wanting to be violated by noise and palpitation, and still being shocked by the unbrute brutality of the thrusting pistons. Even the most wanton wrenchings of the natural world – wild dogs in a tug of war with a baby gazelle, for instance – are tender and proper beside the violence of a bus or a train.

A fox can hear a squeaking vole 100 metres (109 yards) away and rooks winging across plough half a kilometre (a third of a mile) off. To lie ten metres (eleven yards) from a speeding van must be apocalyptic: like living inside a tornado. Even the sneezing, snoring, grumbling, humming, moaning, turning, deep night of the inner city is a cacophonous fairground.

It's the fox's plasticity that so daunts me. I can get an intellectual, or at least a poetical, grip on acute sensitivity in another animal. But acute sensitivity *and* intense toleration: that's hard. And it's not as if it is mere reluctant toleration for the sake of survival, as with the badgers who, because suitable habitats are hard to find, might put up with a rather suboptimal railway embankment. Foxes seem to *enjoy* being outrageous. They flaunt their thriving in conditions that are objectively wretched. They don't want my loud, tree-hugging sermons on their behalf, and I feel not only miffed but mystified. They are the true citizens of the world. I'm not, and I rather resent them for bettering me. I also don't understand how they do it, either physiologically or emotionally.

You'd expect a truly cosmopolitan creature to make some costly compromises: to give up some hearing in return for better eyes, or some smell for some sight. Surely generalists can't be great specialists? But they are. I'm in awe.

I hated the East End. 'This place is an offence', I wrote bitterly in a notebook.

> It was built on water meadows as a refugee camp and is now a workhouse from which, because of poverty or wealth, few can afford to escape. Few would say these days that it's home, and even fewer would say so gladly. Few people really live *here* at all. They beam their thoughts in from outer space, fly their food in from Thailand and their fripperies from China, and their furniture sails in a steel box from Sweden. I suppose that's not really so far. We are, after all, made of star dust.

Though foxes are made of star dust too, and eat Thai chicken curry, they're genuinely local. They know the taste of every square inch of concrete; they've looked from a range of about three inches at every spreading stain of lichen up to eighteen inches from the ground; they know that there's a mouse nest under the porch at number 17A and bumblebees by the cedar wood decking at number 29B. They've watched the tedious adulteries of Mrs S, Mr K being carted off to die, and the psychosis of the M twins blossoming from petty backyard cruelties into much worse. They know the flight paths of jumbo jets and greylag geese. Under the shed they nestle among the oysters that gave the local Victorians typhoid. They walk around the area for nearly five miles a night, and they do it with everything switched on.

But they're not around for long. Being an urban fox is an intense, dangerous business. Sixty per cent of London's foxes die each year. Eighty-eight per cent of Oxford foxes die before their second birthday. They know bereavement. There's only a 16 per cent chance that both animals of a fox pair that have raised cubs in their first reproductive year will survive for a second breeding season. They don't just know the fact of bereavement; they feel it – apparently as I do, and they make similar sounds.

David Macdonald, who has conducted, from his base in Oxford, much of the most significant work on fox behaviour, kept pet foxes. (He commented that his landlady found his flat curiously hard to rent when he left it. Not everyone shares my, or his, taste for the smell of fox urine.) One of his vixens was caught in the flailing blades of a grass cutter. A leg dangled by a thread of tissue. Macdonald's distraught wife picked her up. The vixen's mate tried to pull the vixen away as she was carried to the car, and looked after the car as it drove down the path.

The next day the vixen's sister picked up a mouthful of food at a cache and ran off with it, whimpering as foxes do when they're giving food to cubs. She hadn't called like that for over a year. She took the food to the grass hollow where, the night before, her sister had bled. She buried it beneath the bloodstained blades of grass.

This has the pathos of my own story, and it was this that made me more anthropomorphic about foxes than about any of my other animals. I felt more confident about reading them right than about the others.

Foxes and dogs are very, very different. They're in different genera. They parted company about 12 million years ago – a divergence reflected in the number of chromosomes: domestic dogs (evolved wolves) have seventy-eight pairs; red foxes thirty-four to thirty-eight pairs. You needn't put your poodle on the pill if there's a libidinous dog fox oiling around. And yet there's *something* to be learned about foxes from looking at dogs.

Dogs are specialists in getting along with humans: they have been selected rigorously for it over the past 50,000 years or so. Foxes are not: evolution has nudged them in other, less placid, directions. But it's not unreasonable to suggest that foxes have at least the raw mental processing power of dogs. If that's right, by seeing what dogs can do we can get some idea about the resources available to foxes.

Dogs are supreme copiers and bonders. They mimic human actions as well as a sixteen-month-old child, observe closely what humans are looking at or pointing to, read many human social cues and want to work with us.

Some dogs have capacious memories. One should be careful about drawing conclusions about normality from the spectacular tricks of savants, but the ends of a bell curve do indicate something about where the middle lies. So let's consider a Border collie called Rico who appeared on German TV in 2001. He knew the names of two hundred toys, fetched them by name, and learned and remembered words as fast as a human toddler. When a new toy was placed among his old ones, he recognised it by a process which must have been something like: 'I know the others, but I've never seen this: so this must be the new one.' When he'd not seen the new toy for a month, he picked it out correctly in half his trials. The new name had become part of his lexicon: he seemed to slot new words into some Chomskyite template. Another dog, Betsy, tested in a Hungarian laboratory, had a vocabulary of more than three hundred words.

These capacities and tendencies have obvious emotional (there, I've used the word) corollaries.

Dogs suffer separation anxiety when parted from an owner to whom they are bonded. When the owner returns, they race out to greet them, jumping up and dancing; for all the world like a toddler reunited with its mother. Up on the Howden Moors in the Derbyshire Peak District, where I used to roam as a child, a sheepdog called Tip stayed with the body of his dead master for a desolate, dangerous fifteen weeks.

I can't believe that foxes have used their available RAM in so radically different a way from dogs that these traits have no echoes at all in fox heads. We know that foxes have good memories: they recall, for weeks at a time, not only the location of cached food but also the particular food that is cached there – 'There's a bank vole to the left of the twisted oak; a field vole under the nettles,' they say to themselves. We know that they have a significant vocabulary of their own, produced using a sophisticated suite of methods (at least twenty-eight groups of sounds, based on forty basic forms of sound production), and that the call of individual X is recognised as that of individual X rather than that of a generic fox: a monogamous captive male reacted to recordings only of his own mate.

These faculties in the fox translate just as inevitably into relationality as the corresponding faculties do in dogs. It's just that the relation, as of course will be the norm with animals (the dog–man case is a highly unusual one), is with other foxes. Who, having heard Macdonald's story of the mutilated vixen, could doubt it?

Here's another of his. A tame dog fox got a thorn in his paw. Septicaemia set in. The dominant vixen of his group gave him food when he was ill. That's very unusual: adult foxes are usually aggressively possessive about food.

No doubt this is reciprocal altruism. The vixen, at some level, expected a kickback in the event of her being ill. But that label doesn't begin to mean that there isn't a real emotional component. No doubt my love for my children and the sacrifices I make for them have at least a partial Darwinian explanation: I want them to bear my genes triumphantly on into posterity. But that doesn't mean that I wouldn't be genuinely distressed by their non-reproductive-potential-affecting injury, or that my devastation at their deaths wouldn't go far, far beyond the distress caused by the mere trashing of my genetic aspirations.

I prefer the easy, obvious reading of Macdonald's stories and of the lessons from the dogs. Foxes are relational, empathic creatures. And you can shout 'Beatrix Potter' as loudly as you like: I don't care.

This relationality and empathy of fox X is, so far as we know, directed primarily towards other foxes with whom X shares an interest. That's what Neo-Darwin says, and no doubt he's right. But once you've got a capacity for relationality and empathy, it's terribly difficult to keep it tidily in its box. It keeps spilling out over other evolutionarily irrelevant individuals and species. People give money to donkeys and to starving children from whom they'll never get any benefit. They even give it secretly, denying themselves the chance of being applauded and favoured as a mensch. A Nazi with children of his own will find it harder to bayonet the children of others than one in whom relationality has never kindled.

This is what I told myself, on my knees next to the crane flies and the foxes. Those foxes have the ability to connect to me, and I to them. And there's no reason why they shouldn't want to. There have been times (whole seconds at a time) when I've looked at foxes and they've looked at me (in a Yorkshire wood; on a Cornish cliff; in an orange grove near Haifa; on a beach in the Peloponnese), and I've thought: Yes! There's a rudimentary language in which we can describe ourselves to the other, and the other to ourselves. We needn't be as mutually inaccessible as Earth and the Baby Boom Galaxy.

Even when those long seconds have passed, I've still been able to say to the fox: Listen – we've both got bodies, and they get wet as the clouds burst on their way up from the grey sea, and we're both *here*! *I* am here! *You* are here!

I and thou!

Then it's usually time to go to the pub.

When I lived in the East End I'd often give the arrabbiata a miss and shuffle instead at night round the bins, rifling through the bags. A fox's nose has no problem telling, through a thick layer of black plastic, whether there's anything worth its while, but even thin plastic defeated mine. I had to open the bags up.

It was only the instinctive phobia of the saliva of my own species that made eating scraps unpleasant. I cheated. I sprinkled mixed spices on everything. That, absurdly, seemed to sterilise it, or at least personalise it and defuse the threat of the dribbling other.

At first I tried caching like foxes do. I gave it up in disgust when I returned to a cache of rice in a foil box and found three brown rats with their snouts in it like piglets round a trough. A proper fox would have had them for starters.

The takings were good but dull. If the East End is like the rest of the Western world, it throws away about a third of all the food it buys. There was no shortage of pizza, chicken tikka masala, egg-fried rice, toast, chips and sausages. But not much else. In this most variegated of all English societies, everyone eats the same as everyone else, and the same all the time. Foxes, even here, do much better than the humans. They have pizza, chicken tikka masala, egg-fried rice, toast, chips, sausages, field voles, bank voles, house mice, road casualties of all kinds, wild fruit in season and the air-freighted unwild, unseasonal fruit of South America and Africa, cockchafer grubs, noctuid moth caterpillars, beetles, rat-tailed maggots from the sewage outlets, earthworms, rabbits (wild and insecurely caged ones), slow, complacent birds, rubber bands, broken glass, KFC wrappers, grass to snare intestinal parasitic worms and induce therapeutic vomiting, and just about everything else. But, unfortunately, they're not significant cat killers.

As I mooched round the bins I listened and I watched. I found in the houses and the flats what I found in the bags: uniformity. Everyone had a more or less identical cultural diet. One drizzling September night I stood on the pavement, eating an abandoned pie and looking through windows. I could tell from the flickering that seventy-three households were watching TV. Of those, sixty-four (sixty-four!), the coordinated flickering told me, were watching the same thing.

No fox ever looks at the same thing as another fox. Even when a family is curled up together, each fox either has its eyes shut, dreaming about chicken houses or a vole glut or an onion bhaji, or is looking out from a slightly different angle from every other fox, its understanding of what it's seeing modulated by the slightly different precedence each gives to smell and hearing, with those in turn being conditioned by cement dust in the nose from snuffling round a building site, the angle of the ears, or parental instructions from cubhood.

We too have blocked noses and positions in space, but we're such unsensory, unmindful creatures that they make no difference to us: we don't notice them. We have acutely sensitive hands but handle the world with thick gloves and then, bored, blame it for lacking shape.

I'd just about given up on London, but the foxes' faith in it and the intensity of their commitment to it touched me and made me think again. I suspected that if I could get as close to it as they were I'd see it properly, and therefore learn to love it. To hate anything is exhausting. I hoped that the foxes could help me to rest.

When I lived here I was almost anaesthetic. Like the accursed in the psalm, I had eyes but could not see, a nose but could not smell, hands but could not feel, and ears but could not hear. I was constantly being told that this was where it was all happening; where the real business of life was done. Sometimes I could dimly sense that something *was* happening, but it seemed distant, blurred and muffled, as if I were looking down from a great height through cloudy seawater.

Then, still blind, deaf and anosmic, I started to follow the foxes. Eventually they took my collar between their teeth and swam with me to four islands. On those islands my senses functioned. I could feel and describe things there. The rest of the Atlantean world of the East End remained submerged. If I'd stayed longer and persevered with the foxes, they might have shown me more islands, or perhaps even dived down with me, or raised the rest of Atlantis so that I could buy and taste beer in it, or run over its hills and feel it under my feet.

I never got anywhere other than the islands, and never really understood what made the East End tick. Perhaps the genius loci lies deep in the troughs between my islands, forever out of my reach. Yet in describing my islands to myself I mapped an archipelago, and an archipelago has a taste of its own: it can be a nation of which one can be fond.

I wanted most of all to feel fond. I was so tired of resenting. If I'd thought that fondness for a place was different from understanding the foxes that inhabit the place, I'd have wanted the fondness more than the understanding. But the conviction that they weren't different had grown with every sniff and crawl and bin-bag raid.

It wasn't that I experienced *something* on the islands that was better than anaesthesia elsewhere but not as good as normal experience. Not at all. I became convinced that the foxes saw, smelt and heard the real thing, and that on the islands to which they took me I was experiencing the real thing too. The foxes gave me their eyes, ears, noses and feet. But only on the islands.

The foxes were the real East Enders. They inhabited the place in a way that, without their help, I could not, and in a way that reflected what the place itself was. I lived there in a way that reflected me, or my view of the place. I walked round with a mirror in front of me, describing myself into a notebook and calling it nature writing.

If you look into a fox's eyes, you get no reflection of yourself. They have vertical pupils, which deny gratification to the human narcissist. Now jump to the other side of the fox's eye and look out through it at a pool of vomited curry, or a hedgehog, or a stream of four-by-fours on the school run. You'll similarly get no reflection of yourself. You'll see the things themselves, or a better approximation to the things than you'd get with your own drearily self-referential eyes. Eyes are meant to be sensory receptors. In the fox's head they are. We make them cognitive, and ruin them. This is not because a fox has less consciousness and hence there is less to intrude between its retina and its mental model of that hedgehog, but because its consciousness is less contaminated with toxic self and presumption.

None of the fox islands was visible from more than two feet above the ground. One could be seen only with the nose.

These are the islands:

ISLAND 1

There are lots of shops that sell everything, deep into the night. They smell of ghee, soap, cardamom, coriander and lighter fuel. The owners never ever die or get excited. In an alleyway beside one of these there was a pile of crates, stamped with customs ink from Barbados, Bangladesh and some little piles of Pacific rock. It was soft, sweet, damp and alcoholic under the crates. I floated on a raft of fermenting fruit. The wasps were too pissed to sting me when I rolled on them.

I lay on my belly, because foxes normally do. There was a wall a couple of feet ahead of me. Damp had edged up the first foot. The rest of the wall, which climbed up to the billowing net-curtain sails of a taxi firm's masthead, was dry as toast, and as interesting. But next to the ground there was writhing wonderment: silver slug tracery; trundling woodlice, swimming through air as baby trilobites rowed through the Cambrian soup; centipedes armoured in bronze plates, snaking like a file of legionnaires with shields over their heads towards a tower of hairy Goths; lichens flowering the way that scabs would flower if William Morris directed skin healing; moss like armpit hair.

A crack in a box from Lesotho half-framed a bathroom window, and the woman in the bathroom was lovely and the man was not. Why would she stay? But that was not a fox thought. If I lowered my head there was a cauliflower, green with mould and bonny as a horse chestnut in May.

There were worms in the raft; fat, pickled worms with thick saddles like the thick wedding rings of the emphatically faithful. A fox would have sucked them through its teeth like spaghetti: each is worth 2½ calories – $^1/_{240}$ of the 600-calorie-per-day requirement of an adult fox. Although most foxes eat some earthworms, it seems that some are worm specialists, to judge by the soil and worm chaetae in their dung. It's a safe, lazy way to earn a living: like being a probate lawyer.

ISLAND 2

In the park there's a place where concrete meets tarmac. The concrete has broken where the winter has hardened water into wedges. There's a lush tree of cracks. Flash floods, invisible to us but tumultuous wild water to greenfly, have filled the cracks with soil, full of ascarid eggs from unbagged dog shit near the playground. Wind, shoveled by the wing mirrors of cement lorries and white vans, has seeded the soil with grass and bravely straggling ragwort whose ancestors probably killed a horse or two in Kent.

If you walk on this boundary with bare feet, you'll know that the concrete is as hard and sharply pitted as a cheese grater. It doesn't welcome anything. The sun leaves it as fast as it can go. The tarmac, though, is warm and spongy, even in the cold. When it's hot it sends up tar tendrils to grab your feet. They leave tattoos, like black thread veins, on your soles.

Foxes have absurdly sensitive feet. These city foxes, used to pounding the roads for eight hours a night, have pads that feel like velvet which has had milk poured over it and then been put in the oven overnight to get a fragile crust. Their feet, like their faces, extend beyond the fur line: there are small, stiff hairs on the carpus which are buried in a buzzing hive of nerves. When the biologist Huw Lloyd lightly touched these hairs on a young fox sleeping in front of his fire, the fox, without waking, snatched back its foot. Those hairs are stroked lustfully by the grass in any country wilder than a well-managed sports field. Imagine your nostrils being shafted enjoyably with face-high thistles as you walk. That's a fox's progress through a spring wood.

It seems a bit much. They really don't need to be so good. Clumping, club-footed ungulates, their nerve endings locked up in horn boxes, dance perfectly satisfactorily over rough ground and along mountain ledges. You'd expect natural selection to be more parsimonious in dispensing its favours to foxes.

ISLAND 3

We think of small trees as going straight up from the ground and then getting wider like mushrooms or narrower like carrots. They don't. Even the slenderest tree has a big, wide underground life. The parts up in the light are just kitchens for making food.

If you lie on the ground you'll eventually know this. I watched one tree for about three hours before noticing. It had sloping shoulders, hinting at a pale body beneath the paving.

The tree had prised up the stiff skin of the yard and then, tired, slumped on to the fence, pulled down by the weight of its head as a drunk's head is pulled on to a table by the weight of a head full of beer. Ants, beetles and earwigs, each in their own rigidly observed carriageways, poured over the shoulders – streams of iridescent water with legs. They were going to eat dead stuff, or live stuff: it's always one or the other. The boundary between the two isn't very clear.

I couldn't gallop between trees on my hands and knees in the East End. There aren't enough trees. But I've done it as best I can in plenty of other places. The real fox's-eye view of trees is when you're sledging fast downhill through woodland. Foxes have, like most predators, frontally positioned eyes. They'd have had more or less the same view of the beetles as I had, but I'd have been able to identify the tree species at a running speed sooner than the foxes. For them the trees would have been dark columns that would have come at them with that lurching, not-quite-anticipatable violence that you know best when you're driving one of those fake motorbikes in an amusement arcade. Computer simulation of driving or riding doesn't feel like driving or riding, but it's useful for making you feel like a fox.

I tried to run like a fox at the tree in the yard. I skinned my knees, and the woman in the house next door pulled back her curtain and asked nervously if I was all right.

ISLAND 4

I turned over an old slice of pizza with my nose. It was lying in a backyard. I don't know how it had escaped the rats and the birds and the foxes. It had lasted long enough to have soaked up the weather of a couple of weeks. There had been no rain for a week, but it was damp. There was a luxurious green fur over the pepperoni. There were human tooth marks on one side, and the fur was thinner there: presumably the streptococci of which human kisses are a concentrated solution compete viciously with the mould. The underside was a metro system, its tunnels already packed, like a rush hour station, with jostling weevils. Black beetles (which I always think are too downright mechanical to need food – which is a demand of flesh) were there directing the crowds.

But it was the smell that got me. There were physical smell strata in the slice: at the top there was still metallic tomato and the fat of unhappy pigs, shaken up with spores (which don't smell at all of death, though they should). At the bottom there was pasty, yeasty creepingness. The tomato and the metro were separated by about an inch (it was a deep-pan pizza) and a fortnight. But – and this was the point – I got them both in a single sniffing millisecond.

Smell telescopes and packages history. The pizza was a trivial example. Sniff a lump of Precambrian schist and you might get a couple of billion years of sensation delivered all at once to your neurological door. The sensation, in that case, will be faint: most of the scent molecules will have been reassigned to other bodies and structures, and those that remain are wrapped tightly in a sort of archaic cling film.

As a fox trots down the Bethnal Green Road, it takes with every breath an instantaneous transect through the past five or fifty or five hundred years. And it lives in those years, rather than on the tarmac and between the bins. Time, squashed tightly by olfaction, is the fox's real geography.

The piece of pizza wasn't substantial enough to be an island itself. It was a signpost – a floating piece of fresh wood that said that an island wasn't far off. The island from which it came was a tree stump, crumbling and spongy, next to a ruptured bin bag. Like litmus, it had soaked up the run-off from the bag, and like litmus it declared the real nature of the bag and the bag's ancestors. The declaration was in the smell, and the nature was historical and anthropological and commercial and depraved and careless and anxious and just about all the other adjectives there are. *And I got it all at once.*

I think it had been a lime tree, but its own name had been chewed by the rain and the wasps and washed out by curry bleeding from the bag. Because it was porous, it was a safe and capacious bank of the memory of things. Perhaps it was planted a century ago, for no reason that the planners would have been able to explain: there wasn't language then for motives like 'feeding the wild heart beating inside the black jacket'. And it died about half a century later, when its varicose roots were hacked up because they made next door's yard too interesting.

When it died, it started to accumulate scent. When it was alive it had mostly smelt of itself.

I moved the bag and slept by the tree for a couple of nights, with my nose in one of its armpits.

That nose went through three stages. First, it smelt an old tree and moulded the scent into the shape of a cadaver. Then the nose laid out the scent and (it's a big, sharp nose) began to dissect. It cut out a slice of diesel, perhaps from the mid-1970s, and put that in a bowl for later inspection. Then the nose went back, picked up a length of storm, blown in from Russia at the time of the Suez Crisis, and laid it alongside. With those out of the way, it speeded up: last month's menstrual blood, a brave crack at cheering up a nursery, an overambitious and unpopular attempt at a Vietnamese culinary classic, some evidently successful attempts at safe sex. And beans. So many beans. All laid out in the bowl.

The nose roved round the bowl from item to item, proud of its dissection.

And then, very slowly, it began to know that it is murder to dissect. It reassembled the pieces. It got again what it had got in the first, unexamined sniff: the whole bowl at once; a century in a moment.

That, I think, is how a fox does it. But it inhabits a much longer period in a moment than I can, and inhabits that period far more fully. Yes, it focuses on the things it's particularly interested in, as I lock on to one alluring picture in a new gallery. But it sweeps the millennia in an instant, as my eye sweeps the gallery. From the millennia the fox alights on last week's chops or the last minute's vole, but the scan is complete.

Only noses can travel in time quite like this. Our eyes and ears travel too, but we don't recognise it, because light and sound are fast. We see the light from stars that are centuries old, and the light is mixed on the palette of our retina with light that is tiny fractions of a nanosecond old from the nearby chip shop. We use the mixture to paint a picture of the world that we call reality. In fact, reality's a cocktail of sometimes radically different times, shaken and profoundly stirred by the Self.

So those were my islands: a fruit raft, the edge of some concrete, a tree and a stump. Foxes took me there.

As a matter of mere aesthetics I preferred the fox view to my view from the bus or from my study. It was prettier and much more interesting. As a matter of cartography I came to think that the fox view of the East End was more accurate than mine: it took into account more information. It saw both more minutely and more widely. It saw the hairs on ants' legs and, in a moment-to-moment orgy of olfactory holism, everything that had been spilt, ejaculated, cooked and grown since the creation of the world. So there.

The foxes showed me a London that was old and deep enough to live in and be kind about. They negotiated an uneasy peace between me and the East End, and indeed between me and other squalid, wretched, broken human places. It was a great gift.

But I'd got to know only islands, not whole landscapes. The city squirmed mistily below the waters between them. For my metaphorically aquatic foxes there is no mistiness.

STAG BEETLES

Anita Roy

Anita Roy (b. 1965) holds an MA in Travel and Nature Writing from Bath Spa University, and wrote and illustrated *A Year in Kingcombe: The Wildflower Meadows of Dorset* (2020). She is the author of *Gravepyres School for the Recently Deceased* (2020), a fantasy adventure for children, and co-editor of *Eat the Sky, Drink the Ocean* (2017), a collection of speculative fiction for young adults. Along with Pippa Marland, she is the co-editor of the forthcoming collection *Gifts of Gravity and Light: A Nature Almanac for the 21st Century* and her essays have been published by *Granta*, *Guernica*, *India Quarterly* and *Dark Mountain*. 'Stag Beetles' is original to this anthology.

It's 1973. I'm eight years old and there's a stag beetle on the paved path leading up to our front door in Thornton Heath, London. It is the size of a large dog. I rear up and stagger back. It does the same. I burst into tears. It seems unfazed. My brothers arrive to see what all the commotion is. They squat down for a closer look and poke it experimentally with a twig. The stag beetle reverses, warily, and there's a stand-off. Then Mum arrives, and declares it amazing. So now we know.

It's 1976. The long, hot summer of '76. Remember? Kiki Dee and Elton John, hosepipe bans, the sweat sticking the backs of your legs to the chair as the teacher droned on and on. It was a bumper year for staggies – at least in London. 'They were bloody everywhere,' recalls a friend who grew up not far from me in Croydon. 'You couldn't move for them – hordes!' She windmills her arms around to make her point.

It's 2020. I'm fifty-five. I haven't seen a stag beetle for four decades. They are no larger than my index finger – and I would give my right arm to just glimpse one.

Lucanus cervus is the UK's largest beetle. An adult male can measure up to eight centimetres in body length, added to which are those extraordinary antlers that give them their name, *cervus* being Latin for deer. They are fearsome, fantastic beasts: the males look belligerent and dangerous, and both they and the smaller, less weaponized females can – if provoked – deliver a sharp nip. The antlers are in fact overgrown mandibles that the males use in order to fight off rivals during the mating season. There's a famous sequence on BBC Earth tracking a stag beetle's progress up a tall pine tree in search of a mate. Whenever he encounters another male, he reaches around to grab his opponent under the wing casings, prises him off as if he's flipping open a beer bottle, and lets him drop with a soft clatter to the forest floor far below.

The stag beetle I remember from my childhood was black all over except for its antlers, which had a hint of the rich, dark mahogany of a prize-winning conker. Its legs were ridged and sharp, and it held its curved mandibles at the ready like scimitars. It looked impregnable, invincible: an armoured tank of a creature, poised to attack.

Insects in general have a bad rep. Unless you're a cute ladybird or a pretty butterfly, you're just a creepy-crawly, designed, so it seems, to provoke a shudder of disgust. Something to be stomped on, quickly, brutally, before it bites you. The only reason I didn't, I think, was squeamishness at the inevitable crunch and splatter.

What I didn't realize at the time was that the beetle is really just the (sharp black) tip of the iceberg. That what we would immediately recognize as a 'stag beetle' represents just the final 10 per cent or so of the animal's long life. The earlier 90 per cent or so is spent as a soft white grub, hidden in rotting wood, usually underground, munching its way to maturity. It can take between three and seven years for the larva to go from egg to fully formed adult. During this period, the larva will shed its skin as its body grows. After its final moult, it burrows into the soil in order to form a cocoon, which can be the size of a chicken's egg. Inside, an extraordinary metamorphosis takes place as its body reorganizes itself to take the form that we recognize as an adult beetle: an imago (the plural of which, I recently discovered to my delight, is 'imagines'). The adult may remain underground for several more months, emerging during the early summer in order to mate.

If you imagine the whole life cycle compressed into one hour, the flying season would last for about five minutes. Stag beetles are mistakenly thought to attack and damage wood, but as adults they don't eat at all, although some are reported to lick tree sap or fallen fruit. And then they die.

Spending so much of its life invisible, underground, feeding on decay, dung, detritus, the stag beetle – like other scarabs – carries a strong whiff of death. Its element is earth, associated with memory and the past, and most vividly, the Underworld. According to prolific amateur entomologist and stag beetle enthusiast Maria Fremlin, in France it has been known as *cheval du diable* (a name which more commonly applies to the praying mantis), and an old German name is *Teufelspferd* – the Devil's horse. And in Essex and Suffolk they've been known as billywitches (a name also used indiscriminately for the cockchafer) – the spiky silhouette of a flying beetle being reminiscent of a witch on her broomstick. German folktales tell of the stag beetle's talent for carrying smouldering coals in its antlers to burn down buildings: here, in the past, it has been variously known as *Feuerschröter* (fire thresher), *Hausbrenner* (house burner) or *Feueranzünder* (fire lighter).

But they're not all bad. Two thousand years ago, Pliny the Elder described in his *Natural History* how these beetles were 'suspended from the neck of infants by way of remedy against certain maladies'. Stag beetles are sometimes seen flying before thunderstorms, and in northern Europe it was believed that putting a stag beetle on your head would protect you from being struck by lightning. It may work – who knows? Its old Teutonic name *Donnerpuppe* or 'thunder-puppet' links the insect to Donar or Thor, god of thunder. Maria Fremlin suggests that this may come from their favoured habitats: old oaks that have been damaged by lightning.

'My' beetle, though, the one on the front garden path, is inextricably linked to another god entirely: Kali, the multi-armed, skull-festooned bringer of destruction. Our family was basically atheist, but with a Bengali father, my brothers and I inherited a close familiarity with Hindu deities. Being taken to Kali puja at a family friend's house in London is one of my most vivid memories. The festival centred on the image of Kali, wild hair cascading around her, her many arms aloft, brandishing a sickle, trident, a severed head and a bowl to catch the cascading blood. With her jet-black skin shining like a carapace and blood-red tongue sticking out of her mouth, she was the most terrifying thing I had ever seen. My father's explanation that she was sticking her tongue out to say sorry for stepping on her husband – Shiva, lying down at her feet in order to halt her rampage of destruction – sounded highly implausible. She didn't look sorry in the *least*.

And yet. And yet – when my aunt, my father's youngest sister, talked of Ma Kali, a softness and tenderness would come into her eyes. 'She is *beautiful*,' Jolupishi would say when we visited the household shrine in Calcutta, in the same tone of voice as my mother's as she peered at the stag beetle outside our London house, 'Isn't it *amazing?*'

As I was to discover on my first visit back to Calcutta in 1976, India has plenty of its own creepy-crawlies. My grandparents' house was cockroach heaven. The rickety wooden doors to the bathroom scuttled to life when you banged them shut, and squatting over the toilet – a hole in the floor – triggered sphincter-tightening fear of what might be waving its antennae up at you from beneath. My uncles and aunts watched with tolerant amusement as I, aged eleven and still unable to stomach the crunch-splatter of more direct action, rushed around sluicing away the creatures with bucket after bucket of water. The cockroaches didn't seem to mind. I loved India, but was glad to get back to the relatively invertebrate-free safety of an English house where, at least for the most part, the wildlife stayed firmly outdoors.

Since then, in India as in England, houses have been modernized, cityscapes cleaned up, plumbing improved. There's more concrete and steel, tarmac and glass. Parks are neatly mown, dead wood tidied up, and the English countryside has been transformed by the rise of industrial agriculture into an antiseptic green desert. In an environment so devoid of insects, birds are also disappearing at an alarming rate, deprived of their basic food source. Wildlife writer and conservationist Benedict Macdonald puts it in perspective: 'for just one family of red-backed shrikes to survive the summer, they will need over 26,000 large invertebrates. For a small viable population of fifty pairs to survive, you would require almost 1.33 *million large invertebrates* in a single landscape. That is a landscape hopping and crawling with life.'

The thought of living in a world where stag beetles are so numerous you have to keep the windows shut at night, and duck when you walk down the road in summer, seems unimaginable: how can we have ever lived with such abundance? Yet, there we were – not long ago really – swatting away these whirring mini-helicopters.

We are increasingly cut off from the natural world. A recent report announced that most children in the UK spend less than half an hour *a week* outdoors. In his influential book *Last Child in the Woods*, Richard Louv coined the phrase 'nature-deficit disorder', a useful catch-all term to describe a range of mental, emotional and physical illnesses – such as attention difficulties, obesity, stress and anxiety – that result from children's disconnect from nature and their lack of opportunities for unstructured 'wild play'. This has led to what Louv calls a weakening of 'ecological literacy and stewardship of the natural world'. His book has acted as a rallying cry, with forest schools mushrooming, and more and more people gardening for wildlife. Out with Astroturf and Roundup. In with rotting woodpiles, wildflower lawns and frog-friendly ponds. Rewilding has become the new buzzword – and it's not just about reintroducing wolves into the Scottish Highlands. In a paper published in 2017, the Woodland Trust states that it 'would like to see a greater acceptance of wild spaces everywhere. Even within managed landscapes, and urban areas, there are opportunities for wild and unkempt spaces; prescribed management may not always be needed, nature can be allowed to take its own course.'

So what do you do if you meet a stag beetle on the path? The People's Trust for Endangered Species answers the question succinctly: 'The best thing to do… is to leave it alone.' 'Just think,' said my mother, ever the putter-of-things-into-perspective, 'it's more frightened of you than you are of it.' And though I can think of many exceptions, that's not only a good piece of advice for children when encountering a wild animal, it's a basic lesson in empathy. Perhaps those scimitars were not poised to attack after all, but raised in startled horror at my massive size 3 Clark's shoes.

In the split second before Shiva's intervention, Kali dances in a whirl of pure unfettered energy. She is all movement – moving at the speed of light, at the speed of darkness – until her toe touches her husband's prone body, and she stops, mortified. Her image is captured – fast as a shutter click – freeze-framed at that point of stillness, one foot raised, about to trample. And now we can see her in her true form, suspended for a second, frozen in time, poised so that we humans, with our thin skins and limited frequencies, can catch a glimpse of that wild otherness. A chance for us to gaze up at her hard, black carapace with wonder, humility – even love.

Forty-seven years ago, as a child, I saw the stag beetle as through a glass, darkly. Now, if I were to come upon one face to face, my eyes would soften and the words of my aunt and my mother would echo around my head as I gazed at my Kali imago incarnate: *beautiful*, I might whisper. *Amazing…*

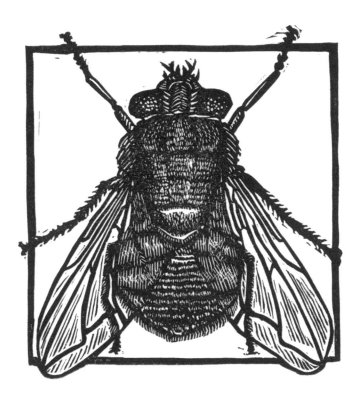

Discomfort, Dystopia, Death

Illustration overleaf: *Blow Fly* (Calliphoridae*)*

from A LINE MADE BY WALKING

Sara Baume

Sara Baume (b. 1984) is a novelist, writer and artist who was
born in Lancashire and raised in County Cork. She studied fine
art at Dún Laoghaire College of Art and Design and creative
writing at Trinity College, Dublin. She has won the Davy Byrne's
Short Story Award, the Hennessy New Irish Writing Award,
the Rooney Prize for Literature, an Irish Book Award for Best
Newcomer and the Kate O'Brien Award. Her debut novel, *Spill
Simmer Falter Wither* (2015), was shortlisted for the Costa First
Novel Award and won the Geoffrey Faber Memorial Prize. Her
second, *A Line Made by Walking* (2017), was followed by her first
non-fiction book, *handiwork* (2020), about her and her partner's
attempts to attract birds to their garden in West Cork.

The chemical blue sky which blazed a backdrop to my hedgehog prevails for the rest of the week. The temperatures tip
over twenty-five degrees for what is the first time – and also
surely the last – all summer. I lie on my back in the dying grass. We
are both turning brown. From the sun room radio, volume turned up
loud so that it reaches my wilderness, I hear a man say: '… clouds are
the facial expressions of the atmosphere…'

I set out on foot for the shop. It's twenty-seven degrees, the radio says
as I am leaving. The road up ahead is a mirage. I think I see a fallen
bird. From a distance, it's hard to tell; maybe only a clump of tawny
leaves in the ditch. But gradually, I am close enough to see that the
clump is flailing, and closer still, that the clump is beady-eyed. I drop
to my knees at the side of the road. I see that my clump is a small

and beautiful and stupid bird – a sparrow – and that it has somehow managed to become fused to the melted tar of a freshly filled pothole.

I should know better than to help. I think of the whales, and of all the wounded creatures I tried to rescue in childhood. I can't remember a single one that survived.

There was a family of thrushes who nested in the dainty woodland, and every spring, our cats would upscuttle the nests, displace the hatchlings. How many times did I try to salvage the peeping babies before they had their bones crunched by cat jaws? I'd wrap them in my mother's linen napkins and feed them pureed worms through a surgical dropper. Once, I successfully nursed two thrush babies to a condition at which they might have been able to fly away, then I locked the cats into the house and left the birds in the woodshed with the doors opened wide. A few hours later, they were gone, and I was overjoyed. But before the end of the week I found a severed leg beneath the silver birch, some feathers caught in its lowest branches, fluttering, and the second thrush baby turned up a week later. It had fallen behind the woodpile and starved to death.

One-legged pigeons, bats with snapped or fractured wings, rabbits with myxomatosis. My sister and I grew up digging tiny graves. Dad had designated us a flower bed in which we were allowed to cultivate whatever we wished, but our plants were few and far between, wild or weed-smothered. Instead we used the flower bed for burying creatures, several deep, until we couldn't dig a new hole without unearthing a crushed matchbox coffin, a ghoulish hamster skull.

I try not to think about the countless lives I failed to save as I prise my sparrow from the pothole, cradle it in my T-shirt, carry it home to my grandmother's house.

Struggling bird clasped to stomach, I tip the gunge out of the basin, refill it with clean, warm water. On the back step, in the basin, in the water, in my hands, the sparrow's plumage soaks and shrivels to nothing, a ball of wriggling gristle.

'I can feel all your bones,' I whisper.

I don't understand why I remember how to distinguish the sex of a sparrow when I've forgotten so many other, more valuable things, and yet, I know from its dark nape that my bird is a male. My male's mouth and nose are bunged, the black glue is everywhere, encrusted with dirt and vegetation. I try for some time before I realise that tar does not come out of feathers, and remember, of course, I knew this all along. Everybody knows this.

I place him in the shade of the garden shed. My sparrow lies, exhausted. And I hope he will die soon.

I forget my trip to the shop, return to my wilderness, the shade of my grandmother's plum trees. But all afternoon, blaring above the words of my book, I can hear him beating his sopping wings, hammering the shrubbery down.

It's almost dark before I fill the basin again. This time the water is nearly scalding. This time I know it's useless; I do it anyway. I manage to clear enough mess from his beak to allow the sparrow to drink. He gulps and gulps, even though it's scalding, and suddenly he goes still, relaxes, floats on the surface without my support.

The state of his plumage is even worse. Coated with moss, with dust, with buttercups. Now my sparrow looks costumed, almost foolish.

In the kitchen, I find an old dishcloth. In the yard, I find a heavy, smooth stone. I place the cloth over my sparrow and wish he'll go quietly, but he doesn't. For a second before I weigh the stone down, my sparrow recognises that his light and air have run out, and he pushes against me with his last shred of useless strength, and eternity passes before the tiny bubbles rising to the surface from beneath fabric and rock and tar and feathers eventually stop.

When I unwrap him, my sparrow's beak is frozen open. Tongue extended, eyes vast with terror. I do not take a photograph. This is the rule, remember? I am not allowed to kill something and then steal its spirit as well. I only bury him in the compost heap. *Bird bones are fine as fingernails*. And back on the step, I sit with my arms folded around my knees and I cry indecently hard. I cry my throat raw and eyes puffed and head sore for a long, long time.

Have I cried out my deadness now?

from THE DIG

Cynan Jones

Born near Aberaeron, Ceredigion, **Cynan Jones** (b. 1975) is a novelist who continues to live in north-west Wales. His debut, *The Long Dry* (2006), won a Betty Trask Award. In 2010 he published *Le cose che non vogliamo più* (Things We Don't Want Anymore) in Italian. His novels are short and he has experimented with removing punctuation such as speech marks in *The Dig* (2014), which won a Jerwood Fiction Uncovered Prize and the 2015 Wales Book of the Year fiction prize. He won the BBC National Short Story Award for 'The Edge of the Shoal' in 2017 and published a short story collection, *Stillicide*, in 2019. He also wrote the screenplay for an episode of the BAFTA award-winning crime series *Hinterland*, and *Three Tales*, a collection of stories for children.

They staked the dogs some way from the sett and poured them water and took a drink themselves. The boy had a queer feeling about the man's mouth being on the water and still did not want to drink it.

The trees had opened up a little and you could see the light finally coming through. There was a moment of greater coldness, like a draught through a door, and the boy felt an unnerving, as if something had acknowledged them arriving there. They had made a lot of noise moving through the wood and when they stopped they heard the birdsong and the early loud vibrancy of the place.

First dig? said the man.

The boy nodded, with that hesitancy. They could hear the dogs lapping and drinking at the water bowls.

The main hole's up there. The big man gestured up the slope. We'll put in the dog, he said. He meant Jip, the big Patterdale.

The big man's own bitch was by his feet, with her distant, composed look against the other dogs.

I want to put her in next. He indicated. Better be a dog goes in first. The big man was thinking of the big tracks and the possibility of the big boar. A bigger dog would have more chance up front. They knew if you put a bitch down after a bitch, or a dog down after a dog, there were problems most times; but if you changed the sex the other usually came out with no trouble.

The boy's father nodded agreement. He was checking the locator, checking the box with the handset.

The boy was thirsty and looking at the water, not wanting to open the other tub in front of the man.

Take him round and block up the other holes. I'll do the other side.

The big gypsy brought out the map he'd drawn of the holes and went over it with the boy's father. The gypsy asked the boy if he understood and the redness came to his throat under the zipped-up coat collar; but he was feeling the rich beginning of adrenalin now. He was dry and thirsty and had a big sick hole of adolescent hunger but he could feel his nerves warming at the new thing and began to feel a comradeship of usefulness to the man.

They unwound the sheets of thick plastic and went off and system-atically blocked the holes with stones and sheets of plastic and laid blocks across the obvious runs with heavy timber and then went back to the dogs. Then they went up the slope with the two first dogs and gathered around the main entrance and stood the tools up in the ground.

There was old bedding around the hole, the strange skeletal bracken starting to articulate its colour in the grey light. Jip started to bounce on the lead and strain for the hole as if he could sense the badgers. The strewn bracken might have meant the badgers had gone overnight, but from the way the dog was behaving there was a fresh, present scent.

The boy looked at the dog straining on the lead and could feel the same feeling in his guts. He felt the feeling he did before the first rats raced out and the dogs went into them.

The boy's father knelt with the excited dog and checked the box and collar over again and Jip let his enthusiasm solidify into a determined, pointed thing and stood stockily facing the hole, a determined tremble going through him.

The boy's father studied the locator once more and checked the signal, then they sent the dog in.

The boy was not expecting the delay of listening for the dog. He could feel his stomach roll though. He could feel a slow soupy excitement. This was a new thing. Then deep in the earth the dog yelped. Then again; and his father was instantly by the hole, prone, calling to the dog, calling with strange excitement into the tunnel.

Stay at him, boy. Good Jip. Good Jippo.

The boy glanced at the man as his father called this out, as if it had revealed what he was thinking about the way the man looked. But the big gypsy seemed to be rapt, a pasty violence setting in his eyes as he listened and watched Messie, his bitch, solidify, focus. Finally, the dog let out a low whimper of desire.

You could hear the barks moving through the ground now and they came alternately sharp and muffled until they seemed to regulate and come with a faraway percussive sound.

The big man moved across the slope. He seemed to swirl in some eddy, then came to a halt, as if caught up on something.

The big man moved again, listening, and the boy's father tracked across with the locator until the two men stood in the same place, confirming the big man's judgement.

Here, he said.

They brought up the tools and they started to dig.

It was very early spring and the bluebells were not out but made a thick carpet that looked newly washed and slick after the rain. They cut through this carpet and cleared the mess of thin sycamore from the place and the big gypsy cut a switch and bent it into a sack mouth and laid the sack down by where they would dig.

The ground was sodden with rain and sticky and they worked with the sharp foldaway spades, cutting through the thread roots. The smell of rotted leaves and dug-up soil strengthened. When they came to a thicker root, they let the boy in with the saw. Then they started to dig for real.

The big man swung the pick and the father and boy shovelled. Within minutes the boy was parched with thirst and hunger and could not shout properly when they called constantly to the dog below. He was dizzy with effort. He was afraid of not being able to keep up with the men. As the hole deepened they shored up the sides of the hole with the plastic sheeting and the work steadied to a persistent rhythm.

The badger was going nowhere and it was not about speed but persistence now.

After two hours they stopped for a drink and ate some of the paste sandwiches. The big man ate nothing. The dry soil on the boy's hands was tide-marked with water from the blisters that had torn and were flaps of skin now and there was a type of dull shock in his back. He had been expecting more action, not this relentless work, and he didn't understand it.

The dog had been down for two hours and had continually been barking and yelping and keeping just out of the badger's reach for that time.

Every so often, the boar rushed the dog and the dog retreated and the badger turned and fled; and Jip went after him through the tunnels and junctions until they reached the stop end.

Then the badger turned and ran at the dog again. It was nearly two and a half times the weight of the terrier and armed with fearsome claws and a bite that would crack the dog if he landed it properly. But the dog was quick and in his own way very dangerous. Jip kept barking. Yelping. The badger faced him down and every now and then turned to try and dig himself into the stop end. But then Jip moved in and bit his hindquarters, and the big boar swung round again in defence.

In the confined tunnel of the sett, the constant yelps were deafening and confusing like bright lights in the brain of the badger and it was unsure what it could do. It was then a stand-off. A matter of time.

They sent the bitch in and Jip came up. He looked like he was grinning. His mouth was open and flecked with spit. The dog was exhausted and thirsty but gleamed with the event somehow and when they took off the box and collar steam came into the morning air off his body. The boy was confused that they ignored the thick ·obvious blood that came out of the Patterdale and spread down its throat.

The boy kept looking nervously at the exhausted bleeding stubborn dog. The fresh blood seemed a synthetic colour against the dun-green slope.

Messie's good, said the big man. She'll hold him for the rest.

The boy sat and held his blistered hands against the cold metal of the foldaway spade. He had gloves but he did not feel he could wear them. Steam rolled off from the plastic-flask cup of tea and it came off the body of the injured dog. Steam came too off the lifted soil, but no birds came as they might to a garden, as if they knew some dark purpose was at work.

The man's bag hung on the tree and the head of the mink protruded. The boy looked at it. The mouth was drawn and the precise teeth showed. He thought of one of his earliest memories, of his father holding a ferret and sewing its lips together so it couldn't gash the rabbits it was sent down to chase. The mink had the same vicious preciseness as the ferrets.

Get your dog on it, the big man said. The boy immediately felt the redness at being talked to.

He nodded.

She on rats?

The boy nodded again. He had a panicky lump in his throat.

Good rat dog should take mink. Start them early.

The boy felt the swell of pride come up and mix strangely with his nervousness.

Nice dog, commented the man.

They'd gone through finally into the roof of the tunnel and it looked now like a broken waste pipe and it was mid-morning when they lifted the terrier out. There was still an unnerving composure to her, a kind of distant, complete look.

The boy did not understand the passivity of the badger and that it did not try to bolt or to struggle. He had to develop an idea of hatred for the badger without the help of adrenalin and without the excitement of pace and in the end it was the reluctance and non-engagement of the animal which drew up a disrespect in him. He built his dislike of the badger on this disgust. It was a bullying. It was a tension, not an excitement, and he began to feel a delicious private heartbeat coming. He believed by this point that the badger deserved it.

The big man was in the hole alone now, his shape filling it. The boy's head pumped hotly from the work and finally his nerves sped.

Have a spike ready, his father said.

Then the badger came out. It shuffled, brow down as if it didn't want to be noticed. It sensed them and looked up and the boy looked for a moment into its black eyes, its snout circling. The boy was expecting it to have come out snarling and fighting with rage, but it edged out.

It had been trapped in three or four foot of pipe for hours and it edged out until it was by the opening and the big gypsy took it.

He got it round the neck with the tongs and it struggled and grunted and then the man swung it up and into the sack with this great out-put of strength. Then it kicked and squealed and you could see the true weight and strength of it and the boy didn't understand why it hadn't fought at first, at the beginning.

The badger scuffed and tried to dig and the big man punched the sack and the badger went still. At this, the boy felt a comradeship with the man again and a sense of victory, holding the iron spike there in readiness, as if he was on hand.

We'll hang him while we fill things in, said the big gypsy, stop him trying to dig.

They filled in the hole. Threw in the old roots and stones they'd dug out and finally put back down the sods of bluebells. The place was slick with mud and trodden down and the ground of the area looked like the coat of a sick dog.

from THE SECRET LIFE OF FLIES

Erica McAlister

Erica McAlister is the Senior Curator for Diptera and Siphonaptera at the Natural History Museum and @flygirlNHM on Twitter. She was educated at the University of Manchester and holds a PhD from the University of Surrey, Roehampton. She has carried out research projects on mosquitoes in Britain and Tajikistan, and is contributing to a project on Ethiopian Diptera. She has presented a Radio 4 series on insects and is regularly communicating science via radio, talks and social media. She is the author of *The Secret Life of Flies* (2017) and *The Inside Out of Flies* (2020) and president of the Amateur Entomologists' Society.

THE NECROPHAGES

A friend will help you move, a good friend
will help you move a body.

Steven J. Daniels

According to Benjamin Franklin nothing can be said to be certain except death and taxes. Everything living eventually dies. But what happens to all of the bodies? Humans are generally either cremated or, as with most animals, left to rot away. Can you imagine if this didn't happen? Corpses littering the high streets and countryside! Luckily for us, nature's own gravediggers start working on the dead immediately life ceases. Adult flies locate the bodies, lay their eggs and, for the most part, leave their offspring the job of cleaning up the mess. If it weren't for these little organic munchers we would be knee-high in dead bodies, with corpses floating around in a quagmire of putrefying organs! These necrophagous species, along with the dung beetles, did not evolve until relatively recently – 66 to 26 million years ago – and since they were not around during the age of the dinosaurs, the decomposing fauna and landscape must have looked quite different then. Flies weren't the first to be involved in the clean up then but they are some of the most important insect carrion feeders today in terms of both densities and efficiency. Not only do they munch away on dead bodies but some feed on the dead or dying parts of living ones, which can have a positive or negative impact depending on the situation. The negative is myiasis – a parasitic infection by any fly larvae in a vertebrate host. This often looks as gross as it sounds and I will cover it later. But the positive is a very exciting thing indeed – and one that humans have used for thousands of years to aid our recovery from injuries.

Not too often can one quote the *King James Bible* in a scientific book, but the Book of Job (24:20) states: 'The womb shall forget him; the worm shall feed sweetly on him'. It was not worms but fly maggots that were being discussed here, and this was not the first published mention of maggots feeding on meat. In the 4th century BC, Aristotle, the famous Greek philosopher, proposed his spontaneous generation theory. He argued that some animals grew from their parents while others just appeared – including flies – from either rotten vegetable matter or from the 'inside of animals out of the secretions of their several organs'. This theory was believed to be true from Aristotle's time right up to the 17th century. It was then that Francesco Redi, an Italian physician and nature lover, conducted the first experiments debunking the myth. These were reinforced in 1862 when chemist and microbiologist, Louis Pasteur, conducted his famous swan-neck flask experiment to disprove spontaneous regeneration. When the flasks were sealed nothing grew on the meat but when they were left exposed flies appeared. But the flies' appearance was not a miracle of spontaneous generation. They needed to arrive in the first place and lay their eggs on the food source.

You can understand why Aristotle was confused – where did the flies come from and, more pertinent, how did they get there so quickly? Well, we know that some species of blow flies in the family Calliphoridae are able to detect dead bodies from considerable distances – some have been shown to migrate to corpses from more than 16 km (10 miles) away. Dr Madison Lee Goff, a forensic entomologist working in Hawaii, has also found that they can get there very quickly as well – in some cases taking just 10 minutes. And they have to, because a decaying body is, by its very nature, an ever-changing food source and there will be lots of competition for it from different species at different stages.

There are five main necrophagous (body-feeding) families of flies: the blow flies, house flies, flesh flies, soldier flies and scuttle flies, but there are species from many other families that also turn up to feast. The Calliphoridae are arguably the most important in terms of the numbers involved in the decomposition of flesh. Although the family are commonly called blow flies, they also include the bluebottles or greenbottles, the adults of which are some of the most recognizable flies. They are the 'vomiters' and some of the most despised insects alongside house flies and mosquitoes. They arrive at the scene and get to work straight away, laying thousands of eggs on the body, which, within hours in some cases, develop into larvae. And if you thought sewage was a good source of nutrients, imagine how good decomposing flesh is. Once more it is the larval stage that is the important part of the life cycle as the larvae are the consumers of flesh.

There is a predictable succession of flies that arrive at a corpse, with different species of fly specializing in eating different parts of the body at different stages of decomposition. We have used this to help us solve crimes. Forensic entomology is a very popular subject today thanks to shows like *Crime Scene Investigation* (*CSI*) – in fact the increased popularity of forensic courses is referred to as the *CSI* effect. But this is not new. Blow flies have been helping us poor-smelling species for a long time now. A classic story, often told but worth retelling, is about the first recorded case of forensic entomology in 1235, in a small village in China. A Chinese lawyer-cum-death investigator called Sòng Cí (or Sung Tz'u) wrote up the 'case' in the medico-legal text book *The Washing Away of Wrongs*. One of the farmers from the village had been brutally killed with a hand sickle, and Sòng Cí realized there was a cunning way to find the murderer. He asked for all the farmers to attend a meeting and to bring their sickles with them. He then had them wait. They did not have to wait long as the days were warm and flies soon started appearing. And these flies all went for the same sickle. Sòng Cí confronted its owner, who was so shocked that he confessed immediately. What the killer had not known was that although he had cleaned the weapon of all visible signs of blood, the flies would still be attracted by the minute traces remaining on the weapon.

It was another 800 years before flies were used once again to legally incriminate a murderer, this time in the UK. At the Museum we have a rather famous jar of maggots that was a sample from the first criminal case where maggots helped convict a murderer. The story begins with Dr Buck Ruxton, who was a practising GP in Lancashire, England, during the 1930s. He was generally well-liked and respected in the community where he lived and worked.

Then, in September 1935, two mutilated female bodies were discovered wrapped in newspaper in a small ravine in Dumfriesshire, Scotland, 100 miles north of where he lived. Though the newspaper used was a national one, one of the pages used was from a supplement only available in an area very local to where Dr Ruxton lived. And when it emerged that Dr Ruxton's wife and maid had disappeared suspicion inevitably fell on him. He denied any involvement, claiming that the maid had fallen pregnant and that his wife had gone away with her to assist with an abortion. But two key pieces of forensic evidence found him out. First, a comparison of images of one of the skulls with photographs of Dr Ruxton's wife pointed to one of the bodies being hers (a discipline called craniology). Second, a sample of maggots collected when the bodies were discovered was sent to Dr Alexander Mearns, an entomologist at the University of Edinburgh. He identified them as *Calliphora vicina*, a very common carrion blow fly, and he was able to establish that they were somewhere between 12 and 14 days old, which meant that the bodies had to have been there at least two weeks. This provided vital information as to when the murders took place, coinciding as it did with when Dr Ruxton claimed his wife and maid had gone away and, coupled with other evidence, it was enough to lead to his conviction and hanging.

Our understanding of forensic entomology has increased greatly over the past 80 years. In the USA there are numerous body farms where donated human bodies in various states of dress are placed in various positions and locations and insect succession is studied. In Australia the first body farm has just been set up in the Blue Mountains near Sydney and as yet this is the only other facility not in the USA. In the UK we can only work with decomposing pigs and at the Museum we have our very own maggot man (forensic entomologist) Dr Martin Hall, who, with the assistance of many, is researching various aspects of forensic entomology. Up in one of our famous towers that never fail to impress the visitors as they approach the Museum, the entomologists often have rows of Petri dishes crawling with maggots, all being subjected to different experiments. In days gone by, when the entomologists were in a temporary home near the towers, the occasional fly would escape the laboratory and come down the many flights of stairs to join us for lunch. How did we know that they were from upstairs? They were always the most pristine of specimens, iridescent in our dim common room light, as they had been nurtured in the most perfect of conditions.

Body farms are a perfect way for us to study the various factors affecting decomposition – in the outdoors, out of the way of curious humans and hungry vertebrates – and enable us to understand how long different stages take. A body that has been hung, for example, decomposes differently to one placed in a bin. I once attended a conference that discussed many of these different results in detail, the example of a suspended corpse sticking in my mind. Instead of decomposing the suspended corpse became leathery, almost tanned, with very little maggot infestation even after a lengthy period of time, as the maggots were not able to attach to and infest it. I talked about this subsequently on a radio show, and shortly afterwards received a charming letter from a very fit (she told me) 80-year-old offering me her body, once she was deceased, for research! Very kind, but I had to decline the offer.

As well as position the succession of maggot feasters can be affected by many external factors, such as temperature and other environmental factors, be they local or extremely local. One such modifier is narcotics. Back in the late 1980s, Dr Madison Lee Goff, the Hawaiian forensic entomologist, received a phone call from another entomologist who had maggots from a female who had been stabbed to death. Oddly the maggots were of different sizes and so the implication was that they were of different ages – making the time of death difficult to determine. Now Goff was, at that time, investigating the effect of drugs, specifically cocaine, on maggot development. In his book *A Fly for the Prosecution* he amusingly retells how he had to apply to the Animal Care and Use Committee at his work for permission to give cocaine to rabbits and then go about trying to legally purchase the product! He eventually did get permission but then had to rely on donations from police agencies rather than buying it himself. When he received this call he immediately thought about cocaine but, he admitted later, it was a long shot to ask if the victim had been tested for drugs. Cocaine is a strong stimulant which in humans can initially produce a feeling of euphoria as it mimics adrenaline. Goff found that maggots subjected to cocaine grow more rapidly in comparison to their clean-living companions because of this stimulant. On investigation there were indeed traces of cocaine in the body and the larger maggots were found specifically around the nasal region (snorting this drug is the most common method of ingestion). Thanks to his new research Goff was able to determine post-mortem interval, which in laymen's terms is the time since death, as he was able to work out timings using both the development of maggots under the influence of cocaine and those developing naturally. From this they were able to establish when the victim had died, which had previously been confusing. This new timing did involve her consuming cocaine and was consistent with the other non-insect evidence and so linked her killer's activities to hers.

Forensic entomology is not the only good thing that maggots do for us. As well as helping us determine the time of death, blow flies actually help prevent death in some cases. Species from this family specialize in consuming necrotic parts resulting from an injury or wound as well as decomposing bodies. Open wounds often have necrotic tissue in and around them – commonly called gangrene. If left untreated, gangrene can result in loss of limbs and, if severe, even death.

An ancient but nonetheless effective way of dealing with gangrene was to place live maggots in and around the wound. Legend has it that Genghis Khan always had a caravan full of maggots with his army to enable his soldiers to receive treatment quickly. Moving from a great warrior to a great war, the American Civil War was particularly brutal, with estimates of 750,000 deaths, not just from war wounds but also from many arthropod-borne diseases and poor sanitation. Medical doctors soon noticed though that wounds infested with maggots healed better than those without them and so began adding more to the wounds. In his book *Flies and Disease II. Biology and Disease Transmission*, Bernard Greenberg quotes Doctor John Forney Zacharias: 'During my service in the hospital at Danville, Virginia, I first used maggots to remove the decayed tissue in hospital gangrene and with eminent satisfaction. In a single day, they would clean a wound much better than any agents we had at our command. I used them afterwards at various places. I am sure I saved many lives by their use, escaped septicaemia, and had rapid recoveries.'

There are many other examples, both historical and current, of maggots removing rotten tissue, technically called debridement, and nowadays there are factories globally dedicated to the production of debridement flies. The most common blow fly used is *Lucilia sericata*, the common greenbottle. Research has shown that the maggots of these flies secrete allantoin, an antiseptic compound, the production of which is not just restricted to these flies but is across the animal kingdom and in some plants. This magic compound stimulates healing and cell development and is now used in many products including cosmetics. It has also now been determined that the effective molecule in allantoin is urea, a major component of human urine, a compound which not only stimulates cell regeneration but also keeps infections at bay.

The ability of maggots to release 'healing fumes' has also been shown to be effective in reducing TB and MRSA infections. Around 100 years ago Arthur Bryant, a Yorkshire man who bred maggots for fishing bait, realized that they could be helpful in other ways and set up 'maggotoriums'. If you have a sensitive stomach I will almost apologize for this next bit of the story. Each summer he received on average

18 tonnes of dead animals (usually from zoos) and he would leave these in the woods to attract greenbottle maggots (the smell was apparently detectable three miles away). Once maggots were visible on the meat, it would be removed and transferred to these maggotoriums. Stephen Thomas writes in his book *Surgical Dressings and Wound Management*: 'Consumptives would sit in the maggotorium beside troughs of maggots to inhale the fumes and pass the time reading, chatting or playing card games'. However, mass production of penicillin and sulphonamides and, I am hazarding a guess, the smell, ensured that these maggot factories never really took off. Now that there is widespread resistance to antibiotics, scientists are once more researching the antibiotic properties of maggots, determining the important components of these maggot fumes and finding a way to apply these to bacterial infections that are developing resistance, such as MRSA.

Apart from having this chemical benefit, maggots are just very good at cleaning up dead flesh. Once properly sterilized, they can eat away at the dead or dying flesh in wounds to leave them clean, thus enabling tissue to regenerate. Suppurating diabetic ulcers and other rather grim infections or injuries can be stuffed with sterile maggots and left for a couple of days before the maggot dressings are changed or removed. They do not eat undamaged cells and, even if left in the wound – though not exactly recommended – they do not cause any damage to the patient. Ronald Sherman MD wrote in 2003 about the efficiency of maggots versus conventional therapy: 'Non-healing diabetic foot ulcers account for 25–50% of all diabetic hospital admissions and most of the 60,000–70,000 yearly amputations in the US.' But Sherman found there was a significant reduction of necrotic tissue and amputations when maggots were used instead of standard methods.

You don't need to pour maggots into a wound any more either. Now doctors can order what look like teabags – albeit teabags stuffed with maggots – instead. These maggot-bags enable the maggots to poke their little jaws through the mesh and get at the necrotic tissue, while the mesh stops them wandering off. And, as we already know, their waste products are useful to our wounds. The bags get changed every couple of days, and after five or six weeks you have a beautifully healed wound.

Maggots don't just devour the meat course but also favour the cheese course. There are a group of flies called cheese skippers or Piophilidae, and they all have a liking for animal products, including mouldy cheese and cured meats. A particular type of traditional Sardinian cheese called *casu marzu*, is banned in many countries because it contains live *Piophila casei* maggots, commonly called cheese skippers. The feeding activity of these maggots causes the insides of the cheese to decompose and then ferment, resulting in a soft, liquid centre. You can either leave the maggots or choose to consume them with the cheese as part of the experience. Whether you choose to eat them or not, caution is advisable as, when startled, the maggots can jump distances of up to 15 cm (6 in). They do this by raising their anterior end, bending it forwards in a loop until their mouth hooks attach to the end of their abdomen. When the maggots rapidly straighten their bodies, it causes them to 'jump'.

I have not eaten this cheese, but was prepared to do so in the name of science (and curiosity) until I did a little more research into this delicacy. This species of fly, and similar species, are extraordinarily resilient. They can survive in our digestive tract and its acidic juices, and can often lacerate the gut lining with their mouth hooks. Internal bleeding and stomach spasms, brought about by a cheese, does not sound like a good ending to a meal. Accidental myiasis resulting in diarrhoea, pain, nausea and other gastric symptoms is apparently not that uncommon but something that I would rather avoid given the choice. There have even been cases reported when larvae have pupated inside the body and an adult fly has emerged along with the faeces.

Most adult cheese skippers have rather oddly shaped heads – almost cheese-wedge-shaped. The males of another in the group, the waltzing fly, *Prochyliza xanthostoma*, have quite wonderful heads – almost conical in shape with very large and thick antennae – and they feed on animal carcasses. As their name suggests the males dance to woo the females. But they also have to defend their territories (the carcasses) from other males and can have the most amazing fist fights – they really reign down punches on each other.

Yet another species of Piophilidae is the antler fly, *Protopiophila litigata.* These don't have antlers and should not be confused with the antler flies in the fruit fly family that do. Instead *Protopiophila litigata* are found on either antlers that have been shed or on the antlers of dead deer and similar species. Their scientific name hints at their behaviour – litigious or aggressive. As with the waltzing fly, males can get very physical with each other but they can also cluster together in groups. This conflicting behaviour is the result of the considerable amount of mate-choosing by both the females and, more unusually, the males. The male is looking for a female with a large derrière, holding out for a lovely big one as this indicates that her eggs are very close to maturity and so the chance of him impregnating her is at its greatest. She is looking also for a large dominant male as it's presumed he will be better at protecting her and will have more ejaculate (which she partly expels then ingests after mating). Romance is alive and blooming with these flies.

Two evolutionary biologists, Russell Bondicuriansky and Ronald Brooks, describe the mating behaviour of antler flies as males leaping on to 'the backs of females, briefly tapping the sides of her abdomen with his legs, then stimulating her abdominal top with his tarsi, parameres and gonopods [specialized external reproductive organs] until she extends her genitalia, after which the pair established genital lock'. These two researchers watched these flies having sex for periods up to 10 minutes, to work out the different behaviours and timings. And this wasn't confined just to the laboratory, they also studied the flies outside in their natural environment on antlers.

I have swept flies from this family in Peru, from rotting cow skulls where all that was left were tiny portions of tanned skin stuck to the bones. Harold Oldroyd also wrote about these flies in *Natural History of Flies* in connection with a collection of 17 elephant skulls left outside the window at the Museum to decompose in the fresh London air. Scientists have been using insects for a long time to help clean skeletons of soft tissue, whether for research or display. Nowadays most skeletons aren't left lying around outside but are kept in special enclosures called dermestariums, within which dermestid beetles carry out the cleaning up of the specimens. Oldroyd comments that 'a fine collection of *Piophila* was a small compensation for the smell…'

I am curious to know what the public made of these elephant skulls decomposing in the sun. The Museum has a dermestarium but it is only used for smaller animals.

Another group of flies that have a liking for dead bodies are the Phoridae, or scuttle flies. These have incredibly diverse feeding preferences but one group in this family is referred to as the coffin flies because, indeed, they develop inside corpses. They are able to survive in these unique environments for many generations even when the corpse is buried in a coffin. The most important of these flies is *Conicera tibialis*, which has a global distribution. The larvae start munching away once the corpse has dried out, which can be as soon as a year after death, but specimens have been recorded at post-mortem intervals of three to five years. Daniel Martin-Vega, of the forensic research group at the Museum, and colleagues found fresh adult flies on a corpse exhumed 18 years after death. When we look at the succession of species on a corpse, flies will be some of the first animals to arrive and some of the last to leave. For a fly to get into a coffin buried several feet under is no mean feat, but these flies are never more than 3 mm ($^1/_8$ in) in size. Adult *Conicera tibialis* have been timed descending from the surface and they were able to burrow to a depth of 50 cm (20 in) in about four days. This species has wings, but many other species of coffin fly are apterous, meaning wingless, such as *Puliciphora borinquenensis*.

Puliciphora borinquenensis have not only an interesting diet and female morphology but also several different mating rituals. The female starts courtship with vigorous abdominal pumping which is thought to waft her pheromones around to attract males. She parades around near the original oviposition site from which she emerged as an adult. Males then decide to adopt one of four different reproductive routines. The first, and in my mind the most ambitious, is for the males to remain stationary and grab as many of the parading females in succession as possible to mate with over about 30 minutes. Peter Miller, an entomologist at Oxford University, stated that they mate with 0.66 females per minute over this period. He observed that one particularly successful male performed 45 separate copulations in half an hour. The second option, again with the males just standing still, is to wait at the oviposition sites and grab the non-parading females that had either already copulated or were not yet ready to. The third and fourth options are more amusing, as the parading females are 'airlifted' by the males, while carnally attached, to new egg-laying sites when these can be found, or dumped randomly when they can't! And just when you thought their behaviour couldn't get any more extraordinary, if the males that are carrying females do figure out a good oviposition site they can transport large numbers of females there – as many as 30 at very quick intervals, that's one female every two minutes. What is there not to admire about the behavioural adaptations of flies? The density of individuals and the age of the males determine which of the four reproductive pathways they choose.

Scuttle flies don't just like human corpses. The larvae of several of the *Megaselia* genus (a rich genus of more than 1,400 species that contains nearly half of the described species from this family) have been found feeding on dead snails. Some of these species were initially considered parasitic as the female was seen laying eggs on live insects. But no, the larvae of *Megaselia scalaris* are in fact saprophagous, meaning they eat decaying flesh, and we have determined this by their mouthparts. This species, as with many saprophagous larvae, have pharyngeal ridges in their mouthparts. These ridges sieve out the ingested fluid – the decomposing bodily juices – and enable the larvae to ingest solid rotten patties rather than litres of putrefied juices. Efficient, if a little nauseating. Amazingly, the mothers are able to determine whether the prey is injured or not (we don't know how), and thus select a suitable host for their larvae.

Scuttle flies like both fresh and seasoned flesh and this is not un-common across many families of flies that have necrophagous species. House flies and moth flies are often found grazing on mature and decomposed corpses and so house flies are often some of the first and last to arrive at a body. Forensic investigators need to be very careful about the accuracy of identifications as wrongly identified species may lead to incorrect ageing. The number of families that have been recorded turning up on carcasses is vast. Work by Catarina Prado e Castro, a Portuguese forensic entomologist, with decomposing pigs has highlighted this as she and colleagues identified 43 different families of diptera on corpses.

Whether it is getting rid of the bodies or mending them, diptera are essential in our environment. These flies favour environments that most of us would consider highly unfavourable, and convert the defunct to functional, which makes for a more pleasant world for us all.

from AFTER LONDON

Richard Jefferies

Richard Jefferies (1848–87) is one of the most enduring British nature writers, a prolific author of essays, journalism, natural history and novels. Born at Coate, Wiltshire, and the son of a farmer, his childhood was a great influence on his passion for natural history which was ever-present in his wide-ranging work from *Bevis* (1882), a classic children's book and part of a golden age of children's literature, to *After London* (1885), an early example of science – or apocalyptic – fiction. He left school at fifteen and worked on local newspapers, later moving to Surbiton with his wife and child to more easily find freelance writing work. Essays based on his childhood friendship with a gamekeeper near Coate were collected into a book, *The Gamekeeper at Home* (1878), which was popular and critically acclaimed, with Jefferies compared to Gilbert White. It was followed by *Wild Life in a Southern County* and *The Amateur Poacher* (both 1879) and *Round About a Great Estate* (1880). Sick from tuberculosis, he moved to Brighton and wrote his autobiography *The Story of My Heart* (1883). In his later years, Jefferies moved around southern England, ill and impoverished, publishing his final novel, *Amaryllis at the Fair*, in 1887. More of his writing has been published posthumously and his work has inspired and influenced Edward Thomas, Henry Williamson and John Fowles among others.

THE GREAT FOREST

The old men say their fathers told them that soon after the fields were left to themselves a change began to be visible. It became green everywhere in the first spring, after London ended, so that all the country looked alike.

The meadows were green, and so was the rising wheat which had been sown, but which neither had nor would receive any further care. Such arable fields as had not been sown, but where the last stubble had been ploughed up, were overrun with couch-grass, and where the short stubble had not been ploughed, the weeds hid it. So that there was no place which was not more or less green; the footpaths were the greenest of all, for such is the nature of grass where it has once been trodden on, and by-and-by, as the summer came on, the former roads were thinly covered with the grass that had spread out from the margin.

In the autumn, as the meadows were not mown, the grass withered as it stood, falling this way and that, as the wind had blown it; the seeds dropped, and the bennets became a grayish-white, or, where the docks and sorrel were thick, a brownish-red. The wheat, after it had ripened, there being no one to reap it, also remained standing, and was eaten by clouds of sparrows, rooks, and pigeons, which flocked to it and were undisturbed, feasting at their pleasure. As the winter came on, the crops were beaten down by the storms, soaked with the rain, and trodden upon by herds of animals.

Next summer the prostrate straw of the preceding year was concealed by the young green wheat and barley that sprang up from the grain sown by dropping from the ears, and by quantities of docks, thistles, oxeye daisies, and similar plants. This matted mass grew up through the bleached straw. Charlock, too, hid the rotting roots in the fields under a blaze of yellow flower. The young spring meadow-grass could scarcely push its way up through the long dead grass and bennets of the year previous, but docks and thistles, sorrel, wild carrots, and nettles, found no such difficulty.

Footpaths were concealed by the second year, but roads could be traced, though as green as the sward, and were still the best for walking, because the tangled wheat and weeds, and, in the meadows, the long grass, caught the feet of those who tried to pass through. Year by year the original crops of wheat, barley, oats, and beans asserted their presence by shooting up, but in gradually diminished force, as nettles and coarser plants, such as the wild parsnips, spread out into the fields from the ditches and choked them.

Aquatic grasses from the furrows and water-carriers extended in the meadows, and, with the rushes, helped to destroy or take the place of the former sweet herbage. Meanwhile the brambles, which grew very fast, had pushed forward their prickly runners farther and farther from the hedges till they had now reached ten or fifteen yards. The briars had followed, and the hedges had widened to three or four times their first breadth, the fields being equally contracted. Starting from all sides at once, these brambles and briars in the course of about twenty years met in the centre of the largest fields.

Hawthorn bushes sprang up among them, and, protected by the briars and thorns from grazing animals, the suckers of elm-trees rose and flourished. Sapling ashes, oaks, sycamores, and horse-chestnuts, lifted their heads. Of old time the cattle would have eaten off the seed leaves with the grass so soon as they were out of the ground, but now most of the acorns that were dropped by birds, and the keys that were wafted by the wind, twirling as they floated, took root and grew into trees. By this time the brambles and briars had choked up and blocked the former roads, which were as impassable as the fields.

No fields, indeed, remained, for where the ground was dry, the thorns, briars, brambles, and saplings already mentioned filled the space, and these thickets and the young trees had converted most part of the country into an immense forest. Where the ground was naturally moist, and the drains had become choked with willow roots, which, when confined in tubes, grow into a mass like the brush of a fox, sedges and flags and rushes covered it. Thorn bushes were there too, but not so tall; they were hung with lichen. Besides the flags and reeds, vast quantities of the tallest cow-parsnips or 'gicks' rose five or six feet high, and the willow herb with its stout stem, almost as woody as a shrub, filled every approach.

By the thirtieth year there was not one single open place, the hills only excepted, where a man could walk, unless he followed the tracks of wild creatures or cut himself a path. The ditches, of course, had long since become full of leaves and dead branches, so that the water which should have run off down them stagnated, and presently spread out into the hollow places and by the corner of what had once been fields, forming marshes where the horsetails, flags, and sedges hid the water.

As no care was taken with the brooks, the hatches upon them gradually rotted, and the force of the winter rains carried away the weak timbers, flooding the lower grounds, which became swamps of larger size. The dams, too, were drilled by water-rats, and the streams percolating through slowly increased the size of these tunnels till the structure burst, and the current swept on and added to the floods below. Mill-dams stood longer, but, as the ponds silted up, the current flowed round and even through the mill-houses, which, going by degrees to ruin, were in some cases undermined till they fell.

Everywhere the lower lands adjacent to the streams had become marshes, some of them extending for miles in a winding line, and occasionally spreading out to a mile in breadth. This was particularly the case where brooks and streams of some volume joined the rivers, which were also blocked and obstructed in their turn, and the two, overflowing, covered the country around; for the rivers brought down trees and branches, timbers floated from the shore, and all kinds of similar materials, which grounded in the shallows or caught against snags, and formed huge piles where there had been weirs.

Sometimes, after great rains, these piles swept away the timbers of the weir, driven by the irresistible power of the water, and then in its course the flood, carrying the balks before it like battering rams, cracked and split the bridges of solid stone which the ancients had built. These and the iron bridges likewise were overthrown, and presently quite disappeared, for the very foundations were covered with the sand and gravel silted up.

Thus, too, the sites of many villages and towns that anciently existed along the rivers, or on the lower lands adjoining, were concealed by the water and the mud it brought with it. The sedges and reeds that arose completed the work and left nothing visible, so that the mighty buildings of olden days were by these means utterly buried. And, as has been proved by those who have dug for treasures, in our time the very foundations are deep beneath the earth, and not to be got at for the water that oozes into the shafts that they have tried to sink through the sand and mud banks.

From an elevation, therefore, there was nothing visible but endless forest and marsh. On the level ground and plains the view was limited to a short distance, because of the thickets and the saplings which had now become young trees. The downs only were still partially open, yet it was not convenient to walk upon them except in the tracks of animals, because of the long grass which, being no more regularly grazed upon by sheep, as was once the case, grew thick and tangled. Furze, too, and heath covered the slopes, and in places vast quantities of fern. There had always been copses of fir and beech and nut-tree covers, and these increased and spread, while bramble, briar, and hawthorn extended around them.

By degrees the trees of the vale seemed as it were to invade and march up the hills, and, as we see in our time, in many places the downs are hidden altogether with a stunted kind of forest. But all the above happened in the time of the first generation. Besides these things a great physical change took place; but before I speak of that, it will be best to relate what effects were produced upon animals and men.

In the first years after the fields were left to themselves, the fallen and over-ripe corn crops became the resort of innumerable mice. They swarmed to an incredible degree, not only devouring the grain upon the straw that had never been cut, but clearing out every single ear in the wheat-ricks that were standing about the country. Nothing remained in these ricks but straw, pierced with tunnels and runs, the home and breeding-place of mice, which thence poured forth into the fields. Such grain as had been left in barns and granaries, in mills, and in warehouses of the deserted towns, disappeared in the same manner.

When men tried to raise crops in small gardens and enclosures for their sustenance, these legions of mice rushed in and destroyed the produce of their labour. Nothing could keep them out, and if a score were killed, a hundred more supplied their place. These mice were preyed upon by kestrel hawks, owls, and weasels; but at first they made little or no appreciable difference. In a few years, however, the weasels, having such a superabundance of food, trebled in numbers, and in the same way the hawks, owls, and foxes increased. There was then some relief, but even now at intervals districts are invaded, and the granaries and the standing corn suffer from these depredations.

This does not happen every year, but only at intervals, for it is noticed that mice abound very much more in some seasons than others. The extraordinary multiplication of these creatures was the means of providing food for the cats that had been abandoned in the towns, and came forth into the country in droves. Feeding on the mice, they became, in a very short time, quite wild, and their descendants now roam the forests.

In our houses we still have several varieties of the domestic cat, such as the tortoise-shell, which is the most prized, but when the above-mentioned cats became wild, after a while the several varieties disappeared, and left but one wild kind. Those which are now so often seen in the forest, and which do so much mischief about houses and enclosures, are almost all greyish, some being striped, and they are also much longer in the body than the tame. A few are jet black; their skins are then preferred by hunters.

Though the forest cat retires from the sight of man as much as possible, yet it is extremely fierce in defence of its young, and instances have been known where travellers in the woods have been attacked upon unwittingly approaching their dens. Dropping from the boughs of a tree upon the shoulders, the creature flies at the face, inflicting deep scratches and bites, exceedingly painful, and sometimes dangerous, from the tendency to fester. But such cases are rare, and the reason the forest cat is so detested is because it preys upon fowls and poultry, mounting with ease the trees or places where they roost.

Almost worse than the mice were the rats, which came out of the old cities in such vast numbers that the people who survived and saw them are related to have fled in fear. This terror, however, did not last so long as the evil of the mice, for the rats, probably not finding sufficient food when together, scattered abroad, and were destroyed singly by the cats and dogs, who slew them by thousands, far more than they could afterwards eat, so that the carcases were left to decay. It is said that, overcome with hunger, these armies of rats in some cases fell upon each other, and fed on their own kindred. They are still numerous, but do not appear to do the same amount of damage as is occasionally caused by the mice, when the latter invade the cultivated lands.

The dogs, of course, like the cats, were forced by starvation into the fields, where they perished in incredible numbers. Of many species of dogs which are stated to have been plentiful among the ancients, we have now nothing but the name. The poodle is extinct, the Maltese terrier, the Pomeranian, the Italian greyhound, and, it is believed, great numbers of crosses and mongrels have utterly disappeared. There was none to feed them, and they could not find food for themselves, nor could they stand the rigour of the winter when exposed to the frost in the open air.

Some kinds, more hardy and fitted by nature for the chase, became wild, and their descendants are now found in the woods. Of these, there are three sorts which keep apart from each other, and are thought not to interbreed. The most numerous are the black. The black wood-dog is short and stoutly made, with shaggy hair, sometimes marked with white patches.

There can be no doubt that it is the descendant of the ancient sheep-dog, for it is known that the sheep-dog was of that character, and it is said that those who used to keep sheep soon found their dogs abandon the fold, and join the wild troops that fell upon the sheep. The black wood-dogs hunt in packs of ten or more (as many as forty have been counted), and are the pest of the farmer, for, unless his flocks are protected at night within stockades or enclosures, they are certain to be attacked. Not satisfied with killing enough to satisfy hunger, these dogs tear and mangle for sheer delight of blood, and will destroy twenty times as many as they can eat, leaving the miserably torn carcases on the field. Nor are the sheep always safe by day if the wood-dogs happen to be hungry. The shepherd is, therefore, usually accompanied by two or three mastiffs, of whose great size and strength the others stand in awe. At night, and when in large packs, starving in the snow, not even the mastiffs can check them.

No wood-dog, of any kind, has ever been known to attack man, and the hunter in the forest hears their bark in every direction without fear. It is, nevertheless, best to retire out of their way when charging sheep in packs, for they then seem seized with a blind fury, and some who have endeavoured to fight them have been thrown down and seriously mauled. But this has been in the blindness of their rush; no instance has ever been known of their purposely attacking man.

These black wood-dogs will also chase and finally pull down cattle, if they can get within the enclosures, and even horses have fallen victims to their untiring thirst for blood. Not even the wild cattle can always escape, despite their strength, and they have been known to run down stags, though not their usual quarry.

The next kind of wild wood-dog is the yellow, a smaller animal, with smooth hair inclining to a yellow colour, which lives principally upon game, chasing all from the hare to the stag. It is as swift, or nearly as swift, as the greyhound, and possesses greater endurance. In coursing the hare, it not uncommonly happens that these dogs start from the brake and take the hare, when nearly exhausted, from the hunter's hounds. They will in the same way follow a stag, which has been almost run down by the hunters, and bring him to bay, though in this case they lose their booty, dispersing through fear of man, when the hunters come up in a body.

But such is their love of the chase, that they are known to assemble from their lairs at the distant sound of the horn, and, as the hunters ride through the woods, they often see the yellow dogs flitting along side by side with them through bush and fern. These animals sometimes hunt singly, sometimes in couples, and as the season advances, and winter approaches, in packs of eight or twelve. They never attack sheep or cattle, and avoid man, except when they perceive he is engaged in the chase. There is little doubt that they are the descendants of the dogs which the ancients called lurchers, crossed, perhaps, with the greyhound, and possibly other breeds. When the various species of dogs were thrown on their own resources, those only withstood the exposure and hardships which were naturally hardy, and possessed natural aptitude for the chase.

The third species of wood-dog is the white. They are low on the legs, of a dingy white colour, and much smaller than the other two. They neither attack cattle nor game, though fond of hunting rabbits. This dog is, in fact, a scavenger, living upon the carcases of dead sheep and animals, which are found picked clean in the night. For this purpose it haunts the neighbourhood of habitations, and prowls in the evening over heaps of refuse, scampering away at the least alarm, for it is extremely timid.

It is perfectly harmless, for even the poultry do not dread it, and it will not face a tame cat, if by chance the two meet. It is rarely met with far from habitations, though it will accompany an army on the march. It may be said to remain in one district. The black and yellow dogs, on the contrary, roam about the forest without apparent home. One day the hunter sees signs of their presence, and perhaps may, for a month afterwards, not so much as hear a bark.

This uncertainty in the case of the black dog is the bane of the shepherds; for, not seeing or hearing anything of the enemy for months altogether, in spite of former experience their vigilance relaxes, and suddenly, while they sleep, their flocks are scattered. We still have, among tame dogs, the mastiff, terrier, spaniel, deerhound, and greyhound, all of which are as faithful to man as ever.

WILD ANIMALS

When the ancients departed, great numbers of their cattle perished. It was not so much the want of food as the inability to endure exposure that caused their death; a few winters are related to have so reduced them that they died by hundreds, many mangled by dogs. The hardiest that remained became perfectly wild, and the wood cattle are now more difficult to approach than deer.

There are two kinds, the white and the black. The white (sometimes dun) are believed to be the survivors of the domestic roan-and-white, for the cattle in our enclosures at the present day are of that colour. The black are smaller, and are doubtless little changed from their state in the olden times, except that they are wild. These latter are timid, unless accompanied by a calf, and are rarely known to turn upon their pursuers. But the white are fierce at all times; they will not, indeed, attack man, but will scarcely run from him, and it is not always safe to cross their haunts.

The bulls are savage beyond measure at certain seasons of the year. If they see men at a distance, they retire; if they come unexpectedly face to face, they attack. This characteristic enables those who travel through districts known to be haunted by white cattle to provide against an encounter, for, by occasionally blowing a horn, the herd that may be in the vicinity is dispersed. There are not often more than twenty in a herd. The hides of the dun are highly prized, both for their intrinsic value, and as proofs of skill and courage, so much so that you shall hardly buy a skin for all the money you may offer; and the horns are likewise trophies. The white or dun bull is the monarch of our forests.

Four kinds of wild pigs are found. The most numerous, or at least the most often seen, as it lies about our enclosures, is the common thorn-hog. It is the largest of the wild pigs, long-bodied and flat-sided, in colour much the hue of the mud in which it wallows. To the agriculturist it is the greatest pest, destroying or damaging all kinds of crops, and routing up the gardens. It is with difficulty kept out by palisading, for if there be a weak place in the wooden framework, the strong snout of the animal is sure to undermine and work a passage through.

As there are always so many of these pigs round about inhabited places and cultivated fields, constant care is required, for they instantly discover an opening. From their habit of haunting the thickets and bush which come up to the verge of the enclosures, they have obtained the name of thorn-hogs. Some reach an immense size, and they are very prolific, so that it is impossible to destroy them. The boars are fierce at a particular season, but never attack unless provoked to do so. But when driven to bay they are the most dangerous of the boars, on account of their vast size and weight. They are of a sluggish disposition, and will not rise from their lairs unless forced to do so.

The next kind is the white hog, which has much the same habits as the former, except that it is usually found in moist places, near lakes and rivers, and is often called the marsh-pig. The third kind is perfectly black, much smaller in size, and very active, affording by far the best sport, and also the best food when killed. As they are found on the hills where the ground is somewhat more open, horses can follow freely, and the chase becomes exciting. By some it is called the hill-hog, from the locality it frequents. The small tusks of the black boar are used for many ornamental purposes.

These three species are considered to be the descendants of the various domestic pigs of the ancients, but the fourth, or grey, is thought to be the true wild boar. It is seldom seen, but is most common in the south-western forests, where, from the quantity of fern, it is called the fern-pig. This kind is believed to represent the true wild boar, which was extinct, or merged in the domestic hog among the ancients, except in that neighbourhood where the strain remained.

With wild times, the wild habits have returned, and the grey boar is at once the most difficult of access, and the most ready to encounter either dogs or men. Although the first, or thorn-hog, does the most damage to the agriculturist because of its numbers, and its habit of haunting the neighbourhood of enclosures, the others are equally injurious if they chance to enter the cultivated fields.

The three principal kinds of wild sheep are the horned, the thyme, and the meadow. The thyme sheep are the smallest, and haunt the highest hills in the south, where, feeding on the sweet herbage of the ridges, their flesh is said to acquire a flavour of wild thyme. They move in small flocks of not more than thirty, and are the most difficult to approach, being far more wary than deer, so continuously are they hunted by the wood-dogs. The horned are larger, and move in greater numbers; as many as two hundred are sometimes seen together.

They are found on the lower slopes and plains, and in the woods. The meadow sheep have long shaggy wool, which is made into various articles of clothing, but they are not numerous. They haunt river sides, and the shores of lakes and ponds. None of these are easily got at, on account of the wood-dogs; but the rams of the horned kind are reputed to sometimes turn upon the pursuing pack, and butt them to death. In the extremity of their terror whole flocks of wild sheep have been driven over precipices and into quagmires and torrents.

Besides these, there are several other species whose haunt is local. On the islands, especially, different kinds are found. The wood-dogs will occasionally, in calm weather, swim out to an island and kill every sheep upon it.

From the horses that were in use among the ancients the two wild species now found are known to have descended, a fact confirmed by their evident resemblance to the horses we still retain. The largest wild horse is almost black, or inclined to a dark colour, somewhat less in size than our present waggon horses, but of the same heavy make. It is, however, much swifter, on account of having enjoyed liberty for so long. It is called the bush-horse, being generally distributed among thickets and meadow-like lands adjoining water.

The other species is called the hill-pony, from its habitat, the hills, and is rather less in size than our riding-horse. This latter is short and thick-set, so much so as not to be easily ridden by short persons without high stirrups. Neither of these wild horses are numerous, but neither are they uncommon. They keep entirely separate from each other. As many as thirty mares are sometimes seen together, but there are districts where the traveller will not observe one for weeks.

Tradition says that in the olden times there were horses of a slender build whose speed out-stripped the wind, but of the breed of these famous racers not one is left. Whether they were too delicate to withstand exposure, or whether the wild dogs hunted them down is uncertain, but they are quite gone. Did but one exist, how eagerly it would be sought out, for in these days it would be worth its weight in gold, unless, indeed, as some affirm, such speed only endured for a mile or two.

It is not necessary, having written thus far of the animals, that anything should be said of the birds of the woods, which every one knows were not always wild, and which can, indeed, be compared with such poultry as are kept in our enclosures. Such are the bush hens, the wood turkeys, the galenas, the peacocks, the white duck and white goose, all of which, though now wild as the hawk, are well known to have been once tame.

There were deer, red and fallow, in numerous parks and chases of very old time, and these, having got loose, and having such immense tracts to roam over unmolested, went on increasing till now they are beyond computation, and I have myself seen a thousand head together. Within these forty years, as I learn, the roe deer, too, have come down from the extreme north, so that there are now three sorts in the woods. Before them the pine marten came from the same direction, and, though they are not yet common, it is believed they are increasing. For the first few years after the change took place there seemed a danger lest the foreign wild beasts that had been confined as curiosities in menageries should multiply and remain in the woods. But this did not happen.

Some few lions and tigers, bears, and other animals did indeed escape, together with many less furious creatures, and it is related that they roamed about the fields for a long time. They were seldom met with, having such an extent of country to wander over, and after a while entirely disappeared. If any progeny were born, the winter frosts must have destroyed it, and the same fate awaited the monstrous serpents which had been collected for exhibition. Only one such animal now exists which is known to owe its origin to those which escaped from the dens of the ancients. It is the beaver, whose dams are now occasionally found upon the streams by those who traverse the woods. Some of the aquatic birds, too, which frequent the lakes, are thought to have been originally derived from those which were formerly kept as curiosities.

In the castle yard at Longtover may still be seen the bones of an elephant which was found dying in the woods near that spot.

A FABLE FOR TODAY

Kapka Kassabova

Kapka Kassabova is a poet and writer of narrative non-fiction. *Border* (2017) and *To the Lake* (2020) explore the trans-boundary human geographies of the Southern Balkans. Border was shortlisted for the Baillie Gifford Prize and won the British Academy's Al-Rodhan Prize, The Saltire Book of the Year, the Highland Book Prize and The Stanford Dolman Travel Book of the Year. Kapka Kassabova grew up in Sofia, was university educated in New Zealand and now lives in the Highlands of Scotland. 'A Fable for Today' also appears in the anthologies *Comment faire?* (2020) and *Scotland After the Virus*, edited by Gerry Hassan and Simon Barrow (2020).

There was once a glen in the Highlands of Scotland *where all life seemed to live in harmony with its surroundings*.[1] The river, later to be named Beauly, from the French *'beau lieu'*, sprang from three sources and joined up into the Strathglass, Gaelic for 'grey-green valley'. The valley whispered with oaks and Caledonian pines. Cattle drovers rode over the hills to the Great Glen, retracing the paths of early Christian missionaries. The forest floor was covered in blueberry bushes that turned dark purple in autumn. Wolves, golden eagles, red deer and wildcats roamed. Springs bubbled up from the hillside and waterfalls thundered in springtime. The springs had names – St Ignatius, St Ninian, Morag, Mary – and stories were told of entities and encounters, and healing properties.

Then a strange blight crept over the area and everything began to change. It was the era of dam-building to bring 'power to the glens' whose remote parts were without electricity. Thousands of engineers and labourers came to live and work by the river, including former prisoners of war. A local lord opened up a gravel quarry on his estate to supply the dams with material. New roads and infrastructure were built. The dams turned out an engineering marvel. True, a waterfall or two had to be sacrificed, and houses had to be flooded, but their owners were promised jobs on the dams and free 'power' in perpetuity. The hills where only the outlines of wild animals and chimney smoke touched the skyline were now studded with pylons and power lines. New lochs appeared, the river was altered. Soon, every river of Western Europe would be impounded until the only wild rivers left on the continent would be in the Balkans. But it was the way of the future, it was just after the Second World War when life was kindled from the ashes of apocalypse. You couldn't argue with it. Just as you couldn't argue, earlier, with the felling of ancient forests for empire's shipbuilding and, later, the coffins made to bury the generation of young men sacrificed in the last throes of empire. The original mixed forests were replaced with a monoculture of pine. Earlier yet, crofting Gaeldom had been terminated by clearing the land of people and replaced with a monoculture of heather moor and sheep. The moor was made for recreational deer hunting, and in time, deer became a dominant monoculture. A pattern was emerging. Over time, people would become accustomed to seeing the body of the land shorn, mown, grazed, subjugated. They would even consider it beautiful, and they would no longer distinguish blueberries from poisonous fruit. A day would come when dog turds would be picked up for health-and-safety reasons, and placed in plastic bags then deposited in the forest or in the oceans, in perpetuity.

Decades passed, people didn't get the free power they were promised by the Electricity Board, but they did get used to the changed land-scape. Golden eagles still roamed, if not wolves and wildcats, and salmon jumped in the river.

Then a strange blight crept over the area and everything began to change. Some evil spell had settled on the community. I saw it close up from our house by the river. It was the era of green energy. There was a lot of money in it for large corporations and large landowners. A new mega-power line was built across the Highlands. The first pylon went up by the banks of the river. It was three times bigger than any pylon seen before. At seventy metres, the new pylons were the Eiffel towers of the Highlands, and the construction company commissioned to build them promised that they would soon 'blend' with the landscape. New roads and infrastructure were built. The pylons, the profitable wind farms that came on their heels, the expanded substation the size of a town – it was a marvel of industry. True, ancient landscape had to be eviscerated, more trees were lost, birds were electrocuted, and many people were forced to sell their houses and leave, while the remaining locals who now lived in the shadow of the pylons, the substation, the ghosts of the forest, didn't get any of the electricity because it was exported to the cities in the south, but green energy was the way of the future, you couldn't argue with it. You didn't want a return to nuclear power, did you?

True, the invasion of the pylons also brought the arrival of a con-struction company with almost a billion pounds revenue who bought the old small quarry started for the dams by the well-meaning lord, and began to expand. For this, they needed to fell more of the wood-land, and remove ancient burial cairns. The forest was replaced with a hole until groundwater was reached, then it was replanted with monoculture pine. No birds sang in the broom and gorse weedland that sprang up among the stunted pine. But we all needed gravel and sand, the construction company pointed out when we complained. We needed it for our houses, for our driveways, for the ever-expanding roads. We were all complicit in it, they pointed out, and besides there had always been a quarry here.

Years passed, we got used to the changed landscape, the tinnitus caused by the electricity lines, the migrating pain in our bodies and hearts, the sight of pylon towers everywhere we looked, the thunder of diggers extracting the earth where the woodland once stood with its purple blueberry floor. Our walking path was now on the edge of the extraction pit: on one side was an abyss, on the other the remaining wood of the river whose name means beautiful. The natural land-scape looked dwarfed by the industrial landscape: the billion-pound corporations, the vehicles that came to fell the trees, the lorries that carried away the trees, the vehicles that came to extract the earth, the vehicles that carried away the earth, the roads that had to be expanded to accommodate the vehicles, the vehicles in which representatives of industry arrived, wearing health-and-safety helmets and avoiding eye contact. The dams looked small and quiet now.

Then a strange blight crept over the area and everything began to change. Some evil spell had settled on the community: mysterious maladies swept… Everywhere was a shadow of death. But this time, it had a name: COVID-19. What a relief to have a name for it! For too long our affliction had been nameless. So we stayed home, tried not to do any further damage, and pondered the meaning of our condition.

Truth be told, we had been expecting it. We knew that we had gone too far in colluding with the extraction, extermination and extinction of all that is natural, abundant and alive in our earth and bodies, the two being the same thing (this, too, we have forgotten). We knew that *something* should be done when Australia burns, when the great Amazon is pulped and its cadaver dismembered into pastural monoculture, when Europe's last wild rivers in the Balkans are impounded by mafia states with EU funds, when politicians with white smiles build walls and prisons for people they tell us are *others*, when humans with all their worldly possessions in a plastic bag run from the ashes of their homelands only to be put in prisons – we felt it in our bones that something had to change. And that we would have to give something up for that change to happen. That if we don't do it voluntarily, it will happen to us. And it is. The earth is shutting us down, just as we have tried to shut it down, because *seldom if ever does Nature operate in closed and separate compartments.*

So when this season the salmon stopped jumping in the river and went into sharp decline, we were struck with sorrow, but not surprised. True, we had thought that salmon would be there forever, we had assumed that *we* would be there forever.

During the first silent weeks of the quarantine, when the people of the glen were being good and staying inside like grounded children, a noise was heard. The nearly-billion-pound construction company was felling the remaining forest. It was preparing to expand, again, all the way to the river this time. Nesting birds came to houses and fields, looking for a home. Deer ran across fields and roads. When we came out of our quarantine and walked along the edge of the abyss, on the other side was another abyss in the making.

Grief is felt in the area of the chest. When we are heartbroken, we can't breathe.

We can't breathe because there aren't enough trees left to make oxygen.

We can't breathe because we see on the news that sea creatures choke to death on the health-and-safety plastic in which our food is wrapped, and the coral reefs we dream of seeing one day are also dying.

We can't breathe because the pain of others increasingly feels like our pain and we begin to suspect that we are the others.

We can't breathe because we know: *no witchcraft, no enemy action has silenced the rebirth of new life in this stricken world. The people have done it themselves.*

We can't breathe because the earth's atmosphere is polluted by the construction companies that felled the trees, and their businessmen cousins that you couldn't argue with, because the water is pesticide-toxic and our blood awash with pharmaceutical residue, because the nuclear fallout of Chernobyl and Fukushima is in our endocrine systems and we have pre-existing conditions. We feel divided between and within ourselves, like the split atom that gives nuclear power and in turn splits the human genome because *radiation is an uncoupler, and the death of cells exposed to radiation is thought… to be brought about in this way.* We are the children of the nuclear age whose aim is self-extinction – and we can't breathe.

We can't breathe because we want to awaken from this nightmare and start again, make amends, say sorry, give us another chance, refill the hole and replant it, demolish the wall and the prison built at our expense by plutocratic horsemen of the apocalypse. A woman who was raped during a recent war asked her rapist, a teenaged soldier, why he was doing this. 'Because I am already dead,' he replied.

We can't breathe because we want to say sorry even though we have done nothing wrong. We used to worry that we're running out of time, and now we see that there's nothing personal about it – the world as we know it is running out of time.

We can't breathe because truths are surfacing as the glaciers melt, ancestral memories surge, the earth's ancient places call us and we suddenly yearn to reconnect with it all, we yearn for intimacy, meaning, justice, for a sacred place, just as the sacred forests are being felled and the sacred mountains extracted, and it feels like our own bodies.

And until we change our ways we will be compelled to wear a health-and-safety mask, as if under sedation. Under sedation, you can't speak or think clearly. Not because the mask protects us – nothing can protect us against ourselves – but out of fear, shame and grief. The primitive mask is an apt symbol and end result of our primitive, split-atom handling of our earth.

A memory remains of how one woman from Strathglass had heard hammering noises and men's voices by the river where a massive dam would be built thirty years later. Another woman had heard 'witches singing' where the first electricity lines and pylons would be built – the small ones. They were publicly derided by the Board at the official launch of the first dam, but over the decades, employees of the Board regularly heard voices, singing and laughing in the empty tunnels that the 'Tunnel Tigers' had dynamited, many perishing in the process. When I walk by my thrice-dammed river whose name means beautiful, on the edge between two crashing abysses, under the pylons – the big ones – and the electricity wires buzz above me like an evil spell that once signalled a fast track to the future, what do I hear?

I hear that the future has arrived. We repeatedly did not take *the other road* that was available to us, as the mother of the ecological movement, Rachel Carson, saw it in her pioneering work on how the health of the earth and the health of the human being are the same thing. I have woven my words here with words from her masterpiece *Silent Spring* (1962). Its opening chapter is called 'A Fable for Tomorrow'.

The crossroad where we found ourselves a generation ago, or two generations ago when Carson saw it all, is now behind us, like the ancient woodland. What is ahead of us? Why do I feel strangely drugged? I wake up and tear off the mask.

NOTE

1. The phrases in italics are quoted from Rachel Carson, *Silent Spring* (1962).

FUTURE NATURE

Illustration overleaf: *Wolf*

from TO THE LIGHTHOUSE

Virginia Woolf

Virginia Woolf (1882–1941) is one of the most influential and innovative modernist writers of the twentieth century. Best known for the novels *Mrs Dalloway* (1925) and *To the Lighthouse* (1927), she was also a prolific essayist, diarist, feminist and thinker. Woolf was the child of affluent upper-middle-class intellectuals: Leslie Stephen, the founder of the *Dictionary of National Biography*, and his second wife, Julia Jackson. Raised in London and educated at home (unlike her male siblings and half-siblings), she explored her father's extensive library in childhood and studied classics and history at the Ladies' Department of King's College London. She became an influential member of the Bloomsbury Group which included her husband, Leonard Woolf, John Maynard Keynes and E.M. Forster. Her essay *A Room of One's Own* (1929) explores the position of women in society and Woolf refused patriarchal awards such as the Companion of Honour (1935) and honorary degrees. In her novel *Orlando* (1928), her hero, who was born in the Renaissance and survives until the present day, wakes up one morning to find that he has changed from male to female. The character was based upon her friend Vita Sackville-West. Woolf's mother, father and brother died in a short period and Woolf, who was abused by her half-brother during childhood, suffered from poor mental health as an adult. She took her own life in 1941.

The house was left; the house was deserted. It was left like a shell on a sandhill to fill with dry salt grains now that life had left it. The long night seemed to have set in; the trifling airs, nibbling, the clammy breaths, fumbling, seemed to have triumphed. The saucepan had rusted and the mat decayed. Toads had nosed their way in. Idly, aimlessly, the swaying shawl swung to and fro. A thistle thrust itself between the tiles in the larder. The swallows nested in the drawing-room; the floor was strewn with straw; the plaster fell in shovelfuls; rafters were laid bare; rats carried off this and that to gnaw behind the wainscots. Tortoise-shell butterflies burst from the chrysalis and pattered their life out on the window-pane. Poppies sowed themselves among the dahlias; the lawn waved with long grass; giant artichokes towered among roses; a fringed carnation flowered among the cabbages; while the gentle tapping of a weed at the window had become, on winters' nights, a drumming from sturdy trees and thorned briars which made the whole room green in summer.

What power could now prevent the fertility, the insensibility of nature? Mrs McNab's dream of a lady, of a child, of a plate of milk soup? It had wavered over the walls like a spot of sunlight and vanished. She had locked the door; she had gone. It was beyond the strength of one woman, she said. They never sent. They never wrote. There were things up there rotting in the drawers—it was a shame to leave them so, she said. The place was gone to rack and ruin. Only the Lighthouse beam entered the rooms for a moment, sent its sudden stare over bed and wall in the darkness of winter, looked with equanimity at the thistle and the swallow, the rat and the straw. Nothing now withstood them; nothing said no to them. Let the wind blow; let the poppy seed itself and the carnation mate with the cabbage. Let the swallow build in the drawing-room, and the thistle thrust aside the tiles, and the butterfly sun itself on the faded chintz of the armchairs. Let the broken glass and the china lie out on the lawn and be tangled over with grass and wild berries.

For now had come that moment, that hesitation when dawn trembles and night pauses, when if a feather alight in the scale it will be weighed down. One feather, and the house, sinking, falling, would have turned and pitched downwards to the depths of darkness. In the ruined room, picnickers would have lit their kettles; lovers sought shelter there, lying on the bare boards; and the shepherd stored his dinner on the bricks, and the tramp slept with his coat round him to ward off the cold. Then the roof would have fallen; briars and hemlocks would have blotted out path, step, and window; would have grown, unequally but lustily over the mound, until some trespasser, losing his way, could have told only by a red-hot poker among the nettles, or a scrap of china in the hemlock, that here once someone had lived; there had been a house.

from A LAND

Jacquetta Hawkes

The childhood home of **Jacquetta Hawkes** (1910–96) was on the site of a Roman road and an Anglo-Saxon cemetery. The daughter of a Cambridge academic, at the age of nine she declared she wanted to be an archaeologist in a school essay. Later she enrolled at Newnham College, Cambridge, and became the first woman in the country to take a degree in archaeology and anthropology. Her first book, *The Archaeology of Jersey*, was published in 1939 and Hawkes worked as a civil servant during the Second World War. She became secretary of the UK National Committee for UNESCO until 1949. During the first UNESCO conference in Mexico City in 1947, she fell in love with the writer J. B. Priestley; they married after their earlier marriages were dissolved. Frustrated with the lack of imagination in traditional archaeological inquiry, her literary geological history *A Land* (1951) was a convention-busting bestseller. She wrote other archaeological books, collaborated with Priestley, published a volume of poetry and was involved in the founding of the Campaign for Nuclear Disarmament.

LAND AND MACHINES

Many landmarks have been recorded during the course of these memoirs, but now the Industrial Revolution appears not as a mark on a continuous road, but an abrupt turning-point. For an incalculably great length of time men had been relating themselves more and more closely and effectively to the land. For the past four or five thousand years they had laboured as farmers, clearing the forests, reclaiming waste and swamp, hedging and ditching. The struggle of two hundred generations of cultivators had its culmination in the high farming of the eighteenth and early nineteenth centuries.

Now those thousands of years of wooing fertility under the sun and rain were to be half forgotten in a third way of living which resembles the first, that of the hunters, in its predatory dependence on the natural resources of the country.

From this time the pattern of settlement was no longer to be decided by the character of the soil, the surface features of the land and the climate, but by the distribution of the deposits which time had left far below the surface. Huge numbers left farms and villages and swarmed to the places where coal and metal ores lay hidden; once there they showed an extraordinary fecundity. The population doubled and doubled again. By the middle of the nineteenth century half the people of Britain were living in towns, a situation new in the history of great nations.

Those town-dwellers, cut off from the soil and from food production, soon lost all those arts and skills which had always been the possession if not of every man, then of every small community. The sons and daughters of the first generation of town-dwellers were not taught how to use eye and hand in the traditional skills, and, a loss of absolute finality, they could not inherit all the traditional forms, the shape for an axe handle, a yoke, for a pair of tongs; the proportions of cottage doors and windows, the designs for smocking, lace-making, embroidery. Some of these forms, because they had achieved fitness for their purpose as complete as the unchanging bodies of the insects, had remained constant for centuries or millennia, others were always evolving yet maintained their continuity. Now all of them, or almost all, were to fade from the common imagination, to become extinct. I know of only one traditional form for an everyday tool which has been adapted without loss to machine production; this is the exquisitely curved and modulated handle of the woodcutter's axe.

With the extinction of ancient arts and skills there went also countless local rites, customs, legends and histories. All these, whether or not they had been adapted to the Christian myth, were survivals of a paganism that helped to unite country people with nature and their own ancestors. Stories and names for fields and lanes recalled men and women who had worked the land before them; legends still commemorated local deities who had lived, in wood, water and stone;

many customs recognized and assisted in the main crises of individual lives; rites helped to harmonize these individual rhythms with the greater rhythms of nature – they celebrated the return of the sun, the resurrection of the corn, harvest, and the return of death.

Without these immemorial ties, personal and universal, relating men to their surroundings in time and space, the isolation of human consciousness by urban life was a most violent challenge. It gave opportunity for the heightening of consciousness and the sharpening of intellect, but human weakness and material circumstances made it impossible for any but the few gifted or fortunate to respond. The urban masses, having lost all the traditions I have just named which together make up the inheritance which may be called culture, tended to become, as individuals, cultureless. The women were in better case, for all except the most down-trodden could rear children, clean, launder, sew and cook after a fashion, though all their work was dulled and robbed of distinction by the standardization and poor quality of their materials. (It is one of the more bizarre results of industrialism that the rich will now pay great sums to obtain goods that were once taken for granted by quite humble people. Such things as real honey, fresh butter and eggs, hand needlework, tiles made of real stone, reed thatch.) For the men it was far worse. Usually they could do only one thing; and that without direct relation to their own lives; when they returned from the set hours of 'work' there was nothing for hand or imagination to do. So, when at last leisure was won for them, it proved to be a barren gift.

I do not wish to suggest that there was any lessening of man's dependence on the land, of his struggle to extract a living from it; that is the stuff of existence and cannot be reduced. It is not true either that industry is lacking in its own bold regional variations; the collieries with hoists and slag heaps, the steel furnaces, the clustering chimneys of the brick kilns, the potteries, all create their own landscape. But the individual life, the individual culture, was not sensitively adjusted to locality and the nature of the relationship was profoundly changed. It ceased to be creative, a patient and increasingly skilful love-making that had persuaded the land to flourish, and became destructive, a grabbing of material for man to destroy or to refashion to his own design. The intrusion of machines between hand and material completed the estrangement.

By this new rapacious treatment of the land, man certainly made himself abundantly productive of material goods. But he cannot be sure of getting what he wants from the great cauldron of production. Meanwhile the land, *with which he must always continue to live*, shows in its ravaged face that husbandry has been succeeded by exploitation – an exploitation designed to satisfy man's vanity, his greed and possessiveness, his wish for domination.

As a starting-point for the Revolution I shall choose the time about two hundred years ago, when men began to smelt iron with coke. Earlier attempts to use coal instead of wood had failed, but now, largely through the efforts of generations of one family, the Darbys of Shropshire, the new process was mastered and the coal-and-iron age of Victorian England was already within sight. It is, of course, possible to say that the real revolution, the tipping of the balance from agriculture to manufacture, took place later than this. Equally, or indeed with more justification, it can be claimed that it began much earlier with Tudor commerce and the scientific ferment of the seventeenth century. I would agree, I would even willingly push it back to the depths of the Carboniferous forests; there is never a beginning. But I prefer to select the mating of coal and iron, for with the thought of it the weight and grime of the Black Country, the bustle and energy of material activity, at once take shape in the imagination. Besides, it was a time when the intellect, sharpened by the new scientific, analytical modes of thought, was achieving many other of the devices that made industrialism possible. In one year, 1769, Arkwright gave the water frame to the cotton industry and Watt patented the steam-engine. Within another ten years the gorge of the Severn which had been cut in the Ice Age by the overflowing waters of Lake Lapworth was spanned by the first iron bridge to be built in the world. Together these closely consecutive events well represent the new forces of the Revolution; coal and iron, mechanical power, mechanization and the corresponding development of transport.

The Industrial Revolution was certainly in part brought about by the scientific mode of thought that had grown from the Renaissance intellect. Yet it was not itself a rational episode. To me it seems an upsurge of instinctive forces comparable to the barbarian invasions, a surge that destroyed eighteenth-century civilization much as the Anglo-Saxons destroyed that of Roman Britain. No one planned it, no one foresaw more than a tittle of the consequences, very few people said that they wanted it, but once begun the impetus was irresistible; more and more individual lives became helplessly involved, drawn into the vortex. It went forward as irresistibly as the evolution of the dinosaurs and in it was included the roaring of *Tyrannosaurus*. It seems indeed that *Tyrannosaurus* and Apollo of the Intellect worked together for the Revolution and no combination could be more powerful or more dangerous.

It lent to its instruments an astonishing strength. It enabled this chip of the earth's surface, the small fund of human mind, will and energy that it supported, momentarily to dominate the whole surface of the planet and in so doing, like a gigantic, slow explosion, to disperse fragments of itself all over that surface. It seems possible that had there not been this association of coal and iron, growing population and intellectual ferment within the bounds of a temperate island, the industrialization that in two centuries has totally changed human life might never have assumed its present forms.

They were there, and the new way of life developed with a speed that is almost unbelievable when it is compared with any other experience of human history. In South Wales, South Yorkshire and Tyneside, all those regions where past events had left iron and coal in close proximity, there sprang up foundries whose crimson glare by night repeats something of the volcanic furies of other ages. With them there grew to colossal stature the manufacture of metal goods, a manufacture centred on Birmingham in a region that had remained longer than almost any other under the peaceful covering of the forests. On the moist western side of the Pennines the cotton industry, the first to be wholly dependent on material produced outside the island, grew up in obscene relationship with the trade in African slaves. The little mills once turned by the Pennine streams, family cottage manufacture, were soon abandoned for the factories of Manchester and the neighbouring towns that were growing round it. Away on the east of the central mountains, the ancient conservatism of the wool trade long resisted the new methods; in time, however, first spinning and then weaving left the rural valleys and moved to towns like Bradford, where the foamy white wool is combed and spun in mills of blackened rock, and to Leeds and Huddersfield, where it is woven on looms whose descent from those of the Bronze Age it is hard to credit. The salt that the evaporation of the Triassic lakes and lagoons had left under the Cheshire plain became the source of a chemical industry, a thing new even among so much innovation. One other industry there was which I will mention because it shows how, exceptionally, a few individuals may impose themselves on the land, creating something from their own wills that is not dictated by circumstances. There was no material reason beyond a supply of coal for his furnaces why Josiah Wedgwood and his family should have built up the pottery business in Staffordshire. Much of his material was dug in Cornwall (where the glistening white heaps of kaolin look so alien, so improbable among the soft, warmly coloured granite moorlands), and his kilns were inconveniently far from the coast for the carriage of both the raw clay and the finished china. However, Wedgwood lived there and started his work there and so the existence of the Five Towns was determined. The craft that even in Britain had a history of four and a half millennia now went into mass production largely through the inspiration of one man. It was appropriate that for a time his name was identified with that of the clay he manipulated – that 'common Wedgwood' should become the accepted term for the people's crockery. Because of their history, the Potteries have remained more patriarchal in organization, more personal in feeling than other industries, just as from its nature the work itself remains exceptionally individual and unmechanized. I will not leave the Potteries without commenting on the extraordinary forethought that nature seems to me to have shown in the formation of kaolin; nearly two hundred million years after its deposition, it has proved that this substance can be used for making china, for fulling cloth, for keeping the shine from women's faces, for paper-making and as a cure for diarrhoea.

Transport was of course one of the keys of industrialism. Upon it depended a state of affairs in which men no longer made things for local use and in which a locality no longer provided the food for its people. By the eighteenth century Britain was more closely unified by roads than it had been since Roman times and soon this was reinforced by the canals, a quiet, deliberate form of carriage that came to have its own nomadic population. Then down the ringing grooves of change came the railway engine begotten by Watt and Stephenson on the iron-and-coal age. Gangs of navvies were moved about the country embanking, cutting, tunnelling, bridge-building; thousands of tons of metal were laid across our meadows, along our valleys, round our coasts. The incidental result of this activity in stimulating consciousness in its search for its origins has already been demonstrated in the life of William Smith, the Father of Stratigraphy.

The shift in population was the fourth and infinitely the greatest that had taken place since Mesolithic times. The north of England and southern Wales, formerly rather thinly settled, soon had the bulk of a sharply rising population. As mills, factories, foundries and kilns multiplied, the little streets of the workers' houses spread their lines over hills that belonged to wild birds and mountain sheep, and up valleys where there was nothing busier than a rushing beck. Without intention or understanding the greater part of the people of Britain found themselves living in towns, uprooted, and in a strange, unstable environment. The growths of brick and stone, later of concrete, whose ragged outer edges were always creeping further might coalesce one with another in urban areas so large that it was difficult for the inhabitants to set foot on grass or naked earth. The results were grim, but sometimes and particularly in the Pennine towns they had their own grandeur. Where houses and factories are still built from the local rocks and where straight streets climb uncompromisingly up hillsides, their roofs stepping up and up against the sky, they have a geometric beauty that is harsh but true, while the texture of smoke-blackened lime- or sandstone can be curiously soft and rich, like the wings of some of our sombre night-flying moths. Nor do such cities ever quite lose the modelling of their natural foundations. On my first visit to the industrial north I rode on the top of a tram all the way from Leeds to Batley and all the way I rode through urban streets. In the last daylight it seemed a melancholy and formless jumble of brick and stone, but as darkness closed and a few smoky stars soothed and extended my thoughts, the lamps going up in innumerable little houses restored the contours of hill and dale in shimmering lines of light.

At least much of this nineteenth-century building showed the force, the ruthless purpose of its age. The railways, too, served to concentrate it and to keep it truly urban. Far more pitiful are the housing estates, the ribbon development and all the flimsy scattered new building that our own century has added as a result of the internal combustion engine. The railways took far too many people to certain places, the motor-car takes rather too many people everywhere. The dormitory housing estates on the outskirts of cities are a limbo created by the combination of meanness with theoretical good intentions. The little gardens that man's incurable love of earth has obliged the council or the speculative builder to provide, soon make a ragged wilderness of broken fences and sheds. The streets wander aimlessly about, representing either simple chaos or the whimsy notions of a planning officer. Nothing has grown; nothing is inevitable. All over England the houses are the same; for they are built of materials that are not local but cheap. A house at Bradford, a house at Dagenham, will show the same silly stucco, the same paltry composition roof. Since 1945 there has been an improvement, and the sight of these better houses, flats, schools, is the most hopeful thing to be seen in Britain, more convincing than ten million optimistic words. It is the only thing that suggests that new roots are going down and new sources of vitality being found.

Perhaps what is worst in the effects of motor transport and of the partial shift of the balance of population back to the south and the southern Midlands, has been the wreckage left in its wake. When the uplands so thickly peopled in prehistoric times were deserted, the scars that human activity had left upon them were so slight, so readily healed, that soon they melted back into the scene and enriched it. The gentle knolls of chieftains' graves adorn the horizon, fortress walls become grass banks for lovers' meetings. But once men had taken to using chemical change on an immense scale to convert the natural substances of the land for their own purposes, this natural healing could hardly again take place. Iron and concrete are not readily softened. A robin may nest in a rusty kettle but that is about the largest scale on which adaptation is possible. The present derelict parts of industrial Britain assume a degraded ugliness never before known. Who can ever express the desolation of these forlorn scenes? The grey slag heap, the acres of land littered with rusted fragments of machinery, splintered glass, tin cans, sagging festoons of barbed wire; vile buildings, more vile in ruin; grimy stretches of cement floors, shapeless heaps of broken concrete. The air about them still so foul that nothing more than a few nettles and tattered thistles will grow there; not even rosebay and ragwort can hide them with a brief midsummer promise. This is the worst that has happened to the land.

One curious result of the Industrial Revolution can claim a special place in this chronicle of the relationship between men and their land. For the medieval peasant eight weeks in the year were holy days, days when a service in the parish church was followed by freedom for rest and celebration. Each chosen black- and red-letter day, each Church festival, was a part of the wheel of the year and served for rites so much more ancient than Christianity as to be almost as old as the consciousness of man. No countryman could have celebrated them away from his own cottage, fields and animals, his neighbours and his church, for they were important threads in the fabric of life where all these things were woven together in a single design.

Now the sharp division of work from play and the natural from the supernatural has turned holy days into holidays, and the compelling restlessness and ugliness of towns has made holidays an occasion for escape from home. So there is this new form of mass migration – no longer to pursue game animals or pasture domestic ones, no longer for fishing or fowling or the visiting of shrines. Instead a flight from a man-made world too hard, dirty and hideous to allow its inhabitants to rest, to lie down on the ground or to dance upon it, to turn back to their surroundings for refreshment. Three hundred years ago how impossible it would have seemed that England should be cumbered with towns built as an escape from towns, that half its south and east coasts should be encrusted with red bricks, walled behind concrete, the sea itself grasped after with iron piers. If the migrations have largely defeated their purpose by spreading more hardness and a new ugliness, at least the resorts are clean, and human beings can find just room enough to stretch their bodies on the sand.

Elsewhere in the country, as has already appeared, crowds make for wide views, for wild country, for unusually dynamic manifestations of nature or ancient manifestation of man, feeding themselves while they may on something which they most urgently need, some nourishment quite lacking in urban existence.

Where did all the men and women come from to fill the towns of the Revolution? What was the cause of the endless fecundity that lent it impetus? I read that it was due to improvements in medicine, to a drop in the death rate. I cannot believe it. Instead I believe that just as the audience in a theatre can become a single being responding as one consciousness to the emotions of the play, so a whole people can be caught up and respond to some drama of which it is aware in its own life. However, it happened, this prostitution of the Great Goddess to the industry that was her bane, wombs conceived, death fought a losing battle and the towns, the factories and the mines were filled, the railways and the ships were manned.

At first the cultivation of the soil almost kept pace with this multiplication of mouths. The enclosure of the old open fields so long delayed in all the Midland shires was rushed ahead; the hedges imposed their rectangles on strip fields that had been cultivated for a thousand years, and the last of the peasants, with their poor husbandry and tenacious love of the soil, were dissolved, scattering readily among the big farms and estates and into the towns. As Arthur Young saw before the end of the eighteenth century: 'A country fellow, one hundred miles from London, jumps on a coach box in the morning, and for eight or ten shillings gets to town by night… and of course ten times the boasts are sounded in the ears of country fools to induce them to quit their healthy clean fields for a region of dirt, stink and noise.' Soon a country fellow could jump onto a railway train even more cheaply and then all was decided.

Under the big landlords and tenant farmers the land was splendidly cultivated. Country mansions, dignified farms went up, modest farmsteads were enlarged; wealth coming from industry flowed into the land. A few great improvers like Thomas Coke of Holkham transformed English agriculture. Through their enterprise simple equipment that had been good enough since the Iron Age was thrown aside; the weight of sheep was doubled; men had never dreamt that cows could yield so much milk. Above all the more skilful handling of grass and the cultivation of roots ended the great autumn slaughter of livestock that had been a necessity since the Stone Age. So great was the increase in cultivation that the conscious lovers of a more natural countryside could even lament it. Matthew Arnold wrote of the change in the Oxford countryside that had taken place since his youth:

> I know these slopes; who knows them if not I?—
> But many a dingle on the loved hillside,
> With thorns once studded, old, white-blossomed trees,
> Where thick the cowslips grew, and, far descried,
> High tower'd the spikes of purple orchises,
> Hath since our day put by
> The coronals of that forgotten time.
> Down each green bank hath gone the ploughboy's team,
> And only in the hidden brookside gleam
> Primroses, orphans of the flowery prime.

What would this high soul have said could he have seen Lord Nuffield following in the ploughboy's furrow?

Coke's column at Holkham stands as a monument to these days of high farming. Surrounded by a park that is still a proof of the creative force possible in a single man, and with a village that keeps a few lingering memories of feudalism, this monument looks from far off like a military trophy. But a closer view shows that on the corners where one expects cannon, there are sheep, cattle, a plough and a seeding machine; the low reliefs on the walls show not battle but agricultural scenes, while on the top of the column the object that might have been a hero in uniform proves to be an imposing sheaf of corn.

But even the new fecundity of the land could not hope to keep pace with that of the new labouring classes. If I have arbitrarily chosen the smelting of iron with coke as marking the beginning of the Industrial Revolution, I will for the purpose of these memoirs choose the time when the country ceased to produce enough food nearly to feed its people as representing its crisis. From that time Britain forfeited the reality of its life as an island, the meaning of the outline that its coasts drew upon the sea. From that time it must always sell overseas not only to be prosperous but to live; it could never retreat into itself to recuperate its powers. The little trade in the things of luxury and privilege that had begun in the Bronze Age had grown to this circulation of the life blood through a score of huge ports.

Yet for the first half of the reign of Victoria, the bringing in of foreign grain did not damage native cultivation. The two Britains flourished side by side, the swarming cities with their new relationships between rich and poor, and a sparsely populated but well-farmed countryside with its great houses, its country towns and its whole aristocratic structure little changed since the eighteenth century. This countryside, too, could still inspire and maintain its painters – Cornelius Varley, Cox, de Wint, men of the second rank, but all still turning out charming water colours of rural England and Wales round the middle of the century.

In reality dangers were already massing against this prosperous world. There were, of course, the material forces; the American pioneers ready to tear the heart out of the prairies for quick gold, and with railways and transatlantic steamships at their command. But even more dangerous, perhaps, was the weakening of resistance from within. The centre of gravity of English life had shifted very far towards the cities; the land was defended by no deeply rooted peasantry and its cultivation had become a way of making money rather than of living. This in turn was no more than one aspect of a pervading materialism – let me represent it by saying that for men their ancient symbol of gold no longer had any hint of the sun or of harvest about it, but only of material wealth. Moreover, there reigned in many places a faith in the new deity of Progress that helped to make men blind to all that was evil, or dangerous, in change.

In the end it took no more than a few bad harvests in the seventies to open the gates. American grain poured in, the future dust bowls were prepared and all the centuries of the loving husbandry of the land of Britain betrayed. The Great Goddess was seen in her aspect of Cinderella, with soot in her hair and dust on her skirt; those who understood her, however, did not doubt that she would wait for retribution.

It is no part of the intention of this book to pass judgements. I applauded the appearance of the trilobites; I did not deplore the fall of the dinosaurs; I freely accepted the progressive virtues of the placenta and even beyond that mammalian *tour de force* have been almost equally acquiescent. This has been due not to a Victorian confidence in progress, but to the fact that my intention was no more than to celebrate the creation of Britain and in so doing tacitly to express a love for the result. If, then, words of judgement begin to appear in this chapter, it is only because my narrative has now reached a point beyond that of the recollections of a general consciousness to one where my own moment of consciousness is touched upon. The following words, in short, must be read not as an expression of the purpose of the book, but simply as murmurings representative of a consciousness subjected to the conditions of the year A.D. 1949.

Seeing the Industrial Revolution as something comparable to a barbarian invasion, I assume that, as after other incursions of violent intuitive forces, it must be followed by a civilizing period – that energy must now be subject to control. I assume, too, that State Socialism has come in response to this need, to impose form and order on the waning exuberance of revolution. But whereas, for example, after the Anglo-Saxon invasions the Christian Church succeeded in slowly civilizing each individual and small community from within so that all became part of a vigorous, organic, but unselfconscious nation, the present State seems in many ways to come closer to the Roman pattern. Although the controlling intellects are not those of foreigners, and Britain is not a remote province of a great empire but very much a nation, yet there is the similarity of deliberate intellectual control from a distant centre, the imposition of plans alien to the local community. The reasons for such control are totally different. Industrialization had so crushed the culture of the individuals composing urban masses that the necessary form and order could only be imposed. Yet as a result we have an urban culture which is in a sense highly complex, yet is not creatively embodied in the people themselves. Everything is supplied for them from outside, whether by the State, the merchant or the purveyor of entertainment. The individual, especially the man, does not possess culture, cannot express it, but merely receives a doubtful mixture in a spoon, paid for from his purse. The greater the improvement in material conditions the more complete this passivity becomes.

It may be that the centralized State represents the logical perfection of the growing selfconsciousness of the land which I have followed by such steps as Domesday Book and Saxton's maps and the unification of the English language. Today the State has catalogued every man, woman and child within our coasts, has mapped every foot of the ground. Not only is there a unified language, but one voice can unite the consciousness of listeners from end to end and side to side of the island; one film can be seen in a hundred towns at once; identical tins are opened in every county of Britain.

When, underneath all this, culture is no longer sufficiently embodied in each individual, the contrasting delights of locality, the poetry of a people delicately adjusted to varied surroundings, finding their new but always fitting responses, must blur into a grey uniformity. Men, and to a lesser extent women, are living in the topmost attics of the mind receiving instruction and information. They are cut off from the nourishment of the past both physically and in the depths of their own minds where the images of experience have formed in darkness since the first stir of life in pre-Cambrian seas. So, too, they are cut off from these deep sources of creative force, and ugliness pours from them, flooding the lowlands, seeping more slowly among the moors and mountains.

It may be the logical development, but like many other evolutionary trends already chronicled, this one has gone too far.

If in some ways the State has far exceeded what is desirable in the imposition of conscious order on the chaos of the Revolution, in others it has failed utterly in the necessary task of civilization. No intellect in command of power has stood back far enough to judge the upshot of this blind surge of energy, selecting what is hopeful for slow development, condemning what is abominable for gradual elimination. Too many of the conditions of life which it imposed without their being anyone's intention or wish, have been accepted as inevitable. This is because its basic value has been accepted, a materialism which has been exposed in all nakedness now that the energy and pioneering enthusiasms which inspired it have died away. Once men were concerned with the quality of life as a whole and with their relation to the universe; they could assume, for example, that the ritual and revelry of the Twelve Days of Christmas were of infinitely greater value than the small material gain to be won by working for those twelve days. Now a man who makes a comparable choice must be called an absentee and seen as a traitor. Production and more production of goods has become an end for which the land may be turned to a wilderness, while individual lives are sacrificed as readily as the victims of the Aztec gods.

There is a new fetish, the Standard of Living, a material measure hardly related to the enjoyment of life. Its worshippers believe that the 'dirt, stink and noise' so long ago recognized by Young, with the additional massive ugliness of the nineteenth century and the shoddiness of the twentieth, are of no importance when set beside this artificial measure. So far have we in Britain been enslaved to this fetish that when we go to another country and see people with light in their faces and beauty all round them we dare not think them fortunate if at the same time we see they have not very much money. Yet here in this once most lovely island people will spend all that they have been able to save and their few most precious days of holiday in flying from the dirt, stink, noise and ugliness in which they must spend the other fifty weeks of the year. Surely it is time to recognize not a standard of living but a standard of values, in which beauty, comeliness and the possibility of solitude have a high place among human needs? It must be established that it is not sentimental to value a fine stretch of farming land more highly than the five thousand tons of iron ore which can be snatched from it, or to believe that life and amenity should not be sacrificed to production, to the rapacity of the machine. In America vast stretches of countryside have the lack of form and sanctity which shows it only to have been tilled since the age of exploitation; the American people, the most successful materialists in the history of the world, are now often to be found speaking with loathing of their own life and with nostalgic envy of the happiness of primitive peoples.

If the memories brought together in this book have any meaning, men must still need to live in some direct and creative relationship with the land from which they have come. They cannot fail to be the poorer for its impoverishment, to be scarred by its mutilation. The people of this island should put their hearts, their hands, and all the spare energy which science has given them into the restoration of their country. At the beginning of the Industrial Revolution gangs of navvies moved about like shock troops embanking, tunnelling, bridge-building. Now such forces could be mustered to clear the filthy litter which the Revolution has left in its wake. Instead, wealth is spent on patching minds and bodies damaged by 'dirt, stink and noise', and in attempting to educate children who are condemned to live in surroundings which would make the educated profoundly unhappy. No matter if such an achievement would take a few points off the standard of living or an acre or so from the desert of industrial leisure. They would not be grudged.

Once materialism had been so far denied, it should be possible to go further. What men produced from the stuff of their land could slowly be brought into the service of good living; satisfaction in the work itself would be recognized as a positive aim. Ruskin may be repudiated for vain fishing in the waters of the past, but he was sane among madmen in insisting on the importance of the nature of work, of giving an opportunity to individual creativeness. Only by accepting this value and by striving to achieve it wherever it is suitable can the growth of standardization be checked, the possibility for the revival of local culture be established.

Such values are too expensive. This country cannot afford to give its wealth to enrich the quality of human life. Britain must export or die! Is it not far more likely that Britain will export and die?

At present with the excess of human beings created by the Revolution and a land, in spite of all contrary pretence, still only partially cultivated, perhaps we cannot afford to seek these values. But is there any coherent plan to bring them within future reach? Controlling intellects could justify their power by using all social and scientific means to increase the amount of food raised from the land, while at the same time encouraging a deliberate reduction of population. The reality of this island s outline, lost only a century ago, would be restored when its people could feed themselves if need arose. Yet there is no sign that the consciousness armed with power which is the State is starting on this path to salvation. When conflict arises agriculture (as well as beauty and amenity) is still sacrificed to industry; the State supports measures to increase the population.

A man can enjoy good relations with other men only if he is a whole being, reasonably secure within the boundaries of his personality; so, too, a land is only ready to join a community of lands if it has this fundamental self-sufficiency and confidence. It is easy for the intellect to conceive higher forms of organization for mankind, but the intellect, that most distinguished creation of life, is always far removed from the forces which move life itself. I know at least that my own love for Britain, for the land and people contained within these coasts, is only heightened by my delight in other lands, each with its own distinctive creation and being, each shaped by its outline of coasts, mountains and rivers.

I have allowed my inheritance of consciousness to argue and posture. It is – it must be, for here it is – the simple reaction of a consciousness exposed at a particular point in time and space. I display its arguments, its posturings, as imprints of a moment of being as specific and as limited as the imprint of its body left by a herring in Cretaceous slime.

from OUR PLACE

Mark Cocker

Mark Cocker (b. 1959) is an award-winning nature writer, naturalist, tutor and environmental activist. He has been a regular country diarist for the *Guardian* for more than thirty years, writing dispatches from the countryside of Norfolk and Derbyshire. His twelve books include biography, history, travel writing, literary criticism and memoir. *Crow Country* (2009) won the New Angle Prize in 2009 and *A Claxton Diary* (2019) won the East Anglia Book Award in 2019. His epic *Birds and People* (2013) is a global cultural history of birds and a collaboration with the photographer David Tipling. *Our Place* (2018) has proven an influential history of the environmental movement in Britain. Cocker grew up in Derbyshire, studied English at the University of East Anglia and has worked as a creative writing tutor. His environmental work includes co-authoring a wildlife policy document for the Green Party. He writes and reviews regularly for the *New Statesman*, *Spectator* and *Guardian*.

Hope is written into all our connections with the rest of nature, and it is a two-way process. The other parts of life are our deepest sources of hope; and hope is part of the very fabric of our encounters. It begins the moment you open the door to go outside. You have only to have the sun on your back, the wind in your face and birdsong in your heart to know their rivet-bursting powers of liberation. It is perhaps partly what Henry Thoreau was tilting at when he wrote the words for which he is most famous and which are among his most ambiguous: 'In Wildness is the preservation of the world.'

It explains why we cling so tenaciously to the myth that this country continues inviolate. We don't want to hear that our final redoubt, the place where we go when our human condition is overwhelming, is itself in need. Alas, it is. In the twentieth century, the British drained their landscape of wildlife, otherness, meaning, cultural riches and hope. Yet because it is central to our purposes and to our relationships with each other, we continue in denial. And what we have done to our country becomes the truth that dare not speak its name. However, hope lies, surely, not in perpetuating any myth, not in doctoring the facts, but in owning them squarely and with the whole of ourselves.

I list here ten interlocking Truths that are fundamental to the story of British nature in the twentieth century. They help to explain what happened, why it happened and, as far as possible, what needs to be done. They bear equally on the agents of destruction and those who oppose it. They are arranged, with a single exception, in a kind of chromatic scale from dark to light. They are, in my opinion, the antithesis of all the platitudes about a green and pleasant land.

1. In the twentieth century the British people devastated large areas of their environment, largely through the instrument of farming and forestry policies. Not only have the citizens of this country had to witness the processes, they also paid for them through subsidies. The losses took place largely over two generations, from 1940 to 1985, though their full effects span a century from 1920 to 2018. In that time 99 per cent of 4 million acres of flower-rich meadow were destroyed and 44 million breeding birds vanished from the countryside.

The loss is not evenly distributed. Our coastlines are still relatively intact, partly because of the National Trust's extraordinary Operation Neptune. Also parts of what Oliver Rackham called the 'Ancient Countryside', which includes a swathe from south Norfolk to Kent and westwards through Sussex and Hampshire, and then due north from Dorset to south Lancashire, have escaped some of the worst effects. Surrey and Kent, despite the large human population of the south-east, retain some of the highest levels of woodland, and Kent has more ancient woodland than any other county.[1]

Density of occupation is a significant factor, and since England holds all but 11 million of Britain's population, it has borne the brunt. Loss of landscape, however, is not necessarily always about human numbers. One need only drive through the sparsely occupied Borders areas from Alnwick in Northumberland to Lockerbie in Dumfriesshire to see a hill country burnt out and minimised to a continuous, sheep-grazed grass monoculture punctuated with conifer plantations. Yet to see in full the twenty-eighth most denatured landscape on Earth one should take the M6 or the A1 south of Cumbria and Northumberland. Then you can really bear witness to the hollow heart of this country, pretty much all the way south to Bristol or London. The arable areas are stripped bare of wildlife. In fact, it is now commonplace for bumblebee numbers and species diversity to be much greater in suburban and urban areas than in the countryside. So much so that it is almost meaningless to talk of it as *countryside*, and one recalls Tony Hare's prophetic words: 'Whenever people talk to me about the British countryside, I ask, "What countryside?"'

Finally, we must acknowledge that some of our agriculture land-scapes – south Lincolnshire and south-west Essex spring instantly to mind – offer a vision of what the entire country will look like if the processes of intensification continue undiminished. It brings me to the next Truth.

2. Things are bad, but there is very little in present public life to suggest that they will not get worse. As a society, so far, we have done too little to turn the environmental ship around. The fundamental drivers of further loss are all intact. The fragmentation will continue: the implications of island biogeography are still in train. No single generation since the First World War has bequeathed a healthier British countryside than the one they inherited. What special efforts have we made in recent years for us to assume that things are different today? They are not. The *State of Nature* report indicates a direction of travel, not a final location.

It is not just that the same forces are in play and bearing down on what remains of our wildlife. It is that we are facing new pressures, not least the need to build a million new houses to accommodate the large population increases mainly since the beginning of the millennium. The scale of demand has led to a loosening of planning regulations, so that new developments contest with the old environmental protections.

One of the most telling is a plan of Medway Council and Britain's biggest property developer, Land Securities, to erect 5,000 homes on the outskirts of Rochester, Kent, in an area called Lodge Hill. The site is Ministry of Defence land, long neglected and in transition from scrub to full-canopied woodland and perfect, it would appear, for nightingales. Today it holds 84 singing males and Britain's largest single population of the species, which since 1970 has declined by 90 per cent.

Each side is claiming that their need for the place is of overriding significance: 5,000 homes as opposed to one per cent of the British nightingale population. It is in many ways a rerun of the Cow Green reservoir debate about industrial water versus wild flowers. One precise difference, however, is the intervening precedent that involves a half-century of destruction that has brought the nightingale to its present plight.

Each side has supplementary arguments. The developers, who have cross-party support in the local council, point out that there are 20,000 local people on the housing waiting list in the Medway area. Lodge Hill is, according to them, the only large site where infrastructure can also be created, including three primary schools, a nursing home and a hotel, creating 5,000 jobs.[2]

The RSPB staff who are leading the challenge point out, meanwhile, that it is not just about nightingales. The place has 19 bat roosts as well as significant scarce reptile and plant communities and rare breeding butterflies, all of which are strong indicators of its wider importance for biodiversity (this MOD location is so little known because access has been highly restricted for a century). Most significant is that it is already an SSSI and thus, theoretically, protected by legislation. The developers, however, are claiming that they must build there and nowhere else and its legal status should be overridden in the national interest. For those championing wildlife in this dispute, Lodge Hill is an acid test of the very framework on which conservation has been based since the Second World War.

Regardless of the eventual outcome at Lodge Hill, which is only a trifling part of the full national impact, when all these fresh inroads into surviving biodiversity are audited in a generation's time they will reveal nature's inexorable decline.*

3. The third Truth is about understanding nature. Ecology as a formal scientific discipline has only been in existence for about 150 years. That is a short time for it to have influenced the ways in which we think and function. What ecology tries to bring into focus is the dynamic structures of natural systems – habitats, biomes etc. – which are infinitely complex. Essentially, ecology exposes how everything in an ecosystem impacts upon everything else. The usual form invoked to illustrate this level of interconnectedness is a sphere, rendered at its most simple in the circle of life in *The Lion King*, which, for all its Disneyfied triviality, is still an ecological parable.

A circle may be an inadequate representation of ecological complexities, but the real issue for the British environment is that the dominant pattern in our thought processes is not a circle, but a straight line. Look at the page you are reading to appreciate the fundamental line-mindedness of our species. Recall the plough lines running through the Flow Country that Magnus Magnusson likened to claw

---

* To give a small sample sense of developments that typify the ongoing erosion of remaining wildlife areas, there are proposed motorway developments in the Gwent Levels, where a road would cut through five protected areas and across Lough Beg in Northern Ireland, one of the regions most important wetlands. Phase one of the HS2 rail link between Birmingham and London will pass through fifty ancient woodlands, four Wildlife Trust reserves and ten SSSIs, as well as numerous local wildlife sites. Since this chapter was written, one positive development has been the withdrawal of the planning application at Lodge Hill in Kent. Environmentalists now hope that the original scheme to build 5,000 new homes will be permanently dropped. However, they expect at the least that smaller applications will be submitted in the future that will affect parts of the site.

marks made by an angry god. Recall Vermuyden's dead-straight ditch from Earith to Salter's Lode right through the middle of the Fen. Recall those machine-drilled GPS-spaced regiments of daffodils at Gedney. Among our various capacities to express ourselves, only music, and possibly painting and poetry, come close to the complex interconnectedness of an ecosystem. *The Lark Ascending* or the song of a blackbird say more about the British landscape than any words ever written. Yet what we need to acquire is something that might be called ecological thinking: an ability to approximate, through our imaginations, to the processes of a real ecosystem. We need a way of thinking that apprehends the rhizome-like multiplicity of impacts that work through and upon land and nature. Farmers used to practise it because they managed a complex ecosystem – a blend of multiple, fluctuating, simultaneous harvests including hens, cattle, sheep, root crops, vegetables, fruit, pasture, hay and cereals – in one land unit. For four generations they have been urged to abandon complexity and ecological thinking in favour of the 'logical' straight line.

Straight-line thinking connects too few truths to be of value in appreciating ecological processes. The spraying of pesticides and the use of nitrate fertilisers are linear approaches to ecological issues. The assumption is that once the chemicals have fulfilled the single intention of a user – once they have gone away – they will cease to operate within the ecosystem to which they were introduced. As Clark Gregory argues in William Bryant Logan's masterful book *Dirt*, 'There's no such place as "*away*" [my italics].'[3] We, the chemicals, the land, are part of a single system. The fertilisers continue journeying through the physical environment interacting in complex ways, fulfilling their unleashed ecological destinies.

While they boost crop production they also accumulate in the aquifers and must be stripped at high cost from our drinking water. They convert to nitrous oxide, a greenhouse gas 200 times more potent than carbon dioxide. Ecological thinking tells us that the true costs of that 'logical' and linear application of nitrogen is a downstream bill of between €70 and €320 billion per annum, double the value of the original boost to crops. The damage that we have inflicted on the land of this country in the name of logic requires that all of us acquire a capacity for ecological thinking.

Ecological thinking entails that we see ourselves *within* nature, and that we understand how everything we do has ecological consequences. We can, in truth, *never* escape nature. A convicted murderer, held in a concrete-and-steel cell in solitary confinement in the bowels of the most secure prison, encircled by nothing but razor-wire and linear arrangements of man-made material, who barely has the opportunity over several decades to see a square of natural daylight, let alone walk upon the soil and enjoy all its manifold bounties, still lives within nature. Everything that he eats and breathes, all that he evacuates, everything about him, is part of an ecosystem. Ecology requires that all of us understand the privileges and blessings of those unending connections and the remorseless, possibly terrifying, scale of our responsibilities.

As our material and interior lives become supercharged with new sources of stimulation we have compensated by succumbing to another linear simplification. Our entire value system, the ways in which we think and talk about life, society, morality, etc., in any public and most especially in any political forum, have been rendered subservient to a single dominant scale as the capitalist model intensifies its hold on all parts of ourselves. It is as if the only qualitative measure of human happiness and experience is money. The entire national political conversation has been canalised into one debate. Yet the economy of a country is nothing but a way of disguising or, rather, one should say, a way of talking about, ecology – since all money comes *only* from nature. It is just ecology entirely devoid of responsibility for the rest of the living system.

We need somehow to recover a sense of responsibility for the nonlinear structures of real life. We live on a planet where life is only to be found in about a fifteen-mile-deep veneer that is wrapped around the surface of the Earth. As far as we have been able to establish in the last 4,000 years, this is the only planet that bears life. We spend our days among the greatest event in all the galaxies; but many people would seem to prefer to play with their iPhones. Isn't it time that we built an appreciation of life into the very foundations of who we are?

—ᴍ—

4. The fourth horseman of the environmental apocalypse in our island is something identified in Oliver Rackham's *The History of the British Countryside*, where he wrote of 'all the little, often unconscious vandalisms that hate what is tangled and unpredictable but create nothing.' Among the list of hateful measures, he included the destruction of ivy-tods or 'misshapen trees', the annual cutting of hedges down to the ground, the levelling of churchyards – and here I cannot help but recall the regime at St Mary Magdalene's in Gedney – and what he described as pottering with paraquat.[4] The real problem is that an ever-expanding arsenal of chemicals and equipment allows us all – not just farmers – to intervene almost to the point of nature's annihilation. In short, we are, as an entire people, guilty of excessive tidiness.

It is this that drives much of the sterilisation of Britain's public space, because what it aspires to is uniformity and, invariably, uniform lifelessness. The classic location is not farmland, but our gardens. The signature sound is the seemingly innocuous drone of the Sunday-morning mower, whose use is ritualised almost to the point of piety. Recall the sit-on mower near Gedney reducing ten acres to a short-back-and-sides of rye-grass monoculture. Ten acres could, correctly managed, support thousands of species of organism, in an explosive mix of colour and texture, across the full spectrum of life.

However, it must be added that lawnmowers are now possibly at risk, because the latest must-have of the tidy-minded is plastic grass, which is spreading with viral intensity. In London, where 3.6 million domestic gardens occupy about a quarter of the entire city area, an estimated third are already obliterated under concrete or other synthetic surfaces. And what happens in the capital happens everywhere. I have relatives who have just laid plastic grass.

If plastic grass is not ubiquitous already, then it soon will be, judging from the state of so many of our civic and public spaces – road verges, roundabouts, the curtilage to municipal institutions such as schools, offices, hospitals, churches and sometimes even our recreational parks, which all obey the same deep concern for rectilinear design and abiotic uniformity.* It is not uncommon to see, in such places, maintenance staff in white space suits, chemical drums upon their backs, spraying herbicides on the minute creases of green life that dare extrude from the cracks between concrete slabs. The closest thing that these outdoor spaces resemble is not anything in nature, but the interiors of buildings, which is presumably the largely unconscious intention.

As a result of the broad interpretations placed upon the word environment, which is taken to mean anything and everything connected to our surroundings, it is often assumed that tidiness is an important *environmental* goal in its own right. It finds expression in the mania for litter-picking and keeping Britain tidy, etc. Not that anyone should condone thoughtless litter; it is not just illegal, it is morally disgraceful, especially fly-tipping. Yet in a list of ten important environmental issues, litter would be tenth and in a list of twenty it would be twentieth. The perfect cure for this 'environmental' concern would be a visit to West Thurrock Lagoons and Canvey Wick nature reserves in Essex. They are two of Britain's most famous biodiverse brownfield sites, which are smothered in flowers and packed with rare bumblebees and beetles, but which are also described in Dave Goulson's recent book as a paradise of 'dog faeces, graffiti, discarded beer cans and broken bottles'.[5]

Litter may be a social problem, but it is seldom a real enemy of biodiversity. Excessive tidiness, however, entails a massive loss of potential wildlife. If we could free ourselves as a society from this neurosis then it offers an extraordinary and, as yet, barely tapped dividend for nature. We may have destroyed 4 million acres of flower-rich meadow. We could recover at least half that figure if only our gardens, both civic and private, were freed from chemical interventions and turned back primarily to native flowers and shrubs. Instead of the work-intensive grass monoculture, we could have virtually labour-free pocket-sized

---

* But not, it must be added, the sides of many modern roads and motorways, which have been planted with rich varieties of perennials and now represent some of our most visible and even most beautiful flower-rich environments. There are glorious examples around Norwich and on the A11 through south Norfolk, which point to a brighter, more colourful, more nature-tolerant future. Such measures should be fast-tracked in all civic spaces.

meadows that require only a single cut in late summer. Instead of fitted grass carpets we could have zones of colour and diversity, rich in pollinating insects such as bumblebees, butterflies and hoverflies.

One final observation is that our reluctance to live with nature's creative disorder is an attempt not just to subordinate the life around us, but also to control something within ourselves. This moral imperative is present on the first page of the Old Testament:

> And God said, Let us make man in our image, after our likeness: and let them have dominion over the fish of the sea, and over the fowl of the air, and over the cattle, and over every creeping thing that creepeth upon the earth.

As troubling in its way, for me, is that these issues play out even in the branding of the RSPB, which illuminates how human dominion over nature is, in the words of John Livingston, concreted into 'the very foundations of western thought'.[6] The organisation's present strapline is 'Giving Nature a Home'. One can understand the very positive intent. Permitting presence may be the absolute inverse of enforcing absence, but both rely on the same basic solipsism that we are the agents and nature is the passive external recipient of our agency. We cannot *give* nature a home: nature is a home – *ours*. We live within it. As long as we see ourselves as outside it, then in those powerful words of John Fowles, 'it is lost both to us and in us'.

5. Environmentalism is part of what you might call soft politics in Britain. Even writing this line of words is a form of political activity. But hard politics in this country converges in a very specific form of psychological architecture, which we know as the Houses of Parliament. Those structures were designed to fulfil an eighteenth- and nineteenth-century process, whereby two relatively similar landed communities exercised power in their own interests. These tribal groupings were known as the Whigs and the Tories, or the Liberals and the Conservatives. Much later, at the beginning of the twentieth century, there was a process of displacement as the Labour Party supplanted the Liberals as the broadly progressive grouping in parliament. The pattern has obtained until today.

Its fundamentally binary structure is indisputable. The very vocabulary of our system – both sides of the House, yah-boo politics, the benches opposite, upper and lower chamber, Her Majesty's Opposition and Her Majesty's Government, divisions, the ayes to the left and the noes to the right, the contents and the not contents, the two-horse race – reinforces the essential kinesis of our public life. If you cannot hear the central dialectic in those words then conjure its physical analogue: two rows of raked wooden benches in diametrical opposition.

At the heart of the process is a winner-takes-all, first-past-the-post arrangement. It squeezes the body politic of a twenty-first-century nation into an eighteenth-century whalebone corset. Some say this is beneficial since it delivers strong, disciplined government and has avoided internal civil conflict for the last 330 years (if one discounts the Jacobite uprisings of the eighteenth century). And we had a chance to change it by referendum in 2011. By more than two to one we rejected the most basic form of proportional representation. Yet no one can doubt that our peculiar political dispensation acts as a powerful drag upon change in Britain.* Recall how it took 114 years and more than twenty separate submitted bills before people acquired a legal right simply to walk on non-productive land. Should we really

---

* One cannot help noticing in a post-Brexit, post-Trump age a profound sense of broken politics among the English-speaking communities on both sides of the Atlantic. One can also see a shared trend towards increasing voter apathy. In the six US elections from 1896 to 1916 the average turnout was 67.25 per cent, compared with 53 per cent in the six elections since 1996. In Britain, the average voter turnout in the six general elections between 1951 and 1970 was 77.1 per cent, but 66.85 per cent in the six between 1992 and 2015. Does the downward pattern in each country – and in the USA only a little over half those eligible now bother to vote – indicate a pervasive sense that binary two-party politics changes nothing? And if it does, is it time that we addressed how the deepest reflex patterns in Anglo-Saxon thought, which seem rooted in the idea of an eternal antinomy between two equal forces, and which is perhaps also manifest in the dominance of the iambic poetic metre, are blocking modern politics?

believe that this legislative entanglement was a clear expression of the will of the nation?

The same restrictive process acts as an immense, regressive filter upon our entire imaginative life. It is very difficult to find ways to talk about environmental issues except outside the main architecture of hard politics because of the binary clamp that the system places over us. For 150 years 'green' politics have remained in the margins of our national conversation or have tried to adapt to the prevailing conditions. As one small illustration of the contortion that this entails, at the 2015 election it took 34,343 votes to elect each Conservative MP and 40,290 votes for each Labour MP, but 1,157,613 votes to elect a single Green MP. And spare a thought for the United Kingdom Independence Party, which needed 3,881,099 votes for its solitary representative.

6. This political system dovetails with another part of the country's political mindset, which we can call 'land-blindness'. As we have seen, the British, more than almost any other country in Europe, are a landless people. In excess of 53 million of us possess an average of just seven one-hundredths of an acre. In 1072, at the drawing up of the Domesday Book, 4.9 per cent of England's eleventh-century population controlled 99 per cent of the land. Today just 0.3 per cent of Britain's 65 million own 69 per cent of it all. In Scotland, which has the most concentrated pattern of land ownership in Europe, three-quarters of the entire country is held in estates of 1,000 acres or more.[7]

Land is the business of a tiny minority, and because it has been outside the mental horizon of so many people for so long, it seems not to register with the British public. How else can we explain the inertia and lack of a sense of injustice that for the last seventy years we have had, in the form of farm subsidies, a feudal system of transfer from the poor to the wealthy? At its worst this process delivers huge amounts of taxpayers' money to millionaire landowners for no other reason than the fact that they are millionaire landowners. In the twelve years to 2011 just fifty Scottish farmers received £230.6

million in subsidy between them, an annual average of £383,000.[8] Should we not even ask why?

It is odd that in all the brouhaha about Brexit, neither from the remainers nor the leave campaign has there been much if any discussion of the 40 per cent of the EU budget which still goes in these feudal payments. Kevin Cahill, in *Who Owns the World*, pointed out that at the heart of the annual giveaway of €46 billion are the 77,000 landowners in the EU area, who own 112 million acres and receive an annual €12 billion of taxpayers' money.[9] Nor is the CAP the only measure of our land-blindness. As Andy Wightman observes, 'Rural landowners have successfully secured the abolition of all taxes on land and, despite professing to be rural businesses, still enjoy exemption from business rates.'[10]

We have somehow contrived to discount land as a significant subject for public debate, yet continued to view land ownership as an instinctive measure of social and cultural merit. The landed lord it over us still. Until the early part of this century, 750 hereditary peers sustained a central place in Britain's political life. Even now ninety-two of them – unelected and unrepresentative, except perhaps of the peculiar interests of their community – retain this same inexplicable privilege. Yet we seem embarrassed to talk about it.

Our land-blindness meshes perfectly with a peculiar characteristic of the landed themselves. It is their land secrecy. They, by contrast, jealously guard the precise details of their territorial possessions just as they might resist public knowledge of their private incomes or their personal sex lives. Recall the shadow Conservative minister who observed that the tax scam at the heart of forestry might attract the attentions of 'the *envious* and *malevolent*'. Recall also how the Forestry Commission, unlike comparable institutions in other European countries, publishes nothing and collects minimal information on the ownership structure of private forestry in Britain. Kevin Cahill has pointed out how, in a manner very similar to the latter agency, the UK government refused to reveal the names of those getting public farm subsidies from the public purse, despite being in breach of the EU's own Constitutional Convention.[11] Today one-third and possibly as much as half the acreage of England and Wales is still not recorded in the Land Registry. One estimate in 1999 suggested that just 25,000 acres of the 11.2 million acres that are unregistered, when they were released as building plots to the construction industry, were worth £40,000 an acre, with a total value of £10–17 billion.[12]

We need as a nation to end the bizarre taboo that nourishes our land-blindness. We should challenge the vested interests who would wish us *not* to be aware or to understand the uses and abuses of our countryside.

7. The discipline that has revealed the inner workings of the more-than-human parts of life is science. Ecologists and biologists were also the community who devised the system of land assessment that is at the very foundations of British conservation and which is elegantly articulated in the *Nature Conservation Review*.

None of this should change. In fact, I would go so far as to say that the only meaningful designations about land quality should be those rooted in an appreciation of biodiversity, and all others that rely upon aesthetic ideas about landscape – the designation of Area of Outstanding Natural Beauty springs to mind – should be scrapped or radically reorganised. But these issues belong under Truth 8.*

Unfortunately, however, the dominant roles accorded to science and scientists in the ways that society ascribes importance to nature have led to a major undervaluing of nature's multiplicity of roles. For scientists have constructed all the arguments for nature in their own image. The Site of Special Scientific Interest is the classic motif of their mindset. The process was writ large in the battle to stop Cow Green Reservoir.

---

* I will add, however, that I once spoke with a Nebraskan farmer, whose 500-acre farm of GM corn was one continuous monoculture, on which, in 2008, he sprayed an estimated $500,000-worth of chemical fertilisers and pesticides annually. The farmer also thought his farm was beautiful, although he could not explain why. The point I would make is that 'beauty', while profound and real to its beholders, is a near-worthless measure of landscape quality.

Setting aside that the other parts of marine and terrestrial life are the source of all the air we breathe and all the food we eat, nature is the regulator of human health. Recently the Wildlife Trusts have expressed these ideas through its Nature and Well Being Act, a proposed piece of legislation that places nature at the heart of the planning process and which takes account of the increasing evidence that access to nature is a crucial element of much preventative and treatment-based healthcare. Yet that ascription of central importance to nature says nothing about its fundamental place in all cultural activity.

What has also been overlooked is the way that diversity in nature is a primary driver for our creativity. Our relationship to the rest of life nourishes the sciences, the visual arts, sculpture, photography, poetry – indeed, all forms of literature, dance, music and cinematography. We are accustomed to the physical connections that flow through the web of life, but sometimes its impacts are immaterial. Our imaginations are, in part, a result of ecological processes. Soul and soil are genuinely and fundamentally interconnected.

Recall George Trevelyan's words: 'By the side of religion, by the side of science, by the side of poetry and art stands natural beauty, not as a rival to these, but as the common inspirer and nourisher of them all.' The only thing I would change would be to substitute *nature* for 'natural beauty'. 'Beauty' is unnecessary. The wings of a house fly, the eyes of an adder and the carapace of an edible crab are beautiful if you look at them for long enough.

The French anthropologist Claude Lévi-Strauss wrote of Amerindians that they found birds not only good to eat but also good to think with.[13] The same principle should be extended to include all nature and all peoples. Other life forms supply the basic fabric of our inner worlds. It is evident in the earliest human forays into what we now call art, especially the spectacular Palaeolithic cave frescoes involving images of aurochs, reindeer, horses, rhinoceros, bears, lions and owls.

Aldous Huxley once suggested that if you took birds out of English poetry you would have to dispose of half the nation's verse canon. I would go so far as to suggest that the single most important natural motif in all world poetry, yielding deeper and more profound insights into the quality of human experience, is the nightingale (see *Birds and People*, pp. 476–9). Tim Dee, chair of the judges for the Forward Prize for Poetry in 2005, noted how there were far more poems on blackbirds in that year than there were on the Iraq War or the 9/11 bombings of the Twin Towers.[14] Nature matters perennially. And these examples merely glance at the totality of our cultural indebtedness.

Go into any British village hall to look at any local art exhibition and you will find a very high percentage of the works depict the other parts of life. At the other end of the artistic continuum, if one had to redact the references to nature from William Shakespeare's collective canon, then one would have to disfigure virtually every single page he wrote and ruin whole plays.

What happens when a country destroys the very basis of its creative responses? We may well find out. But I suggest that, along with the biological deficits inflicted by the self-destruction of our land, we will incur systemic cultural loss. Go to South Lincolnshire if you want to experience what denatured landscapes do to the human spirit.

At present, there is a vector in our cultural life that seems to contradict this statement. It is the massive growth in what one might call environmental art, of which nature writing is a component. Never has the field been richer. Yet we must be careful not to assume that this upsurge of creative responses to our vanishing natural environment is an organic part of some societal awakening and perhaps the vanguard of corrective action. The danger is that it is a compensatory, nostalgic and internalised re-creation of what was once our birthright and is no more: the nature that we knew and are trying to retain through cultural re-imaginings. Ultimately, without the thing itself, without the underlying biodiversity, these responses will be like the light from a dead star: they will persist for a while, may be even decades, but they will travel onwards into the darkness that will eventually consume them.

8. In the sections on north Norfolk and Kinder Scout I discussed at length the confusing multiplicity of landscape designations that have grown up in a thicket around the enterprise of environmental

thought. Not only have we gone on adding additional layers as each new initiative sweeps us briefly away, but British environmentalism has also been dogged by what is called 'the Great Divide', which was instituted with the establishment of the national parks in 1950.

Essentially it turned on a particular question about nature. Do we cherish it for its manifest beauties measured by some arbitrary aesthetic code? Or do we value and protect wildlife diversity? At that time, we allowed two fundamentally separate systems to grow up. National parks were an answer to the first question, and SSSIs and national nature reserves were intended as the answer to the second. Recall the words of historian Michael Winter when he suggested that the division was intellectually flawed and a debilitating feature of the British arrangements.

At present in the British landscape, places are classified as national parks, national nature reserves, areas of outstanding natural beauty, Ramsar sites, biosphere reserves, special protection areas, special areas of conservation, sites of special scientific interest, local nature reserves, county wildlife sites and so on. The truth is, it is maddeningly complicated. And is it really necessary? Could we not call them just one name, from the most important to the least, from the World Heritage Site or biosphere reserve as designated by the UNESCO programmes, to the county wildlife site like my own Blackwater?

My version of that name would be special places for all nature (merely as a token to allow discussion of this issue), with an acronym SPAN that recalls for us in perpetuity that the location's importance *spans* what it does both for the more-than-human parts of nature and for us. It would remind us that the process is a dual one: for people and for the other parts of life. And all constitute one thing. So, Blackwater would be a SPAN site. But anywhere that was previously an SSSI would become a SPAN1 site. If a place were an SSSI, but also an SAC and an SPA it would be SPAN3. And if it were additionally a Ramsar Site and a Biosphere Reserve it could be SPAN5. But there would be only one designation for all places important for nature. Whatever anyone thinks of this idea, the underlying truth is incontrovertible: environmentalists have constructed a barrier to the general public's understanding of nature and of environmental activity. It should be pulled down to make life simpler. Naturalists and environmentalists need to recover the art of speaking plainly.

One other classic expression of the way in which environmentalists have functioned like the legal profession or a medieval priesthood – using language to ring-fence their profession – is in the matter of scientific nomenclature. Scientific Greek and Latin and the nomenclatural system originally devised by Linnaeus in the eighteenth century are undisputed cornerstones of all natural history. Unfortunately, many organisms are still unknown outside this complex vocabulary, and it inserts a major obstacle between the layperson and the other parts of life. British spiders (650 species), flies (>7,000 species) and lichens (>1,600 species) are especially shut out from our ken, partly because of this issue.

Just to give another small example, until very recently it was difficult to find any publications that use common English names for the 10+ British species of sphagnum moss. They are still invariably referred to with titles such as *Sphagnum capillifolium* subsp *capillifolium*, or *Sphagnum denticulatum* or *Spahgnum fimbriatum*.* Yet they are, arguably, among the most important wild plants in all of British nature.

Not all life forms can be incorporated into public knowledge. Some groups are just too complex, and reference to them only in scientific nomenclature is an unavoidable technical necessity. Massive strides have also been taken to introduce accessible names for all sorts of organisms that were previously behind the Latin wall. Fungi and moths, especially micro-moths, are two such large groups that have been rescued from oblivion. Both are now mainstream parts of British natural history activity. There is no more communal, nor more enjoyable wildlife excursion than a foray in search of mushrooms. I have been party to outings that comfortably accommodate scores of people. They are caravans of sharing and laughter and learning and intimacy with the October landscape.

On the other hand, there is a section of the community that wishes to cleave to the old ways. So often it is a matter of pride. It

---

* There are mercifully common names for these species. The three listed are acute-leaved, cow-horn and fringed bogmosses.

arises out of a mindset which insists that 'since I have mastered these complexities, so must you, in order to join the club.' I once attended an excellent entomological course focused on hoverflies, one of the most beautiful and important insect groups, which plays a fundamental role in pollination. When I suggested that common names should be devised and promulgated for the 280+ British species there were unanimous howls of opposition. How could they possibly function without the primacy of *Sphaerophoria scripta* or *Helophilus pendulus*. Both these species, which are in their ways as attractive, engaging and harmless as butterflies, probably occur commonly in your garden. I am guessing, however, that many will never have even heard of them.

9. The creation of common names for all parts of nature is probably the biggest low-cost change that environmentalists could implement. The most important single measure to improve all environmental effort would be to forge genuine systemic unity among all parts. All too often there is discussion of the 'environmental movement' or the 'green lobby', as if there were harmony and accord among its various constituents. The ninth Truth is that there is not.

The inability to combine over the course of the twentieth century and until today, is the cardinal failure of environmentalists in this sense: all parts of its resolution are in the hands of those who are all apparently on one side. There needs to be an NEU – a National Environmentalists' Union. The present government talks about our generation leaving a countryside richer than the one it inherited. If it is serious then the NEU needs representation at the highest levels equal to that of the NFU (National Farmers' Union).

The environmental campaigner George Monbiot has pointed out in his book *Captive State* that almost all the major industries that have an impact upon the British environment employ sector-wide lobby institutions to fight their case in parliament and beyond. These collectives have names like the Construction Clients Forum, the Construction Industry Council, the Construction Confederation, the British Quarry Products Association and the National Council of Building Materials Producers.[15] Is it not odd that environmental organisations have no such voice?

There are indisputable alliances that have been long established and which yield major dividends. The organisation Wildlife and Countryside Link has provided a platform for collaboration in key campaigns. The ability of the different organisations to act in concert is seen by environmentalists elsewhere in Europe as a distinguishing feature of the British scene.[16] Equally, the *State of Nature* reports show an increased recognition of the need for collective impact and offer in themselves a vision of a more united future.

Yet it is not enough. There is no round table that regulates and intensifies the collective impact of the nature lobby. There is no evolving blueprint that sets out a common policy. There is no social forum that allows for the parts to mingle, to appreciate shared values, to forge common bonds. On the contrary, sometimes there is a sense of go-it-alone individualism and even competition.

Sometimes one sees how separate parts of the movement function in ways that even look contradictory. A longstanding initiative for the Campaign to Protect Rural England is to safeguard the Green Belt, the encircling boundary between town and country that has curtailed the outward sprawl of development for decades. Dogged resistance to building on the outer green spaces has been a central plank of CPRE work almost since its foundation. The question that now hangs over this old fixture is what exactly is being safeguarded in the process, and where is the development directed if not into the countryside?

Alternative sites for development are commonly found in what are known as brownfield sites, the pockets of unused or under-used land lying within the urban boundary These are part of the CPRE's answer to safeguarding the Green Belt. Such places, however, have often been shown to be rich in wildlife, and occasionally very rich. In 2008 BugLife, Britain's leading conservation charity for invertebrates, surveyed no fewer than 576 such places in the London and Thames Gateway region and found that half held significant biodiversity. A few, including the West Thurrock Lagoons in Essex, may be, proportionate to area, among the most biodiverse places in the entire country. Some environmentalists now question the value of kneejerk defence of Green Belt when such intensively managed agricultural land, which is what Green Belt land often is, can be nearly worthless for wildlife, irrespective of its greenness or its open character.[17] Protecting Green Belt only adds to the pressure on brownfield areas.

The two parts of this environmental conundrum should speak to one another and harmonise a common position.* A perennially attended round table of the NEU would allow this to happen.

The other loss incurred because of a divided house is well illustrated by the present efforts to halt a six-lane, 22,000-cars-a-day highway across one side of the marshes at Lough Beg, County Derry, which is a reserve protected not only as an ASSI (the Northern Ireland equivalent of an SSSI), but also as an SAC, a Ramsar site and a Natura 2000 site. It is, incidentally, at the heart of the bog landscapes that inspired Seamus Heaney's poetry.

A remarkable couple, Chris and Doris Murphy, at their own expense and initiative, are seeking to overturn the decision in the courts after all the major NGOs have failed to contest the construction. What the Murphys want is not to prevent the road, which all agree is necessary, but to re-route it in a way that accords with the long-established environmental legislation. It is as much a test of the principles governing the development of the British countryside as the other 'hot issue' at Lodge Hill in Kent, discussed in Truth 2. Yet the RSPB, along with the Wildfowl and Wetland Trust, Birdwatch Ireland, the Joint Nature Conservation Committee and Ulster Wildlife (a Wildlife Trust affiliate) have offered no visible public support for the Lough Beg campaign.

In short, the Murphys are pretty much alone, although they have received backing from musicians and from poets and writers outraged

---

* This division in opinion over Green Belt versus brownfield biodiversity is, incidentally, a classic expression of the Great Divide in British environmental thought. The healing of this split between those concerned with landscape beauty and those prioritising biodiversity would be a primary goal for any round table.

at the idea of Heaney's poetic landscape being violated. One of the central functions of an NEU round table would be to ensure that each campaign could be eligible for support from the collective 7 million members of conservation groups.

10. The American farmer and writer Wendell Berry, in an essay from 1969 entitled 'Think Little', suggested that in matters of wildlife loss none of us is innocent. 'A protest meeting on the issue of environmental abuse', he wrote,

> is not a convocation of accusers, it is a convocation of the guilty. That realization ought to clear the smog of self-righteousness... and let us see the work that is to be done.

Every one of us is to blame. And there are no exemptions; not even Sir David Attenborough. Britain's contemporary capitalist society, from which it is impossible to disconnect, is a shared enterprise. It implicates us all. We *are* the problem. 'Nearly every one of us, nearly every day of his life,' according to Berry, 'is contributing *directly* to the ruin of this planet.'[18] No amount of opposition to it in our heads or on our Facebook pages will change those basic facts.

Berry's larger point is that, while we may be responsible, every one of us is, therefore, potentially part of the solution. We *merely* have to act to make a difference. It returns us nicely to the matter of hope, with which I began the chapter, because its supply is in direct proportion to the individual efforts made by any person. To have real hope is not to smear over the facts a higher gloss of optimism, as if the problems can be resolved merely by thinking about them in a particular way. The measures we take have to be ecological in nature; that is, they must travel from the head and heart to the hand. In Matt Howard's magnificently simple line of poetry, each one of us has 'to act with the whole body and mean it'.

The answer to our environmental problems may be societal in nature, but the solutions will not come if we wait until all of us resolve to act together. Change happens when individuals have the courage to do something independently, regardless of the opponents and even the indifference of supposed colleagues. We have only to contemplate the example set by Chris and Doris Murphy in their attempts to halt a motorway across Lough Beg to realise this. Octavia Hill was another such individual. Think also on Benny Rothman or Margaretta Louisa Lemon or Jake Fiennes. In truth there are thousands, if not tens of thousands of individuals acting as well as thinking in ways that can change the world by changing one small part of it.

Yet it is not all about founding momentous societies or attending dramatic court appearances. Most of the key decisions in matters of the environment are literally kitchen-sink choices: they are about which washing-up liquid we use, which shampoo, which detergent, what transport we employ, what food we eat, what pension fund we have, which energy source we pick and the level of acquisitiveness of our lifestyles. Wendell Berry further points out that most of the vegetables needed for a family of four can be grown on a plot measuring 40 × 60 feet. Our gardens are potential sources of high-quality food and of diverse habitat. How we manage them, he argues, can change 'a piece of the world'.

We all need to do more. For my tenth Truth is not really a truth at all, but a question. If the British – with all the privileges of our technology and our historical wealth, with our traditions of democratic government but also our long intricate attachments to nature and our self-proclaimed love for a green and pleasant land – if we cannot sustain a country equal to the love we bear it, then who on Earth can?

NOTES

1. Rackham, Oliver, *The History of the British Countryside*, Phoenix, London, 2000, p. 3.
2. https://www.theguardian.com/environment/2014/sep/25/-sp-nightingales-lodge-hill-sanctuary-conservation-britain.
3. Logan, William Bryant, *Dirt: The Ecstatic Skin of the Earth*, W. W. Norton, New York, 1995, p. 47.
4. Rackham, 2000, p. 28.
5. Goulson, Dave, *Bee Quest*, Jonathan Cape, London, 2017, pp. 156–79.
6. Livingstone, John, *The John A. Livingstone Reader*, McClelland and Stewart, Toronto, 2007, p. 69.

7. Wightman, Andy, *The Poor Had No Lawyers: Who Owns Scotland (And How They Got It)*, Birlinn, Edinburgh, 2013, p. 107.

8. Wightman, 2013, p. 243.

9. Cahill, Kevin, *Who Owns the World: Hidden Facts behind Land Ownership*, Mainstream, Edinburgh, 2006, p. 80.

10. Wightman, 2013, p. 107.

11. Cahill, 2006, p. 80.

12. Cahill, Kevin, *Who Owns Britain*, Canongate, Edinburgh, 2001, p. 14.

13. Lévi-Strauss, Claude, *Totemism*, Beacon Press, Boston, 1963, p. 89.

14. Dee in anon, 2006, p. 9.

15. Monbiot, George, *Captive State: The Corporate Takeover of Britain*, Macmillan, Edinburgh, 2000, p. 150.

16. Matt Shardlow interview, 26 February 2014.

17. Goulson, 2017, pp. 156–7.

18. Berry, Wendell, *The World-Ending Fire: The Essential Wendell Berry*, Allen Lane, London, 2017, p. 50.

from FERAL

George Monbiot

George Monbiot (b. 1963) is an influential environmental activist, columnist and writer. He studied zoology at Oxford and is the author of polemical and bestselling books about politics, the environment and global warming, including *Captive State* (2000), *The Age of Consent* (2003), *Heat* (2006), *Bring on the Apocalypse* (2008), *How Did We Get into This Mess?* (2016) and *Out of the Wreckage* (2017). *Feral* (2013) won the Thomson Reuters Award for Communicating Zoology and the Society of Biology Book Award. *Feral* has been particularly instrumental in popularizing the rewilding movement in Britain, leading to the creation of the charity Rewilding Britain. Monbiot's weekly *Guardian* column has shaped many environmental debates. A portion of his TED talk on the impact of wolves in Yellowstone National Park in the United States has been watched forty-two million times on YouTube. Earlier in his career, he wrote investigative travel books about environmental destruction in Indonesia, South America and Africa, including *Poisoned Arrows* (1989), *Amazon Watershed* (1991) and *No Man's Land* (1994).

GREENING THE DESERT

> When through the old oak forest I am gone,
> Let me not wander in a barren dream
>
> John Keats
> *On Sitting Down to Read King Lear Once Again*

All Hallows' Eve. *Nos Galan Gaeaf.* Early frosts and still days had engineered a blazing autumn. The birches looked like a shower of gold coins. An occasional beech tree flamed against the pale ash leaves and the mauve-brown oaks. The sun was a pewter gleam behind the clouds, the air was almost still. There was a thickness to the day, as if it had been laid on with oil paint, or as if air and leaf and ground were the flesh of a single organism. The berries of the hawthorn exuded from the woods like specks of blood.

Beside the track the dying willowherb had sprung white whiskers. Rills trickled through saxifrage and honeysuckle. Late caddis flies rose from the water and oared the thick air. From across the valley I heard an ancient sound, now rare in these hills: a farmer calling and whistling to his dogs. I left the path and stepped up into the last scrap of woodland before the desert began.

The woods climbed a gentle slope. As I walked towards the light, sheep clattered away from me. I startled a jay and a great spotted woodpecker, which swooped off through the autumn trees with a long, high note. The forest floor had been scrubbed clean. Beneath the fallen leaves there was nothing but moss, sheep shit and mud. A single wood hedgehog mushroom had been turned over by the sheep, and showed its long fine teeth. There were no leafy plants, no saplings, no tree younger than around a century, no understorey of any kind. Many of the oaks had fallen or were close to death. The old wood was dying on its feet. By eating all the seedlings that raised their heads, the sheep were killing it.

The wood petered out into birches, bracken and the odd rowan tree, then into spongy pastures. As I walked up the bare hillside, I could see the mossy domes where trees had fallen: the burial mounds of what had until recently been a larger forest. I hacked through bracken and yellow grass and over anthills covered in red moss. The bracken soon gave way to moorgrass, now greying after the sharp frosts. The last of the waxcap and *Inocybe* mushrooms had flopped over on their stems.

I climbed to the top of a small hill. To my east was Bryn Brith, the speckled hill, whose name suggests that it lost its trees long ago. The yellow grass was still mottled with patches of blue-green gorse. Beyond it were the long blurred slopes of the hills surrounding Pumlumon, the highest mountain on the plateau, grey-brown and treeless. To the south, the hills graded from yellow to green to blue as they stepped away, deep into Ceredigion and Pembrokeshire. Beyond them I could glimpse a grey blur of sea.

Though I could see for many miles, apart from distant plantations of Sitka spruce and an occasional scrubby hawthorn or oak clinging to a steep valley, across that whole, huge view, there were no trees. The land had been flayed. The fur had been peeled off, and every contoured muscle and nub of bone was exposed. Some people claim to love this landscape. I find it dismal, dismaying. I spun round, trying to find a place that would draw me, feeling as a cat would feel here, exposed, sat upon by wind and sky, craving a sheltered spot. I began to walk towards the only features on the map that might punctuate the scene: a cluster of reservoirs and plantations.

Out of the woods, the day felt colder. It had seemed still among the trees. Here there was a cutting, damp wind. I followed a path that took me along the line of a fallen drystone wall, now replaced with posts and wire. No bird started up – not even a crow or a pipit. There were neither fieldfares nor redwings, larks nor lapwings. With the exception of the chemical monocultures of East Anglia, I have never seen a British landscape as devoid of life as the plateau some local people call the Cambrian Desert. In most places the nibbled sward over which I walked contained just two species of flowering plant, the two that sheep prefer not to eat: purple moorgrass and a small plant with jagged leaves and yellow flowers called tormentil.

I followed the Bwlch-y-maen – rocky hollow – trail over bare hills and down bare valleys until it brought me to a point overlooking a wide basin, cradling a small reservoir called Llyn Craig-y-pistyll. I sat on a rock and felt myself slumping into depression. The grass of the basin was already dressed in its winter colours. There were no tints but grey, brown and black: grey water, cardboard-coloured grass, a black crown of Sitka spruce on the far hills. The occasional black scar of a farm track relieved rather than spoilt the view. My map told me that if I walked for the rest of that day and all the next, nothing would change: the plateau remained treeless but for an occasional cluster of sallow or birch, and the grim palisades of planted spruce.

As I glared at the view, the weather front passed in a litter of cloudlets and the sun broke through. Far from enlivening the scene, it brought the bleakness into sharper focus. Now I could see the grey wall of the spruce trunks and the green battlements that surmounted them. The emptiness appeared to expand in the sunlight. I trudged down to the lake. Five Canada geese sat on the far bank, the first birds I had seen since leaving the woods, two hours earlier. They waddled into the water when they saw me, and floated away, grunting softly. Sheep scoured the far bank.

The water was surprisingly low for autumn, exposing the shaley rubble of the banks and the black mud of the reservoir floor, rutted with sheep tracks. I sat by the water and ate my lunch. From where I sat, the tops of the spruce trees looked like an approaching army edging over the hill, pikes raised. I realized that, though this was a Sunday, I had not seen a soul. I leant against the exposed bank of the reservoir, mentally dressing the land, picturing what might once have lived there, what could live there again. Then I rose, stumbled up the hill and ran back along the track. When I returned to the glowing hearth of the ruined wood, with its occasional bird calls, I almost wept with relief.

The Cambrian Mountains cover some 460 square miles, from Machynlleth in the north to Llandovery in the south, Tregaron in the west to Rhayader in the east. They are almost uninhabited, almost unvisited: two friends of mine once walked across them for six days without seeing another person. They begin 300 yards from my home. I see them from my kitchen window, rising through *fridd** and birch woods to a bare skyline.

Before I moved to Wales, I lived for several years in a densely peopled quarter of a city. Whenever I heard the wild cry of gulls, and looked up to see them crossing the narrow strip of sky, I felt a small tear in the cloth of my life elongate a little more. At those moments I knew that I was in the wrong place. Where they were going, I wanted to be.†

When I arrived in Wales, and found myself living between two of the least-inhabited places in Britain – the Cambrians on one side of my valley, Snowdonia on the other – I felt almost overwhelmed by choice. Like a battery chicken released from its cage, at first I ventured

---

* *Fridd* is the land between the enclosed fields of the valley bottoms and the open moor at the top of the hills. It tends to cover the steep slopes of the hillsides and to be dominated by scrub and bracken.

† Unless it was the municipal rubbish dump!

into the mountains tentatively, not quite believing that I could step out of my front door and walk where I would for as far as I wanted, and seldom encounter a road or a house.

But as I began to explore these great expanses, often walking all day over the hills, my wonder and excitement soon gave way to disappointment; the disappointment gave way to despair. The near-absence of human life, I found, was matched by a near-absence of wildlife. The fragmented ecosystems in the city from which I had come were richer in life, richer in structure, richer in interest. In mid-Wales, I found, the woods were scarce and, in most cases, dying, as they possessed no understorey. The range of flowering plants on the open land was pitiful. Birds of any kind were rare, often only crows. Insects were scarcely to be seen. I have walked these mountains for five years now, and with the exception of a few small corners, found no point of engagement with them. Whenever I venture into the Cambrian Desert I almost lose the will to live. It looks like a land in perpetual winter.

It is seen as disloyal, especially in this patriotic nation, to talk the landscape down. Some people say they find it beautiful. The Cambrian Mountains Society celebrates its emptiness. It describes the region as a 'largely unspoiled landscape',[1] and approvingly quotes the author Graham Uney, who claims, 'there is nothing in Wales to compare to the wilderness and sense of utter solitude that surrounds these vast empty moorlands'.[2] To which I say, thank God. What he extols as wild, I see as bleak and broken. To me these treeless, mown mountains look like the set of a post-apocalyptic film. Their paucity of birds and other wildlife creates the impression that the land has been poisoned. Their emptiness appals me. But I also recognize that it is a remarkable achievement.

For the Cambrian Mountains were once densely forested. The story of what happened to them and – at differing rates – to the uplands of much of Europe is told by a fine-grained pollen core taken from another range of Welsh hills, the Clwydians, some forty miles to the north.[3] A pollen core is a tube of soil extracted from a place where sediments have been laid down steadily for a long period, ideally a lake or a bog in which layers of peat have accumulated.

Each layer traps the pollen that rains unseen onto the earth, as well as the carbon particles which allow archaeologists to date it.

The Clwydian core was taken in 2007 from a mire in which peat has settled for the past 8,000 years. At the beginning of the sequence, the plant life was still affected by the cold, dry conditions following the retreat of the ice. Trees – hazel, oak, alder, willow, pine and birch – accounted for about 30 per cent of the pollen in that layer, grass for much of the rest. As the weather became wetter and warmer, elm, lime and ash trees started to move in. The woods became deeper and darker. By 4,500 years ago, trees produced over 70 per cent of the pollen in the sample. Heather pollen, by contrast, supplied around 5 per cent.[4]

Farmers began to colonize the hills in the Neolithic period (between 6,000 and 4,000 years ago). Over the millennia, they gradually cleared some of the land for crops, ran their sheep and cattle on the hills and burnt the remaining trees. The clearing and burning and grazing stripped the fertility of the soil, encouraging heather – which thrives on poor land – to grow. Until some 1,300 years ago the peat still contained pollen from most of the trees of the ancient wildwood. The ash and elm disappeared from the sequence soon afterwards, then the lime and pine, then – but for a few relict stands – the other species.

As the trees retreated, the heather pollen began to rise. The pollen core marks a brief recovery of forest during the plague and economic collapse of the fourteenth century, and the turmoil caused by Glyndŵr's revolt in the fifteenth century. But the regeneration did not last long. By 1900 the proportions of 1,000 years before had been inverted: trees supplied just 10 per cent of the pollen in the core, heather 60 per cent. The forest had been replaced by heath. Over much of the British uplands today, particularly the Cambrian Mountains, the heath has now given way to grass.

Heather took longer to dominate the Clwydian Hills, where the soil is relatively fertile, than most of the uplands of Britain. Where the soil was thinner, it became the dominant vegetation as early as the Bronze Age, between 4,000 and 2,700 years ago. I think of the Bronze Age as the period in which the hills turned bronze.

This record, and similar evidence from the rest of the country, shows us several things. It shows that the open landscapes of upland

Britain, the heaths and moors and blanket bogs, the rough grassland and bare rock which many people see as the natural state of the hills, which feature in a thousand romantic films and a thousand advertisements for clothes and cars and mineral water, are the result of human activity, mostly the grazing of sheep and cattle. It shows that grazing and cultivation have depleted the soil. It shows that when grazing pressure eases, trees can return.

The word woodland creates a misleading impression of what the ecosystem of these hills would have looked like after trees returned in the early Mesolithic, and until they were cleared by farmers. From Scotland to Spain, the western seaboard of Europe was covered by rainforest. Rainforests are not confined to the tropics. They are places wet enough for the trees to carry epiphytes, plants which grow on other plants. A few miles from where I live I have found what appears to be a tiny remnant of the great Atlantic rainforest, a pocket of canopied jungle, protected from sheep, in the Nantgobaith gorge. The trees hanging above the water are festooned with moss and lichen. Polypody – the many-footed fern – slinks along their branches. Through the forest canopy move troops of long-tailed tits, goldcrests, nuthatches and treecreepers. Walking up Cwm Nantgobaith one autumn day, I noticed something unmistakable, but so unfamiliar that it took me a moment to process it. It shone like a gold sovereign against the brown oak leaves on the path. I picked it up.

It was a leaf of *Tilia cordata*, the small-leaved lime. Daffodil yellow, onion-shaped, it filled only the indentation in my palm. I looked up the path and saw another, then another. I followed the trail to two great trunks, forking from one stool and twisting up into the canopy above the path. I had walked beneath them many times but never noticed them: swaddled in deep moss, the trunks were indistinguishable from those of the oaks, and the leaves appeared only far above my head. Since then I have found several more limes in the gorge. This is a tree of the ancient wildwood which is now rare in Wales. Its presence there suggests that this fragment of rainforest might have grown without interruption since prehistoric times.

Heather, which many nature-lovers in Britain cherish, is typical of the hardy, shrubby plants which colonize deforested land. I have seen similar landscapes of low scrub in Brazil, Indonesia and Africa, where logging, burning and shifting cultivation have depleted the soil. I do not see heather moor as an indicator of the health of the upland environment, as many do, but as a product of ecological destruction. The rough grasslands which replace it when grazing pressure further intensifies, and which are also treasured by some naturalists, are strikingly similar to those whose presence we lament where cattle ranching has replaced rainforests in the tropics. I find these double standards hard to explain. I wonder whether our campaigns against deforestation elsewhere in the world, commendable as they may be, are a way of not seeing what has happened in our own country.

This is not to say that there was no open land. In some places the soil was too poor or wet for trees to grow. On the tops of the highest mountains the weather was too cold and harsh. But these open habitats were small and occasional, by comparison to the great tracts of wildwood which covered most of the hills.[5] Nor is this to suggest that if human beings and their domestic animals were suddenly to vanish from Britain, our ecosystems would soon revert to those that prevailed in the Mesolithic. The uplands have been so depleted of nutrients* and their soils so compacted by sheep that they are unlikely to support continuous forest. For a few centuries after rewilding began, they would be more likely to host a patchwork of rainforest, covert, scrub, heath and sward.

The ancient character of the land, the forests that covered it and the animals that lived in them – which until historical times included wolves, bears, lynx, wildcats, boar and beavers – have been forgotten by almost everyone. The open, treeless hills are widely seen as natural. The chairman of a trade association called Cambria Active describes the scoured acid grassland it is trying to promote to tourists as 'one of the largest wildernesses left in the UK'.[6] The Countryside Council for Wales, the nation's official conservation agency, calls its Claerwen nature reserve, a bare waste of sheep-scraped misery in the Cambrian Mountains, 'perhaps the largest area of "wilderness" in Wales today'.[7]

---

* Nutrients are lost as animals are removed from the land for consumption in other places, and as soil is leached or stripped by erosion.

Spend two hours sitting in a bushy suburban garden anywhere in Britain, and you are likely to see more birds, and of a wider range of species, than you would while walking five miles across almost any open landscape in the uplands. But to explain that what we have come to accept as natural is in fact the aftermath of an ecological disaster – the wasteland which has replaced a rainforest – is to demand an imaginative journey that we are not yet prepared to make. Our memories have been wiped as clean as the land.

There is a name, coined by the fisheries scientist Daniel Pauly, for this forgetting: 'Shifting Baseline Syndrome'.[8] The people of every generation perceive the state of the ecosystems they encountered in their childhood as normal. When fish or other animals or plants are depleted, campaigners and scientists might call for them to be restored to the numbers that existed in their youth: their own ecological baseline. But they often appear to be unaware that what they considered normal when they were children was in fact a state of extreme depletion. In the uplands of Britain, naturalists and conservationists bemoan the conversion of heather into rough grassland, or of rough grassland into fertilized pasture, and call for the ecosystems they remember to be restored – but only to the state they knew.

The main agent of these transformations is an animal which, like the flayed hills, we have come to accept as part of the fabric of British life: a woolly ruminant from Mesopotamia. No wild animal resembling the sheep has ever existed in Britain or western Europe. (The musk ox, which belongs to the same sub-family as sheep and goats, probably comes closest, but it has a different ecology and set of habitat preferences.) The mouflon, the 'wild' sheep of Corsica and Cyprus, is in fact one of the earliest examples of a feral invasive species: a descendant of animals which escaped from domestic herds during the Neolithic.[9]

Because they were never part of our native ecosystem, the vegetation of this country has evolved no defences against sheep. In the uplands they rapidly deplete nutritious and palatable plants, leaving behind a remarkably impoverished flora: little beside moss, moor-grass and tormentil in many places. The sheep has caused more extensive environmental damage in this country than all the building that has ever taken place here.

NOTES

1. www.cambrian-mountains.co.uk/

2. Graham Uney, 1999, *The High Summits of Wales*, Logaston Press, Hereford. Quoted by the Cambrian Mountains Society, http://www.cambrian-mountains.co.uk/documents/cambrian-mountains-sustainable-future-low-graphics.pdf

3. Fiona R. Grant, 2009, *Analysis of a Peat Core from the Clwydian Hills, North Wales*. Report produced for Royal Commission on the Ancient and Historical Monuments of Wales, http://www.rcahmw.gov.uk/media/193.pdf

4. Ibid.

5. See for example, R. Fyfe, 2007, 'The importance of local-scale openness within regions dominated by closed woodland', *Journal of Quaternary Science*, vol. 22, no. 6, pp. 571–8, doi: 10.1002/jqs. 1078; J. H. B. Birks, 2005, 'Mind the gap: how open were European primeval forests?', *Trends in Ecology & Evolution*, vol. 20, pp. 154–6.

6. Richard Tyler, 17 December 2007, quoted in the *Western Mail*.

7. Countryside Council for Wales, 2011, 'Claerwen', http://www.ccw.gov.uk/landscape--wildlife/protecting-our-landscape/special-landscapes--sites/protected-landscapes/national-nature-reserves/claerwen.aspx

8. Daniel Pauly, 1995, 'Anecdotes and the shifting baseline syndrome of fisheries', *Trends in Ecology & Evolution*, vol. 10, no. 10, doi: 10.1016/S0169-5347(00)89171-5.

9. Derek Yalden, 1999, *The History of British Mammals*, T. and A. D. Poyser, London.

from THE WOLF BORDER

Sarah Hall

A novelist and poet, **Sarah Hall** (b. 1974) was born in Carlisle, Cumbria. She studied English and art history at Aberystwyth and creative writing at the University of St Andrews. Her debut novel, *Haweswater* (2002), about the disintegration of a hill farming community as a result of the construction of a new reservoir, won the 2003 Commonwealth Writers' Prize. *The Electric Michelangelo* (2004) was shortlisted for the Man Booker Prize and *The Carhullan Army* (2007) won the John Llewellyn Rhys Prize and the James Tiptree Jr Award. Named one of Granta's twenty best young writers in 2013, she also won the BBC National Short Story Award that year. *The Wolf Border* (2015) tells the story of a wealthy philanthropist who is determined to reintroduce wolves into the Lake District. She is also the author of *How to Paint a Dead Man* (2009), *Madame Zero* (2017) and *Sudden Traveller: Stories* (2019). She is a creative writing tutor.

By the end of the month they are fit to travel and everything is ready for their arrival. Rachel drives to the airport to meet the cargo flight. She breaks the journey overnight, stays in an industrial Travelodge. She cannot sleep. She checks the weather app on her phone. Sunny. 15 degrees. She is restless, not tired. A mania has arrived, a combined excitement. In her belly, when she lies flat, there is faint movement, or the boding of movement. Flutters. At 4 a.m. she turns the light on and tries to read but can't concentrate on her book. She looks at the list of contacts in her phone, thinks about calling Kyle; he will still be up. Should she now tell him? Shouldn't he know? For courtesy's sake, if nothing else? She switches the phone off and turns out the light.

In the morning the sky is mackerel-dappled and serene. She checks the airport website – there are no delays. She receives a text message from the transport company – Vargis – the driver has been dispatched and is on his way to the airport. She showers, dresses. She leaves the top button of her jeans undone.

The coffee in the breakfast room gives her heartburn as usual. At the buffet she selects oily eggs from a metal tin, and larvic tomatoes, which scald the inside of her mouth. She eats as much toast and jam as she can. The wonders of a returning appetite. She checks out, puts her bag in the back of the Saab. In the boot is a kit with extra sedative darts, though only a delay or extreme stress will warrant using them, and the transport company is also equipped. At 7.30 she calls Stephan in Romania. He shouts into the hands-free.

Bună ziua? Bună ziua?

She can hear the engine of his truck, and the radio blaring; he is already driving back to the centre, through the alpine meadows.

I wonder if you can help me, she says, I'm looking for two missing wolves.

Rachel, he shouts. I have sent them to you with my greatest love! Are they OK?

Yes, yes, he says. Being rocked in arms of Morpheus. Let me tell you – next time I'm flying wolf-class too. They've got it the best. Like celebrities. They're going to be a great pair.

I know. I can't wait to see them.

You have to come visit us soon, he says. You won't recognise the place – we're getting very high-tech now! It was a generous donation your employer made to us.

Good – he can afford to be generous. And you must come and see them here.

Of course!

They finish speaking and hang up. She texts Huib with an update, sets the GPS, and drives the rest of the way to the airport. Rush-hour traffic eases. She follows signs for British Airways World Cargo. She is early, but the flight is also scheduled to arrive early. On the link road an Airbus roars overhead, tilting and straightening, its wheels locked, its undercarriage close enough to see scratches in the paint. If everything goes to plan they will be back in Annerdale by the early afternoon. The sedation is strong enough that they will not have been disturbed by the flight and the transit north, but she does not want them under for too long.

It does not seem long ago she was arriving at the same airport: her inglorious return home. She parks at the side of the cargo terminal. There are various haulers and transport companies. The Vargis men are waiting in reception, dressed formally in company jackets, carrying cases in which are plastic suits and masks. She too is equipped with a quarantine suit. She greets them and they exchange a few words. They are polite, professional – ex-military, she suspects. She spends twenty minutes with the airport officials. The paperwork is all in order – waybill, licences, CITES, and veterinary documentation. Payment is made. The crates, IATA standard, have been inspected in Romania, but will be inspected again by UK staff, for correct ventilation, bedding; the wolves are not harnessed inside: if they woke under restraint, they would damage themselves trying to get free. While the flight's cargo is being cleared, she waits in a small lounge. Other consignees are waiting too, for what freight, it is impossible to guess. Mammals, plants, alien matter. Or the prosaic family pet.

Soon she is called through. She changes into the suit and goes into the disinfected unloading zone. The crates are brought in, the two Vargis men wheeling them slowly, unfazed by the contents of the covered structures. In bold print the labels read: LIVE ANIMALS – DO NOT TIP. The blue transport van is being reversed into the secondary loading bay, the back doors opened. Rachel gently lifts the overlay on the first crate and opens the small viewing hatch. She shines a torch. The female. Darkness, portions of a hind leg, long, crescent-shaped claws. Her breath sounds are even. Thomas has suggested not naming them until they arrive, almost superstitiously, like a father with newborns. *Let's see what their personalities are.* But Rachel has already christened her, after seeing the photographs sent by Stephan and noticing an uncanny resemblance to a particular starlet. The thin nose, tilted eyes, and lupine brows; a face from Hollywood past – Merle Oberon. Merle. She pulls the cover back down. She moves to the second crate and checks the male. He is big – bigger than she anticipated – pale fur, with long black guard hairs. He was lucky to make it out of the trap alive, lucky there was no infection in the bone.

She listens, then briefly shines the torch inside. The glimmer of a slit eye, atypical blue. The Rayleigh effect. Somehow it is harder, even than with humans, to remember there is no real colour. He is not alert. There's enough meat and water. She takes the docket out of the waterproof shield, scans and signs it.

They are brought out to the truck and loaded carefully. The Vargis men keep the crates level, moving swiftly but carefully. The transport company is top of the range. Bullet-proof glass, armoured siding. She would not be surprised if they were equipped to carry nuclear arms, presidents. The crates are secured to the bed of the van and the doors shut.

On the way out of the airport she follows at a safe distance. The van keeps to sixty-five miles per hour. She checks her mirrors with tense regularity, for idiotic drivers, problems, the police. The journey could not be more regulated, but it still feels like a bank robbery, a crime – like the van is filled with explosives. As they drive, her mind flashes through worst-case scenarios. She imagines a crash: the van tipping, its doors swinging open, and the crates smashing on the verge; the wolves limping into the road, horns blaring as they shake their heads, cut through the wreckage, and lope off. They could be halfway up the country in forty-eight hours, disappearing like ghosts.

The van brakes moderately, keeps its distance from the traffic in front. In some part of their brain, even drowsing, they will comprehend motion. Through the seals in the van doors they will detect traces of passing substances: clays, flints, grasslands, under diesel and bitumen, exhaust fumes. And humans nearby – perspiration, hormones. They are intelligent analysts. In those in captivity, she's witnessed incredible responses to human conditions: aggression towards drunks, defence of pregnant staff if a threat is perceived. If they are starting to rouse, they will be communicating with each other, low-toned, almost whistling. But the sedation has been finely administered and should last.

Warning signs flash overhead. Roadworks around Birmingham – long delays. She follows the Vargis van onto the M6 toll road, which is glossy and empty. They pass through the Midlands. Black Country residue. Towns bleeding together along the river basin. It would have been easy to have taken them from visitor centres in Norfolk or Reading, but they must be unhabituated. They must understand range, be able to hunt, or the project will not work.

She sips water from a bottle, not much – she does not want to have to stop at a service station. Neither does the driver of the van pull over for a break – probably they have helpful devices to relieve themselves. The country rolls by. She indulges in a dark daydream, imagines the Vargis men stopping in a layby, stepping into the nearby bushes to urinate. When they return the vehicle is gone, opportunistically stolen. Miles away in a lock-up its doors are pried open. She imagines the shock of these particular spoils – the thieves recoiling. *What the hell? Is that a…* Then incremental bravado, goading the animals with a stick or a piece of pipe through the crate hatches – bragging and phone calls. Either they'd be kept by some thug on a chain in an outbuilding, or dumped in the fly-tipped hinterlands of England amid old washing machines and corrosives. Worse: they'd be pitted against some trained brute of a dog in a gore-smeared ring. A mastiff. A cross-hound. Such things do occur. She's seen appalling Spanish footage of a wolf matched against a Presa Canario, the most hellish of breeds, 160 pounds of thick-packed muscle, its ears illegally cropped. The fight was brief. A torrent of snarling, spittle flying, eyes filling with red – both of them up on their hindlegs, heaving against each other like boxers, their heads shaking. Within seconds the dog's brindle was muddied with blood, its jowls torn, and the wolf's side rent open. The onlookers cheering and exchanging bets, chanting the name of the dog, *Rafa, Rafa, Rafa*, which would, given the extent of its injuries, still have had to be shot. People look at her with surprise when she says that hunting is at least an honest sport.

The thought passes. The blue van makes steady progress. By Manchester she begins to relax. The roads are relatively clear. She turns the radio on, then off again. The tarmac hums under the wheels. Her phone rings – the number unlisted. She does not answer. Probably Thomas, who was hoping to be present for their arrival, but is sitting in the House. Traffic slows over the ship canal. The road rises and falls, then everything speeds up again. There are multiple lanes around Preston, a cavalcade of undertaking and overtaking. She grips the wheel tightly, flashing her lights and cursing as a car veers between her and the transport van, across three lanes, onto the slip road. The northern cross motorways draw much of the traffic off. After Lancaster the way is clear. They exit the motorway and take the dual carriageway along the county's southern edge. Oyster-coloured skies above Cumbria. The estuary glimmers in the sunlight. Shallow waves traverse its surface, moving both directions at once – a Janus tide.

She concentrates. It will take another hour to get to Annerdale. She signals to the van, overtakes, and leads the convoy – it is unlikely they will get lost but she doesn't want to take the chance. They continue on, into the mountains, sedately, like some kind of royal procession, the diplomatic arrival of a crowned couple. And it is historic, she thinks. It's five hundred years since their extermination on the island. They are a distant memory, a mythical thing. Britain has altered radically, as has her iconography of wilderness, her totems.

Once in situ, she knows they will divide the country, just as they will quarter the imagination again. Always the same polar arguments. Last year, during documentary filming at Chief Joseph, two hunters had shouted in her face. *They devour their victims alive, while their hearts are still beating! They revel in death!* As if the animals were some kind of biblical plague – many do believe it. She had calmly explained on camera the hierarchy and tactics of the hunt, the fact that eighty per cent of hunts fail; the fact that herds, after the culling of the weak by predators, are always healthier. Facts versus fear, hatred, and irrationality. As for glee during a kill, such a thing cannot be ascertained, though females seem to express great excitement the first time they hunt after a new litter has been weaned.

Ahead, the mountains seem to smoke, white clouds pluming above as if they were not dead volcanoes, but live. The new bracken is electric green in the lower valleys. She leaves Alexander a message, so that he will know to set off. She slows for a humpback bridge and sounds the horn to warn oncoming traffic, checks her rear-view mirror. The van is close behind, carefully navigating the narrow structure, its wing mirrors only inches from the stone walls. The screen is tinted; she cannot see the drivers. Its hold might be carrying anything: gold bullion, masterpieces, the body of Jesus Christ. There has not been a public announcement about the arrival – she does not want to risk any controversy. The Annerdale wolves are being brought in, to all intents and purposes, secretly, under the radar, like contraband.

In the quarantine enclosure, Rachel and Huib stand next to the crates, boiler-suited and disinfected, their hands placed on the sliding-door mechanisms. Outside the fence, Sylvia is filming. Alexander is with her, observing – he will do so every day for the next week and then weekly. Michael is not in attendance. A new deer carcass lies at the far end of the pen, wet, aromatic, freshly cut. After six months they will be freed into the main enclosure with the herds, as close to a hard release as possible.

The crates are silent, but the sedation will be lifting. Huib looks over at Rachel. He holds up a thumb – ready. Rachel signals back. They open the doors and step quickly behind the crates. In no more than a second or two the pair has bolted, the male a fraction faster, startlingly pale, with Merle hard at his heels. Huib punches the air.

Boom!

The wolves divide round a stack of logs, make for the end of the pen, and are lost from sight behind a cluster of bushes.

Let's leave them to it, Rachel says.

She and Huib wheel the crates backward towards the gate, where they are stowed. They step into the disinfectant zone and change shoes, strip out of the boiler suits. Rachel shuts and locks the inner gate, which is screened. Although they can no longer be seen, they are well within the auditory and olfactory field, and will always be detected when this close to the pair. They wash down, strip out of the suits, exit the outer gate, and join Alexander and Sylvia in the viewing area. The pair have gone to ground and remain hidden from sight. The group speak in low tones, almost whispering, congratulating each other. Sylvia keeps the camera still and trained through the hide's panel. Alexander nods to Rachel.

Looking good, very alert.

Let's see if they eat anything, she says.

They take up their field glasses and wait. After five minutes, pointed ears come up out of the grass, then heads emerge. The wolves step out from behind the bushes, cautiously, sniffing, a forepaw held aloft. There's a cold austerity to the male's blue-fired gaze, a rarity. Merle is quietly confident in the new surroundings; she beings to lope towards the carcass, investigates it, but does not eat. She returns to the male and he licks her muzzle. They make short forays, close together, in the bottom half of the pen, criss-crossing scent trails to the fence and back, keeping their noses to the ground, lifting them and reading the air. The enclosure is big, several hectares, though as quarantine progresses it will seem limited, Rachel knows, and will induce lazy behaviour, habituation. She has prepared a series of preventative tactics. In the centre of the pen is a pile of dead wood where it is likely they will den. They move closer, towards the hide. For a long while the male stands looking in the direction of the screen where the humans are hidden. The strong April sunlight renders his fur brilliant, pale gold and silver-white, like the blaze of a matchhead. He could almost set fire to the trees. He's going to vanish, Rachel thinks, against the snow and the limestone pavements on the moors, against the blonde sward of the grassland.

I think he knows we're still here, Sylvia says.

Ja. I feel like he knows what I had for breakfast, Huib says.

Alexander laughs quietly.

Muesli, and he's not impressed.

He is going through a health checklist, ticking boxes, the first of many formal documents. They are inquisitive, their tails are up; there is no lethargy. A good score. Sylvia keeps recording.

I wish Mummy could have seen this, she says after a time. She was the one who first suggested the idea to Daddy. She'd be so, so happy.

Rachel glances over. This is the first mention of the project's conception she has heard, and was not aware of the memorial aspect. Sylvia is dressed as a standard volunteer: T-shirt and jeans, a fleece jacket, work boots. Her face is not made up; her hair is tied back, though there is still a quality of refinement to her, a strange Martian beauty. She has spent her first full day on the project, preparing the carcass with Huib, answering the phone. There has been no cause to doubt her commitment, and now Rachel understands why. She is doing it for her dead mother, the most banal and powerful of all motivations.

The pair lope softly to the bottom of the enclosure again and disappear. Sylvia lowers and switches off the camera.

I'll upload this when I get back to the office, she says. I'll send it to Border News and the BBC. Daddy left us some champagne, by the way, if anyone feels like it.

This day gets better and better, Alexander says. Merle is a great name, by the way, Rachel. I saw *The Dark Angel* when I was a kid. I think I would have sent my best friend off to his death for Kitty Vane.

Ja, me too! Huib agrees. Good job you didn't call her Kitty, Rachel.

Alexander snorts.

Kitty the wolf.

I didn't have you two down as film nerds, Rachel says. But we should think about a name for our boy. Anyone?

Sylvia holds her hand up, eager as a schoolgirl.

May I suggest something?

Rachel thinks back to the welcome party, her assumptions about Sylvia's mettle and her tastes. They can always vote on it if needs be. But the mood is high, it is a celebratory day, and she does not want to dampen the spirit by penalising a member of the team. She will have to learn to trust the Earl's daughter.

OK. Go on.

Well, he's just so very bright and brilliant. What about Ra?

As in the sun god? I like that, says Huib. I like that a lot. Our creator!

Sylvia's smile broadens; she is lit up with keenness, and looks a tiny bit smug. Rachel nods.

Actually, I like it too.

Alexander is bent forward, peering through the viewing panel again.

Hey up, he says. Action stations.

They take up their field glasses. There is movement in the enclosure. Cautiously, Merle is approaching the carcass for a second time. She stands over the downy body, sniffs, assessing the state of decay. Scavenging is not the preferred mode, or perhaps she is still suspicious after the recent poisoning. As Stephan Dalakis pointed out, she was extremely lucky the incident did not permanently affect her stomach and bowel. Whatever the meat was laced with left her desperately sick. Another way of killing them. Over the years Rachel has seen several cases along Idaho's sheep superhighway where the hunters use Xylitol, which is easy to buy and toxic to their livers.

Merle looks towards Ra. Her ears rotate forward, black-tufted. Her eyes are tear-shaped, dark-ringed, her expression quizzical. The eye might be drawn to her big, pale mate, but she is more than beautiful, Rachel thinks. Ra arrives and they begin to tug at the flesh. The legs of the deer jerk as they pull it about. Another tick in Alexander's boxes. After feeding, they retreat towards the dead wood, and lie down in the grass. Merle inches over and they lie close together. Ra yawns. He is not yet fully interested in the advances; she is simply practising until he is. She yawns too, puts her head on her paws. She may not have a godly name, Rachel thinks, but she is the vital one, everything rests on her ability to breed. She is the true grey, true to the name; she is tawny as the landscape, and utterly congruent.

from ON EXTINCTION

Melanie Challenger

Melanie Challenger is a writer and librettist who studied English at Oxford University. In 2003, she adapted the Anne Frank diaries for a choral work by James Whitbourn, which was premiered in 2005. Her first collection of poems, *Galatea*, won a 2005 Eric Gregory Award. She also edited *Stolen Voices* (2006), an anthology of young people's wartime diaries with Bosnian writer Zlata Filipović. From 2007 to 2010 she was a Fellow at the AHRC Centre for the Evolution of Cultural Diversity at University College London. Her first non-fiction book, *On Extinction: How We Became Estranged from Nature*, was published in 2011 and won the 2013 Green Award. As the librettist for British composer Mark Simpson, she provided the text for his Manchester International Festival oratorio, *The Immortal*, which won the 2016 Sky Arts/South Bank Award for classical music and received its London premiere at the 2017 BBC Proms. Her latest book is *How to Be Animal: A New History of What it Means to Be Human* (2021).

As I steadily and deliberately gathered my knowledge of the Cambridgeshire flora, I was mindful of the fact that this was not the countryside of my birth and childhood. I was a fleeting inhabitant of this landscape and I knew that I had no intentions to remain here. There were other places I wished to visit, to which I might prefer to belong. My explorations of extinction had made me question how the origins of a person's understanding of nature affected their motives for safeguarding it. Even more so, I had come to recognize that different aspects of our efforts to survive were sometimes irreconcilable.

On the one hand, knowledge of nature might be inherently localized and limited in its scope, like that once possessed by the people of Whitby and still remembered by the Inuit elders. Those endowed with such intimacy with a particular place sensed that the natural world ordinarily altered through slow, almost imperceptible processes – 'the old succession of days'. One person's brief life afforded the luxury of natural knowledge gained at birth and confirmed through growing up in a single landscape. Successive generations could capture the incremental alterations occurring to such a place and the occasional hiccups of its seasonal variation, establishing the illusion of changelessness without shattering it. Such expertise would pass down through the generations, each new generation ensuring that the inherited knowledge still matched the reality of the world.

These traditions were destroyed when the environment changed too quickly, when societies grew too large or technological developments caused sudden deficiencies. Then the old knowledge was thrown into chaos, and a sense of approaching ruin only encouraged people to pull away from place and tradition, in the hope of stealing a march on extinction.

With the advent of the first industrialized societies, debates about the animal nature of humanity gave rise to the notion that one's birthplace was associated with primitiveness, whereas escape into both adulthood and elsewhere was the trajectory of civilization. Industrialization tended to dissolve rural traditions, along with dialects, vernaculars and nature lore of people largely enclosed in their own worlds. In industrialized societies, another kind of natural knowledge gained currency. Francis Bacon and similar thinkers considered the purpose of natural knowledge to be the governance of nature. This 'New Philosophy' of the seventeenth century in Britain grew into the Royal Society for the Improvement of Natural Knowledge, the scientific institute now known simply as the Royal Society. In 1890 the biologist Thomas Henry Huxley defined natural knowledge as a scientific understanding of the world. 'Our business was... to discourse and consider of philosophical enquiries, and such as related thereunto: – as Physick, Anatomy, Geometry, Astronomy, Navigation, Staucks, Magneticks, Chymicks, Mechanicks, and Natural Experiments.' These enquiries galvanized technological improvements that required new knowledge of the world.

Enterprises like the *Oxford English Dictionary* or *Webster's The-saurus* documented the invention of new words in the English language. According to the *OED*, the word 'robot' was introduced in 1922, derived from the Czech word *robota*, for 'forced labour'. Later, as the technology of robotics advanced, it came to mean 'a machine capable of automatically carrying out a complex series of movements'. Meanwhile, novel words predicted as future additions to the dictionary betrayed the emphasis of new knowledge: 'insourc-ing', 'made-for-mobile', 'pay by touch', 'softphone', as did those words already added, such as 'prime time', 'radiophysics', 'clonable', 'wire speed' and 'blogosphere'. These language changes signal the shift of natural knowledge in industrialized societies from the organic to the man-made environment.

This move from distinctive cultural knowledge born of the varied attributes of landscapes to the universal cultural knowledge of tech-nologies available worldwide is akin to the disappearance of diversity in nature. The gardens of people's minds have been writ large in the physical realities of their surroundings. Landscapes bereft of their distinctiveness reflect human habits that have become indistinguish-able, regardless of where people live.

The first page of my notebook was for the month of April at Fidwell Fen. My list of identifications read, 'Cuckoo flower, ground ivy, red dead nettle, white dead nettle, common field speedwell, common chick-weed, lesser trefoil.' Later, in May, on my walks around Clayhithe, I added, 'Creeping buttercup, medium-flowered wintercress, silverweed, slender speedwell, nipplewort, honesty, herb Robert and greater peri-winkle.' The flowers jotted down in my book were all common varieties, most especially the nettles, which have colonized great swathes of the British countryside. My discoveries reflected the spread of similar lifestyles across the world, undermining the idiosyncrasies of nature, increasing homogeneity. At the time of writing, over half of the nearly seven thousand unique human languages are endangered, their traditional cultures carved by experience of special places now under threat.

Aristotle raised the spectre of equality both in his *Nicomachean Ethics* and in *Politics*. *Isos*, the Greek word for equality, was closer in meaning to the concept of fairness. It was the giving of what was due in correspondence with an individual's occupation or social situation. Equality, in this sense, was always relative. But Aristotle's notion of political justice suggested a different kind of equality, one born of participation in a common life. Justice could exist only among those who were free and equal in their capacities and intentions as citizens. This idea of political justice lent modern civilization its grounds for equal human rights. Following the horrors of the Second World War, the newly formed United Nations drafted and adopted the Universal Declaration of Human Rights in the winter of 1948. The thirty rights to which every person in the world was deemed to be entitled included:

Article 3. Everyone has the right to life, liberty and security of person...

Article 9. No one shall be subjected to arbitrary arrest, detention or exile...

And so on. Many of the articles were sustainable as universals across societies and time, but some articles raised a dilemma. Could all people have equal rights to some pursuits, if their destructiveness varied around the world? Could societies justify actions now known to cause short-term and long-term damage to the natural world, if the relative damage depended on population size or the kind of technology? Article 27 stated that everyone had the right 'to share in scientific advancement and its benefits'. Could all humans have equal rights to a technology if this right, when exercised by every person, would devastate nature? The notion of equal and universal rights to all technologies enshrined in Article 27 depends on a kind of consistency across the Earth. It assumes that such rights can exist without relative impact in different landscapes and societies.

The diversity of landscapes, materials and life forms across the Earth has yielded an extraordinary range of products to aid human survival, but their universal application by all societies around the world, regardless of population size and their unique surroundings, requires an essential denial of the fragility of such diversity. Increasing the similarity of environments, as industrialized societies have done through the years, has eroded the natural variety of the world, largely through humanity's reliance on technological progress, now deemed a universal right of our species.

Occasionally, I speculated on whether scientists might find genetic ways to persuade societies and individuals to preserve nature. Knowledge of the human genome along with technologies like pre-implantation genetic screening could allow an interference at the biological level with human nature, an intrinsic transformation of our species that previously only natural selection could achieve. In designing our own nature, what would we choose to keep or abandon from our animal past? Could we eradicate the natural traits that lead to the destructiveness of large, technological civilizations? Could we breed into children an altruistic sensitivity to nature that might guard against its future ruin? Or the self-command necessary to exist more contentedly with finite resources? Leaving aside the moral conundrums of such an intrusion, would genetic engineering pro-duce different results to the arbitrary trials of life? Would interfering with children's genetic make-up be different to endowing them with information from birth? Meeka said that the Inuit had no hunting 'laws', for they believed that experience of nature would moderate behaviour naturally. But as modern lifestyles separate the majority of people from the natural world, such mechanisms might never come into play.

I began my thinking for this book with an intense sympathy for nature but little or no understanding of it and a growing sense of alarm at my own ignorance. While the textures and shades of my native English landscape were strongly familiar to me, I had not grown up knowing its distinctive plants and animals. As I concerned myself with the grim history of extinction, my findings began to alter my own behaviour – at first almost imperceptibly but later in conscious and deliberate ways. I began to grasp my own place in the natural landscape, particularly the landscape in which I was living.

In writing of his own interest in wild flowers, Richard Jefferies said that he did not recognize 'whence or why it was joy'. In the nineteenth century, in Jefferies' lifetime, it was still possible to revel blindly in this natural compulsion to enjoy wildlife. But Jefferies' benevolent carelessness of experience could not be mine. While my pleasure proceeded from an intrinsic desire to discover and understand my landscape, I knew why it was joy, and knew – more significantly – why it *had* to be joy. Although the beauty of wild flowers may have made me notice them, it was my sense of their impediment that inspired my knowledge of them, and the more I knew of both the flowers and the wildlife around them, the more I was motivated in my occupation. This was a profoundly nostalgic way of behaving. It was recognition of the environmental destruction of the age into which I was born that provoked a further recognition of my own loss of any inherited understanding of the Earth from former generations. My observation of wild flowers and the pleasure I took in them was intimately bound to a conscious and moral reclamation of knowledge.

Growing up in Britain, the first nation in the world to become industrialized, I lived amid the ghosts of former wildness. While disappearances had occurred over the millennia as people became more and more skilled at exploiting and modifying nature, industrial processes accelerated their destructiveness by orders of magnitude. In the late 1980s, while I was still at junior school, the United Nations' Ad Hoc Group of Experts began discussing a possible international protocol to slow the rate at which humans detrimentally affected the natural world. By the time I returned from the Arctic, nature continued to be blighted, despite the efforts of conservation organizations and the promises of governments. The extinction of species remained many times higher than natural levels, and diversity was still declining along with habitat loss. In the past century, Cambridgeshire alone had lost nearly seventy species of wild flower that formerly flourished in the county.

The ghost orchid was emblematic of all endangered wild flowers. This fragrant, leafless orchid, its flower a crookedness of pale pink and yellow, once grew in the beech woods of several English counties but was declared extinct in 2005. Last recorded in Britain in some woods in Buckinghamshire, it was discovered again several years later by a wild-flower enthusiast one autumn as he walked among some old oaks. With just one secret flowering each season in Britain, the orchid was more haunting than if it had been lost to extinction. It called to mind a few beautiful lines from Yeats's poem 'All Souls' Night':

A ghost may come
For it is a ghost's right…
His element is so fine,
Being sharpened by his death.

Our species' nutrition is given as the paramount reason to conserve and strengthen the variety of life on the Earth, as we require a rich source of food and our own capacity to yield this variety is limited. The other persuasive reasons given are our health, the security of our homelands against natural disasters, and our ability to exploit the materials of the Earth for manufacture. In this way, these arguments place the wildness of the Earth inside the garden of human concerns. Underlying these justifications is the old presumption that living things and landscapes exist for our sake.

The laudable efforts of governments, conservationists and economists remain pointless without a real, reflective understanding of our behaviour as an animal, uncomfortable though that may be. For much of our history as a species, the pursuit of control has led us to dominate nature, but rationality and inventiveness have also allowed us to make sense of both the recent and the ancient past, steadily condensing information into a much more layered perspective on the natural world. A scientific understanding of nature has afforded insight into the limits of solely generational knowledge, not least because such knowledge relies on our presence. It has enabled us to appreciate our own eventual, unavoidable extinction. This humbling perspective encourages us to harness our rational skills and nostalgic sentiments to more benevolent, thoughtful ends. Our need to exploit nature for our own survival is balanced by an appreciation of the finiteness of our own species and the desire to study imperilled nature and try to salvage it.

The idea of the brutality of our animal nature, which is largely governed by intrinsic genetic traits, makes it hard to know to what extent we can alter human behaviour. However, regardless of the origins of our behaviour, we need to believe that we have the power to act differently. Firstly, by learning as children about our connection with nature and about the wild traits that continue to affect us, we might better anticipate which of these are likely to help or hinder our progress. Such knowledge of human nature ought not to derive only from lessons in classrooms. The findings of science should be integrated with a personal natural knowledge gained by daily closeness to wildlife. This closeness originally derived from use but can now emerge from the importance and attraction of knowledge itself. Effective policies need to be built on these foundations.

A return to a more immediate alliance with nature is essential so that knowledge of how we threaten it can alter our behaviour – reawakening the sense that we live finite lives in a finite world. The spectre of overpopulation remains. For people to return to a reasonable knowledge of nature while still reliant on it for survival, our societies will have to agree on a means of fairly and peacefully controlling the size of the world population, along with the size of societies relative to the fragility of the environments in which they live. Some may dream of colonizing other planets. Such escapism ignores the fact that nature endures beyond our ideas or the Earth's bounds. We will simply perpetuate damage elsewhere. Others may look a long way forward to a time when our history as a species is fossilized in the Earth's annals like the remains of a scrapped car, a perspective that may blunt their belief in contemporary action. Instead, by closing the gap between the natural landscape and ourselves, a direct understanding of nature can govern people's motives, rather than responding to a world made in the image of human desires. By returning to a daily closeness with the natural world, and learning about species other than ourselves, we might strengthen the moral sense that derives from our own origins in nature. My hope is that, in this way, nostalgia and inventiveness can come together to counteract our species' destructive tendencies.

I took the boat through the overgrown lock and up the narrow waterway of Wicken Fen, taking note of golden irises and water forget-me-nots like queens and paupers on the riverbank. The flitting psychedelic flight of a kingfisher left a vivid vein of blue across my vision. Two marsh harriers in black shadow fulfilled their tryst of appetite, the male slung beneath his mate as if the air was his bed, offering up his catch. Perched on the roof of the boat, my legs dangling into the engine room, my hand vibrating on the tiller, I had time to make these observations. I'd come to Wicken Fen precisely to bring wild nature to the fore.

Progress in a narrowboat is slow, especially through cramped or shallow waters – a brisk walker could easily outstrip me. The mind slows, too, thoughts drifting through the landscape like the languorous wake of the boat. I scanned the fields, softly umbering in the setting sun, and allowed my ideas to reel backwards and forwards between past, present and future, occasionally snagging on something physical, like a fly-fisher's line spun in and out. In the kitchen below deck, Ewan was preparing our evening meal, occasionally bobbing up at the bow to study something through his binoculars. We felt like émigrés among the wild inhabitants of this place, stripped back to the bare essentials of what we might have in common.

Living on the boat, I became more and more alert to the countless alterations of life around me. The first thing I had noticed was the hatching spiders, when it was not quite spring. Sunlight daggered the banks of the river but the light was pale as buttermilk, not strong enough to burn or to rouse. Traditionally, spring arrives in Britain as the sun crosses the celestial equator on 21 March. This is the vernal equinox, from the Latin *vernalis*, meaning 'spring', associated with *verno*, the Latin verb 'to bloom'. For most of my life, this date – automatically printed in calendars – was all that spring meant to me. But the river and its wildlife were challenging this view. The obstinate complexity of the natural life that surrounded me had ruptured the idea of spring into dozens of smaller, subtler seasons that I had never before perceived. For the first time in my life, I was living close enough to the elements to witness on a daily basis the arrhythmic strains of the natural world. A number of weeks before the traditional onset of spring, I experienced the thrill of discovering changes to which others around me seemed oblivious. People walking along the riverbank still bemoaned the winter and longed for its end. I wanted to open my windows and call out to them, 'Can't you see? It's already over! Spring is here!' Once the river had offered up this first secret,

I was bound to the landscape by fierce curiosity. The presence of the spiders signalled the return of insects to the skyline of the greenery. I couldn't put a name to any of this diminutive, darting life but I was wide awake to its agitation among the green dimness of the hedges and banks. Questions popped into my mind. From what kind of incubation had the various flying creatures emerged? And what kind of courtship could they hope to take to the air? I wanted to understand something of what I was seeing. The feeling was one of both elation and daring, each morning sprang up with possibilities.

In early English, the strong verb 'to spring' was *springan*, from which derived *sprengan*, the causative verb 'to break'. But the word 'spring' encompassed more than this: a sudden leap, the motive of an action, the emergence of life, the first stage of life, and the means of escape. All this meaning welling up through the ages from that first, pristine, violent word for a break. On this first spring on the river, I took to heart a break of sorts. As the wind reconsidered the world outside the cosy narrows of my boat and the distant sirens reminded me that I was moored between an urban and rural world, my mind was jolted out of passivity.

That afternoon, Wicken Fen told me two different stories: there was the landscape I could see and the landscape that had disappeared. Properly known as Wicken Sedge Fen, it is a flood plain bounded by clay banks and the watercourse through which I had cruised. When the Celtic tribes began populating Britain, the Cambridgeshire Fens were wild, salty marshes. The landscape remained this way until it was drained by Dutch engineers in the seventeenth century. Thomas Babington Macaulay referred to the inhabitants of the fens as 'a half-savage population… who led an amphibious life, sometimes wading, sometimes rowing, from one islet of firm ground to another'. Those living on the marshes could live a subsistence lifestyle, supporting their family from a single boat or drained swamp, selling cheese, butter, fish and timber to London merchants. It was a hard life. In *A Tour through the Whole Island of Great Britain*, Daniel Defoe joked that some of these farmers married ten or fifteen women in their lifetime, as the wives often died early. Once a lush forest, the ancient woodlands were drowned as the last Ice Age retreated, forming a rich peat soil that was later harvested for fuel. Sedge colonized the land after the removal of the peat, which people then cut to thatch houses.

By the end of the nineteenth century, the disappearance of thatch in favour of tiles brought an end to sedge cutting. Wicken Fen became worthless, the preserve of naturalists. It was just an island of unwanted ground amid the wider fenlands. Drainage had made them highly profitable, the prime agricultural region of the country, producing a third of England's potatoes and a huge acreage of cereals. This transformation of the landscape caused considerable losses of species. By the end of the nineteenth century, the bittern, spoonbill, greylag goose, marsh harrier, ruff, black-tailed godwit, avocet, black tern and Savi's warbler were lost from the landscape as breeding birds. The exquisite swallowtail butterfly became extinct due to the decline of its food source, the Cambridge milk parsley. The fen orchid disappeared with the cessation of peat cutting, and the delicate fen violet began to flower less often.

The moorings at Wicken Fen were before a small bridge at the end of the lode, beset by cow parsley. Nobody else was there. The blurred light of the evening was like a dark purply bruise. As night fell, man-made sounds dimmed, and a different communication became perceptible, as exotic as hearing a new language for the first time. The few evening visitors retreated from the Fen and the bird calls, the teasing sounds of insects, the whistle of tiny mammals replaced the footfall of humans. From the darkness came the muscular slap of fish on the water, the chirrups of the moorhens, the crackle of swans inside their beds of reeds, and the quavering nightly cryptogram of the barn owl. Thrillingly, for the first time in my life, I heard the boom of a bittern, its deep-throated, aspirated *who-who-who* echoing across the fen. A poem from the First World War, Francis Ledwidge's lament for the Irish nationalist Thomas McDonagh, who was executed a year before Ledwidge died in Flanders, told of the drowned sounds of nature amid his own extinction:

He shall not hear the bittern cry
In the wild sky where he is lain

Nor voices of the sweeter birds
Above the wailing of the rain.

Listening to the bittern's cry, Ewan told me that the strange hoarse
song belonged to the male as he courted his mate. He happened to pass
me his binoculars at just the moment that the bird took flight across
the pond. For four or five stolen seconds, I watched the ordinarily shy
bird with its mud-coloured coat of stars glide from sight. Although
the wonderful and peculiar lowing of the bird could travel for miles,
it seemed to have come from somewhere nearby. It was exciting to
imagine us as neighbours. The bittern became increasingly rare across
Britain as the reed beds where it fed and mated began to disappear
through the intrusions of agriculture and the sea. Due to hunting
and the drainage of the fens, it became extinct as a breeding bird
in Britain in 1886. The keen eyes of an amateur birder called Emma
Turner, who lived on a houseboat on Hickling Broad in Norfolk,
spotted the first returning bird from the continent in 1911. Since
then, the bittern has maintained a perilously tenuous existence in
England, ill-fated by its reclusion among the reeds.

As I lay in the dark with the sound of ducks pecking the reeds on
the underside of the boat, I had one thing on my mind. I wanted to
see if I could find the fen violet, a wild flower endangered in England
whose hint of pale purple as thin as moth wings made it the most
beautiful plant I could imagine. I wondered, too, as I drifted into
sleep, why it was knowledge of wild flowers that most fired my mind.
Carolus Linnaeus, the Swedish botanist who revolutionized the
categorizing of life on Earth, argued that plants were fundamental
to everything, with their regular cycle of blazing adolescence and
fruitful death. They spring up, he said, they grow, they flourish, they
ripen their fruit, they wither, returning to the earth again. Over the
years, plants had come to stand in my mind for the spring of diversity, the flowering origins of the clashing, propagating mishmash of
life. And so, at the end of all these journeys, it still bothered me
that I had no favourite wild flower. Perhaps the fen violet would
become the one closest to my heart, I reassured myself, if I could
discover it.

Darwin visited Wicken many times, and most likely made an exciting find in the region. In a letter written in 1846 to Leonard Jenyns, he described his discovery of the crucifix ground beetle. 'I must tell you what happened to me on the banks of the Cam in my early entomological days,' he wrote. 'Under a piece of bark I found two carabi (I forget which) & caught one in each hand, when lo & behold I saw a sacred Panagæus crux major; I could not bear to give up either of my Carabi, & to lose Panagæus was out of the question, so that in despair I gently seized one of the carabi between my teeth, when to my unspeakable disgust & pain the little inconsiderate beast squirted his acid down my throat & I lost both Carabi & Panagæus!'

A daring blend of orange and black, the beetle is one of Britain's endangered species, found at only three remaining haunts. Recently, someone spotted it at Wicken Fen, over fifty years since the last sighting. I felt heartened by the reappearance of the crucifix beetle. Perhaps the violet might return too, despite its absence the previous year. The following morning, I began my walk by enquiring in the Wicken Fen Visitor Centre if I might see the fen violet. Armed with their advice, I headed off into the nature reserve.

An obsolete and puzzling meaning of the word 'wilderness' is an area of ground in a large garden or park, planted with trees in fanciful forms such as a labyrinth. In his *Journal of a Naturalist*, John Knapp wrote in 1829 of a summer's day at Hampton Court, where 'on the opposite side of the palace there is a large space of ground called the Wilderness, planted and laid out by William III'. The idea of paradise originated in the Old Persian word *apairi-daeza*, an orchard enclosed by a wall. When translating the word 'garden' for the Septuagint, the scribes used *paradeisos*. Paradise was a fantasy of freedom from the strains of survival in nature. The Greco-Roman tradition celebrated a golden age in which humans lived in a blessed state, free from toil and deprivation. In Greek myth, after death heroes went to the Elysian Fields, where life was unencumbered by storm and plague. Descriptions of voyages blended myth and fantasy with the blurred edges of the known world. Sailors like Iambulus reputedly reached the wondrous Happy Isles. Here, he claimed, inhabitants lived in a state of blissful nature, in a landscape of permanent and effortless fecundity. In the *Odyssey*, Homer described the gardens of Alcinous, on the island of the Phaeacians, whose trees fruited eternally, never showing the welts of overripeness, and whose fields were gilt with corn that grew without the labour of farmers. These were idealized and imagined landscapes. These pagan myths of blessed and abundant nature were seeded in the Christian vision of the garden of Eden, where the first humans lived amid serene and unthreatening nature. Almost immediately, people began to debate the geographical location of this perfect place. In the east, exclaimed Hippolytus in the third century, to be rediscovered by the righteous and adventurous. At the crossroads of the Tigris and the Euphrates rivers, argued Bishop Epiphanius. St Augustine, too, was convinced that Eden was a historical place. How might people reach it again? When Christopher Columbus sailed towards the Orinoco river on his third voyage, he speculated that a vast summit or uncrossable waters impeded his further progress. 'For I believe that the earthly Paradise lies here,' he wrote, 'which no one can enter except by God's leave.' Paradise became a garden into which we could never hope to pass again.

From the Middle East, the tradition of the prince's garden spread around the world as the Arabic rulers occupied new lands. The famous Rusafa garden near Cordoba in Andalusia was constructed as a nostalgic memory of the Emir's homelands in Syria. Such gardens were oases of life amid the relative poverty of a barren landscape and crippling heat. They flowered in defiance of the deserts of the Middle East, where nothing grew and drought always threatened. These gardens were always hemmed-in worlds, governed by people, the first nature reserves, perhaps.

One of the earliest reserves, created in 1899, Wicken Fen was the place with the highest diversity of species in Britain. *The Entomologist*, edited by John Carrington in 1880, noted that 'Wicken still retains its virgin soil and flora, unspoilt by drainage or cultivation.' It became synonymous with hunts for rare butterflies and insects. 'An apparently good night frequently produces little or nothing, while sometimes those collectors who have had the patience or perseverance to stay through a wet and windy night find that suddenly the moths begin to come and many rarities are unexpectedly taken.' In 1895, an entomologist called Herbert Goss approached the newly instituted National Trust to save Wicken Fen and its exceptional range of species. At the close of the century, the Trust purchased several acres of the fen for ten pounds. It was a curious oasis in the black soil of Britain's principal area of farmland. The survival of endangered species like the crucifix beetle or rare wild flowers most probably depends on such sanctuaries for diverse life. But how can people gain native knowledge of them if they exist only within the confines of a nature reserve? The abundance of nature has been restricted to these sanctioned, bordered realms, into which people tiptoe within the allotted hours.

The light was beginning to go across the fen, gilding the tips of the rushes. I had failed to find the fen violet, but I didn't mind. I had made two pure and childlike discoveries of a more modest variety. Standing at a crossing of three paths, I had stopped to orient myself. I could see the green brows of a stand of tall trees further along one path and, beyond these, a flickering stretch of water. Somewhere near here, I guessed, was the hiding place of the bittern I'd heard the night before. Taking this little alleyway down past some willows, I spotted a buff-brown bee that I'd seen once before in Cornwall. Its three tiers of reddish fur made it easy to identify. The books I had to hand told me it was not a bumblebee, but a solitary bee, a tawny mining bee that made its home alone in the earth. I liked the idea of it softly humming, hunkered in a dusty burrow, its minute heart drumming within the darkness of its body.

In my excitement, I somehow believed I would chance across the fen violet, as if enthusiasm alone might rush me towards its discovery, just as young children, in sickening desire, truly believe they might one day see a ghost. A little further along, I came across a flower similar to the delicate violet, with a bluish heart and rounded petals. My heart jolted. But as I flicked quickly through my wild-flower book, I realized it was only a relative of the fen violet and the common dog-violet, the flower my grandmother loved most. It resembled both but was touched with a little golden yoke of the summer to come. This was heartsease. It had other names in English, love-in-idleness, kiss-me-at-the-garden-gate, and was the flower whose juice Oberon squeezed on the eyes of Titania in *A Midsummer Night's Dream*, an amorous tonic to soften the hardest heart and renew admiration for the world. Even Darwin found the flower intoxicating. He undertook a study of its propensity to shimmer through different hues when planted in other soils, slowly and stubbornly returning to its traditional colours by the summer's end. My guide classified it as *Viola tricolor*, the wild pansy, common and uninspiring, perhaps. But at that moment, I didn't want to savour what was dying out. I wanted to revel in the familiar, in something that I might be sure of greeting again. Not a ghost but an omen I could wait in hope for each spring.

The Joy of Nature

Illustration overleaf: *The Skelligs*

from BRENDON CHASE

BB

Denys Watkins-Pitchford (1905–90), who wrote under the name
'BB', was a nature writer, artist and children's author inspired by
the Northamptonshire countryside in which he was raised and
lived. Aged four, he believed he saw a gnome and his enduring
belief in the 'little people' led to his Carnegie Award-winning
saga, *The Little Grey Men* (1942). *Brendon Chase*, an escapist
fantasy following three brothers who run away from school to live
wild in the woods, followed in 1944. Watkins-Pitchford studied
at Northampton School of Art and the Royal College of Art
before becoming an art teacher at Rugby School for seventeen
years, until he became a full-time writer and illustrator. He was
a keen naturalist who also enjoyed the country sports of fishing and shooting. It is claimed that he invented carp fishing;
he was also a keen wildfowler (BB was the size of the lead shot
he used), and wrote a *Shooting Times* column for nearly sixty
years. He illustrated more than thirty books and wrote sixty of
his own – mostly non-fiction for adults and fiction for children
– including the popular Bill Badger series. He is also widely credited with successfully reintroducing the Purple Emperor butterfly
into Northamptonshire.

Robin was a strange boy, at least to many people he would
have appeared strange. He loved best to be by himself in the
woods, he liked to hunt on his wild lone and wander just
like this, for a whole day, in some leafy secret place where nobody
bothered to come. It was his idea of Heaven. When, as now, he would
come upon something which took his fancy and then time would
cease to be for him, he would be lost in a kind of ecstatic stupor.

As he lay looking down into this miniature pool his sharp eyes
took in every detail, even the minute shadows of the sticklebacks
were noted. Each fish had a shadow beneath it on the sandy floor.

After a while, as he kept very still, they became bold and emerged from the shaded water under the hazel leaves and went about their business in their own watery kingdom.

He could see their minute fins trembling, and what perfect fins! These fishes in miniature were truly fascinating. The Creator must have had eyes like a watchmaker, thought Robin, to have made such delicate fishes, and he smiled to himself. The cock fish were very pretty with their bright blue backs and red throats.

They did not glide along in the water, they seemed to progress in jerks. Sometimes a cock stickleback would chase another away and then it moved with great speed, like an arrow, coming to a sudden full stop, opening and shutting its mouth, puffing out its lips.

On this same pool were water skaters or fiddlers. When Robin had come up to the pool these insects had all darted into the grass and ferns at the edge but as he lay quiet they emerged again and began skating about the surface. He saw the tiny dimple made in the water by their feet. They seemed to run about with as much ease as if they were on hard ground.

After a while a fly fell off the hazel leaves, a greenfly. It landed close to the edge but in a minute quite half a dozen water skaters had seized it and the largest bore it away in its jaws with all the others jumping after him.

Then a buzzing sounded in Robin's ear. It was a wild honey bee. He knocked it with his hand and it, too, fell into the water in front of him where it buzzed round making a circular fan of minute ripples. Several fiddlers immediately came skating up. They seemed at first rather afraid of the bee, but one, bolder than his fellows, darted in a rapier thrust. The bee's struggles grew weaker and finally its attacker began to run off with it wedged across his jaws. Robin never realised what savage little insects they were, they reminded him of a pack of hounds.

The bee vainly tried to sting its captor but it was held fast. As Robin watched these fierce little creatures he noticed some were fighting, now and again one would fall over on to its back and show its silver underside, they skipped about each other like crickets.

It was delicious lying there among the cool bracken but the water seemed more inviting still. So he stripped off his shirt and the skin kilt and rolled off the bank. The pool only just covered his body when he lay down full length; it was a natural bath.

The water was warm in the full sun's glare, but when he sidled under the nut leaves it was quite chill. What a fairy-like little pool it was! Then he turned over on to his stomach facing upstream and watched the ripples hurrying round the bend towards him. He stretched out his arms – they looked blue under the water – and raised his fingers so that streams of silver bubbles came past his ears and nostrils.

He scrabbled the stones on the stream-bed and the water clouded for a second, but it soon ran clear again so that he could see his fingers showing bluish-white against the pied stones and silver sand.

Overhead a dragonfly passed to and fro, a bright blue dragonfly with dark spots on the ends of its wings like those he had seen by the Willow Pool at Cherry Walden. It settled on a reed in the full sun with its wings cocked high above its back. There were mayflies on the wing too, dancing up and down with their long graceful tails cocked up behind. When Robin was smaller he used to be rather afraid of them, he thought those long thread-like tails were stings.

It was so dreamy and cool and summery in that miniature paradise that Robin felt he could stay there for ever, and ever. But at last he had to get out and lie on the warm bracken to let the sun dry him. The green fronds felt quite hot against his body after the cold embrace of the limpid water.

When he had dressed again he suddenly felt terribly hungry. You may have noticed that after a swim one often has a good appetite. And he had brought nothing with him to eat. They only had two meals a day, breakfast and supper. It was all they wanted and they were invariably ravenous for either.

It was quite an effort to tear himself away from this little fairy glade with its amber pool, but soon he was pushing down the streamside again, his body still tingling and delightful after the bathe. It had not been a *real* swim, he would have liked to strike out into deep water and oar himself along like a very fat carp and nose among green water plants. Perhaps he could do this when he found the Blind Pool, if there *was* such a place.

Then, quite miraculously, the trees thinned and he saw the object of his search. It was a long narrow pool, dark and very still, with beds of white water-lilies growing near the banks. High oaks surrounded it on three sides, on the fourth were some tall and very gloomy pines whose tops were lit by the late afternoon sun so that their red branches seemed to be artificial, almost painted, or stained with blood.

At the far end, backed by the dark trees, stood a heron, its head sunk in its shoulders. It was standing on a mossy log which was protruding from the water. The pool was so still that a faithful reflection of the bird was visible, perfect in every detail.

Robin crawled through the bracken right up to the edge of the water and stared down into the depths. It was deep, so deep that he could see no bottom, and the water was a very, very, dark green. By staring hard he could at last make out the steeply shelving sides diving down into the gloom. Robin saw his own reflection, curiously dark, so that his eyes were almost invisible and behind his head an indigo sky such as one sees in an old Umbrian painting with the few white clouds which were passing slowly overhead, mirrored very soft and dim. It was like looking at a richly-coloured picture through a smoked glass.

As he lay screened by the reeds and fern, staring down, down, into the green depths, a dim movement attracted his attention below and a grave procession of massive bronze fish passed silently by, some five feet down. In weight and girth they were larger than any fresh water fish he had ever seen, with the exception of a pike. They were tench.

Robin was enthralled – bewitched! This place was even more magical than the tiny pool he had discovered away back down the trail! He lifted his eyes again and saw the heron had come to life and was walking rather awkwardly down the mossy log, clasping it with its long green claws and bobbing its head. It had not seen him, so well was he hidden in the reeds.

Several moorhens, which have the sharpest eyes of any wild bird, were feeding on a little grassy bank on the shore opposite to where he lay in hiding. They quested about like chickens, flirting their white tails. Moorhens are good to eat and so far Robin had shot nothing for the pot all day.

So he raised his rifle and took a steady sight on the nearest bird through the 'scope. It was not an easy shot for the moorhen was moving slowly forward, pecking as it went.

But Robin chose his own time and at the right instant the finger obeyed the brain and the crack was followed by the welcome thud of the bullet going home. The bird rolled over, flapped a wing once, twice, and lay still.

At the report of the rifle, muffled as it was, the heron sprang vertically into the air as if stung and came down again on the log. A moment before it had been hunched, now it was like a long slender grey reed and even from where Robin lay he could see its circular eye staring about it in the most comical manner. It had heard the muffled crack of the rifle but did not know from which direction it had come. Then it launched itself into the air and flapped away over the trees on wide cupped wings. One moment it was a grey bird against a wall of dark foliage, the next it was soaring into the sunlight and had vanished over the tops of the oaks.

All the other moorhens had run for cover when Robin had fired and now the pool was deserted, not a movement anywhere save some ripples on the water where a moorhen had dived. These came wheeling out towards him, breaking up the dark green shadow reflections.

He did not retrieve his bird at once. He still lay hidden among the thick reeds watching and listening. On the far green bank he could see the dark sooty spot of the dead moorhen. It would be delicious roast. Robin was so hungry he almost felt he could eat it raw with the greatest of gusto!

After a while he was aware of another bird moving among the sturdy reed swords at the far end of the pond, close to the sunken green log where the heron had stood. For some time Robin was puzzled as to what it could be and after a while he tried to see through the telescope of the rifle. At last he made out what it was, a mallard duck. Close behind her swam a lot of cheeping striped babies. She was threading her way in between the reed palisades. What a heavenly place! How the others would love it! The white water-lilies so perfect and waxy, looked as though they were artificial. And those fascinating flat circular leaves! Strange fleshy leaves like dishes, how they seemed the very spirit of the water itself! There was a very faint smell of

wild thyme and heated pond water. Earlier in the day the sun must
have been shining full on the pool for when Robin dipped a finger
in it was quite warm. Another time they must come here and swim
and fish. Alas! Robin Hood's day was nearly over. Why did the sun
sink so soon? He had a long weary march back to camp. He must
be starting. But as the sun dipped lower and lower behind the trees
the powerful magic of the scene held him all the more. This place
was surely far more lovely than Thoreau's pond he talked so much
about. There was something mysterious, almost a little sinister about
it. Why should it be set away in the heart of this ancient forest?
The deer drank here perhaps, and all the woodland creatures, foxes,
badgers, stoats, and the like, pheasants, too, and all the wild forest
birds. When Robin looked again in his magic mirror he saw no white
clouds sailing, he saw a sky of rarest aquamarine and, as he watched,
against that background a bird swam into view, a wide-winged bird,
which wheeled and wheeled in vast circles.

Robin looked up at the sky above and saw the whole scene, only
more distinctly and in clearer and more vivid colours. The bird was
wheeling like a buzzard, the sunlight shining on the spread fingers
of the wide-extended rigid wings. Could it be a honey buzzard? If so,
perhaps it had a nest somewhere in the forest!

At last it soared from view behind the oak tops and was gone.
He knew what he wanted to complete the picture of this dark green
lake, set among the trees, starred with ivory lilies. Why, of course, it
wanted this one thing, a moose, a huge black moose, pulling at the
water-lilies! He could imagine it so clearly, the loose pendulous lips
dribbling sparkling drops, its echoing sloshings, as it moved about in
the shallow water of that remote and silent place.

Sadly Robin turned back upon his trail, the moorhen safely in his
pocket. He took one last look at the Blind Pool. It was the loveliest
thing he had so far seen in the forest, and he had enjoyed this day
more than any other they had had so far.

He did not know then that years afterwards he would remember
that picture; the dark pool set among the trees, so still, so calm, starred
with those wax-like lilies, and the grey heron sitting on the log. Some
things we see pass out of the mind, or, at least, are forgotten; others,

little things, little glimpses such as this never depart. And the memory of that first view of the Blind Pool would still be in his mind forty years afterwards, rather faded, perhaps, like an old photograph in an album, but still there, an imperishable masterpiece.

from RUNNING FOR THE HILLS

Horatio Clare

Horatio Clare (b. 1973) was born in London and grew up with his mother on a sheep farm in rural Wales. His childhood experiences are described in his memoir *Running for the Hills* (2006), which won the Somerset Maugham Award. He has written a novella, children's fiction, and about travel and nature, including *A Single Swallow* (2009) and *Orison for a Curlew* (2015). *Down to the Sea in Ships* (2016) won the Stanford Dolman Travel Book of the Year; *Icebreaker* (2017) described his journey around the Bay of Bothnia. His first children's book, *Aubrey and the Terrible Yoot* (2015), which tackles the suicidal depression suffered by Jim, the father of 'rambunctious' young Aubrey, was the 2016 Branford Boase Award winner. Depression was also tackled in his writing for adults, including *The Light in the Dark* (2018) and *Heavy Light: A Journey Through Madness, Mania and Healing* (2021). Clare is also a regular radio broadcaster and teaches creative writing (non-fiction) at the University of Manchester.

Around this time, in the first hot yawns of full summer, we went badger watching. The conditions had to be just right: a warm, still evening after a sunny day, with no wind to carry our scent.

'Would you like to go badger watching, boys?' my mother asked, knowing the answer.

'Oh yeah!' we chorused.

'Don't say yeah, say "yes". We'll need to be camouflaged. Go and put on something dark green or brown, nothing pale, and meet me in the yard.'

We assembled and set off down the track, remarking on the wild roses which later in the season would carry vermilion berries, like clusters of balloons, each stuffed, as my brother and I well knew, with feathered seeds which made the most vicious itching powder. We stuck to the track and ignored the sheep, Jenny ducking their greetings like a film star trying to go incognito. Down the lanes, under the hazels we went, watching our step, avoiding prematurely fallen nuts. At the bottom of the first pitch we paused by the gate to the Horse Fields.

'From now on no talking,' Jenny whispered. 'Tread where I tread, and go very slowly. When we get close, do what I do. We'll crouch down and keep very still, like statues. We'll have to wait, but it'll be worth it if they come out. The cubs will be big enough to ramble about, but they'll start off playing around the setts, I should think. We might be lucky. Are you ready?'

We nodded.

One after another we followed her, cautiously climbing the gate at the hinge end and holding it steady for each other. Jenny stuck to the line of the fence, pointing out fallen ash twigs to be avoided. The sun had turned well over the skyline and the blackbirds were pink-pinking in the hedges, confirming their claims on the world. The cooling land sent up the first twinges of breeze to nudge the treetops, but Jenny had anticipated it and correctly guessed its currents; we were downwind of the badger setts.

The wood was a dimming, brooding thing. The different heights of the trees formed spires and aerial alleyways above the narrow gully which divided the land. The drop was so steep that we were level with the crown of the canopy; the curly whispering of the stream was barely audible, two hundred feet below.

As we drew nearer the setts Jenny bent double, trying to keep her silhouette below a badger's horizon, and we went slowly after her, copying every move. We inched up a swell in the ground, then crept down, just over the lip of the bank.

Twenty yards from the setts we stopped. Our mother placed us just in front of her and we all sat, settled, and tried to keep completely still. There were more than a dozen holes ahead of us, each with its raised stoop where grass had covered mounds of excavated earth, but Jenny pointed wordlessly to two where the earth was fresh and scattered with the dried grass of badger bedding. We fixed our eyes on these.

As all our human motion drained away we became as still as stumps, and sank slowly into a kind of trance. Our ears brought us every tiny rustle and scuff of the world in its lengthening moments; the distant exchanges of a mountain ewe and lamb; the buzz of a motorcycle from the valley; the pillow talk of wood pigeons. As the light lowered to nocturne blues and lacquering greens all our senses stretched; we felt the dusk's harmony like concert-goers – its mystery, melancholy and promise seemed to spread outwards from the wood. It was as though we were almost invisible, our bodies forgotten, leaving nothing but a set of senses, like a family of ghosts, until a sudden flurry of loud chiming cries burst out of a bush nearby, as brash and outraged as a burglar alarm.

'Blackbird,' Jenny mouthed in our ears. 'He'll leave us alone, don't turn a hair.'

We willed him away, defying him with our stillness. After a series of ringing accusations, during which I sent him a stream of psychic abuse, he relented, and dived away to investigate something else. The first rabbit appeared, conjuring himself from a patch of nettles, motionless at first, as if engaging us in a keep-still competition. A minute passed before he lopped forward and sniffed the grass, whereupon the rest of his tribe began appearing, bobbing and hopping, their white scuts amazingly bright against the shadow-gathering field.

And then, materialising as suddenly as the rabbit, a large grey shape appeared at the mouth of one of the setts. A long face, with a beautiful silky black nose, black eye mask and white cheeks contemplated us with what seemed like great solemnity.

We barely breathed. The badger's snout lifted as she tested the air. She seemed to gather more than scent; she seemed to sniff the atmosphere of the quiet evening, the spirit of it, as though she knew there was something about, but could not detect threat in it. After a few moments of peering at us she emerged, followed by first one, then another, then a third snuffling cub. She nuzzled and sniffed them, grunting softly as if reminding them of dos and don'ts. They were adorable, like fat little bears, full of play and trepidation. Soon they were tumbling around, venturing out and dashing back in, pratfalling and beetling about. I knew my own expression was reflected in the faces of my mother and brother; we watched with disbelieving, delighted smiles. The cubs squeaked and wrestled and rolled, until their mother marshalled them, and for one moment paused, looked straight at us, as if cautioning us not to move. For a few seconds two families regarded one another, then the badger turned, her cubs went with her, and they vanished into the wood.

We gave them a couple of minutes, then stood, stiffly, and backed away as quietly as we had come. We joined hands as we went back up the pitch, and tried to keep our thrill to whispers. 'Magical!'

'Amazing!'

'Did you see them! Did you see those cubs!'

It was a shared epiphany. Having approached so reverently, in the hope of merely seeing our wild neighbours without alarming them, we had, for a few moments, experienced the world as they did. We sped back to the farm, vigorous with happiness. The dew-smell rose in the meadows and we were as light as if we had all been blessed. We had known the edge of an evening wood as a badger knows it. For that twilight time we had slipped the separation between us and the world. We were of the mountain, and of the wood, and it was as though the animals, the wild creatures, had allowed it. It was bewitching.

from SKELLIGS CALLING

Michael Kirby

A writer, poet, painter, folklorist, local historian, farmer, fisherman and environmental thinker, **Michael Kirby** (1906–2005) spent all but three of his ninety-nine years in County Kerry, Ireland. (Those three years were spent working on the railroads in the United States during the Great Depression.) His first poetry collection was published when he was seventy-eight. He wrote eight books in his native Gaelic under the name Micheál Ua Ciarmhaic. A trilogy of memoirs, *Skelligside* (1990), *Skelligs Calling* (2003) and *Skelligs Sunset*, published posthumously, reveal his schooldays, local characters and the folk tales, customs, wit, magic and natural beauty of western Ireland.

THE SOFT SOUTH WIND OF SKELLIGS

Never was a day more to my liking than when soft zephyrs sang from the south, blowing gently across the bay of Skelligs whose waters reflected an azure sky adorned with the fluttering white of the gull's wing. It was the threshold of a new summer, a time to be glad. I could feel the life-giving energy of the great ocean, which seemed to enter my very being, calling nostalgically – come away… come away…

Glittering rays of morning sun sparkled, spilled and splashed from wavelet to wavelet and onto the back of a slow heaving billow that arose lazily from the depths of a mighty bosom. Lesser gulls wearing white aprons and little black caps, were scattered like 'sea daisies' across the blue-green fields of the bay. Some birds seemed to hang suspended above the waters, their wings a special whiteness unlike the whiteness of snow – a colour which stood out to me and could be seen flashing against a background of blue. Even away in the distance their wings seemed like a glint of white lightning in the sky. Black guillemots and razorbills called in shrill voice, singing or composing poems, diving and reappearing from the spume white froth, their bills laden with silver sprat.

On a day such as this could be heard the music of the ocean, the deep throated husky laugh of that fickle monarch of the deep, the sea god Poseidon, who might fume and fluster into a raging tempest or wear the smile of an infant in the cradle of a May morning.

As the sail filled with a belly full of freshful fragrance, I could feel the tautening of the canvas when the little boat comes alive, leaning her shoulder against the sudden rush of water from her bow wave, leaving a furrow in her streaming wake like a ploughshare in the blue field of the bay.

Congregations of screaming Arctic terns with scissor-pointed wings swooped, plunged and dived for their share in the fruits of the kingdom, where myriads of silver sprat had surfaced, much to their excited delight.

Puffins with their multi-coloured beaks, like circus clowns breaking the water, and little auks and crossbills all feasted at nature's free table, provided for their survival.

Little white clouds like puff balls of thistledown danced ballet across the blue ceiling of the sky. All things alive and life in all things. Praise the Lord for the resurgence of life I felt around me and in my very soul that morning when the soft south winds sang across the bay of Skelligs.

The molten mirror of the sun trundled its fiery wheel across the southern sky, climbing the ladder of infinity and marking the milestone of yet another day. The grey blue rock of the holy hermits, Skellig Michael, standing sentinel by the Kerry headlands came into view, as we swept by the wild head of Bolus out into open sea, where the south wind took on a more lively singing note, causing the boat to dance and increase in speed, tossing her bow over little hummocks of water which laughed and sparkled in her sea way, throwing white blossoms of spray aboard as if to bless her.

Out here all things lived. Ronan the seal played and revelled in the churning surf. An ugly, hook-beaked cormorant pointed its tail feathers heavenwards disappearing beneath the green waters. Manx shearwaters skimmed the surface. Together with the swallow-like flight of the grey fulmar, the great solan goose, mighty bird of the Atlantic, flew towards Little Skelligs, bearing a long streamer of bladder wrack in its great beak, the building material of a new nest, in expectation of this year's offspring. Little dolphins puffed and played, racing alongside, looping, bending and curving their sleek forms, perhaps in wonderment of man and his little boat.

On a morning such as this what would I wish for? Swallow wings! Yes, swallow wings, wished for by a mere mortal who would feign divest himself of all earthly inhibitions.

I have looked upon the great water asleep like a smiling infant in a cradle, only to awaken to a rosy dawn to watch white horses charging across the bay. I have witnessed sunsets leaving a golden staircase painted on the wave, leading to a flaming crown of molten gold hanging momentarily on the horizon. I can only say – who is the artist? If it be you, oh God, then thank you!

ACKNOWLEDGEMENTS

Thanks to Head of Zeus editors Richard Milbank for his calm wisdom and Christian Duck for her unceasing attention to detail and creative suggestions. Thanks to Rachel Thorne for her speed and professionalism over seeking permissions. For ideas of who I should read, I am indebted to many random conversations over the years, some of which have slipped my mind. So thank you, readers everywhere, and particular thanks to Neil Belton, Stephen Moss, Giles Wood, Dan Milmo, Sean Clarke, Matthew Oates and Robert Macfarlane for their advice. Thanks also to Karolina Sutton at Curtis Brown, and the staff at the British Library for their – shhh – quiet efficiency.

LIST OF ILLUSTRATIONS

Internal illustrations are all original linocuts by Sarah Price.

EXTENDED COPYRIGHT